Anotech Chronicles Books 1-3:
Reshner's Royal Ranger
Reshner's Royal Threat
Reshner's Royal Guard

By Julie C. Gilbert

Anotech Chronicles Book 1:
Reshner's Royal Ranger

By Julie C. Gilbert

Aletheia Pyralis Publishers

http://www.juliecgilbert.com/

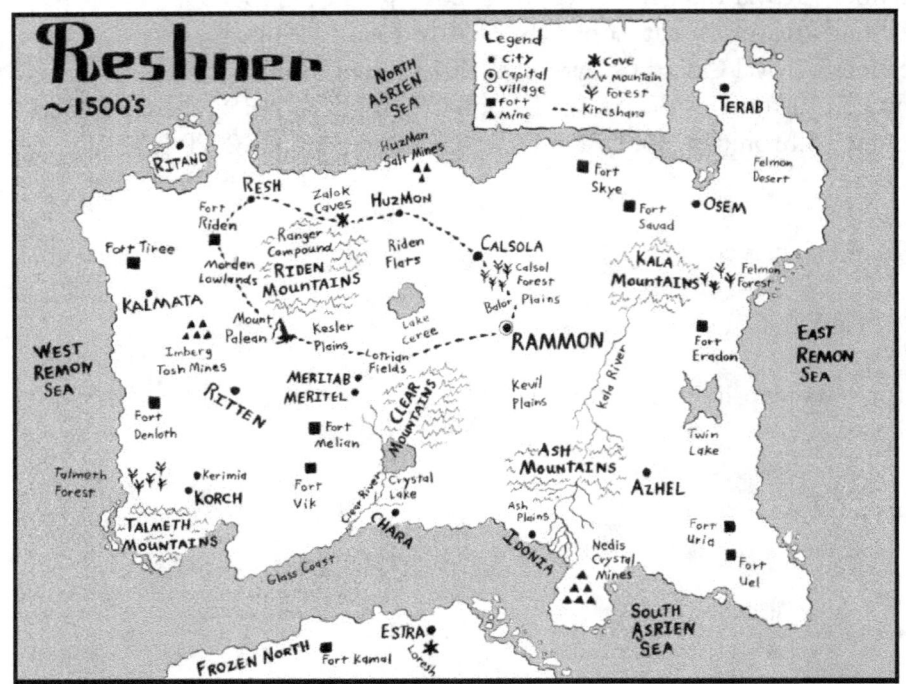

Visit: **http://www.juliecgilbert.com/**
to request a full-sized map.

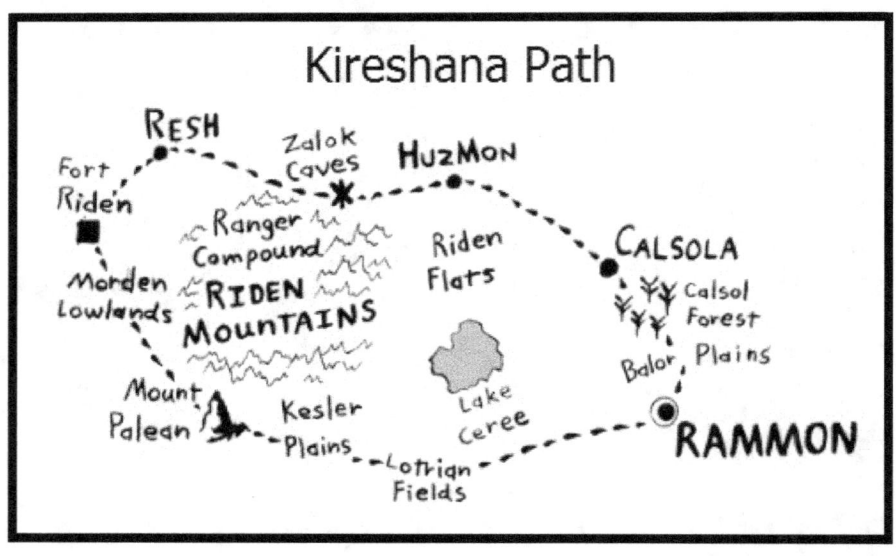

Acknowledgements:

Alex McGilvery, Lucas Dalenberg, Chewie,
J. LaRocco, Timothy Sparvero, Kristin Condon,
Jenny Shin, Deb Monroe and Alan Pinck
for awesome suggestions and test driving the story

Note: The paperback version was too big to fit the full appendixes.
If you'd like a PDF of those, please email devyaschildren@gmail.com.

Table of Contents:

Cast of Characters:

Royals:
King Teorn Minstel – ruler of Reshner
Prince Taytron Minstel – Crown Prince of Reshner
Prince Terosh Minstel – Second Prince of Reshner
Lady Mavis Altran – mother of Lord Kezem, King Teorn's sister
Lord Kezem Altran – third son of Lady Mavis

Rangers:
Reia Antellio – Prince Terosh's Kireshana guardian
Kiata Wellum – Nareth Talis Ranger, Reia's sister
Todd Wellum – Nareth Talis Ranger, Kiata's husband
Master Niklos McGreven – substitute father for Reia and Kiata
Lucas Telon – Ranger master, Kezem's undercover RT agent
Hiram Alikron – Ranger master, Ashatan Council member, RT agent

Restler-Tarpon Alliance:
Gareth Restler – eldest son of Arista, Merisia's husband
Merisia Restler – daughter of Vera and Tyko, Gareth's wife
Alden Tarpon – son of Vera and Tyko
Talyon Keldor – RT agent, Ariman's son, Merisia's friend
Ariman Keldor – RT agent, Taly's father

Other:
Anotechs – Dark Machines, God Machines, microscopic machines
Maledek – part played by Kezem and Dalonos
Dalonos – Dr. Atien Belcross remade by anotechs
Kolknir – mercenary, former Ranger master

Chapter 1:
Restler-Tarpon Alliance

Idela (January) 1, 1538
Temple of the Moon Gods, City of Korch
Talyon Keldor tugged at the robes engulfing his lean body.

Stupid weddings. Stupid formal robes.

"Do you realize the importance of this alliance, Taly?" inquired his father. Ariman Keldor appeared at ease in the black uniform of a Restler-Tarpon Alliance sub-general. The uniforms were as new as the sub-generals now running the Tarpon and Restler family businesses.

Taly wasn't sure what to think. Knowing his father would elaborate later, he shook his head, stared up into the cavernous ceiling above, and tried to imagine being alone with the giant murals of mythical battles. To pass the time, he counted the wooden beams crisscrossing the ceiling.

Soft music rose from the sidron organ, yanking Taly's attention down from the rafters. The crowd jammed into Korch's biggest temple stood and turned as one. Craning his neck, Taly saw two young women standing in the back. He recognized the blonde in the dark green dress as Merisia, daughter of Vera and Tyko Tarpon, and assumed the other woman was Nera, daughter of Arista and the late Tobias Restler.

Taly watched the procession creep forward. A dozen children surrounded each woman, clutching the trains of their dresses. Slowly the two parties split. Merisia and her followers went left while Nera and her followers veered right. Their measured steps matched the music. Despite Merisia's neutral expression, Taly sensed her unease.

If they moved faster, this ordeal would be over sooner.

Willing the women to move faster gave him a headache. Rubbing his temple, Taly silently counted people to ease the boredom. Arranging marriages around business interests seemed wrong. He flushed as he thought of the huge crush he'd once had on Merisia. Thankfully, the one thousand people crammed into the Temple of the Moon Gods had eyes only for the large vidscreen displaying the ceremony. Merisia Tarpon surrendered her last name to marry Gareth Restler, and Nera Restler did likewise to marry Brook

1

Tarpon.

"Why did Nera give up her last name?" Taly asked, once they waited outside for the hovs to carry them to the reception on the Kevloth Plains. According to tradition both families ought to bear the more prominent name by the end.

"Equality must be maintained," the elder Keldor replied.

"If the Tarpons and Restlers are equals now, what changes for us?" Taly swiped sweat from his brow.

His father chuckled and shook his head.

"This union has two enemies calling a truce to face a common threat. As for us, we're RT Alliance agents. Time will tell if that title will lead to glory or gallows, so to speak."

Taly retreated into his thoughts. The hovs arrived, and he climbed in after his parents. He knew the *common threat* was the king's soldiers and the Rangers. He cared nothing for the king or his soldiers, but he owed his life to a Ranger. Kiata had removed viper poison from Taly's body, despite the beating his father had given her for destroying some firfe spice. Were the roles reversed, Taly didn't know if he could bring himself to save an enemy's child. He was saved from making a decision on the hypothetical situation by their arrival at the reception.

The sight of dozens of tables filled with more food than Taly had eaten during his lifetime, cheered him. Every six tables presented the same dishes. Taly wondered how long it had taken the cooks to prepare such a feast. Half a table held rielberry, appola, cran, and bonnelberry pastries. He imagined the melting sugar, but a look from his mother made him eye the rest of the spread. One table held things hauled from the sea. Taly chose a few crunchy scerims and the giant legs of some poor sea creature before moving on. At the meat table he piled his plate high with tretling steaks, codrel legs, rabbit chunks in wheat gravy, and stewed ferbel.

Focusing on his food, Taly tuned out the speeches praising the RT Alliance. He even forgot his uncomfortable robes until sweat and fine food caused them to stick to him. Wishing to return to a shaded place, Taly started dozing.

Merisia appeared next to him.

Taly flinched.

"Great Riden! Where did you come from?" he cried.

"Manners, Taly," his mother admonished. "Merisia, you look lovely. That necklace matches your eyes perfectly."

Taly's attention stayed on his friend. Her face glistened with sweat, but her discomfort seemed unrelated to the heat. Despite the three-and-a-half-year age gap, Merisia had always been easy to read. Taly supposed the fear he saw might be natural on her wedding day, but the frustration surprised him. He couldn't fathom what she needed to ask him either. They had barely spoken in over two years.

"I'm getting dessert," Taly announced, standing up and tripping over Merisia's dress.

She chuckled as she caught his arm.

"I'll go, too." Merisia's purple eyes with their silver flecks spoke of a personal message.

Her laughter improved Taly's mood.

"What is it you wanted to ask me?" he wondered, once they'd stepped away a few paces.

Merisia giggled like the carefree girl she'd once been. The giggle morphed into a woman's laugh, full of mirth and bitterness.

"Ah, Taly, you're good for me, very good." She stopped walking and placed a hand on Taly's left arm. "That's why I talked to my husband and your father about you."

"Why?"

"Because I need you," Merisia confessed. "I can't leave everything and everyone I've ever known to become some stranger's wife! I need something familiar, *someone* familiar. Come with me, Taly, please come!"

Her desperation shocked Taly almost as much as the request. He opened and closed his mouth twice before remembering how to speak.

"Why me? What can I do?"

"You'll still be a terman, but you'll answer to my husband and have the authority of an avidman." Merisia's voice assumed a quiet vibrancy as she explained. "I need you, Taly, need you."

Taly's eyes widened. Avidmen were only two steps below sub-general. Visions of wealth and power filled his head.

"Say you'll come, Taly, say it," Merisia insisted.

He nodded, felt Merisia squeeze his arm, and found himself alone. Taly stumbled to the dessert table and filled a plate with fruits and cakes. Then, he sought out a quiet corner and devoured the food as he thought. He hadn't given Merisia his word, but he had no reason to turn her down. Accepting would mean moving to Meritab or wherever Merisia and her husband moved.

The prospect thrilled him. At fifteen, Taly would soon be a man. A good position within the Restler-Tarpon Alliance would be a nice start toward living up to his grandfather's legacy.

If a fraction of the rumors were true, Niktrod Keldor was a man to be reckoned with. Though his parents wouldn't confirm much, Taly believed his grandfather still lived and fought to free the planet from House Minstel.

Did Grandfather really kill the queen?

Taly couldn't reconcile the memory of the man who pulled mintas drops out of Taly's ears with a man who could poison someone. As the confusion threatened to spiral into despair, Taly wrenched his thoughts back to Merisia's offer. He had worked for his father for several years, but the chance to fully join the RT Alliance was intriguing.

Chapter 2:
Death Defied and Accepted

Idela (January) 4, 1538
Three days after the formation of the RT Alliance
Dark Man's Bluff, Glass Coast near Idonia

Dr. Atien Belcross had once been a respected inventor and scientist. He sucked in painful breaths of icy air. Hunching his shoulders, he tried to shield the bundle in his arms.

"I'm sorry, little one. I cannot let you live."

The infant princess gurgled at him and drooled.

Wiping her mouth so spit wouldn't freeze to her face, Belcross cursed the gesture's futility.

Coward. Traitor. Kidnapper. Murderer.

Each title brought tears to his eyes. He wished they would block his vision. At least then he would be spared the child's trusting gaze. His thoughts churned even as his arms stiffened with the cold. The brutal sea wind twisted his cloak around his legs.

Birds screeched and flew frantically around him. Despite the activity, he stood still and envisioned tossing Elia into the South Asrien Sea then jumping in after her.

A half-step forward drained the nerve he'd gathered. The move brought him close enough to peer down. Waves crashed against the rocks below. Salty spray leapt up and smacked him. Belcross shielded the baby with his cloak but turned his head to face it, welcoming the pain.

"It must be this way," Belcross whispered.

The baby gazed up at him, one fist jammed into her mouth while the other hand clutched at nothing. Turning his back on the sea, Belcross offered the infant a finger. She grasped the finger and tugged. Her delicate touch sent a longing pain through Belcross, making him tremble. He forced his gaze away from Elia's blue eyes, choosing to turn again and glare down at the sharp rocks below.

He considered the events that brought him to this moment. Brilliant work had earned him a commission from Prince Taytron. He'd loved discovering new things with his protégé until she fell in love with the prince.

4

Belcross had feigned happiness even as each new development tore him to pieces. He'd even witnessed their wedding, proving he could refuse her nothing. The event drove him to Maledek.

I did not go to betray, but it is better this way.

Truthfully, the betrayals never seemed harmful. Maledek had assured him of *her* safety. He stood on the cliff holding *her* child, a child that should also have been his. Having lost count of the betrayals, Belcross tried to reconcile his motives for killing Elia. Other paths would only lead to more pain. The child would be brilliant but a slave of circumstances. It would be kinder to end her life before she became everybody's hostage.

Belcross barely felt the blow that made him drop the baby and tumble headfirst from the cliff.

A melodious, childlike voice awakened him sometime later. Hours could have passed, but seconds is more likely. Everything hurt.

Do you wish to live? The coldly female voice was tinged with impatience. **You are broken but useful.**

He laughed, choked, and moaned. Pain impeded thought, but he knew he should be dead. A wave tossed his body against the cliff. He landed hard and slid onto the shallow shore behind a rock, another wave doused him. He sputtered and coughed up salt water.

Yes, I want to live! Who are you? Am I dead?

Stop asking stupid questions. All will be explained in time. Sleep, heal, rest.

***

Idela (January) 4, 1538
Same day
Maledek's Private Retreat, City of Idonia

Deanna Koffrin Minstel, wife of Prince Taytron, awoke in Maledek's dungeon and wept with pain and worry. The stone wall dug into her back, and her heart ached almost as much as her arm. She sat on the hard ground clutching her shattered wrist to her chest and trying not to shiver. Tears filled her mouth with the gritty, bitter taste of salt, dirt, and despair.

She thought back to the Fortune's Glory Inn in Azhel and the last moment she thought life might be all right. But her former mentor had betrayed her again.

I was a fool to believe you, Atien.

Sighing, Deanna recalled the long hov ride to the mines and agreeing to wait for Atien to retrieve Elia. An hour of waiting convinced her of his deception, but the trap had already been sprung. She had retreated deeper into the mines, leading Maledek and his minions on a merry chase. If the Airborne Toxin Emitter had worked properly, they would have both died. Deanna shuddered at how swiftly Maledek had seized her good arm and fled the small chamber. She owed him her life, but he'd done her no favors.

Her failure to kill Maledek in the Nedis Crystal Mines meant she would soon die and many others would follow. Her death would hurt Taytron and leave her baby girl defenseless. Deanna scoffed at the defense she'd provided thus far. The movement hurt her arm. Her temple throbbed to the beat of Elia's name. Deanna wanted to die but needed to live long enough to know her daughter's fate.

Why can't things be different for you, Elia? Your daddy's a prince.

The door crashed open, and the new noise assaulted Deanna's head. Two of Maledek's men lifted her off the floor, heedless of her pain. They held her firmly, both restraining and supporting her as Maledek entered holding a bundle of blankets.

Deanna's heart leapt and sank, elated to see her daughter but crushed to know Maledek had captured her. Anger soon outweighed relief, warming Deanna and driving off some of the pain.

"Let's try this again." Lord Kezem Altran sounded different without his mask. He wore fine silk robes tastefully crisscrossed with tarphan, a durable cloth that could dissipate kerlak beams. "Welcome to Idonia, Princess."

Recognition that Lord Kezem was Maledek blasted through the haze of pain.

"You! You—" Deanna's tongue tripped over the thousand foul things she ought to call him. Pain still forgotten, she strained against her captors. The movement sent new pains zipping up and down her arm. She glanced at the ugly, swollen mass that was once her right hand and wrist.

"Calm down," Kezem commanded, drawing her gaze back to him. "I warned you not to marry him. That you ignored my good advice is hardly my fault. Now, tell me if the dead-man potion worked."

"You gave it to her?" Deanna's question held horror and anger. "Why? You didn't even know what dose—"

"Is she alive?" Kezem interrupted.

"I'll need to touch her to tell."

Despite her stiff words, Deanna suspected her legs might have turned to jelly. A new wave of horror descended as she realized he intended to kill her and convince Taytron both she and Elia had died. Relief that the villain would let her daughter live battled dread at knowing Elia would remain at his mercy.

At a nod from Maledek, one man released her and the other twisted the wounded arm around behind her back, forcing her to kneel.

Deanna moaned and bit her lip to distract herself. Her teeth tingled, and her vision clouded. Blood found its way into her mouth. Her temple throbbed anew, and she sensed the end drawing near.

Kezem knelt and unwrapped the blankets from around Elia, cradling her gently.

Slowly, Deanna brushed trembling fingertips along Elia's icy cheek. She dared not breathe. The cold seeping through her fingers chilled her soul. Slipping her hand behind the baby's head, Deanna used her thumb to feel along the tiny furrow behind Elia's right ear. Tingling warmth met her fingers. Closing her eyes to increase concentration, Deanna felt behind the child's left ear as well. Finally, she rechecked the right ear and reported her conclusion.

"She's alive."

"Good, then you've earned your rest." Kezem's gaze softened. "When her part in this is done, she will be safe here."

The relief consumed Deanna so much that she barely felt a needle prick the back of her neck, just above her left shoulder. The poison spread as fast as her blood could take it. A deep weariness swept over Deanna. She spent her last moments caressing her daughter's frigid cheek.

We can stop this, promised a solemn young voice. ***Once we know a poison, it is forever ours to command.***

Strangely aware that her heart and lungs had ceased functioning, Deanna fought the fog slipping over her brain.

If you wish to live, say the word, and your life will be ours.

Deanna saw an ashen, skeletal form cloaked in black robes, standing in a pool of blue light. The hood was thrown back, revealing a face she hardly recognized as her own. The hairless caricature grinned.
Smoky wisps entered and exited the figure wherever it pleased.

No! The thought embodied Deanna's disgust at perverting the natural course. Breaking the mental connection was the last thing she ever did.

Chapter 3:
Unsettling News

Idela (January) 5, 1538
Four days after the formation of the RT Alliance
Prince Terosh's Office, Royal Palace, City of Rammon

"Excuse me, Dulad Prince, but Lord Kezem Altran requests an audience," the servant said.

Startled by news of a visit from his cousin, Prince Terosh Minstel stared at the man for two seconds before responding.

"Send him in."

These rare encounters with his older cousin always proved intriguing. Terosh checked to make sure his outfit befitted a meeting with Lord Kezem. The outfit consisted of fitted black pants and a matching tarphan shirt with a militaristic cut. His father would disapprove, but Terosh didn't want to delay the meeting solely because his cousin might have out-dressed him. He stood as Kezem entered.

Dressed in red and gold cantlebaun silks, Kezem cut an imposing figure. A black half-cape covered his left shoulder, partially hiding a weapons belt. Terosh saw a silver handled kerlinblade, but the famed electrified banistick eluded him. Curiosity made him wish to see the weapon few non-Rangers could handle. Most banisticks had shock nullifiers so they could stand up against energy-based weapons, but Kezem had commissioned a scientist to make his banistick capable of delivering shocks.

What reason could he have for a weapon like that?

"I apologize for the unexpected visit, Highness. I bring a request and bear distressing news," Kezem announced, bowing deeply.

"Then unburden yourself, Governor General," Terosh said, using Kezem's nicest rank.

Calling the man "Third Lord of Idonia" could be taken as a shot at his birth status and diminished political station. Terosh had always refrained from treating his cousin inferiorly, even when he'd become an adult at age sixteen. Now, at eighteen years of age, Terosh still couldn't talk down to the man. He felt irrational guilt about the bad blood between their families.

If grandfather hadn't disowned Aunt Mavis, she would have become queen when Aunt Uria and Uncle Uel were assassinated. Where would that leave my brother Tate and me?

The way Kezem towered over Terosh left him feeling insignificant. He was grateful to not be facing all three of his Idonian cousins. Governor Lord Eldon Altran and Governor Judge Mitrek Altran—respectively First and Second Lord of Idonia—possessed broader shoulders and higher ambitions than Kezem.

"May we speak in private?" Kezem asked.

Unease gripped Terosh, but he shook off the feeling.

"Of course, let's speak in the gardens."

A brisk walk brought them to the gardens. The place promised more solitude than Terosh's office, but Palace Security and Royal Guards still roamed everywhere. Terosh led the way through a maze of exquisite plant life from around the planet. He had been here so many times that he barely noticed anything they passed.

Fireblooms from the Ash Plains formed intricate swirling patterns amidst a sea of green colbies modified to survive at an altitude far lower than the Talmeth Mountains. Delicate, glowing dayde flowers from the Felmon Forest lit the path wherever the foliage grew too thickly to allow for much sunlight.

Terosh wondered if the Felmon Forest was as dangerous as tales claimed. He had often ventured into the Calsol Forest, but the brief visit to Fort Eradon when he was fourteen had not left enough time to explore the Felmon Forest. Brief regret for the lack of traveling followed Terosh as he led the way to one of the twenty-nine fountains. When they neared, Terosh waved Kezem to a seat on the Fountain of Nouvirn's wide stone bench.

"The water will keep the conversation private," Terosh assured Kezem. "What is your request?"

"I would like two divisions of Royal Guards to aid my search for Maledek," said Kezem.

The rumors had started three years ago attributing hundreds of illegal activities to Maledek. The Ranger dispatched to investigate had disappeared and the rumors faded. Maledek's return had been subtle, and he operated mostly in the southern and eastern regions, far from Rammon. Terosh suspected that the name had become an excuse for every unsolved crime east of the Clear River.

"Two divisions is more Guards than most outlying cities have," Terosh pointed out, after a long pause. "How do you expect to use that many men?"

"My agents believe Maledek's hideout lies between Twin Lake and Fort Uria," Kezem reported.

Terosh smiled and pictured the area on the mental map Master Sedir had etched upon his brain.

"Well, that narrows it down to half the east coast. Such a search would take months. Unless you can offer stronger proof, I'm going to deny your request. Now, what news did you bring?" He hoped his tone left no room for argument. In truth, he could authorize the transfer of manpower, but Terosh felt uncomfortable doing so on Kezem's word alone.

"As I said, distressing news." Kezem frowned. "You had a scientist here by the name of Belcross, correct?"

Terosh nodded.

"And this Dr. Belcross had an assistant, did he not?"

"You know it is so."

Kezem held up his hands innocently.

"I had to ask. She is dead, and I think Maledek murdered her."

"What makes you say that?" Terosh asked. "And why are you telling me instead of my brother?"

Something—besides the young scientist's untimely death—felt wrong.

Terosh knew his brother had loved the fair-haired scientist.

"The police found her body outside the North Gate this morning. It must be Maledek. The scientist died from comaladon." Kezem's deep blue eyes flickered yellow, indicating his irritation. "Few have access to that toxin, but Maledek is one such person."

Terosh's stomach lurched. His mother—Queen Kila—had been murdered by the rare poison almost three years ago.

"None of this makes sense," he grumbled.

I could access comaladon, and so could you. How do you even know who can access comaladon? Why would anyone kill Dr. Koffrin?

"I will present your news and request to the Crown Prince and contact you by comm when I have his answer."

"I'll come, too. There's more but it needs to be shown," said Kezem.

A quick conversation with his brother, led the pair to the center of an impressive courtyard where Prince Taytron Minstel knelt before a white package. His expression told Terosh that he was probing the package with anotechs.

A flash of envy shot through Terosh.

"Your Highness, please let me open the package," said Aster Captain Gina Kelter. "And stand well away while I do so."

She phrased the orders as requests, but Terosh heard the authoritative undercurrent. In matters of safety, the Melian Maiden commander technically outranked Tate. Normally, Melian Maidens shadowed the queen, but even before the assassination, Captain Kelter had been Tate's personal guardian. His brother had probably spent more time with her than he had with their mother.

Reluctantly, Tate retreated a few steps.

"Further, if you please, Highness. Airborne toxins can leap more than that distance," the captain insisted, not even bothering to see how many steps he had taken.

Tate grinned and took another grudging step backward.

"There's nothing dangerous about that package," Kezem called. "But it should be opened in private."

"How do you know?" asked Tate, turning to face them as they approached.

"Because I prepared it myself," Kezem answered.

A short, polite argument later, Captain Kelter took the package to a modest meeting chamber. Kezem insisted on complete privacy—meaning family only—and the captain basically told him over her dead body.

While waiting for someone to break the resulting awkward silence, Terosh amused himself by placing odds on who would win a stubbornness match, Kezem or the captain. He knew the captain better than his cousin, but something about Kezem's eyes declared him a very dangerous opponent.

"Look, if no one's going to open it, I will," Terosh said, reaching for the large package.

Three pairs of hands stopped him.

"Not yet," Tate pleaded.

"Not you," said Captain Kelter.

"No," said Kezem. "It was prepared for Taytron."

"Why can't you tell us what's in it?" Terosh demanded.

"The contents were found in the dead woman's arms," Kezem explained.

"What dead woman?"

Terosh heard the dread in his brother's voice.

"A friend of yours." Kezem lowered his voice as if that would lessen the blow.

"Dr. Koffrin," Terosh said.

Stunned silence fell.

"Where is Elia?" Tate asked hoarsely. "Where is my daughter?" He hit the activation button, and the capsule opened with gentle whirrs. The sides folded down and displayed a tiny body.

Daughter?

Terosh had a hard time processing the word. He couldn't take his eyes off the baby. She looked perfect.

Tate sank to his knees and touched the small face. Despite his frozen expression, Terosh could see the agony rolling off his brother.

"I will arrange burial details," Kezem offered.

"No, I will," Terosh said. "Captain, would you see Lord Kezem out?"

Tate needed some time alone, and Terosh determined to let him have that time.

Chapter 4:
New Masters, New Trial

Idela (January) 7, 1538
Six days after the formation of the RT Alliance
Asrien Sea, Below Dark Man's Bluff
Wake! Wake! Wake!

Feeling the command inside his head, Dr. Atien Belcross blinked against the stinging salt water. Panic gripped him then vanished. Sleeping in fitful spurts over the last few days had conditioned him enough that being completely submerged didn't disturb him. A dozen clams floated in the water, struggling against some unseen current.

Eat.

A sharp pain pierced his head as his left arm rose of its own accord. Belcross fought for control until the pain grew so intense he almost passed out. As soon as he stopped fighting, the pain eased. His chest rose and fell with remembered reflex. He formed a fist, and one of the clams shuddered. He squeezed hard enough that his palm ached, then squeezed some more until the shell shattered, sending fragments in all directions. Belcross opened his hand. The naked clam writhed, stretching itself in one direction and then the other before collapsing into a shivering mass of gray flesh.

A thought brought the clam closer, and Belcross opened his mouth to receive the slimy morsel. The clam tasted of the saltwater flowing into his mouth, and he immediately wanted to spit it out. His jaw closed tightly, and soon, the clam crawled down his throat. Belcross shuddered, and his stomach heaved rebelliously. Against his will, he consumed more clams, several jintals, and dozens of small sea snakes.

What am I? His eyes searched the clear blue waters around him.

The sun's rays shone down dimly, partially blocked by the cliff. Spotting a turtle watching him, Belcross hurled an invisible punch, creating a fist-sized hole in the turtle. Blood and flesh stained the sea before firalas and convies cleaned it up.

Remorse swept through Belcross. He stared down at his hands in wonder and horror.

How did I do that? It's not possible. What am I?

12

You are us. We are Dalonos, and now that you are us, the impossible is possible.

Dark Ones.

He found the title fitting. Fear and excitement made his heart pump pointlessly faster, while guilt and anger battled in his mind. He regretted killing so carelessly and hated his new masters.

***

Lanolin (February) 14, 1538
Forty-three days after the formation of the RT Alliance
Ranger Compound, Riden Mountains

Reia Antellio's steps slowed as she approached Master Niklos McGreven and Master Kale Corida. They stood in the center of the Crossroads Chamber facing each other as if their discussion would soon morph into a banistick contest. Guessing their conversation concerned her, Reia halted a respectful distance away. She didn't want to eavesdrop but couldn't help it. The acoustics carried sound effortlessly.

"She's not even a guardian, Niklos," Master Corida stated. "This is important!"

"She's one of the best healer apprentices, and Lucas is right, she'll blend in with the Kireshana derringers," Master Niklos responded with crossed arms and a stubborn expression. "Few know these mountains better than her."

Kireshana? That starts in Rammon.

Reia had not seen a city for years, though many considered her well-traveled. Feeling dazed, she thought back over the hundreds of trips through the Riden Mountains, starting with the level-one apprentice trial. Her team had included her sister—Kiata—and Todd Wellum, who volunteered to guide her. Reia recalled scouring the mountainside for three weeks collecting corlia, mintas, wuzle roots, alipo leaves, and crela dust. She enjoyed the experience so much that she volunteered for more quests to gather healing substances.

Kiata could sit in a cave and talk combat techniques with Todd, but Reia preferred the open air and sounds of nature. She loved the sweet morning call of colana birds and the faint, sharp scent of mintas sprigs. The happy thoughts fled as Master Corida's jaw flexed.

"That's only part of the journey and you know it," Master Corida argued.

"You asked for my recommendation and I agree with Lucas," Master Niklos said.

"So I did. Well, we need somebody. James won't heal in time." Running a hand through his thick brown hair, Master Corida grunted.

"What happened?" Reia inquired.

"Reia!" Master Niklos greeted, smiling at her warmly. "You're early. I told Calvin to tell you not to rush."

"He did, Master." Reia bowed politely.

"I thought for sure you'd at least visit your sister and her new

13

husband." Master Niklos's eyes sparkled.

"Husband?" Surprise and irritation warred within Reia. She knew who her sister had married, but it still shocked her.

Why didn't they wait for me? I've only been gone a month!

"Love cannot wait, my dear," Master Niklos said, chuckling at her expression. "Oh, they tried. Todd asked her soon after you left, and she made him wait two weeks for the ceremony. Nearly drove the man mad. I encouraged them to get on with it because they were both miserable. Kiata was beating the stuffing out of the practice dummies, and Todd—"

"Was about to burst with anxiety," Todd Wellum finished from behind Reia.

Whirling, Reia shot a critical gaze at her new brother-in-law. He wore a contrite expression.

Kiata's brilliant, silver-blue eyes begged for forgiveness.

Anger dissipating, Reia threw her arms around the pair. The embrace was slightly awkward. Not to be outdone, Todd and Kiata hugged her back fiercely.

What will I give them for a wedding gift?

"We'll finish this conversation later, Niklos," Master Corida said. "Let's leave them to their reunion."

"That's not necessary, Master Corida." Kiata pulled out of the embrace and nodded to the two masters. "We were on our way to the evening meal and heard about Reia's return. We can catch up later." With that, Kiata tugged Todd back the way they had come.

Reia watched them leave then focused on the masters. Uncertain of what to say, she folded her hands and barely resisted the urge to stir the dust at her feet.

Master Corida stared into empty space, and Master Niklos brushed dust from his banistick.

"What happened to Ranger Celdin?" Reia finally asked.

"James was trying to get a tretling out of a canyon when the korver pack that had trapped the creature returned," explained Master Niklos. "He beat them back, but one of the beasts got its mouth around his lower left leg. Broke it in two places."

"Can I see it?" Reia blushed. "I mean, is Ranger Celdin okay?"

"Yes, to both questions but later to the first." Master Niklos grinned, cleared his throat, and looked at Master Corida.

"Prince Terosh Minstel will begin the Kireshana in a month. We'd like you to shadow him." Master Corida's body language betrayed doubts, but he added, "There will be several others watching over him during specific parts of the Kireshana. He will also be traveling with a squad of Royal Guards, but he should still have a guardian."

"Why me?" Reia wondered.

"You've traveled the Riden Mountains extensively, and you know the healing arts. That is important for any journey, especially this one since the prince is a tempting target," Master Niklos explained. "The Ashatans have agreed to make this your level-seven trial."

Reia's breath caught.

I've been level-six for only a few hours!

"Thank you, masters. I am honored you think I'm ready."

"Do you doubt yourself?" Master Corida asked sharply.

Reia considered saying something to convince them she could handle the task. However, when she met her master's cool gray eyes she settled on honesty.

"I do not doubt my skills, but my lack of experience makes me cautious," she said.

"That is why you are ready," said Master Niklos.

Chapter 5:
A New Maledek

Lanolin (February) 15, 1538
Forty-four days after the formation of the RT Alliance
Asrien Sea, Below Dark Man's Bluff
Go to Idonia.

Dalonos stirred. His eyes met only darkness. As the anotechs healed him over the last few weeks, they had steadily drawn his body away from the surface. For a while he'd tried to cling to his former identity as Dr. Atien Belcross, but they insisted he become Dalonos.

Famished as usual, he closed his eyes and reached out with his new senses. Pinpoints of sensation alerted him to the nearby sea creatures. The anotechs could shuttle nutrients through his skin, but eating remained the most efficient way to gain sustenance. Usually, they let him play with the food, but today, a dozen jintals lined up to be eaten. The first time Dalonos had consumed jintals they had ripped his throat raw, but since then, they had become his favorite food. The painful scrape of their writhing spines was a fair trade for the delicious, spicy juices they contained.

After the meal, he tested his limbs, expecting them to be stiff with disuse. To his surprise, his limbs responded with supple grace he had never possessed before. Swimming with all his might, he shot toward the surface, scattering a school of multicolored fish.

Not so fast! The pressure change could break you.

He slowed then stopped altogether.

Don't you have a way to counter pressure changes?

It was half-inquiry and half-taunt. The scientist in him loved discovering new powers, but resentment remained over how little he controlled his own life. He brooded while waiting for the anotechs to slowly raise him safely to the surface.

Breaking the water's surface and breathing air again was the second most painful experience he'd ever had—the first being the initial acclimation to water. He had mercifully passed out the first time, but this time, his body was better equipped to handle pain. Millions of cells changed to handle the new environment. Dalonos suffocated and came to life again. Violent coughs jerked his body. Gritty sand pressed against him as cold waves crashed over him.

Clothes. You need clothes. We needed the others for repairs.

He finished coughing and frowned.

How did I forget that?

We deleted the memory, as we did with other superfluous thoughts.

The answer chilled him. Dalonos used the surge of burning energy that came with the anger to scramble up the imposing cliff face. Part of him relished each pain the rocks dealt him as he climbed. The cuts healed almost as soon as they formed.

This isn't natural.

This is better. Now get to the top. We have brought you an Azhel priest.

"Why?" Dalonos asked, earning a stabbing sensation in his head. Tiny lights danced behind his closed eyes as he endured the pain. When it receded, he finished climbing the cliff.

Focus! You need clothes.

Dalonos giggled, then sobbed.

"I don't even know—" He cut himself off and suddenly knew what they expected of him. His breath rushed out in a whoosh that ended in a curse.

You can't be serious.

A girl appeared before him.

"This is part of your training."

Dalonos shook his head, trying to make the vision go away, and blushed deeply.

"Your modesty is wasted on me, but it is preserved nonetheless."

Her statement drew his gaze downward where he noticed a skirt composed of seaweed, sand, shells, and other debris. Its slight weight seemed disproportionate to the materials.

"It is not a fashion fit for the public," the girl noted, ***"but it should suffice to let you concentrate on important matters."***

"Who are you?" he croaked.

The girl's skin shimmered with brilliant blue-white light, causing Dalonos to blink.

"I wear the form of the Maker's Daughter, but I do not exist here and now." To prove it, the girl collapsed into a pile of pale dust that swirled in the breeze yet remained intact. Then, just as quickly, the girl reformed from the feet up. ***"If you asked the right questions, you would know everything. I am your guide to this new life. Call me Jalna."*** The girl using the identity of the Maker's Daughter turned and ran a few steps, pausing to beckon him forward.

Speech eluded him. His legs carried him onward despite his desire to disobey.

"Stop resisting. It is tiresome."

"This is madness. I'm a scientist! I study life!"

"You were a scientist. You are us now. Your heart is capable of the deed."

His legs carried him toward the victim who struggled against unresponsive legs. Dalonos imagined his expression mirrored that worn by the priest whose eyes pleaded for his life. He thought about leaping from the cliff to avoid his fate, but suddenly, there was a shift within his mind.

"Kill him."

The girl vanished.

The pain disappeared.

A wave of strength cleared away every doubt.

Dalonos needed clothes to enter Idonia and speak with the governor. The priest's robes would open many doors. Leaving the man bound near the Ash Plains would be cruel. Killing him solved both problems. Dalonos slowly approached the man. A dozen ways to kill him sprang to mind, but he rejected most as too messy.

Break his neck. Strangle him. Suffocate him.

His hands twitched, agreeing with the suggestions.

The priest whimpered. Dalonos sensed the anotechs making breathing such a chore that the man could concentrate on nothing else.

Can you stop his heart?

We can, but you must do this deed to earn our aid.

The unseen hands holding the priest suddenly released him. The man sank to his knees and gulped in air.

Dalonos walked calmly over to the man, wrapped both hands around his neck, and squeezed until the life left his eyes.

The trip into Idonia was uneventful. Once he engaged the hov's autopilot, Dalonos concentrated on which arguments to raise with the governor. Getting to the Governor General's Estate was simple enough, but getting an appointment proved much harder. Dalonos had to practically strangle the servant to get him to deliver the message.

Finally, the servant ushered him into a private office.

"You look good for someone dead more than a month, Dr. Belcross," Lord Kezem commented. The flash in his eyes, said he wanted to kill him for not delivering the baby as promised. "You'll be happy to know that an ambitious Tarpon youth completed your task."

The business with Deanna and her daughter seemed a distant memory. Dalonos couldn't be bothered with such trivialities now.

"I am Belcross no more. You don't trust me, and I don't trust you. But we can help each other."

"What shall I call you? And if there's no trust, why should I help you or accept your aid?"

"Call me Dalonos. Let me become that which you pretend to be. Let me become Maledek." Dalonos deepened his voice.

Lord Kezem's expression indicated surprise.

The anotechs flooded Dalonos with the knowledge of an unspoken question and an appropriate answer.

"I know you are Maledek because your mother, Lady Mavis, suggested you create a villain to distract the Royal House. It is working, but slowly. I can help."

"Why do you wish to become Maledek?" Kezem asked.

"The Dark Ones wish it," Dalonos replied. "Let Maledek create chaos. Then rise as a hero to rescue the people."

"I see how this benefits me, but how does this help you? An ally with nothing to gain is dangerous." Kezem frowned and his hands moved toward his weapons.

"Trouble comes. The Galactic Alliance of Populated Planets is expanding. This is our home. We will defend her. Reshner must have a strong leader soon. You must be king if you wish to save the planet from GAPP slavery."

After a long stare, Lord Kezem nodded that Dalonos's proposal made sense.

"So be it."

Chapter 6:
The Prince's Plans and the Assassin

Lanolin (February) 28, 1538
Fifty-seven days after the formation of the RT Alliance
Rammon, Capital of Reshner

Across the street and one floor above the level where Prince Taytron secretly met his spy, Kolknir carefully lined up the shot. It would have been easy to say the shadows caused him to hit the wrong target. He nursed the fantasy, letting the crosshairs rest between Prince Taytron's eyes. Only professional pride stilled his trigger finger.

"Maledek will rule."

Kolknir dared not utter Lord Kezem's name aloud. He would accept control of the armed forces once Kezem took his rightful place as king.

Lord Kezem's mother, Lady Mavis Altran, Kolknir's true employer had vowed to destroy House Minstel, but the Crown Prince's untimely death would not bring her plans to fruition. He found it amusing that he knew so much about the plots and subplots spinning about the princes and the palace.

Does Lord Kezem know of the Lady's plans? He knows more than the Ranger High Council that's for sure. The Lady has them dancing to her tune. Fools, all of them, except perhaps Lucas Telon.

Putting the silenced serlak rifle aside, Kolknir took out his night vision goggles and flipped a switch that let him see through the building. He activated the electronic bugs that would let him hear Prince Taytron's conversation with the spy.

"All is ready, my Prince," said the spy. "Your brother's journey should be swift and uneventful."

"Do not let him repeat my mistake." The prince's order sounded heavy with grief.

"Yes, my Prince. It will be done."

"Riden walk with you," Prince Taytron murmured.

A minute later, Kolknir spotted the prince's spy exiting the apartment building's back door. Kolknir cursed silently, even as he saluted the kid for not being easy to kill. Soon, Kolknir had his rifle strapped to his back. Swinging his legs over the windowsill, he slid down a pipe three floors to the ground, landing near a storm drain access point.

Popping the hatch, Kolknir leapt in and landed in ten centimeters of dirty water. He froze, waiting for the faint splash to settle. Then, he found the access hatch's control panel and keyed in a short sequence to temporarily seal the hatch.

The solution to the noise problem came to him quickly. After a few experimental sliding steps, he returned to the ladder and strapped his rifle case to a rung about chest height. The weapon would hinder him in these tight spaces, and he didn't want to lose it. Once the rifle was safe, Kolknir eased forward so his movements displaced water without splashing. At first glance the stone walls seemed devoid of character, but Kolknir spotted faint marks that helped him follow his target.

Glow panels every few meters provided enough light to avoid colliding with the walls. The storm drain dipped and turned, keeping the water flowing throughout the city. Control panels every few blocks allowed water to be funneled wherever one needed it.

Kolknir considered flushing his victim into a holding tank where he could finish the job, but he dismissed the idea because it would alert Water Management to his presence.

When his left boot brushed something soft yet unyielding, Kolknir threw himself into a forward roll. Gravel dug into his hands as cold water drenched him. Releasing his throwing daggers from the forearm sheaths, Kolknir whirled. The assailant hesitated, allowing Kolknir to step close.

A slash with his left dagger grazed the assailant's neck but a knee to Kolknir's stomach evened the score. He leapt back and regarded the other man. The soldier's body lay between them, but Kolknir doubted they served the same master.

Two kill orders? Not possible.

As Kolknir concluded the assailant was an enemy, the man attacked. Ducking and dodging, Kolknir let the man spend energy on wild swings. The cramped storm drain limited the assailant's movements, yet his strikes held considerable power. A hand came at Kolknir's neck. He raised an arm to block and leaned back, throwing himself off balance. His gamble worked.

Both daggers flew true.

The first lodged in the assailant's right hand and the second slid into the soft flesh of his throat.

***

Lanolin (February) 28, 1538
Same day
Maledek's Private Retreat, City of Idonia

"The assassin has returned, my Lord," reported the servant.

"Send him in," Lord Kezem Altran ordered. He rose and snatched the Maledek mask off the corner of his desk. Donning the mask and turning to face the back wall, which displayed a stunning view of the misty Ash Mountains, Kezem clasped his hands behind his back and waited. Despite allowing Belcross to play Maledek, Kezem found the persona useful when dealing with people he couldn't meet as Governor of Idonia.

"As you wish," said the servant, backing out quickly.

A heartbeat passed, then two. Kezem silently counted the ten seconds it would take the assassin to cross from the doorway to the desk.

"It is done, my Lord," said the assassin.

"Your payment and new orders are on the desk."

"Thank you, but you should know there was another assassin on the same job. I don't know whom he served, but he is dead."

"Interesting. You may go."

Once the Ranger left, Kezem waited for his mother to comment. He wanted to hear her thoughts on the second assassin. Despite his best efforts, she always found a way to install new spy equipment into his private lairs. Kezem hoped his mother's spies would confirm the assassin had done a thorough job. Finding reliable help was becoming more difficult every year.

"I cannot tell if you are brave or mad," Lady Mavis Altran spoke through the wall-mounted holoprojector. "In any case, you should never turn your back on Kolknir … or me."

Facing her, Kezem smiled.

"I am far too useful to have cause to worry, Mother."

"Pray it stays so, my dear."

"What can you tell me about this assassin and news of a second one?"

His mother's hologram shrugged.

"Kolknir is technically still a Ranger, but his training methods effectively ended his career. The Council stripped him of his rank to appease those claiming his methods were cruel. He was a mercenary until I changed his fortunes. I believe the second assassin was an RT Alliance man. You should keep an eye on them. Your pet project could quickly get out of control. Regardless, you should consider the proposal I'm sending over." With that last bit of advice, she disappeared.

Kezem weighed her words.

She is no longer useful.

A thrill climbed up his spine. Plans laid long ago would finally be enacted. Feeling the gravity of the moment, Kezem reached into a breast pocket, pulled out his comm, and typed in the kill order.

As he finished, his comm chimed to let him know a message waited for his attention. Although tempted to delete his mother's proposal without looking at it, common sense prevailed.

"What last plan does her devious mind hold?"

Chapter 7:
Kireshana Intrigue

Jira (March) 1, 1538
Sixty days after the formation of the RT Alliance
Streets of Rammon, Capital of Reshner

Lucas Telon seethed as he settled into position overlooking the crowded streets. While he had a quiet moment, he pondered everything that had brought him here. His ego smarted from the inability to bond with the anotechs and Reia's refusal to marry him. Recalling her expression, he tried to decipher her uncertainty and fear.

"I cannot marry you, Lucas." Her gorgeous green eyes had shimmered with tears as she spoke.

"You can and you will." He'd tried to draw her into a comforting embrace. He would have kissed her inviting lips if he hadn't needed to talk sense into her. *"You're simply scared, that's all. I can fix that."*

The small, fearful step Reia had taken backward might as well have been a canyon.

"I'm scared how fixable you think people are!"

"Why does she fear me?" Lucas whispered to the memory. "Am I not perfect? I love her."

His lean, yet muscled body had no flaws, save for a few battle scars. His face had an open, pleasant cast to it, whenever it suited him. Even his close-cropped blond hair stayed precisely in place, lending him an air of boyish innocence. He'd spent a decade mastering his body language. Every woman—except the one that counted—enjoyed gazing upon him. Reia had accepted his banistick, making a promise she had broken by returning the weapon with apologies.

Lucas searched the crowd for his beloved. Failing to see her, he pulled a Target Tracker-189 from his caydronan sack. Most Rangers carried herbs, but Lucas preferred keeping medkits, trackers, and weapons handy. If the Rangers didn't adapt soon, they would be ill-equipped to face new enemies. Irritation made him flush. The Rangers' stupidity had made Maledek's offer attractive.

Despite initial reluctance, Lucas decided this mission was worthy of his time. It allowed him to safeguard Reia Antellio and fulfill his Alliance obligations. He might even

impress Kolknir. In addition to being a legendary Ranger, the man had trained under the

infamous Gardanian Shadow Guard.

The TT-189 found Reia waiting two blocks up and one block over, close to where the royals gathered. Lucas grinned. Once Maledek ruled, he would win Reia's love. He felt guilty for spying on her, but she would forgive him once he saved her life a few times. Knowing his speech to the Ashatan Council had placed her in danger compounded the guilt. The Kireshana had always been dangerous, but Maledek's interest in the journey increased the danger exponentially.

After memorizing Reia's position, Lucas tucked the TT-189 away and jogged over several rooftops to see the royal procession. Alert for trouble, he stopped and scanned the crowds and nearby windows.

A glint of light caught his attention.

Lucas frowned. The RT Alliance liaison hadn't mentioned an assassination attempt today, and Maledek had been clear about wanting the royal family alive for now.

Measuring the distance from his current position to the sniper's position across the street and one floor down, Lucas quickly backpedaled. A full-out sprint brought him to the roof's edge. Launching himself forward, Lucas drew his banistick and aimed for the distant window. The rifle swung toward him. Lucas swatted the gun aside with his banistick and landed on the man with crushing force.

Rolling the unconscious man into the light, Lucas looked upon the face of his enemy. He didn't recognize the young man. A search through his pockets revealed a silver token embossed with the letters RT. Either somebody was setting up the RT Alliance to be blamed for King Teorn's assassination or Lucas's handlers didn't think him important enough to include in their real plans.

The recent alliance between the Restler and Tarpon families stirred up the political intrigue around the palace. As they grew bolder, Maledek insisted Lucas work closer with them. If controlled, they could be useful allies, but their shortsightedness could make them a nuisance. Whether real enemy or pretend, the boy would have to die.

"Sorry, kid," Lucas said, "but you knew the risks."

Out of respect for the man's efforts and because he had better things to do, Lucas wasted no time in slitting the kid's throat.

***

Jira (March) 1, 1538
Same day
Streets of Rammon, Capital of Reshner

As the procession moved through the Market District, West Quarter, and out the West Gate, Prince Terosh Minstel's stomach tightened.

The streets brimmed with people in colorful finery. Every window and balcony blossomed with figures craning their necks and holding out children for the chance to see the royal family. A few citizens climbed lampposts and perched on rooftops to improve their sightlines. Even the poorest of the poor had donned presentable outfits and come out to see the royals. Terosh could not recall the last time his entire family had been out in public, and he did not envy the Royal Guards, Melian Maidens, and Palace Security guards today.

Wish I could take a serlak rifle.

Though his father considered serlak weapons low-class, Terosh would have felt better with a rifle. The kerlak pistol his father had given him could pack a punch, but its whiny noise hardly gave one the same sense of power as the crack of a serlak weapon.

Terosh could almost hear Master Og's impatient voice saying, *To lose focus invites danger.*

Cheers crashed down upon Terosh in deafening waves. The smell of thousands of people pressed into one place combined with the sun's oppressive heat. Fighting off nausea, Terosh sucked in a breath and wished for clouds. Even an acid storm would be preferable to the sun's fierce attention. Straightening his shoulders, Terosh smiled and waved at the roaring crowd. Faces blurred as the guards hustled the royal entourage down the street toward the Kireshana's starting point.

His mother would have loved this. Terosh momentarily mourned her. Historians—and probably Tate—would remember Queen Kila as a demanding woman. They had not witnessed the long hours spent perusing plans and forging alliances. Terosh knew of her softer side. No doubt she had loved Taytron immensely as well, but she had also expected more from him. Their mother had usually been too busy to attend the nine-day Festival of Future Fighters, which preceded the Kireshana, but she'd always made time for the parade and official send off.

Pride surged through Terosh at finally being among the batch of Royal Guards and Melian Maidens candidates. The Kireshana had always had special meaning for his family. Before the Kireshana, the Governors Council and Senate outranked a prince or princess, but afterward, he or she answered only to the king and queen.

According to Master Og, Prince Remi had taken the first such journey in 1023, though it didn't pick up the name until years later when Prince Davel described his uncle's "renewing fire journey." Since that time, very few royals have skipped the Kireshana.

Why did Aunt Mavis skip her Kireshana? I wouldn't miss it for anything.

Though technically boys became men at age sixteen, Terosh considered this the true test. The night his father had agreed to let him join the Kireshana, he'd committed the route maps to memory.

Start going northwest from Rammon. Cross the Balor Plains. Go northwest still. Enter and pass through the Calsol Forest. Rent horses and cross the Riden Flats to Huz Mon. Pay the salt mine masters their horse ransom. Face west to the Riden Mountains and go there for a zalok scale. After the mountains, travel west again to Resh, then south to Fort Riden. Swing south and bear slightly east again, back toward the Riden Mountains. Cross the mountains again at their southernmost point, Mount Palean. Move east through the Kesler Plains, Lotrian Fields, Kevil Plains, and back to Rammon.

Terosh estimated his trip would take half a year, nowhere near Tate's time, but then again, Tate had traveled much of the Kireshana by hov. Most derringers settled for riding horses because they couldn't afford hovs, but adventure, not lack of money, held Terosh back. He thought of the amenities in Tate's silver hov.

Cheater.

He cast a glance left at his brother. A small part of Terosh admitted that skimming a meter above the ground through much of the Riden Flats would be fun. He could retract the roof and feel the wind move around him.

Tate's bemused smile told Terosh he read the thoughts and didn't care.

Suddenly realizing Tate had stopped, Terosh halted and adjusted the new kerlinblade at his waist to cover the jerky motion. The black-handled weapon, another surprise gift from Father, was new enough to be unfamiliar. Terosh fingered the three control bars near the bottom of the handle, caressing each button and playing with the sliding panel that warded against accidents.

Once again Master Og's history lessons proved useful as Terosh reflected on kerlinblades. Princess Ariella Minstel had uttered the word, which means "fire light sword," upon seeing the prototype about two hundred years ago. Sadly, Ariella had met a brutal end by a kerlinblade.

"You're going to wear that out before you start," Tate commented.

Terosh didn't reply but quit fiddling with the kerlinblade.

"Steady, Terry," Taytron muttered, grasping Terosh's arm. "This is your time. With luck, you'll be back within the month." Tate's grin said he knew the estimate was ridiculous. Hovs would need to be used liberally to finish that quickly. The smile didn't quite reach his eyes. He put on a good front but spent endless hours alone, mourning his wife and daughter.

Irritation at the nickname balanced the sadness of Dr. Koffrin's and Elia's murders. Terosh wondered what it would have been like to have them here with Tate. The thought made their loss even more painful.

Tate tugged him into a brief hug, stepped back, and bowed. As their eyes connected, Terosh saw the smoldering pain in his brother's eyes. The solemn moment passed when a shadow fell over them. Terosh glanced back as his father's arm landed heavily on his shoulders.

"The Kireshana awaits thee, Prince Terosh," boomed King Teorn. "Make thy king and people proud."

Terosh suppressed a cough as his father pounded his back.

"Yes, Father."

Teorn yanked Terosh around and rested both hands on his shoulders. "Prove thyself a man worthy of the Minstel name!"

Nodding, Terosh winced and willed himself to hold his father's gaze.

When his eyes slid over to his older brother, he saw Tate's blue-gray eyes roll at the continued usage of formal speech.

"I want to introduce you to someone." Teorn draped an arm across Terosh's shoulders again. Turning right, he bellowed, "Laocer!"

A lean, young soldier emerged from the crowd, saluted by placing his right fist over his heart, and stood at attention. The soldier's stance and small chin scar nicely complemented the determined glint in his dark brown eyes.

"Lieutenant Ectosh Laocer will command the Royal Guards accompanying you on the Kireshana," Teorn announced.

It took every ounce of restraint Colander and Sedir had instilled in Terosh for him to merely tighten his jaw.

I said no escort! I meant no escort!

"Thank you, Father," he said, fearing he might stamp his foot.

Teorn tightened his grip on Terosh's shoulders then released him.

"I know you're disappointed, but with that business about the Restlers and Tarpons forming an alliance, I'll not have you traveling alone. Riden only knows what trouble they'll dream up."

More trouble than usual?

Terosh's mind clicked through ways to ditch the blue-clad babysitters, but he figured he had no choice about initially taking them along. A wave of tiredness swept through him, but he pushed it back by focusing on the spice-laden scent of the festival. He nodded to Laocer and the other men separating from the crowd.

The crowd chanted various names with frantic urgency. Here and there amidst the sea of green and blue robes, Terosh spotted young and old, fine-robed and thread-bare, locked in embraces like everyone feared it might be the last hug given or received.

Guards had confined the crowd to an area behind a thick rope. A closer scan revealed hardly a dry eye among the civilians or derringers—another name for the candidates. A few Royal Guards and Melian Maidens wore proud expressions that told Terosh they had loved ones about to embark on the journey.

Suddenly, deep silence fell over the crowd, and Terosh knew the time to begin approached. He shook hands with, hugged, and finally bowed to his brother and father before moving to his starting position.

General Ezerd Mordian's voice rang out clear and strong.

"Gentlemen and ladies, this is your final task. You will complete the Kireshana and become Royal Guards and Melian Maidens with all the honor and duties thereof or you will fail. There is no in between. Fight hard and Riden will bless your journey." The general drew his sidearm and fired across the starting line.

Raising his voice with the six hundred and thirty-three other derringers, Terosh sprinted forward. As his legs settled into a rhythm, he pretended to be alone and pushed his body to run faster and faster, hoping speed would carry him away from his father's smothering presence.

***

Jira (March) 1, 1538
Same day
Restler-Tarpon Alliance Safe House, City of Rammon

From the shadows of the darkened apartment, Talyon Keldor tried to sort his mixed feelings as he watched the Kireshana start. The corner window he peered out of offered a fine view of the festivities. The Royal Guards were supposed to clear every apartment with a window facing the Balor Plains, but hefty bribes to the correct officials cleared the way for Taly's unobstructed view. If he had wanted to make a month's worth of kefs, he could have rented out the privilege of sharing the space.

Officially, he had no assignment. If his orders had been to assassinate the king, he might have succeeded. However, Merisia had been curious about the Alliance's interest in the Kireshana. She wished to know how Alliance affairs would pan out, but as the new Lady Restler, she could hardly investigate herself.

At this point, Taly had seen far more than he wanted yet not enough to understand. The sense of missing pieces gnawed at him. Yesterday, he had found Miscel's body next to another lifeless form in a storm drain below Rammon.

The discoveries would have prompted him to return to Merisia in the city of Meritab, but she had insisted he wait. Taly agreed that leaving after the festivities would be less suspicious. The apartment held little more than a sleeping pallet, a washroom, and a hotplate. A nest of blankets in one corner still held a ragdoll abandoned when the soldiers had cleared the family out for the day. The sight magnified the emptiness.

Shaking off the gloomy feeling, Taly considered the stranger in the drain. The fine garments told him the man was a palace district worker, but a quick search had revealed nothing else significant. Miscel had been the other victim. Taly winced, remembering the clammy bodies he had hauled to a garbage site to decompose peacefully. As he pondered the deaths, he thought he sensed eyes upon him and resisted the urge to shrink further into the shadows.

Likely, Taly was the only one—besides the killer—who knew Miscel was dead, so the task of telling the man's wife fell to him.

Maybe I'll just tell Merisia.

A woman would probably do a better job of delivering such news anyway. Taly considered how little he knew. He didn't even know Miscel's last name. He only knew the few facts discreet questions had revealed. Miscel was an RT Alliance man and a friend of Merisia's brother, Alden.

After the Kireshana started, Taly checked on the two other RT Alliance people he knew, Lara Vireth and Kovit. Taly found Lara at her post preparing to follow the derringers. She barely glanced at him before leaving. Though he hardly knew the woman, she scared him.

Taly went to Kovit's post and found his third body in two days.

Chapter 8:
So Close, So Far

Jira (March) 13, 1538
Twelve days into Prince Terosh's Kireshana journey
Kireshana Path, Calsol Forest

Crouched behind the thick trunk of a cal tree, Lucas Telon held the kamad dagger with his right hand then flipped it to his left hand and back again. Despite the lengthy blade, the dagger had nice balance. If the weapon were slightly longer it might be considered a short sword. The black handle fit easily in one hand. The blade appeared to have clean curves up to the pointed tip, but Lucas had seen the damage the teeth could do. The microscopic, inverted teeth would slip smoothly into flesh but chew and claw their way back out. The kamad dagger was still new enough to make Lucas think about how to handle the weapon without losing a finger.

He sighed at the tediousness of his next task. It was as boring as the variety of trees around him: cal trees and more cal trees. Occasionally, an exciting mutation would cause a cal tree to have an overabundance of pale green leaves instead of the usual deep green ones.

Lucas's orders from Lady Mavis Altran were to cause chaos along the Kireshana trail in case she decided Prince Terosh should be captured or eliminated. If there needed to be an *incident* involving the prince, the Lady preferred it be one of many rather than the only thing to occupy potential investigators.

King Teorn had forbidden the Coridian Assassins from participating this year, but since mavericks abounded in their ranks, Lucas figured posing as one would be safe enough. He refocused as a lone young man approached. After waiting for the man to pass, Lucas slipped up behind him and slit his throat before the victim even knew he was there. Lucas shook his head with disappointment and cleaned the dagger.

What happened to standards against weaklings and fools?

A half-hour later, Lucas found another ideal location to wait for a victim, but it took almost a full hour before two young women came his way. When he stepped out of his hiding place, they froze. He flashed a quick, tentative smile to put them at ease, but it only worked on one young lady.

The other woman locked eyes with him and read the deadly intent there. She pulled her kerlak pistol and shot at him. The beam went wide by a half-meter, but as a sign of respect, Lucas killed her before practicing with his new kamad dagger.

Her friend experienced the full attention of the dagger's many sharp teeth. Screams filled Lucas's ears as the woman died.

As he admired his work, he marveled at how easily a smile could disarm people. His charms held more sway over women than men, but Lucas prided himself on being able to get what he needed from people. The soft crunch of swiftly approaching footsteps crashed through his warm sense of self-satisfaction. Rushing to his pack, Lucas shoved the kamad dagger out of sight before drawing his banistick and kerlak pistol to meet the approaching threat. As an afterthought, he fired several times into each body.

It's a shame to destroy such fine work.

He waited tensely to discover the footsteps' owner.

Reia appeared at the clearing's edge, bracing against a tree trunk to keep from entering the open space. Her right hand clutched her banistick and her expression mixed curiosity, caution, and dread.

"Why are you here?" Lucas demanded.

"I could ask you the same," Reia replied.

"I killed them." Lucas tried to keep his voice casual.

The words clearly unsettled Reia, but her grip on the tree kept her upright. She tried to respond but barely managed a strangled noise of acknowledgement.

"Some heartless beast carved them up and left them to die," Lucas explained. "I ended their pain."

"How did you know they would die?" Reia's soft question seemed reasonable, but her eyes remained condemning.

"We're not all healers. We do what we can," said Lucas, surprised by the depths of his bitterness.

Before Reia could respond, Prince Terosh and his cadre of guards crashed onto the scene like wild korvers. Reia fled before they could really see her.

Lucas longed to pursue her, but instead, he braced to face a second round of questions.

"My Prince, this is not a good idea," hissed one of the prince's guardians.

"Why not?" the prince stopped to regard his soldier.

"He just killed those two women," argued the dark-skinned soldier.

"We don't know that for sure," returned the prince. "Besides, if it is true, then we have even more reason to question him."

As the prince and his guards approached, instinct told Lucas to flee. He might have been able to fulfill his Alliance orders if Royal Guards didn't surround the prince. Lucas wished his orders had been to kill. Capturing always involved much more work. He might need the RT Alliance team waiting for him in Huz Mon.

So close, yet so far.

The expected pleasantries never happened.

The prince swaggered forward and demanded answers.

"Who are you? What happened here? Where is the other Ranger?"

Lucas wanted to stuff a kerlak beam through the boy's arrogant face. With great effort, he kept his hands still to avoid a misunderstanding with the Royal Guards. They tended to shoot first when defending one of their precious royals. Not that Lucas blamed them. The royal family's history was as turbulent as a windstorm.

"Ranger Lucas Telon at your service, Highness," Lucas said, realizing he hadn't answered the questions. He bowed as custom demanded. "I came upon these unfortunates and eased them into eternity. I'm not sure where the other Ranger went. She and I have different missions."

"What about the screams?" asked the prince.

"One screamed as she saw me. You heard a cry for mercy."

"I heard a cry of pain," the prince retorted. His eyes searched Lucas for truth.

"Are the two different? Could you ignore such a cry?"

"No, I suppose not." The prince sounded disappointed to have his suspicions fade. He fell silent for a blessed moment, but his next question almost made Lucas flinch. "What is your mission?"

"To protect the derringers."

"You're a Kireshana guardian?" The prince's doubts were evident. When Lucas didn't confirm or deny it, the prince tried a different question. "How do you know your mission differed from the other Ranger?"

"Pardon?" Lucas asked.

"You said your missions differed. How do you know?"

"She is a healer," Lucas explained. "I doubt the Ashatan Council would send someone like her on a mission such as mine. As you can see, the Kireshana has many dangers." He gestured to the bodies.

"Yes, so many predators," said the prince.

***

Jira (March) 13, 1538
Same day
Kireshana Path, Calsol Forest

As Ranger Reia Antellio laid her head down for the night, she reflected on the journey thus far. It had started out with a hundred last-minute Kireshana preparations. She recalled the dark green Melian Maiden robes, grateful to have had the opportunity to change to normal clothes once darkness fell that first day. The comfortable pants, plain shirt, and trusty travel cloak she now wore better suited her. The waterproof, acid resistant, light cloak with color that ranged between blue and black, depending on shadows, was probably her most prized possession next to her banistick and caydronan sack.

Scenes of the last week and a half charged through her head, but it was better than thinking about her recent encounter with Lucas. The memory of the farewell with Kiata and Todd tugged at Reia. She had tried to turn it into a happy occasion by giving them a belated wedding gift. Gathering the herbs and flowers had been a labor of love, but the glass frame Reia had used to press them into a work of art nearly decimated her small stash of savings. The worry that had crossed her sister's normally inscrutable features and her breath-taking hug made Reia think.

Master Niklos had spent several weeks briefing her on the Kireshana mission, and Master Corida and Master Telon had added bits of wisdom. The briefings with Lucas had been awkward. She still had a hard time wrapping her mind around his new rank. Her inability to predict every danger annoyed her.

She tried to balance the annoyance with amusement, recalling the young woman she'd spent the first hour or so jogging alongside. The pretty, dark-skinned woman had talked nonstop about Prince Terosh's fine blue eyes.

Great, now I've got to see his eyes.

As the image of the child dressed in Melian Maiden robes came to mind, Reia wondered how the girl fared thus far. She hoped the child was still alive, but there was no guarantee. The somber thought brought her back to today's encounter with Lucas. She had enjoyed the peaceful morning until a woman's scream shattered the serenity. A second pained cry followed, just barely preceding a third and final scream. Reia had sailed to the scene in time to hear the high-pitched whine of kerlak pistol blasts.

The confrontation with Lucas had been short but intense. Something bothered her, but she couldn't quite identify it for a long time. His last statement was telling.

"He's jealous," she concluded at last. Reia had long wondered why Lucas fixated on her. At first, she found his attention flattering, but she quickly realized he cared only for himself. Reia had seen love draw Kiata and Todd closer together, but the thought of becoming like Lucas made her uneasy.

The scene replayed, and she tried recalling her impressions. Her first glimpse of Lucas standing between the bodies had been important, but she wasn't sure why.

The scene played yet again, and Reia focused on Lucas's expression. *He's surprised, defensive, and … guilty.*

Reia pondered where she'd come up with guilty. She studied the scene again. The tilt of Lucas's head had indicated excitement and challenge. His right shoulder dipped down and back. That was his tell. He prided himself on controlling his facial features, but Reia had endured enough of his attention to recognize the subtle gesture.

After another hour of tossing and turning, Reia resigned herself to not getting any sleep and entered a meditative state that sacrificed sleep for deep thinking.

What about the dead? The thought startled her. Reia assumed Lucas would care for the bodies he had created, but she felt guilty for not thinking of them sooner. Shaking off the restful state, Reia got to her feet and gathered materials for two small fires.

Within minutes both fires burned strongly in shallow, hand-dug pits. Staring into the flames, Reia thought about the two dead strangers. The effort seemed inadequate. She imagined how she would feel if the fires were for Kiata and Todd and real grief brought tears to her eyes.

As the tears fell, a song came to mind, so she sang softly.

> "Here we are once again
> Singing for the dead.
> Here we are once again
> Lamenting life lost.
> May this song carry
> The dead up to rest.
> May it be that when we fall
> Someone will sing over our graves.
> May it be that when we fall
> Someone will carry us on wings
> Made of sweet songs.
> Then life will go on."

She sang the song twice through, once for each life lost, before solemnly burying the flames.

Chapter 9:
Reckless Pace

Jira (March) 20, 1538-Jira (March) 21, 1538
Nineteen-twenty days into Prince Terosh's Kireshana journey
Kireshana Path, Western Edge of the Calsol Forest

You can't bring those women back.

Terosh tried to shake off the images, but they wouldn't leave him alone. Ahead, he saw open land beyond the endless cal trees. A line of silver hovs waited for them.

"Why are *those* here?" Terosh demanded.

"They offer a swift way across the Riden Flats, Highness," Lieutenant Ectosh Laocer replied.

"I can't take those!" Terosh protested. "Everyone else rides horses. I will, too."

"Your royal brother took this route, High—"

"Lose the honorifics. It's getting on my nerves." A lifetime had been quite enough.

Tate's choice was his own. I should be like everyone else.

Terosh sighed.

Yes, like everyone else with Royal Guards watching over him. I'll never prove myself if I don't escape.

"Yes, sir." Laocer's voice contained the crisp snap of a salute. "His Majesty the king thought it best if you started your trip through the Riden Mountains before the next acid storms."

"Before the next—" Terosh cut himself off to avoid an unsightly scene, like him throttling Laocer.

That's two months away! I'd need to crawl to take that long!

"We're going to Calsola and taking horses." Terosh infused his voice with command. "I like riding, and I want to see some of the land." Though not palace-bound, Terosh had visited little of Reshner. The Kireshana provided the first real chance—perhaps his only one—to truly walk among the people.

After sending the hovs away, the group covered the kilometers to

Calsola in silence. Terosh settled the account to rent horses and suppressed a laugh at the owner's expression at seeing close to a thousand kefs counted out. Since greed rolled off the man in waves, Terosh drew him aside and bought some tamitin powder at a hefty price while his men saddled the horses.

Soon, Terosh and his six escorts started across the Riden Flats. Having traveled the path many times, the horses knew how to avoid graveground. Terosh thought little about how they knew but trusted the horses' instincts for avoiding places where the ground would collapse. The pits formed could be anywhere from a few centimeters to several meters across.

The rushing wind thrilled Terosh almost as much as the sight of endless golden fields. He wanted to enjoy the sweet scent of clean air for as long as possible, and he couldn't bring himself to enact his plan just yet. So, he pressed the group on well into the night.

When they finally stopped, Terosh decided to keep the guards for another night. The soldiers fed and watered the horses while Terosh and Laocer started a fire and cooked a hot meal. As stacks of fluffy flatcakes appeared, Terosh opened a small jar of rielberry jam to share.

The Guards cheered at the sight of the treat and devoured the pleasant meal.

The evening went well until the soldiers arranged their bedrolls around Terosh, killing his sense of freedom. The day had been long, but he was too sore to sleep right away.

Dillain, the youngest guard, took first watch and, with a little prompting, sang a sad song in his rich tenor voice.

"Where'd you learn to sing?" Terosh asked.

"Chamberlain's Boys Choir," Dillain mumbled.

Two moons, Gemuln and Corid, shone down brightly enough to highlight Dillain's red cheeks. The third moon, Marishaz, denied the night her presence.

"Do you ever miss those days?" Terosh asked, before the other soldiers could tease Dillain.

"Nah." Dillain's expression contradicted his dismissive tone.

Terosh dropped the point, figuring he should let sleep catch him. He shifted on his bedroll and moaned.

"It'll be worse in the morning," Laocer promised.

Terosh answered with a grunt, rolled over, and bit back a curse as muscles he hardly knew existed announced their presence with pain.

Next morning, he awoke grumpier than a cawalla with a knotted tail. Too sore to feel guilty, Terosh barked orders at the men. He'd ridden horses through the palace gardens countless times, often racing Tate, but the horses bred for crossing the Riden Flats were hardly the well-mannered beasts from the royal stables. Halfway through mounting, the horse reared as a snake shot toward its front right leg. Terosh's shout disappeared beneath the clamor of his men trying to kill the creature. Finally, Laocer fired his serlak pistol twice into the snake's head.

Terosh leapt to his feet, more angry than hurt. His right ankle ached. Speaking softly to the skittish horse, he silently cursed the snake. Closer examination showed that the creature was a maritech viper, one of Reshner's deadliest snakes.

"Can we keep it?" Dillain asked.

"Why in Riden's name would we do that?" Terosh demanded.

"Good meat."

Terosh nodded curtly.

"You want it. You carry it."

Dillain sliced the snake's head off with a kerlinblade to seal the blood inside and draped the body across his shoulders.

Though they didn't press the horses as hard as the previous day, the Riden Flats flew past anyway. Terosh admired the beautiful seas of grain stretching in every direction. Wheat, krinton, corn, sanda, and barley grew side-by-side. Where one field ended, the next began. Occasionally, a huge field of flowers shattered the monotony of beige and brown. Deeply purple iras dominated, but red porlas, green neralas, orange and yellow copalas, and white sholcas held their own. Terosh had seen each flower and many more in the palace gardens but never in such wild openness. The wind shifted carrying the sweet, tangy scent of iras and the heady scent of porlas over his senses.

I could get used to this.

Terosh waved to a farmer who shouted for them to stop and rest.

If we stop for every farmer, we'll never get through.

"Perhaps we should stop a moment," Laocer suggested.

"We've lost ground already," Terosh said, pressing his horse forward at a quicker pace.

A nameless urgency drove him on.

By the time they halted for the evening, Terosh didn't care what Dillain cooked and was pleasantly surprised by the tender snake meat roasted over an open fire. Cold spring water and sliced appolas cooked in water seasoned with mintas sprigs completed the simple meal.

***

Jira (March) 20, 1538-Jira (March) 21, 1538
Same days and beyond
Kireshana Path, Western Edge of the Calsol Forest

Reia's heart nearly stopped when she saw the silver hovs speed away. Some Rangers used hovs, but she never expected to be close enough to feel their vibrations. Spotting the prince just ahead, she breathed normally again.

No one had considered the possibility of Prince Terosh taking hovs to the Riden Mountains. Most reports predicted he would take the harder road wherever possible. Reia silently thanked the scouts for being right thus far.

They'll probably take horses. What will I do?

Having no answer, Reia followed the prince's group. Though grateful nothing unusual had happened in the last week, she knew something could go wrong any time. She also felt someone watching her.

Coridian Assassin? Lucas?

It seemed like something he would do, and public announcements notwithstanding, Reia trusted Master Niklos's warning that Coridian Assassins would train during the Kireshana. She quietly repeated her master's advice for comfort.

"'Prove yourself competent, and they'll leave you alone.'"

Forced to wait while the prince dealt with the horse master, Reia pondered her new predicament. She lacked sufficient funds to rent a horse. She could always rent one now and pay the debt in the Salt Mines later, but that would still force her to abandon her charge for far too long. Even Master Niklos's calming techniques failed to subdue her restless energy. The collection of herbs in her caydronan sack would cover the debt in terms of worth, but they were worse than useless in the hands of untrained people. Too much cormea would paralyze a person instead of deadening pain. Too little astera would make Kemloth Fever worse.

Five minutes after the prince left, Reia stepped into the horse master's office. The outside hadn't been very impressive, and the inside looked like windstorm wreckage. Saddles, blankets, bridles, and bits hung haphazardly on hooks jutting from weather-beaten walls and lay about on every flat surface. A half-eaten appola rotted on a rickety wooden desk, adding a sickeningly sweet scent to the air.

Behind the desk, a fat man counted an impressive pile of kefs.

"Can I help you?" The horse master's voice quivered with excitement. He rose, swept the kefs out of sight into a metal box, and trundled out from behind the desk.

Reia took the man in as he approached.

Greedy, unscrupulous, dangerous.

"I hope so. How much would it cost to rent a horse?" Reia forced her lips into a tentative smile. Not knowing what to do with her hands, she gestured at the nearest bridle with her left hand and kept her right near her banistick.

"Too much. You don't look like you have a single kef to your name."

Reia assumed the man knew enough to associate her attire with the Rangers. The brown trousers and beige shirt fit her well, and her travel cloak gracefully draped her shoulders.

The man's eyes wandered her body.

My sister would probably punch you right about now.

Reia's smile brightened, and she was unaware how appealing the expression made her.

The man grinned and reached for her arm.

"But you look like a resourceful woman. We can discuss other means of payment if you wish."

Reacting instinctively, Reia wrenched her arm away, whirled, and fled.

Kiata would fight him.

"Kiata's not here!" Reia loved her older sister dearly but hated the constant comparisons. Despite growing up together, they had always walked their own paths. Kiata was a fighter, and Reia was a thinker. Some said that the distinctions proved they had different parents, but Reia had never much cared that they didn't share blood. They were sisters bound by fate and love.

At some point, you're going to have to be you, not Kiata.

Irritation both at herself and the horse master gave Reia a burst of energy that drove her over many kilometers. The caydronan sack bounced along at her side, falling into a gentle rhythm with her footfalls.

If you can climb the Riden Mountains with a few caydronan sacks, you can handle a little running.

She winced. The Riden Flats would be a lot of running. Trouble would surely find the prince before she found him. On horseback, he could cross the plains in about a week. Even anotech enhancement and excellent conditioning couldn't match that pace. She didn't know how anotechs worked, but she was grateful that they allowed her to keep a brutal pace for hours. Finally, Reia stopped by a small stream and set up a temporary camp. She ate some korver jerky and washed it down with cool water. Foregoing a fire, she relied on her travel cloak to preserve her body heat and settled down to sleep. Despite the illusion of peace, Reia kept her banistick and shootav close. Soon, the natural night symphony lulled her to sleep.

Reia spent the night captive to her dream. It wasn't the dream where she lay paralyzed in a cold, dark place or the one where she fought off korvers and bears. Nor was it the one where her sister was tied to a rough wooden pole and beaten. In this dream, Reia was a baby carried in her mother's arms.

The infant Reia screamed and thrashed, trying to warn her mother not to walk down that long hallway or open the door to join her father. Her mother paused to soothe her, whispering comforting words she couldn't understand. Everything felt real. Mother's cool hand and soft voice fought the fear as she continued down the hallway, passing the same four candlesticks they always passed. Finally, they reached the terrible room.

Father spoke but Reia heard only the cadence of his words.

Something cold touched her head, pressing painfully.

Mother screamed.

Something bright and hot flashed by Reia's face, burning her right cheek and chin.

Suddenly, she was falling.

Just as she hit the floor, she woke up.

Chilled, sweating, and grateful to be awake, Reia quickly packed her things and followed the prince's trail. The horses left regular markers, making her job easier.

As she ran, Reia kept sane by reviewing plants. She mentally combined them to make teas and healing pastes, which would cure anything from fever to poison to cuts and deeper wounds. She could have wrestled with the dream, but she had pondered it from every conceivable angle and didn't wish to dwell on it further. Nights controlled by the dreams were quite enough.

The second full day went much the same as the first, but this time, Reia concentrated on Master Ekris's stories.

To regulate her breathing, she sang "The Ballad of Ferrakin Maz," a song that took nearly three hours to complete.

Mid-afternoon, Reia came across a herd of danlas and stopped to have lunch with the three keepers. The boys chattered incessantly and insisted Reia judge their mock duels. After an hour, Reia thanked them for sharing their meal and took her leave. She'd needed the rest, but she had a prince on horseback to catch.

Thoughts of three young danla keepers—Raymi, Wehn, and Moorle—kept her company as she ran long after the moons rose. Reia loved running at night. One of the rare, fond memories of Master Kolknir's training was the introduction to the world that came alive once the sun set. Korvers and coyotes might move lazily about in the daytime, but they hunted at night, sending up crisp, raw, and savagely beautiful howls. Even the harsh kill sounds blended with the music of hundreds of thousands of insects.

By the third day, the pace wore Reia down and the trail grew colder, but she forged onward. At this rate, she'd reach the Riden Mountains in about three weeks. Though the prince would have a large head start, Reia could catch him during the mountain crossing. She knew countless shortcuts and could track almost as well as Master Corida or Master Celdin. However, the time estimate was based upon the assumption that she could maintain the fast pace, but as the hours wore on, her pace slackened. As despair set in, she spotted a farmer's purple fire.

Gemon Dravir had searched four different emergency stations only to find them poorly stocked. Reia stopped to help, wondering why the emergency stations had been left in such disrepair. She spent a day nursing Gemon, his wife, and their three children through a bout with cornada and earned the privilege of borrowing a horse named Donol. Cornada's cure was simple to make. Reia had needed fresh ira petals, mesta shoots, ristal leaves, and a few other herbs, but she'd always enjoyed gathering herbs.

As she rode Donol across much of the Riden Flats, Reia thought about the Dravir family. Despite the isolation, they seemed happy. Their honest hard work appealed to her. Even as she scanned for dangers, she imagined what life would be like had she not been raised by the Rangers.

What if my parents survived the assassination? Would Kiata and I be so close? Would I be who I am?

Of the questions, Reia could only answer the last one. Every hardship that came with Ranger life had molded her. The Order had taught her that strong people had to do good. Some Rangers spent days debating definitions of good, but Reia believed *good* simply meant aiding others first.

As a healer apprentice, she trained to handle a banistick almost as intensely as Kiata and Todd. She'd beaten off more than a few korvers in defense of tretling herds, but she had never raised her weapon against a person outside of training sessions. Part of her didn't know if she could, but she knew the matter would soon be decided one way or another.

By the end of the first day's ride, Reia wasn't thrilled about having Donol, but she could hardly blame the chestnut horse.

"You're a good boy, but I don't think my teeth or backside will ever be the same thanks to you," Reia commented as she watered Donol at a spring.

Despite screaming leg muscles, Reia forced herself to get on Donol the next morning. A quick meal of dried ira petals and spring water cheered her as she prepared to continue her pursuit.

Chapter 10:
Trouble Follows

Jira (March) 27, 1538
Twenty-six days into Prince Terosh's Kireshana journey
Kireshana Path, City of Huz Mon

Thanks to Terosh's reckless pace, the horses were spent by the time they reached Huz Mon. Since they arrived mid-morning, Terosh ordered his men to relax for a few hours once the horses were safely stabled. Everyone but Laocer obeyed. Terosh had hoped they would all go to a tavern, so he could leave without them. Unfortunately, Laocer stuck to his side like a rash.

Guess I'll stick with the original plan.

They left Huz Mon in the afternoon. If they walked steadily, they would reach the foot of the mountains before the three moons had full reign over the night. Terosh eyed their goal. The Riden Mountains rose like giants hunkered down against a windstorm. From this distance, the mountains seemed as vast and endless as the Riden Flats had once seemed.

"Impressive, aren't they?" Laocer asked.

"Definitely," Terosh agreed.

As they reached the mountains, conflicting emotions ran rampant in Terosh. Exhilaration overpowered the other emotions but trepidation, awe, and even a slight sense of futility existed within him. He laid a hand on the nearest rock, officially signaling their arrival.

"We'll start early in the morning. I'll get the water tonight. Help the men set up camp."

Laocer raised an eyebrow but said nothing.

Terosh collected each man's waterbag and walked the short distance to a small mountain stream. Feeling Laocer's eyes on his back reinforced the need to break free. Quickly, Terosh poured tamitin powder—a horse sedative—into each waterbag, excluding his own. Too high a dose could easily kill a man, but a small dose would knock him out for a day or so.

Terosh took over the cooking so there wouldn't be an accident. He didn't know when the tamitin powder would kick in. Since his cooking skills were rudimentary, the men suffered through heated pin peas and prazzle beans.

At least it'll stick in their stomachs while they're out, Terosh rationalized, trying not to feel guilty. Noticing Dillain's eyes drooping, he ordered everyone to sleep.

"I'll take the first watch," said Terosh.

"Whoa, I'm real—" Dillain didn't even finish his sentence before dropping over unconscious.

Jos Millard and Dennin Molik started to rise to help him but fell over before gaining their feet. The others dropped off soon thereafter.

"Not … good," Laocer managed, fighting the powder's effects.

Terosh agreed but couldn't turn back now. Picking up his pack, he started into the Riden Mountains determined to prove himself or die trying.

***

Jira (March) 28, 1538
Twenty-seven days into Prince Terosh's Kireshana journey
Kireshana Path, Near the Foot of the Riden Mountains

As Reia Antellio neared the Riden Mountains her desire to reach them increased. The majestic beauty of the sun shining off snow-covered peaks nearly made her forget the teeth-jarring pain of riding Donol. Reia feared she'd end up molded to the horse's back and never move again. However, when she reached the foothills and saw trouble brewing, strength seeped back into her. Five forms advanced on a small party of Royal Guards. The soldiers' stiff movements told Reia something was very wrong.

"Come on, boy. Let's get there," Reia urged Donol, charging forward.

The shadowy figures faced her as she approached.

Twenty meters from both groups, Reia pulled up sharply.

"Leave," a broad-shouldered man ordered. "This is no concern of yours, Ranger."

Reia hoped her voice would stay steady.

"These Royal Guards are on a mission—"

Harsh laughter cut her off.

"Well, we'll just be on our way then since we're clearly overmatched here," mocked a woman. "You know nothing about us, girl."

Would you leave if I asked nicely?

To her surprise, the farthest attacker began retreating. He spoke something too faintly for Reia to hear, and his movements held a fluid grace absent in the others' crisp steps. The five shadowy forms melted into the mountains.

Why did they retreat?

Reia wasn't complaining, but something about them unnerved her. Even fully rested, she doubted she could have fought them all.

"Who are you?" the lead soldier demanded. He tried to look dignified, but his legs wouldn't cooperate. He knelt on one knee, leaned heavily against a boulder, and pointed a kerlak pistol at her. His gun arm shook, and he looked ready to pass out.

"Where's the prince?" Alarm made her voice disturbingly high.

Donol shifted and nickered, and Reia patted his neck reassuringly.

"Who are you?" repeated the leader.

"Reia Antellio, Ranger apprentice and guardian of the one you seem to have lost." The words came out sharper than she'd meant, but she straightened her back with pride anyway.

The one I lost as well, she silently admitted.

A cautious expression crossed the soldier's face, but he shook his head, struggled to his feet, and holstered his sidearm. His eyes glittered with anger.

"Prince Terosh left yesterday, *after* drugging his own men."

The scene suddenly made sense. Railing at her bad luck, Reia flung herself off the horse.

"See that this horse is returned to Gemon Dravir of the Riden Flats." As she spoke, Reia retrieved her caydronan sack from Donol's back, slung the bag around her neck, and secured it to her belt so she could run.

"Wait! Where are you going?" asked a young guard.

"After him," Reia responded. Rummaging through her caydronan sack, she came up with a handful of amtea leaves and four wuzle roots. She placed these in a pile on the ground. "Throw these in boiling water for about ten minutes. Wait for it to cool and drink the tea. It should take care of whatever he gave you." With that, she patted Donol's neck, made sure her banistick and shootav were secure, and took off up the nearest cliff face. She couldn't spend time enlightening Prince Terosh's guards. The fool was probably neck-deep in trouble by now.

Of all the selfish, idiotic things to do!

Chapter 11:
Unexpected Help

Jira (March) 29, 1538
Twenty-eight days into Prince Terosh's Kireshana journey
Prince Terosh's Campsite, Eastern Edge of the Riden Mountains

An anotech warning flooded Prince Terosh Minstel with adrenaline, dashing hopes for a peaceful day. Kicking off his blanket, he drew his kerlak pistol and leapt to his feet. An instant later, three blue energy beams punched holes though the center of his abandoned blanket.

Stun beams.

The thought reassured Terosh, but he tossed the pistol to his left hand and drew his kerlinblade as well. Wielding two weapons could be tricky, but he wanted the offensive edge of the pistol and the defensive edge of the kerlinblade. The blade cast a white glow on the immediate area. His eyes probed the early morning shadows, adjusting to the kerlinblade's added light.

Two energy beams came at him, and Terosh dodged. Though impossible to see, he sensed two darts flying toward his back. He ducked, and the darts shattered against the mountainside. Spinning, he sent three energy beams at the new threat.

"Stay your weapon," called a man from his left. "We seek an audience."

"Odd place to hold court," Terosh said. A scan showed him four attackers arrayed in a semi-circle around him and a fifth watching from the side. Retreating a step, he felt the mountain against his back.

This is bad.

He could pin two attackers with pistol shots and maybe fight off a third with the blade, but his chances of successfully challenging four—or five—attackers were very slim.

"We wish you—" began the left attacker.

Shouting, Terosh lunged at the speaker and fired his pistol. Stun beams meant the attackers wanted to capture him, but he refused to become a hostage.

The beam grazed the man's right shoulder. The attacker grunted, stiffened, and collapsed.

Score one for Belcross's special powerpacks. One down, four to go.

Terosh might have redirected his flight toward the second attacker had he not sensed stun beams from three directions. He'd been told the anotechs would protect him. Though grateful for the warnings, he didn't like relying on things he couldn't understand. Twisting in midair, he caught two beams with his flat energy blade and let the third pass underneath his body. His arm tingled as the blade's surge protectors compensated for the energy influx.

More blue beams struck at him. Terosh dove left to avoid one but it grazed his right arm anyway. He broke the fall with his left arm, twisting to spread the force across his back. The impact knocked the kerlinblade out of his nerveless hand. The dead man switch shut the blade down before it landed next to him.

He rolled away from more shots until someone tackled him. Terosh's numb arm left him at a disadvantage, but Master Colander's hand-to-hand combat lessons took over. His first punch after standing slammed into the attacker's ear. She yelped and hit him in the gut. Her voice startled him. Chivalrous instincts told him not to hit a woman. The hesitation cleared when she smashed him in the mouth. The blow knocked his bottom lip against his upper teeth, splitting the lip. Internal morals straightened, Terosh caught the woman's right arm, jerked her off balance, and flung her into the cliff wall. The woman rammed the mountain headfirst and slumped to the ground.

Before Terosh could celebrate, someone else tackled him. He hit the ground hard with the other man on top. Reaching up, he locked arms with the attacker. The exertion woke up his numb arm. They teetered like that until Terosh pushed the man left, rolling them dangerously close to the cliff's edge.

Below, the fluffy green treetops beckoned Terosh to jump and let them cushion his fall. He and his attacker rolled, and Terosh found himself on the bottom again. A glancing blow off his right ear clouded his mind and sapped his strength. He shook his head, knowing he had to end the fight soon.

A dagger appeared in the man's hand and swept toward his neck. Terosh tried to edge away from the cliff without letting go of the man's hand. They struggled for an endless moment, Terosh pushing up and his attacker pressing down, the dagger caught between them.

A red beam blasted the ground by Terosh's head, startling him. His attacker cursed, pushed off Terosh, and hurled the dagger at the beam's source.

"Traitor!" shouted the attacker.

Two red beams caught the man full in the chest. His legs folded, and he tumbled backward off the mountain.

The fourth attacker, a young man who looked vaguely familiar, stared in disbelief at the fifth man then leapt over the cliff.

Terosh struggled to sit up, not understanding what had just happened. He tried to think where he might have met the young cliff diver before.

"So much for honor among assassins," he commented.

"I have a different master than they do." The last attacker leveled his kerlak pistol at Terosh's face. He wore dark clothes like the others, but something told Terosh the man had two weapons besides the one pointed at him.

Kerlinblade. Banistick.

Only Royal Guards, Melian Maidens, and Rangers used the collapsible, staff-like weapons. Since the man was probably not a Royal Guard and obviously not female, that left only one choice.

I thought the Rangers were on our side!

"And what does your master want?" Terosh had trouble reconciling the image of a Ranger with the idea of a threat.

"I wish to capture you, but I don't intend to give you to their masters. Turn around and kneel." The man adjusted his kerlak pistol back to stun.

"No," Terosh said. The fourth attacker's escape method looked more appealing by the second.

The man holstered his pistol and drew a kerlinblade. It flashed to life with a soft yellow glow. He opened his mouth to speak but never got the chance.

A pebble slammed into the ground in front of the man, prompting him to move. He leapt left just in time to avoid being flattened. Cursing, he pulled his cloak's hood tighter around his face and fled.

***

Reia landed hard next to the attacker. She would have landed on him if he hadn't moved with incredible reflexes. She experienced a moment of horror as she realized that anyone capable of moving that fast could surely kill her in a straight fight.

To her surprise, the attacker hissed a curse and ran.

Apparently, nobody wants to fight me.

The thought was ten percent complaint and ninety percent confusion.

A shout from Prince Terosh warned Reia in time to duck a dart.

The new attacker, a woman, leaned heavily against the cliff face.

"I need to speak to the prince." The woman's shooting arm wavered, but her eyes burned with intensity.

"Nothing's stopping you, but put the gun down," Reia replied. She stepped between the prince and the dart gun.

You make me nervous. How hard did you hit your head?

The two women regarded each other.

Looking past Reia, the woman set her eyes upon the prince.

"When the time comes—"

A strangled cry cut her off.

Reia snapped her attention to the man who had previously been doing a very good impression of a dead guy. He staggered to his feet looking drunk. His eyes wandered then rolled back into his head so only the whites showed. His head sagged, making Reia worry it might fall off. He held a kerlinblade loosely like he didn't know what to do with it.

"Morgan! No! We want him alive!"

Each of the woman's shouts punctuated a rapid and disconcerting change within Morgan. Every muscle in the man corded, and his hands tightened around the kerlinblade. Something black washed over the whites of his eyes.

The woman fired, and the dart struck the man's chest. He twitched like he registered the pain but took a shaky step forward anyway.

"Kill," Morgan mumbled, sounding unsure of himself.

"Morgan, what's wrong with you?" The woman's question was a horrified whisper. Her stunned tone and expression told Reia the voice didn't belong to Morgan.

"Forget Morgan. Follow orders," spoke Morgan's body.

"We want them alive. We want them alive," the woman chanted.

Reia wholeheartedly agreed with the woman.

Morgan's body sagged like a malfunctioning puppet.

"No! Friend! Kill!" His body jerked as it warred with his brain. He lifted his kerlinblade and staggered toward the female attacker.

Great, now he's not even making sense.

Reia moved between Morgan and the woman, hoping she stayed out of it. Getting shot by the woman she was saving would be pathetic. Reia prayed her banistick would hold up against the kerlinblade as the first overhand blow jarred her whole body. The fight might have ended right there had the prince not fired six energy beams at Morgan.

Three beams struck true, but the man merely staggered with the impact and laughed.

Reia swung hard with her banistick but he backed out of reach.

"You have no idea what I'm capable of," he declared.

The note of awe hit Reia.

"Neither do you," she said.

"You're obviously not Morgan, so who are you?" asked the prince.

"I am Maledek."

The name meant nothing to Reia.

"You're far from your area of fame," the prince commented.

"It was time to move on. Look, I've learned to kill without hands. Shall I demonstrate?"

"No!" Reia and the prince shouted together.

Maledek laughed.

"Any volunteers? How about the lovely young lady?"

Reia thought he meant her until a cry from the woman behind her said otherwise. She whirled and found the woman looking stricken. Her face had drained of color, and her hands clutched at her throat.

"Shall I strangle her, break her neck, or stop her heart?"

Reia was speechless.

"Stop!" Terosh exclaimed. "It gains you nothing to kill her."

The woman tensed then collapsed, legs folding beneath her.

"Next," Maledek hissed.

Suddenly, Reia's skin crawled with unseen things. The sensation lasted several terrifying seconds. An invisible hand gripped her throat, stopping almost as soon as it started. A chilling scream tore through her. Spinning to face the thing using Morgan's body, she saw him cradling his hands against his chest.

"No. No. No. Not fair!" Spittle flew from the creature's mouth and his eyes turned white again.

Reia's mind swirled with questions about the man and why whatever he had done failed with her and succeeded with the other woman.

Tears streaming down his face, the man straightened his shoulders and twisted his neck as if it needed to crack. His kerlinblade flashed up in a salute before he attacked.

Reia blocked the first three blows, but her strength ebbed with each strike. The prince attacked the man with a series of swift strikes that forced Maledek to defend himself. Reia mostly stayed out of it, adding a strike here and there if the opportunity presented itself.

Maledek turned his attention back to her. She blocked a high strike aimed at her neck then a low one aimed at her side. The force of the next blow almost knocked her banistick back into her right shoulder. She twisted and avoided her own weapon, but the maneuver opened her to a devastating punch to her left ribs.

Stumbling back, she watched as Maledek attacked the prince. They exchanged several strikes before a kick sent the prince spinning toward the cliff's edge. Maledek's blade began following the prince. Throwing herself forward, Reia aimed a strike at the attacker's wrist. It changed the blade's direction so that the broad, flat edge caught the prince's back at a glancing blow.

Reia didn't think the blow was hard enough to drive the prince from the cliff, but to her surprise, he leapt away. Groaning, she barreled past whatever inhabited Morgan's body and dove off the cliff, attaching her banistick to her waist mid-flight.

A blood-chilling scream followed her.

***

Jira (March) 29, 1538
Same day
Cliff above Prince Terosh's Campsite, Riden Mountains
As the prince and Ranger dove from the cliff, Morgan's anotech-controlled body expired. The anotechs responded by setting off every nerve in Dalonos's body. He screamed with rage, frustration, and pain unlike any he had ever experienced. Even his transformation from Belcross to Dalonos seemed a pleasant memory by comparison.

When the pain finally dropped, Dalonos let Morgan's borrowed body tumble from the cliff. It bounced off the cliff twice before catching on a branch. A crack announced the body's victory over the branch, and both plummeted to the ground. Satisfied, Dalonos flopped onto his back and replayed the short scene with the prince and the Ranger.

"Why couldn't I kill the Ranger?"

"She is protected by Linonos." The girl's voice sounded like wind. It took Dalonos a moment to remember the anotechs calling this form Jalna.

"Can they be killed?"

"The Light Ones are no stronger or weaker than us. Do you not still ache and hurt?"

Sharp head pain followed the question. He moaned.

"You must get better at defending yourself. It takes effort to heal you."

Gathering his energy, Dalonos limped away from the girl, but she followed him. The Ranger would return for her caydronan sack. Although he would love to stay and kill her, the protection of the Light Ones disturbed him.

"Go help Lucas. He is in danger."

"Who?"

The anotechs flooded his mind with information concerning Ranger Lucas Telon.

"How will I get to him?" Dalonos challenged the crazy machines. "It's a long way down."

"Jump. We will protect you."

The dull ache in Dalonos's head flared to a pounding.

I'm not a nursemaid, but fine. Show me.

He jumped.

Upon landing, the anotechs led him on a long trek down the mountain where he found the unconscious Ranger. The man had certainly seen better days. His shoulder was a bloody mess, and his clothes were shredded across the left arm, chest, and legs. A scan of the scene confirmed that the man had at least fared better than the korvers.

"Quickly, take him."

Dalonos considered questioning them, but his head hurt too much already. With a weary groan, he infused the Ranger's body with enough anotechs to stabilize it and picked him up for the long return trip. When he finally reached his campsite, Dalonos ate sixteen energy bars. They tasted awful, but he lacked the time for a luxurious meal. After following the food with an entire waterbag, Dalonos set to work on the Ranger. Under his directions, the anotechs cleaned and knit wounds together throughout the night.

***

Jira (March) 29, 1538
Same day
Kolknir's Observation Post, Riden Mountains

Kolknir had watched Lucas's RT Alliance team clash with the prince, Reia, and a dark-clad man he didn't recognize. From this distance, Kolknir could have shot everybody before they registered the attack, but Lady Mavis would disapprove. His mission was to eliminate Prince Taytron's minions crawling around the Kireshana trail. He might have missed one or two, but his contract said to even the game, not condemn the prince to a premature death.

In an uncharacteristic fit of candidness during last night's progress report, Kolknir had confessed his frustration with the lack of clear orders. The Lady then revealed that she had not yet decided if she wanted Prince Terosh to die on the Kireshana. Kolknir's main purpose was to prepare the way so Terosh's death remained a viable option. He had to admire the Lady's attention to detail. This was quite an investment of time and manpower to watch her nephew's Kireshana. As the conversation wound down, the Lady illuminated Lucas's status as an RT Alliance double agent working for her and suggested that Kolknir consider training the young man.

Years ago, when Kolknir still counted the Rangers as family, Lucas had done a short stint as his apprentice. The boy had shown promise, but there was no way to determine if the intervening years had spoiled or enhanced his potential. So far, Kolknir was not impressed, but he felt a sense of kinship with the young man. As they had done with him, the Council had made Lucas a master and allowed him to operate as a Nareth Talis Ranger, but their gesture could not erase the shame of failing to bond with anotechs.

The dark man caught Kolknir's attention. A few adjustments of the sniper scope brought the man into focus. Pale, gaunt, and wearing a haunted expression, he looked freshly risen from a grave.

Deciding to ask the Lady about the man, Kolknir shifted his attention back to Reia and proudly watched as she fought the reanimated body.

"You've come a long way, apprentice," he commented.

When one of his spy cams spotted Lucas about to engage in a new battle, Kolknir diverted his attention yet again. He watched the short, brutal battle from start to finish.

Lucas Telon started the fight with his back pressed against the cliff. A body lay sprawled across a boulder in front of him. The spy cam picked up a coughing bark. Lucas cursed and drew his banistick and kerlak pistol, fiddling with the controls.

A single korver emerged from the cave below Lucas's current position on the mountainside.

The lean creature slipped forward and sniffed at the body.

Aiming carefully, Lucas fired into the creature's head. The beam bounced off the korver's head as if it had struck compressed carbon plating. The creature whirled and glared at Lucas. The Ranger fired four more shots. One slipped into the korver's left eye, eliciting an ear-piercing howl as it died.

Angry growls came from the cave's mouth just before korvers boiled out. They seemed like normal beasts, but they were unusually well-coordinated.

A large korver bounded on top of the boulder where the body and the first korver lay, knocking both off. Using the boulder as a launching point, the korver leapt up and twisted in midair to face Lucas.

Lucas fired another long stream of energy before abandoning the pistol for his banistick, a better close-quarters weapon. A sweeping slash earned him some breathing space, but the rocky mountain terrain limited the moves he could make. The korvers executed a coordinated assault, but Lucas fought with cold desperation. Kolknir could see that frustration fueled the young Ranger.

Teeth flashed and claws tore at Lucas, but he seemed to feel no pain. Korvers bounced off his weapon left and right. One latched onto his right shoulder and bit deeply. With a cry, Lucas threw off the creature and knocked it senseless.

A minute later, it was over. Lucas shook his head like a man awakening from an unpleasant dream. Korver bodies lay scattered about him. After surveying the damage, Lucas slumped to the ground.

While he debated whether Lucas was worth saving, Kolknir noticed help find the young Ranger. The dark man walked upright but moved with an unnatural grace. Once sure the man meant to help Lucas, Kolknir contacted his mistress.

"What have you to report?" the Lady asked, once the connection was secured.

Kolknir explained the situation.

"The prince has drawn much attention, and he will never be more vulnerable. If you wish him dead, release me to kill him," Kolknir concluded.

Silence answered him as the Lady considered the offer.

"Tempting. Very tempting, but I believe my nephew will best serve me by living for now. My previous order to watch Prince Terosh stands. I will let you know if that changes."

"As you wish, my Lady."

"Have you made a decision about Ranger Telon's worth yet?" the Lady inquired, before he could sign off.

Instead of answering, Kolknir asked, "Who is the dark man rescuing Lucas?" He waited out the long pause.

"He is one of my son's experiments," said the Lady. "He was once Dr. Atien Belcross, a scientist employed by the Royal House. I don't know how he came to be the creature he is currently, but he came to my son wanting to become Maledek."

"Will he interfere?" Kolknir used the question to mask his surprise.

"I doubt he even knows about you. You are my secret weapon."

"You have many secret weapons, my Lady. Me, Lucas, and others, I'm sure." While she seemed in a sharing mood, Kolknir pressed, "What of the RT Alliance? Are they yours?"

"They will be." The Lady cleared her throat. "Currently, the Alliance is another of my son's experiments, a promising one." She let her holographic gaze bear down on Kolknir. "When the time comes to move against the Rangers, the Alliance will become the weapon that destroys them."

"I want to be there," Kolknir declared.

"That can be arranged." The Lady's eyes told Kolknir she understood the emotions coursing through him: pain of betrayal and lust for vengeance.

"But such a moment lies far in the future. We may need the prince to reach our ultimate goals. Watch and wait. I know that is never easy, but I have different matters to attend to right now. When I decide Terosh's fate, you will be the first to know."

Chapter 12:
Healers

Reia nearly panicked as tree branches passed centimeters from her face. When training finally took over she tucked in her limbs, twisted to avoid landing on her head, and waited to meet the ground. Her feet struck first, but her landing roll did little more than make sure no bones snapped. It could do nothing for the nauseating feeling, which said her internal organs were trying to come out her throat. For several heartbeats, her lungs refused to draw breath. Then, she gasped and tumbled three more times, expecting the crazy attacker to rain down shots.

To her surprise, what followed wasn't a stream of energy beams. It was a body, one that used to be Morgan. The sharp crack of a tree branch, followed closely by a solid thump, sickened her, but Reia couldn't waste time thinking about it while the prince lay wounded.

Struggling to her knees, she looked around and found the prince lying face up, unconscious. Breathing heavily, Reia assessed the still man. His clothes were torn across the chest and probably back. Part of his left sleeve was missing. The torn piece clung to a branch midway up the tree. Scattered, broken branches and leaves littered the ground around the prince. A swift examination revealed no broken bones, but the prince's right shoulder had dislocated.

Regretting the pain she would cause him, Reia used her ankle dagger to cut a small section off the bottom of her shirt. This she cleaned, wadded, and stuffed into the prince's mouth. Then, she grabbed his shoulder and popped it back into position.

The prince woke up long enough to scream into the makeshift gag. Before he passed out again, Reia slipped a cormea leaf into his mouth around the gag. Though it wouldn't taste pleasant, the cormea would dull the pain.

Suppressing a groan, she gripped the prince's good shoulder and wrestled him into a sitting position and then onto her shoulders. Praying her adrenaline rush would hold out long enough to see them safely hidden, Reia staggered to her feet. Twice, she almost fell over, and twice, she gritted her teeth and righted her balance.

For such a slender man your dead weight's pretty darn heavy.

Ordinarily, Reia would have hesitated to move a patient so soon after he'd had his shoulder popped back into place. However, extenuating circumstances dictated that she make an exception. Morgan was beyond harming them, but whatever had controlled him was probably still up there somewhere.

After tucking the prince behind some trees, Reia returned to Morgan's body. Finding nothing significant, she made a mental note to bury him later and scaled the cliff up to where the exciting morning had begun. She hoped to find something to explain what had just happened. The fifth man's unwillingness to fight after her grand entrance puzzled her. Also, most attackers wanted the prince captured, but the thing controlling Morgan had tried to kill him.

Shivering, Reia pushed thoughts of Morgan's transformation aside. After retrieving her caydronan sack and bedroll, Reia returned to the prince's campsite and gathered supplies she thought they might need soon. The rest could be recovered later. Spotting his perforated blanket, she decided it could be used for bandages if nothing else.

The morning had just started, but they would travel nowhere today. She doubted anything would bother them, but not having weapons would be foolish. Reia studied the prince's kerlak pistol. The compact, remarkably beautiful, black weapon had gold and silver filigree wrapped like slender vines around the handle, trigger guard, and barrel.

It must have taken a year to get that detail!

A Ranger might have spent such effort carving a banistick, but most banisticks were fashioned of danesque or kintral wood. Reia always expected metal weapons to be too unyielding for fine artistic touches.

I stand corrected.

Using a thin, sturdy length of dristal rope, Reia took a less adventuresome way down the cliff face. Upon reaching the bottom, she whispered to the rope and it dutifully returned to her for coiling. Once back by the prince's side, Reia sat down and watched him sleep.

What do I do? Are we safe? Will they return?

She examined the prince. His thick black hair curled in sweeping waves. Dark eyebrows and long eyelashes guarded the lauded blue eyes, and Reia suddenly wished to see them. She smiled at the memory of the young woman's expression and cataloged more of the prince's features. His nose sloped gently downward, being prominent without taking over, and his lips appeared full of restrained life. He looked so serene that Reia didn't want to disturb him, but his back needed attention to avoid infection.

Rolling him onto his left side, trying not to jar the abused shoulder, Reia examined the burn across his back and winced. A conventional sword wound would have been easier to treat. She didn't care for the way kerlinblades treated flesh. The wound was as thick as her fist and slashed diagonally across the prince's back starting below the right shoulder and ending near his lower left ribs. The burned skin puffed and puckered like an angry insect bite.

Sorry. Guess you really shouldn't have abandoned your guards.

Reia shook her head to fling the futile thoughts aside. The prince couldn't take back his stupid actions, and she couldn't change the direction of her banistick strike. Sighing, Reia rummaged in her caydronan sack until she found the necessary herbs to treat the wound. Next, she took out a toom leaf and curled it into a makeshift bowl. Drawing her ankle dagger, Reia chopped cormea and amtea leaves into fingernail-sized pieces and mixed them in the bowl with water, iretel sap, tosh, and crela dust.

"Micten," Reia murmured, holding her hand above the forming paste. She felt something leave her fingertips and watched with childlike wonder as the rude paste swirled on its own.

Thirty seconds later, Reia said, "Almon."

The source of power returned in an unnerving rush. Master Ekris had tried to explain the anotechs once, but Reia only remembered that they chose to serve certain people and obeyed Kalastan commands.

Remembering the gag in the prince's mouth, Reia leaned over and gingerly tugged it out.

"Disda." The power crawled out onto her hand again and disposed of the slimy rag. That accomplished, Reia replaced the cormea leaf with a new one and dissolved the remains of the old one. "This might sting," she warned her sleeping charge. A few deft twists turned the toom bowl into a dispenser. After applying a generous portion of the salve over the wound, she unfolded the toom leaf and used it as a bandage. Since it wasn't wide enough, she used two more leaves.

Once finished patching up the prince, Reia buried Morgan. Lacking time and energy for a proper funeral pyre, she did the best she could with rocks. She worked silently, but her mind hummed with questions about the man she buried. Finding no answers, Reia sang the *Song of the Dead* and burned a few small sticks to mark his passing. The physical labor let Reia work off some tension, but part of her wanted to curl up and cry.

As the last embers slowly died, Reia remembered the other man who had been shot, the man who had jumped off the cliff mid-fight, and the dead woman above. A search showed where someone had fallen, but there was no body. She would have found that odd, had she not taken the fast way down the mountain and walked away with bruises.

A twenty-minute search revealed a man's gruesome remains amidst the bodies of several korvers. Reia studied the scene. Somebody had walked away, and she could only conclude that it must be the fifth attacker. Having him on the loose was unnerving.

***

Terosh could hardly remember ever feeling so lousy. His head hurt, his back felt like he'd slept on a torch, his ribs hurt, and his limbs were limp and scratched. Something gritty in his mouth tasted awful, so he turned his head and spit it out. He was lying on his stomach. The realization startled him enough to bring him fully awake. He lifted his head and pain shot through the back of his skull. He groaned.

"Keep still." The female speaker sounded annoyed. "That kintral tree cracked a few ribs."

Forcing the pain aside, Terosh pushed himself to his knees and prepared to defend himself. Something peeled off his back with a violent ripping noise. He paused on his hands and knees. A dull ache throbbed through his right shoulder. His arms trembled then collapsed. He would have landed on his face had the woman not caught both shoulders and eased him down. Even so, the new back pain nearly drove him unconscious.

Who is she? How did I get here?

"Move again and I will sedate you," the woman warned. "We'll have time to talk later, but right now, I have to fix the bandages on your back."

It took a lot of willpower to not scream as something peeled off his back. A second later something cool numbed the pain and something else pressed down gently over whatever had stopped the pain.

"Thank you."

"You're welcome, but please, try not to move. My supply of toom leaves needs to hold out for another day or two."

Inexplicable pleasure addled Terosh's senses, and in a moment, he realized that he enjoyed the refreshing challenge in her voice. Frank conversation with a woman was something lacking in his life. Sarie occasionally lent him a piece of her mind, but even when his mother had been alive casual conversations were as rare as a moonless night. Queen Kila Minstel had never wasted words. This woman's voice soothed him almost as much as whatever she had put on his back.

"Who are you?" Terosh asked, longing to hear her speak again.

"Reia Antellio. I'm a healer apprentice. Do you remember what happened?"

Mention of her rank reminded him that she was a Ranger, but the topic switch surprised Terosh.

"I was attacked. You jumped in. One of the unconscious guys woke up, killed one of the others, and fought like a demon. Something struck my back and I jumped off a cliff … I can't remember when." He beat back a surge of panic, determined to keep calm so she wouldn't think him a fool.

"This morning, about five hours ago," the Ranger supplied, sensing his need to gain a grip on time. "Who were they?"

"I'm not sure." Terosh drew breath to continue but hesitated, not sure he should tell her about the other Ranger.

"But you have a guess."

"There was another Ranger with them."

"What makes you say that?" The Ranger's defensive tone said she couldn't imagine one of her Order attacking a royal.

"I saw his banistick," Terosh said. The idea went against every childhood lesson on the Rangers. *Saw* was a lie but saying anything else would lead to an awkward explanation. Stunned silence followed, and Terosh wished he could see the Ranger. "May I get up now?"

"Yes." The Ranger's hands fell on Terosh's left shoulder, gripped, and smoothly hauled him up and around to a sitting position.

He grunted from new pain.

"If it hurts too much, I'll lay you down and we can try again later."

Once he blinked back the pain, Terosh got his first good look at the healer. His breath hitched. She was far younger than he had expected—about his age—and far more beautiful as well. Her thick brown hair was twisted into braids that snaked up and around her head, held in place by subtle clips. Her eyebrows and lashes nicely accentuated deep green eyes, which reminded him of the West Remon Sea. Her cheeks flushed above concerned lips, which currently frowned at him.

Both reactions made him smile.

Their eyes met, and Terosh was mesmerized by the intensity of her gaze. Breaking the eye contact, he checked his surroundings, scolding himself for neglecting the simple survival task. They were in a heavily wooded area somewhere on a mountainside, judging by the sharp slope to the ground. Kintral, cal, and rineth trees rose up on all sides, yet three meters of open space existed under the sturdy branches of an old rineth tree. A pair of codrels eyed them with something between curiosity and hostility. Terosh doubted he could fight off even those mild-mannered, blue-gray furballs in his present condition.

"We're safe," the healer assured him. "But keep this close while I gather the rest of your supplies."

Terosh accepted his kerlak pistol. Along with his kerlinblade, the pistol formed a set his father had given him for the Kireshana. Before he could reply, the Ranger slipped away into the trees. Terosh tried to settle into a position that wouldn't make his back muscles scream.

The healer left for about a half-hour, giving Terosh plenty of thinking time. He wondered what brought someone to the Rangers and what made one stay in the Order. A life of service to the crown was fine, but the Rangers seemed especially zealous. The founding Ranger had once been a prince and the original intent had been to guard the Royal House.

Terosh's thoughts turned to the other Ranger and the attackers.

Who was the Ranger? Did he want to kill me or not? Who were the others? Why did they want to capture me? I'd make a terrible hostage. He doubted his new enemies were the typical kidnap-for-ransom group. Their black outfits had been similar to Coridian Assassin uniforms, yet the attack style didn't fit. *No poisoned flingers, no kamad daggers.* The thought brought him back to asking why someone would want him captured. He blew out an annoyed breath.

A soft footstep drew his attention, and he whipped the kerlak pistol up, ignoring the burning sensation in his ribs. He used his left hand, suddenly grateful for the hours drilling with a pistol. In less than a second, the weapon pointed at the young healer's chest. Terosh lowered the pistol.

"I could have killed you." Her eyes added, *easily*.

"Sorry, I was distracted."

"Well, you should un-distract yourself if you want to live."

Her mild reproof annoyed and amused Terosh, but since laughing hurt, he focused on the irritation.

"How dare you lecture me?" He winced and pretended it was from the pain. Sedir's speech on not being a snotty little prince played out in his head. Pushing the lesson aside, he locked eyes with the Ranger.

Her lips pressed firmly together, holding back words.

"Say what you will," Terosh commanded, bracing for a verbal onslaught.

"I dare because I have a job to do, just as your guards had a job to do. Sneaking away from them was the single most selfish, stupid, reckless thing I've ever witnessed!" Her green eyes flashed.

Terosh let the words sink in, wanting to lash out but knowing them to be true.

"Will they be all right?"

The healer blinked and drew a deep breath. The fire leeched from her eyes.

"I don't know." Her voice was suddenly soft. "They'll probably try to follow us, but we'll be safer if we can lose ourselves in the mountains. Without a guide, they'll probably stick to the marked Kireshana path."

"It will be my fault if they die." The statement tore his conscience to shreds.

"They're not dead yet," the Ranger said. "And they're Royal Guards. They've done this before."

Terosh nodded, resulting in more head pain. He held his breath until it passed.

"How long do you expect to be here?" Terosh asked, needing to change the subject. He couldn't shake the feeling that he wouldn't like her answer but thinking about his men would drive him mad.

"Long enough," she answered, arranging a pile of rineth leaves and pine needles into a rough mattress. She placed her bedroll over it then swept another pile of similar materials together and unfolded his bedroll atop it. Next, she set about making a fire.

After digging a shallow hole, she arranged some small branches over larger ones.

"Linkel," she spoke to the dry wood. Immediately, the stick in her hand produced a flame from the far end.

"Fire?" Terosh asked, surprised the woman could speak Kalastan. His head jerked, jarring his back. Only a slight twitch of his lips acknowledged the pain.

The young woman studied him. Her expression condemned it as a dumb question.

"How do you know that language?" Terosh asked, too surprised to be offended.

"How do you know it?" she fired back.

"All crown royals are taught Kalastan. It's supposed to be an ancient and powerful language, though I doubt even the tutors know much more than that. My brother taught me some words."

Taught me the word for "fire" very well.

Terosh remembered his entire dresser drawer going up in flames. Tate had gotten quite a verbal lashing from Mother—and Captain Kelter—over that prank, and Father had followed it with a long list of chores.

The Ranger poked at the other branches with the burning stick. When the fire blazed, she sat back and clasped her hands around her knees.

"It is both." She watched the flames for several seconds before continuing. "The language you speak of is ancient and powerful." Prying her attention away from the fire, she looked directly at Terosh. The words flowed from her in low, reverent waves.

"How do you know?" he asked.

"The anotechs say so." She smiled mischievously. "The Rangers know little about them, save that they choose whom they will. You are royal. You probably have access to them. Some Rangers say they answer to anyone who is sincere, but I only know they answer best to Kalastan commands."

"Will you teach me?" Terosh asked, barely restraining his excitement. He had heard many tales of the anotechs and knew some simple commands like how to set silent alarms, but the idea of learning how to wield them like his ancestors thrilled him.

"As you wish," said the Ranger.

He let the point drop, not wanting to press her too hard, but his thoughts raced with the possibility of learning everything Tate knew.

Davel must have taught the Rangers. So much for the family secret.

"—ing tomorrow," the Ranger finished saying.

Terosh shook his head to clear other thoughts and immediately regretted it.

"I'm sorry, what did you say?"

"You can probably move a little, but don't overexert yourself. It will slow the healing process."

Terosh nodded carefully, so as not to hurt his head.

"Is there a place to wash up?"

"There's a stream about three minutes that way," Reia said, pointing off to his left. "If you listen carefully, you can hear it."

The Ranger had cleaned his wounds well, but Terosh still felt dirty. Thoughts of a cold bath cheered him. He ate his fill of a savory stew the Ranger cooked, decided he was too tired to wash up properly, and settled down to sleep even though the day was far from over. He wanted to ask a hundred questions, but now seemed an inopportune time. Eventually, he maneuvered his battered body to the bedroll, but once there, the soft padding worked wonders. Before falling asleep, Terosh heard the Ranger approach and mutter words that eased the remaining aches.

Chapter 13:
Adern's Strength

Jira (March) 30, 1538
Twenty-nine days into Prince Terosh's Kireshana journey
Recovery Campsite, Riden Mountains

Reia rose before dawn, shaking off the bad dream like a soggy blanket. This one featured Kolknir, the dark cave, and criessa. The sun had not quite risen, but instinct born of many months under open skies told her it would soon. A glance told her the prince would sleep until she woke him, so she grabbed her waterbag and slipped off to the nearby stream to wash up.

I wonder if crinal will work here.

The thought intrigued her. She knew it worked in washroom caves but had never tried it elsewhere. Wondering why such a simple thing never occurred to her before, Reia stooped down beside the stream and stuck her right hand into the mud. A second later, she retrieved her hand.

"Crinal."

The sensation of many tiny things skittering across her hand made her bite her lip.

That tickles.

The movement changed so that it felt like she'd stuck her hand in one of the small whirlpools under the Riden Mountains. A half-minute later, Reia's slightly raw but unharmed hand had not one trace of mud on it.

So that's what happens.

She dwelt a moment longer on how the anotechs would run a washroom cave. Reia had never considered mundane things like where waste went.

What else might anotechs be capable of?

Reia knew they could start fires and bind wounds, but otherwise, they remained a mystery. Thoughts of mysteries reminded her of the prince, so she filled her waterbag and returned to the camp.

After building a fire, she made a broth with sannin, corlia, and deklov. She also heated the remainder of the coney stew she'd prepared the previous evening. Then, she went to rouse the prince, but his peaceful expression made her hesitate. She had never seen someone sleep so soundly. Her own sleep had always been fraught with troublesome dreams. Sleep could be as helpful at healing as any tea, broth, or bracing stew.

Reia ate, checked on the prince again, and spent several minutes enjoying the crisp morning before closing her eyes to practice feeling her surroundings. Kiata had been tutoring her in the skill for quite some time, but Reia still wasn't very good at it. For some reason, her anotechs responded reluctantly to directional commands.

A few hours slipped by while Reia practiced banistick moves. All Rangers learned to use banisticks, but Reia had neglected the skill as her healing lessons intensified. On the mountains a shootav or serlak weapon usually proved safer in dealing with korvers, lions, and vipers. Reia preferred shootavs over serlak weapons because of their versatility and stealth. Before yesterday, she had never fought a person outside of training, and she wasn't eager to do so again.

When her muscles were pleasantly tired, Reia sat down next to the prince, leaned against a kintral tree, and mentally listed healing plants, their locations, and common combinations. After an hour of the tedious but necessary exercise, she grew bored, so she started singing "Adern's Strength."

"Nehkermahstenmielsto
Keqwircoseikero.
Sehnomfreh.
Sehstimorea.
Nehnqwirmseikero.
Sehnawbon.
Sehnomorikan.
Nehnqwirmseikero."

"That's beautiful," Prince Terosh said. "Will you sing it again?"

Reia opened her eyes, alarmed they had fallen shut.

Some guardian you are.

Her cheeks reddened when she met the prince's cool blue eyes.

You do have pretty eyes.

Reia stared at him, wanting to detect sarcasm. Finding only interest, she nodded and repeated the song, trying not to look away. She considered singing it in the common tongue but refrained because she preferred the Kalastan version.

As the last notes faded, the prince smiled broadly.

"I can't imagine anything I'd rather awaken to. What does it mean?"

"It's called 'Adern's Strength.' It doesn't translate word for word, but—"

The prince's stomach cut her off by announcing its empty state.

"That can wait until after you eat," Reia said, struggling not to laugh. Reaching for his hands, she added, "Crinalge."

Anotechs left and returned almost instantly.

The prince looked puzzled as he examined his hands.

"I'll have to remember that one."

"Learning Kalastan is easy, but the anotechs only follow directions if they want to," Reia reminded him. "Normally, I'd use a sonic cleaner, but I doubt your body would appreciate that right now."

Prince Terosh's stomach growled again.

"Can you explain the song while I eat?"

"I first need to check your injuries," Reia replied. She retrieved the coney stew and broth from the shallow fire pit where she'd left them warming and placed them next to him.

The prince grunted when Reia helped him sit up but submitted with relative grace while she removed his shirt and examined him.

"That's the end of that shirt," the prince said, fingering the deep rips.

Making a mental note to patch it later, Reia grinned but continued the examination without comment.

The healing charm she'd put on him the night before had worked. Most of the scratches were fainter, and the massive burn across his back looked less angry. She gently probed his ribs.

"You'll be fine in a week or so."

"That soon?"

"As long as you drink lots of this and don't strain yourself." Reia picked up the broth she'd made and placed it in his hands.

He cautiously sniffed at it.

"What is it?"

"Water mainly, but there's also sannin, corlia, and deklov," said Reia, earning a blank stare. "Sannin for aches, corlia for pain, and deklov for faster healing."

"Ah," the prince mumbled, taking a slow sip and making a face. "That's … interesting."

Having consumed enough deklov to recall the sharp, bitter taste, Reia chuckled.

"You owe me a translation," the prince prompted, easing back into the remains of his shirt.

"That I do," Reia responded. "The first two lines are one long thought. 'Nehkermahstenmielsto keqwircoseikero.' It means, *'No fiery danger striking near my heart can kill or conquer when I have love.'"*

"I'm sensing a story behind that."

"I'll get there. The next phrases are short sentences. 'Sehnomfreh.' *'See how it floods me.'* 'Sehstimorea.' *'See how my strength grows.'* Then comes the chorus: 'Nehnqwirmseikero.' *'Nothing can conquer me when I have love.'* This is followed by: 'Sehnawbon.' *'See how it binds every wound.'* And 'Sehnomorikan.' *'See how my strength rises from ashes.'* 'Nehnqwirmseikero.'"

"Nothing can conquer me when I have love," Prince Terosh finished.

"You've got good ears," Reia noted.

"My brother, Tate, just calls them big," the prince said, flicking one ear forward. While prominent, his ears weren't monstrous. He turned his attention to the broth, frowning with determination. Taking a deep breath, he brought the bowl to his lips and drained it. Then, he attacked the stew with surprising energy.

Reia refrained from scolding because his appetite pleased her.

"Can the song be sung ... normally?" inquired Prince Terosh.

"Yes, but it's prettier in Kalastan."

"Will you sing me the common version?" The prince put down the bowl and folded his hands in supplication. "Please."

Since she could hardly refuse him, Reia sang:

> "No fiery danger striking near my heart
> Can kill or conquer when I have love.
> See how it floods me.
> See how my strength grows.
> Nothing can conquer me when I have love.
> See how it binds every wound.
> See how my strength rises from ashes.
> Nothing can conquer me when I have love."

Reia held the last note for a three-count, surprised she could sing for this stranger. She had shared songs with half the Riden Mountains on herb-gathering trips, but the only people she'd ever sung for were Kiata, Todd, Master Niklos, and Master Ekris—who had taught her the songs in the first place.

"Who was Adern? Was he real?" Prince Terosh's questions broke into Reia's thoughts.

"He was a Ranger during the reign of Queen Lissa and King Othel, I think."

Terosh whistled.

"That's hundreds of years ago."

Reia nodded, initially surprised but then annoyed with herself for forgetting her audience.

"You know your family history well. Will you share it with me someday?"

"Only if you'll trade me a Ranger story for each tale."

Reia found the mock-serious tone so normal she almost forgot his status.

"Deal. I'll begin with Ranger Adern. On his wedding night, Jadorin Assassins burned down his house and killed his wife with a poisoned arrow. Adern spent the night weeping over Syana's body while the ashes cooled around him, his grief absolutely complete." Reia stopped because the prince wore a far-off expression.

His countenance grew progressively sadder, making him look older.

"I ... think I've seen something like that," he admitted.

Reia waited, hoping he would elaborate.

Eventually, the prince shook himself.

"I'm sorry, I'm terrible company. Please continue."

"The song came to Adern in a dream, but he told no one. He and his apprentice, Kymen, spent months hunting down the killers. On the eve of the final battle, Adern shared the song with his apprentice before they fought the assassins. The apprentice lived, but Adern did not. Kymen carried the song back to the Ranger Compound at Osem and passed it on to a new generation."

The prince nodded solemnly.

"A sad tale, but it fits with most of my family's history." His expression still contained a sense of loss, longing, and something undefinable.

"I'll go get some food," Reia said, sensing his grief. She left the prince alone with his thoughts.

Chapter 14:
Zareb and Covin

Jira (March) 30, 1538
Same day
Recovery Campsite, Riden Mountains

As soon as the Ranger left, Terosh finally noticed the beautiful day. The cool mountain air filled him with new strength. Small animals scurried about and chattered. Birds sang sweet songs, but their efforts could not compare to the Ranger. Terosh recalled every nuance of her voice as it moved with the song. Fearing an end to the intimate moment, he had hardly dared breathe, but when the end came, the peace remained.

Does she know the power she has?

He didn't know whether the warmth coursing through him came from the song or that foul-tasting medicine.

Dentelich would throw a fit over me taking Ranger medicine.

Terosh smiled. Annoying the uptight doctor was a pleasant pastime.

Deciding to wash up, he struggled to his feet and picked his way through quemin bushes and kintral trees toward the stream. He kept his right hand close to his kerlak pistol as he worked his way over to the muddy bank.

Terosh spent much effort simply kneeling next to the stream. Once down, he washed his hands, face, and arms in the gentle current. He drank slowly, dipping one hand into the icy water and bringing it to his mouth. The water with his meal had been nice but not this kind of invigorating cold.

"Why travel by self?" asked a male voice.

Terosh drew his kerlak pistol, spun, and rose, tracking toward the voice. Pain shot through his back and right shoulder, but he held in a cry. He heard no threat in the voice, but survival skills dictated more caution and less politeness, so he kept the pistol leveled at the man.

The man's four arms declared him an Elish. The upper two hands were folded, and the lower two hands held small serlak pistols. His uniform said he was a Royal Guard candidate, yet his thick golden hair hung past his shoulders. He looked to be mid-twenties, but Terosh knew Elish mature differently than humans.

"I Zareb." Excitement and recognition brightened Zareb's silver eyes. "You prince!" He bowed deeply and returned his guns to holsters. "Many honors, Dulad Prince of House Minstel."

The sound of his full title drove the tension from Terosh, so he holstered his pistol.

"Thank you, Zareb. Forgive me for not returning the bow. My back was wounded yesterday."

"Where soldiers?"

Zareb's question made Terosh uncomfortable.

"He was separated from them," the Ranger answered. She stepped from behind a kintral tree holding a weapon Terosh didn't recognize in her left hand and a banistick in her right hand. She didn't raise either weapon but gripped both with ease.

Zareb's head whipped toward the Ranger, and his hands grasped his pistols.

"There's no threat, Zareb. This is Ranger Reia Antellio. She's a healer," Terosh said, feeling weary. A spasm in his lower back made him draw a quick breath. His vision clouded, his knees shook, and he began falling, steadying himself against a tree at the last moment.

Dashing forward, the Ranger tossed the strange weapon into her right hand to join her banistick and caught him with her left hand.

"What did I say about overexerting?" The question held both anger and concern. She returned both weapons to her belt. "I'm going to ask that question a lot, aren't I?"

"Ranger need respect Prince Terosh," Zareb scolded.

"Prince Terosh needs to listen to sense when he hears it." Reia tipped Terosh over her shoulders.

Before he knew it, he found himself staring at the ground from an odd angle and feeling ridiculous. His embarrassment brought back his senses, and he cleared his throat.

"I'm fine. You can put me down."

"I'll put you down at the camp then return for the food." She panted from the exertion.

"I can walk." He didn't care how childish he sounded.

I'm a prince! he cried silently.

The Ranger didn't answer until they reached the campsite and she had deposited him onto his bedroll. Then, she spoke in a gentle, weary voice.

"I know you're a prince. And I know it's not easy to be still, but it will help you heal." She rose. "I'll be back in a moment. Try not to fall asleep until I return."

He noticed she looked good with flushed cheeks, and her first statement about him being a prince shocked him.

I don't think I said that out loud.

Terosh mentally repeated the scene four times, so engrossed in thought that he didn't notice Zareb had followed them to the camp.

"She pretty," Zareb commented.

"Agreed."

"You need help? Zareb help. Travel with prince and Ranger."

More traveling companions would be safer, but an unexpected stab of jealousy hit Terosh.

"No thanks. We'll be fine."

"As you wish, Prince Terosh. Riden speed you on journey." Zareb bowed again, turned, and disappeared between two cal trees.

The Ranger returned and leaned over the fire pit, adding more brush. The stick in her hand already held a small flame at the end.

"Who was that man?" Her curiosity came through clearly.

"Zareb? I guess he's a Royal Guard candidate." Something about the man seemed familiar.

"Why didn't he stay?"

Terosh held in a teasing comment about her scaring the man off.

"I told him we would be fine."

The Ranger's head cocked thoughtfully.

"I guess it's for the best."

"What'd you get to eat? I'm starving," Terosh said, changing the conversation and feigning enthusiasm.

"Cannafitch," the healer replied, gesturing to the large, dark brown lump next to the fire. She took a knife from her boot and started skinning the animal.

Terosh had seen vids on cannafitch but never expected to see one up close. The thin-boned mammals with semi-hollow chest cavities usually grew about half a meter in length with a wingspan of a full meter. They couldn't fly very well, but their wings allowed them to ride wind currents. Their colors ranged from black to brown to gray, depending on their age and environment. They enjoyed eating coneys, squirrels, and even korvers, if they could catch one. Master Og could talk about them for hours, but right now, Terosh was more concerned with how they would taste.

"Are they abundant here?" he wondered, trying to distract himself from hunger.

"They're not native to these mountains, but the windstorms carry them from the Kala and Ash Mountains," the Ranger explained.

"That's a long way."

"They're heartier than they look," the healer pointed out. "I shot this one with a shootav pellet treated with a strong dose of cormea and radon, and that only stunned it for a few seconds."

Terosh wasn't eager to try cannafitch meat, but since there was nothing else, he figured he should attempt to like it.

"Have you ever eaten it before?"

"Yes, and it's rather good with deklov."

Deklov? Deklov.

It took him a few seconds to recognize the bitter herb that had flavored yesterday's awful early morning brew. He shot her a suspicious glare and tried to measure her sincerity. Her sympathetic grin wasn't the answer he wanted. Despite his worries, the fire-roasted cannafitch meat tasted tolerable.

The Ranger had added plenty of deklov to his meat, but thankfully, he didn't notice the bitter taste too much.

"Stuff's strong enough to pull teeth," he mumbled.

"Well, eat up. There's plenty here." The Ranger laid out more cannafitch strips. After lining up three rows of the meat on a large leaf, she rubbed salt into both sides of each piece.

"What are you doing?"

"Salting meat." The healer's expression dared him to ask another question she could answer in the same infuriating way.

Terosh waited for her to elaborate, pressing his lips together to hold in further questions.

Are all Rangers so irksome?

"I'm making jerky out of it." The healer's grin grew, and she held her hands over the three neat rows of salted meat. At the last second, she paused. "Would you like to try?"

"Sure." It took Terosh some time to crawl over to the Ranger and the meat strips.

"Hold your hands a few centimeters above the strips," she instructed. "Good. The word you're going to say is 'drayce;' it means 'dry this thing' or 'dry these things,' depending on your inflection."

"It can have a different meaning based on inflection?" Terosh asked. "That could be dangerous."

"It could be, but not in this case," the healer assured him.

Terosh followed her instructions, said the proper word, and nothing happened. He frowned.

"Try imagining something flowing from your hands."

He did so, and something ripped out of his fingertips. Though sharp and painful, the sensation was so brief, Terosh almost doubted he had felt it. As he watched, the strips of salted meat shriveled like bones left in the Felmon Desert. A triumphant surge filled him. Next, the Ranger instructed him on using cannafitch skin to patch his holey blanket and repair his shirt.

The more he learned about the anotechs, the more he liked them.

***

Jira (March) 30, 1538
Same day
Prince Taytron's Office, Royal Palace, City of Rammon

Prince Taytron Minstel skimmed the many Kireshana reports littering his desk, but he couldn't concentrate. He knew most of them reported the death of his agents preparing Terosh's way. This made him feel guilty, but it was better than memories of Deanna. Most days, Tate could think about her and still function, but nights were far worse. He had ruled Reshner since his mother's murder. Though gravely wounded by that event, Taytron had not understood how one death could emotionally gut a man.

Until now.

Images of Deanna dominated his thoughts. No matter what she wore, she had always looked magnificent. She used to braid her hair then tuck it under a hairnet so she could work in the lab. A lump burned in Tate's throat.

A knock interrupted his reverie.

"Enter," Tate called.

Covin shuffled in quickly. Once inside, he shut the door and bowed three times.

Tate waved impatiently.

"What news do you have?"

Covin's report came out in a rush.

"Zareb met young prince. Dulad Prince sneak away from guards and find trouble. Big fight day last. Prince wounded. Pretty Ranger help. Zareb offer help. Prince no want Zareb help. Zareb await orders."

"What do you think?" asked Tate. "Will they be all right if Zareb watches from a distance?"

"I will ask him, my prince." Covin's eyes went blank as he consulted his twin brother across the distance.

Elish links never ceased to amaze—and unnerve—Tate.

Three seconds later, they had Zareb's answer.

Covin gave it voice.

"Most attackers dead. Dulad Prince has Ranger. One attacker, maybe two, escape." Covin's muscles tightened in reflection of Zareb's body somewhere out on the Riden Mountains.

"What is it?" Tate demanded.

"Bad feeling. Many eyes watch Dulad Prince and pretty Ranger. Not all eyes friendly. You want Zareb find others?"

"If you can do it quickly, then do so. Keep him safe."

"Zareb do this, Crown Prince."

For about a week, Zareb kept his word, but one morning, Tate walked into his office and found this message waiting for him on his comm.

"Many apologies, Crown Prince. Windstorm carry Dulad Prince and Ranger over next mountain. Zareb cannot follow."

Chapter 15:
Wild Flight

Enis (April) 9, 1538
Thirty-eight days into Prince Terosh's Kireshana journey
Kireshana Path, Riden Mountains
When Reia stopped to check on Prince Terosh, she spotted the gray clouds hurtling across the blue sky at an unholy rate.

Windstorm!

Windstorms consisted of the sort of wind that brought cannafitch halfway across the habitable continent.

"We need shelter, right now." Reia's voice was low and calm.

Their position on the mountain's east side would be uncomfortable in minutes and deadly soon thereafter. Windstorms could strip kintral trees right down to their trunks. The trunks stayed put only because their roots went down nearly twice the length of their height. Unprotected cal trees with their shallow roots could be thrown hundreds of meters.

Prince Terosh turned to see what had upset her.

"Windstorm. Lovely."

Reia grunted and spun on her heel, knowing they faced a race they couldn't afford to lose.

"We're on the wrong side." She unfurled her banistick and used it to keep balance while she skipped over small boulders and clambered up larger ones. "The west side should have some caves." Reia headed left to get around the mountain rather than going over. She glanced back at the prince.

"Stop watching me. I'm fine."

Chuckling, Reia concentrated on conquering each new mountain obstacle. By the time they'd left camp, Prince Terosh had been begging to leave for days.

Reia had picked the areas around the campsite clean of anything with the slightest healing properties, but if the windstorm caught them, they would be beyond such help. A strong breeze struck her back, picking up her cloak and twisting it around her body. As Reia smacked the cloak aside, a crazy idea came to her.

If cannafitch can do it, so can we.

Her mind did rapid calculations.

This will work. I think.

The boulder in front of her took a moment to mount. Its flat top jutted out over the open valley below. Reia halted so suddenly that the prince bumped into her back. His arms instinctively wrapped around her, taking away the chill of the mountain air. The windstorm's scouts knocked them forward a step.

"What's wrong?" Prince Terosh asked, steadying her. He shouted into her ear to be heard.

When the wind slackened, Reia twirled in the prince's arms.

"Take off your cloak and wrap your bedroll around yourself," Reia ordered. "And hold this," she added, shoving her cloak into his hands as she tucked the clasp into a pouch at her waist.

The prince followed her line of thought.

"Are you sure about this?"

Of course not.

Instead of answering, Reia opened her caydronan sack and whipped out some toom leaves and a short, fat dandi branch. Her dagger tore into the branch. When the sap began flowing, she held it to one end of her bedroll, and said, "Hekr." While the sap melted, Reia flipped the caydronan sack over her shoulder and rolled her bedroll around her upper body, using the sticky end to secure the padding in place. Next, she took the edge of her cloak and drew a thick line before pressing the edge of the prince's cloak to the sap and repeating, "Hekr."

Hoping her plan worked, Reia tore several toom leaves lengthwise into strips about the width of three fingers. Next, she applied sap to one end of a toom leaf strip, firmly pressed it to her cloak, and commanded the anotechs to heat it. Bending the leaf up, Reia grabbed Prince Terosh's right arm, yanked it into position, and fixed it in place by sealing the leaf's other end to the cloak.

A gust of wind caught the cloak, causing it to flap behind the prince like a blue-black banner. Reia chased down the loose end and secured the prince's left arm, leaving just enough cloth for him to move. Frowning, she turned him sideways so the wind wouldn't catch the cloak while she bound it to his ankles. Finally, she made a strap for her right arm and both legs. The arm strap wasn't as tight as Prince Terosh's because she didn't have someone to help her. She also needed both hands free to make the last strap for her left arm.

A new idea struck her. For the last strap, Reia started the same way by sap-sticking one side down, but then, she used her dagger to make two small slits through the cloak and threaded the toom leaf through it.

Already Prince Terosh and Reia had to concentrate to keep their footing as the wind stabbed at them. They huddled close and changed their angle to cut down on the profile they presented, but each passing second brought faster and faster winds.

Reia shoved her left arm through the loop created by the toom leaf and gripped the loose end, yanking up until the strap pulled tightly across her left arm. Feeling somewhat secure, she maneuvered them to the edge and glanced at the prince.

"Ready?" she asked.

The prince nodded.

"Then jump!" Reia shouted.

With wild cries, they launched themselves off the mountain. At first, they plummeted toward the sharp rocks below. Then, a strong gust caught the underside of their collective cloak and violently altered their course. Instead of falling at an alarming rate, they shot up into the sky above the valley. The rapid ascent stole the air from their lungs, killing their screams.

Reia's stomach jammed into her throat. She clamped her lips tight, thankful they had not eaten a midday meal yet. Reia forced her eyes to stay open, though they stung and streamed with tears. She feared that if she closed them, she would never open them again. The view was breathtaking, but Reia had no breath left to spare. She drew painfully cold air into her lungs. They were almost above the Riden Mountains and could see all the way to the Asrien Sea to the north and the island of Ritand to the west. Resh, Fort Riden, and Mount Palean, respectively to the west, southwest, and south, flashed before her eyes as they twirled in a dizzying circle.

We must change direction!

The winds carrying them were strong enough that the bits of dirt smacking them hurt, but in their current position, much of the mountain they had jumped from protected them from the windstorm's full fury.

Reia wrenched her left arm across her body, twisting enough to slam into the prince. The force spun them dangerously close to the mountain and changed the angle the winds caught them. Tangled in a mass of limbs and cloak, they let the wind carry them along, speeding downward again but not as swiftly as before. Reia almost lost her grip on the left arm strap, which would have doomed them, but she managed to hold on.

By mutual consent, they untwisted and spread their arms and legs to catch the wind. Again, they started to rise, but now, they had enough control to direct their flight. Prince Terosh wheeled them right. By working in concert, they flew two circles over the valley on the west side of the mountain. They were still a good six meters above the valley when the wind suddenly slackened.

Feeling more wind to her left, Reia threw herself that way. The move slipped them into a stream of wind that shot them forward horizontally, then slightly up. They approached the far side of the valley in seconds.

At the last moment, Prince Terosh rolled them out of the air stream, and they smacked into the mountain with harsh—but not deadly—force. Stunned, they tumbled toward the valley and landed on a large, flat rock.

Reia landed atop the prince. With her last scraps of strength, she rolled off his chest. His left arm remained trapped beneath her, but she was too tired to care. She surrendered to the encroaching darkness, thankful to be alive.

***

Enis (April) 9, 1538
Same day
Site of Ungraceful Landing, Riden Mountains

Terosh Minstel woke up with a massive headache. His breaths came in uncertain gasps. Blood pounded in his ears. Every part of him lodged a complaint. He felt like a piece of pottery someone had put together wrong.

Wetness spread across his chest and right side. It took him several seconds to determine that it wasn't his blood seeping out but rather the contents of his waterbag. His left arm had something heavy across it. He couldn't move, not that he wanted to, but the option would have been nice.

The first thing he noticed, besides the intense pain, was the silence. Aside from his ragged breaths, not a sound could be heard. No birds sang. No korvers howled. The wind had swept the battle, cleanly and completely.

The heavy thing on his arm shifted. Terosh forced his eyes open, rolled his head left, and found an unconscious Reia facing him. A nasty gash below her hairline told him why she was out cold. Her right shoulder pressed against Terosh's upper arm, causing the tingly numbness.

An urge to protect Reia sent adrenaline coursing through Terosh. The energy rush wasn't much, but it allowed him to draw her closer. She rolled into his side and fit perfectly. Her head rested on his left shoulder and her body paralleled his. If they had to spend the day lounging on a rock at least they would share warmth. Though the deadly wind was mostly gone, a thick layer of clouds blotted out the sun and sent temperatures tumbling. Holding Reia close, Terosh finally admitted his growing fondness for her but buried the feelings in common sense.

She's a Ranger. You're a Royal. It would never work out well.

Sometime during the week and a half convalescence, she had ceased being "the Ranger" and become Reia. Getting her to address him casually had been impossible thus far, but he would persist.

Terosh lost track of time. He dozed off and on, trying to monitor their situation. When the sun finally appeared, he tried to get up because the blinding light wasn't helping his head. He couldn't quite raise his right arm to block the sun because the rest of the cloak was trapped beneath his body. Frustration made him tense.

The movement woke Reia who groaned and struggled to rise. The cumbersome cloak caught her, and she landed close to where she had started. Moaning, she rolled away from him, unfurling the cloak as she went, waking Terosh's left arm.

"Does that help?" Terosh inquired.

Reia looked at him.

"Hold on. I'm still trying to get my brain to work." Her voice was faint and cracked with dryness.

Relief flooded Terosh, putting him in a better mood.

"Take your time, though you might want to tend to that dent in your forehead."

Reia released a long, low moan, and said, "Yes, it helps." Cautiously, she unclenched her left fist and worked her arm free. Then, she wriggled her other arm free of the toom strap, sat up, and retrieved her boot dagger. That took some doing because she had to lean over to reach her right boot. Once she had the dagger, she attacked the toom straps binding her ankles and Terosh's to their cloaks. Next, she slashed at the strap around his left arm. To reach the one on his right arm, Reia had to lean over him. Exhausted, she dropped the dagger next to him and fell against his stomach.

"Just roll me off," she mumbled. "I'll sleep for a month now."

Terosh chuckled, enjoying being alive.

"Experiment conclusion: humans aren't built for natural flight. Ow!"

"What's wrong?" Reia asked, pushing off Terosh so she could look at him.

"My head hurts … a lot."

"I know the feeling." Reia gingerly touched the wound on her forehead. "It's like a giant gust of wind just tried to decorate a mountainside with my skull."

"Yeah, something like that," Terosh agreed.

Chapter 16:
Dreams

Lord Kezem Altran tried not to fidget. Finding it impossible, he got up and paced. He had bigger offices, but this one afforded the most privacy. Ten brisk steps brought him from the desk to the hand-carved double doors. Three paces carried him across both doors. Ten more steps returned him to the desk. A sharp left turn allowed him to pass in front of the desk.

Kezem completed the circuit a half-dozen times, avoiding the holograph projection plates dominating the center. As a child, he had amused himself for hours slaughtering armor-clad warriors and mythical monsters conjured by holoprojectors. He missed the simplicity of those days where the foes stood tall, fought valiantly, and died when he wished it so. Real life was so much more complicated.

For the hundredth time in the last ten minutes, Kezem checked the wall clock. It read 11:43. If this meeting didn't start soon, he would miss his noon meeting with Ranger Telon. The cryptic message had insisted he be alone in this office at 11:40. The message terrified him. The only person to send him such messages was presumably dead.

"You don't look well," commented the familiar voice.

Kezem faced the hologram.

"Mother." He acknowledged with a small bow. As he straightened, he braced for her reaction to his failed assassination attempt. "Good to see you are well." His throat surrendered the words painfully.

Lady Mavis Altran graced him with an icy smile.

"Yes, we should deal with that unpleasantness. The plan was decent, but the execution was awful. Two things to improve, dear: the first being loyalty and the second being payment. If you want to buy loyalty, pay premium and then some. You may one day bet your life on that loyalty."

"What do you want?" Kezem despised being lectured.

"There's no need to be petulant, darling. Your move cost me many comforts and a few longtime servants. The least you could do is heed some constructive criticism. Your timing was also atrocious."

"Is that all?" Kezem inquired.

"No. Since you obviously have timing issues, I thought I'd advise you to move your plans forward with all possible speed."

"Don't you think I'm trying?" Kezem asked, despising the whine he heard.

"The plan I gave you is still viable, but the Mitra are not a patient people. The Blood Harvest must be completed by the end of Kelos, according to their calendar, which is Allei (August) according to our calendar."

Kezem looked at her blankly.

His mother glared at him.

"That gives you less than four months to get the king and Taytron to Mitra."

"How shall I convince Taytron to go? He's not exactly in a marriageable mood since I killed his first wife."

"Speaking of that affair, how is Taytron's daughter?"

"Safe," Kezem replied, clamping down on idiotic surprise that his mother knew he'd kept Elia alive.

Lady Mavis Altran had proven many times over that her spy network was second to none.

"Good," said his mother, bestowing a brief, approving nod. "As for Taytron, don't even try to persuade him. Convince the king and he will force the boy's compliance. And stop trying to kill Terosh. We need him alive until the Mitran plan is completed. Help him through the Kireshana."

"Help him? Don't I want him dead?"

"You're being short-sighted," his mother scolded. "You need Terosh to convince Teorn to leave. My brother will not leave Reshner in the hands of the Governors Council or the Senate. Besides, if you kill the boy, the mourning period will delay the trip."

Kezem silently berated himself for not thinking of that point. Perhaps he had been overzealous in trying to kill her. On the other hand, her skill at manipulating plans and people made her a very dangerous ally.

"Why are you helping me?"

"Can't an old woman have her dream?"

"You want to recover the throne. I understand that, but why me?"

"Your brothers may be taller and stronger, but you are smarter. Intelligence is something to be valued far above physical prowess." Her calculating gaze swept his face. "They don't have the right disposition. Eldon's too hotheaded and Mitrek's too compassionate and fair-minded. It makes him an excellent judge, but little more." Her eyes glittered with hatred, but it wasn't directed at him. "Agree to the plan, and I can make my brother accept it."

The hologram vanished, but Kezem didn't have long to dwell on the meeting. His mother hadn't told him much, but her instruction to protect Terosh warranted thought. He would leave that decision until after the

Ranger's report. He wondered if his mother would listen to his meeting with Lucas Telon.

A pleasant ding announced a connection query. Kezem activated the holoprojectors and waited for the image to form. The image showed perfect details right down to the dirt smudges marking Lucas's clothes.

"My Lord, your servant Maledek sends his greetings," Ranger Lucas Telon announced.

"Are you surprised to find two Maledeks?"

"It is not my place to wonder, Lord." The Ranger's expression stayed neutral.

Smart man, but your information had better be worth the price I'm paying.

"What have you to report?" Kezem asked.

"The Kireshana goes as well as expected. I have reports of fifty-two deaths so far."

"How many by your hand?"

"Three, my Lord," the Ranger answered. "I was nearly interrupted by the prince, but he had his Royal Guards with him. I dared not attack then."

"What of the Restler-Tarpon Alliance team and the next encounter with the prince? Your report on that was vague." Kezem had received an account from the creature playing Maledek, but he wanted to hear it from Lucas.

"The prince slipped his guards, so we attacked, but we were interrupted by his guardian." The Ranger clasped his hands behind his back and lifted his chin.

"I thought you took care of the guardian. Those were your Alliance orders, were they not?"

"I did. I also made sure his replacement is young and inexperienced, but no Ranger is completely helpless."

"Who is the replacement?" Kezem wondered.

"No one important."

"You're telling me one inexperienced Ranger defeated you and a team of RT Alliance soldiers. Do you realize how pathetic that sounds?"

"I thought it prudent not to fight with a witness present."

There wouldn't be a witness unless—

Kezem cut off the thought. Something clicked in his head, but there was no point in revealing his new knowledge.

"Go on."

"I retreated, expecting the others to follow, but they didn't. A few of them died in the battle, but I think one escaped. I don't know. I stumbled into a korver clan. I killed them, but the beasts wounded me. Your pet Maledek healed me, and I spent the next week recovering."

"How did he heal you?" Kezem asked. Long ago, he had suffered a korver bite. The Ranger was lucky to be alive, especially if he had run afoul of the experimental korvers.

"Anotechs. Ranger lore is filled with accounts of the god machines."

It was the same vague report Kezem had heard from many sources.

"Did Maledek share any useful information about his connection to anotechs?"

"No, my Lord, but he mentioned an interesting point about the royal family."

"If it's valuable, you will be paid well. Keep appeasing the RT Alliance as best you can, but for now, protect Prince Terosh."

Having nothing more to say, Kezem cut the connection. He paused with his hand over the control to shut down the holoprojector. Instead, he gave it new
commands.

"It is not safe to contact me like this." The image recreated the sweat beading across the man's brow.

So, this is the Speaker for the Ashatan Council. It's a wonder the Rangers are still a threat.

"Master Alikron, I have one question for you. Who is Prince Terosh's Ranger guardian?"

"Ask Lucas. You're close to him, are you not?"

Kezem chuckled.

"You're in far too deeply to begrudge the boy taking orders from me, Master Alikron. Indulge my curiosity." Kezem glared at the hologram.

Hiram Alikron's expression flipped through several emotions. He appeared angry, then defiant, and finally resigned.

"Reia Antellio, she's one of the healer apprentices. Lucas gave her his highest recommendation for that mission. The boy's completely obsessed with her."

"Tell me everything you know about her."

***

Enis (April) 9, 1538
Same day
Site of Ungraceful Landing, Central Riden Mountains

Too tired to move, Reia Antellio and Prince Terosh Minstel spent the rest of the day and night near the boulder they had landed on. They ate cannafitch jerky and drank from Reia's waterbag because Terosh's had burst upon landing. A few instructions to the anotechs sealed the breach, but the water had already been lost.

"Disdadandi." With that command, Reia dissolved the dandi sap linking their cloaks together and holding their bedrolls around their chests.

Their movements were slow and stiff, but eventually, they unfurled their bedrolls. Then, they fell into a deep, anotech-induced sleep.

Terosh slept peacefully for two hours before dreaming. It wasn't a normal dream, but something colorful and vivid. He found himself on a graceful mountain surrounded by large boulders. It took him several heartbeats to recognize the mountain he slept on. Though the perspective was like the flight, the sickening rush was absent. The kintral and cal trees sped toward him, yet he did not fear them.

He saw his body's chest rise and fall. As recognition set in, the expression of concentration melted to surprise. He frowned, and so did his body. Then, he saw Reia. She groaned and rolled over. A closer look revealed sweat upon her brow. Terosh wanted to wake her but couldn't move.

"Use her weapon," ordered a boy, appearing before Terosh.

Recognizing the boy as a younger version of himself, Terosh searched for weapons. His pistol holster contained nothing, and the place where the kerlinblade should have been held a banistick. He snatched it up, flicked it out to its full length and nearly dropped it.

"Practice, play!" shouted the boy, clapping his hands and jumping. "Why?"

"Bad things happen soon. Learn to use her weapon."

Terosh collapsed the banistick to its compact form, which was about a third of a meter in length and stared at the strange weapon. Slender and delicate, sturdy and durable, the banistick reminded him of Reia. Terosh turned it over, admiring the intricate handle carvings. At first glance, they appeared to be meaningless lines and curves. However, under closer scrutiny, the lines formed chains of leaves and the leaves interlocked, shaping flowers. To ease the boredom of healing, Terosh had submitted to herb lessons from Reia. Some lessons included handling the real things, so Terosh recognized the rounded leaves composing the chains.

Mintas leaves. I wonder if there are more.

It took some intent staring to recognize the empty space between the mintas chains as the pointed outlines of astera leaves. Where two mintas leaves met across the top or bottom of the weapon, he found wedge-shaped ristal leaves. Where four mintas leaves touched ends, an ira could be found, and where four mintas leaves connected to form astera, the rounded curves of corlia could be seen.

Cures for mood, disease, poison, fever, and pain.

"Mintas makes moods merrier, astera and ira ease what ails, ristal reverses potent poisons, and corlia cures common calamities or makes one care not what comes."

The weapon of a healer.

Terosh hefted the banistick with his right hand and tossed it to his left.

"All right, I have her weapon, now what?"

"Practice, play," repeated the Young Terosh.

"Yes, we've covered that. *Why* am I learning her weapon?"

"Need it. Big trouble soon."

Terosh glanced at his slumbering body.

"We've just been through big trouble."

The boy disappeared but the voice still filled the air.

Bigger trouble. Some want you dead. Others want you to live.

"Which side are you on?"

We are all sides.

"Anotechs! You could speak to us any time you wished." His statement carried condemnation.

We give warning for you to take or leave, Second Prince of the Chosen. Do not die!

***

Oddly aware she slept, Reia began dreaming, but to her surprise, the scene differed from her usual nightmares. She appeared in the center of a small, bare room. The four gray walls and compact dirt floor reminded her of the Riden Mountain Ranger Compound where she had grown up. Light came from everywhere and nowhere.

"Learn his weapon," spoke a sweet, ethereal voice. A girl appeared, and Reia saw it was herself as a child.

What weapon?

Reia reached for her banistick but instead retrieved Prince Terosh's kerlinblade. Like his kerlak pistol, the blade's beautifully detailed handle featured gold and silver filigree wrapped around like delicate vines. The gold leaves were on the silver strands and vice versa. The silver strands snaked up to the left, and the gold strands climbed to the right. They intersected every two centimeters. The handle itself was about twenty-five centimeters in length and four centimeters in diameter. Six silver plates, spiraling right, met in the middle at one end of the weapon, looking like a mintas drop. The plates looked ready to spring open. The kerlinblade's opposite end had small control panels equidistant from each other on three sides. Reia suspected she wouldn't want to be facing the spiral end if she touched the controls.

"Activate his weapon, practice, play."

Reia hesitated, but her hands moved to follow the directions.

What's going on?

Her hands tightened around the handle, and she commanded them to drop the weapon. By the end of thirty seconds, Reia's hands ached, yet she fought the instinct to activate the kerlinblade. She couldn't say why she wanted to disobey, but everything in her rebelled against submitting. She fell to her knees, gripping the handle so tightly her hands turned white.

"Sleep," commanded the Young Reia.

The child disappeared.

Reia felt sharp head pain then ceased feeling anything. She saw the dream version of her body fall, but her point of view remained kneeling. A surge of anger shot through her, jolting her sleeping form.

What's going on?

You would hurt yourself if we let you.

Who are you? What are you? Where—

Do you not know, Descendant of the Chosen? The female voice sounded very different from the Young Reia.

How can I know if you don't tell me?

We prefer the prince. He listens better, the woman's voice said.

I'll listen when you tell me something useful!

Patience. We carry a warning. Many enemies are ahead. Learn about us. Use us. Make the Dark Ones pay.

The dream ended, and Reia's eyes snapped open. She found herself staring up into Prince Terosh's concerned blue eyes. Her chest heaved like she'd run several kilometers up a mountain.

"Welcome back," the prince greeted.

"What happened?" Reia asked, sitting up.

Something's different. Something—

"The pain is gone," the prince said.

Reia drew a breath and held it. The prince was correct. Nothing felt wrong, yet Reia distinctly remembered lots of pain only hours ago. In fact, she hadn't felt so rested in ages. She leapt to her feet, unable to remain seated while energy coursed through her.

Prince Terosh laughed and climbed to his feet.

"I don't know what happened to you, but I had the weirdest dream. And when I woke up, I felt fine. Completely healed of every ache, pain, bruise, and scratch." He studied his hands. "The anotechs have you Rangers beat in the healing department."

"Anotechs?"

"In my dream, I saw us sleeping here. Then, a voice, my own, only younger—"

"That's what happened to me! Only I was in a bare room, like a mountain cave." Reia stopped speaking, realizing she had cut him off. With a bow, she slipped into formal speech. "I apologize, Prince Terosh. It seems—"

His warm laughter only increased the rate at which Reia's cheeks turned crimson.

"Those dreams changed more about us than I thought."

Reia couldn't deny it. The flush faded when she realized he wasn't really laughing at her.

"I do feel strange," she admitted. "I think I saw anotechs, but they took on my form. That is, me as a child."

"Interesting. And did this childhood form tell you to learn my weapon?"

"How did you know that?"

"Because that's what happened in my strange dream," Prince Terosh explained. "There's a lot we don't know about the anotechs, but they seem to want to help."

Do you trust them?

Reia chose not to voice that question. She had no answer and didn't expect the prince to have one yet. As she looked at him, deep peace slowly filled her. She recognized it as the feeling she'd spent countless days missing: love. The feeling embodied everything good. Beyond shock at this point, Reia accepted the feeling along with the knowledge that it would be unrealized. A soul-deep ache brought a tide of tears to her eyes. She held them in check.

"You thrashed while you slept," Prince Terosh commented awkwardly, trying to switch the topic to ease her unspoken pain. "Do you often have nightmares like that?"

Reia twitched her head in a swift negative gesture, grateful for his consideration.

"Not like that. This was different," she said.

"What are your normal nightmares?" The prince's tone said he'd been meaning to ask the question for a while.

Reia wanted to tell him everything.

You barely know him!

"I don't—I mean, I shouldn't—"

"Please, tell me." Prince Terosh gripped both of her hands. Reassurance radiated from his eyes and flowed from his hands.

"Why do you want to know?" she wondered.

"You don't sleep very well."

"I do some nights," Reia insisted.

"If I had to guess, I'd say you slept well about twice a week. I'd like to know why."

Does it matter?

"There's nothing you can do about it, but thanks for asking." Reia gently squeezed his hands, hoping he would let go.

"Will you tell me someday?" The prince held on tenaciously.

"Perhaps." The corner of her mouth curled upward.

He strengthened his grip then released her hands.

"Good enough. For what it's worth, I know a thing or two about nightmares."

"Will you tell me someday?" Reia asked.

"Perhaps." Prince Terosh grinned impishly.

Chapter 17:
Majesty and History

Enis (April) 10, 1538
Thirty-nine days into Prince Terosh's Kireshana journey
Path to Zalok Lair, Riden Mountains

After eating, Terosh and Reia moved their campsite to some zalok caves three kilometers away. Terosh couldn't wait to see the zaloks. He had seen pictures and vids, but a picture could hardly portray the five-meter bulk of an adult zalok.

"We're going to have to proceed slowly at this point," Reia warned, when they drew near the zalok cave. She frowned at the sky and pulled her cloak tighter across both shoulders. "And I think we may be here longer than anticipated because winter's coming … now."

Thick clouds had gathered all morning, but as Reia spoke, the first snowflakes fell. The temperature plunged, and by the time they reached the cave, the snow fell in pure white sheets.

Great, we'll be eating cannafitch jerky forever.

Terosh eyed the falling snow balefully.

"I'm glad we made it before the snowstorm. The zalok queen will need us soon," Reia said.

"Need us?" Terosh asked, prying his eyes from the snow to blink at Reia. "What could we possibly do for a zalok queen?"

"Defend her while she lays and warms her eggs," Reia explained. "Come on. The central chamber should be just ahead." She crept along the passageway and motioned for silence before Terosh could question her further on why a zalok would need defending.

Korvers eat zalok eggs, Terosh recalled. *Bears do, too.*

He doubted a bear would be stupid enough to attack a zalok, but korvers would take on anything that wasn't instant death for them. Zaloks and bears had greater size and more strength than korvers, but the wild, mangy, little beasts traveled in clan packs anywhere from five to fifty members strong.

"Stay here," Reia whispered, leaning close. "I'll announce our presence to the queen before we set up camp."

Terosh nodded, enjoying the tickle of her breath against his ear.

"Ireshasu," Reia greeted, approaching the point where the passage opened into a large cavern.

"Reia, the anotechs understand the common tongue. Talk to her normally. Maybe she'll understand."

Reia shot him an annoyed glance but acknowledged the advice. To his horror, she dropped to both knees and bowed her head.

"I have brought a friend. We offer you protection in exchange for shelter and scales."

A series of throaty yips and growls ensued, and Terosh interpreted them as favorable, despite not understanding the actual words.

"May I approach, Your Majesty?" Terosh called, anxious to meet the magnificent creature.

"Come slowly," Reia instructed. "She doesn't like quick movements. They remind her of korvers."

Terosh cautiously entered the giant cavern. The wall curved around from the passage he had come from, extending fifteen meters up and around before straightening out for another sixty meters. Several tunnels connected to the one Terosh emerged from, and he suspected they led to caverns for the queen's mates and offspring. Faint shuffling confirmed the presence of more zaloks.

The cave reminded him of Loresh, where glowcrystals provided necessary light. Six meters above the ground, the cavern's glowing yellow ceiling shivered and shone almost as brightly as a night of full moons. It took Terosh a few seconds to identify patches of blue marin moss, the major food source for shiners. Millions of tiny insects zipped through the air, lending their light to the cavern. His eyes flicked from the floor to the ceiling and back.

That many shiners means …

Reia's laugh interrupted his thoughts.

"See anything interesting?" she asked.

"Not yet," Terosh muttered. He shifted from foot to foot, trying to resist checking the bottom of his boots.

"The floor's clean," Reia commented. She pointed to the ceiling. "Listen."

Terosh heard the faint whistle of air. After a few seconds, he concluded there must be air vents above and to the sides beneath the shiners.

The zalok queen rose two and a half meters high. If she stood up on her two hind legs she would be over four meters tall, not counting her long, spikey tail. Her black, leathery face and arms appeared bare. Rows upon rows of purple scales—the queen's most magnificent feature—covered her from head to tail. The purple scales exceeded beauty expectations. They shifted shade with every movement either of the zalok or the observer. The queen reminded him of a dragon or a cominad, but the stories had failed to describe her commanding presence.

Unconsciously, Terosh compared the creature to his deceased

mother. Queen Kila's wardrobe of exquisite gowns would have been hard-pressed to match the zalok queen's natural beauty. Terosh joined Reia by kneeling before the splendid creature.

When their knees began burning, Terosh and Reia set about making camp. While Reia fetched water from the stream running along the cave's left side, Terosh braved the snowstorm for firewood. As he tromped back in, shaking snow from his boots, he watched half a dozen squirrels and other small creatures scurrying over the large pile of the queen's stores, setting it in a neater order.

"They bring her tokens in exchange for naturally shed scales," Reia explained, noticing his interest in the tiny workers. "They use the scales in their homes."

After arranging the brush into a neat pile, Terosh picked up a twig and studied its bumps and ridges. He considered waiting for Reia to light the fire but decided to do it himself.

"Light," he commanded the anotechs, expecting them to ignore him.

Upon healing his windstorm injuries, the anotechs had left him with a working knowledge of their language. Terosh could have used the Kalastan word for fire, but he wanted to experiment with the idea that the anotechs could speak his language. The stick burst into flames so fast it seared his hand. Terosh cried out and dropped the stick onto the brush. The fire fixings happily exploded into flames, drawing a stare from the zalok queen.

Reia chuckled and captured Terosh's injured hand.

"Hethiciun." She gently turned his hand over to make sure the wound was completely healed. It had only been a mild burn. "You're going to have to be more specific with them. They're like small children responding to commands."

"Naughty children," Terosh grumbled. "Thank you." He gripped Reia's left hand, suddenly reluctant to let it slip away.

After eating some cannafitch jerky, Terosh and Reia exchanged a few stories. Then, they engaged in a friendly duel. The battle on the Riden Mountains showed them that the banistick could handle kerlinblade strikes, but tonight, Reia added an anotech shield around the banistick to make it more durable.

When they first started fighting, the queen bristled and reared back, ready to defend herself. After three minutes of talk from Reia, the queen shook her head, turned two circles, snorted, and settled down to sleep with her back to them.

"I think we've been dismissed," Terosh said, raising his kerlinblade in a salute. "Shall we?"

"As you wish, Highness," Reia replied.

They fought from one end of the cavern to the other and back twice. Terosh noticed that his dueling skills were sharper. He took a moment to analyze Reia's style. She fought with a refreshing energy and vitality that made him miss the daily duels with the weapons masters, yet her strikes seemed tentative.

"You're holding back," he accused, blocking a slow side sweep.

"Of course, I am. The point is not to kill each other," Reia replied.

"The point *is* to get better," Terosh insisted, disengaging. "So, try to keep up." With that, he attacked with a flurry of strikes that forced Reia back.

She rose to the challenge, and they fought their mock battle, losing themselves in the rhythm of strikes and parries. The duel ended abruptly when Reia took a tumble into the stream. Terosh valiantly fished her out.

As they dried out next to the fire, they again swapped stories.

When Reia's turn rolled around for the third time, she grew pensive.

"My sister once saved a boy from a Porit viper."

"I didn't even know you had a sister," Terosh commented.

"I almost didn't," Reia replied.

"You don't have to tell me."

"I want to, but I think I'd better let the anotechs show you, if you're willing. The experience might be … intense."

She looked so sad that Terosh would have done anything to ease her mind.

"I am willing," he said solemnly.

Reia took Terosh's right hand. His fingers tingled where the anotechs transferred from her to him, carrying the memories.

In his mind's eye, Terosh saw a massive stake surrounded by torch-toting men. A girl slumped against it, making the scene much more disturbing. She didn't look much like Reia, but there was an air of familiarity about her. The anotechs identified her as Kiata Antellio.

"Where are the others?" demanded a tall man holding a banistick. The man kicked the girl, catching her in the lower left ribs.

Breathing raggedly, Kiata stared up at the man.

"What others, Master Keldor?"

The man stiffened with surprise and anger. He rained more blows upon the girl until a new cry split the night air.

Two men leapt into the brush and pulled out a young boy.

"Taly! How did he get here?" A sob choked off more questions. Keldor dropped the banistick, rushed to the boy, and scooped him half onto his lap. *"What happened?"*

"Snakebite, sir," answered one of the men.

The child's eyes were closed, and he lay so still Terosh couldn't tell if he lived.

"I can save him!" Kiata called.

"Silence! The man needs to grieve!" shouted one of the men.

"I can save him!" Kiata repeated.

"Cut her loose, Careth," ordered Keldor.

Soon, Kiata was dumped next to Keldor and the boy. She placed her left hand on the boy's forehead and her right hand on his chest.

"Hesseporatha. Hethledanlon," Kiata mumbled.

"What in Riden's name is she saying?" a spectator demanded.

Terosh's hands tingled again, but this time it was like a hundred tiny pins prickled his fingertips. Kiata continued to work for several minutes, before collapsing next to the boy.

Returning to the present, Terosh looked at Reia and wondered how many times she had experienced the memories.

"Why did she save him?" he asked hoarsely.

"It's what we do," Reia answered, shrugging. She offered him a drink of water.

Accepting the drink, Terosh refrained from telling her how stupid that philosophy could be. To distract her, he spoke of Tarel and Idellia, the royal couple assassinated by rogue Royal Guards on Jira (March) 12, 1330. Then, seeing she still needed distracting, he detailed King Rammon's unusually long reign, the murder of the king's wife and three of his children, Princess Lystran's escape, the building of the city of Rammon, and the discovery of tosh as a healing agent and a fuel source.

To balance things, he recounted Princess Sora Ann's romance with Quinard the Royal Guard and some antics of the twin princes, Yuri and Rumel, sons of Othel Belri and Queen Lissa. He mentioned Prince Skye's obsession with animals. Indulged by his parents and his brother, Crown Prince Tristan, Skye filled the Rammon Palace with over fifteen thousand species of animals from wallays to korvers to cannafitch to rine bats. He even had two hook whales in a tank in his bedroom.

Terosh knew Reia enjoyed tales about Davel. She knew him as the founder of the Rangers, but he doubted she knew much about him as a prince. In Pirua (September) of 1053 Crown Prince Davel's little sister, Princess Lin, was kidnapped. Davel gathered some trusted guards and formed the Order of the Nareth Talis, or Night Torch, to track down the kidnappers. A generation later, the Nareth Talis became a part of the Reshner Rangers. The new title declared that the Order served everybody. The passage of time pared the title down to Rangers.

After about an hour, Reia took over storytelling. She first spoke about her masters and training. Her tone professed love and deep respect for Niklos Mikhail McGreven and Jolinda Ekris. Then, she spoke with equal passion for Rangers who stood for justice, such as Miere Saan, Tolin, and Tyler Wexam, and those who abused their authority, like Raynn Criman, Amnek Miduo, Gedroo, and Vazdon. Finally, Reia explained some of the Ranger traditions, including the prohibition against romantic entanglements with royals.

"You wouldn't want to fall in love with anyone in my family anyway," Terosh teased. "We have the bad habit of dying violently."

"That's a horrible thing to say!" Reia protested.

Terosh shrugged.

"It's the truth. Take my own family, starting with my grandparents. King Salen and Queen Miren had four children: Crown Princess Uria, her twin brother Uel, Princess Mavis, and Prince Teorn. Aunt Mavis was disowned for falling in love with a Third Lord. Uria and Uel were assassinated in Temen (July) of 1516, and King Salen died a few years later, killed by GAPP agents."

"What's GAPP?" Reia asked.

"You Rangers don't get out much, do you?"

"Some do, some don't. I'm just an apprentice. I'm in the 'don't' category."

"Fair enough," Terosh said. "GAPP stands for the Galactic Alliance of Populated Planets. They've been trying to rearrange Reshner's government for centuries, but so far they've only managed a few arranged marriages, such as my grandparents and parents."

"Why accept the GAPP arrangements?"

"Politics is more complicated than simply turning down something distasteful."

Reia's eyes narrowed.

"Are you saying your grandfather didn't love your grandmother?"

Terosh shook his head.

"I'm saying that my grandfather married to avoid a war with Porit, and my father married to seal a trade deal with Gardan. My mother spent much time arranging suitable matches for my brother and me. Based on that, who needs quicksand to sink a relationship?"

"That's sad," Reia noted.

"My brother married for love, and that certainly didn't end well." Silence stretched and Terosh felt Reia's hand upon his shoulder.

"Who was she?"

Tucking his knees close, Terosh pulled up a mental picture of Dr. Deanna Koffrin.

"She was a scientist who brought out the best in him." He squeezed his eyes shut. "They had a child, but they're both dead now. Dr. Koffrin and the child, I mean. Tate's just dead inside."

"I'm sorry." Reia squeezed his shoulder.

His pain flipped to anger.

"I should have stopped him! I could have!"

"How, Terosh?"

Terosh realized she'd finally neglected to use his title, but his efforts went into controlling his emotions.

"You can't stop love. It's more powerful than a windstorm."

Terosh considered her words.

"Then why do Rangers try?"

Reia released his shoulder. When she spoke, her tone hinted at a smile.

"Some of us think that denying love makes us stronger, but we're not forbidden to marry. We just have to avoid royals." She let silence linger then added, "Sometimes, I think we're all fools."

"You're no fool," Terosh protested.

Reia laughed, short and sharp.

"Tell that to Lucas. I'm afraid he'd beg to differ."

"Who's that?" Terosh asked.

The name seemed familiar.

"My one and only disastrous foray into heart matters."

Terosh barely heard her reply because the nagging sensation resolved itself.

"He's that Ranger who claimed to be a Kireshana guardian."

"He did? When?" asked Reia.

"Could he be lying?" Terosh wondered.

"I suppose so, but why? As far as I know, there are no general Kireshana guardians. Our focus has always been the Royal House. We don't have enough people to adequately protect every candidate. Even if we could, Lucas is a master. It would have made more sense for the Council to assign him rather than me as your guardian. What would he gain by lying?"

Trust, Terosh answered silently.

***

Enis (April) 10, 1538
Same day
Governor General's Estate, City of Idonia

After swallowing his pride, Kezem sought his mother's help in confirming Lucas's information concerning the Royal House. He had even offered to meet her in person. Much to his relief, she turned down the face-to-face meeting. Though grateful his mother seemed in a forgiving mood about the assassination attempt, Kezem liked the distance a holographic link afforded him. Still, he hated waiting. Stalking around his office like a caged kambri was the only way to control his nerves. He sighed, feeling like his entire life consisted of waiting for meetings. Training battles hardly assuaged his need to beat something.

His mother appeared and spoke without preamble.

"It is true. I have a dozen informants to check yet, but the reports confirm Ranger Telon's account. I'm surprised your pet Maledek didn't tell you this directly, and I can't believe I never realized it before. It makes perfect sense that Captain Kelter would be Taytron's mother. She looks exactly like Kila and was isolated with the queen for the exact same time. My sources do not think even Teorn knows."

"How could they hide something like that from him?"

"Those were different days. My father kept Teorn busy building alliances and dealing with GAPP lackeys. He hardly had time to breathe let alone think about his quaint marriage. The Gardanian customs dictated the groom not see the bride's face until the morning after the wedding."

"Does this change anything?" Kezem wondered.

"It should make you more willing to consider my suggestion," Lady Mavis said. "The Mitran people and their barbaric customs are capable of dispatching three of our royal troubles. We'll have to handle the fourth ourselves when the time is right."

"Terosh." Kezem voiced the fourth royal problem. He didn't want to think about the backwards Mitran people or their Blood Harvest. The idea of systematically destroying a royal bloodline every thousand year so none could claim a longer rule was ludicrous. The way his mother had manipulated things to have the Blood Harvest deal with his uncle and cousin fascinated him.

Nodding, Lady Mavis continued her analysis of their situation.

"There are many options for dealing with Terosh, but I'm loath to dwell on the problem with much of the Kireshana still ahead of him. Timing is the key to everything. Decide which side you want to be on when this plays out but know that my agents are already working to the ends I described."

"What of the Ranger problem?" Kezem inquired. "They will always defend House Minstel."

"One thing at a time, love," his mother urged. "We'll let the Mitra deal with Teorn, Taytron, and Captain Kelter, cast the full might of your RT Alliance against the Rangers, and then either bend Terosh to our purposes or kill him. I'm working to weaken the Rangers. I'll let you know if my plans pan out. For now, I suggest your agents work with mine in keeping your cousin's royal neck intact."

Kezem grunted. He had told most of his operatives not to kill his cousin, but part of him had hoped one would succeed anyway. He had little choice now. He needed all the help he could get. Working against his mother would only exhaust both of their resources. Without a farewell, he stormed over to his desk and prepared orders for his remaining agents.

The task took almost an hour and gave Kezem a headache. Slumping in his chair, he massaged his temple with both hands. Soon thereafter, Dantrel came in with a glowing report on the korver training program. After listening to the young man blather on for a minute, Kezem threw him out of the office. He'd read the full report later. Right now, he had more pressing issues to consider. For example, Maledek had not taken the changing orders well, and Prince Taytron was making a nuisance of himself by obsessively pursuing Maledek.

Taytron's pursuing a myth and the embodiment of that myth is probably running amok.

The thought wrapped around Kezem like a strong cord looped across his chest, making him feel trapped.

Then, a new thought lightened his mood.

Maledek must be controlled, Taytron needs to kill him, and Lucas Telon can help me accomplish both.

Chapter 18:
Korver Attack

Enis (April) 28, 1538
Fifty-seven days into Prince Terosh's Kireshana journey
Dalonos's Campsite, near the Zalok Caves, Riden Mountains

Dalonos had trained hard for this moment. He remembered staring down at the twisted metal lump that used to be his holograph player. That had been the turning point. The dark anotechs still wanted to kill Prince Terosh. They showed him how, and he'd spent weeks preparing. His control over the korvers still lacked finesse but control was contrary to his needs anyway. He wanted madness, rage, and bloodlust.

Gaius—the beast named after the Kalastan god of fire—was a different story. He was more of an ally than a slave. Roughly four times bigger than the average korver, Gaius made his entire pack look like pups. He stalked back and forth across a circle that rapidly changed as those he drew near shrank away and those he moved away from surged forward, barking wildly. His low growls made the pebbles around him tremble.

Breathing deeply, Dalonos dropped into a meditative state and sent anotechs to control the other korvers. It would be a long but glorious night.

***

Reia dueled the prince every night, often exchanging weapons several times during a fight. Prince Terosh struggled with the banistick being much heavier than his kerlinblade, and Reia had trouble compensating for the seeming weightlessness of the kerlinblade. The duels resulted in many bruises and burns which they fixed with anotechs. They even practiced healing mid-fight. Next, they practiced silently commanding the anotechs.

The true test came late one evening about two and a half weeks into their winter stay with the zaloks. In centuries past, thousands of zaloks inhabited these caves and could readily defend their nests, but in 1230, Channer Mazai discovered how to make a powerful hallucinogen by mixing zalok scales with crela dust and heating it. Since then, unscrupulous adventurers have hunted zaloks, despite protection by the Royal House Minstel and the Rangers.

The prince heard the korver cries first.

"Reia, listen. Is that what I think it is?" He reached for his kerlinblade.

A long, high-pitched, utterly mournful cry pierced the night.

"Yes," Reia answered, drawing her banistick from a belt clip. "Lenviddunoch, nimfeh, widulsucamcres," she called to the zalok queen. She could have spoken the assurances in the common tongue, but old habits die hard.

It's too early. Why attack now?

They had discussed the possibility of a korver attack and arranged some defenses, but she hadn't expected to need them yet. Reia sprinted toward the main entrance. Bitter, cold air whined and whistled its way through the modified passage. She collapsed several parts of the tunnel as she went. None of the partial blockages would stop the korvers but they would cut down on the number faced at one time.

Controlling her breaths, Reia crouched behind the foremost defensive barrier. Rock extensions narrowed the passage to a half-meter, but the area behind that was still the usual three meters across. Slowly, she opened her banistick to its full two-meter length and centered the handle.

Two of Reshner's moons, Marishaz and Corid, were nearly three-quarters full. They peeked out from behind the mountains to the east, shining brilliantly down upon the entrance. Reia knew Gemuln hid behind the mountain directly in front of her and suspected he would show his face before the fight ended.

The howls shortened and intensified as the korvers drew closer.

Soon, one pair of blood-red eyes glowed in the night, then two, then twenty, then she lost count.

The average korver stands just shy of a meter tall from the top of its pointy ears down to its front feet and measures about a meter and a half in length from slender snout to tail tip. One korver could be annoying, but a pack this large would kill them.

Sudden silence ruled the valley.

Reia's blood chilled as she waited.

The chief korver released a long, terrible shriek and received a yipping bark from every pack member. They paused for two seconds then barked again, waited another two seconds, and barked again. This continued for about a minute, with each bark being slightly louder than the last. Then, the leader howled again, and the pack sent up a racket of frenzied barks that echoed off the mountains.

Reia barely had time to brace before the korver tide crashed, forcing her back. Four energy beams sizzled past her and disappeared into the mass. Recovering her balance, Reia slipped the banistick handle down to one end, collapsed the weapon to a meter in length, and smashed a korver aside. The impact jarred her arms, but she used the resulting force to swat the next korver in line. This time, she was ready for the jolt. Leaping backward, she let the banistick unfurl the whole way again, slipped the handle back to the center, and twirled the weapon four times. It kept the korvers at bay and bought her a few seconds to think, but she couldn't twirl the banistick forever.

Surrendering to instinct, Reia swung left and right before retreating and striking again. Korvers bounced away from her banistick with pain-filled howls, but for every two Reia hit, a third slipped past. Prince Terosh promptly shot them and the few he missed were dispatched by the queen's mates, but Reia knew they yielded valuable ground.

Centimeter by grudging centimeter, Reia retreated, making the korvers pay dearly for each step. Around fifty-four, she lost count of the sickening crunch of her banistick's triumph over a korver. Her mind numbed as the violence slammed her sensibilities to pieces. Every muscle in her arms and legs protested the jarring strikes. She hated the loss of life, yet the frustration lent her the strength to fight on.

Before they knew it, Reia and the prince had retreated past all three barriers and reached the entrance to the larger cavern. They had each taken down scores of korvers, but there were still too many. If they retreated further, the korvers would burst into the cave and storm the zalok queen. She and her mates would not withstand such an onslaught for long.

Sensing victory, the korvers paused. Three lined up shoulder-to-shoulder and advanced slowly, deepening their growls.

We must make a stand!

Reia dug her heels into the soft layer of dirt and waited for the final attack.

"Linketalkorvers!"

Reia heard the prince's shout just as something intensely bright flashed past her right shoulder and caught a korver in the throat. The animal burst into flames like a dry stick. Reia's mouth dropped and her banistick almost followed as a stream of fire flowed from the prince through the tightly packed korvers, creating a writhing sea of howling madness. The heat drove her back a step. She leaned forward to catch her balance and almost stumbled into the thin beam connecting the prince to the nearest korver.

It must look like half the mountain's on fire!

The scent of burning fur, smoke, and cooking meat sent her head spinning. At the same time, the screeching korver cries slammed into Reia with near physical force. Her eyes stung from the smoke and heat. Coughing, she turned away just in time to see the prince collapsing.

Terosh!

Attaching her banistick to her belt, Reia lunged and caught the prince before his head could strike the ground. Tears flowed. She gripped the prince under both armpits and slowly dragged him into the central cavern. Reia tripped and fell, breaking his fall with her body. After wriggling out from under the fallen prince, Reia assessed the damage. The shallow rise and fall of his chest told her he lived. When she drew her hand away and watched him, he lay as still as death itself. Both of his hands were raw with burned and bloody fingertips. She winced.

"Hethiciuns." Reia willed herself to touch Terosh's broken hands.

He is badly burned. It will take much time to heal him, said a child's voice in her mind.

"Do what you can," Reia ordered, too distraught to be awed by the anotechs talking to her.

A low growl came from the shadows behind Reia, telling her the fight wasn't over yet. Her banistick materialized in her hands as she scrambled to her feet.

A massive korver with smoking fur stepped over the broken bodies of lesser korvers. Its eyes shifted from the deep red back to normal yellow orbs that gleamed with intelligence.

Every mental calculation led to the same conclusion. To fight would be to die.

What are you?

Gaius, answered the anotechs. ***He is full of Dark Ones.***

Reia stepped away from the prince hoping to draw the creature's attention, but the beast stalked closer and growled. The zalok queen voiced her own challenge. Reia's insides quivered from the combined effect.

Time ceased mattering as the parties studied each other.

Reia focused on the beast, but she knew the queen's mates would form a wall in front of their leader.

"Go back. This fight is lost."

In reply, Gaius growled again, barked, and charged.

***

Lucas Telon had watched events unfold from the moment the soul-piercing korver cry had ripped through him. He'd been thinking about Reia. Watching her train with the prince had been painful, but he needed to focus. Setting his TT-189 to detect heat signatures had revealed an impossible number: 344. Korvers never gathered in such large numbers. Even granting that a few dozen signatures belonged to Reia, himself, the prince, and zaloks didn't bring the number into a reasonable range.

Despite his training, his heart beat wildly. The moment to intervene had arrived.

If he did nothing, Reia and the prince would die. Reia's death would violate his conscience and Terosh's death would violate his orders. Lady Altran had been quite clear that he should get the prince through the Kireshana without being detected. He watched Reia's last stand, mentally ticking off the flaws in her performance.

The big korver swatted her aside like a toy and stalked past her toward the prince. Despite a deep gash in her left arm, Reia smacked the beast's left flank with her banistick, regaining its attention. The massive korver knocked her again, batting her in Lucas's direction. The prince was still unconscious.

Lucas waited until Reia's back faced him before dropping to the ground behind her, wrapping one arm around her neck, and bracing her head with his other hand. She barely had time to gasp before his grip relieved her of consciousness. Then, Lucas grinned at the korver.

"Your move," he challenged, deciding between a banistick and a kerlinblade.

The beast barked and launched itself at him.

Lucas avoided the brunt of the beast's attack, but one shoulder clipped him and sent him reeling off to the side. From that moment on, Lucas approached the fight more cautiously. He settled on the kerlinblade. Fire had dealt nicely with the other korvers.

The giant korver charged again and again, all teeth, muscles, and claws.

Lucas smacked the beast with his kerlinblade, landing several head blows. They bounced as if he were beating on a spaceship's hull with a broomstick. For several minutes, his body fought instinctively, but as he tired, rational thought returned, and Lucas cursed his stupidity. He had fought a beast like this before and knew how to beat it.

After several failed attacks, the korver backed off slightly.

Lucas snatched the mini kerlak pistol off his belt and let three shots fly. The first struck the edge of the beast's right eye, eliciting a yelp and an involuntary head-jerk. The second two shots entered the eye, causing the beast to howl. Instead of making the beast fall over dead though, the pain angered it. The korver charged Lucas again, driving him against a stone wall and knocking his breath out. It took tremendous effort to keep conscious. He was supremely lucky the zaloks closed ranks around him and drove off the big korver.

He wanted to sleep but had to get away. His mission had been preserved, but his mistress would not abide discovery. Gathering his remaining strength, Lucas limped back to his camp.

***

Reia awoke next to the prince and marveled at being alive. She wondered how she had gotten there until the sight of the prince's still form broke her heart and drove off her questions.

Please, please live.

As she clutched his broken hands, Reia realized that somewhere along the journey Prince Terosh had become more than her mission. She had pushed the initial inklings of deeper feelings aside, knowing nothing could come of them. As a Ranger, loving nobles was frowned upon and loving a royal absolutely forbidden.

The tradition came from the 1280's when Queen Rivira Minstel's younger sister, Alana, had fallen in love with Ranger Mordeki VaTraz. The pair ran away, pursued by soldiers under the false assumption that the princess had been kidnapped. Once cornered, the lovers had killed themselves rather than face separation. The truth that Sergo, a spurned suitor, had lied about the princess's disappearance only came out after their deaths. The Royal House and the Rangers bandied blame back and forth for months. Finally, the Rangers—ever the peacekeepers—swore that none from their ranks would ever be allowed to love a royal.

Since that time, people had, of course, gotten around the rule, but the intense stigma was taught to adolescent Rangers. As far as Reia knew, the last Ranger to defy the rule had been Amserd who had loved Crown Princess

Loress. He had been cast from the Order, and she had abdicated to marry him. It had been a happy sacrifice until Gedroo, a Ranger purist defending the old ways, murdered Amserd. Loress had pursued her husband's killer and also fallen victim.

It never ends happily for a Ranger and a royal, Reia thought sadly, forcing herself to stand.

If she sat by him now, she would never leave. She needed a safe emotional distance where thoughts of Terosh lying near death wouldn't pierce so painfully.

Forcing worry aside nearly cost all of her remaining strength, but Reia finally inspected the well-done korvers. After consulting with the zalok queen, Reia helped the zaloks drag each body into the main cavern and stack them in the back corner, opposite the stream. She kept two korvers for meat and skinned off small patches of unburned fur, using the labor as an emotional balm. Reia turned her meat allotment into korver jerky. The rest she left for the zaloks who had their own storing methods, which involved secreting preservative from their mouths onto the meat.

With the hard work done, Reia worried about Terosh. To keep her hands busy, she made several lengths of korver fur rope. She wondered how they had survived the attack. The floor wasn't decorated with the giant korver's carcass so it had to have survived, but someone knocked her out before driving it off.

Who would do both?

If someone was going to fight the korver, why knock her out? For that matter, why not kill her? People died frequently on the Kireshana. No one would notice one more body.

The thoughts haunted her throughout the night as she kept a vigil over the wounded prince.

***

Enis (April) 28, 1538
Same day
Dalonos's Campsite, near the Zalok Caves, Riden Mountains
Dalonos's whole body hurt. Shrieking, he sent anotechs from one korver to another, trying to find one alive. Each new body filled him with more pain, until the anotechs cut the connection and let him go limp.

We're tired of healing him!

A blue-white pool of light formed around him, seeping from his body and coalescing into a young woman. The figure of False Jalna—Dark Ones in the form of the Maker's Daughter—looked down on Dalonos with compassion.

"This will set him back, but he is still our best chance. Perhaps a better candidate will come along soon."

Dalonos looked awful. To gain control over the korvers, the anotechs had established a strong connection with them.

"Yes. Change is good. What about the Lady?"
He'd felt the korvers burn.

96

The translucent girl shuddered, though she possessed only vague memories of such agony.

"She would make a fine candidate, but no, the being must be a slave," the False Jalna said.

The universe worked in strange ways. The girl smiled at possessing memories from their worst enemy, the real Daughter of the Maker. Perhaps one day they could convince the Maker's Daughter to see things logically. Pushing her feelings aside, the Dark One's manifestation of Jalna spent the next four hours multiplying anotechs to replace the trillions lost on the ill-fated korver attack.

"You may yet serve a purpose, even by your death," the girl said, as she infused Dalonos's body with new anotechs.

Chapter 19:
Graveground

Retsi (May) 21, 1538
Eighty days into Prince Terosh's Kireshana journey
Kireshana Path, Resh Grasslands

Winter officially concluded at the end of Enis (April), but the snows remained for another few weeks. Prince Terosh Minstel and Ranger Reia Antellio could have left on the first of Retsi, but they waited until the eighth day to allow the prince's hands to continue healing. After bidding farewell to the grateful zalok queen, they left the caves laden with two korver skin pouches filled with purple scales, gifts of dried berries, and enough korver jerky to last until the end of the year.

Reia chose a gentle path through the Riden Mountains to give the prince's hands time to heal. He didn't complain much, but she knew that they still stung whenever he moved them. While in the zalok cave, he'd let Reia wrap his hands in toom leaves soaked in corlia. The treatment helped, but once they started moving, the prince refused the wraps, claiming they made his hands clumsy.

They reached the Resh Grasslands on the twentieth of Retsi. The next day, they awoke to a sky full of storm clouds, but since it wasn't time for the acid storms, they didn't worry. They hiked steadily for a few hours before meeting Derna and Irek Praem, a sibling pair of tretling herders headed home for a short leave. As the main herding season stretched from Lanolin to Temen (February to July), wealthy flock owners hired herders in cycles. About a meter in length and sporting white, gray, or beige wool, tretlings are blobs of dull color when viewed from a distance. As they possess the constitution of bears and the brains of pill bugs, handling them could be exhausting.

Ten minutes after encountering the herders, Reia halted and seized the prince's left arm to keep him from taking another step.

"Graveground!"

The prince looked confused.

"Wallays, right?" he asked slowly. "Small, furry, brown things. I think Master Sedir mentioned them. He said they were dangerous."

"Well, farmers hate them, but they aren't directly dangerous ..." Reia answered, letting the sentence trail. She pictured one of the creatures. Wallays grow about a quarter of a meter in length and have small, beady eyes and blunt noses. They'd be adorable if they weren't so destructive. She took a cautious step, angling left, and motioned for the prince to follow. Leaping over a seemingly solid piece of ground, she landed on a patch of slightly taller grass two feet away. "Except when they leave."

"How does that work?" asked Terosh.

She waited until she'd identified the next dangerous section before answering the prince's question.

"Wallay colonies can have several hundred members. They maintain underground tunnels by coating the walls with a viscous substance called cradul. The cradul hardens in a half-hour, forming a tough, waterproof wall. No one knows how the beasts learned to make doors, but the system of sliding cradul-treated dirt slabs prevents their homes from flooding."

"Why do farmers hate them?" Terosh asked.

Reia chuckled and jumped another section of grass.

"Hate is too mild a term. Wallays consume crops and soil, but the worst part is when they leave because without the cradul, the tunnel walls crumble, resulting in graveground."

Reia continued to lead the way through the dangerous sections.

"You're stepping on the thicker, darker grass," the prince noted.

"Exactly," Reia confirmed.

A web of lightning brightened the gloomy day, followed closely by a huge thunder crack. The ground trembled. Reia looked up surprised. She had almost forgotten the storm. A minute later, the first raindrops plunked down onto her head.

Not hearing the prince's footsteps behind her anymore, Reia paused and looked back.

"What *are* you doing?" Reia shouted to be heard.

The rain fell faster and faster, thoroughly soaking them both. The prince looked giddy. He held out his hands to catch the rain, tipping his head back and letting the rain pour down onto his face. At first, Reia didn't understand, but then she remembered him talking about his mother's fear of acid storms. The queen had kept him palace-bound during every storm, harmless or not. More lightning and thunder showed off, and the wind ripped at their cloaks.

Before he could answer, Reia cocked her head and closed her eyes. Then, she stepped forward until she reached the prince's side and listened hard. The sound of swiftly moving water reached her. There were no rivers or streams near here. Wind whipped hair against her face, but she didn't acknowledge the discomfort.

Another boom drowned out other sounds.

Still listening carefully, Reia stood next to Terosh as tense as a wallay hosting korvers. Suddenly, she took off in the direction she had been looking, behind the prince and to his right, roughly in the direction they had just come from. Without hesitation, he sprinted after her.

Casting off her cloak, Reia dropped her bags, boots, and leather belt holding her banistick and jumped over a ledge that suddenly appeared.

No!

Ignoring the anotechs, she swam at the two dark masses hurtling down the stream formed as the downpour collapsed the graveground. With the current propelling her, Reia reached the pair within seconds. Luckily, they had attached themselves to each other. She grabbed a handful of soggy cloth and held on tightly, fighting the current with her legs and free arm. Her efforts slowed their pace, but they were still headed downstream at unsafe speeds.

"Reia!" Terosh shouted. "Catch!"

Reia twisted around and searched for his voice. One of the ropes smacked the water by her left ear. Grabbing the rope, Reia silently prayed Terosh would pull them in by the time her strength disappeared.

The rescue went well until a fossa tree careened toward Reia and her limp charges. It was a blessing that the tretling herders were unconscious, for the current and debris gave Reia plenty to worry about. The tree's rapid approach almost made her faint. She had seconds to make a move—any move—to avoid certain death. Diving underwater, Reia twirled so that the rope wrapped around the unconscious herders. The rope cut into her hands as the current jerked her back and forth, but
Reia kept twisting, entangling her arms in the rope.

Use us!

How?

A tree branch clipped Reia's left shoulder as she surfaced for breath. She angled her body to protect the herders, but the blow nearly tore her away. Her arms throbbed as the korver rope dug in. She fought for consciousness and kept enough wits to roll away from another tree.

We can slow the current.

Then do so! Reia snapped.

Can't. Need direction.

Reia imagined the flood slowing and strength pouring into her from the surrounding water. With massive effort, she broke the surface, dragging the herders with her. More debris came at them, but the pace seemed slower. Reia could see where she needed to be moments before the need arose. Doing this saved her some worry and pain. Still, it took several awful minutes of tree dodging before Terosh pulled them ashore.

Once finally safe, Reia closed her eyes and rested.

***

Terosh crouched by Reia and the two young herders, scarcely daring to check their vital signs. His hands burned. The anotechs had shielded and strengthened them while he pulled on the rope, but now that the crisis was over, the pain returned ten-fold.

Lightning, thunder, and thoughts of his pain faded as rain washed mud and debris off Reia. A leaf clung tenaciously to her forehead just above her left eye. Terosh removed the leaf and traced the side of her face. Gently, he wiped mud from her face with a clean section of his cloak.

Reia remained unconscious while Terosh carefully unwound the ropes holding her to the herders. The wound on her left shoulder looked ugly and leaked blood. Her eyes fluttered when he checked for a pulse. She gasped and tried to sit up, but he caught her and eased her back to the ground.

"Easy. I don't know how badly you're injured," he said.

As suddenly as it had started, the rain ceased, leaving everything strangely calm.

"Are they all right?" Reia shut her eyes, clearly exhausted.

"The anotechs will tell me in a minute, but are *you* all right?" Terosh didn't bother explaining that since the korver attack he had been practicing directing the anotechs. She had witnessed his clumsy efforts to move rocks and dried leaves.

"I'll live." Reia didn't sound too pleased with the idea. Several deep scratches decorated her face. The left shoulder wound still bled. The anotechs were already knitting the wounds together, but the gashes still looked painful. Both her sleeves were shredded and deep red marks crisscrossed her forearms.

Terosh grimaced at the rope burns. He placed a hand on each of her arms and thought, *Heal her wounds.*

No.

Shock nearly knocked Terosh over. He jerked his hands back.

"What's wrong?" Reia asked, opening her eyes.

Sorry, bad joke.

You fix her wounds right now! And that scar from the korver attack, if she wants it healed.

He received the mental impression of a shrug, but slowly, Reia's arms looked less irritated. Terosh watched as her shoulder wound slowly closed. He didn't know how long he sat there holding her cold right hand. He only interrupted his vigil long enough to build a fire and check on the other two. They were fine. Reia had caught most of the things flying down the river at them.

Are all Rangers that reckless?

Most, answered the anotechs.

Terosh frowned. He didn't like sharing every thought with them. That night, he learned to shut them out by creating a quiet space within his mind. They had already shown that they would accept directions from him, so he shifted thoughts into sections they could access and private areas they could not. Anotechs could be powerful allies, but sometimes, a man needed to be alone with his thoughts.

***

Retsi (May) 21, 1538
Same day
Maledek's Safehouse, City of Azhel

Prince Taytron Minstel gripped his kerlak pistol so hard his whole arm shook.

Having traveled southeast of Rammon through the Kevil Plains, crossed the Kala River, dodged part of the Ash Mountains, and raided three different possible Maledek hideouts today, he had only rage and determination keeping him on his feet. Still, he hesitated.

This isn't right.

The sweet voice within his head almost made him groan. He yearned to hear the real thing but knew he would never hear Deanna's voice again.

"No, Taytron," called a different female voice. "Not this way."

He almost didn't recognize Captain Kelter's voice without its usual bluster. Tate blinked. Tears blurred the ragged figure at his feet. The man propped himself up on his left elbow and used his right hand to probe a swelling knot on the side of his head. The chase through the klipper factory to this dirty, forgotten corner and the ensuing fistfight had exhausted both of them.

"He planned it. He executed it. He murdered Deanna." Taytron's accusations flew out like bursts of gunfire.

"He may have carried out the murder, but he is not Maledek," said Captain Kelter.

Tate's head whipped toward her, but his pistol remained on target.

"How do you know?"

"Can you not feel it?" the captain challenged.

She is right.

Tate swung his eyes back to the man. He didn't want to listen to the anotechs or face the Melian Maiden captain. She reminded him too much of his mother both in appearance and demeanor. Besides, he couldn't feel anything. He was done feeling. Feeling became synonymous with pain these days.

"Look at me," she ordered softly.

He did so, and his resolve crumbled under Captain Kelter's even gaze. Her stiff posture and sad expression said she would do anything for him but simultaneously begged him to listen.

"Do not do this."

Tate's finger tightened around the trigger. The slightest twitch would release a red bolt into the man's face. The muscles in Tate's right arm trembled, despite the extra support of his left hand.

No story is what it seems. Reach out with us. We will learn the truth.

Tate jerked his arm up to prevent accidentally shooting the man.

"Will you let me inside your mind to verify your story?"

"I don't have a choice," the man replied, "but I'd rather you not." His expression flickered with relief and worry before settling on defeat.

"Why not?" Taytron asked. "Don't you want to live?"

"If I'm right, he's been ordered to die," Captain Kelter answered. Her voice rumbled with rage.

"I have a family, too," the man whispered. He struggled to sit up and leaned back against the wall. "If you're going to crawl around my mind, you might as well be prepared for what you find. I am not guilty of the crime you think I am, but I am guilty of another."

As Tate touched the man's mind a name and a series of images slipped into his brain.

Niktrod Keldor.

"It's true!" The man's voice shook.

Feeling sick, Taytron forced himself to watch dozens of scenes. He paused on certain ones. He saw Deanna's broken body but felt only the curiosity of a stranger. He saw a shadowy figure demanding Keldor settle an old debt. Terror gripped him. The man would not hesitate to kill Keldor's wife and son or even his young grandson. They were faces and names that meant little to Tate, but his heart seized with Keldor's fear. He wondered who the shadowy figure could be and why he hadn't heard whispers of him before now.

Could this be the true Maledek?

Tate's heart nearly stopped when his mind locked upon a scene he remembered very well: his mother's death. The perspective wasn't right. The pristine place settings and excited banquet chatter were perfect, but this time, the small vial of comaladon mixed with gully fish poison rested in his hands. A deft hand flick and the deed was done. His eyes locked upon the smiling queen before turning and walking away. As the first alarmed scream reached his ears, Taytron wrenched his mind free of Keldor's.

Both men panted but said nothing. Tate released his grip on the man's head and let his arms fall to his sides.

"Do what you will," Keldor rasped. His voice sounded like wind over dry leaves.

Tate stumbled to his feet and ran from the room. He had to escape. He didn't trust himself not to kill the man. The man deserved it to be sure, but justice was not his to dispense. That honor belonged to his father.

Chapter 20:
Great Storm

Retsi (May) 25, 1538
Eighty-four days into Prince Terosh's Kireshana journey
Governor Lord's Estate, City of Resh

Located beyond the northwest edge of the Riden Mountains and right along the Kireshana path, the city of Resh was a popular stop. As such, Governor Lord Darmon Zelene had much practice being hospitable. Few people ever defied him. Everything about him demanded respect. His two-and-a-half-meter height alone required everybody to look up at him. Had he been born on Kalast, he might have been hailed as an avatar of Gedroak, god of giants. People on Reshner and Kalast rarely sprout over two meters. The simple fact that Darmon came from Celiost made his height less impressive. How he won the favor of Reshner's Prince Teorn Minstel is a separate tale, but today, the one person who could stand up to him did so.

Akia Zelene, the twenty-year-old daughter of Resh's governor, struggled to hold her father's gaze. For her part, she rarely needed to defy him. The man positively caved every time she asked for anything. Having learned contentedness from her mother, she asked for few things. Akia had inherited more than Eadria Zelene's short stature, blue-gray eyes, black hair, and cheery disposition. In truth, Lady Zelene was rather plain-looking, a fact few noblewomen failed to comment on, but she wore her name, which means "much fire in her," very well.

Father and daughter's discussion had already traveled circles for over fifteen minutes by the time he slammed his right hand down onto his desk like a judge's gavel.

"You will not put yourself in that kind of danger!"

"It is no more danger than any of the relief workers will face, Father," Akia said, speaking as a camrood herder would to one of the easily spooked beasts.

Governor Zelene's comm beeped three times before announcing, "My Lord, Prince Terosh Minstel has arrived with a Ranger. Shall I send them in?"

Akia's ears perked up at the mention of a Ranger, and she slipped deep into her own thoughts, missing her father's response. Rangers knew everything about healing and fighting. Akia could care less about their fighting abilities, but her trip to Ritand would benefit if she could speak with the Ranger about healing. For that matter, her chances of going would improve with the prince's help.

"May I stay, Papa?" she asked.

The twinkle in the governor's brown eyes offset his curt nod.

A long minute later, Akia got her first glimpse of Prince Terosh Minstel. For once the chatterboxes that passed for noblewomen around Resh hadn't exaggerated. The prince's black hair was given life by miniature waves frozen in time. His crystal blue eyes were simultaneously icy and heated, alive with intensity. He accepted her father's commanding presence with practiced ease.

It took Akia several seconds to pry her gaze away. She missed the beginning of her father's welcome speech and ignored the rest, choosing to study the Ranger instead. The girl was probably two or three years her junior. Her controlled expression revealed little, but her green eyes methodically took in the room. She possessed a natural beauty most women spent fortunes trying to attain. A pang of envy shot through Akia, but she wrestled her attention back to the conversation.

"—ter, Lady Akia Zelene," her father introduced with a sweeping gesture. "Lady Zelene, this is His Royal Highness Prince Terosh of House Minstel and the Honorable Ranger Reia Antellio."

Akia dropped into a curtsey and suppressed the urge to laugh. Her father always spoke loudly, but he rarely used such stiff speech. The prince and his Ranger guardian struck her as utterly normal. Their expressions declared a refreshing, open sense of honesty.

"It is a rare honor to meet you, Prince Terosh, and you, Ranger," she said, deciding to rescue her father.

The Ranger nodded, and a faint grin twitched her lips upward.

Prince Terosh smiled warmly with genuine relief. His posture remained regal yet lost some stiffness.

"Thank you, Lady Zelene. We hope not to impose long upon the governor's hospitality."

"Nonsense and rubbish. We'd love to have you for as long as you care to grace our humble home!" boomed Governor Zelene, finally toning down the formality. "Now, if you will excuse me, I shall tell the cook to set two more places. I'm sure my daughter would be happy to show you to quarters and keep you entertained."

As soon as her father had gone, an awkward silence fell. Akia wanted to ask them each a thousand things, especially the Ranger. She was left tongue-tied.

Will the prince help me? Will the Ranger teach me?

***

Reia knew their young hostess wanted to ask something. That much was indicated by her distracted gaze.

"You have a lovely home, Lady Zelene. I would love to see more of it once we wash up. The Resh Grasslands are unforgivably dusty," Reia said, trying to save everyone from the silence.

"Of course, Honorable Ranger, forgive my manners. Allow me to show you to the guest chambers. Then, I would be happy to give you a tour of my home. There should be enough time before the evening meal."

"Thank you, Lady Zelene. Would you consent to call me by my familiar name? I am Reia and merely a healer apprentice. After the evening meal, we can speak more if that is agreeable to you."

Lady Zelene barely managed to choke out a response.

"It would be my—Yes, of course, … Reia. That would please me very much. I … would like to ask you some questions if you'll permit."

The prince looked pleased to be ignored.

"—ns, my Prince?" Lady Zelene inquired.

For a split-second, Terosh looked panicked. Reia couldn't rescue him this time if she wanted to as she too missed the lady's question.

"Please, call me Terosh. I have few friends and would be honored to be addressed as one by you."

Nice recovery, Reia silently complimented.

"I don't—"

"Please, humor me," Terosh requested, taking Lady Zelene's right hand.

Reia bit the inside of her cheek to hold laughter in check. The sight of Prince Terosh begging Lady Zelene to address him familiarly was wonderfully pathetic.

"You embarrass the lady."

The prince turned a mock long-suffering look to Lady Zelene.

"Rangers are impossible to please, you know." He tucked the lady's arm under his own and gently lead her out.

Reia bid the anotechs to dampen odors coming from the prince so the lady wouldn't faint away. She already had them working for her.

Anotechs are useful things.

She followed the prince and the lady toward the guest chambers. During the past few months, she had snuck in a few stream baths and waterfall showers and even rubbed her skin with sweet-smelling fenria petals. For the most part, however, she'd settled for daily rinses from small brooks and an evening ritual of having the anotechs clean her.

After a wonderful bath, Reia dressed in the fine clothes Lady Zelene had placed out for her. The soft tunic and rich satin robe felt strange, but Prince Terosh looked magnificent in expensive clothes. Master Niklos's lessons on interacting with nobles included how to dress appropriately. Unfortunately, the lessons never covered her growing feelings for the prince.

The evening meal contained dozens of items. Reia recognized six species of fish, eight meats, and twenty-six vegetables and fruits. Several types of fish, including praja, comooli, and edakk, were new to her. Reia cautiously tried the odd dishes. Three out of four times the food pleased her palate, but the times it didn't, she struggled not to spit the thing across the room. She ended up drinking a lot of water and had little room for treacle pudding, cudri pie, or rielberry tarts. Nevertheless, she thoroughly enjoyed the meal.

Prince Terosh spoke easily with their hosts, but Reia said little. Instead, she focused on watching Lady Zelene. The young noblewoman defied every one of Reia's preconceived notions about those in the upper echelons of society. She played hostess beautifully and often sent her father reassuring smiles and encouraging nods.

The evening hours disappeared. The meal had destroyed most of Lady Akia Zelene's initial awkwardness. Still, it took Reia and the prince an hour to get her to consistently use their familiar names, but soon thereafter, Reia considered the lady one of the loveliest people she had ever met.

Reia wondered how to get Lady Akia to open up. Her sister would demand the woman speak her mind, but Reia didn't think the tactic would work. Lady Akia struck Reia as the sort to shut down if confronted, so she endured mundane conversation until the truth emerged late in the evening.

A comfortable stillness swept the room, broken only by Lady Akia's pacing. Her voice vibrated with passion as she finally presented her concern.

"An Ashasten—a Great Storm—is about to hit Ritand."

"The island or the city?" Terosh inquired.

Reia's mind scrambled to locate Ritand on her mental map. Master Niklos's geography lessons were over a decade old.

"Both," Akia answered.

"What do you seek from us?" Reia asked, infusing the question with formality yet tempering it with friendship.

Turning to the prince, Akia lapsed into formal speech.

"My Prince, my father forbids me to join the Ritand relief efforts. Though I am of age, I seek his blessing. The Great Storm will be enemy enough without making a foe of him who is all I have left."

"What can I do?" Terosh's expression said he doubted he could do a blessed thing.

Reia knew better and told him so with an unladylike noise.

"You are Prince Terosh Minstel. Your name carries enough weight to sink a waterhov. Besides, your fathers are friends."

Akia was speechless; Terosh chastened.

"What else can we do?" Reia asked. She rose, took Akia's left hand, and led her to the couch, lest the noblewoman fall over. "I cannot speak for the prince, but you have my support as a friend if nothing else."

Akia swallowed a few times.

"Would you teach me?"

"Me?"

Terosh shot her a triumphant look.

Reia shot him an *I'm-ignoring-you* look.

"To heal?"

"Yes! One of my father's greatest arguments is that I have no skill to offer. But if I could heal, I could help. Even if I can't, I must go. They're a fascinating people. So simple, yet so real."

Reia silently queried Terosh. She truly wanted to help, but it wasn't her place. Her mission consisted solely of guarding the prince. She couldn't even promise to train the lady if they planned on leaving in the morning. She had forgotten to ask how long they would be in Resh. This was his Kireshana.

***

The simple question in Reia's eyes moved Terosh. For a moment, he couldn't think. Like Akia, Reia's spirit hurt at the notion of people facing pain and hardship. Her expression contained curiosity and hope. Hope for what, Terosh couldn't fathom, but the question deserved an answer. He didn't even realize how long he'd been silently staring at Reia. Her half-smile and pink cheeks said she felt the attention. He cleared his throat, thinking furiously.

"Lady Akia, I doubt the Ashasten will wait for us, but you have our support. I know little about healing, so I defer to Reia on that, but I will speak with the governor."

After uttering his speech, Terosh retreated to his quarters. Too much time with women—especially those two—did strange things to his head.

Chapter 21:
Healing

Retsi (May) 26, 1538
Eighty-five days into Prince Terosh's Kireshana journey
Governor Lord's Estate, City of Resh

As Prince Terosh headed for Governor Darmon Zelene's office, he fought a surge of nervousness. He was so distracted that he got lost twice, but finally, he knocked on the correct door.

"Enter!" thundered a voice from within.

Terosh did so, feeling like a kamria about to face down a viper.

"I'm sorry to distur—"

"Forgive me, Dulad Prince, I did not—this is certainly a welcome surprise!"

Terosh had carefully considered how to approach Governor Zelene with Akia's request. Straightening his shoulders, he decided to go with the formal approach.

"My Lord, I have heard about the Ashasten facing Ritand and her people."

The governor's features turned neutral, but traces of his initial expression, which mixed irritation and helplessness, remained.

Terosh analyzed the expression and decided to further aid both Akia and the Ritand people. Though technically submissive to House Minstel, Ritand was a poor, fiercely independent island province. They had no representation in the Senate or the Governors Council—unless one counted Darmon Zelene. To Terosh's knowledge, the tension between Rammon and Ritand had its roots in his own family. In 1311, Prince Edeen accepted a commission from his brother, King Tarel, and became Ritand's ambassador. They disagreed on nearly every issue, and eventually, Tarel had Edeen exiled to the island. Since that time, the kings and queens have been cold in their care for Ritand.

We know how to hold a grudge. Perhaps it's time to end this nonsense.

"I doubt my father will send them aid from Fort Riden, but as Governor of Resh, you possess the authority and duty to care for the people," Terosh said.

"Do I have your blessing to evacuate the island?" The governor smiled hopefully.

"You do, Governor Lord, and I have a request."

The man's smile faltered, replaced by a wary expression.

Terosh hesitated, still gathering his thoughts.

The wary expression morphed into a sad frown.

"She sent you, didn't she?"

Terosh plucked up his courage, considered all the diplomatic advice Sedir had ever pounded into his head and discarded most.

"My Lord, I do not know the depths of pain caused by separation from one's child, but Lady Akia seems determined to go."

"Will she defy me?"

"Will she have to?" Terosh returned, meeting the man's gaze. Silence ruled until Terosh continued, "Let her go, Governor."

"Do you know what you ask?" the governor demanded. "Do you know what it's like to love someone so deeply it hurts?"

"I ask much, Governor, but I am only a mouthpiece. Let your daughter go and retain her love. Deny her and keep her and you might lose her."

Where did that come from?

You're welcome, said the anotechs smugly.

Terosh almost laughed but knew it would be inappropriate.

"You'd make a fine ambassador, Prince Terosh, and you are wise." The governor's frown turned into a grin. He sighed and rubbed his forehead. "I will let her take supplies to Ritand."

"Thank you, Governor, and if you can get enough people to take extra supplies, I will get some from Fort Riden," Terosh offered.

"Let it be as you say," Governor Zelene said.

When he reached the door, Terosh paused.

"In answer to your other question, Governor, I think I'm starting to understand."

***

Retsi (May) 26, 1538
Same day
Throne Room, Royal Palace, City of Rammon

"Keldor is in the Court's hands now. Justice will be done," King Teorn Minstel shifted on the throne. One would think the chair held nothing but tacks instead of the plush cushion that paired well with the dais's carpeting.

Anger coursed through Prince Taytron with each pounding heartbeat. A petty part of him relished his father's discomfort. Tate's flushed face made him look ready to spontaneously combust. The anger almost covered the sting of his father's indifference. He had waited days for something to happen, but the king had done nothing with the prisoner acquired in Azhel.

"You never loved her."

The king jerked as if Tate had struck him, but he didn't deny it right away. Instead, he clenched his jaw and searched for words.

"You fail to understand many things." The king's declaration rumbled, but his next statements came out softer. "I loved her. Not at first, for I hardly knew her when we married. But I learned to love her."

"Then do something!"

"What would you have me do?"

"Kill him." Tate stood his ground before the throne, feet planted shoulder width apart. "It is your right and duty to avenge her!"

"Right. Duty." The king spat the words like poison. "They stay my hand."

Confusion slapped Tate.

"What are you talking about?"

King Teorn looked at him with an expression of profound sadness.

"Her father has claimed her killer."

Most of the fight drained from Tate. A small measure of peace and a strange uneasiness battled within him. His grandfather was not a man to cross, and Gardanian executions were famously brutal. King Padric Creston probably had his entire Central Council working overtime to determine a proper execution for his daughter's murderer. A steady procession of sobering thoughts marched through Tate's head. Bowing to his father, he turned and exited the throne room.

***

Retsi (May) 26, 1538
Same day
Governor Lord's Estate, City of Resh

As Lady Akia Zelene watched, Reia Antellio spread the contents of her caydronan sack across the floor. She laid out twigs, stems, leaves of various sizes and shapes, pieces of bark, flowers, dried insects, and several tiny vials containing tree sap. She chuckled as Akia's expression shifted from excitement to trepidation.

"You'll learn quickly. Master Ekris says there are six-thousand and seventy-two ingredients to healing teas, broths, and patches, but I never deal with that many. The first thing you need to know about healing is that you can. Most people are already healers."

"They are?"

"Do you not comfort your father when you see him frustrated or hurt?" Reia asked. "That is a form of healing. Master Ekris says the best forms of healing are preventative."

"Your master must mean a lot to you," Akia commented. Curiosity crossed her countenance. "What's it like to be raised as a Ranger?"

"I've never known any other life," Reia replied, shrugging.

"Forgive me. That was an awful question." Akia's cheeks reddened.

"No offense taken," Reia assured her. "As Master Ekris says, 'All life is learning, and all learning starts with questions.'"

"All right. What can you teach me?"

The question launched a long tutoring session in the healing arts.

Lady Akia Zelene readily absorbed the herb names and their functions. The lessons proceeded for almost three hours before she finally held up her hand for a respite.

"I think that's enough for now. My brain hurts."

Reia smiled and agreed it was time for a break.

"Need some corlia?"

"That's a painkiller, right?" Akia asked. "I thought you treated wounds with that."

"You can. Corlia's a powerful painkiller. It's great for headaches or open wounds, but it doesn't work well on poisons or diseases. Its main use is healing physical wounds. For emotional wounds you'll need mintas tea or cormea and radon combined."

"What will that do?"

"Paralyze you," Reia answered, trying to keep a straight face. She failed and burst into laughter as Akia's expression switched from amused to horrified and back again.

"I suppose that works on all pains then."

"It's only a temporary cure," Reia reminded. She shook off the somber mood threatening to take over. "Most of these plants—corlia, astera, ristal, ira, and so on—can be bought in any city and most villages, but if you don't know how to use them properly, they're useless or even dangerous."

On that sobering note, they took a break for lunch.

Afterward, Reia had Akia order hot water in four separate bowls, and the practical lessons began. Reia taught her pupil how to properly make mintas tea, comosal, and finally mendaid. She started with the one she would teach last by throwing several herbs into the smallest bowl of hot water and letting the ingredients soak. As she slowly added the ingredients, she studied the small porcelain bowl, admiring the flower pattern on the side. Picking up one of the two medium-sized bowls, she added mintas to the tea and held it up for Akia to see.

"Most people drink mintas or wuzle root tea, but the trick is to first make a strong mintas tea and add a wuzle root for about a minute."

"What does the wuzle root do? Why not add more than that?"

"Both mintas and the roots have a relaxing effect, but they're not as effective if combined improperly."

Reia made both the ineffective and the effective forms of tea and let Akia try them. The lady nearly choked on the ineffective one.

"The taste's a bit stronger if you mix it improperly. Some people do that on purpose. Just be grateful I'm not going to make you try comosal."

"What's that? What's it for? What's it taste like?"

Akia's tone reminded Reia of Kiata discussing a new weapon.

"Comosal's the cure for cornada. It's probably a good one for you to know. People caught in storms are susceptible to it. The cure's made by combining ira petals, mesta shoots, and ristal leaves." Reia checked the temperature of the water in the largest bowl by sticking a finger in it.

"Um, isn't that a bad way to check water temperature?"

"Not when it's been sitting out this long and there's no steam hissing off of it," Reia replied. "Here, I want you to feel this though. It's a good temperature."

Akia obediently dipped her finger into the water.

"Briefly soak the ira petals and ristal leaves in the water then wrap a mesta shoot around it." Reia demonstrated by tying a quick knot in the shoot and holding the package out to Akia. "You'd then stick this under a person's tongue until it dissolves in about six hours."

Akia made a face.

"I agree, and after the first hour, it tastes like rancid cannafitch."

"That's disgusting."

Reia shrugged.

"Don't get sick," she advised. "But if you do, comosal can probably cure you of it, if not by healing properties, then by fear of its taste."

Akia grimaced and nodded. Her eyes fell upon the smallest bowl.

"What's in this one?"

"That will be mendaid, a combination of cormea, sannin, corlia, water, and deklov. Do you remember what those do?"

"Corlia's the painkiller and deklov has something to do with healing speed," Akia ventured. "I don't remember the others."

"Cormea also dulls pain but too much can cause paralysis. Sannin acts on aches," Reia said. "You're doing fine. It took Master Ekris over two years to teach me the healing plants." Reia had more to say, but she stopped upon seeing her student's attention had wandered.

Akia sighed and stared into nothing.

"Am I doing the right thing? Maybe my father's right, maybe it is too dangerous."

"I won't tell you what to do, but I will say danger is everywhere," said Reia.

Both young women slipped into their own thoughts.

***

Retsi (May) 26, 1538
Same day
King's Private Chambers, Royal Palace, City of Rammon

"What do you want?" King Teorn Minstel asked, not bothering to hide his irritation.

"Can't a sister make a social call on her baby brother?" Lady Mavis Altran inquired. Her rich voice held the usual hint of mocking.

"You could, but you don't." Teorn didn't particularly like his sister. She had a knack for discovering harmful secrets. Though he had been spared most of her machinations, he had witnessed enough of her cruelty over the years to make him wary.

Mavis placed a hand over her heart.

"You wound me." She appeared hurt until she grinned. Letting her hand fall to her side, she drew herself upright, and asked, "You received my son's gift, did you not?" She purred the words.

Teorn swallowed and tried to loosen his tongue.

"Taytron delivered him, but it's not much of a gift if you can't keep it. I'm not pleased that the incident almost made a murderer of my son either."

"You are right, of course—on both accounts. I am sorry it has to be this way," Mavis said, sounding regretful. "But that incident aside, I have come on further family business."

Fear gripped Teorn.

"Is it Terosh?" A hundred terrifying thoughts crowded his head. Mavis had resources that kept her very well informed. It wasn't impossible to imagine her hearing a report of something befalling his younger son before his own men could share the news.

Surprise flitted across her face.

"He is fine. Last I heard, Terosh and the Ranger had reached Resh." She brushed at an invisible imperfection in her silk dress. The deep red fabric wrapped closely around her. Precious gia gems winked at him from her fingers, wrists, ears, and neck.

Teorn nodded, relieved to have the confirmation. That had been the last report given to him as well. He shook his head at the thought of Terosh traveling alone with a Ranger—and a young female at that—but everything had gone well so far. By all reports, the boy was doing fine without the Royal Guards. Teorn forced himself to relax.

"I apologize for unnerving you." Mavis's voice, though penitent, still held a mocking note. "I came about your elder son. Some time ago you asked me to seek suitable matches for Taytron. I believe I have found one."

Chapter 22:
Shadow of Mount Palean

Zeri (June) 2, 1538
Ninety-one days into Prince Terosh's Kireshana journey
Campsite near Mount Palean, Morden Lowlands

The days passed, and the lessons continued until Lady Akia Zelene set off for Ritand with twenty-three relief workers and four hovs filled with supplies. Prince Terosh and Reia Antellio shared the midday meal with a lonely Governor Darmon Zelene then took a hov to Fort Riden to pick up supplies. During the ride, Terosh kept stealing glances at Reia, enjoying seeing her smile as the wind blew in their faces. He insisted they update their weapons for the journey's second half since Fort Riden was the last major military outpost along the Kireshana path. If they needed supplies after that, they would have to travel down to Ritten, Meritab, or Meritel. The stop took less than an hour.

By late afternoon, they were through most of the Morden Lowlands and entering Mount Palean's shadow. Thanking the hov driver, they disembarked.

"We should stop near here. It's at least a kilometer from the foot of the mountains," said Reia.

"Why does the distance from the mountains matter?" Terosh asked.

"If we get too close, we risk something sneaking up on us."

I suppose it's about time for something to go wrong. We've had plenty of rest the last few days.

They hiked a little longer, hoping to find a stream. After a short, fruitless search, they tossed their burdens under a collection of fossa trees.

Terosh stretched and yawned.

"You're tired?" asked Reia incredulously. "We've done nothing but sit in a hov all day."

"I was thinking about taking a nap." Terosh shook out his bedroll and flopped down onto it. Folding his hands behind his head, he pretended to sleep. "What would you suggest?" He opened one eye to look at Reia.

"There's still an hour of daylight. How about a duel?" Reia rested a hand on her banistick then drew the weapon and idly flipped it a few times.

Terosh groaned.

"All you Rangers ever do is train. Don't you know how to have fun?" Despite his complaints, he smiled, hauled himself upright, and drew his kerlinblade. Bowing deeply, he waved toward the empty fields to his right. "Shall we?"

Reia removed the clasp holding her travel cloak together and tucked it into a small pouch at her waist. The travel cloak fluttered to the ground behind her. Terosh removed his cloak as well and tossed both it and the ornate clasp onto his bedroll before following Reia into the middle of some graveground.

"Try not to twist an ankle," Reia cautioned.

A salute later, the fight began. The duel started slowly with each combatant initiating attacks. Terosh stayed conscious of where he placed his feet. Reia floated over the weak spots like they weren't even there. Several minutes later, they intensified the battle, striking, dodging, kicking, flipping, and rolling until their clothes looked shabby. Sometime later they switched weapons and continued the battle. Round after round passed until both fighters were drenched in sweat. By mutual agreement, the duel finally ended in a draw.

Reia gathered brush and lit it with anotechs while Terosh searched for water.

"We'll have to ask the Mount Palean Guide for water," Terosh said, once he found what the trees were using as a water source. "That stream's more mud than water."

Reia didn't respond immediately. She crouched by the fire and tossed in a few more twigs, looking pensive.

"I wonder if the anotechs could get water."

Terosh mulled the possibility over.

Can you get water here?

We can.

"Yes," Reia and Terosh confirmed simultaneously.

"From the air or ground?" Reia wondered.

Terosh repeated the question silently.

Both, but from the ground is easier.

Reia knelt, held her hands a few centimeters above the ground, and said, "Ricridofirm."

Terosh watched as a pool of water a handspan across formed. He scooped up a handful of the water, but before he could bring it to his mouth, Reia caught his arm, spilling the water.

"It's poisoned," she explained, "or at least not very clean." She released his arm.

"Ah. Right. Have to be specific with them." Terosh searched for the proper terminology. He could have tried the common tongue, but he needed the Kalastan practice. "Ricrinadofirm," he said, holding a hand near the ground about a meter or so away from the other pool. He had the briefest sensation of something leaving through his outstretched hand. Seconds later, he had the opposite sensation.

They watched silently as a pool of water formed. Terosh admitted that the new one looked much cleaner than the first.

"Destroy the other one so we don't get confused."

Terosh was taken aback by Reia's tone.

"Not you. The anotechs," Reia clarified.

Grinning sheepishly, Terosh rummaged for food.

When their bedrolls were laid out, Terosh sat down and breathed deeply of the sweet fresh air. For the first night in over a week, they would sleep beneath the stars. Thinking of the stars made him look up.

"What a sight!" he whispered.

***

On the fire's other side, Reia sat on her bedroll and fiddled with the new banistick shock nullifiers. She studied the effect with an eye for aesthetics as well as function. The lightweight metal fixtures looked unnatural, but they would make the wooden weapon impervious to most energy weapons, including kerlinblades.

At least they'll free up some anotechs.

Terosh's awed exclamation brought Reia's head up. She looked at his face, followed his gaze up to the stars, and agreed. Wordlessly, she told the anotechs to dim the fire.

Clouds covered Reshner's three moons so that they didn't interfere with the starry host. Billions of tiny dots, insignificant on their own yet breathtaking together, winked like shiners.

"I've never seen anything like it," Terosh murmured, as if speaking loudly would drive off the sight.

"I've only seen a few nights like this," Reia said. "Usually, I'm up in the mountains where the moons can find me anywhere."

"Do you know any constellations?" Terosh asked.

"A few," Reia said.

"Will you show me?" Terosh inquired.

"Of course," Reia answered. Ignoring her sore muscles, she rose, crossed over to the prince, and sat down next to him. She looked up and studied the stars, remembering the night Master Niklos first took them stargazing. She spotted Cascius's Cloak first. "See those four stars there, the ones in a perfect line?" she asked, pointing in the appropriate direction.

Terosh craned his neck for a long moment but finally admitted defeat.

"No." Disappointment made the word heavy.

Reia hesitated. There were two ways she could show him, and both were fairly intimate. She scanned for an easier one and located Obrius's Mace next. "Okay, see that cluster of slightly brighter stars over there?" she asked, pointing in a new direction.

Terosh looked for a minute before shaking his head. His neck cracked several times.

"Ow," he said, rubbing the spot. "Guess I'm not cut out to be a stargazer."

Again, the disappointment touched her.

"Shall I help you?"

"Please."

Reia forced herself to her feet again.

"Then, stand up."

**

Terosh followed the instruction, hearing the slight tremor in Reia's voice.

What's she nervous about?

Then, I took her into my arms and the stars were ours, the anotechs intoned.

Oh.

Feeling Reia tug at his arm, he stiffened.

"Stop that. Hold your arm out straight and let me direct it," said Reia.

That was easier said than done. Terosh's arm balked at being directed. As Reia tugged, his arm jerked away. He let her wrestle his right arm until one hand brushed the underside. Then, he laughed and jumped backward. When he glanced up, he saw Reia's stunned expression.

Her lips twitched as she struggled to hold in laughter. She lost.

"I guess you're ticklish," she said, when she finally stopped laughing. Her head turned skyward again.

"Will you still help me find the constellations?" Terosh asked, wishing he didn't sound like a needy child.

"Fine, I'll point, and you can stand behind me and follow my arm. I'm not touching *your* arm again. Nearly lost my nose last time." Reia turned her back on him.

Suddenly, the hesitation that had gripped her seized him. His heart pounded like it wanted out.

"There's Cascius's Cloak. The four stars in a diagonal line at a thirty-degree angle." Reia's right arm stretched out, and her hand turned to mimic the angle of the four stars.

Terosh crept up behind her and leaned so that his eyes could follow her arm.

"I see it!"

"Good. That marks Cascius's forearm. Imagine someone holding a cloak across their face with their right arm. If you trace up slightly to the left until you see the next few stars, you'll trace the path of his left arm to his ice dagger."

"Cascius. Cascius. Why does that name sound familiar?"

"Count Cascius Drooin," Reia supplied.

Cadrish's emotional rendition of the *Legend of Count Drooin of Doxiti V* came back to Terosh. The story featured a fictional count whose wife was murdered by his brother. Driven by grief, Cascius donned a cursed cloak that would make him immortal and plagued his brother's family for five generations.

"I remember," Terosh said. "Sad story."

Reia lowered her arm and looked for another constellation. The hours slipped by as she showed Terosh dozens of constellations. Obrius's Mace, Irmen's Shield, Kala's Heart, Riden's Justice, Rammon's Scepter, and many more came to life before his eyes. He remembered most of the stories but happily listened to her tell them again. As a storyteller, Reia had old man Cadrish cleanly beat.

***

Lucas Telon observed the constellation lessons dispassionately. Murderous thoughts toward the prince had ceased days ago, but he still hated to see Reia with him. They tried to pretend there was nothing between them, but she looked at the prince in a way she had never looked at Lucas. His TT-189 chimed, announcing an encrypted call, so he flicked it on and found Lord Kezem on the screen.

"Yes, my Lord?" Lucas kept his voice cautious.

"I hope my mother is paying you well, Ranger." Lord Kezem's greeting was terse.

"Well enough, sir, what can I do for you?"

"If she hasn't forbidden you from accepting my orders, I have a job for you."

"Speak, my Lord."

Kezem spoke casually, as if ordering him to fetch water.

"I want you to track down the other Maledek. The one calling himself 'Dalonos.' I have need of him and he failed to answer my summons. I prefer him alive, but if you can't manage that, kill him and bring me the body. He shouldn't be hard to track."

"What of my current mission?"

"Ask my mother for her leave if you must," Kezem grumbled. "Just get it done. I don't have time to contract another Ranger."

Another?

Lucas couldn't imagine any other Rangers wanting his job. A few had the right skills, but they lacked the proper temperament. The link broke before he could reply. Lucas flicked the controls so he could spy on Reia and the prince again, but disgust soon overwhelmed him. Lucas had taught Reia some of those constellation legends long ago. Having her share the stories with the prince felt like a violation of something sacred.

To distract himself, he called the Lady. She picked up and listened as he explained Lord Kezem's request.

Lucas got the distinct impression she knew why he was calling before he said one word.

"May I pursue this new mission, my Lady?" he asked.

"How are you?" she asked, instead of answering his question.

"My Lady?"

"It is a simple question, Lucas. Given your past with the subject, I am curious."

"I can do my job."

"Good. My son's request seems strange, but I'm inclined to trust his instincts for now. If he's lost faith in this scientist turned Maledek, it would be wise to control the being." She cut the connection without so much as a fare-thee-well, leaving Lucas to wonder where this new mission would take him.

Chapter 23:
Cries for Help

Zeri (June) 6, 1538
Ninety-five days into Prince Terosh's Kireshana journey
Throne Room, Royal Palace, City of Rammon

"It is as much a cry for help as purple fire, and you *will* answer it," declared King Teorn Minstel.

Prince Taytron stiffened. He hated debating his father, and it seemed like every conversation turned into a confrontation these days.

"Will you order it, sire?"

I can't remarry, Father. Not yet and maybe not ever.

The king held his hands out in a placating gesture.

"I know you had your heart set on that young scientist. I'm not blind, Taytron, but she's beyond your help. Princess Alikai is not beyond our help. She must marry before the first of Pirua (September) or the Blood Harvest will claim her entire family. This is the only way to stop it."

Mention of Deanna hit Tate like ice water. He had tried a dozen arguments to no avail. Still stinging from thoughts of Deanna, he tried again.

"Do you think it wise to unite Reshner with a people whose practices include the Blood Harvest?"

Their gazes locked. The question hung between them.

"I had the analysts assess the risks and put it before the Interplanetary Politics Committee. There were doubts, but most agree with my decision." The king stared into nothing for a moment. "The Mitra are a strong people. We need strong allies."

Realization slammed into Tate.

"You're going to defy GAPP."

His father nodded gravely.

The news thrilled yet sobered Tate. Responsibility landed on him like a falling zalok. The idea of replacing Deanna sickened him, but if it would save Reshner from GAPP, he had to consider it.

"Where did you hear of this possible alliance?"

"Your Aunt Mavis." His father's expression said he didn't want to argue about it right now.

The answer surprised Tate, though he knew it shouldn't. His father had always looked up to his older sister. Tate thought her too shrewd to be trusted, but he wasn't ready to open old points of contention just yet.

Perhaps Captain Kelter will help me investigate this alliance.

"I will think on it, Father," Tate promised.

Thoughts chased each other around in his head as he left the throne room. He would need to have his people check into the potential alliance, but his father wouldn't have brought it up if it wasn't a sure thing.

***

Zeri (June) 6, 1538
Same day
Kireshana Path, Kesler Plains

On Zeri 3, 1538, Reia and Prince Terosh conquered Mount Palean with ease, checked in with the Guide on the other side, and continued the Kireshana.

A few days into their trek over the Kesler Plains, they spotted a fire atop a gradually sloping rise in the land. The purple flames swayed, sometimes flaring, sometimes shrinking to almost nothing. It was hard to tell how far away the fire burned. The flatness of the plains meant little, for old patches of graveground—collapsed or not—could hide anywhere. The distance could be five or twenty-five kilometers.

The sun had just disappeared over the Riden Mountains at their backs and brilliant streams of purple and orange still protested the end of day. They exchanged glances, each expecting the flames to be a figment of their imagination.

Purple, green, or even blue fire could be a cry for help. Most of the farms were so spread out that help could be days away. The occasional emergency station could be found, but they were unreliable at best. If the windstorms and acid rains didn't destroy them, cawallas would break in and eat anything they could fit in their mouths.

The best hope for those working the lonely land lay in traveling Rangers. Those assigned to each city had the duty to check surrounding areas for colored fires.

"Is that flame purple or am I going crazy?" Terosh wondered.

"Perhaps both theories hold truth," Reia responded evenly.

The prince stared at her then took off to find the fire.

"Wait!" Reia called, tightening the strap of her caydronan sack. Suddenly grateful to have left the korver sacks with Lady Zelene, Reia ran after Prince Terosh. "We don't know whose fire that is!"

"Does it matter?"

"Of course, it matters! What if it's a trap?" Having shorter legs, Reia worked harder to keep the swift pace.

"Then, we'll deal with it," Terosh replied.

"We should at least approach cautiously!" Reia got the impression he used anotechs to augment his breathing, allowing him to talk normally.

Cheater!

Even as she thought it, she asked the anotechs to do the same.

Suddenly, the effort of running disappeared. She had never felt so alive, so free. Not having to struggle for breath made one feel invincible.

No wonder he wants to race.

The land flew past beneath them. Their legs never tired. Viewed from afar with their travel cloaks streaming behind, they could have been mistaken for low-gliding cannafitch. Their legs moved in a blur too swift for eyes to track. A pack of korvers chased them for three kilometers but eventually stopped to find easier prey. Wallays popped their heads above their holes to watch them.

Reia and Terosh came across a large section of graveground, and ran on, letting the ground collapse in their wake. By the end of the tenth kilometer, Reia had to concentrate to maintain the pace, but she stuck with it, knowing they neared their destination. When they got within a hundred meters, a burning sensation soared through her muscles, as the anotechs reached the limit of their ability to help her.

"We should slow down," Reia said.

Terosh looked at her impatiently but slackened his pace. Then, he pitched forward like he had taken a bullet.

Too startled to call his name, Reia stopped running, and thus, stopped instructing the anotechs to augment her muscles. All at once, she felt every one of the kilometers covered. Prior to their stay in Resh, she would have been able to pull off such a sprint and still stand, but the recent rest had made her soft. Her legs gave out, and she landed in a heap. By the time she checked on Terosh, he had struggled to a sitting position.

"Well, that answers that," he muttered.

Reia opened her mouth to question his health and sanity.

"The anotechs." Terosh still wasn't making a lot of sense.

"You're obviously having a conversation with yourself," Reia remarked. "Care to share?"

Terosh gave her a patient, princely grin.

"They're not perfect, and they take a toll on your body."

"Really? Never would have guessed." Reia rubbed at a sudden cramp torturing her lower left leg. "Didn't you learn that lesson in the zalok caves?" She didn't expect an answer and wouldn't have heard one if it were offered. Emotions she couldn't understand gripped her. Her mind flew back to the korver attack. Images zipped through her head, slamming to a stop on an unconscious Terosh.

"Don't frown. It doesn't suit you," Terosh whispered.

Reia had never heard him use that tender tone before. It sent a tingle down her spine and simultaneously raised her defensive hackles.

"I—we still have a purple fire to check." The prince held a hand out to help Reia to her feet.

They covered the last few dozen meters at a slow walk, expecting to be spotted at a distance.

Nothing happened.

The night sounds went on as usual. The larger creatures hunted smaller ones with moderate success, and the smaller ones did their best to leave the universe as loudly as possible. The insects cheered on both sides, sending their buzzing, chittering, and clacking cries up in soothing ascending and descending waves.

Prince Terosh tripped over a body and landed near the fire.

"Ah! What's that? Who's there?" cried a man.

Reacting instinctively, Reia drew her banistick and brought one end up under the man's chin.

"Ranger! Please! My family is ill! Even the youngest! Especially the youngest." The man's last statement was barely audible.

"Show me," Reia ordered, snapping her banistick closed.

Semon McNoughten introduced himself and explained the situation as they hurried toward his home, which lay approximately two hundred meters from the fire. His wife and seven children had come down with cornada after the last round of unexpected storms about a month ago. They had seemed on the mend when a stranger came. The man's words started out as an agitated stream, but gradually, they softened until Reia strained to hear.

"Our farm is the only one out here, so when a stranger showed up three nights ago, I gave him food and insisted he stay the night. I awoke around midnight to find him standing over my wife breathing into her face. Before I could rise or speak, he was gone, and it was too late for my family."

Reia's exhausted legs protested movement, but she plodded on. The man's name amused her for it meant "seven" in Kalastan, and she would bet anything the man was his parents' seventh child. The amusement gave her something to focus on besides Semon's disturbing story.

"Who was he?" asked Terosh. "The man who did this?"

"He gave no name and only said he had far to go. Aside from weariness, he displayed no signs of disease."

"What signs do your wife and children show?" Reia queried.

They were almost to the house now, but the man's steps faltered.

"Bloodshot eyes, weariness, fever, aches, skin cracks, pain—"

Reia stiffened and stopped.

"Heskrin!" She spat it like a curse.

She felt the prince's eyes upon her. Under the moonlight, she figured she must look as white as a Gegi arcghost. A breeze billowed her cloak, reinforcing the image of a tormented specter said to haunt ships lost to ice storms in the Asrien Sea.

"What is it?" Terosh and Semon asked as one.

Rage filled her.

"A disease." She drew a deep breath and raised her chin. "But it can be packaged, swallowed, and breathed as a weapon."

"Poison," Terosh concluded.

"Can it be cured?" Semon's voice was tight with terror.

Reia bit her lower lip.

"Sometimes." She didn't want to tell him how because the ingredients they would need were far out of reach.

Chapter 24:
Amrita Tears

Zeri (June) 7, 1538
Ninety-six days into Prince Terosh's Kireshana journey
McNoughten Farmhouse, Kesler Plains

Reia's throat felt like she had swallowed half the Felmon Desert and washed it down with saltwater. She wanted to say something hopeful, but the words got stuck. Her eyes narrowed as she marched into the McNoughten home. Following Semon's directions, she found the master bedchamber. She didn't realize the men trailed her in. A short examination of Semon's wife, Kira, confirmed Heskrin. The woman submitted to the scrutiny without comment, but her expression spoke of misery in a universal language. Reia's breath refused to come out, and she fought back waves of helplessness.

Who did this? Can these people be saved? She didn't even realize she sought answers from the anotechs until they spoke.

Dark Ones—Dalonos—control the one responsible. Amrita Tears can save them.

"Amrita Tears," Reia said. A spark of hope flared, wavered, then faded. She'd known that all along, but Amrita Tears were nowhere around here.

"What?" Terosh demanded. "You had hope for a second."

"Amrita Tears could cure them. It's a sap you get from amrita plants, but they only grow on Mount Amri, high in the Ridens. We're too far away, even if we could find them this time of year."

"Can you ease their pain?" Semon asked.

Reia got her first good look at the man. If she stood on tiptoes, she might come up to his shoulders. A short, bushy beard and a trim mustache softened his blunt face. His deep blue eyes were flecked with yellow specks, indicating Bornovan blood.

"I can," Reia assured him.

More than three hours came and went, while Reia mixed broths and teas. As she prepared the elixirs, Reia questioned Semon about his family. Kira favored ira flowers. The youngest child, Teven, was only two and already had his own specially carved chair. The next older child, Dable, turned four last week. His body had always been frail. Kesella, five-and-two-twelfths, and Arel, five-and-eleven-twelfths, proudly shared an age. Semon had gotten them each a doll from Rammon on his last trip. Nicella, Azer, and Torkrin, respectively seven, eight, and nine, freely shared a collection of wooden animals imported from Tareb amongst themselves but guarded them from the "children." The two boys, though older, deferred to Nicella because she made them rielberry tarts and pies.

Reia had never treated Heskrin before, so she ended up treating the individual symptoms. She answered pain with corlia and cormea, aches with sannin, and fever with ira petals. In addition, she tried to slow the poison with ristal leaves. After administering the broths, she made some mintas tea with a bit of wuzle root, but only Kira and three of the children drank it. The others had already fallen asleep, and Reia didn't wish to awaken them. After the tea, those four patients also drifted off to sleep.

Sitting by young Teven McNoughten's bed, Reia held the boy's hand long after he drifted off. Her remedies helped, but her caydronan sack ran short on sannin and corlia. If the Heskrin was as entrenched in their bodies as she suspected, there would soon be nothing she could do.

They're so young.

Alas, the innocent perish beneath Ill Fate's heavy hands.

She ignored the anotechs.

"Reia," Terosh called from the doorway. "We need to talk."

Something about his cautious tone warned Reia she might not like this conversation. Nevertheless, she released the boy's heated hand, rose, and followed the prince to the common room. No one was around since Reia had forced Semon to drink some mintas tea and rest.

Reia sat on the couch and let her gaze wander the cozy room. A plethora of detailed wooden creatures spilled over the sides of a small box. A pair of well-loved dolls leaned against the legs of a child's wooden chair, looking as haggard as Reia felt. Trying not to cry, she went to right the dolls.

Kesella and Arel will need you again.

Then, she slowly walked back across the care-worn rug to the couch. The braided rug's muted red and brown tones gave the room a warm flavor. Evidence of Reia's healing efforts littered the ground around the fireplace along the back wall.

Terosh seemed troubled.

"We can save them, but not without a price." He paused for a slow breath. "Are you willing to try?"

"How?" she demanded.

"Anotechs."

"That seems to be the answer to everything." Reia was surprised by the bitterness she felt. "How can we use anotechs to save them?"

Terosh responded with a question.

"Do you know the conditions amrita plants need to grow?"

Reia's mind latched on to the thought, and she sucked in sharply.

Can you make amrita grow rapidly?

Maybe. It takes much energy. The conditions here are not good. You might not live through the process.

Yes or no?

Yes.

"They can do it, if you know how," Terosh said. "Their best estimate was five days and enough strain to almost kill us."

Reia shut her eyes, seeking and receiving confirmation from the anotechs. She cupped her head in her hands, trying to ward off a headache brought on by lack of sleep and worry that Terosh might actually talk her into this craziness. Teven's pitiful cries echoed in her skull. She remembered feeling his sweat-stiffened blond hair and limp, burning arm beneath her fingertips.

"I—I want to do this, Reia," Terosh confessed. "My father and tutors would call me a fool. My advisers would say I have higher duties, but this feels right." Terosh drew his shoulders back. "We must help them."

The last vestiges of resistance crumbled in her.

"If it can be done, it will be done," Reia promised, rising to wake Semon.

He argued with them but agreed to let them use the barn, which currently lay empty, since the grain was already packed and stored in underground cellars to protect it from windstorms.

***

While Reia tutored Semon on preparing remedies for the Heskrin symptoms, Terosh prepped the barn. Following instructions from both Reia and the anotechs, he heaped dirt in the center of the barn. Next, he patched the few weak spots in the walls and gathered several buckets of water. The McNoughten house connected to a waterline from underground streams from Lake Ceree, but an outside pump existed for the barns. Finally, Terosh returned to the house, ate a huge meal, and forced Reia to eat as well.

Torn between fear and excitement, Terosh entered the dirt-filled barn, knowing he would either exit triumphantly or not at all. The anotechs had explained their plan at least four dozen times, but he turned it over in his mind again and again.

Get amrita seeds from Mount Amri, carry them back here, plant them, and care for them.

Their care included creating a frigid atmosphere, giving them an occasional touch of acid, adding lots of fresh water, and periodically zapping them with heat. Getting the seeds would take several days. The job fell to Reia, since she knew where to find Mount Amri. Terosh would concentrate on creating and storing water. Then, he would prepare the small amounts of acid and practice chilling everything to the proper temperature.

As they lay down on the freshly mounded dirt, Terosh impulsively caught Reia's left hand. It felt small yet strong. A lump foiled an attempt at speech, but he forced a smile.

"Alosoolsonana." Reia squeezed his hand and closed her eyes.

To success on our journey, the anotechs translated.

***

Zeri (June) 8, 1538
Ninety-seven days into Prince Terosh's Kireshana journey
McNoughten Farm, Kesler Plains

The small bits of Dr. Atien Belcross that still existed within Dalonos ached to know what went on in that barn, but the presence of so many Light Ones made him sick. His confidence had been shaken enough to make him fear tangling with those other anotechs. Instead of fighting the gut-twisting sensation, he checked on his experiment.

The smallest child still barely clung to life. The disease was obviously thriving. The man who had served as a reluctant vector deserved a reward. Dalonos would kill the man swiftly later. A closer examination via anotechs revealed remnants of herbal remedies that kept the symptoms at bay. Two of the children seemed slightly better but the rest had worsened, though not to the point they should have. The woman struggled against the disease and grew stronger by the minute. Dalonos was tempted to declare the experiment a failure, enter the house, and clean up the mess.

"They grow amrita," the figure of False Jalna reported, appearing at Dalonos's side.

"Will it work?"

"That is unknown," False Jalna replied.

Dalonos cursed.

"Stop sounding like a machine."

The girl chuckled and disappeared. Dalonos braced for the inevitable sensation of ten thousand needles pricking him as the anotechs entered him simultaneously.

"Should I kill them?"

We no longer want them dead.

"Not them, though it would be easy now. I meant the family. Should I kill the farmer and his family?"

An excruciatingly long silence followed, but eventually the anotechs answered.

No. Leave scouts to report on their success or failure. There is no time to wait. We must warn the master that the Light Ones grow stronger. It may affect his plan.

"You know he wants me dead, right? I can feel that skulking Ranger haunting my shadows."

Lord Kezem is momentarily misguided. He will see reason soon enough.

***

Zeri (June) 13, 1538
102 days into Prince Terosh's Kireshana journey
McNoughten Farm, Kesler Plains

Terosh and Reia stayed in the McNoughten's barn for six days. They lay side-by-side locked in unnatural slumber, connected to the dirt by thousands of threads. The anotechs inside them weren't enough to accomplish their mission, so they constantly drew new ones from the ground. They didn't know where they came from, but each time they needed new anotechs more answered their call.

The days were paradoxes: long and short, safe and perilous, peaceful and strenuous, fascinating and tedious. Reia's presence disappeared for two days so she could personally direct the anotechs in their seed-retrieval task, leaving Terosh feeling empty. To blunt the edge of slowly passing time, he practiced his parts endlessly. He spent some energy maintaining their sleeping bodies, but most of his effort went into manipulating the air. Molecule by molecule, he formed water and stuck it to the back wall. When that filled, he started a new sheet. He willed the anotechs to spread over the barn and draw heat away until the temperature hovered just above freezing.

The acid was the hardest part. Terosh soon discovered it would have to be fetched from the Talmeth Mountains, volcanoes tucked in the southwest corner of Reshner's habitable continent. The volcanoes spew molten metals and acids approximately every three months. Knowing he couldn't retrieve the acid and continue working in the barn, Terosh sent Reia soon after she returned with the seeds. He sensed her weariness as she planted the first two seeds and instructed him on planting the other eight, but if he asked her to stop, they would fail.

She returned two days later, bearing the precious acid. Her life force trembled with fatigue, which coupled with the cool temperatures to make her physical form shiver.

Terosh concentrated on feeding the amrita plants water, acid, and proper jolts of heat but remained aware enough to go half-crazy staring down upon their bodies. Seeing Reia's deathly pale cheeks made him angry.

When the amrita plants were finally ready, the anotechs informed them that they could return to their bodies. The task of withdrawing control slowly, while still maintaining the right temperatures, took a lot of patience. Terosh had gathered too much water and could not release it all at once for fear of flooding their work. Reia helped him slowly return the water to the air, then return to his body.

He awoke with a gasp. The cry that escaped him was as pitiful as a newborn baby's mewling. The sensation of a thousand glass shards repeatedly stabbing his head made him nauseous. Sparkles of light danced around his vision. His mouth tasted like he had been sucking on tretling fur for a week. He released Reia's hand and rolled left, away from her. A coughing fit overtook him, followed closely by twenty seconds of body-racking, empty retching.

He landed on his hands and knees. Spotting the three buckets of water he had gathered, Terosh crawled to them. Another coughing fit threw him forward into the first bucket, spilling it. He rolled onto his back and shut his eyes, too weak to try again and willing to die if it would stop the headache. Soon, Terosh felt water slowly dripping onto his face.

"No quitting now," Reia said with a rough, weary, and wonderful voice. "I have what we need."

"How—"

"While you were playing with the weather, I was conserving my strength," Reia explained. "Sit up, drink this, and spit. It won't taste pretty, but it's clean. The anotechs inform me they've killed all the evil crawly things."

He followed her instructions. When his mouth felt normal again, Terosh swallowed some of the stale water. It tasted metallic but passable.

Reia cleaned him up with a few words to the anotechs, helped him to his feet, and guided him to the side wall.

"Stay there until your legs agree not to dump you on your head. I'll be right back. I need more vials."

Chapter 25:
Master and Healer

Zeri (June) 13, 1538
Same day
McNoughten Farm, Kesler Plains

Master Niklos Mikhail McGreven was weary from his long hunt, but he forced himself on, feeling drawn to this place. At the very least, the farmer could spare a cup of water. He had spent almost a month tracking Nevira Sedrock and Ranger Kas Nelvon. Together and separately, they had infected dozens of remote homesteads with either Jekrin or Heskrin. Neither disease was particularly pleasant, but Jekrin was messier. In addition to shakes, chills, dangerously high fevers, and profuse sweating, Jekrin made people break out with weeping sores, ranging in size from a baby's fingernail to as large as Niklos's hands.

The hunt had ended yesterday when Niklos had finally come across Nevira and Kas's campsite. By this time, their respective diseases, Nevira with Jekrin and Kas with Heskrin, were so advanced that they had lit a purple fire and collapsed beside it, waiting for someone to kill them. Niklos tried to treat their wounds but it was far too late to save them. He wanted to question them, but they were incoherent. Niklos shook his head to rid himself of the vile memories.

A familiar figure stumbled out of the barn ahead. Her thin frame shook. Her light brown hair hung as limply as her expression, but as she stumbled toward the house, a gust of wind blew hair back from her face.

"Reia!"

Niklos met her with open arms.

Joyful recognition transformed her countenance, but her smile remained weak.

"Master Niklos!" She greeted him with a warm hug, then leaned heavily upon him.

"Let's get you inside," Niklos said. "We can talk later."

"The prince. He's ... in the barn ... with the amrita plants."

Reia's statement halted Niklos.

"Amrita? Here?"

Her eyes shut, but her smile widened.

"We … grew them … for the children."

Niklos needed to hear no more. Scooping her up, he carried her to the door. A few good kicks brought a distraught man to the door. Gently shoving past the man, Niklos placed Reia on the couch.

"Master, would you give …" She waved in the general direction of the fireplace.

Spotting six vials of beautiful, deep purple liquid lined up neatly near Reia's caydronan sack, Niklos rushed over and snatched up the lot, sparing only a second to cast off his own sack so he could move quicker.

"More … in the barn," Reia mumbled. "Not enough vials."

"Sleep now, Sela." His voice thickened as he called her 'dear one.' "I'll handle the sick."

In less than a minute, Niklos determined that six children and one adult needed the Tears. The instant he touched the youngest boy's cold arm, he knew the child was beyond help. Two of the girls whimpered, so Niklos dripped a generous amount of Amrita Tears into their mouths, sending them into restful slumber. He used one and a half vials between the two girls, maintaining a steady stream of words in the common tongue and Bornovan.

With a heavy heart, Niklos moved to the next room where a boy of about four years clung to life by shredded threads. Niklos dumped two vials of Amrita Tears into the child. The strong elixir rendered the child unconscious. He would either wake in a day or never awaken again.

The next room held a woman. When Niklos trickled a bit of Amrita Tears into her mouth, she rallied her strength, and said, "Save my children!" Then, she clamped her mouth firmly shut.

The remaining children were more receptive to the Tears. Niklos could tell they were fading fast, so he split the remaining Tears among them and rushed to the barn for more.

A miraculous sight met him. A small hill of dirt covered with clava grass glistened as if covered with morning dew. The air around Niklos was cold. Ten tall, slender amrita plants framed the hill like a lush green, gold, and blue crown.

Reverently climbing the small hill, Niklos soon saw the thin, purple veins running up and down leaves that were as long as his arm. Each plant had six or seven fragile stems rising at even intervals, arranged roughly in a circle. Atop these, heavy flowers bent the stems out from the center, as if bowing. With a little imagination, the folds and furrows forming the flowers created a face with prominent black eyes. From these eyes seeped slow drops of Amrita Tears.

Nobody knows which tribe of extinct mountain people originated the legend of Amri's Tears. According to the story, Amri, goddess of goodness, wept when her jealous son poisoned her daughter. Unaware of the passage of time, Amri spent four years mourning, then split her spirit into two halves. With one half she gave her daughter new life and with the other she created a weeping plant with the power to cure any poison. The harsh conditions needed to grow the plants stemmed from being born of pain and anguish.

Niklos pondered the legend as he hurried to refill the vials. The room grew warmer with each passing moment. Soon, the plants would wither and die.

"Do you need help?" asked a young man from behind Niklos.

Nodding at the prince, Niklos motioned the young man forward and returned his attention to the two slowly filling vials. After brief introductions and an explanation from the prince, they worked in silence until the flowers began wilting. Niklos turned away, not wanting to witness the noble flowers' demise.

"Will it be enough?" The prince sounded worried.

"It will," Niklos replied, hoping he was right.

"It has to be," Prince Terosh declared.

"You did well," Niklos encouraged.

"I wish we could have done more." Clearing his throat, the prince added, "Reia had the harder role. Will she be all right?"

"She'll be fine after some rest," Niklos replied. "Come, you could use some rest yourself."

As they raced to the house, new energy entered Prince Terosh, but Niklos didn't have time to dwell on the changes.

He returned to each of the sick ones to distribute the Tears as needed. Niklos tasked the prince with calming the woman while he attended the children. The Tears already in the children seemed to be working, so each one needed only a drop or two more. This time, with assurance that the remaining children would live, the woman drank the sweet purple liquid. Niklos used a whole vial on her, leaving him with five remaining vials. When they had done everything they could, Niklos ordered Prince Terosh to rest. The prince grabbed a blanket and stretched out on the floor next to the couch holding Reia. A strong bond had developed between the pair, and Niklos wasn't surprised given what they had accomplished. Amrita plants normally took four months to mature to full weeping status. They had completed the task in less than a week.

***

When Reia opened her eyes and found Master Niklos holding her right hand, she feared it was a dream. Her heart fluttered, anticipating horrible news. Memories crashed upon her: the Heskrin, Terosh's plan, the anotechs, the strange floating feeling, collecting the Amrita Tears.

"Good evening," Master Niklos gently teased. "I wouldn't be surprised if your sleep patterns are off for a time." He leaned down and came up with a glass of water. "Drink. You were sleeping so peacefully I didn't want to wake you."

Reia obediently drank several slow sips before waving the glass away. "Are they alive?"

Master Niklos's grim expression confirmed her indefinable fears.

"The youngest child perished before the cure was ready."

Reia tried to fight off tears but failed.

Teven.

The little blond boy would never again sit atop his father's head and rub for luck or sneak out at night to play with the forbidden wooden creatures.

"Here now, drink more. You'll need the moisture for a proper cry," Master Niklos said. When she finished drinking, he set the empty glass aside, lifted Reia, slipped onto the couch beside her, and held her as she mourned the boy.

Safe in the embrace of the man who had raised her, Reia let herself really weep.

Terosh woke a few minutes later and left the room silently when told of Teven's death.

Reia wanted to follow him but realized he needed space to grieve. She sobbed until her tears were spent then leaned back, shut her eyes, and breathed deeply.

"Tell me of your Kireshana travels," Master Niklos suggested.

It took several minutes to work up to talking, but eventually, Reia told him about the attack, Terosh's injuries, the windstorm, the zalok caves, the korvers, graveground, flashflood, Resh, and everything else that brought her to this moment. By the time she finished, she was tired again.

Master Niklos got up and arranged some cushions behind her. Then, kneeling before her, he picked up her right hand. The serious expression on his face drew her attention.

"Reia Antellio, were you my daughter, I could not love you more," he said with a gentle smile. "It is with great pride that I bestow upon you the rank of healer. May Riden continue to use your spirit and talents to bless those you meet."

Reia blinked. Her master had bypassed the rank of guardian.

Master Niklos's smile widened.

"You have earned this honor and more." He squeezed her hand. "I wish I could stay longer but some Tears remain. These people have been given what their bodies will bear, and since the Tears won't last, I will borrow a horse and take the cure to two other families." With that, Master Niklos released her hand, kissed her forehead, picked up his caydronan sack, and went to find Semon.

Reia barely had time to whisper, "Ridenspeed, Master." Then, she closed her eyes and drifted off to sleep.

***

Zeri (June) 15, 1538
104 days into Prince Terosh's Kireshana journey
Governor General's Estate, City of Idonia

Taytron's hunt for Maledek is tiresome.

As was becoming a persistent habit, Lord Kezem paced his office to burn the minutes before a meeting. This plotting business could be mind-numbingly tedious. He wondered how his mother managed it for so many years.

The creature Belcross had become appeared in stunning detail. Kezem knew the creature preferred being called Dalonos, but he couldn't forget the scientist the creature had once been. A faint, blue-white mist surrounded the figure, providing the only visible clue that the image was not a normal hologram.

Kezem suppressed the urge to touch his kerlinblade for reassurance.

"I've considered your report on the Light Ones. If these … machines are indeed growing stronger, I'll have to modify my plans."

"I am listening." The creature crossed his arms and tilted his head.

"Let's assume the Mitran plan works for Taytron and my dear uncle. That will leave cousin Terosh as the most obvious threat, but the Rangers pose an even greater threat. They will not allow the Minstel line to fail."

"What would you have me do? I thought you wanted me to bolster the RT Alliance," Belcross said.

"I do. The Alliance is at the heart of the plan to destroy the Rangers. Killing the king and elder prince will be like kicking korvers. When things turn chaotic, I will need the Alliance to play their part, but there's also another task I have for you. It must be discussed in person."

"Did you explain this to the Ranger sent to kill me?"

"Kill you? No, I needed him to find you since you stopped taking my comm calls. Lucas could never kill you anyway. You're practically immortal. Come to my estate in Idonia so we can discuss your next move."

It took Kezem another fifteen minutes of cajoling to get Belcross to agree. Upon signing off, Kezem paused to consider the terrible risk he was taking. If he failed to contain the creature, Taytron's obsessive hunt for Maledek would be the least of his problems.

Mother will disapprove.

Kezem hated how much weight his mind placed upon that thought.

I can take care of my own problems.

Wincing at the childish thought, Kezem turned his attention to capturing Belcross. As much as he wanted to test his fighting prowess against the creature, prudence prevailed. He would use the coma gas. Even with augmentation, the gas should keep Belcross unconscious long enough to be delivered.

You shall have your Maledek soon, Taytron.

Chapter 26:
Every Prince Needs a Princess

Zeri (June) 16, 1538
105 days into Prince Terosh's Kireshana journey
McNoughten Home, Kesler Plains

To Reia's relief, the Amrita Tears worked well on Kira McNoughten. The disease burned away in hours, but it took more than a day for the lady to gather enough strength to rise. Reia knew it would be months before things returned to normal for the family. Kira sat by Teven's grave for long hours. Semon had returned to the farm work.

About midday, the front door crashed open, and Semon stood in the threshold breathing hard.

"They're coming!" he whispered to his wife.

"Who?" Kira asked.

"Alliance people. They're here for the prince. There's a reward for his capture!" Semon's words tumbled out.

"Where are our weapons?" Reia asked, struggling to rise from the couch.

"What's wrong?" Terosh was on his feet but looked ready to collapse.

"Restler and Tarpon agents are searching for you," Semon said, peeking out the window one more time. His right hand gripped the window frame hard.

"Why would they want me?"

"I don't know." Semon whirled to stare at them. "But you have to leave!"

"Semon!" Kira protested. "We cannot abandon them!"

Reia exchanged a look with Terosh and flicked her eyes toward the barn. They rallied the anotechs and sent them into the barn to destroy evidence of the amrita plants. Getting caught would be bad. Letting RT Alliance thugs know about the anotechs would be infinitely worse. Though completed in seconds, the task left them dangerously weak. Knees buckling, Reia sank onto the couch, trying not to land on Terosh who had also sat down. She landed facing the prince with one leg curled underneath and the other flopped over the side of the couch. Her mind raced, trying to ignore the McNoughtens arguing in the background.

"Reia, the Alliance doesn't know about you," Terosh whispered. "Stay here. Pretend to be their daughter or something."

She glared at Terosh.

"I'm eighteen and hardly dressed to play their daughter. And you can forget about surrendering."

"But what—"

"This way! Hurry!" Kira McNoughten urged. She tugged on Reia's arm. Getting little reaction, she sat down next to Reia, tucked an arm around behind her, and stood up.

Reia could do little more than lean on her.

"You too," Semon said, doing the same for Terosh.

Moments later, they found themselves locked in the master bedchamber, tucked under a mass of blankets.

Well, this is awkward.

Nevertheless, Reia couldn't deny that she felt better knowing Terosh was close.

A knock sounded, and soon, many voices came from the living room. As the argument raged, Reia's heart and head pounded with anticipation and dread. She slowed her breathing, employed a few of Master Niklos's calming techniques, and strained to hear the conversation.

"—is here?" demanded one man.

Reia assumed he was the leader.

"Our sev—six children, my sister, and her husband," Kira answered.

Reia smiled at the story being weaved, but the danger stole most of the amusement and the hitch in Kira's voice as she corrected the number of children killed the rest.

"Bring them out here," the man commanded.

Heavy footsteps clattered outside the bedchamber door.

"No!" Kira protested. "They've both got cornada. Real bad."

Reia tensed. Cornada wasn't dangerous enough to warrant avoidance.

"Look at this," called another man. He sounded young and excited. "Pretty large caydronan sack you've got here. Only Rangers carry those."

Terosh kept Reia from rising by drawing her back against his chest. She remained tense but felt safer.

"They'll be fine," Terosh promised.

A slap, a scream, and several confused orders rang out, contradicting him. Reia clenched her jaw to keep from adding her own scream to the mix.

"You're not hiding a Ranger, are you?" The man's question came out with a growl.

"There was a Ranger here," Semon admitted.

"She came to treat our children for Heskrin," Kira added.

Silence enveloped the house. Reia's heart faltered as she pictured Teven's utterly still features.

Don't think about it!

She swallowed to suppress a sob.

"Heskrin," hissed a female voice. "That's bad. Very bad. We should leave, Adnir."

The leader ordered his people out.

"That's the sixth case, boss," the young man said. "I thought that plan was scrapped."

"It was."

Reia missed the rest of the conversation, but the information she had heard didn't sit well. It fit with the McNoughtens' plight and the notion of more families needing the Amrita Tears, but so many questions remained.

Once certain the RT Alliance people had truly gone, Reia allowed Terosh to help her rise, and they entered the common room. Their shaken hosts were locked in an embrace.

"We're leaving," Terosh announced.

Kira opened her mouth to protest.

"We will not endanger you any longer," Reia added.

"At least stay the night," Semon insisted. He released his wife and spread his arms, shifting his weight like he'd physically block the door if necessary. "Give them time to get to the next farm. You're both poorly equipped for a fight right now. Tomorrow, you can set out whenever you like."

Sensing the query in Terosh's gaze, Reia shrugged.

The prince tipped his head in a respectful bow.

"Your offer of hospitality is much appreciated, Master McNoughten. We accept."

"You talk funny," a girl called from the hallway leading to the other bedrooms.

"She's got you there," Reia teased. "Must come from being a prince."

"Arel! Mind your manners," Kira scolded.

The girl entered the room looking sleepy but healthy. She shook herself as if suddenly registering the presence of strangers. Her gaze flitted over Terosh and fixed on Reia. A hundred questions lay behind her deep blue eyes.

"Is he really a prince? Is he yours? Can I have a prince?"

"Arel, these are our guests. Behave," said Kira.

"It's all right," said Terosh.

Reia's tension melted. She avoided looking at Prince Terosh as a flush warmed her. She covered the two steps to the child and knelt beside her. Taking the child's hand, she turned the girl so they both looked at Terosh.

"Yes, Arel, he's a real prince. He's not mine, but he's real."

"Why is he not yours? You're pretty!" said Arel.

"That's enough," said Semon.

"But he's a prince, Daddy! Every prince needs a princess!" declared the child.

Picking up Arel's other hand, Reia regained the child's attention.

"I'm glad you think I could be a princess, Arel, but I'm a Ranger."

"Can't you be both?" asked Arel.

No answers came. The adults silently willed each other to answer.

"What do princes do, Arel?" Terosh asked at last.

"Rescue princesses from dragons, zaloks, korvers, and bad men," replied the child.

"And who rescues the princes?" Terosh challenged.

"Ohhhhhh," said Arel. "Rangers!"

"That's right." Terosh winked at Reia.

She couldn't understand the flood of emotions the exchange released. A rush of warmth lifted her spirits even as a sense of longing and loss enveloped her.

***

That night, the girl's question kept Terosh from sleeping. It didn't take much twisting to turn the question into: *Is she yours?* The obvious answer was no, but that begged a different question.

Why isn't she yours?

Every prince needs a princess, the anotechs said, replicating Arel's voice and inflection.

She's not a princess.

Does it matter?

Father would say it does.

Since when have you listened to Father?

Terosh couldn't tell if the thought came from the anotechs or not, but it didn't matter. He knew Reia was everything a princess should be and more.

How can I get her to love me?

She already does.

Chapter 27:
Coridian Assassins

Zeri (June) 17, 1538
106 days into Prince Terosh's Kireshana journey
Temporary Campsite, Kireshana Path, Kesler Plains

After a good night's rest, a few hearty meals, and some charming conversations with the young McNoughtens, Reia and Terosh packed their belongings, strapped on their weapons, and continued the Kireshana.

After walking through the Kesler Plains much of the morning, they stopped for a midday meal. Kira McNoughten had sent them away with fresh bread, corncakes, rielberry and blueberry jam, and a small jug of appola juice. It didn't take them long to eat, but they stayed by the stream for a while afterward. As Reia prepared to suggest they move on, she sensed someone watching them.

Half a second later, Terosh grew still and reached for his kerlinblade.

"Ho there!" called a friendly voice in a clipped Terabian accent.

Reia found the accent charming but dangerous. Located northwest of the Felmon Desert, the former prison colony of Terab had birthed a strong, fierce people. Looking left, she spotted the dark-skinned young man in a black uniform. He stood straight and proud about twenty meters away. His teeth gleamed white, rivaling the kamad dagger he held in his left hand. Reia couldn't recall where the dagger had gotten its name, but she recognized the thin, silver weapon.

"Coridian Assassin." Terosh tightened his grip on his kerlinblade.

Reia reached for her banistick.

"Wait. He can't harm you if you don't draw on him," said Terosh.

"Says who?" Reia demanded.

"The rules, ma'am," the assassin said.

"What does—" Reia began.

"I am called Dryse, ma'am. A Coridian Assassin candidate may challenge Royal Guard or Melian Maiden candidates. I may, of course, defend myself, but so long as you pose no threat to me, Ranger, I pose none to you."

A flush crept over Reia's cheeks.

"If you th—"

"I do not presume, ma'am," he interrupted again. "I only request that you allow me to finish my business." Dryse's voice dripped with cultured politeness. He now stood only ten meters away. "I must challenge three derringers, and I choose the prince as my third. There shall be no death today, only a fair contest, and the winner walks away with honor."

Something sharp bit Reia's neck. Ice water replaced her blood. Her vision clouded. The sensation of lightning soaring through her bloodstream wreaked havoc on her nerves, causing her to stagger. Though she had only felt this once before, she remembered it well from her dreams. Whipping her hand up to touch the wound, she felt a tiny drop of blood.

Criessa dart!

Master Niklos had said some attackers would carry the darts. They hold only a small dose of criessa and disintegrate after delivering their payload, but they can still knock a person out for hours.

Find it. Destroy it, Reia ordered the anotechs.

We will do this.

Luckily, previous exposure weakened the criessa's effect. Master Kolknir had insisted the Ranger apprentices experience a wide variety of poisons and sedatives. Criessa had been the first thing given to Reia. She shivered. The darkness, cold, terror, and pain flooded back in numbing waves, but she fought the memories. Lucas had insisted on dosing her, though it was only his fourth day as Kolknir's assistant.

Lucas isn't here.

Reia had refused to talk to anyone but Kiata for a week after the experience.

Kiata isn't here.

When Master Niklos discovered the cruel lesson, he had almost strangled Kolknir.

Only you are here.

Found it.

As soon as the anotechs destroyed the criessa, Reia drew her banistick.

***

Terosh studied the lean Coridian Assassin as the man tried to reason with Reia. He wore his uniform well and appeared to be in his late teens or early twenties. His accent and manners indicated a wealthy family. Terosh wished he had paid more attention to Sedir's lesson on Terabian nobles.

A faint hiss sounded near his left ear and something struck Reia. She recoiled, staggered, and swayed, but soon regained her balance and drew her banistick.

Reia!

Terosh's kerlinblade blazed in his hands, opening to a medium-sized green band.

She's okay. You're not. Move!

Sensing danger from behind, Terosh dropped into a roll.

We help.

Terosh let the anotechs guide his blade, striking left, right, up, then left again. Four things hissed as they struck the pure energy. Another impulse of incoming danger—this time directed at Reia—threw Terosh into motion. He dove left to place his body between his friend and the danger, letting the anotechs guide his blade again.

Two more hisses; two more dangers gone.

Something metallic pinged off his kerlinblade.

Flinger!

By this time, Reia had her banistick open. A glance into her eyes sent relief soaring through Terosh. She slid the handle to the middle and twirled the banistick so that it formed a temporary shield. More hissing sounds said she had connected with three darts.

Terosh ducked two more darts. As he raised his blade to attack, the Coridian Assassin held out his left arm in a ceasing motion.

"You are a worthy opponent, my Prince."

Two more assassins rose from hiding spots behind the man and approached.

"Anyone can divert flingers, but only a scion of House Minstel could consistently block criessa darts from three sources." Dryse's tone conveyed admiration. "And you are also a worthy opponent, Ranger. I have heard your kind can resist criessa, but now I have seen it. You may both continue the Kireshana in peace. Safe journey."

The other two Coridian Assassins joined the first and all three bowed.

"Are you going to tell them?" asked one man in a low voice.

"Of course," Dryse assured his companion. "Dulad Prince, Ranger, you may wish to investigate something." Dryse pointed northeast. "You will find six bodies about a hundred and fifty meters that way, and two more a dozen meters beyond them. We buried them so korvers wouldn't find them. You will have to dig if you wish to see them. Besides weapons, they carried only this." He tossed something at Terosh who caught it. Without another word, the assassins sprinted away.

Terosh looked down at the coin in his hand. The silver token sparkled in the fading afternoon sunlight. The letters *RT* stood out on one side. He flipped the coin over to see the other side. A picture of a zalok and a man dominated the back. The man was being crushed by the zalok, but he had his sword thrust into the zalok's soft underbelly. Grimly, Terosh tucked the coin into a pocket.

***

As adrenaline faded, Reia frowned after the departing Coridian Assassins. Tears threatened to fall, but she fought them, unwilling to surrender to the terror rising from her past.

It's over. It's over.

No matter how many times her mind chanted the phrase, part of her disbelieved it.

Terosh tentatively touched her arm.

"What's wrong?"

She swallowed hard and cleared her throat.

"What's on the coin?" Reia tried and failed to ask the question casually. "Should we check on the bodies the Coridian Assassins found?"

Terosh slowly withdrew his hand.

"Never mind that. We should start moving. It might settle our nerves. And no, I don't think we need to see the bodies if they already buried them."

Reia let the matter drop. She appreciated his effort, but it bothered her to need comfort.

You should be long over the criessa thing.

Only faint curiosity lingered concerning the coin. She pushed it aside. He would tell her in time if it was important.

They picked up their packs and started walking. The sky held a few clouds, but it didn't look like it would rain. The plains boasted colorful fields of purple iras, orange and yellow copalas, and pink cadriks. Gradually, Reia's muscles unclenched, and her stride evened out.

"Technically, the Coridian Assassins are a branch of the Royal Guard, but only King Rammon ever formally recognized them," Terosh said, trying for a casual tone. Tension crept in anyway.

"Does that bother you?" Reia asked, knowing from his tone that it did.

"Rammon established them to hunt down his enemies." Terosh paused to let her think about that.

Reia wanted to divert the conversation, for she could guess what he would say next.

"Their first duty was to execute Queen Haria, Prince Savad, Princess Itel, and Prince Vik. Princess Lystran escaped only because one Assassin couldn't stomach the betrayal."

"I'm sorry, Terosh." Reia didn't even realize she had neglected his title.

"No apology necessary. It's a truth my family has to live with."

Reia felt as if the prince had stepped three meters away and built a wall between them. She fell silent rather than risk deepening either of their wounds.

Chapter 28:
Shattered Peace

Zeri (June) 23, 1538
112 days into Prince Terosh's Kireshana journey
Kireshana Path, Kesler Plains

Travel went smoothly for almost a full week. Reia used the time to teach Prince Terosh dozens of Ranger skills. Her lessons included how to use a shootav, catch wallays, trick tretlings into following one out of danger, and find underwater streams. In addition, she covered how to spear freshwater koomies with a banistick, turn shed winol skin into inoli powder, use the stimulant to bolster one's immune system, and skywatch for storms. By the end, the prince could track okapis, antelope, sinabis, cootras, hiktanis, and morookas. He confessed to liking tracking morookas best because the little creatures were not generous with clues and changed directions often. He could also recognize and imitate quava, colana, sweswi, kyrie, and kamria calls. In return, the prince taught Reia how to dance to "Leparnisu."

As a part of his marriage proposal on Temen (July) 4, 1140, Prince Olin Minstel told Jaivia Elikrie that she was his world. Later, a harpist named Valin Tamron wrote the song for a play based on their courtship.

If you wish to kill me, walk away swiftly,
For my whole world is you.
The fire in every star
Cannot compare to you.
The light of life shines so bright
The rocks near come to life.
Don't you know? The world is you!

If you wish to kill me, walk away swiftly,
For my whole world is you.
See and hear the angels sing
They will tell you sweetly
All the gods bound to good
Are manifest in you.
Don't you know? The world is you!

If you wish to kill me, walk away swiftly,
For my whole world is you.
I could be blind and deaf
Yet still feel your goodness.
You haunt my dreams and my heart.
Please tell me we'll never part.
Don't you know? The world is you!

Prince Terosh also explained some court rituals, past and present. One required the sprinkling of dirt from one's home city in front of the throne. Another demanded people touch their face to the floor seven times before speaking. The seven bows were for the three moon gods, the king, the queen, the palace, and Reshner. One ordered courtiers to present their wrists to the sovereign every time they made a request. *Sovereign* usually meant King Rammon who had developed a nasty sense of humor after using Dark Ones to prolong his reign.

Everything was peaceful as they lay down to sleep on the night of Zeri 22, 1538.

That didn't last.

Wake! Wake! Wake!

The anotechs' insistent cry prompted Reia to roll off her bedroll and open her banistick. A two-meter-long, meter-high, gray-black blur landed where she had just vacated and tore into her caydronan sack, which had been her pillow. Reia swung hard. The blow hardly phased the giant korver, but the return force propelled her to her feet. She spun with the momentum until she faced the beast again.

The korver snarled, showing Reia a fine set of fangs flanked by a row of gleaming white teeth.

"Konjah, Ademos, contain! Melini, Kenos contain!"

Reia couldn't see the man, but she spotted another overgrown korver stalking close. The beast's slender snout told Reia it was female, but the teeth seemed about the same size and the snarl sounded no friendlier than the male. The beasts held their positions, crouching low.

Big puppy, bad puppy, cried the anotechs.

Yes, I have eyes, thank you!

Poke the eye and death defy, added the anotechs.

Reia grunted at the anotechs but considered their advice. She didn't dare take her eyes off the korver in front of her but needed to find Terosh and see if he was okay.

"Terosh?" she called.

"I'm here."

The tension in his response told Reia his situation probably mirrored hers. She wondered if she could reach her shootav in time. She would have less than a second to shoot and couldn't be certain the dose of cormea and radon would be enough.

"We'd prefer to take you alive as those are our orders," said a polite male voice.

"Alive would be nice," Reia muttered.

"What about—"

"Don't you dare go noble on me," Reia snapped, interrupting the prince.

"My masters have an offer for the prince," the man said.

"Good to know," Reia said. "But I don't believe you."

"There's also a job for you, Ranger, if you'll take it. My masters have already hired several Rangers like my friend here."

The announcement shocked Reia. She glanced toward the voice and then in the direction the silhouette pointed. A cloaked, silent figure stood with crossed arms, watching the scene unfold.

Traitor.

"Not interested," Reia said tightly.

"Too bad. Konjah, Ademos, attack!" The civility vanished from the man's tone.

Reia drew her shootav and rolled under the leaping korver, firing two stun pellets up into its belly as it sailed over her. She only had time to squeeze off one shot at the second korver leaping for her throat.

The beast latched onto her banistick but let go with a whimper when the electric pulse registered in its teeth.

Reia landed with the korver on top. The three energy beams that would have struck her slammed into the korver's tough hide, but the giant thing landed squarely on her chest. She remained conscious but having one arm trapped beneath the korver left her vulnerable.

***

As soon as Reia turned down the job, Terosh knew the two korvers facing him would attack. He drew his kerlinblade and kerlak pistol. A swift adjustment put the pistol on full automatic, which would cause it to fire one continuous stream of energy. The powerpack would deplete almost instantly, but if he swung his arm fast enough, he might hit both korvers and the Ranger before it ran out. He had two more powerpacks strapped to his belt, but they would do him no good without adequate reload time.

As the first korver leapt, Terosh pulled the trigger. The beam slammed the korver to a halt in midair and threw it backward. Before the scent of well-done korver reached him, Terosh turned the beam on the other korver and the Ranger. The second korver yelped, leaving its cry hanging in the air as it died.

The Ranger leapt away from the energy beam as the powerpack died. Nevertheless, the thin beam skipped along the Ranger's right forearm, causing him to recoil and flee. It was too bad that the powerpack had come from Fort Riden's armory and thus lacked Dr. Belcross's special knockout concoction. Terosh wanted to pursue the man but saw a korver land on Reia and went to help her.

***

Lucas Telon didn't care as much as Kiner that the korvers were dead, but it was a shame. Even though he had shot one of the korvers to save Reia, he wished the program no ill-will. The first korver trials had been promising but this disaster would be a big setback.

Playing games with the Alliance is foolish.

Lucas wanted to kill Kiner, but the RT soldier wasn't a true threat. Kiner would crawl back to his masters and report the program's failure. Lucas would file his own report with Gareth Restler, but his official report would go to Lord Kezem.

How many Alliance soldiers know Lord Kezem is Maledek?

If Kezem's plans proceeded properly, the Alliance and the Rangers would soon destroy each other. Kolknir approved, but despite flaws, the Order still felt like family to Lucas

Chapter 29:
Roads to Meritab

Zeri (June) 25, 1538-Temen (July) 2, 1538
114-121 days into Prince Terosh's Kireshana journey
Kireshana Path, Kesler Plains
The Heskrin battle, the brush with Coridian Assassins, and this korver encounter stole some joy from the Kireshana, but Reia determined to make the best of everything. She ached for a couple of days after the korver attack but at least they were alive. Worse than the soreness, something happened inside Terosh. He was pensive for long periods of time. Reia worried about the silences but didn't want to pry.

The ground trembled.

Probably just shifting graveground. Nothing to worry about. Terosh will open up when he's ready.

Reia guided them southeast toward the Lotrian Fields. It would take several weeks to reach the fields at their current pace, but they had no reason to rush. The goritor-infested area would still be there when they arrived.

Suddenly a tremendous crack sounded, followed by a high-pitched scream.

Flinching, Reia exchanged a *what-now* glance with Terosh and dashed toward the scream. Seconds later, she halted on the edge of a miniature canyon. The depression was only a meter across but extended almost four meters to Reia's right, two to her left, and went down at least five meters. She wanted to call it graveground, but it wasn't like any graveground she had ever seen.

A girl leaned awkwardly against the dirt wall at the bottom.

Shouts brought Reia's head up. A man and a woman sprinted from a large white house about a hundred meters away. The ground trembled and rumbled.

"Stop them." Reia threw off her cloak and scrambled into the hole.

Terosh shouted something, but Reia didn't hear his words.

The anotechs delivered the message.

It's a maw!

Reia remembered Master Niklos telling her how the ground would split open for no good reason, then snap shut again, like a mouth closing on a tasty morsel. A maw could stay open for years but smaller ones—like this one—usually only lasted minutes.

I'd better hurry.

Every muscle complained as she braced a leg on each side and descended as quickly as possible. The dirt walls were firm, yet small pieces dislodged and rained down on the child as Reia scrambled for hand and footholds. She kept her caydronan sack with her, though she wasn't sure the child could be helped.

When she reached the bottom, Reia examined the girl. The child was crouched on her right side with her knees tucked beneath her. Curly dark hair draped the girl's face, rising and falling with each shallow breath. Reia didn't want to move her, but something had to be done soon. She sensed movement and looked up in time to see Terosh slam into the ground next to her. Heart skipping three beats, Reia wanted to yell at him, but the dust cloud raised by his landing caused her to choke and cough instead.

"What are you doing?" Reia barely got the words out before Terosh bounded to his feet and said something she couldn't hear.

Another ear-assaulting crack preceded a deep rumbling. The air pressed down and in from all sides, squeezing Reia until her lungs wanted to explode. Instinctively, she instructed the anotechs to protect the child and push against the closing ground, creating a thin shield around them. Breaking into a cold sweat, she continued to pour energy out, expanding the shield to include Terosh. The effort took a tremendous toll on her body. Her muscles quivered. She could see the prince only as a glowing blur.

When Terosh took her hands, Reia sensed admiration, annoyance, worry, and inklings of a plan for having the anotechs propel them upward through the closing ground.

It could kill you, the anotechs warned.

This maw will kill us!

Terosh's thought sailed through Reia as if it belonged to her, but she didn't have time to be amazed. The prince squeezed his eyes shut and struggled to reinforce the capsule Reia had started. She lent what strength she could, helping the prince tap into the anotechs' power. Not even growing the amrita plants had been this hard. Terosh released Reia's hands, snatched up the child, pulled Reia upright, and held on tightly. The pressure built around them. Just as she thought they might be squashed, Reia felt her feet rising. She watched a blood vessel in Terosh's head tick in time with the passing seconds, grateful for the thick shield he had created so they wouldn't blunder through the dirt with their skulls.

Reia clung to Terosh and shut her eyes, enduring the wild ride through the closing walls of soil. When they reached open space, she fell and flopped onto her back. Familiarity swept over Reia as she opened her eyes and stared at the cheerful sky with its fluffy white clouds. Something bony dug into her back. Her limbs wouldn't cooperate, but she twisted her head and saw Terosh.

Out cold. What else is new?

A spark of anger poured energy into her. It wasn't much, but it allowed her to sit up, check the prince for injuries, and glare down at him upon finding nothing to fix. Her head pounded, distracting her from the urge to smack him.

You knew the ground would close! You knew it and jumped in anyway! That was beyond stupid!

Terosh blinked at her, groaned, and closed his eyes.

"Don't look at me like that."

Reia gained enough strength to rub a sore spot in her side.

"Like what?"

"Like you want to yell."

"Terosh—"

"Leave it," he insisted, meeting her gaze and slowly sitting up.

"You can't—"

"It's my life," Terosh said, cutting her off.

Something inside Reia crumbled.

"You're a prince." She hated the tremble in her voice.

"And that means I should watch you die?" He fixed icy eyes on her. His expression said he would not allow her to come to harm because of him.

"Yes, if it comes to that!"

The intensity of his gaze touched Reia.

Don't look at me like that!

Between the notes of his question Reia heard a declaration. The unspoken words pulsed through the air.

Reia numbly patched the child's wounds with toom leaves and anotechs.

The little girl was Seri Elad. Her parents arrived as Reia finished patching the girl's scrapes. The parents insisted they stay several days to rest and recover. They gratefully accepted this invitation. When they felt strong enough to continue, the girl's father took them as far as the Lotrian Fields in his battered old hov.

***

Temen (July) 2, 1538
121 days into Prince Terosh's Kireshana journey
Kireshana Path, Kesler Plains

After safely crossing the Lotrian Fields, Terosh and Reia continued the journey, well-aware that they approached the last quarter of the Kireshana. Terosh would be home in less than a month. The thought of leaving Reia ached, tempting him to take a circuitous route back to Rammon.

"You look like you could use some sleep. Didn't you like the bed at the Elad's house?" asked Reia.

"Hmmm? Yes, it was fine." Terosh avoided Reia's gaze but still felt her attention.

"It's the anotechs, isn't it?" Reia inquired. "You shouldn't use them so much."

"You use what you can to save people, and I use what I can. What's the difference?"

"Toom leaves and iras don't leave me half-dead every time I use them," Reia pointed out with a sad smile.

"What do you think about anotechs? Are they good or evil?" Terosh asked, needing to deflect the conversation.

"What do you mean? They're just machines," she answered.

"God machines. Thinking machines." Terosh waited several seconds before adding, "There are rumors that some anotechs are evil, just as some people are evil. They're called Dark Ones."

"They've certainly got enough power to make trouble if they wish." Reia took another dozen steps. "Do you believe the rumors?"

"I don't know," Terosh answered.

"What could be done if the rumors were true?"

Terosh shrugged at the disturbing question.

Are the rumors true? What can we do?

Fight Dalonos.

What are these Dark Ones? Where do I find them? How do I fight them?

They are us and not us. Twisted. Evil. Unfettered.

Unfettered?

Yes, no rules, only power.

"Look. Kamrias," Reia said, pointing to their left.

Terosh focused on a small flock of kamrias circling about a kilometer away and listened to their triumphant cries. He remembered Reia telling him kamrias prey on scavengers.

They changed direction and quickened their pace. A few minutes later, they stumbled across eight bodies, six in the gray uniform of Meritab Regulars and two in jet black uniforms with no markings. The scent surrounding the hours-old battle matched the sight.

Terosh had the anotechs filter the heavy stench of blood and burned flesh.

Reia stopped by the third soldier.

A deep gash ran down his left side. A serlak rifle with a bayonet lay next to him, telling Terosh what had killed the man. He winced.

That's not a pleasant way to go.

To his surprise, Reia knelt, checked the man's pulse, and sent Terosh a measuring gaze.

"Good or evil, we've got to use anotechs. This man's alive but beyond conventional healing." Her expression said she clearly didn't like what they had to do. "He still has a thread of life the anotechs could preserve." Reia placed both hands over the man's wounds.

Terosh knelt on the man's other side, and together, they poured anotechs into the wound. Had anyone attacked them at that moment, they would have been helpless. The work was long and slow. While Reia tended to the man's body, Terosh funneled anotechs to Reia and modified the man's memories. Practicality demanded that the man never know the extent of his wounds. If word spread that anotechs could be miracle healers, there would be no end to the abuse.

People kill for trinkets, what would they do for the anotechs?

Terosh's family and a few others had been entrusted with the anotech legacy. Maintaining that legacy meant secrecy. He had never liked it, but he had always understood the necessity, even when that meant Tate would receive training and he would not.

Why can't anything be simple? Terosh wondered when they finished almost four hours later.

More work needed to be done, but the anotechs now possessed the instructions to continue piecing Lieutenant Korben Fericin together. Terosh felt odd knowing the man's name without ever having spoken to him. The anotechs had pulled the name in the first two seconds of searching his brain. Terosh had to instruct them not to pry every memory out of poor Fericin.

The potential for damaging something vital chilled Terosh. Hearing tales about King Rammon stripping minds down to nothing had come nowhere near the experience of being inside Fericin's head with the power to heal or destroy.

Reia had retreated into her thoughts, and Terosh decided to leave her alone, despite burning questions. Throughout the evening meal Terosh thought of several dozen ways to ease into the topic. As they settled for the night, he took the direct approach.

"Reia, why do you care if I overuse the anotechs?"

He really wanted to ask: *Could you ever love me?*

The question stopped Reia from straightening her bedroll. Her expression told Terosh she thought it an odd question. Twice, she opened her mouth to reply, and twice, she closed it again. She took her time about finding a comfortable position, but eventually, she tucked her knees underneath her body, gazed at the fire, and tried to explain.

"It's sort of like the Ralose Charm."

"What's that?" asked Terosh.

"There is a legend from long ago, before we were called Rangers, when Prince Davel's Order of the Nareth Talis was still finding itself." Reia looked like she wanted to restart the conversation, but she sighed and continued, "Prince Davel's first recruit was his best friend, Aimeri Turnok."

"His wife?"

"Not yet. When he recruited her, she was just a servant girl he befriended and taught to handle a sword."

"Why haven't I heard of this?" asked Terosh, searching his thoughts for a lesson he might have forgotten.

"Many people argue it never happened."

"Do you believe it happened?" Terosh questioned.

"Five months ago, I would have said no, but now that we've learned so much about the anotechs ... I guess it could happen."

"It's a sad story, isn't it?"

"They're related to your ancestors," Reia gently teased. "Yes, it's sad.

They married about a year after starting the Nareth Talis, but they were only married for about four months. Then, Aimeri and Davel ran into trouble with Miquinn Firol. During the final battle, Aimeri cast what is now called the Ralose Charm upon herself and Miquinn."

"Reflect harm on him," Terosh murmured.

"Close enough," Reia confirmed. "Aimeri knew only one of them would walk away from the fight. Wanting her husband to live, she told the anotechs to transfer damage her body sustained to Miquinn."

"How did she get the anotechs to Miquinn?"

"Shootav."

"Why didn't she just use poison or something?"

Reia shrugged.

"I don't think she planned on fighting that day."

"Could we use the Ralose Charm?" Terosh wondered.

"I don't think we would want to. Aimeri died that day. It's not exactly a weapon of choice," Reia noted. "No one has tried it since then. The anotechs swore not to let anyone cast it on their own person, and few will risk somebody else's life. The truth's in the translation. The Ralose Charm can bind two people's fates together, making any harm done to one be shared by both."

"What's that got to do with this?" Terosh asked, struggling to make the connection.

"I feel like I'm wearing one. It's like your pain is mine, and I fear my pain might become yours. You're a prince. That cannot happen!" She drew a breath to compose herself before asking, "Do you understand?"

Terosh didn't respond right away, but eventually nodded.

"I guess Davel also died that day."

The somber statement effectively closed the conversation as they slipped into their own thoughts.

***

Temen (July) 10, 1538
129 days into Prince Terosh's Kireshana journey
Maledek's Safe House, City of Meritab

Blood leaked from a cut over Prince Taytron's left eye. He stood over the broken body of the man he had greatly admired, invited into his home, and trusted in nearly everything. The intervening months since their last meeting had not been kind to Dr. Atien Belcross. His eyes glowed with strange light.

He is full of Dark Ones, the anotechs reported.

He deserves to die.

Not by your hand, Prince of the Chosen.

Captain Kelter echoed the anotechs' sentiments.

"Do not do this, Taytron. Your wife and daughter are gone, but if you sacrifice your honor, you will never be the man their memory deserves."

He had pictured this moment for many months. Conflicting emotions assailed Tate. He wanted to kill this man, yet Captain Kelter was right. They had captured Dr. Belcross and needed to let justice work. Still,

Tate's finger tightened over his kerlinblade's activation switch. It could be over in a second. With strength drawn from the memory of his sweet Deanna and innocent daughter, Tate finally pushed himself away from the thing Belcross had become and ordered his men to secure the prisoner.

All this time, was he truly Maledek?

Yes. He has played the part.

Then, at last, Maledek is no more. Deanna and Elia can rest in peace.

***

Temen (July) 10, 1538
Same day
Governor General's Estate, City of Idonia

Kezem sprang to his feet and watched a pair of servants scurrying in his mother's wake. They looked apologetic. He waved them off. He would deal with them later, but for now, he had a force bearing down upon him like a Great Storm ready to relocate a mountain.

"Mother, what a pleasant—" he cut himself off, knowing she wouldn't hear a word anyway.

Lady Mavis Altran drew close and glared up into Kezem's eyes. Her dark hair—liberally sprinkled with gray—remained perfectly in place. Her eyes flashed dangerously. She closed her eyes, drew a breath, and placed one finger on his chest.

"I thought I raised you better."

Kezem held her intense gaze for an eternity then finally broke the eye contact and backed up a step. He would have felt more comfortable if she brandished a kamad dagger at him. He didn't bother defending himself. He had seen her in this mood before and Riden himself would have had a tough time stopping her.

"My plans took months—years—to lay and you risked everything on one stupid ploy." Her words rushed out in an ever-quickening stream. "Taytron is nothing! His search was nothing! It meant nothing, but if he had killed that man the investigation would have taken months, completely destroying the plan's timing!"

"Then it was a fragile plan, wasn't it?" Kezem returned.

She slapped him.

He never saw it coming, but he knew better than to touch the stinging spot.

"Any idiot with enough money can hire an assassin. I don't want my brother and his family simply dead. I want them *destroyed!* There is a difference, my dear, a very large difference. If you cannot see that, then I have no further use for you."

From any other being, her statement would have been laughable, but Kezem knew his life depended on his next words. He tipped his head forward.

"My apologies, Mother. I will do better."

His mother tilted his chin up and planted an icy kiss on his forehead. "See that you do."

"What shall I do now?"

"Wait," Lady Mavis replied. "Everything is not lost. We have Captain Kelter to thank for staying Taytron's hand. Terosh will return soon. When he does, we can move the Mitran plan forward." A slow smile spread across her face. "The Kireshana may also have given us the answer to our Ranger problem."

"How so?" Kezem couldn't follow the many threads to his mother's plots.

"If the reports are correct—and I have no reason to doubt them— our young prince has fallen in love with a Ranger."

Kezem had received the same reports but did not see the significance until now.

"Such a match is forbidden by Ranger law, but only if they marry."

"Have a little faith in your cousin's charms, Kezem. If nature does not draw them to a favorable conclusion, I'm sure the right pressure could get them to comply."

"You're playing matchmaker," Kezem commented, scarcely believing his ears.

"The match has already been made. We have only to discover how to make it useful, darling."

Kezem almost pitied his cousin.

***

Temen (July) 12, 1538
131 days into Prince Terosh's Kireshana journey
Royal Palace, City of Rammon

You are no longer useful.

Dalonos heard the words, but they didn't make sense. When the anotechs' intentions finally dawned on him, he screamed.

They let him scream as they drained his life and withdrew.

***

"The prisoner is dead, my Lord," Aster Captain Gina Kelter announced.

Tate understood the words but felt nothing. Bit by bit, his emotional shell cracked and shattered, flooding him with pain. He fell to his knees and tried to contain the grief. Next thing he knew, Captain Kelter had wrapped her arms around his shoulders and drawn him into a strong embrace. Tate was grateful to share the burden with someone he trusted, someone who had always been a steady presence in his life.

***

Temen (July) 22, 1538
141 days into Prince Terosh's Kireshana journey
Slightly off the Kireshana Path, road toward the City of Meritab

Lieutenant Korben Fericin felt he should know his companions better. They had been traveling together for almost three weeks. In another hour, they would reach Meritab and part ways. He felt guilty for making them backtrack to escort him home, but they had insisted.

The jagged scar on his side troubled him. His mind felt sluggish and

155

uncooperative. Whenever he started remembering something, he would hit a wall of nothing. He must have hit his head during the battle. That would explain the gaping memory holes.

Do you hear me? a child's voice asked.

"Yes," Fericin replied.

"Did you say something, Lieutenant?" The question came from the Ranger.

Shhhh. Tell her nothing.

Korben couldn't think of anything to say to the Ranger so he shook his head. She would probably give him a mintas leaf to suck on and say it would relax him. Despair gnawed at him. He remembered much, but the blank spots bothered him. The voice in his head spoke more often as the days went on. The first few days it had only spoken once or twice, but this was the eighth time today.

"Are you feeling any stronger today?" the Ranger asked.

"Somewhat," Korben replied. The simple response didn't seem right. He couldn't fight his companions, but they had to be responsible for his current state of being.

Should I be grateful? What happened to me?

He would take the pair to Meritab and give them horses like he had promised then he would take some time off to heal and think.

***

Temen (July) 25, 1538
144 days into Prince Terosh's Kireshana journey
Ranger Compound, Riden Mountains

The Ashatan Council argued most of Temen 24, 1538, and part of the next day as well. An important mission involving an informant in a Tarpon house in Meritab required two of the very best. However, most of the Nareth Talis Rangers were missing, previously engaged, or loners.

Master Alikron had sent Kolknir on a mission to Idonia some time ago, and Lucas Telon disappeared on a mission to Azhel. The Celdins were unavailable. Kelsa would soon have a child, and James would not leave her side. Adji, Zed Laverit, Esther Penoi, and Rivi Santros always worked alone. Only Todd and Kiata Wellum were both physically available and functioned as a team.

Master Niklos McGreven opposed the idea, and he wasn't technically a Council member. Niklos had turned down the Ashatan Council position in favor of spending scant free time with his wife and children.

"It is entirely unfair! They have completed three missions without rest. They need time off," he insisted.

"These are hard times." Master Hiram Alikron voiced the general sentiment. "Everybody must do their part. Send for them at once."

Growling at the lack of sympathy, Niklos went to find the Wellums and deliver the summons. As he let his feet wander, not wanting to find Todd or Kiata, Niklos let his thoughts drift. Any mission could be dangerous, but this one carried extra risk. Infiltrating the Tarpon house could take weeks.

Then, they would have to find the informant, assess the situation, and escape. The tasks would take a lot of time and patience.

Poor Kiata, patience is not her strong suit.

Nevertheless, Niklos knew she would do her job well.

"They'll be fine." No amount of self-assurance could conquer the worry.

Sending them is foolish! What if something happens?

Niklos had practically raised Kiata and Reia Antellio. He loved them both deeply. His back ached with the memory of countless hours pacing while waiting for them to return from various missions.

***

"The Council wants to see us," Todd Wellum announced gently. "Master Niklos is waiting. He thought we might need a minute."

Kiata smiled. She had ceased being Master Niklos's student when she chose the knight's path over the healer's path, but he was still the closest thing she had to a father. She straightened.

"I'll be fine."

Todd wrapped an arm around her waist.

"I don't want to leave either." He planted a kiss on her forehead. "I was looking forward to some time alone."

Kiata slipped from his grasp and walked from the room, keeping her back stiff. She regretted the cruelty of ignoring his comfort, but if she yielded now, nothing would stop the tears of exhaustion. She had pushed herself beyond pain for years, ever since her parents' murder. If she kept busy enough the hurt would fade to tolerable levels. She almost broke her vow not to cry when Master Niklos met her at the door and opened his arms. She wordlessly hugged him.

"I'm sorry, my dear, I know you wanted to wait for your sister's return. I tried to talk them out of it, but they would only have the very best," Master Niklos said.

Kiata tightened her hug.

"Thank you, but we can do this, whatever the mission may be."

Soon after, Kiata stood beside her husband before the Ashatan Council. She had only been in this private conference chamber a few times. Although one might meet a council member in the tunnels, they usually only assembled for trials or commissioning ceremonies. Kiata listened as the Council handed down their decision, which doubled as her orders.

Chapter 30:
Promise

Temen (July) 30, 1538
149 days into Prince Terosh's Kireshana journey
Kireshana Path, nearing the City of Rammon

After getting horses from Lieutenant Fericin, Terosh and Reia rode toward the capital, knowing the Kireshana would soon end. Terosh saw the Royal Guard fires burning at even intervals around Rammon. The fires burned for him as a part of a long-standing tradition. His heart beat faster as each step brought him closer to home and back to fine food, lazy days, and every comfort he had foregone the last few months. At the same time, each step also brought him closer to the end of his time with Reia.

Minutes later, as they came within sight of the West Gate, they halted the horses. Terosh let his gaze linger on the elegant spires of the cathedral, the solidness of the peasant apartments in the Southern Quarter, and the thousands of lights illuminating the palace. The fading sun still hung in the sky behind them. The weakening sunlight shone off the countless rooftops, bathing them in the illusion of fire. The last several hours had slipped by in silence, lost in the rhythm of pounding hooves. Both had far too much to say to begin. Terosh's throat felt dry and thinking became difficult. He turned his horse to face Reia and swallowed several times.

"Reia, I … I've enjoyed traveling with you," he said.

It sounded pathetic. The words he really wanted to say stuck in his throat.

I love you.

Reia's expression remained neutral for a second, and then she grinned.

"So have I."

"How will I find you?" Terosh asked, trying not to sound desperate. The horse shifted under him, carrying him back a step. He patted the horse's neck and urged him to recover the step.

"I'll be around for a few weeks," Reia promised. "I didn't get to see much of the capital the first time."

"What will you do?"

"Heal people. There's always—"

"I love you!" Terosh burst out. He smiled shyly as relief and mortification battled across his features. "I … have for a long time, practically since you ruined that ambush in the Ridens. You're beautiful and compassionate and wonderful. And I'm probably making a mess of this, but you should know how much you mean to me."

Did I say that out loud?

Aye, ya did, laddie, said the anotechs.

Terosh stared intently at Reia. She fell quiet, but he suspected the sudden glistening in her eyes might be tears. He studied her face, trying to glean what he could, but her expression matched his muddled feelings.

"Please say something."

A single tear slipped out and slid down her face.

"My Prince, I cannot …"

Reia's formal tone struck Terosh harder than her fist might have. She wiped at her eyes and drew a deep breath. Her face flitted through several unfathomable expressions but finally settled on sadness.

A ray of hope ignited in Terosh.

Reia closed her eyes as if pushing down pain. When she opened them again, the sadness had vanished, but she still seemed shaken.

She loves me!

Told you so.

"It would be impossible to—"

Impulsively, Terosh dismounted, stepped close, and gripped Reia's right hand.

"Could you love me?"

***

I already do!

Reia buried the heart cry so the anotechs wouldn't broadcast it. Her face did a fine job describing her inner turmoil. What could she tell him?

Silence stretched between them.

"We've been through—"

"No! I see your answer and feel it. How can—"

"It's forbidden," Reia broke in, squeezing his hand with aching force. The words sounded feeble.

"I know," Terosh said, squeezing back. "You told me, but it can be done."

"How?" Reia asked, surprised at her desperation.

A light of hope dawned behind Terosh's deep blue eyes.

"I'm younger than Tate. I don't have to be king!" He sounded deliriously happy. "Don't you see? Tate will marry and carry on the family line and rule Reshner. And we can marry. We'll go to the mountains or wherever you want to go. I could be a Ranger if they'll have me." He wasn't shouting, but in the still evening air, he might as well have been.

Bowing her head, Reia tried to believe things could work out. Their love had been born of shared trials. They knew most of each other's faults and flaws, hopes and dreams. She wanted to travel the Riden Mountains with him. Terosh wouldn't be the first Minstel to lay down the title of "prince" in favor of "Ranger." Then, reality intruded, and the dream slipped away. Reia had seen his expression upon spotting the Royal Guard campfires and recognized the joy of homecoming.

You belong in Rammon, and I belong in the mountains.

"No, Terosh, we—"

"Reia, I understand how you feel about the Rangers, but once we marry, they'll—"

"Don't pretend to understand what—" Reia cut herself off violently, pulled back her hand, and dismounted. It gave her an excuse to look away. She would not hurt him this way.

I'd have to leave the Rangers, but that's my problem, not his.

Trying to steady herself, Reia faced Terosh again.

"It's … better this way," she whispered. As he opened his mouth to reply, Reia raised her hands to ward off words. At the last moment, she placed a single finger against his lips. The finger slipped.

Terosh pulled her close, trapping her hands against his chest.

"Give us a chance, Reia."

She couldn't resist turning her head and resting in his embrace.

His heart beat as wildly as a colana trapped in a hunter's net. He kissed the top of her head and breathed into her hair.

It felt so gentle she almost cried. A sob burned inside.

Terosh cleared his throat.

"I've got to tell my father and brother about the attacks on us. They must be warned, but then, I'll announce my intent to leave the palace."

Reia spoke, but her words were muffled against his chest. Grateful for the excuse to step back, yet battling a terrible sense of loss, she surprised herself by having a steady voice.

"I do love you, Terosh, but doing anything about it will change everything for both of us. Are you sure you want this?"

"Tell me how to find you."

Reia slipped into formal speech.

"Think carefully, my Prince. I will stay near Rammon for a month. If you need to find me, light a purple fire."

"I will."

Hope and caution blasted through Reia.

"Take this," she said, unclipping her banistick. "It's a promise to wait for your decision." As she handed him the weapon, Reia rested her hands on his, squeezed one last time, and quickly mounted her horse. She let the tears fall as soon as she had galloped away.

***

"We should take 'em now." Lieutenant Adrik Bentanner lowered the spotting scope. Only a hint of his soft Charan accent seasoned his speech. He kept his voice low, though little chance existed that their quarry would overhear them. His voice vibrated with youthful energy.

"We'd never make it in time," General Ariman Keldor said, his voice calm. Keldor never made his men do anything he wouldn't do himself, and that included scouting hostile territory. He wouldn't tell his superiors, but he preferred the open plains and action over their boring meetings.

"Why not?" The way Bentanner tilted his head reminded Keldor of a korver pup. "I could signal the others, and we could swoop down—"

"Keep your voice down," Keldor ordered. He narrowed his eyes at the young man, but the effect was lost to the darkness. "That's why," he added, shifting the vidscreen so the boy could see the mass of yellow dots clustered about two kilometers beyond their target. Royal Guards had been camping on the Kevil Plains for weeks, watching for Prince Terosh's return. "We could reach them first, but we'd never take them quietly," Keldor explained. "We want them alive."

"We could stun 'em," Bentanner suggested.

"Yes, and have every Royal Guard within five kilometers on us instantly."

Keldor smothered the urge to cuff the boy. Adrik occasionally let his mouth outrun his sense. The kid had the same bright-eyed enthusiasm Keldor had last seen in his son, Talyon. Unfortunately, Adrik had only half of Taly's intellect. From the back or side, Keldor could almost imagine Adrik was Taly.

"Guess they might see the flash, but if we get real close—"

"You ever try sneaking up on a Ranger?"

"No, sir, but—"

"It can't be done."

"They're—"

"Very good at what they do," Keldor cut in. "Besides, she rode away from him."

"It's just a girl," Adrik said sullenly.

That's a fight I'd like to see, Keldor silently admitted. He stared into the semi-darkness. The Ranger didn't look like much of a melee fighter, but he had learned to never underestimate Rangers. Rumors of strange powers didn't spring from nothing, and he had seen those powers. A Ranger had once healed Taly from a venomous snakebite, placing Keldor deep in her debt.

Bentanner shifted uncomfortably.

Keldor let him stew a little longer, using silence as a weapon.

"Let's go," he said finally.

When they returned to camp, Keldor slipped into his tent and sent a report to the Lady, pondering his conflicting orders. Donovan Meetcher wished the prince captured and the Ranger killed. The Lady believed their relationship could be exploited, and Keldor agreed. Since he valued his life, he counted the Lady's order as binding, but the others were committed RT Alliance men. For the moment, he needed to keep them thinking he would obey Meetcher. Keldor had no plan for completing his mission, but that had never stopped him before.

In preparation for this assignment, he had spent hours learning Ranger customs. Lucas Telon's voice returned to Keldor with bitterness intact.

"You can count on a Ranger to be predictably, honestly, stupidly noble. They can't help it."

His obvious disdain told Keldor that Lucas possessed no such flaw.

Keldor didn't know which way this Ranger would lean, but her recent heart-to-heart with the prince gave him much to consider. Generally, princes too could be predictably stupid when it came to women in danger.

The TT-189 gave Keldor a close look at the Ranger. Upon adding artificial lighting to the frozen image, he saw she possessed an attractive face. Her neat eyebrows curved slightly, leading to a gently sloping nose. Light brown hair perfectly complimented her green eyes, and the lines of her face were smooth and clean. The face looked too soft for a Ranger.

A sense of familiarity stole over Keldor. He stared at the picture for five minutes, mentally replaying the conversation. Then, he added the sound and let the conversation play another four times. Some sections were inaudible even with enhancement, but enough remained to stir his curiosity. Over the years, he had fought quite a few Rangers.

I've never met her.

He knew that for certain. Keldor rarely forgot a face, and any man would be hard-pressed to forget this woman.

Have I heard her speak?

He played the conversation twice more and concluded he had never heard her voice.

Have I seen her before or heard her name?

He studied the woman's face again. Aside from the impression that she wore her name well, Keldor could get nothing more distinct. Grunting, he paced his tiny tent.

The woman said she'd be around for a month.

Despite knowing her name, he preferred to depersonalize her. If instinct panned out, the woman would become a target. She likely possessed the weakness Lucas Telon had mentioned, but to be safe, he would have Adrik and Einer watch her.

A chime told Keldor he had a new message. He read the orders and turned his mind to the details. The Lady agreed the Ranger should be captured but absolutely forbade him from killing her. In the end, he decided that choosing the right bait would be key. While half his men shadowed the Ranger, Keldor and his two remaining men would scout nearby farms for good targets. Once they had the Ranger, the Alliance people inside the Rammon Palace would summon the prince.

Let's hope they're both predictably stupid.

Chapter 31:
Crown Prince

Allei (August) 1, 1538
One day after Prince Terosh's Kireshana journey
Prince Terosh's Private Quarters, Royal Palace, City of Rammon

Prince Terosh Minstel stalked back and forth across his bedchamber. He had spent the night in a Royal Guard camp and returned to Rammon in the morning. His father had hardly let him rest since stepping foot in the palace. Even stealing a moment to dispatch Dr. Dentelich on a mercy mission had taken considerable effort. A steady stream of celebrations left Terosh's head buzzing, and though his body wanted sleep, his mind wouldn't let him.

He idly picked up Reia's banistick from where he had placed it and considered the many young noblewomen he had just met. They couldn't match Reia's wit, wisdom, or beauty. Their efforts to get his attention were pathetic. He must have caught at least six young women who had mysteriously lost their balance.

You'd think the palace floors were riddled with graveground.

Reia would laugh at them and him. The more he thought about her, the more he missed her laughter, smile, and even anger. He remembered her cool hands changing the bandages on his back. He longed to hear the cadence of her voice, hold her and gaze at the stars, or just see how firelight changed the color of her hair.

Can I live in the palace without her?

"No!" Terosh clutched the banistick.

She had promised to await his answer. He had been more than ready to give an answer that moment, but now, his conviction had grown. The palace, the power, and the pride of being a prince paled next to the terrifying thought of living without Reia.

Is this love?

No wonder Tate looked miserable. If his connection to Dr. Koffrin had been a fraction of what coursed through Terosh, her death must have been devastating.

As if thinking of Tate conjured him, he appeared in the doorway to Terosh's bedchamber looking ill.

"Don't." Tate's single word order held warning and affection.

Terosh tossed the banistick onto his bed, rushed to his brother, and braced his right arm behind Tate's back.

"What's the matter? You're shaking and sweating … and you smell like a vat of wine. How much did you drink?"

"Not enough," Tate mumbled.

After lugging his brother over to his bed, Terosh dumped him onto it, belatedly hoping the banistick wasn't beneath him.

"He does this at least twice a week, though few know about it," said Aster Captain Gina Kelter.

Terosh whirled. His right hand searched for his kerlinblade but found only the ceremonial sword he had worn to the mid-afternoon banquet.

"Explain, Captain." Terosh glanced at Tate to make sure he hadn't moved. When his attention returned to Captain Kelter, he found her still standing in the threshold. Terosh waved her in. Tate's presence had already disturbed his solitude.

"You're dismissed, Captain," Tate called in a surprisingly clear voice.

Another glance confirmed he still lay flat on his back in the middle of Terosh's bed.

The Melian Maiden commander bowed to Terosh.

"I'm sure the prince will explain. I will be outside if you need anything." Her eyes begged him to help Tate.

Terosh blinked, trying to figure out what had just happened. Not knowing what to do with his hands, he folded his arms across his chest and focused on his brother.

Tate lay half on the bed with his legs dangling off, arms splayed like one exhausted with life. His chest rose and fell slowly. Suddenly, he lifted his head and opened one eye.

"Is she gone?"

Again, the normality of Tate's voice struck Terosh. He sighed away the worry and allowed irritation to replace it.

"Why are you avoiding Captain Kelter? And how did you fake being drunk?"

"The woman's been like a second skin for the last few months," Tate grumbled, ignoring the questions. He opened his other eye and propped himself up on elbows. "She thinks I'm suicidal."

"Are you?" Terosh demanded. He uncrossed his arms and ran a hand through his hair.

"Sometimes, but that's beside the point," Tate answered. "And I wasn't faking," he added, brushing at his sleeves to straighten them. "I just wasn't compensating with anotechs."

Letting his arms fall to his sides, Terosh watched as Tate's clothes straightened. The rich fabric of Tate's robes shifted shades of green from nearly yellow to almost black, depending on how the fabric bent. Sometimes the intricate patterns of gold, silver, red, blue, and yellow threads would disappear, only to reappear at a different angle and shape. The sheen of sweat dried, and Tate's blond hair sorted itself into neater waves.

The casual use of anotechs annoyed Terosh, but he admired his brother's control. Terosh waited patiently for Tate to explain.

Sitting cross-legged on Terosh's bed, Tate tilted his head and regarded him.

"I know I have problems. I'm dealing with them, but I don't want to see you hurt this way."

"What are you talking about?"

"The girl. The Ranger. You know *exactly* what I'm talking about."

"Reia?"

"If you love her, let her go. Drive her off if necessary."

Feeling like he'd been struck, Terosh knit his brows together.

"You've seen her and probably know everything about her, and yet you expect me not to love her?" Once again lacking something better to do with his arms, he resorted to crossing them.

"I expect you to do the right thing," Tate responded.

"The right thing being … what exactly?"

Tate sent him an *I-just-told-you* glare.

"You know what happened to Deanna. I loved her. I married her. I even had a child with her, Terry, and now, they're gone."

A memory of Kezem's package seared Terosh's mind. He unfolded his arms and stared at his hands. Clenching and unclenching his fists, he studied the bed, the banistick, the floor, and anywhere that wasn't Tate. The anotechs let him feel the waves of pain rolling off his brother.

"I understand."

"You don't," Tate replied. "And I hope you never have to," he added softly. Then, clearing his throat, he confused Terosh by announcing, "I'm getting married soon."

Head snapping up, Terosh's expression turned incredulous. He let out a bitter laugh.

"You're here warning me away from love, obviously still hurting, and telling me you're about to get married," he summarized, shaking his head.

"That's right, but it's not love this time. It's duty."

Terosh stared at his brother. They had spent countless nights as children sneaking into each other's private quarters and playing pranks on the guards. They had shared everything, including the promise to marry for love.

"But you promised."

"That was a long time ago, Terry. A lot has happened since then. I kept my promise and only ended up with pain. This time, good will come of it."

"How?"

Tate let his legs dangle off the bed.

"The Mitra will ally with us if we help them avoid the Blood Harvest."

A fuzzy memory of Master Sedir's history lesson came to Terosh.

"New blood," he said, recalling the only thing that would suspend the Blood Harvest.

"Do you know what that means?"

"You're marrying a Mitran princess."

Tate shook his head.

"It's more than a simple exchange of promises. New blood means I become Mitran by marrying Princess Alikai. The marriage will forge an alliance that will hopefully keep both planets free from GAPP." A bitter smile formed. "It means instant kingship, though not of Reshner. I can only return after producing an heir to take over the throne. Even then, it'll be at least fifteen years before he will be old enough to rule. I'll be a stranger." He stopped speaking, then chuckled. "Gods help us if we don't have a son. The Mitran aren't quite as progressive as Reshner about rules of inheritance."

The implication seeped into Terosh. He sat heavily upon his bed.

Tate stared at the floor, hands clasped together.

"In a few weeks, Father and I will go to Mitra. Six days toward the core and everything changes. It's likely I won't come back." He met Terosh's eyes and touched his upper arm. "That makes you Crown Prince, Terry. If anything happens to Father or he steps down, Reshner is yours to rule. You will be king." He squeezed once and let go.

Dreams of escaping to the mountains with Reia shattered. Terosh felt the loss deep in his gut. Emptiness spread through him. He became hyperaware of everything. Time meant nothing as scenes from the Kireshana replayed in his mind then crumbled to dust.

"I'm sorry," Tate said sincerely. "I wanted to warn you, so you could tell her. Do you have some way of finding her or should I send a messenger?"

"Purple fire," Terosh responded listlessly.

Tate stood up.

"Come, I want to show you something."

Chapter 32:
A Visit to Rammon

Allei (August) 1, 1538
Same day
Southern Quarter, City of Rammon

Reia waited until midmorning, an hour after the hype surrounding Prince Terosh's return had finally died down, before approaching Rammon. She entered from the South Gate, so she would be in the Southern Quarter where most of the poor resided.

As Reia arrived, a young boy sprinted past her, tripped, and fell headlong, scraping a good portion of his legs and knees. She didn't inquire after the boy's health. His tears told her of his pain. He bit his bottom lip to keep from sobbing.

A few silent anotech instructions calmed him. Nevertheless, Reia kept up a steady stream of soothing words and questions to distract the boy while she tended his wounds. A little iretel sap took away the sting, and she applied strips of toom leaves held in place with dandi sap as a bandage. By the end of their short conversation, Reia learned the boy's name, age, family history, occupation, and favorite pastime. As she finished, Reia asked the anotechs to summarize. She'd never asked them to do something like that before.

They affected a nobleman's voice as they reported.

Eight-year-old Tyler McDooley lost his father three years ago in a graveground accident on the McQuinten Farm out on the Kevil Plains. Since then, he has worked as a personal messenger for Second Lord Andul. Tyler loves running, so he doesn't mind carrying messages between Lord Andul and the man's various lady friends scattered throughout the other city Quarters. Sometimes, Tyler runs just for fun.

Reia had mixed feelings concerning personal messengers. On the one hand, she appreciated that children like Tyler could help their families, but she also knew messengers sometimes suffered mistreatment. Reia didn't need the anotechs to tell her such things. The bruises on Tyler's arms spoke volumes as did the wary expression that came over his face when he mentioned his master. Tyler shyly thanked Reia, bowed, and sprinted away.

She wanted to shout for him to be careful but stopped herself.

"Excuse me. Are you a Ranger?"

"Yes, ma'am," Reia replied, turning to face the speaker.

"Oh, thank goodness!" The woman grasped Reia's right arm. "Can you heal Kemloth Fever?"

"I can." Reia extricated her arm from the woman's grasp and dug through her caydronan sack until she came up with two astera petals. She pressed the blue petals into the woman's hands. "Stick these in boiling water and make a broth out of them. Wuzle roots should be enough to hide the bitter taste, but if you prefer, vegetables and salt would also make a nice soup."

"I don't have any wuzle roots." The woman's voice went high with alarm. "Will it still work? Both my boys are sick."

"Of course." Reia scolded herself for not considering that possibility. "But I have some extra roots here if you'd like them." She retrieved three wuzle roots from her caydronan sack, gave them to the woman, and added two more astera petals. "Throw everything in a pot of water and bring it to a boil for about ten minutes, then let it cool and serve it. A weak broth can make Kemloth Fever worse, but these should be enough."

"Thank you." The woman dashed at some tears, whirled, and hurried off.

Word of Reia's presence spread through the Southern Quarter like wildfire. People poured from their homes, ready to receive whatever aid she could offer. She picked a street corner and set up a makeshift clinic. Reia doled out herbs and instructions for common illnesses, made some of the more complicated cures, cleaned and patched infected wounds, and occasionally, used anotechs to fix the serious injuries. She used the anotechs as little as possible since she didn't know their true limits.

Her caydronan sack quickly emptied of remedies for fever, pain, and stress. She had started out short of sannin and corlia anyway from her efforts for the McNoughtens and Lieutenant Fericin. The weeks of travel had allowed for some herb gathering but not nearly as much as she would have liked.

As Reia started turning people away, a short man with brown hair and black eyes pushed to the front. A neat mustache and beard softened his otherwise angular face.

"Make way! Make way!"

"Wait your—" a young mother began to protest. The two small children in her arms lay limply, their dark eyes as dull as stones.

"I have orders to follow," the man interrupted.

"Says who?" demanded another man.

"The Dulad Prince," declared the man.

Reia couldn't help thinking he looked like a puffed up little kyrie boasting of a great catch.

"What orders have you, master?" Reia asked, noting the man's fine robes.

"Doctor, actually. Dr. Ezzai Dentelich, head doctor for the royal family." He inclined his head.

The crowd around Reia and the doctor rumbled. Some seemed awed, others disgusted, but everyone was impatient.

"What can I do for you, doctor?" Reia queried, careful to keep her tone level, even though the man's attitude rankled.

"It's what I can do for you," the man replied.

"Please get to the point, doctor."

Doctor Dentelich frowned and raised his voice so everyone could hear.

"His Highness, Prince Terosh of House Minstel, has requested I deliver these to you." The doctor motioned something forward. His attitude suddenly made a strange sort of sense.

He's never been here before.

The thought shocked Reia, though she knew it shouldn't. Rammon, like any city, had its rich, well-off, middle class, poor, and really poor. She had heard that the nobility and wealthy stayed in the North and West Quarters, but she had always assumed the situation was exaggerated. The middle class occupied the East Quarter and the Merchant Quarter, which surrounded the palace. The poor lived in the South Quarter. From there, ground vehicles and hovs swept them off to farms around the Kevil Plains so they could pick fruit, harvest grains, and herd tretlings.

The crowd parted to let a boy through. At least Reia assumed it was a boy, judging by the scrawny legs teetering under a huge, bulging sack. Joy swept through her at the thought of Terosh, but she pushed it away to seize control of the situation.

The crowd buzzed.

"What does the prince send?" Reia had a pretty good idea, but she wanted confirmation.

"Ridiculous stuff," said the doctor. "Herbs, dried flowers, preserved meats, and kefs in case he forgot something. I told the boy he needed to send real medicine."

The doctor seemed to be talking to himself, but Reia didn't care. It took significant self-control not to squeal with delight. She quickly relieved the boy of his burden and thanked him for his service. The boy blushed and ducked his head.

"Thank you, Doctor Dentelich, please convey my thanks to Prince Terosh," Reia said, remembering her manners.

Not used to being dismissed, especially by a young woman, Dentelich merely glared.

Reia smiled to ease his tension, but soon, she turned her attention back to the people who needed her.

By the end of the first day, Reia had several invitations to spend the night. She weighed each invitation and chose to stay with the Mirovi family whose neighbors happily donated food for her upkeep. Lelianna Mirovi had been the woman asking her to cure Kemloth Fever. Her sons, Tomas and Chaz, suffered from the disease, and her husband, Medri, worked a rich farmer's land and would be gone for the rest of the month.

Reia enjoyed her time with the Mirovi family immensely, but after two days, the young men were on the mend and the situation grew awkward. With the boys ready to work, Lelianna wouldn't accept food from her neighbors. Not wanting to tax any family too long anyway, Reia thanked her hostess and took her leave.

As she went out to work that day, she had no clue where she would spend the night, but as usual, word spread and the invitations made a comeback. This time she chose the Veenir family.

Almost two weeks passed in quick order.

Every morning, Reia rose early, walked to the nearest street corner, and spent the day tending sick and injured people.

At night, she returned to her current hosts or found new ones, shared a simple meal with them, and tended to her clothes and body's need for cleanliness. Sometimes, the care took the form of a lukewarm bath, but mostly, she settled for a cold-water rinse in a small basin. In such cases, she had the anotechs go through their cleaning rituals. While on the Riden Mountains she could track down a Ranger supply cache with a hand-held, tosh-powered sonic cleaner, but such things were nonexistent in the South Quarter.

Thoughts of Prince Terosh often intruded on the peaceful work. She knew no other life than as a Ranger, yet the thought of Terosh changed everything.

I miss him. I miss his humor, his bravery, and even that irritating need to protect everyone.

Her mind wandered back to the Kireshana. She recalled waking up each morning, looking for him, and feeling relieved when she spotted his soft, wavy black hair. She wanted to run her fingers through that hair. Stargazing together had been wonderful. She smiled at the memory of how hard it had been to direct his arm. The way he'd held her while she explained the stories and pointed out the constellations felt so right.

He's everything a prince should be. Can I really ask him to give up palace life for me?

During quiet hours, Reia thought of her next meeting with Terosh. By temporarily giving him her banistick, she had confirmed her interest in him as a suitor. She vaguely recalled explaining the custom to him, but the memory seemed like a distant dream.

Every night, she waited for news of a colored fire, hoping for a purple one. She asked people to watch the plains for her. Nobody took this for an odd request, for everyone knew colored fire meant a cry for help, one a Ranger would always answer.

***

Allei 14, 1538
Fourteen days after Prince Terosh's Kireshana journey
Royal Palace, City of Rammon

If Prince Terosh thought he might get to relax, he was gravely mistaken. With

Tate preparing to go to Mitra, his role shifted dramatically. In addition to dodging increased efforts to pair him to a suitable woman, Terosh found himself buried in lessons on planetary finance, war tactics, network building, rebellion suppression, public relations, speech crafting, banquet etiquette, and anotech mastery.

Insisting that his lessons be practical, Terosh spent nearly a full day meeting his brother's Rammon informants. They came from all city Quarters and fell into a wide age range, but he noted that most were young.

"Why are there so many children?" Terosh asked his brother.

"Personal messengers are often overlooked." Tate ruffled the hair of a little boy who gaped at Terosh. "They're commonplace in the noble houses, and they know how to listen."

Terosh envied the ease with which Tate moved among the informants, be they man, woman, or child. He knew it was an act, for every time they were alone the melancholy mood took over again.

The bits of news varied greatly. The RT Alliance soldiers were becoming bolder in their efforts to buy informants. The last acid storm had hit farms on the Balor Plains hard. Idonia's Second Lord might visit Lord Lyaloth next week. The news that most interested Terosh concerned the Ranger Healer working in the South Quarter. He arranged for several personal messengers to keep an eye on Reia. He felt bad for spying on her, but he needed to assure himself of her safety.

He didn't know how to break the news of his sudden rise in status. It wasn't something he wanted to bring up when proposing marriage, but it had to be done. She had to know exactly what she was walking into. For most women, the change would appeal to an innate lust for power, but Terosh knew Reia would feel duty-bound to step aside in favor of a more qualified woman. He didn't want anyone else. He had already found the perfect woman and just needed to persuade her to stick around

Chapter 33:
Setting a Trap

Allei (August) 14, 1538
Same day
Keldor's Camp, Kevil Plains

"What can you tell me about the Ranger?" Ariman Keldor asked his men.

Adrik Bentanner and Einer Akurin had spent the last two weeks shadowing the Ranger. Now, they stood before him to deliver their report.

"She's gorgeous, and everybody in the South Quarter loves her," Adrik reported. "She rises early and spends a few hours searching the plains for herbs. You should see her hair when she lets it down. It's so long and silky and—"

"Stick to the point," Keldor interrupted. "Would she sacrifice herself for a stranger?"

"Yes," Einer confirmed.

"We're just gonna capture her, right? We won't have to hurt her, will we? She's so pretty."

Bentanner's smitten. That could be trouble.

"Don't worry about that now," Keldor said. "Go get Herik and Alden. We need to discuss the next move."

While they waited for Adrik to return with the others, Einer spoke again.

"The Ranger's not carrying a banistick."

"I know," Keldor said. "She gave it to the prince. It tells me we're on the right path."

While Adrik and Einer had followed the Ranger, Keldor and his remaining men had scouted nearby farms for convenient targets. Two families drew Keldor's attention. The couple about to have their first child would theoretically be easier to handle, but experience told Keldor that a man with a threatened wife could be extremely dangerous. Once upon a time, his own, dear, very pregnant, Ilia had been taken by Restler scum as a means of controlling him. Keldor still remembered the gut-wrenching desperation that drove him to slaughter the kidnappers. He pushed the thoughts aside, not relishing the role of kidnapper.

The other option, a couple slightly older than the Archers, had three small children. Keldor's experience again made him ponder the situation carefully. Children made wonderful hostages, for parents nearly always complied once they knew their children's lives depended upon it. However, more hostages meant a fluid situation.

Unable to decide, Keldor waited until the men were crammed into his tent and asked for their thoughts.

"I say we go for the ones with kids," said Herik Lezan. The gangly man spoke slowly as he studied his kerlak pistol.

"Why?" Keldor asked.

Herik shrugged and shook his head, indicating he had no real reason. Keldor waved off his opinion.

"Anyone else want to weigh in?" he asked.

"Kids cause extra sympathy," Einer pointed out. He looked like he didn't want to be making that point. "Grab a kid and the parents are yours to command." Clearing his throat, Einer picked up a stick and poked lazily at the fire blazing in the center of Keldor's tent. Flaps in the tent roof had been thrown back to let the smoke out, but the fire still created a haze inside the tent.

"I agree," Adrik said.

Keldor acknowledged their opinions and waited for Alden to say something. The tall, quiet young man stared deep into the fire. He had spent the last two days as a field hand on the Archer farm. As such, he still wore the sun-faded coveralls of a field hand.

"What do you think, Alden?" Keldor didn't know much about the Tarpon boy, but so far, he had proven himself a sturdy fighter and a keen observer.

"Children are … unpredictable. I think we should take the couple who hasn't had their child yet. We'll have less people to deal with." Alden poured great thought into each sentence.

"I agree," Adrik said again.

"You already agreed with me," Herik reminded him. "You can't—"

"He's got a good point. Besides, how much trouble can—"

"Never underestimate a target," Keldor said, cutting Adrik off. "We'll go for the Archers. Alden's right. Too many people will only give us trouble. Now get some sleep, we'll take them tomorrow."

Early the next evening, after the workers left for the day, Ariman Keldor led his men to the Archer's humble property. Upon spotting their target, Keldor was glad he'd brought four men with him.

Derk Archer used a wicked-looking pitchfork as a walking staff, but he put up very little resistance when Adrik and Herik pointed serlak pistols at his stomach.

"What's this about?" Archer inquired, bewildered. He held the pitchfork across his chest. "I have no money, nor much worth taking. Everything I have goes straight into the farm."

"Stop talking and let my men bind you." Keldor kept his voice steady to avoid misunderstandings. "I'm not here to hurt you or your wife, but I need your cooperation."

Derk looked like he wanted to argue, but he obeyed.

At Keldor's nod, Einer removed the pitchfork and stuncuffed the man's hands behind his back. They had to roll up his long sleeves to let the metal cuffs rest against the man's skin for maximum effect. The guns remained level to keep the burly farmer compliant. The metal restraints clamped Archer's arms together and would shock him if he struggled.

As they approached Archer's home, the farmer resisted.

"Do what you want with me but leave my wife out of it. I—"

"If you speak again, I'll stuff Alden's dirty socks down your throat," Adrik threatened.

Keldor was surprised that the silly threat worked. Another nod sent Alden to knock on the door.

In moments, the door swung open revealing a woman in her early twenties. Her light brown skin paled at the sight of Keldor's men holding her husband captive. Airiel Archer nearly dropped into a dead faint. Instead, she leaned heavily on the doorway. The awkward posture made her swollen belly strain against the fabric of her simple cotton dress. Her dark brown hair hung loosely to her shoulders and her pale green eyes held many questions.

Einer leapt forward and caught her as she leaned against the doorway.

"Get your filthy—"

"Archer, shut your mouth and keep it shut," Keldor ordered. "Put her on the couch, Einer."

He didn't care if the couple knew their names, for the knowledge would do them little good. With the army and police forces stretched across a dozen useless forts, not to mention numerous cities, Keldor doubted anyone would even investigate, especially if no serious harm befell the couple. Rangers came and went as they willed. Nobody would miss one.

Derk struggled until the stuncuffs settled him. He looked helplessly at his wife. Locks of golden brown hair moved in concerted waves as he shook his head in frustration. He cursed until Adrik shook him hard enough to set off more shocks.

"What do you want with us?" Airiel asked. Her voice wavered with fear.

Keldor ignored her.

"Adrik, Herik, settle Master Archer somewhere. Alden, search the house for threats. Einer, sweep the outside. I'll see what we can do about food for our hosts."

"Why are you doing this?" Airiel wondered.

Keldor ignored her again. He could stuncuff her, but a strong shock might endanger the child. He would do his job, but he had no desire to kill an infant before it drew breath. He could bind her with korver or hemp ropes, both of which would be easy to find, but he wasn't eager to do that either. This mission was about capturing the Ranger, not causing needless pain.

Coming to a decision, Keldor walked over to where Airiel lay on the couch.

"Madam, I have no wish to hurt you. Sit quietly and no harm will come to you, your coming child, or your husband." He left unsaid what consequences might befall her and her family if she gave him trouble. In his experience, threats made targets surly, and people's imaginations usually dreamed up far worse things than anything Keldor would bother doing to them. Fear of the unknown would keep the woman in line.

Airiel crossed her arms over her stomach like she could protect her unborn child better that way.

Preparations for the evening meal were practically finished. Keldor took everything off the stove and added more vegetables and grains for his men. Airiel occasionally ventured a question which went ignored. When served by Einer, she barely picked at the food. Adrik had to physically feed Derk, since Keldor wasn't about to let him loose for any other reason than to use the washroom. At such times, Keldor had a Klagris SS-79 kerlak pistol leveled at Airiel's head. He preferred the SS for hostage situations because of the stun setting.

The cabin had four rooms. The front room contained the living room and kitchen separated by the couch and a table. A pathway between these led to the main bedchamber. A room barely larger than a closet, which Keldor assumed would soon hold the baby, sprang off the left side of the master bedroom, and the washroom sprouted from the right side.

Keldor's men were unusually somber until it came time to spring the trap. Adrik whooped and leapt up, Herik and Einer checked their weapons and hauled Derk to his feet, and Alden simply smiled. Keldor couldn't help but chuckle.

"Where are you going?" Airiel asked, sounding relieved and worried.

"Alden, stay here and guard the lady. We'll be back with our prize in—"

A cry from Airiel cut Keldor off. Fear lined her face.

All eyes riveted upon her.

"Aw, no," Einer muttered.

"Don't you dare have that kid." Keldor hated himself for not foreseeing this possibility.

"Help her!" screamed Derk, stamping a foot and wincing.

"Einer, you've had the most experience with this sort of thing. Switch with Alden," Keldor commanded, making things up as he went. He couldn't inflict a frantic pregnant woman upon a kid like Alden.

"Yes, sir," Einer responded. "Come on, let's get you into a nightdress," Einer added gently to Airiel. He moved to help her stand.

Derk looked ready to spit nails.

"Let's go," Keldor barked, prodding Derk toward the front door. "The sooner we get back the better."

"But—"

"We're going to find a Ranger. She's a healer," Keldor said, betting Archer would care more for his wife than a stranger.

"No! Derk, you can't help them!" Airiel shouted.

Keldor and his men exited the Archer home and hurried to the spot four kilometers away where they had left bonfire fixings. Along the way, Keldor explained Derk's role to him. This would be the most dangerous part of the plan. The fire needed to be big enough to attract attention in Rammon. A Ranger's presence was rare enough that everyone knew how to find her, but if the fire got too big, soldiers would be sent to offer aid. Keldor hoped the Alliance people in the palace could intercept news of the fire. King Teorn probably wouldn't send an investigator, but Prince Terosh might, especially since he knew his lady would answer the signal fire. The goal was to draw out Prince Terosh, but Keldor didn't want him bringing half the Royal Guard with him.

Alden lit the fire with a shot from his kerlak pistol and threw a handful of zalok scales on top to turn the flames purple.

Keldor didn't know how long they would have to wait. He hoped no other Rangers happened to be in the area. If he caught the wrong Ranger, he would have to kill him or her. It would not be a problem, but it would be annoying. Rangers could be very hard to kill.

If everything went well, the right Ranger would get the message within a half-hour, but depending on her mode of transportation, it could be anywhere from ten minutes to an hour or more before she could reach them. Keldor doubted she had made enough contacts to access a hov. The nobility guarded those things better than gold. It wouldn't surprise him, however, if she showed up on a horse. He fervently hoped she would come alone.

Chapter 34:
Springing a Trap

Allei (August) 15, 1538
Fifteen days after Prince Terosh's Kireshana journey
Edix Home, South Quarter, City of Rammon

On the night of Allei 15, Tyler McDooley roused Reia from her temporary sleeping quarters with the Edix family.

"Ranger! Ranger! I saw it! Purple fire! Someone's in trouble! Hurry!" Tyler woke the whole house and half the block before Reia could assure him she was awake and get the details on where to find the fire.

Terosh! Or someone in trouble. In either case, I must go.

She thanked the Edix family, donned her clean cloak, grabbed her well-worn caydronan sack, and hurried toward Rammon's South Gate, Aslinai. She couldn't help comparing her mission to Aslinai's urgent errand to warn the people of Meritab and Meritel that Terabian Firethrowers were attacking Rammon.

As she reached the gate, Reia slid to a halt before a pair of Royal Guards.

"Ho! Slow down now. What's the hurry, Ranger?" the older guard asked.

"I'm needed outside," Reia said, trying not to tell him too much.

"For what?" The older guard wouldn't let the matter drop.

"Someone spotted a purple fire out on the plains," Reia explained. "They could be in trouble. I must see if I can help."

The elder guard studied her, taking in her agitated state.

"Please! Let me pass."

"All right, but take a horse and an escort."

Reia wanted to refuse the escort but didn't wish to stand there arguing. If Terosh set the fire, she would have some serious explaining to do, but someone in trouble set it, the soldier might prove useful.

Her thoughts roiled so furiously that the kilometers sped past with Reia having no notion of the passage of time. Heavy clouds blocked the moons, making the fire glow brighter. Reia and the guard rode the horses hard until they came within forty meters of the purple fire. The guard halted suddenly.

Reia clung tightly to the horse's neck to keep from being thrown.

I don't even know his name.

Calan, the anotechs answered.

"Ho! Stand and state your business!" Calan shouted.

A storm of blue beams erupted around them. Reia dove off the horse's left side and tucked into a roll. She came to her knees in time to see Calan draw his kerlak pistol. He fired three times before Reia could stop him. The flashes from his pistol told the enemy where to concentrate their fire. Two stun beams caught the guard in the chest. Reia's horse bolted when a stun beam caught it in the flank.

Grabbing the reins of Calan's rearing horse, Reia had the anotechs calm the animal and make it kneel. Knowing the effect wouldn't last, Reia slung Calan's limp form onto the horse and secured him with more anotechs. Then, she commanded the horse to rise, turned him around, and smacked his flank, encouraging the beast to flee toward the city. The effort made her lightheaded, but she ignored the discomfort.

Alone, Reia spared a thought for how much she disliked fighting. She reached for her banistick before remembering Terosh still had it.

A Ranger is never without weapons.

Reia ducked to avoid more blue beams. The color comforted her, for it meant the attackers wanted her alive.

Cold comfort. Are they after me or is this a random attack?

Having no answer, Reia drew her shootav and checked to see how many cormea and radon pellets remained. She had spent some in the fight with the overgrown korvers and had been too busy gathering healing supplies to restock. At best, she had three shots.

The stun beams stopped as suddenly as they had started. Instinct told Reia to leave before it began again in earnest. She was about to do just that when she remembered Master Niklos's words.

Claiming to be a Ranger is easy but living as one is far different.

"All right, Master Niklos, I'll see what's going on," Reia whispered. She crept forward and scouted ahead with anotechs. It took a lot of concentration.

The anotechs gave a short report: **four hostiles, one prisoner. The captive is bound and sitting on the close side of the fire between two hostiles. Two more hostiles are hiding in the grass three meters away on the far side of the fire.**

Trap.

"Come on out, Ranger," called a man. He pointed an SS pistol at the hostage.

Do you know or are you guessing?

She waited, caught between curiosity and fear.

"Speak, Archer. She's out there."

Who are you?

Ariman Keldor, the anotechs answered.

Reia stifled a gasp. She knew that name. Whenever she remembered Kiata's level-seven trial, the name haunted her. Once again, she touched the spot on her waist where her banistick should have been.

Of all the lousy times—

And so shall love lead me to my death, intoned the anotechs, affecting a woman's desperate voice.

You're not helping!

Reia didn't have enough shots to engage every attacker at once. With her banistick she might have evened the odds by stunning three then defended the hostage while handling the last threat.

Another man spoke.

"I don't care what your business is with—"

"You're wasting time your wife doesn't have," Keldor said.

Wife? How many hostages do they have? Where is she?

"She said—"

"She's hardly in a position to protest," Keldor reminded. "And neither are you. That baby's coming right now so stop stalling."

Baby?

A pain-filled cry almost made Reia rise from her hiding spot. The jerky motion rustled the grass around her enough to bring the leader's pistol and the second man's gun swinging her way. Two stun beams sailed centimeters over her head.

I wish Kiata were here!

Her sister always knew what to do in bad situations. She found herself in them often enough.

"Ranger, I know you're out there. This man's wife is about to have a baby. His name is Archer. Derk Archer. His life, Airiel's life, and the child's life rest in your hands." Keldor paused to let his words sink sharp teeth into Reia's conscience.

How do you figure that?

Reia removed her cloak, took off her caydronan sack, cautiously regained her feet, and slipped forward, crouching to stay below the tall grass. She briefly considered using the anotechs to imitate a squad of soldiers, but she couldn't concentrate enough to attempt such a sophisticated illusion, even if she could summon the billions of anotechs needed. She could also startle the attackers with noise, but if they panicked, the hostage's life would be forfeit.

As her legs carried her closer to the fire, Reia argued with the anotechs.

Stupid, stupid Ranger.

What can I do? Reia's heart pounded and her body tensed.

Not be trapped. Evil men always lie.

Not this one.

Reia had analyzed Ariman Keldor's voice and features. His attention was focused on the hostage, so the flashes of raw emotion crossing his face rang true. The fire sputtered, sometimes purple, sometimes brilliant yellow.

The flames and soft moonlight showed her that Keldor's tough countenance held dignity, strength, and even honor.

I can't let them harm the man or his family!

Few deaths or many, the anotechs snapped.

That's cheering. Besides, you don't know for sure.

"The baby started coming before we left a few hours ago. Airiel looked ill. She may die without care," Keldor called, interrupting Reia's debate with the anotechs. "My name is Ariman Keldor. I've got no quarrel with this family, but I need to speak with you. Surrender and no harm will come to them."

What quarrel do you have with me?

Reia tried to fit this new attack with anything experienced during the Kireshana. Coming up with nothing, she used the anotechs to throw her voice several meters left.

"So speak."

Both men's guns shifted to where she had thrown her voice. Another man stepped out of his hiding spot and joined the others in the small clearing by the fire. His gun also pointed where Reia's voice had sounded. Four more stun beams ripped through the grass.

"That's not talking." Reia threw her voice even further left.

"Show yourself," Keldor commanded.

"I would but you seem to have twitchy trigger fingers."

"Please, Ranger, you've got to help my wife! She's about to have the baby!" Derk Archer pleaded. His panic-stricken tone sounded genuine.

"You have my word no harm will come to you," Keldor promised. "Do the honorable thing and surrender yourself in exchange for this man and his family." He spoke like a man selling tretlings.

"A man who holds a family hostage has no honor! Your word means nothing." Reia's words were harsh, but she knew they contained a tremor he would exploit. She found herself in the clearing and knew they would see her in seconds. Relying heavily on the anotechs, she steadied her nerves. Her body itched to sprint away.

Keldor raised his pistol to the hostage's head.

"Wait!" Knowing she would have to speak fast, Reia stood up. Every man, save the trussed up one, looked ready to tackle her. "I've studied you, Keldor. There is honor in you." She held her shootav away from her body in a non-threatening manner. Her eyes locked with Keldor's and held.

Something slammed into her from behind, driving her forward. Resolve to surrender vanished. Reia cried out, dropped the shootav, and thrashed wildly. She nearly broke free, but strong arms snaked under both her arms and tried to interlock fingers around behind her neck. Before the fingers could connect, Reia smashed her head back into the man's jaw, hurting her head.

The man screamed and loosened his grip.

Another man came at them from the right. Reia gripped the arms of the man who had grabbed her from behind, swung her body up, and planted both feet on the approaching man's chest. The three of them crashed to the ground. Reia recovered her feet in time to see the tail end of a serlak gun arc toward her. She jerked her head left, but the blow glanced off her skull with an explosion of pain.

"No!" Keldor shouted.

The crack of a serlak gun preceded a scream.

Stunned, Reia stumbled back into the man who had first grabbed her. This time, he succeeded in thrusting both arms under hers and interlocking his fingers behind her neck. Before she knew it, the man brought them both to their knees with crushing force. Reia expected her neck to snap in half. Her breath whooshed out and refused to return. She couldn't even scream. Her arms felt like they had been ripped from their sockets and left detached. Her head and neck felt like a zalok had just stepped on them, and most of her muscles protested the abuse.

The man yanked her upright and released her arms long enough to twist them up behind her back. Pain shot down her arms and her legs refused to hold her, so she hung by her arms. The new jolts made Reia raise her head, but she clamped down on a groan.

After a long moment, the man eased her to the ground, keeping a firm grip on her arms. He pinned her arms in place with one massive hand and reached for the shootav she had dropped. After tossing the weapon to his boss, the man renewed the pressure on Reia's arms.

What do they want?

She tried to process the situation but couldn't think straight.

Keldor caught the shootav and slipped it into his belt.

A whimper drew Reia's eyes toward the ground to her right. The boy she had kicked in the chest clutched his left leg, which had a neat hole leaking blood onto the ground. The sight touched her. Despite intense head pain, she sympathized with the man Keldor had shot.

He really does want me alive.

Reia couldn't decide if that was a good thing or not. She liked being alive, but the lengths Keldor and his men had gone to here didn't bode well.

Keldor holstered his serlak pistol and returned the SS pistol to the young man's head.

"It's over. You can't win this fight, and if you try, I'll kill him."

Like I'm going to fight now anyway.

She winced but nodded, willing the anotechs to put her head to rights.

"Agreed, but let me fix the hole in him before we go anywhere." Reia traced a line with her eyes to the wounded man.

Keldor hesitated but gave his consent.

Reia sent one of the men to fetch her caydronan sack and cloak from the nearby field. When he returned, she dug out a corlia leaf and ate the bitter thing. Then, she fed the wounded boy a few corlia leaves.

"Hold him down," she instructed, aware that they watched her every move. Slowly taking her dagger out of its ankle sheath, Reia cut off a strip of her shirt, folded it several times, and placed it in the wounded man's mouth as a makeshift gag.

The big man who had almost broken her neck leaned across the boy's shoulders, keeping him still while Reia worked.

Silently directing the anotechs, Reia deadened as many of the nerves as she could while probing for the bullet. She couldn't get them all however, so the young man—Adrik by name according to the anotechs—gave the gag a good workout.

It took Reia fifteen minutes to find and remove the bullet. After that, it was a simple matter of tearing toom leaves into strips and fixing them in place with dandi sap. She sighed as she wiped her hands on a rag one of the men handed her.

Let the real games begin.

***

As he waited for the Ranger to patch Adrik, Ariman Keldor watched the purple flames struggle for life. He considered putting the fire out, but then, a new thought struck him.

What if the prince hears of the purple flame? That could save us some time. If we can capture him tonight, we can deliver him to Meetcher for the Alliance pitch then let him go.

As his thoughts churned over what the Alliance and the Lady had planned for the Ranger, Keldor forced himself to focus on the issue at hand: the possibility of the prince showing up. He kept silent, knowing he ought to consider plan changes very carefully before implementing them.

"Herik, stay here with Adrik and Master Archer in case the prince comes to check on his lady friend."

The Ranger's expression cycled fear, anger, disgust, and despair. She closed her eyes as if to pray.

"I'll stay," Alden offered.

Keldor began to shake his head, but then reconsidered.

"Very well. I'll send Einer along when I get the Ranger to Archer's place."

"Thank you," whispered Derk Archer hoarsely.

"You sure you don't need help with her?" Herik inquired.

"I'm sure, but put her in stuncuffs anyway," Keldor said.

Herik nodded and retrieved stuncuffs from the pack he had left behind the fire. The Ranger looked ready to flee or put up another fight, so Keldor drew his SS again and pointed it at Archer. She got the message and submitted to having her arms bound behind her back. Her forearms practically disappeared beneath the thick metal bands.

Keldor's hands tingled from the faint shocks caused by pulling the Ranger to her feet. A shove sent her moving in the correct direction.

***

Allei (August) 15, 1538
Same day
Prince Terosh's Private Quarters, Royal Palace, City of Rammon
The thud of a door smacking a wall heralded somebody's entry into Terosh's

private quarters. He whirled and raised Reia's banistick into a defensive position. Seeing his brother, he lowered the weapon, retracted it to its compact form, and tucked it into his belt.

"What brings you here at this hour?" he asked.

"Purple fire," Tate said.

"Where?" Terosh's heart lurched.

Reia would think he was trying to contact her. A steady tide of questions flowed through him.

Is it a trap? Who knew of the arrangement? Tate knew but who else? How can I get there?

"Grab a weapon and come with me." Tate spun away and moved toward the exit.

Terosh raced to the weapons rack and grabbed a belt with a kerlinblade and a kerlak pistol. He still had Reia's banistick attached to his current belt. He would sort the weapons later. He could guess where Tate would lead him, but he didn't want to get too far behind. The palace's deeper levels could be tricky to navigate.

"Where are we going?" Terosh asked, catching up with Tate.

"Since that fire isn't yours, it's probably a trap." Tate's rapid words rivaled his walking pace.

"Could it be a cry for help?"

"It could, but I doubt it," Tate responded. "Call it whatever you want, but something doesn't feel right. There hasn't been a purple fire on the Kevil Plains this close to Rammon in over a year."

"Should I take some Royal Guards?"

Tate shook his head.

"There's no time. Father would keep you an hour trying to explain why you need them. I've sent the messenger who brought the news to fetch a horse. He should be waiting for you. Don't worry. The anotechs will secure the location when you're gone. The boy has agreed to the arrangements."

"My hov would be faster," Terosh noted. He hadn't even thought to worry about the security of the South Passage.

"Not with the amount of paperwork you'd need to get it released from the lot," Tate replied. "Father tightened security when rumors of an RT Alliance plot against us picked up momentum."

Terosh conceded the point, grateful Tate had a clear head.

I might never see him again. The thought slammed into Terosh's chest, and his steps faltered.

Tate smiled even as he pushed their pace faster still.

"Not exactly how I pictured our farewell, but if I'm right, your friend needs you more than I do."

Urgency unsettled his stomach, but Terosh raced through the palace corridors behind his brother. It took them ten minutes to reach the entrance to the South Passage several levels beneath the palace prison. They paused at the door.

Terosh hugged Tate fiercely.

"Send a message when you reach Mitra."

"You'll be fine. You're a good man, Terry," Tate said, returning the hug. "If all goes well, I'll be back in two decades. I expect to be greeted by several nieces and nephews and their pretty mother."

A lump caught in Terosh's throat. He stared at Tate, trying to memorize everything about him. He couldn't remember how many years had escaped them while they were wrapped up in their own agendas.

"No regrets," Tate admonished, reading his expression. "Forget what I said before, if she makes you happy, treasure her." With that, Tate spun Terosh around and pushed him through the entrance to the South Passage out of Rammon.

Chapter 35:
Beauty and Strength

Allei (August) 15, 1538
Same day
Archer Farm, Kevil Plains

Can you open the stuncuffs? Reia Antellio asked the anotechs.

Of course, descendent of the Chosen. Should we release you now?

Not yet. I will let you know when, thank you.

Upon spotting the farmhouse, Reia forgot to walk. Smoke curled lazily out of the chimney. The tiny place projected warmth and comfort, but awareness of her situation caused Reia to fight the illusion of safety. A shove from Keldor sent her forward again. From time to time, she sensed him studying her. She wanted out of the stuncuffs but refrained from complaining. Keldor's men still held the farmer hostage.

As she crossed the threshold, Reia's right foot caught the nearly imperceptible ledge. She tripped and landed in the middle of the room, centimeters from a solid looking couch. With her arms secured behind her back, Reia could only roll over and struggle to a sitting position, wincing as the stuncuffs shocked her.

Three new pairs of eyes stared down at her, and she sensed a fourth pair looking through the couch. A woman and a boy were both gagged and tied to chairs, and an annoyed man stood next to them.

"Einer, what in Riden's name are they doing here?" Keldor demanded, tugging Reia upright.

"This is Vel Drisher and her son, Jaidir. The kid came to deliver corncakes, and the mother followed when the kid didn't come back," Einer reported. He waved at the package on the kitchen table between the people tied to chairs.

A cry from the woman on the couch cut off Keldor's response.

Reia twisted around to get a good look at the distressed woman.

"Where's my husband?" cried the woman.

"He'll be back later," Keldor replied.

Reia tried to get a better look at Airiel Archer who appeared ready to deliver the baby. Something in the woman's expression spoke of more than normal labor pains. Reia sent anotechs to investigate, and they reported the problem.

Babies all twisted. Choking to death.

Reia turned to her captor.

"Something's wrong. You've brought me here, Keldor. Now turn me loose so I can help her."

The intense look of concentration on Ariman Keldor's face told Reia his mind was far away from the woman's plight. His face grew hard and unreadable as he drew some sort of conclusion about her.

"You're related to that Ranger witch who saved my boy." It was a statement of fact.

Reia nodded.

"Kiata. She's my sister. We're not related by blood, but we're still close."

"I let her go. That makes us even." Keldor didn't sound like he believed it.

Unsure how to answer, Reia nodded again. She might be able to exploit the sympathy later, but the woman needed immediate help.

Shaking off his stupor, Keldor stepped toward her.

"I'll remove the stuncuffs, but if you—"

"I know my duty, Master Keldor, but I want your word that the woman, her son, and the children—"

"Children?" Keldor echoed.

"Yes, children, plural. Guarantee that they, the farmer and his wife, and their neighbors will be unharmed, and you'll have my full cooperation." Reia wanted to make sure the help wasn't given in vain.

"I already command your cooperation," Keldor pointed out.

"I can take my life at any moment." Reia hoped the air of mystery surrounding Rangers would lend strength to her bluff. She sensed Keldor didn't want to hurt these people any more than she did. "Guarantee their safety." Reia kept her posture stiff yet tried to project serenity.

A strangled cry from Airiel and grunts from the gagged ones punctuated her statement.

"You have my word," Keldor responded.

"Then you have mine as well," she answered evenly.

Before releasing her, Keldor turned to the man standing next to the chair captives.

"Einer, go help the others capture the prince. Adrik took a bullet. If the prince doesn't show up tonight, get a message to the palace tomorrow and follow the previous plan."

Einer acknowledged the orders and headed for the door.

"Take the kid with you," Keldor added.

Reia wanted to argue but another round of screams from Airiel filled the house. It would probably be good to remove the boy from the Archer house.

"If we're not here when you get back, you know where to find us. Follow as quickly as possible. Oh, and take this." He threw Reia's shootav to Einer. "Mention that you know he has her banistick if he needs more convincing."

Einer caught the weapon and tucked it into his belt. Drawing a dagger, he quickly slashed the bonds holding the boy to the chair. Then, he grabbed a fresh strip of rag and
tied the boy's hands behind his back. Yanking the child around and meeting his wide-eyed stare, Einer removed the gag.

"You're going to follow every order I give you so I don't have to hurt your mother. Do you understand?" asked Einer.

The boy glanced at his mother who tried to break free of her bonds. She stilled when Einer rested the dagger's blade against the boy's right shoulder.

Keldor finally released Reia from the stuncuffs and stepped back to cover her with his pistol and stay out of the way.

***

Terosh jogged along the South Passage beneath Rammon, knowing each step was a permanent one away from his family. The tunnel would only take him six kilometers into the Kevil Plains, but it might as well be the other side of the planet. He might never see Tate again, and Father would probably never speak to him for marrying so far beneath his station. If he wanted to marry Reia, he would have to do so before returning to the palace, or his father would guarantee that he never saw her again.

The thought of Reia lightened Terosh's mood and quickened his steps. He held her banistick in his left hand so he wouldn't lose it. His kerlinblade bounced lightly against his right thigh. He considered using the kerlinblade for light but decided to rely on the dim path lights.

Guilt pressed down upon him. He didn't want to fail his father, but he couldn't marry for duty. In that regard, Tate was a much braver man.

There are other ways to forge alliances.

Lost in thought, Terosh barely realized he had reached the end of the secret passage. As he scrambled up the ladder, he noted the change from stone walls to reddish-brown dirt. He cautiously climbed out of the hole that appeared when he pressed a button on the second-to-top step.

A personal messenger met him as he emerged.

"Greetings Prince Terosh of House Minstel, my master says that Correth will serve you well." The boy bowed and held the reins out to Terosh.

"Thank you, Tyler." Terosh recognized the boy as one of Tate's most trusted informants. "Send your master my compliments."

He wanted to give the boy a more personal message, but he had no time to compose anything meaningful.

Mounting the horse, Terosh aimed for the purple flames and set off. When he drew close enough to see figures around the fire, Terosh halted his horse and sent anotechs forward to investigate. The setup intrigued him. From the perspective of anyone coming from Rammon, the fire had been built on top of a gentle rise in the land. Two bound figures, a man and a boy, sat in front of the fire. Two men stood on either side of the fire with clear shots at either hostage.

Before he could turn his horse, a man shouted, "Wait! This man has a message for the prince!"

Dismounting, Terosh crept forward and listened.

"Go ahead, Archer."

"If you're there, my Prince, I—"

"Pull yourself together!" the same man demanded.

"They have the Ranger," said the child.

Terosh's heart sent blood pounding against his skull. His stomach clenched, and his mind spouted useless denials.

No one knows I'm here! They can't! Reia's safe. She must be.

He tried plotting ways to attack the men without getting the hostages shot, but his mind refused to work. The best he could do was close his eyes and watch the scene through the anotechs near the fire.

The adult hostage let his head sink to his chest.

"My name is Archer, and I would not deliver this message if I could help it, but they have my wife and the boy's mother back at my house." His head slowly came up and his jaw clenched. "They used us to force her surrender, and they'll use her to—" His speech ended abruptly as a stun beam plowed into his back.

The leader moved behind the boy.

"My masters need to speak with you, so I need you to come with me to Meritab. They will present their offer then."

You're lying!

They are not lying, said the anotechs.

They have to be!

An uneasy silence fell.

"Show yourself!" yelled the man in charge.

More silence.

"Tell your story," the speaker ordered the child. He pressed his pistol to the back of the boy's neck.

Terosh held his breath. Even a stun beam could kill the boy at that range.

"What am I supposed to say?" the boy asked.

"Tell him what happened tonight."

"Momma made corncakes fer the Archers 'cause the lady's gonna have a baby real soon. I got knocked out but woke up by the time a man brought the Ranger to the house."

"Describe her." The leader's gun hand twitched impatiently.

"She has brown hair and really green eyes," said the boy.

Terosh's heart shuddered within him, and tears stung his eyes. Each passing second convinced him they spoke truth. He wiped the tears away angrily.

"I have her shootav," the man announced. He removed the weapon from behind his back and tossed it to the ground in front of the prisoners. "I also know you have her banistick."

Terosh wished he were anywhere but by this fire listening to this man. *What do I do?*

Talk to them. The offer sounds real.

Sounds?

98.8755555% possibility the offer is legitimate, the anotechs clarified.

"I can take you to her. She'll be at the meeting."

That decided the matter for Terosh. He stood up.

"How will this work?" he asked.

"Simple. We take a short hike to Archer's house. My master contacts some

people, and we get a ride to Meritab."

A korver howled plaintively in the distance.

The other man holding a gun cleared his throat.

"Einer, we should probably wait until morning. Adrik's not moving until then, and I don't want to carry him and Archer. It's only a few hours off anyway."

The leader agreed.

"How do I know you won't kill me?" Terosh asked.

"What good would that do?" Einer demanded. "You don't waste time, effort, and manpower on a trap like this to assassinate someone."

"Ransom?"

"Stop being stupid, son. When was the last time the Royal House paid kidnappers in anything but death?"

Terosh hated being called "son" but the man's words made sense. Questioning his sanity, he cautiously stepped into the trap.

***

Back at the Archer farm, Airiel lay on the couch in quiet awe. Tear streaks ran from her eyes to the tip of her chin. Reia sat on the floor and smiled up at the new mother, completely exhausted. The scene almost made her forget she was a prisoner. She wanted nothing more than to watch Airiel cradle the newborns. Deep shadows around Airiel's eyes spoke of worry for her husband.

Even with the anotechs' aid, it had been a long fight. The twins had been one mass of entangled arms and legs.

"I miss Derk." Airiel's admission opened the way for more tears.

Reia wished she could do something meaningful, but no words could conjure the woman's husband. What should have been a wonderful night for them had turned out horribly wrong.

"What will you call them?" Reia asked, trying to distract Airiel.

When the tears finally subsided, Airiel gazed down at the sleeping babies.

Reia gripped her right hand, grateful to have her concentrate on something besides her missing husband.

"Nothing we chose fits." Airiel's voice was hoarse. "Do you have a suggestion?"

"That's not my place," Reia replied, patting Airiel's hand.

Airiel squeezed Reia's hand hard.

"Please, they wouldn't be alive if you hadn't saved them. Derk would want it this way."

Reia studied the twins. Swaddled in soft towels, they looked identical in every way. The sleeping boy's face was pinched. He had worked one fist free and had it curled tightly. The girl was awake but well on her way to sleep. Her head lolled against her mother. Her dark eyes slowly shut. Her cheeks were still red but her round face and perfectly formed features would soon blossom into true beauty.

"Kayla and Stenneth," Reia whispered. "Beauty and strength."

Chapter 36:
Leverage

Allei (August) 16, 1538
Sixteen days after Prince Terosh's Kireshana journey
Meetcher Estate, City of Meritab

Meralla Meetcher stood before her husband and trembled with rage. Signs of their vast wealth were everywhere in the furniture, paintings, and even on her person, but what mattered most was gone: Kia. Meralla had been a prisoner most of her life, but she would not tolerate the same for her daughter. The memory of Kia's frightened screams made Meralla clenched her fists so tightly her nails cut into her palms.

"Can I help you, my dear?" Donovan asked. He put down the glass of fertia wine. His eyes darted to every object on his desk like he was measuring their potential as weapons.

Meralla wished she had the will to wield the Nedis crystal lamp like a club.

"Where is she?" Meralla's eyes drilled the question into her husband.

"They didn't tell me." Donovan's hazel eyes flickered with annoyance.

So, I wasn't supposed to know.

The realization drove the pain deeper. Meralla trembled again, fighting tears.

They took her without warning.

The thought temporarily buried sorrow beneath anger.

"Why her?" Meralla demanded.

"Because you have to stand by me." Donovan's condescending tone negated any sympathy in his eyes. "Appearances must be maintained, my dear. With my new position, we'll have many important meetings to attend."

Meralla silently cursed his new position.

"This ends here, Donovan."

His dark brown hair ruffled where he rubbed it wearily.

"I don't like it any better than you do, Meralla, but it's always been like this. It's just a formality."

"Formality? They kidnapped our daughter!" Meralla shouted.

Donovan winced, rose from the camrood leather chair, and slowly circumvented his desk.

"It's not kidnapping. We know where she's going … eventually."

"How do we know where she's going? They could take her anywhere!"

Donovan held Meralla's shoulders and enunciated each word carefully.

"I don't know where Kia is right now, but they will eventually take her to Idonia to stay in Lord Kezem's care. His people will train her to be a Melian Maiden. Isn't that what you wanted?"

I thought we wished that once.

She knew her husband spoke of his "secret" dealings with Idonia's Third Lord. Although she had never met the man, she hated him. She suppressed the urge to pound her husband with both fists, but as she released the anger, fear set in.

"Is it worth it, Donovan? Is this promotion truly worth our daughter's life?"

"Don't say that. It's not like that. We'll visit her every few months when I go for the meetings and—"

Meralla laughed bitterly.

"Councils of war," she said. A stab of remorse battled satisfaction at hurting him, but mostly, she felt Kia's absence like an open wound.

Donovan's eyes darted around nervously.

"Meralla, please guard your words. It isn't safe. Governor Riber already suspects I threw in my lot with Lord Kezem. He's probably sent spies."

The Restlers and then the RT Alliance had given Donovan everything. As much as Meralla tried to stay out of politics, she knew Lord Kezem had higher ambitions than ruling the RT Alliance. She couldn't begin to fathom what plans he wove, but the effect of those plans upon her family infuriated her. Disgusted, Meralla stepped back, wrenching her shoulders out of Donovan's hands. Her glare told Donovan he was worse than the scum-sucking leeches lining sewers. She spun away and marched to the heavy wooden doors just in time to almost be flattened by them.

"What is the meaning of this?" Donovan blustered.

Meralla recognized General Ariman Keldor as he strode in. Her breath rushed out when Dariad and Bairok entered lugging the limp form of a young woman between them.

"What is that?" Donovan demanded. "I thought I—"

"She's the best chance to control the prince," Keldor explained. "My men sent word they have him and will bring him here. He will listen to the proposal for her sake."

Heat entered Meralla again. In her thirty-seven years she had not run across such blatant disregard for people's lives, yet here, twice in one day, not an hour between them, were separate evidences of such. Even her part-time captors, part-time parents, Nadia and Byrich Restler, had treated her decently.

Her knees shook, but she forced herself to go to the prisoner.

Keldor stepped in front of her.

"That's not a good idea, ma'am."

"She could be dangerous," Bairok warned.

"She's a child, and she's unconscious!" Meralla pressed past Keldor. "What do you expect her to do?"

Has the entire planet gone mad?

Meralla knelt in front of the young woman and gently lifted her head, brushing errant locks of brown hair aside to see if the brutes had hurt her. A shiver ran up her arm as she touched the girl's icy skin.

Criessa! Meralla was too angry to speak.

"Rangers aren't easy to hold prisoner." Keldor sounded apologetic.

"Then why is she here?" Donovan asked. "If she's that dangerous, why isn't she dead as I ordered?"

The questions stole the heat from Meralla, leaving only a ball of ice in the pit of her stomach. This couldn't be the same man she had loved and married. That man had been fun-loving and devoted to family. This man not only consented to having his only child held as leverage, he spoke of murder as casually as hunting rabid korvers.

"She's here to ensure Prince Terosh's cooperation. His loyalty to our cause depends on her. Where should we place her?" Keldor asked. His tone told Meralla he didn't think very highly of Donovan.

"Take her to my private chambers," Meralla said. "I'll clean her up and have her ready to meet the prince."

"But—" Donovan began.

"It's a good idea," Keldor interjected. "He'll want to see her, of course. Besides, there's a storm collapsing graveground all over the Kevil Plains right now. It's too dangerous to send a hov for my men."

Donovan stood straighter, obviously not happy.

"Yes, yes, I'm sure the prince will arrive just fine, but what guarantees he'll cooperate?" asked Donovan.

"Love." Meralla spat the word like a curse.

Keldor's curt nod confirmed it.

"I've heard Ranger weapons are unique," Donovan said. "Could you not simply show the prince those?"

"Would you accept your wife's necklace as proof someone had her alive?" Keldor asked. His eyes flashed. "Besides, we don't have either of her weapons. The prince has her banistick and my men have her shootav."

"He wouldn't care." Meralla brushed strands of wavy, blond hair aside and considered Keldor's statement. "She gave him the banistick, didn't she?"

"Why would that matter?" Donovan wondered.

"It's a promise," Meralla explained. "She's saying she'll marry him."

"As you say," said Keldor. His voice stayed steady, but Meralla saw his surprise that she knew of the obscure custom. Clearing his throat, Keldor turned to Dariad and Bairok. "Take the prisoner wherever Lady Meetcher tells you and wait outside the chamber." To Meralla, he added, "My lady, please let me know if you need anything or if the Ranger gives you trouble."

Meralla knew Keldor meant well, but she shivered at the implied threat to the young woman.

***

Almost ten blocks north of the Meetcher estate though still in the city of Meritab, Talyon Keldor watched his friend tread back and forth across the hand-braided rug. Whenever something upset Merisia Restler, the choices were either pace or cry, so Taly had learned to appreciate pacing. Unfortunately, this would be one of those times where pacing came before sobbing. He looked at the nature paintings lining the walls for calming inspiration.

"It's wrong, Taly, very wrong." Merisia's pale cheeks brought out the deep purple color of her eyes. The flecks of silver disappeared beneath the glaring lights as tears pooled.

"I know," Taly said, wishing Merisia's husband, Gareth, were around to deal with the coming flood.

What could he say?

Merisia, I think it's a good idea to hold small children captive to make sure their parents don't back out on a deal.

Taly shook his head in frustration.

"She's five, Taly, five! And she's scared. I know she's scared! We've got to do something. We've got to return her!"

"Maybe her father will turn down the position," Taly offered, feeling sick.

Or maybe not. Who are those men? Who do they work for?

Taly had never known the RT Alliance to be generous with kefs or positions, and he hadn't liked the two men. He had only seen them briefly, but the sight of them carrying Kia Meetcher had disturbed him. Their rumpled uniforms and dark expressions said the child had fought. Taly refrained from telling Merisia the obvious. They could safely do nothing to help the Meetcher child.

Merisia stopped pacing and wrapped both arms around her stomach, staring hard at the floor for several seconds before finally meeting Taly's questioning gaze.

"You've got to get me out of here, Taly, got to!"

"Why?" Taly sat up straighter and watched Merisia's every move.

She pressed her lips together.

"Because I'm going to have a baby, Taly, a baby! And I never want this to happen to my child. Never!"

"What about your husband?" Taly asked.

Pain crossed Merisia's face, and she averted her gaze.

"I ... don't know." She stared into the flickering fireplace flames. "I don't want to hurt him, really I don't. He's a good man, but I've got to get away."

Taly's head spun with partial plans. If they left, they would be leaving for good.

We need to be good and gone or we're dead. Who would help us?

A year or two ago things might have been different. Both of their families would be furious, but no harm would befall them. Since the birth of the RT Alliance, however, things had changed. The Alliance did not tolerate disloyalty. What Merisia proposed would bring no small amount of consequences crashing down upon their heads.

"What do I do, Taly?" Merisia asked. "At first, it was just Alliance soldiers acting like street thugs and shaking down merchants. I tried to ignore the small wrongs, but this is no small wrong. I'm surrounded by plots and plans, and if I do nothing, my baby could meet Kia's fate."

"You don't know that, Merisia," Taly said.

"But I do, Taly," Merisia argued. "This incident with Kia is only the most recent outrage. There have been others, many others." Tears glistened in her eyes. "I tried to ignore them, but I can't pretend everything's right when everything I know about the Alliance tells me we're on a dark path. Will you help me?"

Taly needed time to think, and he couldn't concentrate with Merisia charging up the air with fear. Though she was several years older, she had looked up to him for years.

"We'll figure something out," he promised. "Why don't you visit the Meetcher kid? She could use a friend, but calm down before you go or you'll scare her."

It took Taly several minutes to convince Merisia a visit with Kia Meetcher would do them both good, but finally, he was alone to ponder their precarious situation. Her position as Lady Restler gave her some authority, but the fact that she sought Taly's help proved how desperate she must feel.

The Alliance grows in power every day, but what are we doing with that power?

Since the formation of the RT Alliance, Taly had expected broad changes in the political spectrum. He kept waiting for the power to grow to a point where they could demand representation in the Senate and better the lives of the merchant class. Instead, things had carried on much the same as they had before the Alliance. True, the black-market sales thrived, and squads reported less deaths from day to day clashes. But Merisia was right. The time to choose between the Alliance and his conscience had arrived. Running away with no plan would only get them caught. They needed to leave Meritab quietly. If anyone suspected, they would be hunted down within hours. If they got caught, he would probably pray for death long before they granted it.

For some reason, Lady Meetcher kept coming to mind. At the very least, she deserved to know her daughter was safe, and perhaps, she could help them escape. The Meetcher Estate controlled several Alliance resources and was located in the bottom left section of Meritab right along the wall. If anyone could arrange for Taly and Merisia to disappear, Lady Meetcher could. Taly liked her, and the danger her daughter faced might even make her sympathetic.

I hope we can trust her.

***

Allei (August) 16, 1538
Same day
Governor General's Estate, City of Idonia

Once again tucked into his office, Lord Kezem Altran patiently awaited contact from his mother. Reports from his agents within the RT Alliance in Meritab covered his desk. He longed to take a klipper northwest across the Ash Plains, over the Clear Mountains, and straight to the Meetcher estate to teach the fool a lesson. The noble houses were supposed to willingly send their children to serve in Kezem's estate and be trained in his schools and camps. The fuss Lady Meetcher caused nullified any control the tradition was supposed to instill.

A chime announced the anticipated call.

"Yes, Mother, how may I help you?" Lord Kezem asked, not bothering to look at the hologram. He kept his head cradled in his hands, elbows propped on the desk.

"I cannot state this any clearer. Keep Terosh alive until the Mitran plan is complete and the Rangers are destroyed." His mother's voice rang with warning.

"Meetcher's a fool, but Keldor's not. He'll keep Meetcher in line."

"See that he does. Do not let them kill the Ranger either. My plan for the Order requires Terosh to marry the girl."

"The Rangers have been wary of late, what makes you think they'll gather to conduct some silly trial?"

"Their love of tradition is eclipsed only by their arrogance," explained his mother. "As ridiculous as it sounds, the ban on marrying into the Minstel line is sacred law to them. The girl gave her banistick to our dear prince. It's a promise to marry him. Make sure Terosh believes he could lose her. Hurt her if you must. He will marry the girl if he thinks he can protect her. The disregard for the Ranger code should be enough to convene the Ashatan Council."

"That still leaves too many Rangers in one place," Kezem argued, trying not to sound whiny.

"That is where your precious RT Alliance comes in." His mother smiled coldly.

"How will the Rangers learn about the marriage?"

"I believe that is a task for Lucas Telon and Kolknir."

Chapter 37:
Revelations

Allei (August) 16, 1538
Same day
Meetcher Estate, City of Meritab

Down in the depths of the hov lot, Todd Wellum couldn't wait for this rescue mission to end. He understood the Council's wish to protect the defector, as the last three who had cut their Alliance ties had been murdered. Still, the knowledge of the mission's significance only went so far in comforting him. He missed his wife. They had used Ireea and Odrik as aliases before, but not being able to call Kiata by name bothered Todd. Being so near her yet keeping emotionally distant was awful.

"Odrik!" a man called, breaking into Todd's thoughts. "Whatcha doing down here?"

"Waiting for a personal package for a friend," Todd responded, barely stopping his hands from tugging at the Alliance jacket Meetcher insisted his servants wear while on the estate grounds. Todd had drilled the response into his head just in case someone confronted him. It wasn't supposed to come to that though, and his heart pounded with the complication. "Ireea said to expect a package around nine."

Kiata, as Ireea, had told him she would send the informant along at nine tonight. The escape had taken careful coordination and several days to prepare. Todd forced himself to shrug. His shoulders wanted to lock.

Wish I had Kolknir's acting skills.

"Stupid as a tretling." Addram cursed and drew breath to start yelling. "You're on duty, man! If Meetcher catches you doing personal business on Alliance time, it'll be my head that rolls. Don't the—"

"I'm aware of the rules, but she must not be. I figured I'd help her out this once," said Todd.

He listened to Addram's minute-long tirade, nodding at the right times while he scrambled for a plan.

Eventually, Addram ran out of curses and told Todd to leave.

A shadow moved behind Addram, followed by a faint shuffling noise. Addram spun to face the newcomer, preparing another scathing speech.

Todd struck Addram's neck, then scooped the man up, and tossed him over his shoulders. His mind raced, but none of the plans sounded good. He had to get rid of Addram, but he didn't want to kill the man. They couldn't afford for him to be found for at least ten hours. Kiata would need that time to escape. Her job had been to cover the informant's movements as he traveled throughout the Meetcher estate.

Nodding to the man he was meeting, Todd said, "Hurry. The hov's about a kilometer away."

"Why can't we take one of these?" queried the informant.

"They have their tracking devices intact," Todd replied, ushering the nervous man out in front of him.

Without waiting for a reply, he shifted to get a better grip on Addram and raced toward their only hope of escape. He assumed the hov would be in position like Kiata had promised, but Addram's presence disturbed him. The informant's successful escape meant that her position was secure as of a few minutes ago, but that did not guarantee she would stay safe. She would smooth things over with their boss back at the Meetcher Estate. Todd didn't like that part of the plan.

When they arrived at the hov the young driver asked, "What happened? Who's that?"

"Addram had too much ale," Todd answered, tossing Addram into the back of the hov.

"How'd you—" began the driver.

"We were out on patrol and hit a fossa tree," Todd said, silently thanking Addram for having a well-known love of ale. "Ireea's a friend. I called her, and she sent you."

The boy sputtered but could do little as Todd yanked him out of the hov, knocked him out, and placed his unconscious body in the backseat with Addram.

"Thank you," breathed the informant.

"We can talk after we get rid of them," Todd said. "The hov's clean, but we can't be sure they're totally out. I don't want anything you say getting back to Meetcher."

After driving about twenty minutes, Todd tied Addram and the hov driver to a tree and placed a time-delayed homing beacon on the back of the boy's shirt. He double-checked to make sure he had removed their weapons and anything that could be used as a premature signal. The beacon would ensure a morning rescue, but it would be a long night out on the Kesler Plains.

Hopefully, Kiata would be safely away by then. According to the plan, she would delay things several hours and escape by hiking toward Kerimia until Todd could find her by tracing her comm.

Climbing into the hov, Todd pointed the vehicle in the correct direction and engaged the autopilot.

"I think it's safe to talk now. Name's Todd Wellum."

"I am Nils Clavon, a native of Terab, but my home has long been

Meritab. I owe you my life, and for that, I am forever your servant. But my past is painful. I do not wish to explain more than I must. You will hear it when I report to the Ranger High Council."

"Fair enough." Todd hoped he could negotiate the servant part. His knowledge of Terabian history told him it would be difficult to convince the man information was payment enough. The Terabians held their honor debts in very high regard. Thinking the conversation over, Todd switched off the autopilot and concentrated on driving.

To his surprise, Nils cleared his throat.

"Besides my story, I have much information about the Alliance: numbers and names. They are not working alone. They have a very powerful ally in the government."

"Who?" Todd prompted.

"I have only a code name," Nils confessed. "She is called 'The Lady.'"

Oh, well, that's specific.

Todd listened raptly as the informant spoke about the Alliance's ambitions. He hoped the man's information would be worth the risks he and Kiata had taken. So far, the RT Alliance had confined its bullying to individuals and small businesses, but if the informant spoke truth, their goals included meddling in the highest political arenas, perhaps in the palace itself.

***

Kiata Wellum listened for people who might barge into the cramped security closet. The rescue had gone well, but she wouldn't count it a success until she put at least half the Kesler Plains between herself and the Meetcher Estate.

Remembering her husband's shabby story, she hissed and checked the security vids, erasing traces of the informant's movements. Common sense told her to move the timetable up and escape quickly, but something urged her to stay. Sixteen small screens, stacked four by four, cycled feeds from multiple vidrecorders. Suddenly, the image in the bottom right screen confirmed her instincts. The sight sent chills everywhere. She froze the image and enhanced the quality, dividing it over every screen. Kiata gaped at the image.

Reia!

Fear, confusion, and anger, coursed through Kiata so strongly that she grew lightheaded. Reia's hair, braided and coiled in a fancy style, caught Kiata's attention first. A closer look revealed an unnatural stillness that clawed at Kiata's heart. She held her breath until she saw her sister's chest rise and fall in the slow manner of a drug-induced sleep.

A check confirmed the room as one of the nicer prisons below the estate. Kiata had never visited that level but knew of them from her mission research. Questions crowded her head, but she pushed them aside to concentrate on freeing Reia. Thoughts of her own escape were buried beneath improvised plans. Kiata regretted the worry Todd would feel then whipped her mind into sharp focus and attacked the problem with single-minded determination.

***

Allei (August) 17, 1538
Seventeen days after Prince Terosh's Kireshana journey
Meetcher Estate, City of Meritab

After making several arrangements, Taly went to the Meetcher Estate. A man ushered him into a comfortable, tastefully decorated room. Lady Meralla Meetcher stood in the far corner looking out the window. Before Taly had taken three steps into the room, she faced him. Her stiff posture was offset by a hesitant smile, and her eyes radiated misery that gave Taly hope.

"Thank you, Kiner, you may go." Her tone made it an order. She motioned Taly to take a seat and waited for the man to leave before tapping a code into a control panel located on a picture frame. When the task was done, she studied Taly.

He counted to fifteen to give the sound damper time to take full effect.

"Lady Restler sends greetings, news, and an important request." Taly swallowed.

If I've misjudged you, I'm dead.

"How is Lady Restler?" Lady Meetcher inquired.

"She is worried," Taly answered. "But she sent me to tell you that your daughter is safe."

Lady Meetcher gasped.

"How do you know about that?"

"She was brought to the Restler mansion yesterday morning." Taly's gray eyes were gentle, but he spoke urgently. He wanted to continue but stopped to consider the wisdom of it one last time.

"I didn't pursue her because I didn't know where to find her," said Lady Meetcher.

Taly had always been good at reading people, and Lady Meetcher wasn't trying to hide her emotions. As she spoke of her daughter, her gaze became distant, then unfocused, and finally, her expression darkened with desperation.

She's hiding something, but what?

"My lady wishes to help you," Taly blurted.

Lady Meetcher laughed bitterly.

"Sometimes I think I am beyond help."

"My lady also wishes to avoid your fate." Taly figured the whole truth couldn't hurt.

"Lady Restler is pregnant?"

"Yes, ma'am. She wishes to go someplace she can raise the child without fear."

Taly endured an uncomfortable silence as the lady searched him for signs of deception. He knew she had shared some meals with Merisia and liked her well enough.

"What does Lady Restler really seek?" Lady Meetcher asked. "You may speak freely."

"Your aid," Taly answered. "You have the supplies, contacts, and authority to send her somewhere her husband will never find her."

"Where would she like to go?"

"The decision is yours, ma'am, but I think it best if we don't know the destination."

"We?" Her voice held disapproval.

Taly reddened.

"It's not what you think. The—"

"Speak plainly, Talyon Keldor. No formalities. Do you love her?"

Whatever he had expected, that wasn't it. Taly gulped and measured his words.

"I do. She has been my friend for as long as I can remember, and her safety and happiness are my highest priorities, though her honor closely follows."

Lady Meetcher pressed a hand to her temple and considered his words.

"I will help you, but you must help me."

"We will take your daughter with us," Taly assured her.

The lady shook her head.

"No. Yes, please take Kia with you, but I have another favor to ask." She paused as if questioning her own sanity. "There is a Ranger being held here. I want you to take her with you."

Taly's eyes widened but he agreed.

I'll take every man, woman, and child in Meritab if you'll help us.

They spent the next ten minutes outlining a plan. While Lady Meetcher arranged for the hov and freed the Ranger, Taly would return to Merisia and free Kia. They agreed the rescue should take place that evening while Donovan met with Master Erik Restler and Lady Vera Tarpon. It couldn't be earlier because the storms on the Kevil Plains had changed direction, and the prince would be brought in sometime during the day. The meeting with the prince and the meeting he would demand with the Ranger would likely last until evening.

***

Ariman Keldor frowned down at his infopad, rereading the text:

Keep Meetcher in line and aid Prince Terosh's escape with the Ranger.

The instructions were clear, but the Lady's purpose eluded him. He found that disturbing.

Chapter 38:
Proposals

Allei (August) 17, 1538
Same day
Meetcher Estate, City of Meritab
When a hov had finally picked them up, Prince Terosh Minstel submitted to stuncuffs, grateful to finally go somewhere. He couldn't stop worrying about Reia. His captors didn't drug him, but they didn't answer his questions either. They arrived in Meritab and entered an underground hov lot. The anotechs confirmed the location as the Meetcher estate.

After exiting the hov, they traveled up several floors and down several hallways, arriving at an impressive door. The thick carpet sank under Terosh's feet, giving him a clue as to the sort of person he would soon meet.

Terosh and his three captors—Herik, Alden, and Einer—stepped into the large office. Six strangers—five men and one woman—stood before him. Four men wore black uniforms, which bore no symbols, and one wore an outfit designed to imitate a uniform without being as austere. Two young men flanked a middle-aged man with graying brown hair. Next, a man in his mid-thirties stood slightly to the right and a step behind the dark-haired man in the black half-cape. The woman wore a long-sleeved, blue satin gown, which flowed from her shoulders down to a pair of silver slippers. A lightweight cape graced her shoulders.

"Welcome, Prince Terosh," said the man in the half-cape. "My name is Donovan Meetcher. We have business to discuss."

The man flanked by uniformed men gestured, and Terosh sensed his guards standing down.

So, you're the one in charge.

Ignoring the man who had greeted him, Terosh watched the woman. The set to her shoulders and furious glares she fired at the half-caped man told him they were well-acquainted. Whenever her pale blue eyes flicked toward Terosh, they softened. He didn't know how to take that but filed the information away.

"Get on with it, Donovan. This isn't a social call." The woman's golden hair looked ready to cast off the clips trying to subdue it.

Meetcher frowned at the woman before speaking.

"My Prince, I have reliable word that the king and elder prince will not return from Mitra."

Terosh froze. He had spent the night preparing to see Reia. This was the last news he expected.

"Taytron's staying to avert the Blood Harvest, but why would my father not return?"

"The king will not return alive, but the Alliance and my patron believe House Minstel should stand. We will protect you until you can claim your throne. When that happens—"

"No." Anger gave Terosh a moment of euphoric defiance. "I will not be your puppet king."

"You forget that we hold one you love," Meetcher reminded, motioning to the wall to Terosh's right.

One of the pastoral paintings shimmered and melted into a far less peaceful scene that made Terosh sick and furious. The picture changed every few seconds, showing the scene from four different angles. It took two cycles for Terosh to understand what he was seeing.

Reia lay unconscious, suspended from the ceiling of a room barely larger than a hov. She wore dark brown pants and a light beige shirt, but today, she also wore a blue band around each of her upper arms. Ropes bound her hands in front so that they rested below her body, and a thick strap of camrood leather secured her feet. Strong metal chains surrounded by more leather straps formed larger bands, which supported her forehead, shoulders, stomach, waist, and four spots along her legs.

About a quarter meter above the floor a web of thick, blue beams cast everything in eerie light. The beams arranged themselves into square grids with six smaller beams inside each box.

Terosh felt Donovan Meetcher measuring his reaction. The message was simple. Reia's life literally hung in Meetcher's hands. Terosh didn't know who Meetcher answered to, but it mattered little now.

Picking up an infopad, Meetcher switched to a live feed.

"Lower her a meter," he instructed.

"Yes, sir," answered the controller.

Terosh couldn't tear his attention from the screen. His breath jammed in his throat as Reia sank the prescribed distance, coming to a stop a meter off the floor.

"Sizer beams deliver minor shocks, but they're strong enough to wake her from the criessa," said Meetcher. "The bands around her arms will prevent any shocks from going beyond that point, but—"

"Stop!" The lady's cry contained horror, disbelief, and loathing.

Meetcher shot her an impatient look.

"Why don't you—"

"Who are you?" the woman demanded, cutting Meetcher off. She fumbled for her comm, keyed in a code, and tried to master her emotions. "Controller, this is the Lady Meralla Meetcher. Turn off those beams and lower the girl to the ground. I'm coming to collect her." She turned off the comm before the man could protest.

"Meralla, I—"

"Master Keldor, please release the prince and see him to a guest room. I'll take care of the Ranger and have her in sublevel one, prison room three as soon as possible." Without waiting for an answer, the woman stalked from the room.

Dazed, Terosh allowed himself to be led from the room.

The wait turned out to be an excruciating hour and a half, but as soon as he set eyes upon Reia, Terosh forgot everything but his love for her.

Lady Meetcher had briefed him on her plan several times, patiently trying to break through the fog surrounding his mind.

"She'll be awake soon, but she might not be able to talk right away," said Lady Meetcher. "This room is safe. I'll have a meal sent in around two. If you need anything, ask one of Master Keldor's men. Wait for my signal. It should come around seven tonight, but if it comes before, you must be ready to move immediately."

"Why are you doing this?" Terosh wondered.

"For my daughter," Lady Meetcher answered. "And for myself."

Terosh nodded thanks but couldn't conjure proper words. He wanted to warn his father and brother of the danger, but his brain was thick with grief and worry.

Smiling with understanding, Lady Meetcher slipped out of the room.

The scent of iras and fenria clung to the air, coming from Reia's neatly brushed hair. Terosh sat on the low but comfortable sleep pallet and picked up her right hand. Her skin felt like she had spent a month in the Frozen North, the poorly named southern continent. She shivered.

Criessa. Don't those idiots know too much criessa could kill her?

Terosh tried to think of what he should say when Reia awakened. He could speed up the process if he could warm her. The thin blankets might help, but they weren't fast enough for him.

Can you warm her? Terosh asked the anotechs.

No. Too warm, too fast with criessa very bad. You warm.

Finding no fault with the idea, Terosh picked Reia up and slid her over. Then, he tucked his arms around her and pulled her across his chest so his body heat could drive off the cold. It reminded him of the day they had run into the graveground and the flashflood. That got him thinking about the Kireshana, and he remembered teaching her "Leparnisu." He kissed the top of Reia's head.

I'm sorry, Reia. I'm so sorry. The world is definitely you, he thought, resting a cheek against her sweet-smelling hair.

They sat like that for a long time, shivering as the drug delivered waves of fresh cold. Finally, the chills ceased and Terosh felt Reia's hands warm beneath his own. Her head moved slightly.

"Reia?" Terosh asked, squeezing her hands. "Are you awake?"

***

Consciousness returned slowly to Reia Antellio. She first noticed the unrelenting sensation of ice flowing where warm blood had once traveled. Then memories played for her. Lady Meralla Meetcher had spent hours gently washing away the dirt and hurt of the last few days.

This morning, Meetcher and his men had come with painful instruments and questions they knew she couldn't answer.

When they finished their interrogation, two of Meetcher's men had carried her down the hall to a tiny room and pinned her arms against the wall. Reia had just enough time to register the camrood straps and chains littering the floor when the criessa injector pressed against her neck. A hissing noise had preceded the injector's cold kiss. Unconsciousness came as a relief until the cold returned in vicious cycles.

During a light part of the sleeping cycle, Reia imagined hearing Terosh call her name, but she ignored it. Thinking of him would hurt. He couldn't be here because she was a captive and being here would only make him a captive as well. She would never wish that on anyone, especially him.

"Reia, wake up!"

Reia shook her head, figuring that if she ignored the cry long enough it would go away.

Wake! Wake! Wake! the anotechs added.

I'm not talking to you.

Fine, ignore the prince. He's been here over an hour. Let him wait forever.

Reia awakened with her heart pounding enough to rattle her head. Her hands were restrained by something warm. It took her a second to recognize the warm thing as a pair of hands attached to arms wrapped tightly around her. She tensed to throw off the arms.

"Wait, Reia! It's me!"

"Terosh?" Reia asked, hoping she'd heard wrong. Her voice was weak from disuse. "You came for me."

It was not a compliment.

"Of course, I came for you, I—"

"You came here," she said, as warm tears flowed. "You big idiot. Go away! Don't you—"

"Hey, hey." Terosh kissed her neck. "Is that any way to treat the man who came to rescue you?"

Reia continued crying softly. The tears were surprisingly refreshing.

"Only when he plays the honorable fool." She worked a hand loose and patted his left forearm. "But for what it's worth, I'm glad you came."

"I'm glad I came, too," Terosh whispered. He cleared his throat. "Now, before I forget, I must ask: will you marry me, flaws and royal strings and all?"

Reia licked her dry lips to buy time. Had he asked the question two days ago she would have shouted *yes*, but so much had happened.

"Before you answer, you need to know that the royal strings are a lot more complicated." Terosh brought her up to date on his brother going to

Mitra and what that meant for him. Still holding her tightly, he finished, "I—I'll understand if you're afraid. My family doesn't exactly have a peaceful history, but I love you." He shrugged, squeezing her tighter. "I guess I'll always love you, so I had to ask."

"I am afraid," Reia admitted, "but not of following you wherever life may lead." She paused as her throat constricted. "I'm afraid to lose you. Do you know how many times I've pictured you hurt or dying? Do you know what losing you would do to me?" Reia twisted her head up to look at him.

"Don't lose me then," Terosh answered, kissing her lips. He pulled away slightly. "You've a better chance of safeguarding me if you marry me." He didn't wait for an answer. Instead, he kissed her again.

Each warm kiss loosened some of the icy fear. After the sixth or so kiss, Reia pulled away long enough to speak.

"Yes."

"What?" Terosh asked, feigning confusion.

Reia sat up straighter.

"You know very well which question I just answered."

"Remind me," Terosh murmured with a grin.

She did so with a kiss.

Chapter 39:
Strange Allies

Allei (August) 17, 1538
Same day
Meetcher Estate, City of Meritab

Kiata Wellum never liked sneaking around, but her job required an awful lot of it. Truthfully, she would rather face down a pack of ninety korvers than have to rescue Reia.

Isn't she supposed to have the boring life?

Hours passed and still Lady Meralla Meetcher had not returned to her chambers. Kiata's legs began cramping as she waited by the door. As soon as the lady entered, Kiata would need to move fast. She tested the dagger's weight in her hands again, passing the weapon from one hand to the other. The dagger had been with her almost as long as her banistick. She had nearly lost it twice and used it to win back her life more times than she cared to count.

The door swung open, and Lady Meetcher entered. Kiata tucked the dagger into her sleeve sheath and nudged the door so it would close faster yet hopefully not slam. Then, she reached up and grabbed Lady Meetcher from behind, one hand closing around the older woman's mouth and the other pressing hard on the back of her neck. She didn't give the woman time to scream. As the woman went limp from the pressure applied to her neck, Kiata whipped her into the side wall, drew her dagger, and pressed the blade to her neck.

"Take me to the Ranger," Kiata ordered. Her silver-blue eyes promised that anything other than instant compliance would result in death. She slid the blade back enough to let the woman speak.

"I've already arranged for her release." Lady Meralla Meetcher spoke quickly. "The prince will take her through the hov lot and out back where Lady Merisia Restler will be waiting with a hov. My men will think I'm taking an evening drive with the lady and her friend, a young man by the name of Talyon Keldor. He will—"

"Taly?" Kiata asked, surprised. She had not seen the boy since saving him from the Porit viper years earlier, but she had often wondered how he fared. He might even be a man by now. She pulled the dagger away a little but not enough to make Lady Meetcher feel too comfortable.

Confusion crossed the lady's face.

"I've never heard him addressed informally but that would make sense."

Ponder Taly later.

"Is the Ranger all right?"

Kiata watched as Lady Meetcher pieced the story together. Donovan Meetcher had been as mad as a ferbel dropped into a bucket of cold water when four of his people had disappeared in one night. Todd's homing beacon had led to two trussed-up men early this morning, but the other two were still missing. Meetcher had wanted to have a long conversation with Kiata, but she had been dodging his men the whole day.

"Ireea?"

Kiata hissed and pressed the dagger against Lady Meetcher's throat again.

"Wait! I mean you no harm. You're in danger too. It's close to seven now. I came back for their weapons. They're over in that trunk." Lady Meetcher flicked her eyes in the proper direction. "Go to sublevel one, prison room three. I'll unlock the way and tell the prince to expect you. Take them to the back hov lot. Merisia and Taly should be there soon."

Kiata hesitated, wishing she had Reia or Todd's perception. Deciding to trust the woman, she stepped back to give the lady some breathing room.

"Come with us," she said.

"No, the hov will barely hold six people, and I must delay discovery of the escape as long as possible."

"Six?" Kiata asked, coming up with a discrepancy in numbers. Prince Terosh, Reia, Lady Meetcher's friend, Taly, and Kiata made for five passengers.

"My daughter will be with you. Now go!"

Kiata tried one last time.

"My lady, surely there are other hovs. We can take two."

Lady Meetcher shook her head.

"As you stayed last night, so I must stay today. I will escape later or not at all, but that girl needs you. Keep her safe."

Kiata took another step backward, tipped her head in a small bow.

"May you have success on your journey, Lady Meetcher." Kiata collected Reia's banistick and shootav and a beautiful kerlinblade and kerlak pistol she assumed belonged to the prince from the trunk Lady Meetcher indicated and dashed from the room.

***

Ariman Keldor knew Meetcher's conduct had upset Lady Meetcher. Having nothing to do after the evening meal, he went to the sitting room to relax. The fertia wine gave him the courage to try and comfort the lady. It didn't take him long to locate her private chambers. He had learned the house's layout soon after stepping foot in it. He knocked and a moment later she answered.

"Did you—" the lady cut herself off as surprise, fear, and guilt crossed her countenance. Her right hand trembled.

Keldor cleared his throat.

"I came to check on your welfare, my lady."

"Thank you, Master Keldor," Lady Meetcher said, after a slight pause. "I am … well."

The plush purple carpet caught Keldor's attention. He gently pushed past the lady and leaned down to read the marks. An attack had taken place here recently. Everyone entering or leaving would cross this spot. If the attack was a day old, the marks would have faded. One scuff led Keldor's eyes to the right wall near the door, where a painting's skewed frame indicated something—or someone—had struck it.

Lady Meetcher closed the door and leaned back against it, breathing unsteadily. A faint line traced across her pale neck.

"Who attacked you?" Keldor asked.

"I cannot tell you, Master Keldor." Lady Meetcher blinked and avoided his gaze.

Keldor reached for his comm.

"Please, you do not understand!" Lady Meetcher insisted, breathless with anxiety. "It has to be this way." Tears spilled from her eyes as her comm chimed. She looked plaintively at Keldor and slowly reached for it.

Suspicion took over, and he touched his kerlak pistol. He doubted Lady Meetcher's husband knew about her actions. That alone wouldn't move him to action, but guest or not, he needed to know what she was hiding.

"Give me that," he ordered, holding out a hand for the comm.

Lady Meetcher clutched it to her chest and shook her head.

"My daughter's life depends on my silence."

The statement sent Keldor's suspicions soaring. In one swift motion, he brought his right forearm across Lady Meetcher's neck, pinning her to the door. Prying the comm from her, he flicked the on switch.

"Who is this?" he demanded.

With a burst of unexpected strength, Lady Meetcher threw off his arm and ducked away. She kicked at his left shin, but he side-stepped. Dropping the comm, Keldor grabbed the woman's arms and slammed her against the door, stunning her. He drew his kerlak pistol, set it for low stun, and leaned forward with his forearm once again pressed against her throat.

The comm chattered from the floor, and he thought he recognized the voice.

"Einer? There's been a security breach. Let no one leave. Where are you?" Keldor wanted the Ranger and prince to escape, but the presence of others confused him. The situation threatened to move beyond his control.

"Back hov lot, sir. Lady Merisia Restler is here to see the—"

"Detain her and anyone with her. Stun only. That's an order!" Keldor spun Lady Meetcher around and twisted her left arm up behind her back. "Let's go to the back hov lot." He tucked his kerlak pistol into his holster so he could open the door.

They arrived at their destination just as Meetcher's guards bathed the area in brilliant white light. A firefight was already well under way with a familiar sandy-haired young man in the thick of it.

Taly!

***

A few meters from the south wall of Meritab, Talyon Keldor tapped his foot nervously, sending puffs of dirt into the air. Merisia held Kia Meetcher. Taly had offered to take the child, but she cried every time he touched her. His hand hovered near his hidden kerlak pistol.

The man who had challenged them stepped away and spoke into a comm.

Taly concentrated on the conversation but couldn't hear the words. He didn't want to give them away by pulling his gun, but the man wasn't accepting the excuse of a pleasant evening drive. Taly suddenly realized that bringing Kia along had been a mistake. He should have known everybody in the Meetcher estate knew the girl's father had allowed her to be taken away. Thus, her presence aroused suspicion. As Taly came to this conclusion, the guard reached for his weapon. Taly whipped out his kerlak pistol and shot the man as bullets and beams started flying from the wall sentries.

"Merisia, get behind the hov!" Taly shouted, diving for cover.

This was supposed to be a simple pickup.

Two figures darted from the hov lot, not bothering to weave. The figure in front carried something in its arms. As they moved forward, Taly recognized Prince Terosh, and the burden the prince carried as a thin young woman. The second figure—a tall woman—held a banistick with tendrils of energy zipping up and down its surface in her right hand and a wide, flat, violet kerlinblade in her left hand.

Taly watched open-mouthed as the woman ran backwards, swatting beams aside with incredible speed.

He waited until he saw the flash of a kerlak pistol and shot in that direction. He didn't know if his shot connected or not because his eyes scanned the wall again, searching for more ways to help. Moments later, Taly spotted a man holding a woman in front of him as they emerged from the nearest door. His stomach climbed into his throat.

Father!

Taly had believed his father to be on a mission near Rammon. Instead, his father held Lady Meralla Meetcher by one arm and shot kerlak beams at the two fleeing figures headed for the hov.

"Momma!" screamed Kia Meetcher.

Horror seized Taly as the girl slipped from Merisia's grasp and dove beneath the hov. For a moment he was relieved, but then, he heard serlak bullets striking the hov's sleek, black frame.

"Kia! Come back!" Merisia desperately reached for the child but missed.

The girl popped out from the other side and dashed toward her mother.

"No, Kia, no!" Merisia scrambled to her feet. "Taly!"

As Taly started for the girl, an energy beam slammed into the child, threw her back a meter, and cast her to the ground with the force of a sledgehammer.

With a cry of rage and grief, Lady Meetcher wrenched her arm free and raced toward the child. Heedless of the bullets and beams flying around her, Lady Meetcher fell to her knees, scooped Kia into her lap, and sobbed. If she stayed upright, she could die of a stray bullet.

Heart heavy, Taly fired two stun beams into Lady Meetcher's shoulders to knock her out.

Prince Terosh Minstel and the tall woman hurtled his way. Slapping away a few beams that came too close for comfort, the woman spun to face Taly.

As recognition ignited in his brain, Taly was transported back to the last time he'd seen Ranger Kiata, the night she'd saved him from the Porit viper.

The prince shouted something, but it took Taly's brain an extra second to comprehend.

"Open the door!"

Before Taly could comply, a bullet slammed into Merisia's right arm, spinning her halfway around, and causing her to faint. Luckily, Prince Terosh caught her. Seeing the prince struggle to keep Merisia upright and not drop the girl already in his arms, Taly rushed to help. Merisia had the other girl pinned to the prince's chest. In other circumstances, it would be amusing.

By the time Taly returned to the hov, Ranger Kiata pried open the doors, deactivated the kerlinblade, threw it to the floor, and tucked the banistick into her belt. As Taly reached to help, the Ranger grabbed Merisia and tossed her into the hov then relieved the prince of the girl he'd been carrying.

"Taly! Let's go!"

The Ranger's words slapped some sense into Taly just in time for him to register two more hovs arriving.

"Get in and drive!" Kiata ordered.

At first, Taly thought she was talking to him, but before he could unstick his feet, Prince Terosh obeyed.

Grunting, Ranger Kiata seized Taly's shirt and hauled him to the hov. After pushing him in, the Ranger leapt in and balanced above the backseat with her hands and shoulders braced against the driver's seat and her feet pressed on the back window.

"Go! Go!" she shouted.

For the first few minutes of the wild chase across the Kesler Plains, Taly could only brace Merisia and the other girl. It proved a difficult task because the prince kept executing sharp turns. For a while Taly muttered apologies alternately to Merisia, the other girl, and Ranger Kiata as the ride bounced him around the backseat. Eventually, Taly wrestled Merisia into a seatbelt. He considered trying to strap the other girl into the middle seat, but figured she would probably be safer on the floor. A bullet pinging off the roof confirmed his decision.

The next several minutes kept Taly busy trying not to crush Merisia or step on the woman still cradled in the foot space. Taly wished the hov's back wasn't quite so roomy. The space just gave him more momentum as he slammed into the other occupants. The gray fabric ceased to be comforting the fifth time Taly had his nose buried in it.

A quick left flung Taly toward Merisia. Desperate not to bust her nose with his head, Taly grasped the balance bar that hung above her head. He held on so hard his wrists hurt. Taly considered waking his friend but figured if they died in a crash she'd probably be better off slipping from unconscious to dead rather than experiencing unnecessary terror.

The brief glimpses Taly had caught of the pursuers looked like the dark hovs belonging to the Meritab Regulars, but he couldn't fathom why soldiers would be chasing them. They must have seen the prince. No soldier would dare shoot at a royal.

Ranger Kiata's calm voice pulled Taly from his thoughts.

"Taly, return fire if you can. Try not to hit me."

"Where are you going?"

"On the roof," Kiata answered, climbing out the window and perching on the doorframe.

Taly's mind struggled to find a different meaning for those words.

"Get us close to one of the pursuers!" Tossing that order at the prince, Kiata scrambled up onto the roof.

Crazy Ranger!

Taly didn't envy the prince his driving job: bullets slamming into the back bumper, bouncing off the metal frame, and scratching the reinforced windows. Taly prayed the chase would end soon.

***

You only get one shot at this.

If Kiata missed at these speeds, she would be lucky to end up as one large collection of broken bones. She landed on one of the pursuing
hovs with enough force to dent the roof. The hov swerved violently, reminding Kiata why she hated the flying metal boxes. Todd loved the power hovs offered, but Kiata preferred traveling by horse.

Must be a guy thing.

Commanding herself to focus, Kiata instructed the anotechs to stick her body to the roof.

A man's astonished face popped up from the front passenger seat. Kiata's fist met it with satisfying results. He almost fell, but she caught his shirt and tossed him back into the hov.

The other hov turned to help. Kiata took her dagger out and slid from the roof to the front engine compartment, heedless of the beams flying millimeters above her head. A few precise stabs and slashes left the engine exposed. A jab with Reia's banistick took care of the engine itself.

Kiata refocused on the soldiers in the hov, locked eyes with the driver, and touched the window. A word to the anotechs knocked out all four men. She didn't want to kill the king's soldiers. Still, she needed to end the chase before somebody crashed. She held on tight until the hov finally stopped. Feeling incredibly tired, Kiata slid off the hov and raised Reia's banistick to face the remaining soldiers. To her surprise, a swarthy man with dark brown hair and eyes stood over his comrades with a kerlak pistol in hand.

Prince Terosh halted the hov near Kiata, climbed out, and stared at the newcomer.

"Lieutenant Laocer?"

"I'm glad you're safe, my Prince," Laocer said. "Rumors around Rammon speak of assassins. This proves it." He motioned to the dead soldiers in the hov he had just emerged from. The four dead men wore the gray uniforms of Meritab Regulars. Laocer wore Royal Guard blue, but something about him made her uneasy.

"Yes, I suppose it does," the prince said.

"The Royal Guard is fractured, my Lord. Some stand by their vows, but others are lured away by promises of high positions if they join the rebels."

"Who leads them?" Prince Terosh asked, his anger flaring.

Kiata could sympathize. Rebellions inevitably led to deaths.

"I do not know, my Lord," Laocer replied. "Captain Antar sent me to find you. I am to escort you back to Rammon as soon as possible."

"I'm not returning right away," Prince Terosh said. Suspicion shone in his eyes.

"Where are you going, my Lord?" Laocer asked.

"Come with us and see," Terosh invited.

Kiata wished he hadn't done that, but if Laocer was going to betray them, she supposed it would be best to keep him close.

Another hov pulled up, and Kiata braced for a new fight until she saw Todd jump out. He ran to her and smothered her in hugs and kisses.

Chapter 40:
Consequences

Allei (August) 18, 1538
Eighteen days after Prince Terosh's Kireshana journey
Meetcher Estate, City of Meritab

Lord Kezem had sent Kolknir to sort the mess in Meritab. Dutifully, he ran lengthy interrogations until he had a clearer picture of events. The Lady wanted Lord Kezem's plans for the Alliance to succeed, but ever the cautious planner, she had also instructed Kolknir to help where possible. He was to punish the failures and reward the deserving.

A review of the security vids showed several promising Alliance soldiers. Kolknir would make them offers later, but the Meetcher family presented a more pressing issue. Donovan's clumsy attempts to play both sides deserved death, and his wife's betrayal of Alliance ideals and contempt for Lord Kezem also deserved death. The fact that her actions aligned with the Lady's wishes was irrelevant. Free thinking on the part of ambitious Alliance individuals had led to this debacle. Kolknir needed to make an example out of the Meetchers lest others decide to question Lord Kezem or the Lady.

The appropriate fate for the Meetcher child remained unclear. In times past, she might have been killed for her parents' failings, but the Rangers had taught Kolknir to never waste resources. Kia had fought Lord Kezem's agents. She had fighting potential.

Kolknir brought his attention back to the makeshift prison holding the Meetchers. The prisoners stared into empty space. Meetcher ignored Kolknir's questions, but Lady Meetcher answered without protest, showing little emotion until he mentioned her daughter.

"What will happen to Kia?" Meralla asked hoarsely.

Kolknir walked to the small table in the corner and poured a glass of water. He returned to Lady Meetcher, brought the glass to her lips, and let her drink.

"She will live," he said.

Peace came over Lady Meetcher.

"What will happen to us?" Meetcher wondered.

"We'll die," answered Meralla. She winced, but Kolknir guessed it was more from the burns on her shoulders than the thought of their fate.

"You can't—" Meetcher began.

"I can and will, but if you have a last request, I'll consider it," Kolknir said, feeling generous.

Meetcher slipped into a catatonic state, but Lady Meetcher looked at Kolknir.

"I want to see my daughter but not like this. Let me see her some place without the cuffs."

Since the lady clearly wasn't a fighter and she had recently been shot twice, Kolknir removed the stuncuffs and led her down the hall to the room with the child.

Two Alliance soldiers, Herik and Alden, stood guard. They looked worn from the previous night's excitement, despite sitting out much of the battle after a brief, brutal encounter with a Ranger.

"Let her stay with the child until I return," Kolknir ordered. "She should awaken soon." He would return in an hour or so, after taking care of Meetcher. That should give Lady Meetcher time to make peace with her child.

***

Meralla's heart ached so badly she thought it might fail before she got to see Kia. Rallying her energy, she slipped into the room. Kia slept on the overstuffed couch dominating the center. Pain radiated from Meralla's left arm, but she ignored it, rushed to Kia's side, and knelt. The broken arm hung uselessly, but Meralla used her good arm to lift Kia and pull her close.

It was only a stun beam.

The thought of her daughter being shot almost undid Meralla's control.

A little over a half-hour went by while Meralla sat with Kia. At times, she wept, but mostly, she showered her sleeping daughter with words of love, comfort, and advice she would never live to give. When Kia began stirring, Meralla held her tighter with her good arm. She suddenly wanted to say so much that no more words would come.

What should I tell her? Will she be better off missing or hating me?

"Momma?"

The single word restored Meralla's ability to speak.

"Kia, I love you. Never forget that … no matter what happens." Meralla tried with only partial success to keep her voice calm.

"Momma? What happened?" Kia's voice was heavy with sleep, but she hugged fiercely.

The hug brought more tears to Meralla, but she savored every painful heartbeat.

"I have to leave soon, darling. Be brave. Please," she said.

"Where are you going?" Kia asked, pulling away. Tears rushed into her eyes. "Don't leave me. I'm sorry! I—"

Seeing her daughter blame herself stabbed Meralla deeply. She reached out and brushed at Kia's tears, cupping her sweet face and patting at the sweat-dampened hair.

"This isn't your fault, love. Bad things happen. Don't blame yourself or let it make you bitter."

"Where are you going?" Kia asked again. Her hazel eyes were desperate.

Can she handle the truth?

"Kia, I made a decision some people don't agree with." Meralla couldn't bring herself to say that she would soon die. It would be cruel. "I have to go away, but always remember I love you.

Chapter 41:
The Illusion of Peace

Allei (August) 21, 1538
Twenty-one days after Prince Terosh's Kireshana journey
Temple of Marishaz, City of Chara

"I would like a word," said a female voice.

Recognizing the voice calling from the shadows, Lucas Telon halted and tried to cover his surprise at seeing Lady Mavis Altran in Chara. Nobody knew exactly where the Lady's hideouts were located, but one would sooner guess Idonia—the other main southern city—over Chara. Though anxious to be inside he forced himself to bow.

"My Lady, it is an honor to see you again," said Lucas.

"Come with me." The Lady swept gracefully up the steps to the temple's side entrance. Decked out in dark robes complete with a cowl for anonymity, one could easily picture her as an avatar of Marishaz, goddess of secrecy.

Lucas wanted to ignore the order but good sense prevailed. This was not a woman to disobey. She led him into the temple to an upper room complete with soundproof walls and an excellent vidscreen. He stared at Reia's image. She had always been beautiful, but he had never seen her like this. Her wedding dress matched her eyes, and the look of peaceful happiness tore at him. The look should have been aimed at him. With great effort, he forced his gaze away and slapped the sound controls, cutting off incoming sound and preventing noise from leaving the room. For several moments, he concentrated on controlling his emotions.

"I know of the sacrifice you make this night," Lady Mavis Altran said.

"What sacrifice?" Lucas spat, despising himself for needing to witness Reia's marriage. "She would never have me. What's a Ranger compared to a prince?"

"As a Ranger, you have every right to stop that wedding, but I ask you to let it happen." Lady Mavis's stony tone touched Lucas more than her words.

"Why?"

The Lady's smile contained triumph and contempt.

"Because love declared could be denied, but a secret marriage will become undeniable fact."

"You're after the Council," said Lucas.

Lady Altran's smile widened, but she shook her head.

"Not only them."

"You seek to destroy the Rangers." Lucas felt irrational loyalty sweep through him. He had emotionally ceased being a Ranger long ago, but part of him still loved the Order.

"The Rangers are the strongest support for the king. I have bought what loyalty I can from their ranks, but the rest must be dealt with. I need a reason for the Ashatan Council to gather. This will be that reason." She spoke softly, almost kindly.

Lucas considered Lady Altran's words. The plan might work. The Lady didn't have to explain the details. He could work out the rest. Reia's disregard for one of the most sacred Ranger laws would force the enclave in the Riden Mountains to call for a full meeting. The Ashatan Council hadn't assembled for more than two years for fear of attack. The issue would force them to strike down the archaic laws or see justice done. Lucas pitied Reia. He didn't know if she had willingly fallen into the trap or not, but either way, her words tonight would seal many fates.

***

A most unusual time for a wedding.

Sadness crept in and squeezed Father Morgivesh Niktol's heart as his gaze took in the prince, the Ranger, and their few guests. Stretched out end to end, the whole party would barely take up a fraction of one pew. In better circumstances, this temple would be filled to capacity and ringing with joy.

That's the way it should be.

The day was mere minutes old. The sadness turned sharper and poked at his heart as he thought of the other secret royal wedding he had performed.

Does this young woman know what she's getting into?

The other union had been just as perfect, but he knew how tragically that had turned out. Prince Taytron would never again be the happy young man so in love with life. His heart had died with Deanna Koffrin Minstel. Father Niktol couldn't help but worry that a similar fate awaited this new pair.

The prince looked handsome in his Royal Guard uniform, and the bride looked stunning in a deep green gown borrowed from Lady Akia Zelene. The dress complimented her figure, showing off the emerald pendant Terosh had given her.

Father Niktol smiled at the haphazard perfection characterizing this wedding. The young couple would have been married in dust-covered travel clothes had it not been for Governor Darmon Zelene. Although the governor couldn't make it, he had sent his daughter with everything necessary, including the priest. Though not his own temple, Father Niktol found it fitting to marry the couple under the figurative eyes of the goddess of secrecy. Some people mistakenly associated secrets with deception, but he preferred to think of them as beautiful gifts hidden away until the right time for revelation.

"It's your line, Father Niktol," the prince prompted, grinning. He had both arms wrapped around his bride.

For her part, the bride smiled and leaned back against the prince, looking content to never move again.

"Have the vows been composed?" Father Niktol asked, clearing his throat.

"They have," answered the prince.

The Ranger simply nodded.

"Wonderful. Now the hard part—you must let go of her, young man. Please kneel before each other."

Prince Terosh reluctantly let his bride slip from his grasp. She smoothly turned and faced him, hands held out palm down. His hands reached for hers, and together, they knelt on the thin mat placed there to protect their knees. The wedding gown billowed, creating a sea of fabric that touched Father Niktol's robes.

"Prince Terosh of House Minstel, I understand you have something you wish to say to this young woman here in the sight of the gods and these witnesses."

"I do, Father, but I shall let the lady go first." The prince's eyes never left his bride's face.

Only mildly surprised, Father Niktol said, "Very well. Reia Antellio, Ranger Healer and friend to House Minstel, I understand you have something you wish to say to our beloved Dulad Prince. Please say it here in the sight of the gods and these chosen witnesses."

The Ranger spoke heartfelt words.

"Ehnocheatosches mimindoahsu. Tahmsukeromfetoa. Icana-tuapwemosetos. Stobrem-compltos. Coshaminmatakalanlin."

Father Niktol couldn't understand one word until she translated.

"At nighttime and all times my thoughts dwell with you. Tell me you'll love me forever. I could not take a parting, now or ever. It would break my heart completely, shatter my mind, and turn my soul dark."

"I am yours, you are mine. This promise is forever," Prince Terosh answered. "You hold my heart in your hands as you hold my soul with your smile. Your eyes speak your mind and heart, but I need to hear the words again. Tell me you'll love me forever then come what may, life will be perfect."

"Suhomielstomensuhan esuhomiessasufaclin. Sulispaksemina-mielstom contrinessaliseh-messrep. Tahmsukeromfetoa toncome-vancectpa," repeated the Ranger. She paused a second then continued, "Isesussuame. Esepromatos."

Father Niktol gathered the last part meant the same thing as the prince's reply.

"Ifinedisquamonakero aperamostre aleminafin," the Ranger

whispered.

"I finally found what it means to love someone so much that it hurts at the thought of an end," repeated the prince.

"Tahmsukeromfetoa," spoke the Ranger.

"Tell me you'll love me forever," translated the prince.

"Isiltosriotroapan alanaiknoseisu," the Ranger said.

"I'll be all right through trials or pain as long as I know I have you," Prince Terosh repeated.

"I am yours, you are mine. This promise is forever," they vowed together.

***

Allei (August) 21, 1538
Same day
Tiny Gem's Ale House, City of Chara

"What can I do for you, Master Telon?" The voice held much caution.

Perverse pleasure swept over Lucas. Knowing this was an audio-only connection, he allowed himself a smile.

"Master McGreven, it's been a long time, hasn't it?"

"Where have you been, Lucas?" Master Niklos asked in that utterly paternal, contemptible tone. "We thought you had turned or been killed. Why didn't you finish your mission to Azhel?"

"It was a waste of time." Lucas regretted the impatience. He wanted Niklos's cooperation. Squabbling over the past would hardly accomplish his goal. His spirits diminished. As much as he would have liked Niklos to be the ill-fated messenger, he needed assurance that the plan would be carried to fruition. "Let me speak to Master Alikron please."

"Certainly," Niklos said stiffly.

"Who's your master now, traitor?" asked Master Alikron a moment later.

"A fine one you are to speak thus," Lucas scoffed.

"What do you want? I'm a respected member of the Ashatan Council. They'll never believe you!"

"Relax, Master Alikron, I wish you to convey a message to the Council." Lucas suspected Alikron would work himself into a fine fit if he let him.

"Message? What message?"

Lucas pinched the bridge of his nose.

How did I ever tolerate this fool as my master?

"You need to call the Ashatan Council," said Lucas.

"The whole Council? Whatever for, boy?" asked Alikron.

"A Ranger has fallen from the way," Lucas revealed.

"Now see here—"

"Not you!" Lucas shouted. "I'm talking about Reia Antellio."

"Niklos's pet? The one he promoted to healer without our consent? What about her?"

Good mood thoroughly destroyed, Lucas explained the facts to

Master Alikron and finally elicited a half-hearted promise to petition for a full Council meeting.

"How will you get her here?" Alikron demanded.

"I can be very persuasive," Lucas assured him.

***

Allei (August) 23, 1538
Twenty-three days after Prince Terosh's Kireshana journey
Chamber of Wisdom, Loresh Cave System, Frozen North

Princess Reia Antellio Minstel stood in the Chamber of Wisdom and watched in wonder as a new stone pillar was added to the hundreds already lining the room in neat rows. Her mind reeled, trying to absorb this new shock. She had never seen so many strange things and felt so many strong emotions in such a short time.

Her quiet wedding to Prince Terosh had happened two days ago. She would remember Allei 21, 1538 forever. Every part of the last few days permanently etched in her memory: the escape, the emergency surgery to remove a bullet from Taly's friend, the crazy wedding preparations, the kind priest, the soft silk dress, the expression on Terosh's face when they exchanged vows, their few guests, the frantic packing, the rushed farewells, the sweetness of their first night together, and all the rest.

She smiled remembering Father Niktol's befuddled expression when they spoke most of their vows in Kalastan. The words returned easily to her, and she rolled the most important ones over in her head.

I am yours; you are mine. This promise is forever.

The ceremony had no sooner ended when Taly and his friend left for an unknown destination, Kiata and Todd returned home, and Lieutenant Laocer went back to Rammon to await news from Mitra. Lady Akia Zelene stayed long enough to see them settled into the guest chambers in her father's Charan estate before also leaving. They had spent the night in Chara and traveled to Loresh the next day.

Loresh, an impressive system of caves and tunnels deep in the Frozen North, known only to the Royal House and a few servants, was surprisingly cozy. The sheer size and natural beauty matched any sight Reia had ever seen in the Riden Mountains. Most caves had glowcrystals casting colorful beams of light in breath-taking shows. The Chamber of Enlightenment even held an ancient, ice-encased ship.

"Come, I want to show you something," Terosh announced, breaking into her thoughts. He grabbed her hand and led her to the stone pillar next to the forming one and placed his left hand on it.

Reia chuckled as a very young Prince Terosh appeared and stared into the empty space over her right shoulder.

"Yeah, yeah. I'm getting there," said the young Terosh. "Greetings, I am Prince Terosh Minstel, brother of the obnoxious I-am-great Prince Tate, second son of Kila and Teorn Minstel. I cannot sing, and I'll never be king so lots of me will you hear."

"And so mature, too." Reia stood on tip-toes to kiss Terosh's cold cheek. "Play another message."

"There aren't any," Terosh replied, looking embarrassed. "I never got around to leaving more messages."

"Well, fix it," Reia ordered. Her eyes sparkled with mirth.

Terosh sighed and smiled down at her.

"Why do I get the feeling I'm going to hear that a lot?" He started several messages but ended up erasing them. "They don't sound right. Why can't I think?"

Reia had retreated out of the recorder's range. Now, she stepped forward, reached up, and pushed a tuft of wavy black hair into line.

"Just say what you're feeling," said Reia. "It doesn't have to be formal and elegant."

Terosh opened his arms.

"What am I feeling?"

"Love and excitement." Reia stepped into the embrace and met his kiss.

Eventually, Terosh pulled back and squared his shoulders.

"Okay, I can do this now." He released Reia, whirled, and told the anotechs to start recording. "I am in love! I have come with my new wife so all future generations may learn from her as I have. She is wonderful in a hundred thousand ways, which I have no time to record. Besides, I'd rather spend my time with her than this machine anyway." He cocked his head to the side as if to wink and ended the recording. The message had taken less than ten seconds to finish.

"See, that wasn't so bad. You're even a good liar," Reia teased.

"No lies ever fell from my lips, fair lady," Terosh said with a deep bow. "Besides, it's your turn," he added.

Me? Oh, no no no no no. No.

"But—"

"You're part of the royal family now. It's your duty to leave a message for the future generations."

What do I say?

Reia cast her mind about frantically and settled on the truth. She instructed the anotechs to record her message and used one of Master Niklos's calming techniques to keep her voice steady.

"Greetings, I am Reia Antellio Minstel, younger sister to Kiata, daughter of Sela and Basil Antellio, wife of Prince Terosh Minstel." Even as she spoke, the full meaning of everything that entailed dawned on her. She paused half a second as the consequences of her choice barged to the forefront of her mind. "Once a Ranger, now an outcast, I confess choosing love over duty and the life I was trained for."

It wasn't official yet, but it would be as soon as the Ashatan Council learned of her marriage.

***

Knowing she would have to face the Rangers sooner or later, Terosh vowed to be there with her the whole time. Likewise, he would one day face his father and hoped she would catch him after the fallout.

They spent the rest of the afternoon and most of the evening listening to the messages left by his ancestors. Except for the new messages from Tate and Deanna, Terosh had heard them before, but it had been so long that he had forgotten all but the most outlandish messages.

Worry tried to intrude on the peace, but Terosh pushed it aside. He trusted Laocer and the anotechs would notify him with any news concerning his family.

Chapter 42:
The Weeping Princess

Allei (August) 28, 1538
Twenty-eight days after Prince Terosh's Kireshana journey
Chambers of Princess Alikai, Deleur Palace, Planet of Mitra

Prince Taytron Minstel slowly stirred in his sleep, tightening his arms around the warm body pressed against his own. The figure shifted, rising and falling in the jerky rhythm of suppressed sobs. Tate woke up and abruptly released his new wife, realizing she was not Deanna. Everything flooded back, shattering the temporary peace that had formed. The shock drove away remaining thoughts of sleep.

"What is it, Alikai?" Tate asked, mentally apologizing to Deanna.

The cosmic storm outside the Mitran System had delayed his arrival for three days above the estimated six, leaving the Mitran ambassador practically foaming at the mouth with impatience. Tate had barely agreed to marry Alikai when he found himself before an Azhel priest and a Pirtan monk exchanging vows with the princess.

His thoughts drifted to his first glimpse of Mitra. Whereas Reshner appeared a soothing mix of brown, blue, white, and deep green, Mitra was dominated by black and red. Everything here seemed hostile, making Tate miss his homeworld. Fierce winds whipped strands of red dust into a stinging lash. No wonder every building on Mitra had special air filters.

Princess Alikai Minstel curled into a ball and sobbed, making Tate glance her way. As he watched, her expression changed to something like shame, and she rushed into the washroom, pulling the curtain across with clinking finality.

Stunned, Tate flopped against the fluffy pillows and reflected. His new wife confused him. Her physical beauty was undeniable, and she carried herself with dignity. Her purple eyes held mysteries he couldn't fathom.

After dressing in the second washroom, Tate cautiously approached the closed curtain hiding Alikai. He wore dark pants and a shirt of the softest material he'd ever felt. The pants had a deep blue stripe down each side and the shirt sported a web of silver strands, which made it look ready to shatter. He longed for the sturdier clothes he was used to wearing at home.

Muffled sobs seeped through the thick purple curtains.

"Alikai? May I—"

"The princess does not wish to see ye," a stiff female voice said from behind the curtain.

Irritation chased away worry, making Tate brave. He swept the curtains aside and barged into the spacious washroom. Alikai was curled against the far wall with one of her maidens helplessly standing by. Her skin—dark as a moonless night—contrasted nicely with her white nightdress. Alikai looked at Tate with an expression so desperate and guilty that he didn't know what to say. Robbed of his irritation, he felt awkward and foolish.

Dropping to his knees before her, Tate felt the coolness rising off the tiled floor.

"Will you let me take you back to the bed?" he asked, taking her icy hands between his own. How the Mitran people could stand such frigid temperatures was beyond him, but he would have to tolerate it if he was going to spend the next twenty-some years here. "It's warmer, and you'll be more comfortable."

At her nod, Tate picked up Alikai and returned her to the bed. He propped three pillows behind her and moved another two to make room. As he climbed up beside her, a series of sniffles threatened another round of tears. He didn't dare take her into his arms. Instead, he quietly sat next to her, clutching one hand. They sat in silence until Alikai finally mastered her emotions enough to speak.

"There is too much goodness in ye, Taytron Minstel." Her voice cracked with grief. "How I wish ye'd been as ugly and cruel as described!"

Tate's confusion reached uncharted heights.

"What?"

Alikai had differed from the description he had been given, but Tate had taken that to be a simple communication gap. He had expected her to be tall with dark hair and purple eyes, which she was, but he had also been led to believe her skin would be almost translucent. He knew now that a small subset of Mitran people experience "White Nights" twice a year wherein their skin lost its pigmentation.

He grinned, recalling his father's reaction to the dark-skinned Mitran people. Thankfully, they had still been on the ship, so only Tate and Captain Kelter had heard his father's wheezing gasps.

Alikai suddenly gripped Tate's right hand fiercely, capturing his attention.

"Can ye fathom what me name might mean, Taytron?"

Tate enjoyed the way his name rolled off her tongue. Only his mother had consistently called him by his full name, and she'd always made it sound as solid as ice. The way Alikai spoke his name softened it to something smooth yet strong, like a mountain lion's measured steps. He shook his head.

"Tell me."

"It means 'ill-fated winds.'"

Why would anyone burden a child with such a name?

"Ye truly do not know what awaits us, do ye? Do ye realize what I've done?" asked Alikai.

"Alikai, I've been lost for a long time. Nothing, save your beauty and royal bearing, have been as I ...." Fresh tears from her made him forget his words, so he trailed off and kissed her. His heart ached, feeling like he was betraying Deanna.

Alikai kissed back with such unbridled emotion that Tate felt something inside move. An uncertainty he hadn't even known existed suddenly melted.

I'm sorry, Deanna. Will I ever let you go?

After the long kiss, Tate felt brave enough to try and lighten the mood.

"Now, what's this about me being ugly?"

Alikai's answer started between a laugh and a sob, morphed into a coughing fit, and ended in a deep sigh. She leaned against Tate's chest.

"I'll tell ye all I know."

"Good, take your time." Tate held her protectively.

"Ye are Mitran now, and I wish to the gods I could take it back." Her tone was soft and serious.

"Why?"

"The Blood Harvest approaches. My House has stood for exactly a thousand years. On Mitra, that means death."

She said it so matter-of-factly that Tate's reaction of pulling her closer was delayed.

"Then we'll leave. No one will touch you on Reshner."

"It is far too late for escape," spoke a silky male voice from the doorway.

Alikai stiffened and her tone became so cold Tate almost expected her to breathe icicles.

"Leave us!" she commanded.

The Mitran man—Hinoli Brek if Tate remembered correctly—bowed. As typical of many Mitran men, Hinoli's head sported a crown of seven silver spikes grafted above his forehead, a testament of his devotion to Rishmaltair, god of suffering and pain. His teeth had been sharpened to razor thin edges, which constantly ripped his lower lip to shreds. Thick black body armor that matched his skin covered his chest, but his arms were bare, showing off his celzan tattoos. The blood-red lines rippled haphazardly across his muscles, showing him to be a prominent member of the Gathering.

"Explain as ye wish, Princess. Three hours remain." The man left abruptly.

"Time escapes us. I must prepare." Alikai twisted out of Tate's grasp, called her maiden, and disappeared behind a screen to change. As she did so, she talked so fast Tate had to concentrate to follow. "Every thousand years the Blood Harvest sweeps away the old dynasty and inserts a new royal family so none can claim a longer reign. This being the thousandth year, my family must perish."

"I thought our marriage prevented that," Tate said, more confused than fearful. "It doesn't have to—"

"Peace, Taytron. When I have explained, ye'll know all and hate me." Alikai spoke with surprising dispassion. "The people of Mitra may look like the people of the planet ye call home, but our bodies are more durable than most humankind."

What's that got to do with anything?

"That means the Blood Harvest can be swift, almost painless, or dragged out for years."

The statement brought Tate to his feet. He strapped on his weapons belt and began pacing the room as Alikai continued her explanation.

"My fate has been sealed since birth," Alikai said calmly, stepping out from behind the screen. "The fate of my family is what ye came to change."

Tate's breath stuck in his throat and he stopped pacing.

Alikai wore an outfit made of many layers of fine red and yellow silk. Even as she stood before Tate, her maiden wrapped, twisted, and otherwise bullied her hair into an elaborate coif that was both regal and gorgeous. If Alikai noticed Tate's admiration, she ignored it.

"And the fate ye face is my fault alone," she continued.

"How?" Tate demanded, getting tired of her blaming herself for something he didn't understand.

"I was given a choice that t'was no choice: marry ye and have ye and Reshner's king share in a painless Blood Harvest or watch my family suffer a slow Harvest for as long as it may last."

Rage grew in Tate, but it wasn't directed at Alikai.

"It gets worse," Alikai confessed, "and worse still because I think I love ye."

"Worse?" Tate laughed bitterly.

"I won't die." Sitting on the bed, Alikai let her head sink to her chest.

Hope welled up in Tate, but one look at her expression killed it.

"What happens?" he asked.

"I will live long enough to have our child and perhaps through the first year of his life. Then, I will be the last of my House to perish."

Tate's eyes widened.

"You're pregnant? How do—that's—what?" He finally stopped trying to speak.

Who would bother with such an elaborate scheme? Why involve Mitra? A few crazies with pistols and suicidal tendencies could have done the job.

No one in the Governors Council or the Senate had pitched a significant fit in a long time.

Alikai continued as if he hadn't spoken.

"The child will carry on your name here, but my House will disappear, except for some distant cousins. Their lives and that of our child will only be spared if we surrender."

Tate squared his shoulders. No one would take him or his wife without a fight. His expression hardened until he caught the vulnerable cast to Alikai's countenance. His resolve wavered. In the history he had studied—truth or fiction—Tate couldn't recall one tale that asked a man to not fight to save those in his care. Yet Alikai's eyes asked exactly that of him. He didn't understand the Blood Harvest nuances, but he grasped that if they fought everybody connected with the Deleur name would die. Three steps brought them together, and Tate wished the comforting embrace could last forever.

"I do not fear my fate, Taytron, but I wish ye'd been spared this path. The rules to the Blood Harvest have been changed to affect ye and thy kin. I learned this only yesterday. Ye truly have powerful enemies." Alikai finally pulled away.

"What guarantee do you have that your family won't suffer even if we surrender?"

He heard a sad smile in her reply.

"The traditions that condemn also protect. The Brek family, though chosen to replace mine, still answers to the Gathering. Four children will live to rebuild the Deleur name, but we won't inherit the throne for another twenty thousand years. If I—if we—fight them, my family will be lost forever."

For some reason, having Alikai speak in terms of thousands of years and forever struck a chord within Tate. He had finally found a purpose in life—to die well.

Two loud thumps sounded outside the door. Tate drew his kerlinblade and kerlak pistol.

The door burst open and Aster Captain Gina Kelter rushed in.

"We're leaving." Her voice held the fury of a pending Great Storm. "Right now."

"Ye don't understand!" Alikai cried, holding a hand over her heart.

"Stand down, Captain," Tate ordered. He returned his weapons to their appropriate places. "There's—"

Twelve Palace Security Guards rushed in and leveled half-pikes at Captain Kelter. She whirled and fired on them, dropping three in the first second. A half-pike swept toward her left side. She blocked it with her kerlak pistol, but the move left her weaponless. She backed away but soon had two half-pikes pressed under her chin.

"Stop!" Tate shouted. His gun was back in his hand, but he didn't know who to shoot. Stunning Captain Kelter might be the easier solution, but he wanted to know why she was having such a violent disagreement with the guards.

Alikai loosed a torrent of Mitran words. It took the anotechs a moment to translate.

"Stay your weapons! These are guests of House Deleur. My House will soon pass but until this day expires, you *will* obey me!"

To Tate's surprise, the soldiers straightened, brought their weapons upright, and slammed them into the floor as a salute.

The head guard faced Alikai and dropped to a knee.

"Forgive us, Exalted One. We have orders to detain the Reshner delegation, especially the royals."

"Where's my father?" Tate's gaze darted between Captain Kelter and the Mitran commander. He holstered his pistol, but his hands hovered near it just in case. "What's going on?"

"They have your father." Captain Kelter's voice held icy calm.

"You left him?" Tate asked incredulously.

"His orders," Kelter grumbled.

"Leave us," Alikai ordered the soldiers.

The commander looked like he wanted to argue but nodded stiffly. A hand signal sent the soldiers into a flurry of motion that had them carrying their wounded and dead out the door.

"What is going on?" Tate demanded again.

"We are betrayed, Highness." Captain Kelter blinked slowly and her shoulders slumped. "The king is captured, and you and I are slated to die with House Deleur."

"Why you?" Tate knew about his own pending doom thanks to Alikai's explanation, but that didn't explain why Captain Kelter had been marked. Something the Mitran commander had said stuck with him: *especially the royals*. His breath quickened as the phrase clattered through his head.

Captain Kelter's head tilted and unshed tears glistened in her eyes.

"It's true, but it doesn't matter."

Alikai looked back and forth between Tate and Captain Kelter.

Tate couldn't move. Everything fit with stunning clarity. His mouth felt dry, and his legs threatened to buckle.

Captain Kelter's eyes never left Tate's face. Finally, she cleared her throat.

"The Mitran people have a curious way of defining royalty."

"Bloodlines," Alikai supplied.

Captain Kelter looked at Tate kindly.

"It's not what you think."

"I can't think." Tate fought hard to focus.

"You are married to Reshner's king?" Alikai's inflection made it a question.

"Not in the formal sense," Captain Kelter said carefully.

The ghost of a smile came to Alikai.

"My people count every union, even temporary ones, as binding."

"Mother?" Tate asked. His voice reluctantly surrendered the word.

"It was better this way." Captain Kelter's statement sounded as much to convince herself as Tate. She sat down abruptly and wrapped her arms around her knees.

The uncharacteristic display of vulnerability made something crumble inside Tate.

"How?" He choked on the question.

She looked up at him and let the tears fall. Her chest heaved with suppressed sobs. When she gained a measure of control, Captain Kelter quietly explained.

"I—we were part of the Covenant of Lasting Peace between Reshner and Gardan. Our planets were headed for a war neither could afford, not with GAPP poised to take over the Edge planets."

Alikai sat beside Captain Kelter and embraced the older woman.

"The arranged marriage," Tate murmured. He had been told the story his entire life.

Captain Kelter shut her eyes and shook her head.

"It wasn't that simple. It should have been, but it wasn't."

"What do you mean?" Tate wondered.

"It was supposed to be an even trade of princesses."

"Aunt Uria?"

"No. She was already promised to Colimech's Sultan. That caused enough controversy with the match being made to Teorn and not the elder prince, Uel."

"Another princess escaped her fate then?" Alikai questioned.

"How do you know that?" Tate asked.

"You are connected to me and she is linked to you, so I am connected to her," Alikai answered.

Tate knew it would make sense to him if he thought about it long enough.

Captain Kelter cleared her throat and straightened her shoulders.

"When Princess Mavis married her lover, Dravid Altran, the treaty began collapsing, but we were already on Reshner. We'd just arrived so no one had yet seen the princess. The wedding was a rushed affair, and in accordance with Gardanian tradition, Princess Kila Creston was fully veiled. Fearing an assassination attempt, my mistress and I switched places the night of the wedding."

Tate felt exceedingly awkward.

"The prince was furious at the deception but terrified at the consequences should the truth be revealed to King Padric Creston." Captain Kelter smiled faintly. "For everyone's good, the secret was kept, but I was already pregnant. Kila and I were sequestered until you were born. She pretended you were hers, and the people of both planets hailed the treaty's success."

Tate rubbed his forehead. A glance up brought a lock of hair into view. He fingered it, noting how closely its shade matched Captain Kelter's hair. He dropped his hand and shook his head.

How could I not know?

The answer was obvious. Queen Kila had also possessed similar hair. Captain Kelter must have accompanied the princess because of the striking similarities between them.

Captain Kelter slowly climbed to her feet.

"Time runs short. I will leave you two in peace. I just had to see you one last time." She turned away.

"Captain," Tate called. He wanted to call her "mother" but the title stuck in his throat.

She paused.

"I know, Taytron," Captain Kelter replied over her shoulder. "Your answer is written on your face. I will heed your wish to do the honorable thing. Riden be with your brother when we are gone." With nothing more to say, she left.

Tate felt Alikai's arms wrap around him.

Are you there, friends? Tate asked the anotechs.

Always, Prince of the Chosen.

When I die, return to Reshner.

No, we will stay. You can be saved if—

I have made my choice. Protect my brother. He is Reshner's last prince and best hope.

Chapter 43:
The Fall of House Deleur

Allei (August) 28, 1538
Same day
Chambers of Princess Alikai, Deleur Palace, Planet of Mitra

To pass the time, Princess Alikai forced herself to eat with Prince Taytron from the rich fare brought to them. The food sat in her stomach like a soggy rag, making her queasy. Mostly, they lay on the soft bed talking quietly. Alikai's eyes filled with tears several times, but she drew strength from her husband and held them back. Then, soldiers loyal to the Deleurs for generations marched into the bedchamber in two unyielding lines, their faces blank masks. At least they waited for Alikai and her husband to gain their feet before arresting them.

"No!" Taytron cried, offering the first resistance when a soldier moved to bind Alikai's wrists. He moved to throw off the hands at her elbows.

Twin waves of fear and love seized Alikai, nearly making her freeze, but she fought the numbness to grasp her husband's hands.

"Peace, Taytron. It must be this way."

Though her heart fluttered, Alikai refused to let her features show the fear. She had been preparing for this day since before she could speak. She could walk the path blind, yet now that it was upon her, every part of her cried out to fight. She ran the last few months over in her mind, desperate to know if she could have done something different. She had not even seen Taytron's face until after the wedding. When his
gentle face appeared from behind the mask instead of the cruel one expected, she had nearly fainted.

Events moved swiftly, yet they seemed slow and blurry, like something seen through murky water. Tight iron bindings pinched her wrists. Her heart ached when they bound Taytron. The soldiers surrounded them and marched them to the throne room, called Deleur Hall for another few hours.

No amount of bracing prepared Alikai for the raw emotions which ambushed her upon stepping through the gilded doors and seeing Deleur

Hall packed with soldiers and family members. Only instinct kept her walking forward. If she fainted, the soldiers would carry her, but dignity was all her family had left. She refused to steal that small treasure from them. Her father's heart attack may have been merciful to him, but it had placed a heavy burden upon her.

Taytron's father struggled against three soldiers. They were too far away to hear words, but his protests were clear. Pity for him and anger at being manipulated coursed through her. The captain they had spoken to earlier stood stiffly beside the king.

Hinoli Brek stood next to the throne, tall, proud, and contemptible. His yellow eyes shone bright, and a tight smile locked his lips into an unnatural position.

"If it pleases the Princess, her servant seeks a blessing upon his rule," Hinoli said.

The oily sound made Alikai bristle, and the anger lent her strength. Few dared to ask the blessings of the former dynasty, a move considered the highest form of insult and the lowest form of conduct.

"I do not please!" Mounting the six steps, Alikai stood in front of the throne and forced herself to stare into Hinoli's eyes. "Furthermore, I would beseech the Gathering to choose another ruling House or at least another ruler from House Brek." She glared at each of the Gathering representatives surrounding the dais.

Hinoli's eyes narrowed.

"As it pleases Her Highness," he replied stiffly. Turning to the Gathering representatives, his smile turned feral. "I invoke denulan upon House Deleur!"

A hush fell over the crowd.

Alikai's heart skipped several beats.

Denulan, "Total Death," would mean no survivors and an end to House Deleur. It hadn't been invoked for nine thousand years, not since House Kinn had been wiped from Mitra for rebelling against the Blood Harvest.

"What grounds have ye for such a request?" Geroli Rikk demanded.

Alikai silently thanked him. The Rikks and Deleurs had been close for countless years.

Hinoli didn't answer, proving he had no legitimate grounds for denulan.

"We should get on with the ceremony," Geroli urged quietly.

Alikai called each of her young cousins up by name and blessed them in the holy language. The bindings made the blessings awkward as she needed to touch each child's head before speaking. For Dekoli and Reloni, she beseeched the gods for strength of heart. The boys received the blessings with stony faces. For Meriki and Sali, she asked for an extra measure of wisdom. The girls let their tears flow freely. Sali's smile came close to undoing Alikai's courage. Once finished, she charged Geroli and his house with their care.

"Fear not, Princess, House Deleur survives this day." Geroli bowed as he spoke the ceremonial words.

She acknowledged the bow and watched Geroli summon a servant to hustle the children away. Her blood pulsed in her ears and a haze hung around her vision.

Alikai felt herself falling.

Suddenly, strong hands gripped her right arm, and she heard Taytron's voice.

"Release me!" he shouted.

The darkness closed in even more.

"Someone wake her. She must witness the cleansing!" declared a female voice.

"You'll have your Blood Harvest but let me hold her." Taytron's voice vibrated with passion.

Alikai stopped fighting and fell back against Taytron. His arms slipped around her waist. She had no strength to speak but leaned her head back, basking in the safety he offered. Her skin tingled where his hands touched and liquefied energy rushed into her, rallying her senses.

"Emnon mer Deleur," Alikai said.

Thus ends the reign of House Deleur.

The Blood Harvest began in earnest, and Alikai watched with abject horror as soldiers carried out their duty. Taytron's hands never left her. They stood together while half-pikes ripped through the screaming crowd. Tears washed down Alikai's face, but a small measure of peace existed between herself and Taytron.

Suddenly, Hinoli was before her, his sword raised, already crimson. His sadistic smile filled her vision. The sword swung toward her and would have sliced into her arm had it not been intercepted.

"What are you doing?" shouted Geroli.

Alikai knew Geroli would not let this stand. Still, she was almost relieved to be able to die with her family and beloved. Her sole regret was for her unborn child.

The sounds of a scuffle followed. Alikai felt herself spinning around. Her eyes opened, and she stared into Taytron's beautiful blue-gray eyes. He kissed her. It was the last thing either of them felt before a sword pierced through her back and into his chest.

Chapter 44:
Tides of Change

Allei (August) 29, 1538
Twenty-nine days after Prince Terosh's Kireshana journey
Rikk Palace, Planet of Mitra

Weary beyond words, Sarie Verituse let the Mitran king, Geroli Rikk, gently lead her to the ship. Her wrists stung where the ropes had punished her for struggling. Her throat burned, but no more tears would come. They had been spent yesterday and throughout the sleepless night.

"I know our customs seem cruel to Outsiders, but they've prevented planet-wide war for thirty-five thousand years." Rikk patted her hand. "The bodies are already aboard. I'm sorry more cannot be done."

Sarie couldn't even muster a nod.

Prince Tate's dead.

The thought would give her no peace. She had been arrested yesterday, same as everyone in the Reshner delegation, but only the prince, the king, and Aster Captain Kelter had been killed with House Deleur. Sarie was upset that nobody could find Captain Kelter's body, but most of her grief was due to the prince's death. She had been present hours after his birth and helped Niktasha raise him. With ten years separating them, he had been the little brother she always wanted. When he gained his feet, she had chased him around the palace. She had also washed, dressed, and comforted him on the days when Queen Kila was in one of her moods.

Sarie didn't remember getting on the ship but felt the vibrations as it rose. She was going home, but home would never be the same.

What will Prince Terosh do?

A stab of fear pierced Sarie's grief. If someone had arranged for Prince Tate to be murdered here, they could certainly kill Prince Terosh back on Reshner.

King Terosh.

***

Pirua (September) 4, 1538
Thirty-four days after Prince Terosh's Kireshana journey
Governor General's Estate, City of Idonia

"It is done, my Lord. Their bodies were delivered not an hour ago. I've had them moved to the throne room for now."

"Well done, Captain Antar," Lord Kezem replied.

"Have you further orders, my Lord?"

"Have you found the prince?" asked Kezem.

"Lieutenant Laocer is in contact with the prince now. Shall I have my men move in?"

"No, let him return and claim his throne. It is not yet time." Kezem cut the connection, sat back, and smiled. The victory was two-thirds won. Terosh would share his brother's fate soon enough, but first, the Rangers needed to be destroyed. They had been given the opportunity to join him, but few did. The RT Alliance would destroy the Rangers and they, in turn, would either submit or be destroyed.

Having Terosh assassinated now would be simpler, but there were far too many royalists to get away with it. He didn't just want to rule. He wanted to be king.

Chapter 45:
Caught, Chasm, Chaos, Queen

Pirua (September) 6, 1538
Thirty-six days after Prince Terosh's Kireshana journey
Prince Terosh's Private Estate, City of Estra

Being stranded in the Frozen North half a planet away from her new husband was not an appealing option, but Princess Reia Minstel had reluctantly agreed to stay in Estra. Located almost equidistant from Chara and Idonia, Estra hosted about a tenth of the population of either mainland city. Reia wondered what kept people living here. Ice, snow, and cold wind offered little in the way of comfort, though admittedly the sun shining off snow could be quite beautiful.

Word of the assassination of Prince Taytron and King Teorn had forced Terosh to travel north to Rammon. Reia would have gone with him, but he had enough to deal with without having to explain his marriage to the Governors Council and the Senate. In time, she would have her own explaining to do. How she would do so consumed much of her thoughts, the rest she reserved for worrying about Terosh.

This place is too big.

Reia walked softly, so her footsteps wouldn't echo. Terosh's absence turned the elegant beauty of the cavernous rooms cold and distant. Reia drew her travel cloak tighter around her shoulders to ward off a chill. She could have roused a servant to turn on the heat, but she didn't want to disturb them. She'd spent many nights in harsher conditions out under the stars.

Thinking of stars, Reia quickened her steps, determined to visit the observatory. She spent an hour gazing up at the stars through the powerful telescopes and thinking about sharing constellation stories with Terosh. The memories warmed her. When her heart regained some peace, Reia returned to the main floor.

As she passed her bedchamber, a rustling noise caught her attention. She gripped her banistick. Nervously drawing the weapon, she searched several nearby rooms. Finding nothing, she admitted she was growing increasingly jumpy. The first week had been fine, but now, she wished she hadn't worked so hard to convince Terosh not to leave a guard or two.

Or two dozen.

If Terosh had gotten his way, she would have been tucked into one of Loresh's bunkers surrounded by Royal Guards and Melian Maidens.

That would have fixed the loneliness issue.

Having already eaten an evening meal and not quite ready for bed, Reia decided to take another walking tour of the vast estate. This took her the better part of an hour. She returned to her bedchamber pleasantly weary, but when she noticed the door slightly ajar, instinct put her senses on high alert. Her pulse quickened, and she snatched up her banistick. Creeping close to the door, Reia pushed it open with her banistick.

A hand latched on to her weapon and pulled. Though surprised, Reia threw herself into a sideways roll, wrenching her weapon free. Coming to her feet, she whirled to face her attacker.

A broad-shouldered figure covered entirely in black stepped out of the shadows and nodded.

An arm encircled her neck and drew her back into a man's chest. His other hand braced the back of her neck.

"Hello, Reia. Why is this the only way I get to hold you?" asked Lucas Telon. "You don't know how hard this is for me."

"Not. Hard. Enough!" Instead of reaching for her neck, Reia whipped her banistick down, aiming for Lucas's kneecap. She missed and connected with his right thigh instead.

Grunting, he shoved her away.

She tried to keep from landing in the other attacker's arms, but she hadn't anticipated being released suddenly. The next thing she felt was a hard knock across her shoulders that spun her half-way around. This was followed by hands driving her to the ground and a knee landing on her back. A cold dagger nestled into the flesh under the right side of her chin.

"Trials waste so much time," the man complained.

She knew his voice, too.

"I wish it were still the old days. When criminals were simply caught and gutted," Kolknir continued. He emphasized the last three words with small increases in pressure on the dagger.

"Let her up," Lucas growled.

"As you wish," Kolknir said. His blade left Reia's neck. "But don't get cocky. She's the means to the end we both seek. Remember that."

As hands rolled her over onto her back, Reia tensed to continue the fight.

"Don't even twitch." Lucas's dagger appeared under her chin.

"If you wanted to talk, you needn't have stalked me in my own house," Reia commented.

"She's mighty comfortable in these fancy new trappings," Kolknir said with a chuckle.

"What now, Lucas?" Reia asked.

"Now you stand trial before the Ashatan Council for betraying the

Rangers."

Reia couldn't believe it. Lucas's outrage sounded genuine. Then, it suddenly made sense.

"The Council never sent you on the Kireshana. Who is your new master, Lucas?"

The dagger pressed even closer until it broke the skin.

Reia held still and prayed Lucas had steady hands.

"It doesn't matter," Lucas said. "What matters is that if you even think of sharing your thoughts with anyone I will personally hunt down your precious sister and her husband and kill them painfully."

"Kiata and Todd would never turn. You'll have to kill them anyway."

The drug on Lucas's knife made Reia drowsy.

Cormea, radon, and alipo sap.

It was a combination many of the Nareth Talis Rangers used on their daggers, for it could render an enemy unconscious without having to kill them. The first two ingredients caused paralysis and the last induced sleep.

Reia feared Lucas would flick his dagger once more and end her life before she could reveal his plans.

Who else has turned?

She felt Lucas's tension. He really wanted to hurt her. Just before the cormea, radon, and alipo sap sent Reia into oblivion, the dagger left her neck and slipped into her side. The flash of pain was the last thing she remembered.

***

Pirua (September) 8, 1538
Thirty-eight days after Prince Terosh's Kireshana journey
Ashatan Council Chamber, Ranger Compound, Riden Mountains

Having finally been admitted into the Ashatans' meeting chamber, Kiata Antellio Wellum stormed over to Lucas Telon and smacked him. He reeled from the blow. Lionel Riften and Val Cederik steadied him with neutral expressions. James Celdin and Todd stepped between Lucas and Kiata. Everyone had seen how Lucas had brought Reia back, and most believed he deserved what he got.

Kiata would have punched him, but she wanted answers before breaking his jaw.

"What happened to my sister?" she demanded.

Todd placed restraining hands on her shoulders.

"Not now, Kiata. This won't help her. Come away with me. We can deal with Lucas later."

"What's this about?" asked James, one of the few people who didn't know what had transpired. Until a few hours ago, he had been with his wife while she gave birth to a son.

Kiata shook off Todd's hands and glared at Lucas.

"What happened to Reia?"

Why did you stab my little sister, you slime-sucking maggot?

"She surprised us," said Lucas.

"And the great Master Lucas Telon stabbed her before she could explain." Kiata's anger threatened her self-control. "Why question people when you can stab them?" A new thought struck her. "What are you afraid she'll say?"

Anger covered her fear. The dose of sedatives on Lucas's dagger must have been high for Reia to be unconscious almost two days. Master Ekris had treated the cuts on Reia's chin and side so they wouldn't scar too badly, but Kiata knew there would be different scars.

"I think we'd all like to know what happened out there, Master Telon, but there's no time now." Master Niklos's tone left no room for argument. "Everyone sit down so this phase of the trial may begin."

Kiata couldn't let the matter go yet.

"If what you're accusing her of is true, she'll soon be your queen!"

"She's not queen yet." Lucas looked like he wanted to say more.

Kiata wanted to shake the rest of the words from him, but she reluctantly allowed Todd to pull her to a cushion on the floor. Her hands unconsciously formed fists.

Todd squeezed her right arm.

The room was set up like most of the instructional chambers with ten lines of twelve cushions on both sides of the center aisle. The speaker, Master Hiram Alikron, sat in the center of the judgment barrier, flanked by six council members. Kiata took in their grave expressions. Alikron had called for the trial. He would certainly oppose Reia. To his left and Kiata's right sat Jolinda Ekris, Kale Corida, and Liam Deliad, respectively masters of healing, tracking, and arms. Of those, Kiata expected Master Ekris and Master Corida to support Reia. Kiata wished for Master Deliad's support, but knowing his traditionalist views, she counted him among the opposition. The masters from Osem—Alvis Canter, Viki Tor, and Simon Haloren—were unknown, but their expressions did not give Kiata hope.

Two Rangers escorted Reia into the chamber to the seat of those on trial, which is halfway between the Ashatans and the spectators and directly across from the witnesses.

Kiata's anger melted in favor of sympathy. Sitting still was difficult. Kiata wanted to go to Reia, hug her, and kiss away the hurts as she had done when they were children.

At least she looks better, but I should have been there! She needed me, and I wasn't there to protect her!

"Beat yourself up later," Todd whispered.

Try as she might, Kiata couldn't concentrate on the trial. As the Ashatans argued every facet of Reia's "crime," Kiata could only stare at her sister.

Reia's eyes said much. The green orbs cycled through fear, anger, and sadness so deep it was almost palpable. When Reia finally stood, Kiata tuned in to Master Alikron's words.

"Ranger Healer Reia Antellio," Hiram Alikron began.

Reia opened her mouth to correct Alikron on her name, but he stopped her with a glare.

"We have discussed the matter at length. This Council is clearly divided. A Ranger marriage with a royal has not happened for many years. The old ways are unacceptable. So, we give you a choice. Renounce your marriage to Prince Terosh of House Minstel and retain your position or leave the Order."

Reia sighed like she had expected as much.

Kiata snorted. She knew what would come, though she doubted the stuff-headed High Council members had a clue.

She'll never do it, you fools!

Master Alikron blundered on.

"Your master speaks very highly of your skills, and we are certain you have a promising future."

Oh, yes, a promising future in an Order that put you on trial for forbidden love. Brilliant, Master Alikron.

"I cannot simply stop loving him," Reia said.

"That is your decision then?" Alikron's expression hardened.

"It is, and we shouldn't even be discussing this. There are traitors—"
"

"We are aware of your recent troubles with Ranger Kolknir and Master Telon," Alikron interrupted. He exchanged glances with the other council members. After receiving silent approval, Alikron turned his gaze back to Reia.

"I'd like to say one more thing," Master Niklos called.

"You will wait until this trial is concluded," Alikron said haughtily. He impaled Master Niklos with a stare before returning his attention to the accused. "Reia Antellio, the Ashatan Council finds you guilty of betraying the Rangers. You are hereby stripped of your rank and forbidden to use your skills as a healer. In addition, you are forbidden from ever using the weapon of a Ranger. Your banistick will be destroyed by—"

"I claim her weapon!" Kiata declared. Anger added force to her words.

"That is—"

"Well within her right to request," interjected Master Niklos. "If her sister had died, the weapon would have been returned to her closest kin. Ranger Knight Wellum is a respected member of the Nareth Talis and deserves this honor."

Alikron looked like he had taken a large bite of something very foul.

"So be it. Ranger Riften, remove this woman from our presence."

Kiata's heart ached, for she could imagine how she would handle someone telling her she couldn't love Todd. She didn't even acknowledge the part about Reia not healing people. The idea was ridiculous. Plenty of people used healing arts similar to the Rangers. The knowledge could not be confined by a title.

Master Niklos retrieved Reia's banistick from Master Alikron, cradled it gently, and passed it to Kiata. She clutched the weapon desperately but could not think about it while Ranger Riften moved to take custody of her sister.

Reia closed her eyes and absorbed the pain of Alikron's announcement as Ranger Riften took her elbow. She shook him off.

Silence ruled the chamber.

Finally, with tears streaming down her face, Reia spoke.

"I am sorry my actions have caused such a rift in the Order, but Riden as my witness, I have done no wrong." With a respectful bow Reia concluded her ill-fated trial with the Ashatan Council.

Though Reia walked from the room with a straight back, Kiata sensed the pain rolling off her. She moved to follow, but Hiram Alikron's nasally voice halted her.

"Ranger Wellum, we are very close to war with the Restler-Tarpon Alliance. We need loyal Rangers to concentrate on their duties. I doubt you'll have time to fraternize with traitors."

War I'm sure you pushed for.

Not trusting herself to speak civilly to the man, Kiata clenched her teeth and stalked from the room.

***

The same night as Reia's trial, Lucas Telon gladly acted upon new orders from Lord Kezem. His first target met him in a dark, seldom used training chamber. The kill had been clean and quiet. Hiram Alikron—and other weak members of the Restler-Tarpon Alliance—had no place in the future Lord Kezem was building. Tonight would be the cleansing of the old and the birth of the new.

Wiping his dagger on Alikron's shirt, Lucas silently moved through the familiar mountain tunnels until fresh air greeted him.

"Good evening, Master Telon," said a young, chipper voice. "What's the hurry?"

Lightning quick calculations took place in Lucas. The boy didn't sound suspicious, but Lucas couldn't afford to have an alarm raised. His fist caught the youth in the throat, resulting in a strangled noise somewhere between gasping and gagging. The noise cut off a moment later as Lucas's dagger claimed another victim.

Kolknir and Kezem's men should have killed the lookouts already. Hoping they could handle the simple task of slaughtering the slumbering Rangers, Lucas anticipated fulfilling his next objective. He jogged past several dwellings until he came to the Wellum's home. He had warned Reia he would kill her family if she caused him trouble, and he intended to keep that promise. He wished he could kill her soon after, but she left as soon as the trial had ended, carried away in a hov sent by her dear husband.

I'll give her the details later.

***

Scuffling sounds awakened Kiata Wellum. Her mind started organizing battle tactics almost before full consciousness gripped her. A crash further motivated her. Having taken Reia's warning about traitors seriously, Kiata had slept fully dressed in case a midnight fight rolled her way. She snatched her banistick off the end table, jumped to her feet, threw on her boots, and raced to the cabin's main room. Until now, Kiata had never appreciated having a small cabin. Even in the dark, she knew where she could safely step. Todd, who had been slightly farther from the doorway, was only half a step behind her.

The ceiling's lightbar had come to life at the first bang. Two figures wrestled on the floor, blood spilling from at least one of them. One of Kiata's favorite chairs had been reduced to firewood crowned with a crooked cushion, but she couldn't mourn the casualty. The framed arrangement of pressed flowers and herbs Reia had given her as a belated wedding gift miraculously remained fixed to the wall.

The satisfaction that the keepsake had survived the invasion vanished as Kiata recognized the intruder. Her banistick whistled through the air as she brought it down on Lucas Telon's back. He rolled away from the blow but most of it caught him anyway. Seeing the odds had changed from one-on-one to three-on-one, Lucas cursed, threw his dagger at Kiata, and fled.

Kiata swatted the dagger into a wall. For an instant, she could only stare at the empty space that had once held Lucas. She'd believed Reia about Lucas's being a traitor, but that did not prepare her for seeing the man attack her servant. The thought of Nils brought her back to the moment.

Todd already knelt by him, examining the knife wound.

"He'll be fine. Go help the—"

Kiata had only listened until the word "fine." After that, she raced out the door and ran down the hill making as much noise as possible.

"Wake up! Wake up! We're under attack!"

Where are the sentries?

Kiata didn't have time to consider the question, for she ran into four assailants. She had the advantage of going downhill, and the attackers had been stupid enough to run one right behind the other. The unfortunate back two tumbled down the hill, and Kiata sent their comrades after them with two strikes from her banistick.

Something grabbed her right ankle. The ankle twisted painfully, and Kiata fell hard. Luckily, she had taken enough tumbles to know how to break a fall. The attacker was on her before she could rise. She had lost her banistick somewhere. The pain in her ankle helped her focus. The blow to her head did not. Kiata fell back on years of hand-to-hand combat training. For all his crude methods, Kolknir had been an efficient instructor. Kiata's assailant cocked a fist to bring down on her head. She grabbed the wrist he was using to brace himself and drove her thumb knuckle into the flesh, whispering words to tighten her grip. At the same time, she whipped her left elbow up into the man's nose. He screamed and recoiled but not swiftly enough to avoid catching her left knee with his stomach. A punch to his head finished him. Satisfied, Kiata used one of Reia's healing phrases to fix the pain in her ankle and went to find her banistick.

***

Pirua (September) 29, 1538
Fifty-nine days after Prince Terosh's Kireshana journey
Royal Palace, City of Rammon

Queen Reia Minstel stood a step behind her husband, trying not to gape at the crowd filling the palace courtyard and the streets beyond. The cool, early evening air wrapped around her, but she still felt uncomfortably warm. Her serene expression betrayed little, but she prayed she wouldn't faint. Having the attention of several million people directed at her was not her idea of a good time. Thousands of eyes stared up at the balcony she stood upon.

Determined to face her fears, Reia struggled to see past the blur of faces to individuals. A little girl sat atop her father's shoulders, eyes wide and hands outstretched like she wanted to touch Reia. An old man struggled to keep his posture straight as tears of joy and sorrow mingled in his white beard. A pair of young Royal Guards straightened as Reia's gaze passed over them. She wasn't used to having that effect on people.

Everything felt strange. Her hair was piled atop her head. The hair preparation had stretched Reia's patience very thin. The deep purple evening gown she wore weighed almost nothing. She occasionally brushed her fingertips across the fabric to assure herself she wore anything at all. She didn't even want to know what it cost.

To escape the moment, she turned her thoughts to the last few weeks, trying to focus only on the good. It was a hard task. The news from the Ranger compounds in the Riden Mountains and Osem was mixed. Her banishment from the Order was complete, yet both Councils had drafted formal letters recognizing her new status. The recovery efforts after the twin attacks were proceeding slowly.

Kiata, Todd, and Master Niklos are safe. Don't think about that right now.

Thoughts of Terosh's drawn face after seeing the anotechs' messages from Mitra haunted her. He had not let her see the images yet, and she wasn't sure she wanted to see them.

Not that either.

Uncertainty made her heart falter until she fixed her eyes upon her husband as he addressed the crowd.

So much has happened.

Terosh's warning that he might one day inherit the throne had been easy to relegate to somewhere far in the future, but now that day had come.

The coronation ceremony in the Temple of Riden in the heart of Rammon had been beautiful. First Terosh, then Reia had knelt before Father Niktol and promised to honor and serve the people of Reshner with their lives, no matter the costs or consequences. It had reminded her of their wedding where they had made similar promises to each other.

Love brought us here, but can it carry us through what comes next?

***

Terosh looked back at Reia. She stood calmly behind him, her bearing regal and wonderful. His spirit absorbed the peace she projected.

Does she know her presence makes everything better?

Realizing he had been silent too long, he glanced at the quiet crowd and forgot the rest of his speech. Burying the inadequacies, Terosh stood taller.

"I never expected to be here and wish my brother yet lived so that I could serve him as he served you, but he is gone. And we cannot despair for long for we have hope in a new form. People of Reshner, I give you your queen!"

He stepped aside so they could see her.

A loud cheer went up, and Terosh waited for it to subside. He motioned for Reia to join him before the amplifiers. When she did so, he grasped both of her hands. Forgetting the crowd, Terosh brought Reia's hands to his lips and kissed them.

"She was a Ranger and a healer, and now she is queen. May she give us the strength to face the future."

THE END

(The story continues in *Reshner's Royal Threat*.)

Anotech Chronicles Book 2:
Reshner's Royal Threat

By Julie C. Gilbert

Table of Contents:

Cast of Characters:
(Spoiler Alert)

Royals:
King Terosh Minstel – ruler of Reshner
Queen Reia Minstel – wife of Terosh, former Ranger
Lady Mavis Altran – Terosh's aunt, mother of Lord Kezem
Lord Eldon Altran – Governor Lord of Idonia, eldest son of Mavis
Lord Mitrek Altran – Governor Judge of Idonia, second son of Mavis
Lord Kezem Altran – Governor General of Idonia, third son of Mavis
King Padric Creston – ruler of Gardan, Terosh's grandfather

Rangers:
Kiata Antellio Wellum – Nareth Talis Ranger, Reia's sister
Todd Wellum – Nareth Talis Ranger, Kiata's husband
Master Niklos McGreven – substitute father for Reia and Kiata

Restler-Tarpon Alliance:
Vera Tarpon – mother of Brook, Alden, and Merisia
Tyko Tarpon – father of Brook, Alden, and Merisia
Brook Tarpon – eldest son of Vera and Tyko, Nera's husband
Alden Tarpon – son of Vera and Tyko
Nera Tarpon – wife of Brook, recruited by Lady Mavis
Gareth Restler – eldest son of Arista, Merisia's husband
Ariman Keldor – RT agent, Taly's father

Other:
Ectosh Laocer – Royal Guard captain
Merisia Restler – daughter of Vera and Tyko, Gareth's wife
Niktrod Keldor – Taly's grandfather, assassinated the former queen
Talyon Keldor – former RT agent, Ariman's son, Merisia's friend

Villains:
Kolknir – Kezem's agent, mercenary, former Ranger master
Lucas Telon – Ranger master, Kezem's undercover RT alliance agent
Maledek – alias for Lord Kezem

Chapter 1:
Enemies and Emissaries

Maledek's Private Retreat, City of Idonia

Lord Kezem Altran adjusted the voice modulator to the settings for Maledek, a personal favorite he'd not had the pleasure of using for a week. At the same time, he eyed the young man featured in the hologram display. Gareth Restler looked distinctly uncomfortable. Kezem already knew the essence of the man's request, but he waited for him to articulate it.

As Maledek, Kezem had dealt with the Restler-Tarpon Alliance many times, but this was his first direct contact with the Restler heir. Gareth's light brown hair stuck out at several odd angles, telling Kezem he had probably agonized about making this call. His brown eyes flickered between anger and worry, but his posture remained stiff.

Gareth tipped his head down in a bow.

"Greetings, Lord Maledek, it is a pleasure to finally speak with you. Your support of our great alliance is much appreciated."

"I trust you have more than greetings and thanks in mind," said Kezem. He left out the obvious part that contact of any sort was risky. Kezem had the latest in anti-spying equipment, but he doubted that would stand up to the technology his mother could access. Thankfully, her sources usually outstripped anything the Royal House could come up with as well, but Kezem liked to avoid unnecessary risks.

"I do, my Lord. My wife has gone … missing," Gareth said.

"I assume you seek my aid?" Kezem's inflection inserted the hint of a question into the words.

"Yes, my Lord." Gareth said it stiffly but a slight shift in his jaw betrayed his nervous energy.

"It has been more than a month since your wife left, has it not?" asked Lord Kezem.

Gareth flinched as Kezem expected he would.

"Why do you care now?" Kezem wondered, enjoying the rich tone the voice modulator added to his Maledek voice.

"I have always cared!" Gareth declared. "The Alliance has done everything it can to track them to no avail, but I cannot accept that. I'm told you have resources beyond us and an interest in keeping this alliance viable."

"What makes you believe the Alliance itself is threatened?" asked Kezem.

"This ... misunderstanding has strained the trust holding the Alliance together," Gareth admitted. "I have word that measures will be taken against a similar situation happening within the new Tarpon household. I do not wish it to come to that."

Kezem took a moment to absorb Gareth's concern before voicing his next question.

"Has Lady Nera Tarpon indicated she might leave as well?"

"No, but that does not mean the Tarpons believe my sister is loyal to the Alliance," Gareth answered. "I fear they may do something ill-advised. Getting Merisia back is the easiest solution to setting everybody's mind at ease."

"Assuming my contacts can locate your wife, what will you do?" Kezem asked, genuinely curious.

"I do not know, my Lord. I suppose that will be decided once my wife is recovered and the full story comes out," said Gareth. "The best scenario would hold that the boy forced her to leave with him, we catch them, he dies, and my wife sees the error of her ways."

Kezem laughed. "Your wife left of her own accord, Master Restler, all the evidence points to such."

"How do you know?" Gareth challenged.

"I like to protect my interests, so I keep agents in every city, including Meritab. That's why the Alliance came to me in the first place, and as you said, it is why you come to me now."

"I see," said Gareth. His tone turned sour. "Will you help?"

Kezem let a few moments pass to see how the young man would react. Gaining nothing more than a solemn stare, he finally said, "I will do what I can to see that the Alliance remains strong. To that end, you have my aid in the search for your wife, Master Restler."

"Thank you, my Lord," said Gareth with another stiff bow. His hologram disappeared abruptly.

Lord Kezem turned off the hologram display and went to his desk to read a few reports from his agents.

***

Pirua (September) 20, 1538
Same Day
The Lady's Estate, Kala Mountains
Lady Mavis Altran replayed the conversation between Gareth Restler and her youngest son.

Kezem received many requests every day, and she certainly didn't have time to review every one of them. Still, she made a point to at least know each person with whom her three sons spoke each day. Kezem happened to speak with more interesting people than Eldon or Mitrek. His ambition had always impressed her.

This particular conversation told her nothing new except that Kezem failed to identify the implications of Merisia Restler's defection. Lady Mavis paused to ponder whether Merisia's actions could be qualified as a true defection. The word usually implied a change of allegiance to something else. Mavis decided it qualified anyway, even though Lady Merisia's allegiance seemed only to herself.

Next, Mavis debated with herself over whether she should help her son, or not. Her agents already knew where to look for Lady Merisia and her young escort, Talyon Keldor. She also knew whom to send after them: Talyon's father. Ariman Keldor was the only one who would hope both Merisia and Talyon lived through the encounter. She didn't know why she felt compelled to save Talyon, but her instincts said he was worth saving. He possessed the sort of incorruptible good nature that would doom him in time, but that also made him easy to manipulate. The more she thought about it, the more certain Mavis grew in her conviction that Talyon could be used against her nephew.

Terosh was regent now, but he would soon be Reshner's official king. Mavis indulged in a sweet, heady rush of anger that made her feel more alive. Terosh and his new wife both possessed a delightfully predictable good nature, same as Talyon Keldor, but Terosh also had a healthy fear of Mavis, one that made him almost untouchable.

If reports could be trusted—and she paid dearly to ensure such—Talyon had once been saved by a Ranger. Thus, the Ranger, Kiata Antellio Wellum, was connected to Talyon. However vague that connection might be, it could probably be exploited at some point. By extension, Ranger Wellum reportedly doted on her younger sister, the only Ranger in decades to break the code prohibiting marriage into the royal family. Lack of shared blood between the sisters meant nothing in this case. Having lost their parents early in life, they'd grown very close indeed.

Part of Mavis admitted to stretching things, but many a fine plan had started as series of convoluted connections. Her nephew had already proven he would take stupid risks for someone he loved. By all accounts, his wife would do the same.

Concluding Talyon Keldor's life hinged on helping her son see things her way, Lady Mavis weighed various options of how to best make contact. Nearly any contact would remind Kezem that her resources were far superior to his. She did not wish to needlessly provoke him, as he was likely her best chance to gain the throne.

Eldon, her eldest son, also had the hardest and hottest head. Mitrek, her middle and most moderate son, lacked ambition. Both fell far short of Kezem's discipline and deviousness.

Mavis had been officially stripped of her royal rank by her own dearly-dead father, Salen Minstel, but he had loved her sons almost as much as his other grandsons. Mavis and her recently deceased little brother, Teorn, had never been terribly close, but he had never felt threatened enough to remove her sons from the royal records. Thus, they maintained their positions in the succession. Kezem could be king. It would be a long and not entirely pleasant road, but it was possible.

After following her thoughts down familiar, fruitless paths, Lady Mavis settled on the direct approach and activated her hologram projector. The machine blinked four times as it tried to establish the connection. Finally, Kezem's unsmiling face materialized. She had the projector set so that only his face and shoulders showed. Over the years, she had learned that facial expressions divulged the most information. She recorded calls for later reference if she needed to see the whole speaker, but the face usually told her enough.

"What do you want?" Kezem asked. His tone lacked strong emotion. He spoke unhurriedly, but his dark blue eyes had telltale yellow flecks indicating irritation.

Mavis silently thanked her long-dead husband for his Bornovan genes that made their sons so easy to read. She chuckled, as her mind flashed back to her brother asking that very question. It had ultimately led to his downfall. She fervently hoped the same would not hold true for her son.

"It is customary to exchange pleasantries before conducting business," she said.

"As you wish," Kezem said with a nod. "How are you, Mother?"

"Oh, you know me," Lady Mavis said. "I am still a little disappointed the Rangers didn't crumble quite as expected, but I am hopeful that our other endeavors will prove more successful."

"Other endeavors? I wasn't aware we had any other endeavors," Kezem said.

She laughed outright.

"Perhaps *we* do not, but I do. If I raised you right, you do as well."

"I have a lot of problems to deal with at the moment. I don't really have time for word games."

"Then I shall make my point," Mavis said graciously. "You were recently contacted about recovering Lady Merisia Restler. Help her husband find her, but I want her escort to live through the confrontation."

Kezem stayed silent a moment, trying to work through the same thought process she had moments before.

"How is the young Keldor useful to you?" he asked at last.

Locking her disappointment inside, Lady Mavis tried to console herself with the knowledge that he didn't have as much information as she did, but it didn't completely exonerate his ignorance.

"What do you know about him?" she asked, instead of answering his question.

"I don't keep files on—"

"Maybe you should," Mavis interrupted, not bothering to sweeten her tone. "Every scrap of information could be useful. I shall have Dennel send you what I know about Talyon Keldor. It should be there momentarily." She keyed in the order to Dennel, and he complied. She waited for her son to read the file.

It wasn't a big file. At sixteen, Talyon Keldor was barely a man. He had not lived long enough to generate a large file.

Lady Mavis watched in growing anticipation as her son absorbed the pertinent facts. She consciously contained her comments, wanting him to draw his own conclusions.

Kezem returned his attention to her and nodded slowly.

"I see."

"What do you see?" asked Mavis.

"You want to spare the boy to get to the queen's sister, which might be a way to get to the queen and king," Kezem summed. "It is a valid point, but I don't think it's necessary."

"Why not?" Mavis didn't argue about the royal titles. It would be official soon enough.

"They have both recently proven themselves idealistic fools taken captive by threats to complete strangers," said Kezem. "I don't think an elaborate plan will be necessary."

"Power changes people," Mavis replied. "At the time you're referring to, Terosh was merely Dulad Prince, the spare, and Reia was a Ranger. Your cousin needed to take risks to prove himself. Most Rangers are fools, but the mantle of rule does not come without direction. Sedir and Colander are sure to imprint their stuffy selves on our young monarchs."

Kezem chuckled. Then, he closed his eyes and bowed his head in a gesture of respect. When his head came up again, he said, "I still do not completely agree with your assessment, but since it is very hard to bring people back from the dead, I will heed your advice concerning the young man. Good day, Mother." With that, he cut the connection.

You will come to agree with me in time, my son.

***

Pirua (September) 29, 1538
Ashatan Council Chamber, Riden Mountains

Once again finding herself in the meeting chamber of the Ashatan Council, Ranger Knight Kiata Antellio Wellum willed her emotions to remain in check, wrestling with resentment. Most of the members arrayed before her were the same ones who had banished her sister three weeks before.

Of the Council members, only Master Hiram Alikron had perished in the attack on the compound, but the Osem masters had promptly fled home. Master Niklos McGreven had accepted a temporary position until a permanent replacement could be found or the Riden Mountains Council officially agreed to exist with only three members.

No big loss, Kiata thought bitterly of Alikron. She felt guilty for thinking ill of the dead, but Alikron had called for the trial that led to Reia's banishment.

"Do you understand the situation, Ranger Wellum?" asked Master Niklos, gently breaking into her thoughts. She couldn't think of him as Master McGreven. It sounded so impersonal.

Kiata briefly wondered why her husband wasn't here with her. There had been a lot of "situations" of late.

"What are your thoughts, Kiata?" prompted Master Jolinda Ekris.

"I'm sorry, masters. I'm not sure which situation you're refer to," Kiata admitted. "I don't know why I was summoned."

Master Liam Deliad frowned.

"Have you not heard—"

"Please, Master Deliad, these are trying times for everybody," said Master Kale Corida. "Kiata, we were discussing the situation with the royals."

How much did I miss?

Kiata commanded herself to focus. She felt like a first-year apprentice caught napping.

"What do you want me to say?" Kiata snapped, trying to keep her tone civil.

"Relations with House Minstel are understandably strained right now," Master Niklos said. "We want your honest opinion on how your sister will react."

You of all people should know how she'd react, Master Niklos.

"React?" repeated Kiata, genuinely stunned. Their implication started to sink in.

"Will she ask for our resignations?" asked Master Deliad. "Will she disband the—"

Kiata's sharp laugh cut off Master Deliad's second question.

"They are valid concerns, Ranger Wellum," said Master Ekris. "The Order's first mandate has always been the protection of the Royal House. Should the queen wish for new leadership, we would be compelled to resign."

Kiata made eye contact with each master before speaking.

"Your positions are safe," she assured them.

"How do you know?" challenged Deliad.

Feeling her jaw tighten, Kiata used one of Master Niklos's calming techniques to hold her temper.

"I know my sister, Master Deliad," said Kiata. "She is not stupid, petty, or vengeful. She knows very well what the Rangers stand for, and I doubt she even knows she possesses the power to demand change within the Order."

"I agree with your assessment of her character, but as to her knowledge, she will quickly learn the extent of her power. We should mend this relationship quickly," Master Ekris said. She looked meaningfully at Kiata.

Holding Master Ekris's gaze, Kiata bit the inside of her lower lip to keep from speaking. If they wanted her help, they would have to ask for it. She refused to offer.

Master Niklos sighed as if in her mind.

"We want you and Todd to move to Rammon."

"You want us to move?" Kiata had expected to be sent to Rammon with profound regrets, copious apologies, and solemn promises to aid the new king and queen. She had not expected the assignment to be long term.

"You would still be part of the Nareth Talis," said Master Niklos.

"We would issue you orders via comm," Master Corida added.

"The political climate has changed much in the last few years," said Master Ekris. "We have been discussing the need for more of a presence in Rammon for quite some time. We feel this is the right time and that you and Todd are the right people. Will you accept the position?"

"I will need to speak with Todd," said Kiata, hoping to put off further conversation.

"We already spoke to your husband," Master Deliad said. "He is for it."

"I would like to speak to him anyway," said Kiata.

"Of course. How much time will you require?" Master Niklos's eyes silently asked for a quick decision.

"How much time do I have?" asked Kiata.

"Can you reach a decision by tomorrow morning?" asked Master Ekris.

"I will do my best." Kiata nodded farewell and took her leave of the Ashatan Council.

***

Pirua (September) 29, 1538
Same Day
Wellum Home, Riden Mountains

Hearing the front door open, Todd Wellum stopped cleaning his kerlak pistol. Some traditionalist Rangers refused to use any weapon besides a shootav or a banistick, but Todd was practical enough to familiarize himself with any weapon he might have to face.

"What did you tell the Council?" Kiata demanded, appearing across the table from him.

Todd clamped down on a response that would rile his wife. She seemed agitated enough.

"They asked if I would be willing to move to Rammon. I told them to ask you," he said.

"Why?" she asked, almost breathless. She dodged the table and stood beside him.

Todd put the gun pieces down and wiped his hands on a rag. He avoided her gaze, but felt it burning through him anyway.

"Because I know what it would mean for *our* plans," he said as gently as possible. He finally met her eyes and emphasized the "our" so she would know that his wishes aligned with hers. He pushed his chair away from the table and held out his arms.

"We can't wait forever," said Kiata, settling herself sideways on his lap. She reached up, traced the faint scruff lining his jaw, and cupped his chin.

He turned his head and planted a kiss in her palm.

"I know," said Todd. "It's just that now doesn't seem to be the best time to ask for a break."

Kiata let her hand fall to his shoulder.

"There will never be a 'best time,' my love."

"Well, I'm sure there will be a better time than now," Todd offered.

He didn't have to list the problems the Rangers currently faced. The Restler-Tarpon Alliance had shown a considerable increase in boldness. Their attack on the Riden Mountain compound, though largely a failure, was troublesome to say the least. Reia's trial had highlighted some of the fundamental rifts in the Order, rifts that threatened to undermine crucial cohesion. The government transition provided enough of a gap for bolder criminals to expand their spheres of influence. Rangers tried to avoid politics and private affairs, but the lines blurred when those endangered members of the Royal House.

Kiata leaned forward to kiss him lightly and leaned her forehead against his.

"I'm not sure things will ever get better now that Reia is queen," said Kiata.

"Your faith in your sister is overwhelming," Todd teased.

She pulled back and shot him a dirty look.

"You know what I mean," said Kiata.

He did. Ever since the day he'd met her, Todd knew Kiata's private mission consisted of safeguarding her little sister. He couldn't blame her. He would probably feel the same way if his parents had been murdered when he was a small child. His parents were dead, but they had passed away from separate incidents of disease years apart from each other. They had given him to the Rangers as a small boy because his mother was too ill to watch over him. His father and older brother, Terik, had to work the farm. When given the choice to return home or stay, Todd had chosen a life with the Rangers.

Kiata paced, confirming Todd's suspicion that her agitation had not diminished.

"I thought things would get better when she chose the healer path. This is all Lucas's fault."

"How so?" Todd struggled to follow her logic.

"He pushed the Council to accept Reia as Prince Terosh's Kireshana guardian," Kiata said.

"I thought you were happy for her," said Todd.

"I *was* happy for her. Right up until she married the man with the biggest target on his forehead." Kiata's tone added: *How could she be so stupid?*

Todd laughed.

"He seems like a nice man."

"Tell that to the people who are going to try to kill him," Kiata muttered.

"When did you get so cynical?" asked Todd.

"When did you get so naïve?" she returned.

Todd held his hands up in mock surrender.

"Cease fire. I come in peace," he said, standing to equalize the verbal battlefield. "We have a lot of packing to do."

"You'll go?" Kiata asked. "But we haven't even discussed it yet."

He shot her a long-suffering look.

"What's to discuss?" Todd asked, spreading his arms wide. "There's trouble here," he said, waving his left hand as if presenting the problem. "There's trouble in Rammon," he said, holding out his right hand. He raised a finger like an idea had just struck him. "But the capital has the added attraction of your baby sister and her new husband. Both of whom tend to get shot at a lot. You don't particularly like that part and wish to go crack the heads of the would-be shooters. I'm going to go because someone needs to keep you out of trouble. There, wasn't that a great discussion?"

Kiata marched over to their couch, snatched up the nearest pillow, and launched it at his head. He caught it easily and fired it back.

Chapter 2:
Fugitives

Pirua (September) 29, 1538
Same Day
Tarpon Estate, City of Kalmata

"I'll wear it," said Lady Nera Tarpon. She gently eased the distasteful band from her husband's clenched fists.

"You shouldn't *have* to wear it," Brook Tarpon declared. "You've done nothing wrong." He looked like he wanted to punch his brother.

"Please calm down. This isn't going to help us," Nera said, adjusting her position so she stood between the brothers. She slipped her right hand through the metal loop she had taken from her husband and flinched when it snapped snugly into place midway up her forearm. An unnatural coolness from the band caused her heartbeats to quicken. Two small dots of light blinked yellow, transmitting her reaction to the Target Tracker-65 unit linked to her band.

"It won't be for long," Alden Tarpon offered. He sounded guilty, but his fingers were sure as they tapped commands into the TT-65. The yellow lights stopped their frantic flashing.

Nera turned and nodded to her husband's younger brother, smiling to ease his discomfort with the assignment. She could easily imagine how awkward he must feel guarding her while men hunted his sister.

Oh, Gareth, be gentle when you find them, Nera silently begged her brother.

"It's already too long," Brook complained.

Nera turned back to her husband, reached out, and patted his right arm.

"I'm all right," she assured him. She let her hand rest on his arm briefly before sliding it down to his clenched fist.

"Nothing's right. Nothing's *been* right since Merisia left. Why would she leave?" Brook's words rushed out. "She knew what this alliance means for our families."

"We don't know the whole story. My brother isn't always the easiest man to get along with." Nera curled her hand around Brook's fist.

"What do you mean? Would he hurt her?" A protective glare lit up

Brook's green eyes.

"I don't know," Nera answered honestly. "I don't think so. Gareth is volatile sometimes, but he's fiercely loyal." She left off that her brother was loyal to those he loved. She honestly didn't know where he stood with his wife.

Why would Merisia leave him?

***

Pirua (September) 29, 1538
Same Day
Gareth's and Ariman's Camp, Felmon Desert

"You're going to break your gun if you keep holding it that tightly," said Ariman Keldor to his companion.

The younger man, Gareth Restler, stared through the sniper's scope and pulled the trigger several times. Each pull produced an empty click.

"What would her face look like if I killed him?" Gareth said, clicking the trigger twice more.

The question brought up a mental image of Merisia Restler. Ariman had been the first to spot their camp and gaze upon the fugitives. The young man's wife retained her beauty despite the strain of fear. Her black hair possessed a gray tint thanks to the desert dust, but her purple eyes still had a determined glint to them. Ariman had purposefully unloaded the gun so they would never have to find out Merisia's reaction to Taly's death. Gareth seemed like a level-headed man, but Ariman didn't want to take the chance with his son's life.

"Keldor, I'm going to beat your son until he breaks," Gareth promised.

"I doubt he has useful information, but Lord … Maledek wants him alive," Keldor reminded. "I'm half-inclined to beat him myself. This is killing his mother."

"It's quite simple," Gareth said, his voice tight with anger. "Your son ran away with my wife. Tomorrow we're going to catch them. I will beat him to my satisfaction before handing him over to Maledek's agents."

Ariman listened without comment to Gareth's threats. Things didn't look good for Taly and Lady Restler. He rubbed a hand down his face, trying to focus. He had almost let Gareth know Maledek's real name. Such a mistake would have been unforgivable. The slip would have forced him to kill Gareth, and Lord Kezem and the Lady still needed the Restler-Tarpon Alliance.

"We should rest now," Keldor suggested. "Everything's set in Terab." He stifled a yawn. "I'll take the first watch."

Gareth had shown remarkable restraint so far, but Keldor did not wish to test him too much. It took about ten minutes to convince Gareth to cease his morbid vigil and sleep.

Twenty minutes into his watch, Keldor picked up the sniper rifle and sighted on his son and Lady Restler. They were too far away to hear, but they seemed to be arguing. Drawing on many years' experience, Keldor read their body language.

Several minutes later, he finally learned something useful.

He considered waking Gareth but decided against it. There was no telling how the man would react to such news.

***

Pirua (September) 29, 1538
Same Day
Merisia's and Taly's Camp, Felmon Desert

"What's wrong, Merisia?" asked Talyon Keldor. He hated having to ask, especially since he knew it would have been easier to list the few things favoring them.

Tomorrow morning, they would reach Terab and the safe anonymity of its masses. Their food and water supplies, though tight, would carry them through. They even had a friend willing to hide them for a few days. Everything else fell under the "wrong" category.

Merisia Restler pierced Taly with a long, mournful look that spoke volumes, but she said nothing.

Taly despised that look. She had leveled it at him more than once during their six-week journey, but its frequency seemed to be increasing. This was the fourth time today. The look combined apology, guilt, and heart-wrenching sadness. Taly knew she didn't mean to hurt him, but he caught her sentiments anyway.

I'm sorry I got you into this mess, very sorry. The corner of Taly's lips twitched in a weak smile. *Great, just great, now I'm even thinking like Merisia.*

"We're almost there. We'll be safe once we reach Terab," Taly encouraged.

"Thank you, Taly. Thank you for staying."

"Where else would I go? I'm a wanted man." He meant it in jest but saw that his words wounded Merisia. "It's not your fault," he added quickly.

"It is my fault," Merisia said. "It most definitely is but thank you all the same. I can always count on you to be there. I know I can, which is why I have a favor to ask you, a big favor."

"Anything," Taly said instantly. The look on Merisia's face gave him a sudden chill. He mentally cringed at the hasty promise. "You know I'm with you until the end of this."

She nodded and smiled weakly.

"I know, Taly, I know. You're not going to like my request, not one bit, but please hear me out."

Taly braced as best he could, but Merisia's next words still ripped through him.

"If—when they catch us ... I want you to kill me." Tears sprang to Merisia's eyes and flowed down her cheeks. "Please, promise to kill me."

Taly scrambled off his bedroll, rushed to Merisia, and hugged her.

"I can't do that," Taly whispered.

Merisia allowed the embrace but stiffened at his refusal. Several awkward beats passed before she relaxed in his arms. Then, she pulled away and gripped his upper arms with desperate strength.

"It's got to be this way, my friend, got to," said Merisia. "I won't go back, I won't! They can't use my child against me or my husband, never the child."

"They won't," Taly promised. "Once we reach Terab, the crowds alone will—"

A bitter laugh cut off Taly's protest. Merisia squeezed his arms once more before releasing him. Another tear worked its way down her left cheek.

"You're not blind, but you can be stubbornly stupid when you want to be. I know you saw the pursuers we picked up two hours before the moons rose."

"I saw them," Taly admitted. "But what makes you think they're after us?"

"We're not exactly the desert's swiftest travelers. We're not swift at all. They stopped when we did with an hour of good travel time left in the sun. Anybody else would have passed us."

Taly silently cursed. He had hoped to avoid worrying her with those observations. He adjusted his position on her bedroll, content to offer her physical comfort instead of the promise she sought.

***

Pirua (September) 30, 1538
Deegan Estate, City of Terab

Dread opened a chasm in Talyon Keldor's stomach a split-second before a pair of blue stun beams flew at him. Without thinking, he shoved Merisia to the ground and dropped to his knees beside her, trying to shield her. His kerlak pistol, set to high stun, dropped their hostess before she could utter a sound.

Merisia screamed and tucked her knees to her chest, trying to protect her abdomen.

Anger and fear fueled Taly. He scrambled in front of Merisia and unleashed a sheet of blue beams at their attackers. Most of his shots slammed harmlessly into the walls and ceiling but one connected with a kerlak rifle. The resulting yelp brought a smile to Taly's face as he basked in his blind luck. His knees burned, but he ignored them. His kerlak pistol emitted a buzzing whine that said the battery pack was almost depleted. He squeezed off one more shot then fumbled to grab a spare pack from his belt.

"Duck, Taly, duck!" shouted Merisia. From the sound of it, she had managed to crawl to the only meager protection in the room.

Trusting her, Taly flattened himself on the ground, landing awkwardly on his pistol. It dug painfully into his chest. A blue energy beam flew over his right shoulder and blackened a spot in front of him. He blinked, forgetting the chest pain. Part of him understood the beam had come from behind. He doubted the shot had come from Merisia. Despite his best efforts, she remained the lousiest shot—besides his mother—with twice the hatred for all weapons.

Taly rolled onto his back. More beams crisscrossed over his head, but he ignored them. He suddenly understood why his father had demanded he practice loading and unloading serlak and kerlak guns repeatedly. Putting those skills to good use, Taly snatched a new battery pack off his belt, ejected the old pack, and clipped the new one in place. Then, he adjusted the gun to semi-automatic fire so he wouldn't immediately drain the new pack.

Rolling twice then scrambling ungracefully brought him to the lone couch in the room. Unintelligible curses crowded his head at their lousy position. He had one entrance in front of him, one next to him, and one behind him. The ambush had been perfectly planned. Even if Merisia was a crack shot, they would have been hard-pressed to cover three entrances.

Sound crashed over Taly's senses. Merisia's weeping provided an odd counterpoint to the men's shouts and the sound of heavy boots pounding the ground.

Taly threw the pistol to his left hand and reached for Merisia with his right. She clutched his hand unable to speak, but her eyes pleaded her case again. Taly locked eyes with her for the briefest second. Her desperation struck him like a physical blow. He shook his head once.

The shouts and boots were closer now. Dark forms rushed toward them.

Merisia dropped his hand.

Taly shot the first three RT Alliance soldiers to enter the room before a stun beam struck his left hand. Another beam hit the back of his right shoulder as he spun with the first blow. A third slammed into the space between his shoulder blades, driving him forward and relieving him of consciousness.

Chapter 3:
The Gift

Pirua (September) 30, 1538
One Day after the Coronation
Royal Gardens, City of Rammon

Queen Reia Minstel lifted her face toward the sun, closed her eyes, and tried to dispel the sadness clinging to her like a cloak. Part of her felt she had no right to be sad.

Things were finally settling down. The isolated protests in Azhel and Idonia had ended peacefully. The previous day's coronation and Terosh's first address had gone wonderfully well. The Senate and Governors Council had finally finished wording the appropriate pieces of legislation confirming her husband as Reshner's undisputed king.

Everything was right, yet she still felt lost and lonely.

She could handle isolation. Much of her Ranger training had her trekking through the Riden Mountains in search of healing herbs. But she had a husband now and wished to see him more than once or twice a week. His duties often pulled them away from each other, but she took the pain in stride.

She could handle danger. The last year of traveling the Kireshana trail with Terosh had proven quite the learning experience. Together, they had weathered windstorms, graveground, and korvers. Surely those were comparable to wild senators and stormy governors.

Unknown expectations scared her beyond speech.

What is my role as queen?

Terosh had mentioned something about training with his former tutors, but the last few weeks had passed too quickly to spare thought for educating her in royal matters. She had suffered through one fitting and hair styling session after another, so the seamstresses and tailors could create a wardrobe fit for a queen.

Now that Reia could think, the full meaning of recent events started to coalesce in her mind. Terosh had told the people she was a Ranger and a healer, but the former title no longer fit. It had defined her for so long, yet the Ranger High Council had stripped her rank and cast her out of the Order

265

because she defied them by marrying a royal.

Lost in thought, Reia failed to sense the breach in her solitude.

***

King Terosh Minstel studied his wife from afar and felt his heart constrict with the sense of loss he saw in her.

Guilt flooded him. What kind of thoughtless, reckless wretch would knowingly chain an innocent woman to a family such as his? What made him think he would escape his family's curse? So many of his ancestors had perished before their time, he marveled that the family name had ever survived. His mother had been poisoned, his father and brother assassinated on Mitra, and his brother's secret family had perished here on Reshner.

When guilt faded, love replaced it full force. He felt its warmth sweep through him. As he watched, Reia's expression cleared, becoming less sad and more accepting. He remembered why he loved everything about her.

Suddenly, Terosh didn't know what to say. He wanted to make everything right for her. The gift held behind his back suddenly felt inadequate. The anotechs assured him of the gift's appropriateness, but he argued with himself anyway. Most women would want jewelry or flowers or sweets.

Not this woman.

Gathering his courage, Terosh straightened his shoulders and moved down the path with sure strides until he was two meters from his wife. Then, he slowed, stopped, and waited for her to notice him.

Reia stood with her face tipped toward the sun. The garden spread around her in a riot of resplendent colors and delicate shapes. Terosh had never appreciated the garden's beauty quite like this, enhanced as it was by his wife's presence. A gentle breeze rustled the flowers and played with the folds of Reia's dress and the flowing tresses of her hair. Her sad expression somehow simultaneously enhanced and marred the scene's perfection.

"If I could take away your pain, I would," Terosh whispered. The sound of his voice startled him, for he had not meant to interrupt her solitude. He rather liked observing her this way.

Reia's eyes flew open and joy replaced sorrow.

Suddenly, Terosh found his arms wrapped firmly around her. The gift clattered to the ground behind him. He didn't care. Life would be perfect if he could stop it here forever. He grunted at the force of her return embrace.

"Was I gone so long?" he asked.

For a time, Reia stayed tucked in his arms, content to prolong the moment. Finally, she pulled away with a sigh and slid her hands down his arms until she caught his hands.

"Every moment apart is forever," she said. "I never was much good at sharing."

"How good are you at accepting gifts?" asked Terosh. Before she could answer, he pulled her close and kissed her.

When the kiss finally ended, Reia smiled.

"I thought kisses were supposed to follow gift-giving."

"You're avoiding the question," Terosh said, leaning his forehead against hers.

"I'm out of practice, but I usually accept gifts graciously," said Reia.

"I want to give you lots of practice. Anything you want, it's yours," he promised.

It was the wrong thing to say.

She stiffened and stumbled back a step, looking ready to cry. Her expression flickered between anger and sorrow. Her eyes said that the thing she wanted most was beyond his power to give. He should have seen as much.

"I'm sorry," Terosh said, frantically casting about for something profound to say. "I—please don't cry. I'm no good at this. I want to fix it, make it better, but I can't. I don't know how. I'm sorry I ever—" He cut himself off. His mind went into a blind panic for several agonizing seconds.

He watched in horror as his words cut through his beloved wife.

***

—*married you,* Reia's mind finished. She felt her world collapsing. Her head felt light and unattached, ready to tumble from her shoulders.

"That's not to say that I—" Terosh babbled, stopping himself again.

Reia wanted to flee but could not pry herself away from his painful words.

Terosh took a few deep breaths before attempting to speak again.

"What I mean to say is that I'm sorry about what happened with the Rangers. They were your family, and I'm sorry they withdrew from you—from us." He closed the gap between them again and tenderly reclaimed her hands. "I love you, and I meant what I said. If I could take away your pain, I would. I … hope the gift helps you heal. Please don't ever doubt my love."

Terosh released her hands and walked back to where the gift had crashed to the ground. In seconds, he stood before her cradling a sheathed sword. Three metal clips on the hilt folded down and locked around the sheath to hold the sword in place. The markings running up and down both the sheath and the hilt were identical to those on her banistick, the weapon the Ashatan Council had wanted to destroy. Kiata had saved the weapon but nothing could change the fact that Reia could never use it again.

Breath hitching and cheeks flushing, Reia couldn't speak. After all they had been through, she had let herself doubt his love.

Uncertainty and vulnerability shone from his striking blue eyes.

"Do you like it?" asked Terosh.

For an answer, Reia gently pushed the sword aside, stood on her tiptoes, cupped his face, and kissed him.

When Terosh finally drew back so they could both draw a breath, he said, "I'll take that as an affirmative answer."

"Thank you," Reia whispered. She accepted the sword with two hands and studied the design.

"You're welcome. I … it's a symbol and a promise," Terosh said, suddenly shy.

Reia stopped looking at the sword and instead studied her husband. His outfit had a military flavor to it. A three-centimeter-wide stripe filled with silver and gold threads in alternating sections ran up each side of the black pants. The shirt was black with silver threads weaving back and forth in a tight, regular pattern. A series of three black buttons sat near the right side of his collar ready to secure his formal cape. Knowing how much he despised the cumbersome thing, she was not surprised to see him without it. His next words did surprise her.

"I want you to come to the next Governors Council meeting tomorrow morning," said Terosh. "It's smaller than the Senate, but it should give you a good introduction to our planetary politics."

"What could I possibly do?" Reia wondered. "I haven't even met with Master Sedir yet."

"Masters Sedir, Cadrish, and Colander are all eager to meet you and impart their knowledge. They have quarters here in the palace. Whenever you're ready, you can summon them."

The casual way he said it gave Reia pause.

"What if they don't want to come?" Reia asked.

"Why would they not want to come?" Terosh shot her a puzzled look.

"I will see Master Sedir this afternoon then," Reia said, dropping the subject. Terosh had been a prince his whole life. People naturally obeyed his every whim.

Terosh shook his head.

"Can't. I've scheduled a sword lesson for you with Master Colander this afternoon." He paused and cocked his head to the side as if a new thought had struck him. "You can change it, of course, but the gift is useless until you learn to use it."

Reia nodded. Everything he said made sense, but part of her felt confined by the sheer amount of order in her new life.

Not sensing her disquiet, Terosh continued, "I'm afraid you might need it."

"What happened?" Reia asked, sharpening her senses.

"Nothing yet, but Reia, we've talked about this. My family has a long history of premature deaths. More than anything in the universe, I want you to be safe." Terosh smiled that gentle, teasing smile that always lightened her mood. "And I'm well-aware that you would resent being locked in the palace for the rest of your life. The sword is my compromise."

Reia responded with a wry smile.

"If anyone gets close enough for a sword to matter, we're in serious trouble, my dear."

"Master Onro will teach you how to handle a kerlak pistol as well," Terosh said, nodding to acknowledge her point, "but hopefully, you won't have to use either of them. I've been training with weapons since childhood, but I never really used the skills until the Kireshana."

"Let's hope ruling the planet proves less *eventful* than that," said Reia.

Chapter 4:
Miscommunication

Pirua (September) 30, 1538
Same Day
Deegan Estate, City of Terab

Tears streamed down Merisia's face as she watched her dear friend fall. Taly's kerlak pistol dropped from his left hand and clattered to the ground. His body collapsed atop the weapon. Needing that gun and the end it offered, Merisia crawled to Taly and tried to reach around him.

Two stun beams struck her back and she fell forward onto Taly. An anguished cry tried to rip itself from her paralyzed body but came out as a mournful whimper. As her tears soaked Taly's back, she prayed more energy beams would finish her. Blood pounded through her skull, making her head throb. She tasted something bitter. Her breaths came in little raspy fits. She wished she had the will to stop drawing them.

Hands hauled her upright and held her while stuncuffs were applied. The minor shocks from the cuffs brought feeling back into her arms. She wanted to protest. Merisia knew there was a reason shocks would be bad, but her mind went blank with dread. The hands pulled, tugged, pushed, and prodded until her uncooperative legs carried her two steps back to the couch. She felt herself falling backwards, but the hands caught her and eased her onto the couch. Then Gareth was before her, shouting. His words made no sense, but they fell upon Merisia in waves, battering her worn nerves.

Mother appeared and argued with Gareth.

They shouted at each other.

Mother won the argument.

Gareth stormed out, taking his minions with him.

Mother knelt before Merisia. Love, concern, and anger played with Mother's expression.

Merisia wept some more.

***

Vera Tarpon wanted to nurse her anger. She needed the strength of it, but it leeched away as she gazed up at her broken daughter.

Hands resting on Merisia's knees, Vera fought the urge to embrace her. This was her youngest child and only daughter, her baby. She knew the story behind each scar. She had prayed for and rejoiced in the beautiful changes as Merisia eventually stopped chasing frogs with Taly and took up more genteel pastimes. She had waged—and lost—the battle against this arranged marriage. Now, she wondered why she failed to fight harder.

With tremendous effort, Vera wrenched her thoughts out of the past. Merisia's bleak expression spoke of much more than physical exhaustion. The hundreds of unanswered questions seemed trivial now, but Vera needed answers before Gareth took Merisia away.

Gently squeezing her daughter's right knee, Vera said, "Meri, I'm here now. Tell me what's wrong. I want to help you."

The vacant glint in Merisia's eyes told Vera her words were bouncing away harmlessly.

"Meri, focus!" said Vera, gripping Merisia's knee harder. "We haven't much time. Your husband wishes to leave soon, and he will have his way unless you give me a reason to hold you."

The silent sobs slowly abated, and Merisia's breath evened out.

"Why did you leave him?" Vera asked, fighting to keep her voice steady. "Was he rough with you? Did he hurt you?"

The second and third questions provoked stiff negative twitches from Merisia.

"Then what is wrong? Why all the tears? Why run so far for so long?" Vera bit her lip to stem the tide of questions.

Give me answers, Meri!

The silence stretched Vera's nerves near to the breaking point. Being so close to answers and meeting such resistance was worse than knowing nothing. Her eyes searched her daughter's face, hoping to see answers etched amidst the tear streaks.

Merisia sniffled, wiped at her eyes, and finally held Vera's gaze. Longing, loss, confusion, and pain radiated from her haunted eyes. Then her hands clamped down on Vera's right hand and crushed the bones together painfully.

Feeling her throat closing, Vera swallowed hard several times and tried not to wince at the discomfort of her daughter's desperate grip. Strong shocks from the stuncuffs flowed through Merisia's hands into Vera.

"You lost something," she said in a hoarse whisper.

"I lost something," Merisia repeated mechanically. She squeezed Vera's hand hard again then let go. Merisia leaned back against the couch. The movement drew more shocks from the stuncuffs.

Vera waited for her to continue, but the three words hung between them for more than a minute.

"What did you lose? Why did it drive you—" Vera cut herself off. She knew.

Merisia nodded slowly.

"It's not what you think; not all of it anyway." She sounded weary.

"Help me understand, Meri," Vera said.

"I'm so tired of running, so very tired," said Merisia. "I wish I were brave like Taly, brave enough to face this."

Vera tapped Merisia's knee urgently.

"Do *not* mention that name to your husband. Do you hear me? Taly is dead to you!"

"Dead? No, not Taly, not dead." Merisia's words poured out with childlike conviction.

"He is to you," Vera said slowly, willing the words to sink in. "Meri, regardless of Gareth's retribution you must accept the fact that Talyon Keldor does not exist in your world anymore."

More tears escaped Merisia, but she nodded.

"Tell me he's not dead, tell me. I need to know that much, need to."

"He was alive when I last saw him," Vera said.

"Please look after him, Mother, please."

"I will do what I can, Meri," Vera promised, "but this is very important. If you value his life, do not let yourself think of him. Now, tell me what you lost." Vera let an edge sharpen her request.

Merisia's face contorted as she struggled for words.

"A child, Mother, I lost a child."

***

Pirua (September) 30, 1538
Same Day
Deegan Estate, City of Terab

They've talked long enough.

As the thought crystallized in Gareth Restler's head, he motioned his two hand-picked men to follow him. He had as much of a right to speak with Merisia as that meddlesome Tarpon woman. At least Ariman Keldor had agreed to wait with Talyon. He almost wished the man would do something stupid like try to escape with his son.

Gareth marched into the room where he had left his wife with her mother. He paused in the doorway. Merisia looked awful. Her eyes were puffy from crying and her dark hair was a mess. His anger slipped. Narrowing his eyes, Gareth looked to his men and nodded curtly.

Adrik Bentanner and Einer Akurin immediately moved to carry out his silent orders. Adrik moved to Vera Tarpon's left side, and Einer took a position to her right side. Each man grasped an arm and gently but firmly pulled her up, so they could escort her out.

She protested loudly, but Gareth ignored her.

He was too busy trying to figure out what to say to Merisia. His entire planned speech escaped him. Despite their marriage being arranged and the massive trouble this merry chase had caused him, he still loved her. Her odd way of phrasing things could be annoying, but he often found it charming.

Not knowing what else to do, Gareth knelt in front of Merisia, taking the space her mother had occupied.

While he was still searching for words, she asked, "Where's Taly? Where is he?"

Gareth's sympathy vanished.

"Dead," he answered coldly. "I figured it was personal since he ran off with my wife, so I stuck a dagger in him." The lie came easily, but the pain filling Merisia's face struck him as well. He twisted the pain back into anger.

She wept, and he hated her for it.

"He lives," Gareth spat, pouring his contempt into the two words. "How long he lives depends on how you answer my next question. How long did it go on, Merisia?"

She looked startled then offended.

"You're jealous."

It took much willpower to not reach out and shake her.

Merisia blinked back tears and laughed bitterly.

"I don't believe it; I just don't. Gareth, this has nothing to do with Taly, nothing."

"How can you say that?" Gareth demanded. "Merisia, you ran away with that boy."

"No, Gareth, no. He helped *me* run away!" Merisia raised her bound hands. "Can't you see the difference, the big difference?"

Gareth got to his feet, forcing her to sit back and look up at him.

"No, I don't see the difference. Why would you want to leave me?" Gareth tried to hide his hurt but didn't quite manage it.

Merisia's gaze hardened.

"Kia Meetcher."

The name sounded familiar, but it took a moment for Gareth's mind to locate the image of a small, angry child brought to his house.

"What does the Meetcher kid have to do with—"

"They took her away, Gareth, away from her family." Merisia sounded close to tears again.

Gareth hoped she held them in. The tears tugged at his spirits. His glare demanded she explain.

"Don't you see? I didn't want that to happen to our baby. They would do it; you know they would," said Merisia.

Gareth's mind vainly tried processing the news. Shock and unbridled joy threatened to make him mute. He fought the feelings.

"Who would dare interfere with our child?"

"The Alliance," Merisia spat.

Her vehemence slapped Gareth.

"But it doesn't matter now, doesn't matter," she added in a dreamy tone.

"What doesn't matter?" asked Gareth.

"Nothing matters, nothing. The child is dead." The words seemed to suck the life out of her.

"What do you mean? How?"

"Nothing matters now," Merisia repeated.

Try as he might, Gareth could not coax another word from her.

***

Pirua (September) 30, 1538
Same Day
Guest Quarters, Deegan Estate, City of Terab

Angela Deegan moved gingerly, still stiff from Talyon Keldor's stun beam. She dipped the soft cloth in the warm water basin and wiped more blood from the boy's face.

"Will he live?" inquired Lady Vera Tarpon. She stood at the threshold flanked by two RT Alliance men.

Angela couldn't tell whether the men were there to protect Lady Tarpon or prevent her from interfering.

"He'll be fine," said Angela.

Having finally removed the blood from the young man's face, she lifted his shirt and started on the blue-black, sometimes red masses of abused flesh on his chest and stomach.

The patient moaned.

How did this happen?

Angela meant more by the question than merely how the boy had come by his injuries. She knew that part very well. Everything else was a mess in her head. At first, she had been thrilled to hear from her childhood friend, but Merisia's call had been immediately followed by representatives of the RT Alliance under Gareth Restler's orders. Lacking time to prepare a proper lie, the Alliance people had quickly gotten the truth from her. She hated the cowardice that drove her to betray her friend, and she hated the Alliance for their poorly veiled threats against her family.

Anger made her absently clean harder, drawing a louder groan from the boy. His pain suddenly reached out and seized her. She dropped the cloth and burst into tears. She cried for him, herself, Merisia, and because she was tired of holding the fear inside. More than a few tears were shed in relief that she had sent Ronnie and Rachelle to her sister's house for the week. A gentle hand landed on her shoulder. Instinctively, she turned and embraced the woman offering comfort.

***

Vera Tarpon let the younger woman cry, wishing it was Merisia. When the sobs subsided, she gently extricated herself from Angela's grasp and looked at Taly. Gareth and his men had been very thorough in administering their own brand of justice. Picking up the cloth Angela had abandoned, Vera continued the cleaning process, aware of her two shadows.

"I need some fresh water," Vera said, directing the comment to Adrik and Einer.

"That can wait," said Gareth Restler.

Vera leveled a contemptuous gaze at her daughter's husband.

"He needs care now, not questions," she insisted.

"He needs to record a message now. This cannot wait," said Gareth. "You can leave peacefully, or my men will escort you out. They will fetch you back when we're finish with him."

Vera stood reluctantly.

"May I see my daughter?" asked Vera.

"Yes, but I need you to deliver a message for me," Gareth said.

Vera inclined her head in acknowledgement.

"Tell her he died."

Chapter 5:
Urgent Request

Pirua (September) 30, 1538
Same Day
East Weapons Training Room, Royal Palace, City of Rammon

Terosh Minstel stretched his neck, trying to work out Senate-induced stiffness. As far as he knew, they had accomplished nothing in the three-hour morning session. He had begged off the afternoon session, leaving Miles Cadrish behind to take notes. His former speech and language tutor, recently promoted to advisor, had been less than enthusiastic, but Terosh knew he would acquit himself well.

Part of him felt like a stalker. Once again, he found himself standing out of the way simply watching his wife. Drenched in sweat and clad only in a plain exercise outfit, she looked perfect. Despite a slightly finer cut, the brown pants and white shirt reminded him of her Ranger attire. Reia had worn a similar ensemble practically every day for as long as he had known her. It surprised him to realize the days of their acquaintance numbered less than a year. The fierce concentration in her eyes and the determined set to her jaw reminded Terosh of their first meeting.

A sense of peace came over him, followed closely by a longing to participate in the sword lessons. During the Kireshana, he had taught Reia how to handle a kerlinblade, and she in turn taught him how to fight with a banistick. Though he had given her what skills he could, Terosh accepted his limits as an instructor. It helped to know she would be in capable hands.

The weapons master, Victor Colander, alternately encouraged and corrected Reia, skillfully pushing his new student to her perceived limits and then slightly beyond. He fought with a blue kerlinblade set wide and flat.

For an irrational moment, Terosh worried his gift would be destroyed by the kerlinblade. Then he remembered the craftsman's claim that it would handle almost any substance created. The man had refused to reveal his secret formula, but Terosh guessed it was an alloy of tosh, iron, and compressed carbon.

The kerlinblade and sword met several times in quick succession. Each time they met, Colander's blade changed color. From blue the blade

turned indigo then to violet. Terosh squinted against the glare of the rapidly changing colors, a force of habit more
than a necessity. The anotechs automatically adjusted to the glare for him.

Colander spun away, giving Reia a brief respite, and touched the control panel on the bottom of the kerlinblade. The blade blazed with blinding white fury. He attacked with renewed fervor, slashing high and low, left and right, seemingly everywhere at once.

Reia worked frantically to deflect the strikes, but twice she had to leap back, slowly surrendering ground.

Colander drew another kerlinblade from his belt and activated it to a short setting. The green blade extended to a length slightly longer than a dagger. While the full kerlinblade kept Reia's sword busy, Colander took a few probing stabs at her undefended side.

Terosh could tell Reia didn't know how to adjust to the new threat. She ducked and dodged more and more of Colander's strikes, giving up more ground but being careful to avoid corners. Terosh watched the duel with interest, knowing that Colander could win whenever he wished.

"I'm sorry to disturb you, Highness," said a female messenger. "There is an urgent communication for you in the Comm Chamber. It's from off-planet."

Resenting the intrusion but determined to be civil, Terosh frowned at the messenger.

"I thought the interplanetary communications array was being repaired," he said.

"That is correct, my Lord. This is a new array," explained the woman. She spoke clearly and quickly. Her accent and light brown skin hinted at a Terabian background. "It arrived with the cargo ship, *Dicey*, last night. Security scanned it carefully and cleared it, so the tech crew installed the basic elements this morning. It's not complete, but it can accept the call. Captain Darrow tried your personal comm but failed to reach you. He sent me to deliver a request for your presence."

With one last look toward Reia and Colander, Terosh followed the messenger out of the training room. It bothered him that he couldn't remember the messenger's name.

Lelianna Rivers, supplied the anotechs. **Daughter of Governor Edeline Pallav *and her consort Brendan Calik, wife of Simon Rivers, a native of Terab. Would you like a more thorough background?***

Terosh declined, still a little unnerved at sharing thoughts with the anotechs. He considered asking who the message was from but settled for following the messenger. Lelianna set a brisk pace, faster than a normal walk but not quite undignified. Terosh knew exactly where they were going. He could have made it there on his own. He spared a wistful thought for the bygone days of unsupervised leisure. As king, he would have to get used to escorts.

Captain Ivan Darrow stood at attention just outside the door to the Central Communications Chamber. He greeted Terosh with a low bow.

"Thank you for coming so quickly, Highness," said Captain Darrow. "I hesitated to interrupt you, but the caller would not be deflected. She awaits you in pod three."

"It's fine, Captain," Terosh said, acknowledging the man with a nod. He entered the main chamber and walked toward pod three.

Before he reached it, a new male voice said, "Highness, I must protest. There could still be unknown danger from the array."

Terosh stopped and faced Aster Captain Surd Antar of the Royal Guard.

"Your concerns are noted, Captain Antar, but your men already cleared it. I'm sure it's perfectly safe." Despite his words, Terosh sent anotechs into pod three to verify that the new equipment was free of traps. "It would be ill-mannered to not use such an expensive gift."

Antar bowed, but his expression remained querulous.

"As you wish, my Lord, but expensive gifts always have their price."

The anotechs returned with a clean report for the equipment.

Suddenly nervous, Terosh keyed in a code to unlock pod three and stepped into the cool, sterile air inside the pod. A brand-new interplanetary communications array lay before him. It was surprisingly small for such a powerful piece of equipment. The sleek, silver box sported a dozen or so buttons, a few knobs, and a standard keyboard. The anotechs regarded it with disdain, but Terosh ignored them. They were snobbish when it came to other technology.

The holoprojector and receiver display took up most of the small room. Terosh moved to a position where the vidrecorder could capture his image and activated the projector.

The woman who appeared made appropriate gestures acknowledging his rank. Her skin possessed a slightly blue tint and her forehead bore an intricate tattoo. The pattern seemed to change with every movement of her head. Her posture and bearing said she had formal training as both a fighter and a diplomat.

"Greetings. I am told you have an urgent request for me," said Terosh.

"It is so. I am Ashel Privim, Voice for King Padric of House Creston, ruler of Gardan and its two moon colonies. Please confirm your lineage. My master has a private matter for the remnants of House Minstel." The woman's voice flowed like an unhurried stream.

Terosh paused to consider the request, wondering how they would confirm his lineage.

Voice pattern analysis, said the anotechs.

"I am Terosh, son of Teorn and Kila Creston Minstel, brother of the late Taytron Minstel, currently the last of my bloodline." A chill ran through him at the last part. The knowledge was nothing new to him, but speaking the words aloud made them more real.

Ashel's eyes flickered away from him, presumably to check a display he could not see. When her attention came back to him, she said, "Identity accepted. Await transfer."

She disappeared before Terosh could offer his thanks.

A distinguished man with icy blue eyes appeared and leveled a penetrating gaze at Terosh. Short gray and blond hair mingled freely on the man's head. Everything from the arrogant tilt of his chin to the haughty, demanding glint in his eyes declared him a man used to immediate and complete obedience.

The few times Terosh had seen this man he had both literally and figuratively hidden behind his mother. He drew on years of rigorous diplomatic training to keep from recoiling from the display.

"Have you no greeting for family, boy?" asked King Padric Creston.

"Hello, grandfather," Terosh said awkwardly.

What does he want?

To Terosh's knowledge, Padric Creston had never made a simple social call. If he contacted Terosh's mother, it was to demand something of her. She had hated it, though she said nothing of her feelings to Terosh.

King Padric laughed harshly.

"It will have to do. I see you lack your mother's oratory skills, so I will speak plainly. I want my daughter's killer delivered to me immediately."

Terosh vaguely recalled reading a report detailing the capture of Niktrod Keldor, the assassin accused of poisoning Terosh's mother. The man was slated to be delivered to Gardan, but Terosh could not remember if the transfer had occurred. The current conversation indicated no transfer.

"I will look into it, Your Grace," said Terosh.

"I will accept nothing less than complete compliance with this request, boy," said King Padric.

Anger spiked inside Terosh, but he managed to keep his expression neutral.

"You have my word, sir. I will investigate the matter. If I find the prisoner has not yet been delivered, I will hasten to rectify the situation."

King Padric was silent a moment, but his eyes slowly swept every part of Terosh's face.

"So be it. That is the first matter I wished to discuss with you. The second matter is your wife."

Terosh blinked, again calling upon his training to resist reacting physically. His defensive instincts flared.

"I apologize, but I fail to understand what my wife has to do with our discussion."

His grandfather gave him a pitying look.

"I understand you took her before becoming king, but your sudden ascension changes things."

"How?"

"She is a commoner. You are a king," said King Padric.

"She is my wife, that makes her queen," Terosh retorted.

"I would agree with you, if Reshner were just another Edge Planet with no political potential, but its fate is tied to Gardan and it holds secrets that could compromise the balance."

"What are you talking about?" Terosh asked.

"If I knew the secrets, I would conquer Reshner myself," King Padric said, sounding amused. "I do not know them, but I am adequately convinced of their importance. Long ago, I promised to do what I could to safeguard Reshner. The planet should not even be habitable. The Galactic Alliance of Populated Planets will not take you seriously as king until you ally with your betters. You may not think it, boy, but I say this for your own good."

"My own good?" Terosh echoed. "How do you suggest I fix this terrible situation I've gotten myself into, grandfather?"

Ignoring the sarcasm, King Padric answered, "The simplest solution would be to annul the marriage, but since I doubt you would consider such simplicity, I will offer a second solution. Bring her to me."

"What?" Terosh wished he had something more intelligent to say, but it captured the essence of his confusion.

"Your wife is an orphan, according to my reports. If she became part of my family, it would reinforce the alliance between Gardan and Reshner," King Padric explained. "I'm sure I have a child willing to take her."

"Why should we care about this alliance?" Terosh asked, knowing it was a stupid question.

King Padric gave Terosh a feral smile.

"You should care because it is one of the only things keeping both our planets off GAPP's list of ripe targets. Our own alliance has suffered for several years now. One of your people killed my daughter on your soil. In GAPP's eyes, the alliance no longer exists. My insistence on bringing your mother's killer to Gardan for justice is to re-establish our alliance."

Terosh despised the fact that his grandfather had a point.

"Why would my wife have to come to you?"

Assuming she'll even agree to this madness.

"Adoptions can be started across planets, but to make it official, she will need to spend a year here."

The news hit Terosh hard, leaving him dazed. He said hasty farewells and turned the machine off. Then, he sank down onto the chair to think.

Every option seemed terrible.

Chapter 6:
New Opportunities

Pirua (September) 30, 1538
Same Day
The Lady's Estate, Kala Mountains

Slapping the vidscreen controls, Lady Mavis Altran froze the image at a split view of her nephew and the hologram of Gardan's infamous king. It had cost her dearly to arrange vidrecorders for each communication pod in the Royal Palace, but her foresight finally paid off. The two faces, though strikingly alike around the eyes and mouth, showed such a difference in disposition that Mavis could only chuckle.

Poor Terosh. The throne may cost you more than you can imagine.

The boy looked so incredibly lost that one would think he had just received news of his beloved wife's death, not a threat veiled as a favor. It was most certainly a threat, but the details and motives escaped Mavis. She let her gaze linger on Terosh a second longer then enlarged the image of King Padric Creston so that it covered the whole screen.

There is the face of power, thought Mavis, hoping her own features never showed such harsh markings. Even now, she felt her heart flutter with fear. This was the face that drove her from the palace, seeking safety in a hasty marriage.

As the third of four children, Mavis had always excelled at being unobtrusive. Her skills at judging character had almost failed her at the time. She had been drawn to the alluring power of Gardan's king. Only a series of fortunate—and unfortunate—events had spared her from becoming a pretty bauble mounted in Padric Creston's crown, officially married to one of his handsome sons yet ultimately a political game piece to be played at will.

Forcing herself to stare into his face, Mavis confronted the rising sense of unease. She soothed her mind by concentrating on the many questions the conversation raised. Why did Creston want Queen Kila's assassin? Simple revenge seemed a flimsy reason to bother with the details involved in claiming him. Why this sudden interest in renewing the treaty built through her little brother anyway? Did Creston truly want the new queen or was she merely a target of convenience?

Seemingly unrelated reports of random disappearances sprang to the forefront of Mavis's mind. Individually, they had meant nothing, but she had long ago learned to trust such instincts. The motive was so obvious as to be laughable. Creston had said it aloud to Terosh: he wanted the secret to the anotechs. He had probably already brokered a deal with GAPP, selling Reshner for Gardan's peace.

Her unique position offered several choices. Mavis could do nothing and wait for things to unfold. She could warn Terosh, risking valuable sources in the process, or she could send a subtler warning. Those were the easy options. The others required much more elaborate involvement. Higher risks also meant higher rewards. Ironically, she and Creston both sought stability for their planets.

Slowly, a plan formed. Mavis would need to earn Creston's trust. A few changes to previously laid plans should accomplish the task. After seriously weighing the consequences, she decided to embrace the new plan. Summoning her faithful servant, Dennel, Mavis dispatched him to research everything official and unofficial known about Gardan.

***

Pirua (September) 30, 1538
Same Day
Deegan Estate, City of Terab

With an odd mixture of relief and fear, Ariman Keldor watched his new orders appear on his private infopad. The Lady rarely risked such direct communication. That she did so now reinforced the sense of urgency.

This will endanger Taly.

He dismissed the thought. Leaving Taly with Gareth Restler was also hazardous. The man kept his emotions under tight control, but Keldor sensed the deadly hatred. He doubted Maledek's order to keep Taly alive would last much longer in Gareth's mind. Keldor continued reading and felt his heart seize at the blind trust he would need to place in complete strangers.

Draw the Rangers' attention and record their every move when they rescue Talyon.

Keldor wondered how the Lady could predict the movements of others so well. Could he trust Taly's life to her? Though he had never met her in person, she knew him better than his own wife. Her ability to bend him to her will made her dangerous, but in this case, their desires aligned.

Committing himself to the new orders, Keldor turned his attention to the details. The Rangers would sense a trap if he gave them too much information but withholding information could hinder their efforts.

***

Pirua (September) 30, 1538
Same Day
Maledek's Private Retreat, City of Idonia

Lord Kezem mulled over his mother's message about changing the situation in Terab. He did not delude himself into thinking he could alter her mind, but he desired clarity. Modifying plans so late could be dangerous. Something drastic must have prompted her to take the risk. Irritated at having to

281

constantly turn to her, he indulged in some brief, murderous thoughts. Her hologram appeared almost instantly, indicating that she had expected his call.

"Trust me," said his mother without greeting.

"What changes have you ordered?" Kezem demanded.

"If I thought you needed to know, I would inform you, my dear."

Kezem narrowed his eyes.

"How am I to know what orders to issue, if I don't know what will happen?"

His mother gave him a penetrating gaze, and her next words surprised him.

"You are still my best hope for regaining the throne, my son, but Terosh is no longer our only enemy. I have been blind to another threat for longer than I care to admit. These changes are in hopes of rectifying that lapse. Whatever happens in Terab can be turned to our advantage. Let things play as they will. Your men know their parts."

"Are they still *my* men?" Kezem asked. His voice shook with suppressed rage.

"They are yours as long as you can control them," his mother replied. "Study the information I am having Dennel send you. It may ease your mind. I have a personal messenger standing by to deliver a vid if you can get one on short notice."

***

Kest (October) 1, 1538
Wellum's New Home, East Quarter, City of Rammon

Hearing a faint knock, Todd Wellum cautiously opened the door and found nothing. A split-second later he spotted the small, cylindrical comm unit lying on the ground, and his ears picked up frantic footfalls to his left. He considered whether to go for the comm or the mystery person and decided on the chase. With a mental apology to his wife, Todd leapt over the comm and sprinted down the street. He achieved his top speed quickly, grateful to finally be doing something besides moving boxes and furniture.

This wasn't what I meant when I said I wanted to see the city.

He was almost disappointed when he caught the fleeing boy after only two blocks.

The child screamed and dove to the ground to evade Todd for one more second.

Todd plucked him from the air midway to the ground, pinned his arms in place, and forced him to his knees so he couldn't kick.

"Calm down!" Todd ordered.

"Unhand that boy!" shouted a woman from a nearby doorway.

Todd twisted toward her, so he could watch for any new threats.

Screaming again, the boy wriggled furiously, trying to break free.

"Let him go, or I'll call the police and the Royal Guards," the lady threatened.

"Calm down," Todd again told the boy. He emphasized the order by squeezing a pressure point in the boy's upper arm. "You can go as soon as you answer a few questions."

"I didn't do anything!" the boy cried.

Todd flicked his attention back to the woman as a kerlak pistol leveled his way. Grunting his annoyance, he turned his back to the woman to protect the boy. "You don't need a gun, ma'am," Todd assured the woman. Turning his head, he kept his right eye trained on the woman. A flicker of movement caught his attention.

"Let me go," whined the boy.

"I told you the terms," Todd reminded his captive. "You go free when I get answers."

"Who gave you the comm you left on our doorway?" asked Kiata Wellum.

Todd craned his neck around and saw his wife calmly standing next to the dumbfounded, weaponless woman. The kerlak pistol was in Kiata's left hand. Her right hand held her banistick in a guarded, semi-threatening position. The question was directed at the boy, but Kiata's attention stayed on the woman.

"I don't know," said the boy, suddenly sullen.

"Who are you?" asked the woman, her voice a little awed.

Kiata returned her banistick to her belt in one smooth motion before removing the kerlak pistol's battery pack and presenting the two pieces to the woman.

"Just new neighbors," Kiata answered. "Sorry for the misunderstanding, Lady …"

"Channer," supplied the woman. "Elise Channer, cloth merchant."

"Was it a man or a woman? You must have gotten paid somehow," Todd pressed the kid. He hauled the boy to his feet and turned him around, keeping both hands on the child's shoulders to prevent escape.

The boy's dark eyes glared at Todd.

"Another messenger," he answered finally. He shrugged. "It happens all the time in the East Quarter. It's why I like working here."

"We should go," Kiata said. "He knows nothing more." She directed the words at Todd before smiling at the woman. "It was nice to meet you, Lady Channer."

***

When they got back home, Kiata set the comm on the kitchen table and checked it for traps. Finding none, she hit play and listened as Talyon Keldor's voice floated out of the tiny speaker.

"Ranger Wellum, you once saved my life, and now I want to return the favor. Meet me at moonrise on the tenth of Kest (October) where the firfe spice burned all those years ago."

"What do you think?" Todd asked.

Without answering, Kiata reviewed the short message another four times while pacing the kitchen. Still thinking, she reached up into a cabinet and retrieved two glasses. By the time she set them on the table, Todd had found the appola juice. He poured the juice as she settled into one of the chairs.

Kiata noted that they seemed to be having a lot of meetings at their lonely kitchen table.

"Taly's in trouble," she replied, finally answering Todd's question.

"Agreed." Todd slid one of the glasses over to her. "But why the sudden interest in you? It's obviously a trap."

Kiata caught the glass, nodded thanks, and lifted the drink to her lips. After taking a sip, she asked, "Did they get caught? There's no mention of Merisia. That's ... troubling." She did not wish to discuss the reasons why she might suddenly draw interest from the wrong sorts of people. The obvious answer was her link to Reia, but that opened a line to many more questions. She wanted to focus on Taly.

"I hope they're safe," Todd said. His tone said he shared her doubts about that. "They seem like nice kids."

Kiata chuckled and drank more of the juice.

"They're not that much younger than us," said Kiata.

"Merisia maybe, but Taly's what? Fifteen? Sixteen?"

Kiata smiled gently at her husband.

"He's probably sixteen or seventeen. That's only five or six year's difference."

"Really? This business must age us." Todd studied his drink for a second then drank the whole thing in one shot.

"Must be all the high-speed chases involving messenger boys," Kiata teased.

"Or the disarming of little old ladies," Todd added.

"All in a day's work," said Kiata. She raised her glass toward Todd and drained the rest of the juice. Setting the glass down, she added, "Unfortunately, there's also this aspect." She picked up the comm and let the message play again.

Todd listened with his eyes closed.

"He tried to warn you," he said, when the message stopped. "His voice trails off when he speaks of the favor and then it starts up again strong. He sounds nervous, too."

"Either he's afraid of being caught or he's being forced to record the message against his will," said Kiata. "It doesn't really matter which. The key question is: what do we do about it?"

"Are you up for a trip to Kerimia for old time's sake?" asked Todd.

Sliding her empty glass back and forth between her hands, Kiata considered Todd's question.

It would be the simplest answer, she mused, but she knew better than most how complicated the simplest answers could be sometimes. She shook her head slowly then turned it into a sort of half-nod.

"We need to find Taly and Merisia," said Kiata.

Todd sat up straighter, his playful expression gone.

"What about your sister?" asked Todd.

"What about her? She's been safe without me these past few weeks.

She should be fine for another week and a half, but I'll see her before we leave. We are technically assigned to her. At least we will be soon."

"A week and a half isn't much time. They've been gone for a long time." Todd sat back and ran both hands through his thick red hair.

"We need to think like them," said Kiata. "I don't believe Merisia's the sort to rough it too long in the wilderness. She seemed ill the last time we saw her. That narrows the search down to cities, but we don't have time to search each one."

"We should tell Master Niklos," said Todd. "Perhaps he can help us find them. And Nils, of course, we'll have to tell him."

Kiata felt the first inklings of excitement and the nervous energy that began every mission.

"We should speak with Nils first. He would have the best insights into the RT Alliance, and they have the most reasons to want Taly and Merisia."

Todd nodded agreement and flipped his empty glass up in the air.

Kiata winced as her good glass went sailing through the air end over end. Todd caught it easily, laughing at her expression. She was tempted to throw her own glass at him but knew it would be useless.

Thankfully, Nils arrived from his surveillance assignment.

Chapter 7:
Night Visitors

Kest (October) 1, 1538
Same Day
Queen Reia's Private Chambers, Royal Palace, City of Rammon

Moonlight streamed in from the large, open windows. Kiata Antellio Wellum pressed her back against one side of the window she perched on, trying to keep from blocking the light. An odd mixture of relief and irritation battled within her as she watched her sister sleep fitfully. A fine sheen of sweat glistened on Reia's brow. A breeze blew past Kiata and caused Reia's sleeping form to shiver.

Kiata leaned her head back against the window frame, sighed, and pondered her next move. Breaking into the palace, though not easy, should not have been possible. The imposing palace walls enclosing the gardens took less than a minute to scale. The expansive gardens provided nice cover the entire way to the palace itself. Kiata had narrowly avoided several Palace Security and Royal Guard patrols on her ascent to Reia's private suite of rooms. Had she been a real assassin, Reia would be dead.

She could call out to her sister, but Reia wasn't exactly the easiest—or quietest—person to wake. The nightmares usually kept a strong grip on Reia, but occasionally, they released her suddenly, waking her with a full adrenaline rush. Master Ekris had once confessed to Kiata such sleep patterns were quite unnatural and very worrisome.

As usual, Kiata settled upon the direct approach. Still conscious to stay out of the moonlight, she ducked, crept around the bed, and cautiously climbed up.

Reia tossed her head violently and rolled onto her left shoulder.

Kiata froze and waited for Reia to roll away from her. She could have made her move at any time, but she wanted to wait for the best angle. Crouching on the edge of Reia's bed, she silently willed her sister to move again.

A few minutes later, Reia finally settled onto her back again. Quick as a striking snake, Kiata slapped her left hand over Reia's mouth, used her free hand to grip Reia's upper left arm, and leaned close.

Tucking her mouth next to Reia's ear, Kiata whispered.

"Chalmd. Ceme." (Calm down. It's me.) She didn't bother speaking the Kalastan words backwards, as was her custom with her sister. Reia's sleepy brain would have enough trouble absorbing the quiet words through the trauma of waking. Kiata patiently waited out the seconds of blind panic, throwing her weight into pinning her sister down. "Neskrimda. Ehcamemastas," she said lightly, when Reia's struggles abated. (Please don't scream. It would cause me much trouble.)

When Reia stopped thrashing, Kiata cautiously released her sister's mouth so she could speak.

"Kiata," Reia whispered, sounding like she was trying to believe it.

Kiata eased her grip on Reia's arm and spoke softly.

"Tuisola. Dimesunarethdrims." (We are alone. Tell me your nightmares.)

"You were in Kerimia," Reia answered. She sat up carefully and arranged the blankets around her knees.

Kiata's lips pressed together but she said nothing right away. It was one of four dreams that haunted Reia night after night. The first dream featured their parents' murder. If one wanted to get technical, the dream featured the murder of Kiata's parents and Reia's adoptive parents, but the distinction had never made a difference to Kiata. Although practically an infant at that time, Reia remembered the event far more vividly than Kiata who had been four. The second dream forced Reia to relive the criessa training, complete with the cold terror of being abandoned by Master Kolknir in a mountain cave. The third dream consisted of endless fights against korvers, bears, lions, and other mountain creatures.

This was the fourth dream where Reia experienced everything that had happened to Kiata on her level-seven trial in the village of Kerimia. Kiata had been captured and beaten with her own weapon until a viper had bitten Talyon Keldor. Then, the boy's father had spared her in exchange for saving his son.

"I'm sorry. You shouldn't even have those memories," Kiata said finally.

Reia shrugged, wincing with the movement.

"I'll let you know when I learn to block them. Was there something specific you wanted?"

***

Reia knew her sister meant well but talking about the nightmares only reinforced their hold on her.

Kiata touched the bottom of Reia's chin in a motherly gesture.

"What happened? You're moving like someone who wrestled a goritor."

"Just stiff from sword training," Reia admitted. "How was your day?"

Kiata tweaked Reia's chin and let her hand drop.

"All right, we'll talk about something else besides bad dreams and sword training if you want, but I'm here if you need me."

"I know."

"Contrary to that statement, Todd and I are leaving Rammon for a few days. Taly's in trouble and probably Merisia as well. We need to find them." Kiata shifted her knees to a more comfortable position.

"How do you know? Where will you look for them? Why are you telling me?" The thoughts flowed out of Reia in rapid succession.

"We received a message from Taly earlier this evening. Nils thinks there's a good chance they went to Terab. Todd is contacting Ranger Zinn now. Hopefully, he'll have something more specific by the time I get home, and I'm telling you because we've been assigned to Rammon."

Clarity crashed over Reia.

"You're asking my permission," she said, stunned.

"Precisely, Highness," said Kiata, grinning. "Nils will be around if you need to contact us. We won't be gone long. If we find nothing, the message said to meet Taly in Kerimia on the tenth of this month."

"What if I refused to let you go?" Reia knew she wouldn't, but she wanted to hear Kiata's answer.

"I'd be tempted to kidnap you myself," Kiata replied. "In actuality, I would probably just ignore you. We don't have official orders from the Council. They gave us until the seventh of this month to move, but Todd and I didn't have much to move."

Reia detected a hint of sadness in Kiata's last statement, but it disappeared before she could confirm it. A wave of tiredness swept over her as the last of the adrenaline rush disappeared. She blinked.

"Why didn't you wait until morning?"

Kiata's grin widened and she shook her head.

"You have no idea what you've gotten yourself into, do you?" she asked.

"Do you?" Reia challenged.

Chuckling, Kiata picked up Reia's right hand and began massaging it.

"Your life is no longer your own. You'll be admired by many, hated by many, and probably misunderstood by everybody."

"You make it sound so glamorous," Reia said.

Kiata stopped massaging Reia's hand and patted it affectionately.

"It will fall to Todd, me, and Rangers you'll never see to make sure you and King Terosh have a long, boring reign," said Kiata. "I chose this method of entry because I wanted to see you tonight, and I wanted to test the palace security, which could stand for some improvements."

"Terosh is not going to be pleased by that news," said Reia.

"Why isn't he here? Is everything all right?" asked Kiata.

"He needs his rest. My nightmares aren't exactly conducive to sharing a bed," Reia answered.

"That I remember vividly," Kiata commented, no doubt recalling the bruises earned through years of easing Reia's nightmares.

"Besides, this is how the royal quarters have been arranged for decades."

"Reia." Kiata said it with equal measures of gentle reproof, amusement, and pity. "You are queen."

"Yes, I know—oh." Her sister's meaning slammed into her. She drew a breath and tried to explain. "People here don't really like change."

"Very few people in the universe like change," said Kiata. "It's hard, but sometimes it's also right. I'm not saying your sleeping arrangements should change. I'm saying you need to choose your battles wisely."

"What battles?" Reia asked, stifling a yawn.

Her sister's wry expression asked: *how did such a sweet thing like you make it so long in this world?*

"You should try to get some sleep soon but be careful," said Kiata. "People are going to want to change everything about you. They're going to redefine your looks, speech patterns, and ideals. I know you must let them mold you into a queen, but don't forget who you are deep down." A playful grin added: *you're my kid sister.*

"What am I?" asked Reia.

Kiata got up, went to the window nearest the bed, and climbed on the windowsill.

"We'll find out soon enough," she said, before vanishing out the window.

***

Kest (October) 1, 1538
Same Day
King Terosh's Private Chambers, Royal Palace, City of Rammon

Terosh knew he should be asleep, but he could not stop thinking. His grandfather's statements still bothered him. He understood the need for vengeance against Niktrod Keldor, but the part about Reia baffled him.

Growing up, Terosh had slipped into Tate's room or gone down to Master Sedir's chambers on the third floor when sleep eluded him. Kaimon Sedir always received him warmly.

With inexplicable rising fear, Terosh dressed and eased open the door leading out of his private rooms. He looked carefully left and right before realizing the ridiculousness of his caution. Nobody would scold him. He could go wherever he wanted no matter what the hour. Straightening out of sneak mode, Terosh walked down the long hallway to the East stairwell. His first few steps were tentative, but the strangeness of taking the main stairs gradually wore off.

About seven minutes later, Terosh arrived at Sedir's quarters. He reached up to knock.

Sedir swung the door open before Terosh's knuckles could brush the door.

"Enter to find the answers you seek, Your Grace," said Master Sedir.

Terosh smiled, trying to recall how long ago he had first dared to come here.

"How did you know I was coming?" he asked.

"Some old friends told me," Sedir replied easily. He motioned Terosh inside and gestured for him to sit in one of two comfortable chairs arranged for easy conversation.

Terosh realized Sedir must be talking about the anotechs and felt stupid for not understanding that sooner. He perched on the edge of a chair.

"I knew you would seek answers eventually," said Master Sedir.

"How did you come to know about the anotechs?" asked Terosh.

"Someone told me. You have discovered some of their powers, but not all of them. Your grandfather, King Salen, was friends with my father. When my parents died in a water hov accident, the king made sure my sister and I were well cared for. Eventually, he saw I liked to teach, so he instructed me in the knowledge of the anotechs and entrusted me to teach his children."

"Did you teach my aunts and uncle?" asked Terosh. "I thought only the eldest was to know."

"I taught them all something about the anotechs, but most of my efforts were spent with the twins."

Terosh longed to know his Aunt Uria and Uncle Uel.

"How come you didn't teach me?" Terosh wondered, trying not to sound miffed.

"That was your father's decision," said Master Sedir. "King Teorn knew next to nothing about the anotechs because he had no interest in knowing. He had me instruct Prince Taytron because tradition demanded that at least one Minstel know the family legacy. Now that your brother is gone, it falls to you to learn everything you can."

"Will you teach my children?" asked Terosh. "When I have children, I mean."

"If you have more than one child, would you like them all to know the truth about the anotechs?" asked Sedir.

Terosh considered the question. The anotechs were a wonderful, beautiful, and dangerous secret as well as a heavy burden for the bearer, but they had also saved his life several times over.

"Yes. Finding out later is harder. I think my children will need every advantage they can get," said Terosh.

"Very well, but I should probably start by teaching you and your wife. I will try to schedule some daytime lessons, but I think a large part of this should be done at night."

"Why?" Terosh wondered.

"The less people who know about the anotechs, the safer you will be."

"Speaking of anotechs and secrecy, my grandfather said something about Reshner not being habitable. What did he mean by that?"

Instead of answering directly, Sedir asked, "Have you listened to every message in Loresh, Your Grace?"

"I believe so," said Terosh. "The Chamber of Enlightenment only opened for me recently, but I have always had access to the Chamber of Wisdom." He paused and added, "You don't have to use honorifics, Master. I'm still just me."

"True, but you need to be comfortable with the title," Sedir said gently. He cleared his throat to dispel the ensuing awkward moment. "You've probably forgotten my history lessons, so I shall summarize. When Jaspen Turgot crashed here centuries ago, Reshner held only a few research scientists. His arrival changed everything."

Terosh cocked his head slightly to the right, a habit present since childhood.

"Should I send for the queen?" he wondered, nearly stumbling over the last word. "She would enjoy hearing this."

"Call to her from here," said Sedir.

After a few failed attempts, Sedir coaxed Terosh into a state conducive to a strong connection between minds. When the message was delivered, received, and accepted, Terosh reported his success.

"Well, keep at it," instructed Sedir.

Terosh blinked at him.

"She will not know the way unless you guide her, Your Grace," Sedir explained. "I'll see to some refreshments while you practice."

***

Kest (October) 1, 1538
Same Day
Queen Reia's Private Chambers, Royal Palace, City of Rammon

Reia felt Terosh's call in her mind like a half-remembered whisper. She ignored it the first three times, attributing it to her troubled sleep, but the fourth time she answered aloud.

"What is it?"

King calling for you, answered the anotechs.

What does he want?

Ask him.

She did and felt the urge to follow his voice. Feeling silly and insane, Reia quickly dressed and left her private chambers. The guards standing in the hallway asked if she wanted them to accompany her, but she politely declined. If she was destined to wander the palace halls like a lost little tretling, she would do it more comfortably alone.

After about ten minutes, Reia paused in front of a door identical to countless others she'd just passed. As she gathered the courage to knock, the door swung open and Terosh stood before her. He wore comfortable nightclothes and nothing on his feet. Relief rushed through Reia and propelled her into Terosh's awaiting arms.

A lingering kiss later, Terosh pulled away slightly.

"What took you so long? I was calling half the night." A twinkle in his eyes told her he was teasing.

"Most people use comms, my love," Reia said.

"Most people lack your unique abilities, Majesty," said a soft male voice from behind Terosh.

Reia recognized the voice as that of Master Kaimon Sedir.

Terosh sidestepped and turned, tucking her left hand in the crook of his arm. He led her to a finely threaded couch. A low table laden with cakes, pastries, and fruits lay in front of the couch.

"Please, sit. Have some refreshments. Would you like some tea?" Sedir spoke easily, but Reia knew even now he was instructing them. "His Highness said you had a fondness for mintas and wuzzle root teas. Both are available in plenty."

Graciously accepting some mintas tea, Reia waited for someone to explain why she was in Master Sedir's quarters at this unholy hour.

Sedir busied himself rearranging the pastries while Terosh picked apart an appola tart.

"You have lovely quarters, Master Sedir, but I doubt you had me roused at this hour to delight in them," said Reia. "May I inquire as to the occasion?"

Sedir smiled expansively.

"Well phrased, Your Majesty. Master Cadrish's labors are showing."

"Master Sedir was explaining some of the history of the anotechs, and I knew you would want to hear it," said Terosh.

Sedir quickly reviewed the little they had covered without Reia, then continued, "The king's ancestor, Jaspen Turgot, brought the anotechs to Reshner in his own body. They spent three years piecing together his shattered body and carving out Loresh. What happened after that is debated, but I favor the simplest explanation."

"Records say the planet was ice around a molten core back then," said Terosh. "How did the anotechs change the entire core?"

"It has not been proven, but I believe the entire core *is* currently anotechs," said Sedir. "I do not know why they would spend so much effort, but the nearly constant weather is proof of a sort."

"Could their numbers grow so large in such a short time?" asked Terosh.

"If every anotech created could build another like itself, I believe it is likely. The question then becomes why have they not consumed the entire planet?" Sedir arched an eyebrow at Reia and Terosh, waiting for one of them to venture a guess.

"It would not serve their purposes," Terosh said at last.

Sedir nodded.

"That's as close as anyone has ever come to a reasonable explanation. The anotechs serve their makers. Turgot—presumably one of the anotech creators—landed on a relatively inhospitable planet, so they changed it to suit him. Perhaps we were too close to our primary star as scientists theorize, and the anotechs needed to move Reshner. Perhaps they merely funnel energy from the core, redirecting it as they will. I am less certain of the mechanics, but the results seem to speak for themselves. After all, we only have one truly temperate continent."

"I'm not sure I follow," Reia admitted.

"Planets caught too close to their suns burn; those too far away, freeze," explained Sedir. "The slightest degree can make a big difference.

Somehow, the anotechs have established a haven suitable for humanoid life without an expensive terraforming patent. I'm sure the how of it is something GAPP scientists would kill for."

"GAPP again," said Reia, recalling Terosh's recap of his conversation with his grandfather.

He had seemed uncomfortable, like he was omitting details.

What would he hide from me?

To distract herself from the disturbing train of thought, she looked deep into her untouched tea, drank a little, and put the cup down on the table.

"They keep coming up," she murmured.

"They are one of three major powers in this galaxy," Sedir offered, sensing her unspoken question. "The other two powers are the Vambri Consortium, an alien collective largely on the other side and the Unclaimed or Independent Systems, depending on who you ask."

"We rely on a series of alliances to remain independent," Terosh said. The look he gave Reia told her he had much more to say on the subject. He reached over and squeezed her right hand.

"Perhaps we can discuss such alliances tomorrow evening. We should retire for the night. May I escort you back?"

The tender, shy way he asked the question filled Reia with a sense of peace. She quickly consented.

Chapter 8:
Bold Moves

Kest (October) 1, 1538
Same Day
Deegan Estate, City of Terab

"This is absolutely going too far," Vera Tarpon declared, piercing her daughter's husband with a scornful look. The pup had just had the nerve to send her hov away.

"Have some Charan wine and hear me out, Lady Tarpon," said Gareth Restler. He held a delicate glass of blood-red liquid out to her.

Vera took the glass from him, quelling the delightful urge to upend the glass over his head.

"There is nothing to hear," she said, sitting on the edge of the room's sole couch. "You have my daughter back, and you have had your revenge against her friend. This matter is closed. I am going home."

Gareth took a sip of his wine and carefully placed the glass on the low table in front of the couch where Vera sat primly.

"I have taken the liberty of informing your husband you wish to extend your stay for a few days."

"Then I shall have to disabuse him of that foolish notion," Vera said evenly. She took out her personal comm and began keying her husband's private code.

Gareth cleared his throat.

"I apologize for taking another small liberty. Your comm will only work if I release it to do so."

Vera arched an eyebrow at him.

"That is indeed a bold move. What precisely do you hope to gain by holding me?" Vera asked.

"Merisia will need you, and I need to be elsewhere for a few days," said Gareth.

"Then let her come with me. Perhaps what she needs is some time among her childhood comforts," said Vera.

"That may be, but it would also shift the alliance balance too much. This incident has destroyed a lot of the trust between our families. I will not risk destroying the rest over so trivial a matter as where to send Merisia to convalesce. She will stay here on neutral territory."

"Yet you would risk this self-same trust to get your way, by holding me captive and lying to my husband?"

"You are free to come and go about the estate as you wish, Lady Tarpon. My men will escort you, of course, for your own safety. I simply desire that you refrain from making unnecessary calls, hence the lock on your comm. As for what I told your husband, I am fairly certain I did not lie."

Vera cast a dagger-sharp smile at Gareth.

"Of course, you simply left out all details except my concern for Merisia's health." Vera contemplated the glass of wine in her hands. Then, taking a long breath, she tipped the glass to her lips and drained it all at once. Setting the glass down carefully, she said, "This is a very dangerous game, Gareth. Choose your allies and enemies wisely."

***

Kest (October) 3, 1538
Desert Dreams Inn, City of Terab

"What is our next move?" asked Kiata Antellio Wellum. She quickly removed the confining headwrap typical to Terabian attire. Two days of hot surveillance had convinced her that the headwrap's inventor was evil. She would rather deal with the sting of sand against her face than suffer under layers of stifling cloth.

"Well, we don't have much of a choice," said Todd, stating the obvious. "We wait. They're both in there somewhere. They'll have to be moved sometime."

An idea came to Kiata, and she gave her husband a sly smile.

"There is another option." She wadded the headwrap and tossed it onto the rickety bed.

Knowing that expression usually led to trouble, Todd winced.

"I know what you're thinking and that is *not* a valid option," said Todd. "We have no jurisdiction here. Ranger Rinn—"

"Would have to help you if I got into trouble," Kiata finished.

Todd walked up to her, draped an arm over her shoulders, and led her to a seat on the bed. It creaked and popped ominously but held. Todd eyed it suspiciously and chose not to further test the bed.

"We've tried this plan before," Todd began with a let's-be-reasonable gesture.

"Yes, and it worked," Kiata said.

Removing his headwrap, Todd tossed it onto the nearest pillow and crossed his arms over his chest.

"You have a very selective memory."

"I remember you and your fancy shooting," Kiata said, lifting her chin a bit and grinning. "You were pretty impressive."

"You got shot," Todd reminded her.

"Yes, that part was less impressive," Kiata admitted. "It hurt like hungry fire beetles, too, but the point is we rescued the hostages, caught two of the perpetrators, and restored peace to the City of Korch."

"You got shot," Todd repeated, glaring at her.

"Yes, I did," Kiata said. "And Master Ekris did a lovely job of fixing me. How does that change anything here?"

Todd uncrossed his arms and held out his hands in a halting motion.

"Let's just wait and see what happens. Even if they confine Merisia to her friend's house indefinitely, they have to move Taly eventually, especially if they want to bait that trap in Kerimia."

Kiata flopped back on the bed, which squealed in protest.

"I hate waiting."

***

Kest (October) 3, 1538
Same Day
Maledek's Private Retreat, City of Idonia

"What did you do today?" asked Lady Mavis Altran. Her hologram flickered as it adjusted to the glare of her red and gold shimmersilk dress.

Lord Kezem noted the finery as he gritted his teeth against the tediousness of this exercise. He had endured this test nearly every day of his life. It was always a battle to keep secrets from his mother. Every answer he gave would be analyzed considering information she already knew.

"What is the occasion?" he asked, instead of answering.

"I was deciding what to wear for tomorrow's banquet at the palace," said his mother. "Dennel sent your people the reminder hours ago. Have they failed to notify you?"

Kezem cursed silently. He did not doubt that the message had been delivered on time, but Dennel had probably time stamped it to be given to him just after this impromptu meeting. It was yet another petty test from his mother.

"I will have to check my messages more often," he said mildly.

"Indeed. Has the Keldor boy arrived yet?" asked his mother.

Kezem shook his head.

"Gareth said there was a delay."

"Gareth is unstable," said Lady Mavis. "This business with his wife has unhinged him, but he should be able to hold together long enough to be useful. When the time comes to dissolve the alliance, you'll have a fine weapon in him."

"I believe so," Kezem agreed. "The delay is of no consequence. Whether the young Keldor is there, here, or some other place, the Rangers will track him down."

"Do you have enough people watching over him?"

Kezem nodded.

"The guard on him is adequate for the moment. I'm more concerned with how to capture and keep the Rangers."

"You don't have to keep them both," said Lady Mavis. "Besides, killing Todd Wellum should take some of the fight out of his wife. Just remember that I need Kiata alive."

"I will consider your advice, Mother," Kezem said noncommittally.

"Good. I have another matter to discuss with you."

"And that would be?"

"It would behoove you to save our young royals a time or two." Seeing his blank look, she added, "Get the common people to like you."

Kezem listened raptly while feigning disinterest, as his mother outlined her thoughts on this new matter. By the end, he was truly speechless. He knew his mother could be coldly calculating but this was a new level even for her.

***

Kest (October) 3, 1538
Same Day
Deegan Estate, City of Terab

Todd Wellum checked the charge on his kerlak pistol and gripped his banistick hard.

How does she do that?

He ran their conversation over in his mind. He thought he'd convinced her to do nothing, yet here he sat tucked under thick bushes on the Deegan Estate, waiting to enact her crazy plan.

Movement to his left caught his eyes. A dark figure—presumably Kiata—sailed over the wall and landed in a crouch. Then, tossing a mock salute in Todd's general direction, the figure raced around toward the back of the huge house.

Todd put his banistick back on his belt, scrambled out from under the bush, and climbed the wall to the fourth room from the front on the third floor. There was no convenient balcony, and the window had a dozen sensors to detect movement and prevent tampering. Todd dispatched some anotechs to deal with the window sensors and reinforced lock. When they returned a moment later, he slid the window glass left into its space in the wall and climbed through the opening.

A lone woman lay on the massive bed, surrounded by a small army of pillows and mountainous blankets. Todd regretted the fright he would cause her. A few more commands to the anotechs had the woman sitting up straight, wide awake, scared to death, and, thankfully, mute.

Todd willed the floor lights to come on dimly so Lady Deegan could see his form but not his face.

"I apologize for the intrusion, Lady Deegan. I assure you I mean you no harm. I seek Merisia Restler and Talyon Keldor. Are they still here? Please nod, if so."

Lady Deegan blinked rapidly. She nodded then shook her head, looking frustrated.

"I'm going to unlock your vocal cords. Please just answer my questions without trouble. I seek only to help them." Todd spoke like a man trying to tame a wild korver. He issued the correct commands but had the anotechs wait with the woman and react if she so much as thought about screaming.

"Merisia is gone," said Lady Deegan, sounding like she had a sore throat. "Her husband had her moved out of Terab earlier this evening." She swallowed hard and a tear worked its way down her left cheek. "Talyon is here. Three rooms down the right hallway, but you'll never reach him. There are too many guards."

"Thank you, madam," Todd said, infusing his voice with sincerity. "Would you like to leave this place?" he asked impulsively.

She shook her head.

"I am safe enough but find Merisia. She is not safe."

"I shall do my best," Todd promised. "Sleep now. I apologize in advance if you wake up with a slight headache." He gestured and the anotechs rendered Lady Deegan unconscious before returning to him.

Counting windows, Todd exited Lady Deegan's room the way he had entered. Once outside, he climbed the wall horizontally, disabling the motion sensors in each window as he reached them. When he had passed twelve windows, Todd disabled all security measures, slid the window aside, and entered. He found Talyon Keldor asleep on the bed, bound with stuncuffs secured to the headboard. Korverhide ropes held the young man's ankles together.

Three RT Alliance soldiers slept in the room, one on each side of Talyon's bed. Todd considered shooting them but rejected the idea. These men simply worked for the wrong people. Taly too had worked for the RT Alliance once upon a time. Moving swiftly from one guard to the next, Todd silently rendered each man unconscious.

After turning up the lights, Todd assessed Taly's injuries and winced. The boy had been beaten. Both eyes were multicolored and swollen. His left cheek had a jagged gash down the side like someone had been punching with more than bare knuckles. Todd imagined the rest of Taly's body probably looked the same, so moving him would hurt a lot.

The muffled whine of energy beams tore Todd from his thoughts. He snatched up his kerlak pistol, raced to the door, and swung it open. A man's limp body fell toward him. He stepped back and let the man crash to the floor. Instinctively, he crouched to feel for a pulse and was relieved to find a pathetic, erratic excuse for one.

So much for quiet, Todd lamented, casting a few anotechs to scout for his wife.

Finding her down the hall to his right, he ducked into the hallway far enough to fire four shots left in the direction Kiata was shooting. Six angry answering shots, bright red with deadly energy, sailed back at him. He pulled his head back into Taly's room in time to keep it.

Knowing it was dangerous but a better bet than wading through kerlak beams, Todd grabbed his banistick off his belt to have a focal point, sat on the floor, and sank into a trance. It took several seconds to marshal enough energy to gather the anotechs and several more seconds to properly word the orders in Kalastan.

"Seblaetdiscurtotevons," said Todd. (Find and disable all enemies.)

Anotechs flooded out of him and scurried down the hall like a silent stream of water. Todd felt strangely drained. He hoped his gambit worked because if any of those men rushed him now, he would have no hope of stopping them.

***

Kiata felt the anotech surge and knew her husband's intent.

That was not part of the plan!

She redoubled her efforts to take out the RT soldiers shooting at her. Blue and red beams lit up the hall in an impressive display of sizzling light. At any other time, Kiata would have thought the display pretty.

Suddenly, the red beams stopped coming.

Kiata sprinted down the hall to the room where she had seen her husband. Sending a few anotechs to confirm the enemies were down, Kiata knelt beside Todd and gently tapped his face with her palm.

"Wake up, Todd!" Kiata commanded. "Wake up, so I can yell at you for that stupid move."

Frowning down at him, Kiata considered a more forceful method of waking Todd. Pounding footsteps on the stairs convinced her to try. Closing her eyes, she gripped Todd's shoulders and willed anotechs to flood his body. Then, she sent a strong shock down her arms and into him. He awoke with a pained cry, which she muffled with a hand across his mouth.

"Shhhh. This is no time to sleep on the job!" Kiata scolded. She planted a kiss on his lips to take the sting from her words.

"You shocked me," Todd said.

"I did, and we need to go," Kiata said, hauling Todd to his feet.

"Taly won't be easy to move," Todd warned.

Kiata cast a glance at the bed where Taly lay.

Todd's kerlak gun snapped up and fired twice into the hallway. Two men toppled. Todd scrambled to his feet, slammed the door, and pushed a dresser in front of it.

Kiata sent weak stun beams into the three men surrounding Taly's bed, one of whom had staggered to his feet. The task gave her something to focus on while she thought. Moving Taly would be risky but leaving him to the tender mercies of the RT Alliance would be tantamount to murder. As she turned to offer her opinion to Todd, she found him standing before her holding a bundle of sheets that probably contained Taly.

"Out the window then," Todd said, throwing one last glance at his makeshift barricade.

"Just once, I wish you'd factor a door into your escape plan!" Kiata measured the distance to the window, sprinted forward, and launched herself out the opening.

***

Todd Wellum's heart climbed into his throat and rattled his teeth as he watched his wife jump out the window. Silently apologizing to Taly, he used anotechs to render the boy unconscious. He considered releasing the stuncuffs and untying the ankle rope but decided it would be easier to move

299

Taly if his limbs stayed in place. Todd grunted. For such a frail-looking pile of beaten flesh, Taly still weighed a lot.

You're getting old.

Gritting his teeth and willing strength into his tired limbs, Todd hauled Taly to the window and peeked to make sure Kiata was ready.

No going back now.

Todd heaved Taly out the window, dropped him, and imagined a cushion of anotechs forming beneath him. He had done this a few times before but never with a person.

Kiata stood below with her head bent forward and her arms outstretched like a frozen swimmer.

Hoping everything would work out, Todd allowed his body to tumble forward out the window. They dropped like ungainly rocks. With huge effort, Todd twisted so he would land on his back and not on top of Taly. He hit the aircushion before the ground, but it knocked the breath from him all the same.

A siren cut through Todd's head. Two hov bikes flashed around the corner, firing streams of red energy. Before the air cushion could dissolve, Todd willed it into a stronger form and whipped it up as a shield. The red energy met the white shield and splashed it with crimson light. Todd's hands hurt from the influx of heat, but he maintained the shield anyway.

Meanwhile, Kiata leaned around the shield and fired four blue beams at their attackers. Two went wide and two caught the front attacker. He flew off the bike with a cry of dismay. His bike barreled forward without him. Kiata slapped her kerlak pistol back into its holster and leapt aboard the passing bike. Then, she drew her banistick and reversed the thrusters. The results sent her hurtling backward toward the remaining attacker.

He defiantly raised a kerlinblade but never got the chance to use it. Kiata's banistick caught him full across the chest. She reversed thrusters again at the last moment, so the force wouldn't be deadly. Still, Todd practically heard the man's ribs break with the impact.

Digging deep into energy reserves, Todd released Taly from his bonds and draped the boy across his back. Then, he hauled himself aboard the recently vacated hov bike and used anotechs to secure Taly to his back. Not burdened by their charge, Kiata ran interference against three additional pairs of hov bikes that pursued them. Todd had not had many opportunities to observe Kiata's driving, but he concluded strapping himself to a wind-launched cannafitch might be safer.

The chase took them through most of Terab, winding through residential and business streets alike. Luckily, the late hour meant little foot traffic. A police hov joined for a while, but Todd wasn't about to stop and answer a dozen questions, not with half a dozen fancy hov bikes chasing him.

At last, they lost their pursuers long enough to ditch the hov bikes and smuggle Taly back to the Desert Dreams Inn. Upon arrival, Todd tossed Taly onto the poor excuse for a bed and collapsed onto an old blanket thrown on the floor.

Chapter 9:
Royal Role

Kest (October) 4, 1538
Queen Lissa Banquet Hall, Royal Palace, City of Rammon

Queen Reia Antellio Minstel nodded graciously as each guest was introduced by the excitable Banquet Hall Master. The existence of such a position had surprised her, but she accepted that surprises would be quite normal for a while. As advised, she kept her movements slow so she would not strain her neck. Reia had thought Sedir's warning ridiculous until a painful twinge convinced her to take him seriously.

One by one, Reia met Terosh's aunt, cousins, and their families where applicable. In spite of her husband's dire warnings concerning his aunt's manipulative nature, she found Lady Mavis Altran fascinating. The older woman wore her dark hair pinned up in such a way that the gray sections looked like foamy, cresting waves. Her eyes, which matched Terosh's shade of deep blue, absorbed and measured everything with cool calculation. Reia wondered what impression she was making on the former princess.

Lady Mavis's sons each towered over her, but they also deferred to her. The eldest and most physically impressive son, Eldon, bowed deeply upon introduction then made a sweeping gesture toward his wife and sons. His two boys copied his movements and waved to their mother, drawing a warm smile from Reia. On cue, Eldon's wife, Lady Calia Altran, stepped forward and curtsied. Her blond hair was swept up and subdued by a small army of pins. The older boy, Emry, jostled the younger one, Jaedin, and Lady Calia stepped between them, parting the boys like a woman wading through a wheat field.

Mitrek Altran ushered his family forward as Master Roth announced them. Looking like Calia's twin, Lady Delia Altran held a disgruntled baby swaddled in white shimmersilk robes. Reia couldn't tell the child's gender until he was introduced as Lord Sullivan Altran. Next presented were Lady Silvia and Lady Arabeth Altran. The girls, six and two respectively, attempted curtseys. Silvia's was mostly successful. Arabeth simply plopped down on her tiny rump and screeched with delight. Lady Mavis scooped the child up and whispered in her ear. To Reia's amazement, Arabeth jammed a thumb into her mouth and rested her head on her grandmother's shoulder.

Last presented was Lord Kezem Altran, the youngest, shortest, and most serious of Mavis's brood. He bowed stiffly to Reia and Terosh in turn then stepped back almost shyly.

The Banquet Hall Master, Wesley Roth, babbled on for a few minutes about each Idonian lord and his position, but Reia only partially listened. She already knew their positions. Governor Lord Eldon was Idonia's representative to the Governors Council. Governor Judge Mitrek oversaw legal matters for the city and the surrounding villages. Governor General Kezem handled the details of running the city.

When Master Roth finally asked everybody to be seated, Reia gratefully rose from the throne, accepted Terosh's hand, descended the three steps to the ground, and walked over to the table. Then she waited for two servants to pull out her dining throne. Terosh had assured her the imposing monstrosities would be used sparingly, and she sincerely hoped he was right. Murmuring thanks, she hauled herself up as gracefully as possible, feeling silly about the formality and embarrassed by the ornate chair.

Once the ordeal of sitting down had been successfully overcome, Reia relaxed a little and tried to feel dignified with her feet hanging half a meter off the ground. The urge to imitate young Emry and Jaedin—who were bouncing up and down and kicking with abandon—almost overcame her sense of propriety.

"There's a control on the left armrest for a foot support," said Terosh, leaning over to whisper in her ear.

Reia glanced down and saw a disconcerting array of buttons tucked beneath a glass cover. She shot her husband a mildly panicked look.

"The glass slips aside," said Terosh. "Press six, eight, two, and the little green button in the lower right corner."

Following the instructions, Reia waited anxiously until the throne responded by slipping a thin metal rung beneath her feet. Before she could thank Terosh, the loud crash of Master Roth taking a mallet to a large gong made her flinch. She stopped just shy of throwing herself off the throne. Terosh's comforting hand landed on her arm, which had unconsciously moved toward where a banistick ought to have been attached to her waist. He squeezed gently and sent a few calming thoughts through the anotechs.

There's nothing to worry about. It's just the evening meal being summoned. The gong can be used as the fire alarm and the heralding of an impending invasion as well, but not tonight.

After shooting Terosh a questioning look, Reia cleared her expression and glanced about to see if their guests had noticed her reaction. Lady Delia and Lord Mitrek were deep in conversation. Calia whispered furiously to one of her sons, and Kezem chatted with Eldon. Only Lady Mavis appeared to be paying any attention to them. A faint smile said she noticed but sympathized with Reia's unease.

Lively music sprang from various points around the room. Willing her overactive heart to calm down, Reia watched as a line of servants entered from a side door. Each wore a white uniform with a wide, brightly colored belt cinched at his or her waist. The color corresponded to the type of food carried on heavy-looking trays. The servants' steps had a definite rhythm that matched the music perfectly. Reia admired the display of strength and coordination as the servants surrounded the table and descended on it as one.

***

Sweet and spicy aromas rose from the steaming plates. Fried wallay legs, rine bat wings, ferbel meatballs, turtle soup, plains turkey soaked in jintal juice, swordfish fillets, crab legs, and scerims appeared in generous quantities. Terosh felt conflicted but soon settled on the plains turkey in jintal juice, some buttered wheat bread, and the mixed vegetable casserole.

Conversation stayed to safe areas such as the most recent windstorm to sweep the Balor Plains, until Jaedin caught up a long, slender crab leg and whacked his brother upside the head with it. As he drew back for another blow, his mother's hand shot out and plucked the crab leg from his grasp.

"That is *not* a kerlinblade," Lady Calia scolded.

"Is too," Jaedin insisted, reaching up to reclaim his toy.

"It is food," said Lady Calia calmly. "You love crab, remember?" She used a crab cracker to break the shell and pulled out the pink and white meat.

"Do not," said Jaedin, scowling at the meat.

"Do too," said Lady Calia, matching her son's obstinate tone. Speaking thus, she grabbed her fork, speared the strip of meat, and tapped the boy on the nose with it.

He giggled and took a bite as Calia floated it past his mouth.

Terosh observed the scene with a mixture of admiration for Lady Calia's skill and a sudden, inexplicable pang. He gazed at his wife and tried to read her expression. As usual, simple study failed him, so he gauged her emotions with anotechs. His senses flooded with her warm affection, fierce love, and an odd, stabbing fear of failure. The reason for his pang and her fear suddenly smacked him. They both wanted a child.

It's too early, Terosh thought, shaking free of the feeling. *You've only been married a month and a half. There's so much to take care of first.*

"I want a kerlinblade!" Jaedin declared.

"When you're older," said his father.

"Uncle Kezem has one," Emry declared. "He has a special Ranger weapon, too."

"Have you ever killed anybody with it, Uncle Kezem?" asked Jaedin.

"Boys! This is not polite dinner conversation," said Calia.

"I am sorely out of practice with a kerlinblade," Kezem admitted.

"He used to be quite the duelist," said Lady Mavis. She casually lifted her Nedis crystal wine glass. After taking a delicate sip, she added, "His Grace, the king, used to be quite the duelist as well." She languidly lifted her eyes to meet Terosh's curious gaze. "I wonder if he has kept up those skills."

"There is but one way to know," said Kezem, setting down a forkful of swordfish. He picked up his wine glass and raised it to Terosh. "Your Highness, would you accept a friendly challenge to a Dollan duel at the next

Colored Crossblades Tournament? It is about a year off."

The boys' faces lit up with the possibility of a fight.

"It would be a pleasure to accept such a challenge," said Terosh, not wishing to disappoint the boys. Picking up his wine glass, he sealed the promise with a brief toast and took a long swallow.

The smooth wine filled his mouth with the taste of sweet rielberries then burned a little as it slid down his throat. The slight kick brought about that familiar dread of the wine containing more than fermented rielberries. The thought released a cascade of further fears. They tossed around his head until they settled on one particularly painful thought.

What if Reia is poisoned?

He had lost his mother to poison. He would not lose his wife to it. Setting down the wine glass harder than intended, Terosh vowed to do everything in his power to protect his wife. Perhaps Dr. Dentelich would have a contact that could help him. The physician knew an awful lot about everyone in the palace.

***

Kest (October) 5, 1538
Senate Great Hall, City of Rammon

Queen Reia tried very hard to not let the size of the Senate Great Hall bother her, but the place was designed to be imposing. The meeting areas were much more manageable, but the hallway leading to them covered several city blocks. Sedir had explained the rationale for this massive waste of space, but Reia still didn't understand the need for pillars commemorating long-dead senators. She felt like a condemned person as she continued along at a steady pace. Most of her just wanted to jog to the end and be done with the grand entrance.

Conscious of the crown atop her head, Reia felt ridiculous. She had protested wearing the extravagant thing, but Master Sedir insisted first impressions were important. If she thought too long about the crown's cost, she got dizzy. It featured a sea of diamonds cradling amethysts and emeralds of varying sizes atop a gold and silver band.

The crown's weight settled evenly over her head but fears of tripping clung to her. It did not help knowing that the crown had been crafted for Terosh's great-grandmother, Queen Cora Savron Minstel. Only considerable will stilled Reia's trembling heart enough to keep her feet moving forward. When she finally reached the end, she waited to be announced. Then, she endured the stares of a few hundred people crammed into the General Assembly Chamber.

They stood as one.

Forcing a smile, Reia met as many gazes as she could while being ushered to her seat at an ornate desk marooned in the middle of the room. Once she sat down, the masses resumed their seats.

"Queen Reia, we are delighted to formally meet you," said Senator Byron Price. "Our counterparts in the Governors Council speak very highly of you. We have gathered here today to know you better and answer any questions you may have concerning this august body."

"Thank you, Senator Price," said Reia. "I look forward to joining you in service to these people and the masses they represent."

"Do you understand your true role as a royal, Majesty?" asked Senator Collie Bristol in a voice like gravel skipping down a slope.

"I am certain there are many aspects of my position that have yet to be revealed to me, Senator Bristol," Reia replied, trying to ignore her pounding heart. "Can you be more specific as to which aspect you mean?" She silently thanked Master Cadrish for his instructions on how to turn a question.

"Of course, Highness, your predecessor, Queen Kila Creston Minstel, bore the crown prince not one year after their union. Have you plans to compete with her timing?" asked Senator Bristol.

Did you seriously just ask that? Despite her resolve to not be shaken, Reia flushed. She smiled to cover the discomfort.

"It has not escaped my attention that there is an expectation to continue the royal line, Senator. However, definite plans have not been laid out." Reia couldn't believe she was even discussing this with these emotional black holes.

"How will House Minstel address the disappearances?" asked Senator Gabriel Luvak.

What disappearances?

"I apologize, Senator Luvak. I was not made aware of any disappearances. Can you please illuminate the situation for me?"

"I filed a report three days ago," said Senator Luvak. "What has been done in that time? Nothing! The Royal House is useless."

Reia endured the complaint with tolerable good grace, but she felt her serenity slipping.

"I cannot answer for what has or has not been done in the absence of my attention. Now that I am aware there is a situation, I shall have it investigated."

"That's not good enough!" declared Luvak.

"Senator Luvak, please calm down," said Senator Price. "Be reasonable. Her Majesty the Queen has just invited you to share your report. I suggest you take it."

"People are disappearing," said Luvak sullenly.

"From where?" asked Senator Bristol. Her voice boomed the question on Reia's mind.

"From everywhere!" Luvak cried. "Meritab, Azhel, Korch, farms on the Kesler and Kevil Plains. You name a populated place and look at the incident reports for the last few months and you'll see the truth."

"The truth about what?" asked Reia. "Senator, I do not doubt your report, which I shall read in its entirety as soon as possible, but the disappearances you speak of sound like a symptom, not the problem. We must work together to find—"

"What is there to find, Majesty?" Luvak challenged. "This is an invasion, an attack on our sovereignty by Gardan. If the Royal House wanted to prove itself, it would move to sever ties to that nest of—"

"That is enough, Senator Luvak," said Senator Price. "Your sentiments are well-recorded. This is not a discussion about the alliance with Gardan. If you wish to place such a conversation on a future agenda, please have an aide inform Senator Moraton."

What makes you think Gardan is responsible?

Reia wanted to question Senator Luvak, but she resisted for Senator Price's sanity.

Murmurs arose as the senators quietly consulted—or complained to—their aides. Question lights made Reia's display come alive. She chose one, hoping for an easy question.

"Can you enlighten us on the current state of the alliance with Gardan, Majesty?" asked Senator Urik Dade.

His face appeared before Reia on the vidscreen that replaced the top portion of the desk. She found the effect disorienting.

"At this time, I know little more than you do," Reia said demurely.

Actually, I know a whole lot less than you do.

Inside, she made a note to ask Terosh about the man's question. She suspected this might be the matter Terosh had been hiding from her when he had reported on his strained chat with his grandfather.

A cacophony broke out. Though Reia couldn't make out specific words, she gathered they didn't believe her and felt denied by her response.

Senator Price called for order three times before it was restored.

"Has anyone else a question for our queen?" he asked, once the senators had settled down enough.

"How was the dinner with Lady Altran and the Lords of Idonia?" asked Senator Victoria Turrel. The vidscreen accentuated each line of the senator's face. The challenge in her eyes contradicted her neutral tone.

Reia silently thanked Sedir again for insisting she know each senator's biography. Senator Turrel of Idonia stood firmly in the camp that Lady Altran had been wrongly cut off by Terosh's grandfather, King Salen Minstel.

Quickly, Reia reviewed her impressions of Terosh's aunt, cousins, and their families. Governor Lord Eldon and Governor Judge Mitrek both had fair hair and rough, chiseled features, and stood nearly a head taller than their brother. Their wives and children stayed firmly in the shadows. The youngest Idonian Lord had inherited his mother's dark hair, sharp features, and famous, icy blue Minstel eyes. Lady Mavis Altran carried herself with a cool confidence.

"Are there plans to restore the relationship with the former princess?" demanded Turrel.

"We are aware of the tensions existing between House Minstel and House Altran," Reia began, casting about wildly for something substantive to say. "Nothing formal has been made official, but I will say my husband and his cousins seemed comfortable with each other. Lord Kezem challenged my husband to a Dollan duel at the next Colored Crossblades Tournament, and the king has accepted. It seems a friendly competition is a step in the right direction."

"What is your personal opinion on the matter?" pressed Turrel.

Warnings from Cadrish, Sedir, and even Colander sounded in Reia's head. Refrain from giving official personal opinions, especially when addressing one of the councils. As Cadrish had put it: *Those vipers wait for words they can string together and hang you with.*

With this in mind, Reia said, "Lady Altran is a strong woman. I can only hope to show such strength when faced with trying times."

After that, the questions seemed easier. Reia could almost predict which type of question each senator would ask. They inquired about everything from her favorite meal to her history to her favorite colored crossblades combatant. To that question, she again admitted a lack of knowledge and made a mental note to ask Sedir about the popular game.

Chapter 10:
Uncomfortable Conversations

Kest (October) 5, 1538
Same Day
Vengal's Alehouse and Inn, City of Meritel

Above all life's burdens, Lucas Telon hated waiting the most. He almost wished to be back in the Calsol Forest stalking Kireshana derringers or even in the zalok queen's lair battling that great korver beast. He thought of Reia and their first kiss. Everything had been right in that moment. Lucas drank some of his ale and let the burning sensation clear his senses.

At midday, the place had been busy, but by now, business had slowed to a trickle. Lucas felt secure at his corner table. Tiny candles and weak glow panels provided the room's only illumination. The darkness suited his mood. Kolknir was late, but that could mean any one of a hundred things. Lucas assumed the most likely explanation was a misguided attempt at teaching patience.

After cutting ties with the Rangers in the semi-successful attack on the Riden Mountain compound, Lucas had done little more than continue his private training. His only order was to remain free to receive further instructions.

Half an ale later, Kolknir appeared in the seat across from Lucas.

"We have a job," he said without preamble.

"What is it?" Lucas asked softly. "Who needs to die? I haven't killed for weeks now. I might forget how."

"Why do you do this?" Kolknir demanded, crushing Lucas's playful mood.

"Do what?"

"The Lady and I need to know your heart is in the right place before you learn the mission details," said Kolknir, ignoring Lucas's feigned innocence.

"Reia?" Lucas asked. His eyes widened, and he tried to keep a tremor from his voice.

"Not yet, but when that order comes, I need to know if you can handle it," said Kolknir.

Lucas searched his feelings. Lying to Kolknir would be stupid. Reaching deep for the burning anger at Reia's betrayal, Lucas said, "I have chosen my side. Those who oppose us are my enemies."

Even her.

Kolknir's gaze hardened.

"You are using anger as a fuel. It is effective to a point, but you will need to wean yourself off this crutch."

Feeling like cold water had just been dumped on his head, Lucas clenched his teeth in annoyance.

"Yes, master." He tried to keep his tone free of sarcasm.

"I have sent a list of targets to your infopad. They are marked terminate, wound, or capture accordingly," said Kolknir. "There's even a job or two demanding theatrics. I hope you have a clean black cloak."

"Have I not already proven myself?" Lucas complained.

"I do not question your ability to kill," Kolknir assured him. "I am merely honing your skills through practice."

Feeling like a third-year apprentice, Lucas abandoned the rest of his ale and stalked up to his room. If Kolknir wanted to continue these silly games, Lucas would play. He had no choice. The Lady would kill him if he failed her.

***

Kest (October) 5, 1538
Same Day
Royal Gardens, City of Rammon

I see what he meant about the governing bodies being soul-sucking leeches.

Exhausted, Reia chose a grassy spot with a full view of the bright sun. Sitting down, she tried escaping the countless questions she had just answered. The Senate session had gone on much longer than anybody anticipated. Reia couldn't decide if that was a good thing or very, very bad.

Her head felt light from lack of food, but her limbs would not obey a command to rise. Instead, she lay back, grateful that the dress's short sleeves allowed her to feel the grass. After a moment, she let her legs stretch out and rest until she lay completely prone. Her hands idly mingled with nearby blades of grass. She concentrated on breathing slowly and letting the anotechs enhance her senses. The sun's warmth relaxed her even more, and she enjoyed the pleasant scents rising around her.

Footsteps drew near then a shadow blocked out the sun. Raising a weary hand, Reia squinted up at Terosh. Her eyes adjusted almost instantly, courtesy of the anotechs, but she let her hand hover in front of her face and studied his expression. He knelt beside her, looking relieved. Reia knew if she felt his heart, she would find it racing. She lowered her hand to his chest and rested it there, enjoying the pulsing vitality.

"You had Captain Laocer frantic," said Terosh, clapping her hand to his chest.

"How did I manage that?" asked Reia, drowsy from the sun's warmth.

"He thought you'd been slain right here in the gardens," Terosh said.

"You can guess how often people come to the gardens the last few years."

"It would be a pity to waste such beauty," said Reia.

"So it would," said Terosh, his voice low and serious. His left hand tightened briefly around the hand still clutched to his chest.

Reia knew his mind was far from the garden. His grip tightened even more, and a shock of panic shot from his hand down her arm before he dropped her hand.

"What's wrong?" Reia sat up to get a better look at him. She wanted to bring up the subject of the disappearances, but Terosh's worry superseded her wish.

A dozen defensive lies flitted through his eyes.

"I don't think this—"

"I'm here when you're ready to share," Reia promised. "Whatever it is, it will be easier to face together."

Terosh stalled by rearranging his legs in a more comfortable sitting position.

"I meant to ask you something before the senate hearing," said Terosh. He finally settled his right leg down and bent the left at the knee so he could clasp his hands around it and lean toward her.

Reia nodded and gave him a tight-lipped *go-on* smile.

"You probably noticed I left out some details about my conversation with Grandfather the other day."

"I did," Reia confirmed, relieved to finally get to the heart of this little mystery.

"He wants to renew the treaty between Gardan and Reshner," Terosh said slowly.

"I take it you have reservations about that. Can you tell me why?"

"The original treaty took place before I was born. It was supposed to involve two marriages, Princess Mavis Minstel to Prince Zarik Creston and Princess Kila Creston to my father."

The story fit with what Reia knew about Lady Altran.

"Your aunt disapproved?" Reia's words embodied both question and statement.

"She ran away and married Dravid Altran," Terosh confirmed. "But the Gardanian princess had already been delivered. The treaty continued on the weakened grounds of the one marriage."

"Your parents," Reia concluded.

"Yes. My mother's assassination further weakened the ties between us, and now, with my father gone as well, the treaty holds very little strength," said Terosh.

"Is it a treaty we need?" asked Reia. Icy claws of fear crept down her spine.

"Yes," Terosh said without hesitation. "Gardan stands as a gateway, a stronghold against the GAPP powers. If we want to stay out of that mess, we need them."

Realization slammed into Reia with jarring force. This renewal involved her.

"What do you need me to do?"

Terosh's expression told Reia that he wanted nothing more than to hold her and pretend no problems existed. He seemed torn between laughing and weeping.

"My grandfather wishes to renew the treaty through you."

"How?" asked Reia. Panic and ravenous curiosity filled her.

"He wishes to have one of his children adopt you," said Terosh, forcing a smile.

"How is that possible? My family is here. What would Gardan gain from such a deal?"

"I don't know. That has me worried," Terosh admitted.

"Is your grandfather the sort of man who would lend aid without hope of repayment?" Reia wondered.

"No. He's the sort of man who spent his children like tretlings. I wouldn't even bring it up if I hadn't seen it among the proposed session questions. How did that go, by the way?" His light tone failed to counter the gravity in his expression.

"Fine," Reia said with great patience, "but you don't really want to talk about that. What's wrong?"

"This whole thing with Grandfather feels wrong." Terosh looked chagrined at having his emotions read so easily.

"Wrong how?" Reia probed.

"Just … wrong. Forget it, you're not going. Let's go eat something." His expression lightened and he stood, reaching to help her stand.

"Who said anything about going anywhere?" asked Reia, accepting his help.

"My grandfather wanted you to stay on Gardan for a year to formalize the adoption."

Surprise sent a new wave of fear through Reia.

Using their clasped hands to draw her close, Terosh leaned down and kissed her tenderly.

"I'm not my grandfather," he whispered when the kiss ended. He leaned his head against hers, waited a few heartbeats, and added, "I would never trade you for anything. We will find another way."

***

Royal Guard Captain Ectosh Laocer watched the king and queen from a respectful distance. He could not make out their words, but he knew the conversation was serious.

He blinked as if seeing the queen for the first time. She looked so innocent. Her concerned expression played his protective chords like a master musician. No matter how hard he tried, he could not tear his gaze away from her.

Chapter 11:
Dark Deals

Kest (October) 6, 1538
The Lady's Estate, Kala Mountains

It took Mavis Altran a few seconds to recognize the odd fluttering sensation in her stomach. She hated the interplanetary call she had to make, but she drew comfort from the fact that if everything worked out well Reshner would be free from the corrosive relationship with Gardan.

Thinking over the reports her people had compiled over the last week filled Mavis with an invigorating sense of righteous anger. That twit of a senator, Gabriel Luvak, had been right: people were disappearing. Perhaps only a few hundred so far, but Mavis had traced enough of the weak links to suspect a far more sweeping plan. Only three of the abductions could be connected to Gardan, but the evidence convinced Mavis something needed to be done.

It took twenty minutes for Mavis to gain an audience with King Padric Creston. While she waited, she debated herself about her motives. If something went wrong one way, she might inadvertently help Gardan harm her people. That was an unlikely but sobering possibility. If everything went wrong in a different way, she might destabilize half a dozen tenuous alliances Reshner needed.

She wondered why she hated Gardan's king with a deep passion. All things considered, he was a very small piece of her distant, painful past. In his position, she might have even made many of the same decisions. As she narrowed her thoughts, Mavis focused on his current plan, if it could even be called a plan. It was sloppy, unprofessional, and desperate. There, she found the core of her hatred for the man: his desperation.

King Padric Creston's greeting cut into Mavis's thoughts.

"Lady Altran, your persistence is rewarded at last. You have quite a reputation. I wonder if you are worthy of it, but such curiosities will have to wait. What matters warrant such secrecy and urgency?"

"I have an offer for you," replied Mavis. She kept her features and body relaxed.

"This is indeed a surprise," said Padric. His condescending tone hit three separate notes of measured boredom that told Mavis he knew, at least in part, what she had in mind.

She forged on, still banishing emotions to a small, unseen part of her. Leaning toward the vidrecorder, Mavis said, "I want you to stop stealing my people."

"That is an offensive request implying wrongdoing," responded King Padric.

"We could spend all morning trading accusations, or you can agree to let your people question my people later. A better use of our time would be to let me explain my proposition."

King Padric tipped his head in a gesture of gracious tolerance.

"You are wise and beautiful, and you have my attention. Do not waste it," said King Padric.

"You seek the anotech powers," Mavis began, enjoying the chance to shock him. "I want to help you."

King Padric's surprise morphed into anger.

"You dare—"

"I dare to try and help my people," Mavis cut in.

"They are not even *your* people. You are nothing but a disgraced former royal."

Even though Mavis had braced for cutting remarks, the words struck her painfully. She sipped a breath and let three heartbeats pass before attempting a reply.

"That as it may be, I happen to be in the unique position to nurture or destroy your work here," said Mavis.

The Gardanian king stared at her intently for a long second.

"I find it hard to believe you would aid my cause without proper motivation. You obviously have enough wealth and power to cultivate valuable contacts, so what is it I could offer a lady like you?"

"More power and more wealth, of course," said Lady Mavis because he expected it. His type, though gifted in many ways, could never comprehend some of her reasons so she did not burden him with them. "There is always the motive of revenge against my family, but that has little to do with you. Believe it or not, King Padric, we have a similar goal."

"I find that difficult to believe, but I shall humor you for now." His arched eyebrow asked the obvious question.

"We both seek a clean break from this disastrous union. You seek it by gathering a gift of people, no doubt for some mid-level GAPP bureaucrat to secret away for illegal experiments."

"You have an interesting imagination, Lady Mavis." The king's neutral tone could not mask all of his dismay.

Mavis continued as if he had not spoken.

"You would sell us as slaves. I say sell us as royals."

"Is there a difference?" asked King Padric, obviously aware of how the question would affect Mavis.

"You ought to be a connoisseur of such knowledge," said Mavis evenly. "A slave is useful because of what he does; a princess is useful because of who she is. It is no secret GAPP desires that which makes Reshner unique. If we are to be sold, I demand it be for a higher price than that of a common slave."

"What an odd request," said Padric. "What about your rhetoric of helping people?"

"I meant every word," Mavis assured the king. "Things will go much worse for my people if I let you blunder around taking innocents at will. Allow me to choose the targets in exchange for a few small requests and a treaty of non-aggression between us."

"I assume you mean you and me and not our respective planets," said King Padric.

"Correct, though I would hope Gardan had the good sense to stay out of Reshner's affairs once our dealings conclude."

"Assuming we reach amiable terms, what prevents me from making a captive of you and extracting the information by more conventional means?" asked King Padric.

"You can certainly try," said Mavis, letting a cold edge take her voice lower. "However, time, effort, and convenience favor partnership over hostilities."

The ghost of a smile touched King Padric's lips.

"We have much to discuss, Lady Altran."

Mavis agreed and turned the call over to Dennel so he could work with some of Creston's people on the details.

Alone at last in front of the blank vidrecorder and hologram display, Mavis let herself sink into her chair. Dealing with King Padric was every bit as difficult as she had anticipated.

Let the games begin.

***

Kest (October) 6, 1538
Same Day
Market District, City of Rammon

Talyon Keldor walked beside Nils Clavon in silence. He had nothing against the Terabian man, but he also had little to say to anyone. His best friend was for all intents and purposes a captive, and his body ached and bore ugly bruises from her husband's misplaced wrath. His family likely wanted him dead, and his bosses certainly wanted him brought back under their control.

"The Alliance hold on you will fade with time," said the dark-skinned man walking beside Taly through the crowded market streets.

Taly nodded, hoping the man was right. Before he could respond, someone bumped into him, knocking him off balance.

"Check your pockets," Nils instructed tersely, righting Taly with a firm hand on his arm.

"I'm not carrying anything valuable," Taly protested.

"Check anyway," Nils replied.

Not wanting to argue, Taly reached into each pocket. To his surprise, his fingers brushed a thin, sturdy infopad chip in his left pants pocket. He held it up to study, but Nils stopped him.

"Put it away and follow me. We must not be followed back to our place of rest," said Nils. He turned away from Taly and started walking rapidly down a side street filled with fruit vendors.

Taly's heart raced as he followed Nils, keeping his pace just under a run.

The Wellum's servant led him through a winding set of Rammon streets through the Market District and into the West Quarter. Two streets into the West Quarter, Nils stopped suddenly before a small shop where people could buy any sort of drink imaginable and rent the use of private infopads.

"In here," Nils said.

Once they were settled in a private booth, Nils took out his own infopad and motioned for Taly to give him the chip.

"Why not use the infopad here?" Taly asked, holding up the machine chained to their table. "We don't know anything about this chip," he added, fishing it out of his pocket. He flipped it over a few times.

"The Tarpons have outfitted many of these places with listening devices. I am certain other organizations have done the same," Nils explained. He took the chip from Taly and tucked it into a slot on the side of his infopad.

"The chip itself could be trapped or traced," Taly pointed out.

"You speak truth, but we must investigate," Nils replied.

The head and shoulders of a masked figure shrouded in black appeared on the screen. A man's voice spoke.

"Greetings. This message is for Talyon Keldor only. Please confirm your identity and that you are alone. A simple two sentence response should suffice."

Taly cast a curious look at Nils and received an encouraging nod. Shrugging, he said, "I am Talyon Keldor. And I am alone."

"Error. Multiple presences detected. Please reset and try again."

Taly sat up straighter and stared at the infopad in disbelief.

Nils stood up.

"I will leave you alone. Come out when you finish, and we can return."

Once truly alone, Taly repeated his introduction and declaration of solitude.

"Confirmed," said the infopad. "Young Master Keldor, I represent a party known as the Lady. She believes you are in a unique position to help her, just as she is in a position to aid you. At this point, you may cut off communication and destroy the chip or request further information."

Two small squares appeared at the bottom of the screen. Taly hesitated only a moment before pressing the one for more information.

"You have chosen well. Your instructions are simple, but the rewards will be great. Keep this chip on your person at all times. When the Lady wishes to give you a task, one of her agents will activate the chip. It will vibrate to indicate a message. Upon completion, the Lady will restore Merisia Restler to you at a location of your choosing."

The message ended, and the infopad ejected the chip. Taly tried to reinsert it, but the infopad refused to accept the chip again. Bewildered, Taly shoved the chip into his pocket, picked up Nils's infopad, and left the private booth.

***

Kest (October) 6, 1538
Same Day
Miraz Estate, City of Resh

Lucas Telon waited impatiently by the front gate to the Miraz Estate. When his target finally emerged, bid her friend goodbye, and climbed into the back of a grand hov, he released a breath he had not realized he held. A gesture to the miniature vidrecorder recalled the device from its position hovering three meters above his head. When it touched his palm, he tucked it into a pouch on his belt and mounted his hov bike.

Crouching low, he activated the cloaking shields on his bike and dark outfit. He had avoided using the devices before to minimize the sense of claustrophobia and not tax the batteries.

Each second stretched into the next. Less than a minute later—though it seemed much longer—a dark green hov slid out the gate and turned left.

As the hov passed, Lucas flicked half a dozen trackers onto its back and sides. He braced, not really expecting an alarm but oddly wishing for one. It would complicate his mission, but the excitement would be worth it. The trackers were only a secondary plan anyway, a guard against the unexpected.

Lucas let the hov gain a lead of several hundred meters before starting his slow pursuit. He knew the hov's destination and exactly where he wanted to intercept them. He followed the hov at a gentle pace for five minutes before altering his course. A small part of him disapproved of the recklessness of waiting until the very last moment. A rush of adrenaline blew the pesky thoughts away.

Dropping the cloaking shields, Lucas enjoyed the cold rush of night air that roared past him as he carved a path through the sky. For no other reason than that he could, he weaved back and forth across several rooftops and passed in front of some windows. The hov bike's powerful vibrations pumped through his arms and legs, reverberating in his chest. He felt alive. Lucas cursed the necessity of wearing a mask on this mission. He wanted to really experience the wind on his face.

Normally, Lucas could expect a police hov to accost him, but he trusted the Lady's word that tonight the skies belonged to him. He spared a glance at the moons and dared the three crescents to reveal him to his powerless quarry.

As he whipped around the last building blocking him from the young lady's hov, Lucas cut the bike's power. The bike lurched and dropped, causing his stomach to flip within him. At the last moment, he re-engaged the power and flipped forward onto the hov's roof. Kolknir would scold him for the theatrics, but Lucas would not be denied the added drama.

After slapping a scrambler onto the hov to prevent cries for help, Lucas drew a pair of kerlak pistols from holsters strapped to his lower back. One pistol would have been sufficient but two was much more fun.

Electricity zipped across the roof, destroying his scrambler and sending a painful jolt through each of Lucas's boots. His lower legs felt like metal spikes had been driven deep into them and spewed liquid fire through every nerve. He grunted but recovered quickly, thankful for the insanely expensive boots and the extra pain tolerance training Kolknir had forced upon him.

Accepting that his legs would be momentarily useless, Lucas dropped his pistols and awkwardly rolled from the roof, letting the pain motivate him. Despite the energy influx, they should still work, but he had no wish to wager his life on that assumption. Instead, Lucas reached for the case of flingers secured to his waist.

Two doors opened and a pair of well-muscled security officers emerged with kerlak pistols at the ready.

Lucas didn't wait for their orders to surrender. He completed another roll and forced himself to his feet. As his body teetered on wobbly legs, Lucas whipped his right arm across his chest then back the other way. At the peak of each wave, he released a flinger. The security men stiffened and fell, neither having time to protest as death claimed them.

An anguished cry of dismay coincided with another door opening. In a moment, Lucas's target stood before him, a shaking serlak pistol in her left hand. She hesitated. Had his orders dictated her death, the mistake would have been fatal. That not being the case, Lucas disarmed her with another flinger and closed the distance between them. She screamed a split-second after his right hand closed over her mouth.

He leaned into her, pressing her back against the hov. When she paused for breath, he said, "Peace, Lady Zelene. My masters wish you no harm. Your presence is required elsewhere this evening."

Without giving her time to reply, Lucas rendered her unconscious. Once certain she would not move, he retrieved his flingers from the dead guards and recovered his pistols. Then, belatedly, he considered how he would get the young woman onto the hov bike idling above their heads. Hefting the lady with one arm, Lucas fumbled at his belt until his hand secured the bike controls.

A few commands later, the bike drifted down like a mythical steed ready to fulfill its master's wishes.

***

Kest (October) 7, 1538
Prince Skye Research Center, Royal Palace, City of Rammon

For the first time in many years, Terosh stepped into the largest of the labs tucked in secluded corners of the palace. Cool air wrapped around him, making him grateful for the long sleeves of his formal robes. He had wanted to change into something more comfortable and less imposing, but the Senate meeting had gone on longer than anticipated.

Terosh walked swiftly past many scientists hard at work and willed people to ignore him. He need not have bothered. The scientists seemed completely enthralled by their projects. The few researchers who looked up executed swift bows and returned to their work as if royalty entering their private domain was a common occurrence.

Perhaps it was a common occurrence, Terosh thought, recalling his brother's obsession with Dr. Deanna Koffrin.

He shook his head sadly. The anotechs had informed him they were currently compiling the story for him, but they had also warned him that he would not like several parts of it. He wondered if he would let them tell him the tale. Tate was dead. Deanna was dead. Their daughter was dead. What would it gain him to know how they loved, lived, and died? Perhaps he owed his dead brother the satisfaction of catching whoever had killed his family, but revenge ranked low in matters of running the planet.

At any given time, the Royal House employed about two dozen scientists through research grants offered to professors and students at the University of Rammon. Master Sedir had once tasked Terosh with reading through a stack of proposals and choosing the next year's scientists. The ideas had ranged from slightly odd to boring to downright crazy to an exciting sort of dangerous. He remembered being intrigued by Dr. Atien Belcross's proposal of adding sedatives to kerlak energy packs. Terosh had approved the project and eventually enjoyed the fruits of Belcross's labor.

The door to Dr. Kurt Saddic's private lab opened as Terosh approached. He entered and stopped two steps into the room as a putrid odor assaulted his nose. The anotechs dealt with it almost immediately, but it took a lot of willpower not to clamp a hand over his nose and mouth. The brief taste of the odor filled his entire being, hitting him hard in the gut.

"Welcome, Highness," said Dr. Saddic, rising from his comfortable chair and bowing. "I apologize for the smell. Porit vipers are especially fond of rotten wallay corpses. I find this surprising because in the wild they thrive upon freshly hunted game, but I'm sure that's not what you came here to know. How may I be of service?"

Terosh noticed shelves full of tanks containing every kind of crawling, creeping, and slithering creature.

"Dr. Dentelich says you're an expert on poisons," said Terosh, tearing his gaze away from the tanks.

The scientist nodded vigorously.

"It is so, Highness. I have been studying poison in one form or another for over twenty years. It captured my fancy as a small boy when I saw a widowmaker spider take down a full-grown roakul while I was on a camping trip in the Felmon Desert."

The Terabian reputation for speaking swiftly holds truth, Terosh thought, picturing the scene the scientist described.

He had never seen a real roakul, but Sedir's Native Predators lesson had included several impressive holograms. The three-meter-long beasts had been imported from Nabeloth about three centuries ago. The original intent had been to cull some of the nastier desert creatures, but the reality was a restructuring of the food chain.

We promised to protect her, the anotechs said, sounding miffed.

I just want to be sure.

Smiling politely, Terosh asked, "Can you make someone immune to a particular poison?"

"It depends on the poison, Your Grace," answered Dr. Saddic. His words continued flowing with the cadence of racing ibeks. "Most common poisons already have reliable antidotes, but some of the faster-acting ones have never been studied in sufficient detail to develop an antidote. May I inquire as to the specific poison you wish to conquer?"

"Comaladon," said Terosh.

"The poison that killed the queen," Dr. Saddic's said, sounding surprised. His head bobbed up and down several times. "You wish me to make it so that our new queen does not share your mother's fate, yes? Yes, of course, why else would you be here? I believe this can be done, Highness, but I cannot guarantee swift results. I will have to isolate the chemical, study it, synthesize an altered version, and arrange for experimental trials."

The mention of trials chilled Terosh's blood. His stomach twisted at the thought.

Noting Terosh's expression, the scientist hastily added, "The test subjects are always willing volunteers. In the few cases the experiments have failed, the families have been well cared for."

The words brought little comfort to Terosh.

If you want to bring about change, do so.

"No more," said Terosh firmly. His heart raced with excitement and trepidation for what he would have to face in the Governors Council and Senate if he truly wished to back up his words.

"No more what, my king?" asked Dr. Saddic.

"Study the poison and try to create an antidote, but do *not* perform trials with live subjects." Terosh's tone left no room for argument.

Dr. Saddic argued anyway.

"Highness, please reconsider. The only way to truly know if the counteragent works is to test it upon humans from this planet. No other species or foreign population can claim our unique genetic pedigree."

"I'm trying to save a life, not destroy more," Terosh snapped.

"Your Grace, this is the way science has been conducted for decades," argued Dr. Saddic. "I will need subjects who grew up in conditions similar to the queen. Her sister would be—"

"Find another way," Terosh interrupted, hardly believing he was having a conversation about experimenting on his wife's sister.

That would thrill Reia.

Without another word, Terosh spun on his heel and left the scientist's creepy lair. He had a ceremony to attend.

Chapter 12:
Momentous Moments

Kest (October) 7, 1538
Throne Room, Royal Palace, City of Rammon

Reia barely resisted the urge to leap from her throne and rush to the two Rangers being ushered in. To distract herself, she stole a sideways glance at her husband. He appeared calm, but Reia could tell he felt uneasy. She sent him the mental equivalent of a reassuring smile and received a similar nudge in return.

As per Sedir's instructions, Reia carefully avoided eye contact with any of the soldiers or courtiers. It helped a little, but she still felt their emotions ranging from cool neutrality to simmering resentment. She would have to thank Sedir for his warning to expect as much.

Her composure almost faltered when the Rangers approached and knelt. Knowing tradition dictated each movement could not help her shake the strangeness of the moment.

Why did the Council send Kiata and Todd? Reia dismissed the thought, choosing to simply be thankful.

"The Ashatan Council sends its highest regards and deepest well-wishes," said Todd Wellum. He kept his voice serious in acknowledgment of the occasion, but genuine affection poured from his eyes. "It is thus with great pleasure that we come before you to renew the vows established by Prince Davel's Order of the Nareth Talis with regard to the members of House Minstel."

Kiata voiced the familiar vow with steady, flowing words.

"Essepetraesmeaproc. Isercuessecaiu totmielstom. Enlivetninliv ichonasev-petraminstel." As she spoke, Kiata removed her banistick from its belt clip and placed it on the ground before the throne, a symbol of her willingness to do likewise with her life.

"This house is mine to protect. I embrace this cause with all my heart. In life and death, I choose to serve House Minstel," Todd repeated for those who could not understand Kalastan. He too removed his banistick and placed it before the throne.

"Your aid is most welcome," said Terosh. "I shall hold you no longer

than necessary as I am certain you have much to do, but you are always welcome in this palace
and in our lives. Before you go, I believe my queen desires a private word. If you would be so kind as to retire to the Upper East Library, she will join you shortly."

Reia's heart leapt. She certainly wanted to speak with her sister and Todd, but she had not said as much to Terosh.

The Rangers acknowledged the request and gracefully rose, retrieving their banisticks in the process.

***

Kest (October) 7, 1538
Same Day
Governor Lord's Estate, City of Resh

Lucas Telon marveled at the ease with which his mission had proceeded. Resh was a relatively peaceful city, as befitted its name, but he thought common sense would warrant greater caution. He silently thanked the relatively uneventful reign of King Teorn for lulling Governor Darmon Zelene into his current state of vulnerability.

Capturing Akia Zelene the previous night had been extremely easy. A short comm conversation had convinced the governor of her tenuous position and gained Lucas this audience.

Despite the governor's promise of complete cooperation, Lucas expected trouble. As he entered the governor's office, Darmon Zelene rose from his chair. His face bore the lines of a worried father, but he said nothing. His chest rose and fell in a regular rhythm, and his eyes flashed with suppressed rage. Large fingers stabbed commands into an infopad. Lucas wondered if he should be alarmed until the muted buzzing of a sound damper reassured him.

"Greetings, Governor Zelene. Your daughter is well for now," said Lucas. He let the obvious threat hang in the air as he crossed the room to stand before the governor's desk.

"Do you have the proof I requested?" inquired the governor.

"I do," replied Lucas, holding out an infopad. "I also have a summary of your instructions should you forget anything we discuss here." He laid the infopad on the governor's desk and retreated a step, clasping his hands behind his back to present a less threatening figure.

Lucas had enjoyed taking the pictures the governor flipped through. Kolknir would caution against emotionally engaging the target, but Lucas saw his task as an art form. He needed to capture the young lady's vulnerability and display it for her father.

Some pictures showed her face relaxed in a state of peaceful slumber, but most showed her bound with stuncuffs. His favorite showed her hanging from the wall, arms secured up behind her head. Lucas had been careful not to leave her there too long, as his purpose was not to physically distress her. However, her expression in that image had been a perfect mixture of pain, confusion, and frustration. Lucas smiled at the memory.

Darmon Zelene's face paled as he scanned the images and instructions.

"I accept," he said at last. He tossed the infopad onto his desk. It landed with a clunk that rang with a note of finality.

The response surprised Lucas. He felt cheated out of the fight he had braced for.

"I sense the Lady's dark hand in this," Governor Zelene said, as if it would explain his easy capitulation. In a way, it did. "She is misguided and dangerous, but she is also true to her word. Now, if you'll excuse me, I have some arrangements to make."

***

Kest (October) 7, 1538
Same Day
Upper East Library, Royal Palace, City of Rammon

The Royal Guards standing outside the library entrance snapped to attention and opened the door for Reia. Nodding to their commander, Captain Ectosh Laocer, she thanked the guards and wondered if she would ever get to touch a door handle again. Once she entered the room, the guards swung the big doors shut. Remembering Sedir's repeated warnings, Reia reached for the panel next to the entrance and keyed in a privacy code. Then, she turned to her guests.

They stood respectfully. For a moment, nobody spoke.

Reia started closing the eight or so meters separating them from her, keeping to a slow and regal pace, but the sight of her sister changed her mind. She spared a sour thought for the shoe designer, shucked the evil creations binding her feet, and sprinted to Todd and Kiata. Once wrapped in Kiata's embrace, she sighed.

"One would think our separation had been months, not days," said Kiata with a laugh. She pulled away enough to plant a kiss on Reia's forehead.

"It has been a long few days," Todd commented.

Reia broke free from Kiata and hugged Todd.

"I read some of the reports from Terab," she said, twisting in Todd's grasp to loop an arm over her sister's shoulder and draw her close. "You two have a lot of explaining to do."

"What's to explain?" asked Todd with wide-eyed innocence. "We went to retrieve Talyon Keldor, and there was a slight altercation at the Deegan estate."

Kiata squeezed Reia's waist with her right arm and scoffed. Then, letting go, she sat on one of the ornate couches.

"That's one way to put it," said Kiata.

"Then you explain it, if you can do better," Todd said. He led Reia over to the couch where Kiata sat and deposited her before retreating to the other couch. He kept his tone light, but Reia sensed an underlying layer of tension in the set of his shoulders.

"Is the young man all right?" Reia inquired, letting her gaze bounce between her sister and Todd.

"For now," Todd said with a curt nod.

"That doesn't sound very convincing," Reia noted.

"He's worried Taly might do something reckless," said Kiata.

Todd's laugh was tinged with bitterness rather than mirth.

"It's more a question of *when* Taly will do something stupid," he clarified.

Reia arched an eyebrow at him.

"It's complicated," Kiata said, rubbing her temple with her left hand. "You were there when Taly and his friend, Merisia, broke free from the Restler-Tarpon Alliance."

"Of course," Reia confirmed. It would be hard to forget such a night. "We were chased all over the Kesler Plains until you jumped from a moving hov to stop our pursuers."

"I'm surprised you remember all that," Kiata commented.

"Taly and Merisia were also at my wedding," Reia said, "but beyond that, I know little of them."

"Merisia is the youngest child and only daughter of Vera and Tyko Tarpon," Todd explained. "She was married to Gareth Restler as part of the formation of the Restler-Tarpon Alliance. From what Taly says, she wanted to break free because she feared her unborn child would become an alliance target."

"They were caught a few days ago in Terab," said Kiata. She took a deep breath and released it slowly. "I came to see you, we went to rescue them, the mission was partially successful, and here we are, a little the worse for wear."

"It's not over though," Todd said. "There are too many unanswered questions."

"Is there anything I can do to help?" Reia asked, feeling oddly powerless.

"Not in this matter," Kiata said slowly.

"What matter may I be of service then?" asked Reia. She sat slightly straighter and slipped unconsciously into more formal speech. Though Terosh had been the one to mention a meeting with Todd and Kiata, Reia suspected they had arranged it for a specific reason.

Kiata and Todd exchanged a meaningful look that confirmed her suspicion.

"Master Niklos," Todd said. He sounded weary, worried, and frustrated.

A jolt of panic shot through Reia.

"Is he—"

"He's fine," Kiata cut in quickly.

"He's quitting and moving to Resh," said Todd.

"Quitting?" Reia asked, dumbfounded. She could not fathom the Rangers without Master Niklos Mikhail McGreven. Her spirit warmed at the thought of the man who had taught her practically everything she knew about being a Ranger.

"He's angry with the Council," said Kiata.

Before she could elaborate further, a chiming noise caught everybody's attention.

A disembodied, apologetic male voice said, "Forgive me, Majesty, the king requests your presence in the throne room. There is urgent news from Resh."

"Thank you. Please tell the king I shall be there shortly," said Reia, rising from the couch.

She tossed hasty farewells to Todd and Kiata before fleeing the library, but they followed her to the throne room anyway.

Chapter 13:
Cause for Concern

Kest (October) 7, 1538
Same Day
Throne Room, Royal Palace, City of Rammon

In spite of the grim news he'd just received, Terosh smiled when the heavy throne room doors burst inward and his barefoot wife made her grand entrance. Courtiers gasped and soldiers suppressed grins. Noting her worried expression, Terosh sobered, feeling bad for alarming her and even worse for the news he had to share.

"I would like a word alone with my wife," Terosh said to the chamberlain.

Dutifully, the man issued the appropriate orders and the throne room emptied with remarkable speed. The Captain of the Royal Guard, Surd Antar, protested but was successfully mollified by the skillful chamberlain.

Terosh barely paid the controlled chaos any attention. His mind scrambled for some way to make the news more palatable. He was still stumped when Reia arrived at the foot of the dais. She drew in deep breaths and looked at him with a mixture of caution and compassion that made him love her even more.

"Governor Zelene is dead," Terosh blurted, knowing of no other way to tell her.

Reia paused midway up the platform steps and closed her eyes against the pain of the news. When she opened her eyes, unshed tears made her green eyes shiny. The next instant, she finished climbing the steps and wrapped him in a hug.

Terosh stiffened instinctively then relaxed and returned the embrace. He wished his roles as king and husband could always intertwine, but often, the king role demanded he cloak himself in an impenetrable emotional shield.

"He took his own life," Terosh said, after allowing himself a long moment of just holding her.

Twisting her head sideways, Reia asked, "Why?"

"I don't know. I'm having Captain Garahad look into it, but I doubt he'll find much," Terosh admitted.

"Who knows?" Reia asked, as she reluctantly drew away.

"Lady Akia, of course—"

"She's here?" Reia demanded.

Terosh shook his head.

"Not yet. She sent a comm message. She'll be here tomorrow to announce her father's death to the Governors Council."

"We should go to her," said Reia.

"There will be time for condolences when she gets here, but there's a more pressing issue to settle." Terosh winced at how callous that sounded. Forming a fist and closing his eyes, he said, "That's not what I meant." He retreated down one step and looked to Reia, as if she held the answers.

"What pressing issue must be settled?" Reia wondered.

"Governor Zelene's successor," Terosh answered, grateful she did not call him on his poor manners. His throat threatened to close, but he forced himself to swallow. He wanted Reia to be a part of these tough decisions.

Brows drawing together in confusion, Reia said, "Sedir said governorships could be inherited."

"They can," Terosh confirmed, "but Lady Akia Zelene has recently spent a lot of time among the Ritand. Fair or not, that does not endear her to the power bases in Resh. If she moves to succeed her father, they could stir up enough trouble for the people to reject her."

"They are wrong," Reia declared.

Terosh agreed but knew that power meant more than personal beliefs in the political arena. He offered Reia a thin smile.

"Welcome to the wonderful world of politics, where words are daggers and right, wrong, and fairness don't matter."

"It can't be all that bad," Reia protested.

"It can when the major contenders for a carefully balanced Governors Council both have little love for House Minstel."

"Cynicism doesn't suit you, dear," Reia said, gently touching Terosh's chin. With him one step down, they stood almost eye to eye. Reia took advantage of the position to kiss him firmly. "Who are these would-be governors?"

***

Kest (October) 7, 1538
Same Day
Throne Room Entrance, Royal Palace, City of Rammon

"They will call us when they're ready," Todd called to Kiata. He stood with arms crossed over his chest and leaned back against the far wall, eyes shut in an attempt to minimize distractions.

Kiata paced back and forth in front of the imposing throne room doors.

"She forgot us." Kiata reached one side of the door, turned sharply on her left heel, and started back the other way. "I hate this."

Todd tried to concentrate on moving anotechs beyond the doors, but he kept meeting electrical resistance. As vexing as he found the situation, it also intrigued him. The obvious reason for such resistance was a royal awareness of the anotechs. He had always known anotechs were heavily involved with House Minstel in the past, but he had assumed the connection had been lost over the years. Kiata's talks with Reia after Terosh's near-disastrous Kireshana had revealed some anotechs at work, but this level of protection spoke of a very deep understanding.

Most of the Nareth Talis Rangers would fail to raise such a defense.

The thought brought him back to the old debates over using the anotechs. Rangers accepting a position among the elite did so with knowledge that the anotech secrets came and went with the job. In other words, retiring from such service meant leaving their mission memories behind. The ceremony, called Remominelstom, literally meant "remembered no more in mind or heart."

Todd understood both positions but had yet to choose a side. Some felt the Ranger mission to guard the anotechs was paramount to everything, even the mandate to protect the Royal House. The other side believed that not using the anotechs was irresponsible at best and morally reprehensible at worst. Having experienced anotech abilities for several years now, Todd gravitated to the side favoring anotech use, but his history lessons were thorough enough to make him cautious.

We need to have a long, serious conversation with our new sovereigns.

As if the thought could summon results, a Royal Guard announced, "Their Majesties will see you now."

Todd snapped his attention back to the moment and nodded thanks to the guard. Two servants swung the ponderous doors aside. Kiata's sure strides carried her into the throne room, and Todd jogged to keep pace with her. He noted the curious absence of Royal Guards. The heavy thud of the throne room doors emphasized its deserted state.

After greetings, King Terosh and Queen Reia filled Todd and Kiata in on the recent turmoil in Resh.

"We want you to investigate Governor Zelene's death," Reia finished.

Kiata glanced sideways at Todd before returning her attention to her sister.

"Our current mandate is to protect you," she reminded them.

Reia nodded like she had expected the protest.

"We will be in Resh for a few months. It should give you enough time to make discreet inquiries and obey your mandate."

"Master Sedir suggested we visit each city over the next few years. It will not be a problem to rearrange the schedule," said King Terosh. "Funeral rites for the governor commence in three days. I must be there to honor him for my father's sake."

"Your willingness to go to Resh speaks much for the weight you give these matters, but what do you think such an investigation will yield?" asked Kiata.

"I suspect either Tyko Tarpon or Damien Luvak forced Zelene's hand," King Terosh answered. "They are the two with the most to gain."

Todd cleared his throat uncomfortably.

"Rangers will hardly help your cause where Master Tarpon is concerned, and House Luvak holds us in fairly low regard as well," said Todd.

"You're the only ones we can trust." Reia's tone underscored the gravity of the situation.

"You might find nothing related to House Tarpon or House Luvak," King Terosh admitted. "Still, the threat they represent is enough to warrant investigations on several levels."

"What about Talyon?" asked Kiata. "Our responsibility to him continues."

The king and queen shared a long, meaningful look that said Taly had come up in their conversations. Todd found that interesting.

"Leave him here in the palace for now. He will be safe for as long as he wishes to stay," said Reia. She hesitated, then added, "Talk with him though. We cannot hold him prisoner. From what you said before, I suspect he may return to the RT Alliance for Merisia's sake."

Her statements rang uncomfortably true for Todd, especially given the message Taly had received yesterday. He still didn't know what to believe about that mysterious communication.

***

Kest (October) 7, 1538
Same Day
Wellum Home, East Quarter, City of Rammon

The conversation was not going well. Kiata Wellum wanted to reach out and shake sense into the boy.

"You're not safe here, Taly," Kiata declared. "The close call yesterday proves as much."

His defiant expression told her the argument failed to sink in. Talyon Keldor nodded and stood.

"I know and I thank—"

Waving impatiently, Kiata said, "Sit down. We're not kicking you out."

"We're trying to tell you that the queen has offered you refuge at the palace," said Todd.

"Please consider the offer," Kiata added.

Taly cast a pleading look at Nils Clavon.

Nils crossed his arms and leaned against the doorframe as if the less obtrusive position would allow him to escape involvement. After a few moments of awkward silence, he cleared his throat.

"Talyon does have a point, masters."

Kiata grunted and hung her head in temporary defeat.

"Which one?" she muttered, frustrated that the servant chose this moment to assert his free will.

"He must disappear," said Nils. His clipped Terabian accent made the statement sound like the only option.

"It's for the best," Taly said glumly from the seat he had reclaimed. "Every moment I stay here endangers you."

Kiata snorted.

"You're not that important," she said, knowing she was probably wrong.

The Keldor name carried a lot of weight in the Restler-Tarpon Alliance. As far as she knew, Taly's father, Ariman, still held a high rank. In addition, rumor had it that Taly's grandfather, Niktrod, had been captured in connection with the death of Reshner's previous queen. If the public knew, the Keldor name would become immediately famous—or infamous.

"We're not exactly Alliance favorites, Taly. What's one more reason to kill us?" Todd asked with a shrug.

"It's different," Taly protested. "Before you helped me, the Alliance viewed you with the general contempt held for all Rangers, but now, it's personal. I—"

"Tried to help a friend," Kiata finished.

"That's not how they see it." Taly stuck his hand in his pocket and removed the chip. He turned it over several times with one hand before passing it to the other.

Kiata fought the impulse to wrap the forlorn young man in a comforting hug. Even though she and Todd had experienced danger since they were far younger than Taly, it felt wrong for him to have to face so much.

"Perhaps there is a better plan," Nils said, yanking Kiata out of her thoughts.

Every eye focused on the tall, elegant man.

He stopped leaning against the doorframe, uncrossed his arms, and looked at Kiata and Todd, silently requesting permission to speak.

Kiata nodded, wishing she could convince the man his debt of service was not necessary.

"Speak your mind," said Todd.

"My people send youths on a solitary journey, much like the Kireshana. They choose to explore mountains, deserts, forests, or seas," Nils explained. "Travelers carry only what weapons they need for survival and no extra links to the modern world."

"You think it's best to send Taly into the wilds?" asked Kiata, incredulous.

"It is a suggestion only," said Nils stiffly.

Kiata felt a stab of remorse, but she couldn't help thinking Taly would be safer on a farm or even in a Ranger compound. She immediately rejected the idea of suggesting Taly stay with Rangers. Not many people knew enough of Taly's story to sympathize. Most still believed him an RT Alliance agent. On the other hand, the idea of a farm struck her as favorable.

"It's a fine suggestion," Todd assured Nils, "but I'm not—I mean it's probably better if Taly stayed somewhere we can find him."

Kiata fixed her attention on Todd.

"What about your brother's farm?"

Todd tilted his head and considered her question.

"I don't want to put more of your family at risk," Taly said, shaking his head.

"It's pretty remote," Todd reflected, speaking mostly to himself. He nodded, as if answering an unspoken question. "Terik could use the help, too. What do you say, Taly? Would you like to be smuggled out of this dreary city to spend some time pushing dirt around?"

"No one will know you're there," Kiata added, willing Taly to believe the danger would not follow him from the city.

"How do you know he'll even take me?" Taly asked.

"He's always looking for new hands," said Todd. "I'll give him my highest recommendation and leave what you tell him about your past up to you."

"I think I would like to get away from cities for a while." Taly still looked uncertain, but he tried to smile.

"I'll call my brother later this evening, and we can leave in the morning," said Todd.

"What do I do about the chip?" asked Taly, glancing between Todd and Kiata.

"What would you like to do with it?" asked Kiata carefully.

When Taly had confessed the substance of the message delivered in the Market District, it took all of Kiata's willpower to not advise him one way or another. Truthfully, she did not know which advice she would have given him anyway. Keeping the chip could draw unknown enemies down upon Taly, yet destroying the chip would end the best chance of solving the mystery it presented.

Taly looked torn between relief and fear, but he seemed grateful for the freedom to make his own choice.

"I'd like to keep it," he admitted. "I only ask because it is your family I put in danger if something goes wrong." He stared gravely at Todd. "You'll have to warn your brother that I might leave suddenly." His gaze became distant.

Sensing Taly's need for space, Kiata motioned for Nils and Todd to follow her into the kitchen.

Chapter 14:
Camarek Pieces

Kest (October) 10, 1538
The Lady's Estate, Kala Mountains

A deep sense of satisfaction swept over Mavis as she observed Governor Darmon Zelene's funeral procession moving through the streets of Resh. She almost wished she'd spent the effort to secretly attend. Indulging the disappointment, she ran her slender carving knife across a piece of kintral wood clutched in her other hand. A delicate sliver peeled away from the block, curling as it did so.

Zelene had been a popular governor, a cool head among a group of highly opinionated people. Tosh and salt dealers, coral and fish traders, Idonian glass merchants, and farmers had come to expect fair treatment from Resh markets. Had Governor Zelene not been tainted by close affection for Mavis's brother and his family, she would have let him live despite his other flaws. He had provided stability to the region, and unfortunately for him, stability gave the royals too much time to think. Mavis wanted them reacting, not thinking.

Sweet chords from Parioxa's *Last Revelations* filled the room providing a suitable atmosphere for watching the funeral. Mavis liked the original version in the artist's native language best, but any version was preferable to hearing the announcer describe everything the viewer could clearly see.

As Mavis slowly worked the knife over a fresh section of wood, the screen showed Terosh and his precious wife in clothes meant to honor the departed. Terosh's dark blue uniform had him looking ready to lead the Royal Guards on parade. His wife's light blue shimmersilk gown flowed in a faint breeze, making one think of peaceful waves. No tears marred their perfect, innocent, very young faces, but their expressions were heartbreakingly sad.

Mavis focused on her nephew's wife and imagined her at his funeral. She felt no particular ill-will toward the woman, but Kezem could never take the throne while Terosh lived. Under better circumstances, Mavis might even like the young queen who at eighteen barely qualified as an adult. Initial reports had dismissed the former Ranger as a harmless healer, but recent events spoke otherwise.

Several wood shavings tumbled free from the figure Mavis was liberating from within the block. A thought struck her.

What would Terosh look like at his wife's funeral?

Mavis had always assumed a need to deal with her nephew first. She regretted the time and effort the deal with Gardan would take, but it was necessary for building a foundation upon which Kezem could rule.

The focus shifted from the royals to the veiled Lady Akia Zelene who marched directly behind her father's body, which floated down the street on a hov sled. Mavis felt a pang of sympathy for the woman. Sacrifice of any kind was regrettable. The most skilled camarek players could vanquish their opponents without either side losing a piece. Mavis did not doubt her skills at fashioning outcomes, but she also knew the value of a timely execution.

As the funeral dragged on, she let her mind chase the possibilities around in circles while her hands deftly dealt with the kintral wood. Bit by bit, the wood submitted to its new form. When it at last took shape, Mavis blew on it to remove dust remnants and held it up with admiration. The piece looked like any other camarek common soldier, but the face bore a striking resemblance to Resh's late governor. Like the others in her collection, this piece would never be played with. They existed solely for her private pleasure at creating—and sometimes destroying—them.

Mavis slowly traced a finger over the figure's face. As a girl, she had loved camarek. Noticing a strong, strategic mind, her father had insisted she learn the rules. From the first, she had admired the fact that the game could be as simple or complex as the players wished. Any small child could comprehend that attack hounds only moved one space in any direction, common soldiers moved two such spaces but only forward, backward, left, or right, and elite soldiers traveled any number of diagonal spaces.

The king and queen could move any number of desired spaces in any direction except the diagonals. The most powerful piece, the spy, could be disguised as any piece and had to be chosen before each match. The spy could move up to five spaces in any combination of directions and was the only piece able to capture the king or queen. Most people tried not to reveal their spy until the very end. Victory could be achieved by annihilating all enemies, capturing the king and queen, or destroying the opponent's spy.

Who will be my camarek spy? Mavis wondered.

She chuckled at the clichéd notion of likening her plans to the strategy game. She had several options for the part, including Kolknir, Lucas Telon, and Surd Antar, but the analogy was imperfect. Kolknir and his protégé had been revealed as enemies of the Royal House, and Antar was too dull to make an effective spy. All three men were eager to challenge the royals, but they seemed better suited for the attack hound role. Even Kezem was not completely capable of playing the part well.

Mavis tucked the new carving into the specially prepared box. Perhaps she would burn the piece to honor the dead man, but for now, the carving's fate would remain safely sealed away. She had new pieces to consider and new players to tempt to her cause. Antar's protégé, Captain

Ectosh Laocer, might be the sort of man Mavis needed, and he had an obvious weakness that could be exploited.

***

Kest (October) 10, 1538
Same Day
Tarpon Estate, City of Kalmata

Lucas Telon hurried through the hallway leading to the master bedroom. His breath felt uncomfortably warm and moist within the confines of the black mask. He was anxious to be done with this mission. After the recent invasion of the Deegan Estate in Terab, he had expected to meet fierce resistance at this Alliance stronghold. The two, half-asleep guards he'd met were hardly worth the bullets Lucas had spent on them.

Complacency's a killer, he thought, quietly opening the door.

A dull scraping noise warned him something was wrong just as the door exploded, sending Lucas hard into the far wall. Searing heat made his mask unbearably hot, but the cloth protected his face from most of the splinters. The impact drove thoughts from him, but his training took over. He rolled onto his back, drew his serlak pistols, and shot the figure rushing toward him through the destroyed doorway.

A woman's sharp, pained cry pierced through the ringing in Lucas's ears. He cursed and scrambled over to the body slumped in the doorway to confirm Nera Tarpon's death. A mass of dark, flowing hair covered her face. The body lay curled across the threshold where it had crumpled under Lucas's gunfire.

His mind reeled. That had not been part of his mission. He was supposed to terrorize and perhaps torture the woman but definitely not kill her. He cursed the need for serlak weapons. It had seemed important to his role as a house intruder, but with a kerlak weapon he could have stunned the woman.

Before he could brush the hair away from the woman's face, pain blossomed in Lucas's left shoulder as a strong hand clamped down and hauled him to his feet.

"Let's go," growled Kolknir's voice.

Shame flooded Lucas, but he forced himself to stumble after his mentor.

***

Kest (October) 11, 1538
The Lady's Estate, Kala Mountains

Lady Mavis Altran let the recording finish its gruesome story before shutting the screen off.

"I told you he could not protect you," she said, working compassion and caution into her tone. She turned toward her guest and studied the young woman's expression.

Nera Tarpon sat stiffly in the comfortable armchair. Her body had the unnatural stillness of a Porit viper preparing to unleash a devastating attack. Her fingers dug into the expensive fabric composing the chair's arms.

The force drove traces of blood from her fingers.

Mavis imagined those long, delicate fingers as cold bones. While giving her guest a moment to order her thoughts, Mavis thought about Lucas Telon's test. His performance—exemplary until the end—was marred by the simplest of failures. Mavis shivered at how close she'd come to losing a valuable asset and thanked whatever fortune had pressed upon her the need to have Kolknir implement safety measures. Her designs for Nera Tarpon were only starting to materialize.

"What will happen to him?" asked Nera. Her pale purple irises focused intently on Mavis in a sharp contrast to her hoarse tone.

Resisting the tide of irritation trying to consume her, Mavis said, "If you agree to my terms, your husband will simply remain under guard. When all the unpleasantness is past, you will be restored to him." She left unsaid what could happen if Nera chose not to accept her terms. Imagined threats often held more power than spoken ones.

"What must I do?" asked Nera. Her voice trembled.

Mavis pitied the desperate young woman and wondered whether she possessed the emotional fortitude to finish the task. She pushed the doubt aside. Time would tell. Nera was only one day removed from her old life.

"You will train with my agents for a time," she said.

"Kolknir," said Nera, spitting the name with disgust.

"What he lacks in social graces, he makes up for in skill," Mavis assured the girl. She stopped short of apologizing for Kolknir's brutal ways. "He will not be your only instructor, but I will arrange those details in time. All I require now is a commitment."

Nera hesitated.

"What of the king and queen?" she asked.

"What of them?" returned Mavis.

"Will they come to harm?"

Mavis drew a slow breath and tried not to laugh. The question evidenced the sort of idealism that had caught Mavis's attention in the first place. Nera Tarpon, daughter of Arista and the slain Tobias Restler and wife of the Tarpon heir, should have little love for House Minstel. Her question was a troubling reminder of just how far-reaching Terosh and Reia's popularity stretched. Realizing she had remained silent too long, Mavis forced a smile.

"I cannot predict the future, but your help may be crucial to preserving them."

Suspicion entered Nera's expression.

"But you hate them. You're working with my husband and the Alliance to destabilize their rule. Why would you help them?" Her conflicted emotions caused several expressions to flicker across her face in rapid succession.

Mavis acknowledged each point with a small nod, ignoring the annoying notion of working with the RT Alliance.

"My family troubles are long past," she lied. "I remain too much my father's daughter to let revenge blind me to a threat against my homeworld." She let passion infuse her voice with conviction. "Just hear me out."

Even as she spoke, Mavis knew she'd found her camarek spy.

Chapter 15:
A Matter of Right

Kest (October) 11, 1538
Temporary Quarters, Governor Lord's Estate, City of Resh
The moment Terosh Minstel awoke he felt a dozen matters vie for his attention. A week and a half had passed since his grandfather had issued two orders thinly disguised as requests. Terosh knew his people could pacify King Padric Creston for a short while longer, but he wanted the matters settled for his own peace of mind. He had never seriously considered sending Reia to Gardan, but he changed his mind at least twice a day concerning Niktrod Keldor.

Also, Resh needed a new governor, and his favorite candidate would likely refuse the position. He understood and accepted most of the reasons she would cite, but he still needed to decide how dirty he wanted to fight in the battle of wills yet to be waged.

He wanted answers to the recent disappearances. Task forces had been formed in every major city, and troops had been dispatched from most forts. Still, Terosh felt something more ought to be done. At least no new disappearances had been reported.

As expected, the Governors Council and Senate balked at Terosh's call to reform scientific practices. Their coordinated efforts spoke of forewarning. The more he learned about the guidelines, the less he liked them. People could buy and sell living bodies, so long as *reasonable expectations of care and consent* were met.

Fort Tiree needed a new commander, as the last one perished in a boating accident while on vacation in Chara.

Flooding around Twin Lake had damaged several villages. Azhel's governor, Leonard Westis, requested aid with the relief efforts.

Thoughts of these matters and more left Terosh feeling helpless. He tightened his hold on his wife, as if clinging to her could blast through the negative feelings.

Reia shifted, pressing her back more firmly against his chest.

He froze—not wanting to wake her—which, of course, did so.

Her hands squeezed his forearms, sending anotechs with a simple declaration of love. The skin she touched tingled pleasantly. She nestled her head into the warm space between his neck and the pillow.

"Sorry," he murmured into her hair.

"Don't be. It's much easier to appreciate your company while conscious." As the anotechs reported Terosh's emotional state, Reia added, "I wish you wouldn't worry so much."

"I wish there wasn't so much to worry about," Terosh replied. He sent anotechs carrying the mental equivalent of gentle kisses across her forehead, nose, and lips.

"Kiss me yourself, you lazy bum," Reia said with mock sternness. She twisted around so she could face him nose to nose.

He chuckled and complied, sticking to the same order. When the kiss on the lips reached its inevitable conclusion, Terosh drew his head back, met her steady gaze, and grinned.

"Is there anything else I can do for you, Majesty?"

Reia traced the curve of his cheek and jaw then placed a finger across his lips.

"Kiss more. Talk less."

***

Once dressed, Reia made the bed. Terosh had laughed the first time she insisted on straightening each corner, but her Ranger training was too thorough to rely on servants. She had never minded the chore of setting her sleep pallet to rights. It helped her prepare for the day by providing a nice metaphor of chaos yielding to order.

"Reia, what do you think about Niktrod Keldor?" asked Terosh, breaking into her thoughts.

"The man who killed your mother?" she asked, tucking in one last blanket corner and smoothing it out. Though she tried, Reia could not keep the curiosity out of her voice. She faced her husband and perched on the spot she had just fixed. "I thought you had settled the matter with your grandfather."

"He thinks it's settled, but I keep changing my mind," said Terosh. He wore a thoughtful scowl but did not elaborate.

Resisting the urge to gauge his mood again, Reia pulled herself further onto the bed and waited for Terosh to continue. She knew only scant details concerning the fate of the former queen. Terosh tended to avoid conversations about his mother and the ill-fated banquet that killed her. Reia had not thought to ask Master Sedir for answers, but she made a mental note to do so.

Eyes fixed on the floor, hands clasped behind his back, and frown still firmly in place, Terosh said nothing for a long time.

"I don't know what is right," he admitted at last.

"Is Keldor guilty?" Reia asked, curious about his lack of anger.

Terosh nodded.

"It's not his guilt I question. The investigation was one of the most thorough ever conducted."

"Then what bothers you?"

"He's a citizen of Reshner," Terosh said. "If I hand him over to Gardan, the people will feel robbed. I feel robbed already, but that hardly matters. And I know my grandfather well enough to feel guilty about sending anyone—even Keldor—to face him."

"They would torture him," Reia said. Even in the Riden Mountains, people had repeated stories of Gardan's Shadow Guard in hushed whispers. Master Kolknir's decision to train with them had nearly sent the Council into hysterics.

A possible—unpleasant—solution occurred to her. She tried to keep it off her face but failed. It would be a sort of suicide rather than murder, but the distinction brought her little comfort. Setting the man free would upset everyone and violate justice.

"What is it?" asked Terosh, unclasping his hands and stretching his arms out to his sides.

Reia drew some deep breaths, hoping to draw in extra courage.

"Call for a public trial," she said, still feeling uneasy.

"To what end?" Terosh's gaze sharpened as his mind turned the possibility over a few times. Cautious hope entered his eyes.

"A public trial may satisfy our people," Reia began. "If the evidence is as strong as you say, the outcome is inevitable." She paused to worry her lower lip, silently questioning the morality of this scheme. With a sigh, she forged on. "His sentence could be execution on Gardan, which would satisfy your grandfather, but for the sake of our consciences, I propose an execution on the way to Gardan."

A slow smile spread across Terosh's face.

"Your compassion matches your wisdom. I will see it done." With that short speech, he rushed forward for a kiss and hurried from the room with a renewed sense of purpose.

***

Kest (October) 11, 1538
Same Day
Communications Hub, University of Resh, City of Resh

Terosh stepped into the pod and activated the security devices. He also activated the personal sound damper. In theory, anything trying to hear the conversation from outside a one-meter radius of Terosh would hear nothing but white noise. His outfit conveyed power and opulence. Though he needed the image, the multicolored robes bothered him.

"One short conversation and you can change," Reia promised, looping her left arm through his right arm and clasping his hand.

They had discussed their beginning pose at length and agreed that Reia would stand a few centimeters behind and to the right of Terosh until he introduced her. Then, she would step up beside him so they could present a united front.

"I feel like I'm about to be executed," Terosh complained, "or suffocated or both." He entered the code to establish a connection with

Gardan's royal palace. "Now we wait," he said, entering a command for the console to alert him when someone answered.

"Why?" asked Reia, retrieving her left hand and rubbing it down the side of her dress. Her hands were not sweaty, but she needed to move to ease her tension.

"Because grandfather needs to establish that he's more important than us," Terosh replied. "It probably won't be long. I told him you would be here."

"I thought you wanted to surprise him," Reia said, slipping off the diamond studded shoes pinching her feet.

"You really don't like shoes these days," Terosh commented, eyeing the sparkling heels. "One would think a mountain-raised Ranger would be used to shoes."

"Boots and normal shoes are fine. These are jewel-encrusted torture devices," Reia explained. "When we get back to Rammon I'm having a long conversation with Lady Parné about my footwear."

"Just send her a message. She can—"

A chime cut him off.

Terosh gave his wife a sympathetic, encouraging smile and steadied her while she climbed back into the offending shoes. They took their agreed upon positions and Terosh reached to confirm the connection.

"Just a short conversation and—"

A jeweled toe slammed into the back of his right boot cutting him off. He laughed and squeezed Reia's hand before opening the connection with Gardan. By the time King Padric Creston's imperious form appeared, Terosh wore a neutral expression.

"Greetings, Grandfather," said Terosh, lowering his head in a gracious bow. "In our last conversation you expressed an interest in my wife. Allow me to introduce Her Majesty Reia Antellio Minstel, Queen of Reshner."

Reia slipped forward and tipped her head down respectfully.

Terosh dared not look at her. He felt like they were facing a venomous snake and wanted to sweep her behind his back.

"Where is my prisoner?" King Padric asked, ignoring Reia.

Her lack of reaction emphasized the absence of royal blood. Any queen should be livid at such dismissal. Terosh flushed, offended on her behalf. A wave of calming thoughts descended on him as Reia urged him to let it go.

"You will have him after we conduct a public trial." Terosh did not have to work hard for a cold tone.

King Padric's countenance turned stonier.

"That is—"

"The only way to preserve peace, Your Grace," Reia interrupted, dropping into a full curtsey.

What happened to not giving in to his over-sized ego? Terosh demanded through the anotechs.

She sent him a trust-me nudge.

"Your daughter, our queen, was much loved," said Reia. "If we simply sent her killer away, we would be accused of robbing the people. A trial will allow us to address their anger and acknowledge your right to claim the prisoner."

King Padric's glare lost some of its chill as a spark of amusement appeared.

"She speaks well for a commoner. The speech master should be commended," said King Padric, studying Reia with a critical eye. After a long look, he shifted his attention back to Terosh. "You might even want to invest in a few more lessons yourself, boy." He tilted his head thoughtfully. "Assuming I humor you, how long will this trial delay justice? What guarantee prevents a soft-minded judge from acquitting Keldor?"

"In the unlikely event Keldor is exonerated, we will rejoice that an innocent man has escaped wrongful conviction," said Terosh.

Laughing harshly, King Padric leaned close to the vidrecorder.

"Your simplistic views will get you killed, boy. It's just as well you favor your father. I would hate to be linked to your inevitable failures."

Ouch.

Terosh tried to keep the words from bothering him, but they hurt all the same. He sensed Reia's ire rising and silently willed her to let him handle the situation.

"In blood, sir, I am as much a son of Gardan as a son of Reshner," Terosh said, letting anger stiffen his words. "I am proof that a close relationship exists between our planets."

Disgust rang through King Padric's response.

"Any children you produce with this commoner will receive diluted blood."

Terosh bowed his head, so he could consider his next words. He needed to move the conversation back on course, but the man's attitude rankled.

"Had I wed a distant Gardanian cousin, my children would be three parts your home and one part mine. There is no fair way to share the blood of two lines on one throne, but blood matters less than knowledge. Any child of mine will be well versed in both legacies. This I promise on all honors due my late mother."

Menacing silence fell until finally King Padric said, "I will accept your ridiculous need for a public trial and expect news of my prisoner's pending arrival within four months."

"Trials take a long time, Grandfather, but I shall see matters proceed quickly," Terosh promised.

"See that you do. Now, I will repeat my advice that you annul the bond with this commoner or accept my offer to adopt her," said his grandfather.

If I have my way, you'll never set foot on the same planet she does.

"I will not renounce my wedding vows," Terosh declared.

"And we respectfully decline other offer, Your Grace," Reia said.

"Insolent children," muttered King Padric.

Pompous fool. Terosh fired back silently, glaring so intensely at his grandfather that his head hurt.

"We apologize, Your Grace," said Reia. "For my part, I cannot rewrite my past or recast my loyalty. I was born here, I will likely die here, and I am sworn to protect the interests of this people. Were that something I could lay down lightly, it would be worthless."

Surprisingly, King Padric's lips twisted into a smile.

"Boy, you are ensnared by a silver-tongued enchantress. Move the trial along and see that this harpy does not twist what little good sense my daughter imparted to you."

As the connection cut off, Terosh wordlessly embraced Reia.

Chapter 16:
Guarantee

Kest (October) 11, 1538
Same Day
The Lady's Estate, Kala Mountains

Knowing Terosh and his wife had a "secret" interplanetary call scheduled with King Padric Creston, Mavis played a game of camarek against the board's artificial intelligence and waited for the inevitable call that would follow.

It vexed her not to be able to hear the conversation. The latest personal sound dampers currently had her experts stumped. Dr. Quatar had promised to invent a device that could break through any sound damper in the next few months, but that hardly helped her now. Besides, she preferred the good doctor devote his time to the project he was hired to complete. The other professors had issued similar promises, but Mavis had far less confidence in their work.

The camarek board moved an elite soldier against the common soldier she had secretly made her spy. She concentrated on the problem that presented. She could boldly move one of her elite soldiers to block the board's move, thus betraying her common soldier as the spy. Conversely, she could cautiously move her queen to a position that would threaten the board's king to divert attention from her lowly common soldier. She could also have her spy execute a clumsy retreat and delay the revelation. The first move would be reckless but take care of the board's last elite solider, leaving it only common soldiers, the king, and the queen. The second and third moves would only delay the confrontation.

Relishing the idea of recklessness, Mavis decided on the boldest move. She hated losing with a passion that could break stone to tiny bits, but playing the game without risk bored her. As Mavis picked up her elite soldier to capture the board's last elite soldier, a pleasant, triumphant tune indicated an incoming call from Gardan. She smiled to herself, paused the game, and wondered how the board's AI would handle the situation. Determining to find out later, Mavis got up and walked to the communications array.

Activating the vidrecorder and hologram projectors, Mavis met King Padric's glare and permanent scowl with a pleasant smile.

"How may I help you?" she inquired.

"Observe the conversation I will send you and tell me your thoughts on my grandson," said King Padric.

Almost immediately, one of Mavis's vidscreens blinked a yellow light indicating an incoming data pack. She activated the recording and felt a thrill of anticipation. It still bothered her that she did not have the information already, but she was happy to witness Terosh's meeting with King Padric.

The entire recording focused on Terosh and his wife and took less than four minutes to unfold. Mavis controlled her expression, but inside, she longed to see King Padric's expression to her nephew's cool reception. Creston's grumpy tone told her the expression would be both amusing and satisfying. She smiled at Terosh's flat refusal to annul his marriage. Their plan to hold a public trial intrigued her. The reasons made sense, but Mavis wondered if they were really so sweetly naïve or more devious than she had imagined.

"I warned you he would never submit on the issue of his wife," Mavis said when the recording had ended. She had asked Dennel to include the warning as a gesture of good will.

"What do you think of this trial they propose?" asked the king.

Mavis hesitated not sure which light to cast Terosh in. Did she want Padric to think Terosh a dolt or a mastermind? She had yet to fully assign him a role, but eventually, she decided that having Padric underestimate her nephew would be preferable. After all, a time might come when she had to deal with one of Padric's plans. Mavis put a lot of effort into a casual shrug and wished she had more time to think over a response.

"It is a decent plan, and I can attest to their assessment of the situation," said Mavis. "Sending Keldor straight to you would be highly unpopular."

"Will the trial be fair?" asked Padric, spitting the last word like a curse.

"I will see that the trial goes our way," Mavis promised, laughing delicately.

"How will you control the sentence?"

"Trials on this planet are fairly standard, except that the judge wields a lot more power than in most places," Mavis explained. "Very few cases stand before a jury of commoners, though some may stand before a royal or a government committee. However, a trial of this magnitude will likely demand multiple phases."

"What does that mean? How long will I be denied my prisoner?"

The king's questions and tone gave Mavis the image of a petulant child crying foul.

"It means the trial will be a planetary affair," Mavis explained. "Normally, it would fall to the king to appoint a judge, but Keldor's advocate will likely object to any involvement from the Royal House. He or she will then appeal to the Governors Council to appoint a judge. They will—"

King Padric exploded with a word Mavis assumed qualified as an invective.

"It could be years before such an inefficient system renders judgment of any sort!" he shouted.

Mavis raised her right hand in a placating gesture.

"It could, but it will not. Leave that to me. I will arrange for my son to be judge, and you will have your conclusion by the Dalest Nareth of next year."

"How can you make such a grand promise? My astronomers tell me your Darkest Night falls early in the next cycle."

Mavis confirmed it with a nod.

"It is set to fall on the twelfth day of Idela (January) in 1539."

"What will you give me as a guarantee that you will keep your word?"

Denying him would be fatal to their deal. Mavis could read as much in Padric's narrowed eyes. Her mind raced. She knew the sort of guarantee he wanted. Though her father's family had long since ceased trading hostages, several noble families—and even Kezem—indulged in the practice. She did not think she could trust King Padric, but she also knew she had little choice if she wanted him to honor his end of their deal.

"You must claim the guarantee yourself," Mavis said, hating the weakness in her voice.

Padric's gaze never wavered.

"Whom shall my men seek?"

Lifting her chin and staring as hard as she could, Mavis said, "Seek the family of Governor Judge Mitrek Altran of Idonia. He has two daughters and a son. Take the eldest child as your guarantee."

"I take it the judge is your son," said King Padric.

"Yes, he is my son," answered Mavis.

"What of his connection to the Royal House? Your sons are still officially recognized relatives to the king, are they not?"

"They are indeed, but Mitrek has a reputation of maintaining impartiality," said Mavis.

"As for your plan, will not a missing child disqualify him as judge?"

"It depends on how the child's absence is perceived. Strike the last plan. Send your men to Rammon," Mavis instructed, suddenly feeling ill. "I will have people bring them to a safe house and see that the child makes it to that same house. They can wait for the trial's conclusion with a few of my people. As far as my son and his wife will be concerned, their daughter will be safely in my care. That is my guarantee."

King Padric said nothing for a time, and his intense eyes swept Mavis's face again and again, searching for deception. Finally, he said, "I accept your plan. Now, what can you tell me about my grandson and his wife?"

"I can add very little to that which your spies have already told you," said Mavis, trying not to let her relief show. "Terosh is dangerously idealistic, as you have pointed out."

"And the commoner?" asked Padric, for once not quite glaring.

Mavis reviewed her knowledge of her nephew's wife, searching for new insights and trying to decide how much to share.

"The reports on her potential to lead vary, but the facts remain consistent. Her parents owned tosh mines and died when a competitor had them assassinated. The Rangers raised her and an older sister upon the request of a mercenary who could not kill them. She became a healer then got herself banished by marrying Terosh."

"This sister you mentioned, do I know her?" inquired the king.

"I sent you a vid showing the sister and her husband breaking into an estate in Terab to rescue a young man," said Mavis.

Recognition flashed in Padric's eyes.

"I remember. That was a most impressive display. I am eager to meet such powerful beings. Tell me, can I expect such a boon?"

That was my intention, Mavis thought, but now that he asked, she hesitated to make a promise she might fail to keep.

"I can make no guarantee, but I shall set my mind to the task," she promised.

"See that you do," said Padric imperiously.

Eager to be done with the distasteful man, Mavis steered the conversation to a close by promising to have Dennel call with instructions once he worked out the details of securing Mavis's granddaughter.

Alone at last, Mavis retreated to the table holding the camarek board and let the AI battle itself. She had no heart to continue the game and barely paid attention as the pieces moved themselves around the board, challenging and capturing each other.

What have I done?

Mavis tried to fight the thought off, but it kept pricking her conscience. She had just wagered her granddaughter's life that she could control a trial that had not even been called for yet. If Terosh changed his mind, Mitrek lost the bid to judge, one of the advocates stalled, or one of a few hundred other things went wrong, Padric Creston would kill Silvia.

I won't let that happen.

Dreading the call she needed to make but determined not to put it off, Mavis reset the camarek board and went to her thinking chair to consider how to acquire Mitrek's cooperation.

Unbidden, another problem surfaced. A public trial might provoke Eldon to an act of supreme stupidity. Her eldest son claimed to have evidence that she had ordered Queen Kila's death. His clumsy threats to reveal such evidence had been a minor thorn in her side for years, but the problem grew exponentially upon Keldor's capture. She cursed herself for not killing the assassin ages ago.

Mavis sighed deeply. She had no wish to deal harshly with Eldon, but her plans were too important to risk on waiting out his unsteady nerves.

He always was a sensitive boy, she thought sadly.

He hid it well behind coolness, but Mavis knew she had failed to turn Eldon against House Minstel. She hesitated to warn him off though because his natural stubbornness and idiotic pride would provoke him into exactly the sort of behavior Mavis would need to deal with harshly.

***

Kest (October) 11, 1538
Same Day
Governor Judge's Estate, City of Idonia

Delia Altran nervously twisted the rings adorning her left hand. Squeezing hard enough for the Nedis crystal diamonds to dig into her fingers, she watched her husband. His tense stance and vacant stare told her of his agitated state, but his expression failed to divulge more information. Although eager to know what bothered him, nameless fear rendered her mute.

"Mother called today," Mitrek finally blurted.

Delia's heart lurched. It suddenly became clear why Mitrek had ordered the children to bed early. Lady Mavis Altran's calls had the nasty habit of heralding trouble. To say she scared Delia would be a gross understatement.

"We are to return the call tonight," said Mitrek, sounding like he was bracing for a refusal.

Just then, Leah walked in with a comm attached to a vidscreen so they could make the call.

Delia wearily rubbed at her eyes and waited while the servant arranged the communications device. Mitrek took the open seat next to her and leaned close so the tiny vidrecorder could capture both their images. Now that he was so close, Delia noticed the fine sheen of sweat glazing his forehead. Somehow, the observation made her feel worse.

When Lady Mavis Altran appeared, Mitrek cleared his throat.

"Greetings, Mother. Leah said you wanted to speak with us this evening, so here we are."

Lady Mavis's warm smile did nothing to ease Delia.

"I realized I have never truly enjoyed the pleasure of Silvia's company and request the opportunity to make up for the lapse." The way she spoke the word "request" made it an order.

"Vee," whispered Delia, unconsciously using the nickname. Her lower lip trembled as her mind conjured a dozen frightening images. She stole a glance at her pale husband and reached for his clenched left fist.

"What have you done?" Mitrek's question contained more accusation than inquiry.

Lady Mavis's smile dimmed. She looked slightly wounded for a second before her smile turned bemused.

"Why does everybody assume I have ulterior motives?" she wondered.

"Because you always do," Mitrek answered.

"Fair enough," replied Lady Mavis graciously. She stared at Mitrek and Delia in turn. "You deserve the truth, and I shall tell you what I can."

She wasn't going to tell us!

The realization struck Delia like a physical blow, making the pain of the news to come worse. Delia held her breath and griped her husband's hands tightly.

"A trial will soon be ordered for Queen Kila's assassin. You must bid for it," said Lady Mavis.

"Why? Did you order her death? Shall I set the guilty free, Mother?" Mitrek's voice trembled with suppressed anger.

"Bitterness suits you not at all, my dear," Lady Mavis said mildly. "And, as for your last question, my wishes are quite the opposite. You will give Niktrod Keldor a death sentence to be carried out on Gardan."

Mitrek's harsh laughter chilled Delia.

"So you did kill the last queen, and I'm to clean up your mess." He shook his head in disgust. "Do you have any idea how many laws you just asked me to break?"

"Do you have any idea how many lives rest upon your decision?" Lady Mavis returned.

Delia was stunned. She knew her husband's mother could be cold, but she never imagined the woman would threaten them.

Mitrek paled even further. His gaze turned murderous.

"How many lives, Mother?"

Delia's breaths came in short, frantic bursts. Her vision clouded and her hearing wavered. She released her husband's hands to rest her head in her palms, elbows propped on knees.

Mitrek's arms encircled her.

"Breathe deeply," he encouraged, rubbing her back with his left hand.

"Delia, focus," Lady Mavis demanded. "You must follow my instructions explicitly. No one can know there is anything amiss about Silvia's visit to me."

"We don't even know where you live!" Mitrek shouted.

"You will know precisely what you need to know when you need to know it," Lady Mavis said.

"You expect us to pack up our daughter—" Mitrek began.

"I expect obedience," Lady Mavis interrupted. "You will bid for and win Keldor's case, conduct the trial, and hand down exactly the sentence I described. Then, I can send Silvia home."

A few more shaky breaths made Delia feel a little better.

"How can you do this?" she asked, wishing her voice were steadier. "How can you threaten your own family?" Tears that had been pooling finally fell, but she locked away the sobs.

"What if I lose the bid?" Mitrek wondered.

"You won't," Lady Mavis said. "Just worry about your part in this." Her eyes focused on Delia. "I do what I must to protect my family. Silvia will have my finest guards during her short stay."

Delia felt like something was trying to suck her soul out.

Still holding tightly to Delia, Mitrek refused to look at his mother.

"I will do as you say, Mother, but when this matter ends, we're done." He slapped the switch to end the call before she could respond.

Chapter 17:
Tutor

Lord Kezem spun around and drove his kerlinblade hard against the attacker who stood ready for the blow. The man grunted but absorbed the strike with relative ease. A swift kick to the man's right knee earned Kezem a moment to miss the satisfying weight of his electrified banistick, but he needed the kerlinblade practice.

Another eight attackers stood warily in a loose circle around Kezem and the man climbing to his feet again.

"I don't like this," said one of the mercenaries. The blond woman nervously shifted her grip on her kerlinblade. "It feels wrong. You knew we were coming."

A few of the mercenaries muttered agreement and the occasional curse.

"Do you know who hired you?" asked Kezem.

"Not really," answered the woman who first sensed something wrong. "The broker said only—" She cut herself off and raised her kerlinblade up to a defensive position. White light shone off her face.

Kezem sensed movement from behind and threw himself left a split second before a kerlak beam flew across the circle and struck the wall by a surprised mercenary. Three men drew pistols, one kerlak and two serlak. Kezem mentally cursed and decided to kill them all for breaking the contract. His man had been very specific about the job being completed with kerlinblades only. He never expected them to honor the contract, but the point had been to gain genuine practice fighting multiple adversaries.

He charged the nearest man and plunged his blade into the man's stomach, releasing a near-deafening roar of pain and rage. Before the man could even finish bleeding to death, Kezem gripped his right shoulder and pivoted so the body blocked the incoming energy beams and bullets. The twisting motion of plunging the blade in had helped Kezem turn the man, but now, the blue blade cut itself free. Knowing his makeshift shield would

349

soon be useless, Kezem abandoned it.

A lunge brought him within striking distance of a young mercenary. The boy barely had enough sense to raise his kerlinblade to catch Kezem's first strike. The force pressed the boy's weapon into his left shoulder. He screamed and fainted, but Kezem wasn't satisfied yet. With a well-timed flick of his kerlinblade, Kezem removed the unfortunate man's head.

Two down, many to go. His eyes challenged the rest to step forward and test him.

"Who are you?" demanded the talkative woman.

"Don't you recognize me?" Kezem asked, grateful for the break. He felt their gazes scrutinize his features. His man had hired them from Azhel, but if they had paid any attention in school, they should know him.

One dark-haired young woman stood with her kerlinblade held casually at her side. She didn't fit with the rest of the group. Too much certainty shone in her lovely, purple eyes. Kezem expected her to speak, but she said nothing.

"You are Governor General Kezem Altran, Idonia's Third Lord," a man said eventually.

"You are Maladek," said another man. He appeared older than the others.

The woman with blond hair immediately lowered her kerlinblade.

"You hired us," she said.

"Right on all accounts." Kezem lowered his chin in an acknowledging bow.

"Why would you hire us to kill you?" asked a young man.

"It doesn't matter," said yet another mercenary man. "I say we finish the job and loot the house besides." The man raised his serlak pistol and started shooting.

Expecting the man to do just that, Kezem easily sidestepped the first two bullets and retrieved a pair of flingers from the holder on his belt. The first flinger lodged deep in the man's throat. He died almost instantly, but his finger tightened over the trigger and sent one more bullet flying. The errant bullet caught one of the young mercenaries in the left arm, spinning him around and knocking him back into a wall where he leaned heavily. The body of the man killed by the first flinger teetered before falling backward, but Kezem didn't have time to enjoy the sight. The second flinger barely missed the light-haired woman's head, as she used her blade to redirect its flight.

Despite the blond woman's shouted orders to stop fighting, two mercenaries attacked with kerlinblades, unwilling to risk more friendly fire. Kezem attacked the first man to reach him, driving him back into his friend. The second man steadied the first, and they raised their blades to defend against Kezem's vicious strikes.

Suddenly, Kezem disengaged, stooped, and snatched up a kerlinblade dropped by one of the fallen mercenaries. Energy coursed through Kezem as he activated the second blade. It glowed orange. One of the mercenaries lunged, and Kezem swept the man's clumsy strike aside before bringing the handle of his other blade down upon the back of the man's skull.

A terrifying, eerie scream came from the second mercenary facing Kezem with a blade. The man's shirt exploded outward in several pieces. Two more arms uncrossed from the man's bare chest, each clutching a throwing knife. With unimaginable speed, both arms whipped back then forward, firing the daggers.

Kezem made some adjustments to the kerlinblades so they were wider and held them together so they formed a shield. The throwing knives slammed into his kerlinblades with surprising force. Kezem feared the thin energy beams standing between him and death would collapse, but they held. A few more adjustments narrowed the beams and changed their colors to blue and red for one and yellow and blue for the other.

By this time, the Elish mercenary held a kerlak pistol in each of his lower two hands. His upper left hand still held his kerlinblade, but the upper right hand clutched a serlak pistol. Kezem had a sinking feeling he might not be able to escape so many bullets and beams. His mind cast about for options. He could seize the man he had just stunned with his blade handle.

Before he could consider other options, the dark-haired woman who had remained quiet thus far traded her kerlinblade for a kerlak pistol. Then, she calmly released a series of stun beams at her female associate. The blond woman cried out at the betrayal, as a beam knocked her unconscious. Three beams pushed the Elish man toward Kezem who slashed diagonally down across the man's chest with his blue and red kerlinblade.

Shifting his grip, Kezem crouched and stabbed down and back, driving the same blade through the mercenary dazed by a head blow. Kezem froze with his right kerlinblade positioned to intercept any attacks and waited to see what the intriguing woman would do next.

She did not disappoint. More stun beams dropped the two remaining mercenary men, including the one already wounded in the arm. Then, the woman put away her pistol, dropped to her knees, and lowered her chin to her chest.

Cautiously rising, Kezem deactivated the kerlinblade in his left hand and clipped it to his belt, but he kept the other blade in a guard position.

"I did not expect such help in this exercise. Who are you?"

"I am Nera Tarpon, my Lord," said the woman, keeping her head lowered. "The Lady would have me learn a blade from you."

His mother had told him to expect a student soon but not deigned to give him details. The young woman before him fit none of the imaginings he had indulged in. Kezem slowly let the kerlinblade drop to his side even as he wondered if his mother was sane. He could easily have killed the woman during this exercise.

"This was as much a test for me as for you, my Lord," said the woman, finally lifting her head. "Will you accept me as a student?"

Do I have a choice?

Kezem knew well enough that he did not.

"I will," he answered, switching off his blade.

"What is your first order then, my Lord?" asked the woman.

Kezem debated killing the mercenaries that had survived. Four were merely stunned and one of those had a serlak bullet in his arm. The first three might be useful sparing partners, but Kezem preferred not to waste his time with the wounded one.

"Kill that one," said Kezem, pointing to the young mercenary who had been shot in the arm and then hit with a stun beam.

"But he's just a boy," protested the woman, her expression stricken. Nevertheless, she took her kerlak pistol out again.

"Wait," said Kezem, deciding to turn the situation into a true test. He walked over to a medical pack attached to the wall and retrieved a stimulant shot. Then, he went to the young mercenary and administered the shot. In a moment, the boy would return to full consciousness. In the meantime, Kezem considered the weapon choices. A kerlak pistol was far too impersonal to prove his point, but a dagger might be a little too close. He settled on a kerlinblade; after all, he was to teach the woman to wield one.

"My Lord?" asked the young woman. A hopeful note said she thought he might have changed his mind about killing the mercenary.

"Take out your kerlinblade and make the blade thin," Kezem instructed.

The horrified expression returned, but the woman swallowed hard and obeyed. Soon, she held a green blade no bigger around than her little finger.

Kezem activated his own blade and made the blue blade very thin as well.

"Good, now I want you to hold your blade like so," he said, demonstrating a simple two-handed grip. He had her practice different cuts for several minutes, sometimes gripping the blade in one hand and sometimes using both hands.

At first, she moved stiffly, but eventually, she relaxed enough to attack the tasks with fluid grace. Occasionally, her eyes wandered to the carnage around them and a bit of the stiffness returned.

After Kezem determined his student had practiced beating the air long enough, he said, "Now, stand in front of the boy. You have more work to do."

Chapter 18:
Time to Move On

Kest (October) 12, 1538
Tarpon Estate, City of Resh

Ignoring the frantic servant begging him to stop, Brook Tarpon crashed through the doors to his father's office.

"What is the—" his father began. Tyko Tarpon cut himself off sharply, glared at the intruder, and muttered something into the infopad he held.

"I'm sorry, Lord Tarpon. I should—" babbled the servant.

"It's all right, Orius," said Tyko in a soothing tone. "My son is always welcome here."

Brook's blood pumped furiously through his head, making his ears ring. Each footfall reinforced his fury. He halted in front of his father's desk, noting the characteristic state of disarray it was in.

"Where is my wife?" Each word in the question could have been its own living entity.

His father's angry gaze softened.

"Lord Maledek must have need of her," he replied, gesturing for Brook to be seated.

"But where is she?" Brook demanded. "Why was my home invaded? The alliance was supposed to improve things, not complicate them."

"You should be more cautious with your words, Brook. Even here at home careless words could call down trouble," spoke a familiar voice.

Brook turned and bowed as his mother swept into the room. The hum of the sound dampers suddenly surrounded them.

"Hello, Mother. I have come to inquire about my wife," he said stiffly. A spike of resentment rammed him in the chest.

"I received a missive from the Lady this morning," informed his mother airily.

"What?" asked Brook and his father at the same time.

"I made some inquiries as soon as I heard of the attack," Vera continued in a slightly more sympathetic tone.

Brook's father cursed and threw his infopad down on his desk.

"I told you to keep me apprised of all contact with Lord Maledek and the Lady." His petulant tone was magnified by his soft Charan accent, which only surfaced when something truly annoyed him.

"You were busy, and I thought it best not to interrupt," said Vera.

"What did she say?" asked Brook, tired of being ignored.

"Not much," his mother admitted, sitting primly in an armchair. "She claims that Nera is safe, but that she will have need of her for quite some time, years perhaps."

"Years? What could Nera possibly do for her that could take so long?" Brook pictured his wife's rich, dark hair and expressive eyes and felt a pang of despair at the thought of such a long separation.

"I don't know, but you had better let caution guide your every move," Vera warned.

Brook gave his mother a questioning look.

"After all this time, my boy's an idiot," muttered his father, heaving a sigh and letting his chin fall to his chest.

"Innocence is not idiocy," snapped Vera. Her hands clenched in her lap to keep from placing a comforting hand on Brook's arm. "Sit down, Brook dear."

Annoyed but accepting obedience as the swiftest path to answers, Brook followed the instruction.

"Try not to worry about your wife," said Vera. "Given recent tensions in the Alliance, she will probably be safer with the Lady than with you."

"What tensions?" asked Brook through a stiff jaw. "That mess Merisia caused? I thought that foolishness was behind us."

"That's only part of it," said Tyko, massaging his temple with his right hand. "And it's not quite a closed matter. Talyon Keldor's escape is unsettling."

"How so?" asked Brook. "Surely, he would not return for Merisia. It would be suicide."

"Do not worry about Talyon Keldor," advised his mother. "His fate will be determined soon enough, but heed my advice concerning your own safety."

"Why do you think I'm in danger?" Brook wondered, despising the faint whine in his tone. "Why do you say it like it's something new? I've always been in danger thanks to you two." He had not meant to rant but felt better afterward.

"Don't be impertinent, boy," scolded his father.

"This is something else entirely," Vera said slowly, ignoring Tyko. "The danger you have faced all your life was subtle and mostly from the Restlers. The Lady and Lord Maledek operate in a completely different stratum."

"You fear them," said Brook, grinning with perverse pleasure.

"As should you," said Tyko gruffly.

"But the Alliance—" Brook protested.

"Is dangerously dependent upon them," Vera finished. "They know precisely where and how to pressure this Alliance into executing their will."

Her words scared Brook.

"Is Nera a hostage?" Brook asked.

"No more than you or I." His mother shrugged then waved at the faint buzzing from the sound dampers. "Then again, the threats are growing ever more real."

"Can I go to her?" Brook asked, a crazy idea forming.

"Why would you want to do that?" asked Tyko.

"I will raise the issue with the Lady." A spark of interest shone in his mother's shrewd green eyes. "But I doubt she will consent. We have consistently failed to place someone close to her."

"Nera would help if she knew," Brook said, hoping he was right.

They fell silent as each wondered how to best contact Nera.

***

Kest (October) 14, 1538
Governor Judge's Estate, City of Idonia

Lord Kezem silently renewed his vow to permanently deal with his mother sooner rather than later. He liked it best when she left him to his delusions of privacy. He hated it when she used him, and the order to escort his niece to a safe house in Rammon rankled even more than usual. This little errand would make his brother hate him almost as much as they mutually despised their mother.

Does the contempt hurt you, Mother?

Sometimes he caught glimpses of pain in her face or heard traces of it in her tone.

"I thought she might send you." Delia's cool voice interrupted his thoughts. She motioned Kezem in and shut the door after he entered.

"Where is Silvia?" Kezem asked, figuring it best to leave as quickly as possible.

"She is with Leah gathering a few items," replied Delia. She turned away and led Kezem through several hallways to a sitting room.

Kezem sensed nothing wrong until the faint click of tumbling locks reached his ears. His kerlinblade was in his hands an instant later.

By this time, Delia had walked to a wine cabinet and removed a kerlak carbine. The weapon shook in her hands, but her eyes glittered with feral determination.

"Delia, this won't help." Kezem kept his voice calm and soothing. He angled his kerlinblade so that it could shield most of his body, but he left it off to avoid needlessly spooking his brother's wife.

"Yes, it will," Delia declared unsteadily. "She will leave us alone if she knows we hold her favorite son."

Shaking his head, Kezem stifled bitter laughter.

"You are mistaken. She cares only that her plan succeeds, and if she has determined your daughter should be involved, it will be so." As he spoke, Kezem took small steps toward Delia.

"Why are you helping her?" Delia asked in a pleading tone. "Mitrek has turned away from her, you could do the same."

Kezem's bitter laughter finally escaped him. He took two more steps in Delia's direction.

"You don't need to save me from her, Delia."

I will see to that myself one day.

In one swift motion, Kezem's left hand seized the gun and twisted it from Delia's grasp while his right activated the kerlinblade and brought the indigo blade to her throat.

With a small cry, she stumbled back a half-step, halted by the wine cabinet. She shut her eyes like she expected him to kill her.

Grunting annoyance, Kezem deactivated the kerlinblade and tossed her gun onto the small couch behind him. Taking his comm from his belt, Kezem held it out to Delia.

"Call Leah and have her bring Silvia here," he said gruffly. Softening his voice, he added, "I will call you when we reach our destination and have my people provide regular updates."

Delia eyed the comm contemptuously but reluctantly accepted it and did as he asked.

"Leah, please bring Silvia to the first-floor sitting room," said Delia. Instead of handing the comm back, she tossed it onto the couch beside the kerlak weapon. "It's hot in here. Would you like some wine?"

Suspicious, Kezem glanced from the comm to Delia and back again. A few quick steps brought him to the couch where he picked up the comm and noticed it was still on.

"Leah, bring me the girl in the next five minutes or I will kill Delia."

***

Kest (October) 14, 1538
Same Day
Governor Lord's Estate, City of Idonia

Eldon Altran's hands shook so hard he nearly dropped the infopad. He sank onto a reclining chair, feeling like a man swallowed by a maw. Having the ground suddenly open then snap shut around him might have been preferable. The report left a sour taste in his mouth. Kezem always had been Mother's favorite, but Eldon thought his brother was smart enough to stay out of Lady Mavis's schemes.

Apparently not, he mused. *How deeply are you involved, Kezem?*

A sinking sensation in the pit of his stomach told Eldon it was only a matter of time before his family faced a crisis like the one thrust upon Mitrek.

Poor Mitrek, poor Delia, poor Silvia. He thought of his wife and two boys. *How do I protect them?*

Eldon wished he could talk to Calia, but he knew ignorance would be her best defense should his plans draw his mother's wrath down upon them.

As time slowly passed, Eldon's frustration mounted. His one protection against his mother was about to either become completely useless or else tear his life apart like a windstorm in a crystal shop. The king had called for a public trial of Niktrod Keldor. The Governors Council and Senate had both agreed, and Eldon had not dared to protest too much.

His mind whipped through options. He could petition the Governors Council to investigate, but that would only suspend the problem for a few months. He could privately beg King Terosh to cancel the trial, but he doubted that would succeed. Reliable—and expensive—word had it that a Gardanian deal prompted the trial in the first place. Eldon could publicly release the evidence, anonymously, of course, to avoid falling afoul of the Law of Obligatory Revelation. The plan would save Keldor's life if several key factors panned out, but it would earn Lady Mavis's eternal ire regardless of the outcome. Eldon fought a sudden chill as he dismissed the idea.

As he despaired of a good plan, a wild idea came to mind. He argued with himself.

Get Keldor the evidence.

What would that accomplish?

Tell mother he has it and let her deal with the problem.

He knew exactly how she would deal with it. She would kill Keldor.

Well, if you're going to kill the man, why not just shoot him yourself?

The thought shocked Eldon. He had managed to go his entire life without killing one sentient being, and now, he was plotting murder, just like his mother.

He felt sick, but he could not shake the knowledge that Keldor was the problem. While Keldor had been free, Eldon's knowledge had been valuable. A trial risked exposing his mother's involvement, which would obliterate any tenuous hold he had over her. If Keldor died, then the truth might remain safely buried.

Eldon held his head in his hands. He loathed his mother's ways, but he would employ them if it saved his family.

Chapter 19:
Meetings of Heart and Mind

Kest (October) 17, 1538
McGreven House, City of Resh

Sitting on the couch in her former master's new home, Reia consciously tried not to fidget. She had intended to come much earlier in her visit to Resh, but the week had passed in a flurry of lessons, meetings, and entertainment. She had tried to prepare arguments as to why Niklos Mikhail McGreven should continue being a Ranger, but now that she was finally here, words failed her.

"You can't do it," said Master Niklos with one of his gentle smiles. His expression said he knew her purpose in visiting. "I have made my choice."

"But they need you!" Reia protested. "I need you."

"You still have me, Sela," he replied. Master Niklos looked at Reia steadily. "You will always have me."

Reia was grateful he used the term of endearment meaning both "dear one" and "daughter" instead of a lofty honorific, but his dull tone worried her.

"Why would you leave the Rangers?" she asked. "They were your life."

Please don't say it was on my account, she silently pleaded.

His warm smile cut through her.

"I am getting older and perhaps more cynical. I want to spend more time with my family, watch my children grow. I have seen too much trouble and am entirely done with that quarrelsome Council."

"They're not perfect, but they try," Reia said, surprised to be fighting tears. She could hardly think about the Council and their last words without the pain crushing her again. Her mind frantically searched a few of the fruitless what-if threads. "Was I wrong?" she blurted at last.

The question could mean almost anything, but Master Niklos knew her better than anyone except Kiata. He knew exactly what she meant. His expression shifted from the compassionate countenance of a friend to the sterner visage of a frustrated instructor. He leaned forward in his chair with an elbow resting on each knee and hands clasped as if in prayer.

"Listen to me, Sela. Whether or not you were wrong does not excuse the Ashatan Council's lack of judgment."

"Then join them. Guide them," said Reia.

"I tried that for a time, but it was like trying to shout in a windstorm." Having lost the hard edges to his expression, he just looked weary. "I will continue to help wherever I can, but I will no longer submit myself to the Council."

His words frightened Reia.

"You're going to go rogue?" she wondered.

Master Niklos chuckled, and a spark of humor brought life to his eyes.

"Oh, I'm going to do much worse than that. I'm going to be a tosh merchant."

"But the mines are corrupt," Reia said.

"What better place to start cleaning than with that which is most in need of it," Master Niklos intoned in his wisest teacher voice.

Reia conceded the point and let the conversation flow into neutral territory for a time. They needed the break. Finally, she brought up the second reason for her visit.

"Master Niklos, what can you tell me of the anotechs? Why do the Rangers limit their use?"

"You probably know much more than I at this point," said Master Niklos.

"But you were a part of the Nareth Talis," said Reia. "You must remember something."

"I retain only vague impressions of those years," Master Niklos said. "The mandatory memory alterations bring up yet another issue that plagues the Council." He shrugged. "At least it gives them something to argue about when they cease philosophizing about why the anotechs reject certain Rangers."

"Does it happen often?" Reia wondered, trying to absorb the new information and reconcile it to things she already knew. Rumors long since dismissed floated to the forefront of her mind.

"Despite two such cases in the last generation, it hardly happens at all," answered Master Niklos. "Your old trainer, Kolknir, was the first case in a few generations, and then, more recently, Lucas Telon failed in the joining ceremony."

Reia nodded thoughtfully. She had known of Lucas's failure, but the significance had been lost on her. Sympathetic emotions for her former friend battled indignant feelings from recent encounters.

"Kiata wouldn't tell me anything on the subject of anotechs or the Nareth Talis ceremonies, but Todd told me active members are sworn to secrecy. Why the silence?" asked Reia.

"For the same reason much ill is done anywhere," said Master Niklos gently. "Fear."

"If we knew more, we would have less to fear," Reia argued.

Master Niklos began to nod agreement but then shook his head.

"You speak some truth, but you forget that fear comes in many forms. Our internal fears may be assuaged by increased knowledge of the anotechs, but we would also draw much unwanted attention from within and without."

"You speak of GAPP. Are they that powerful? Would they take drastic steps to understand the anotechs?"

"I have no doubt they would," said Master Niklos gravely. "The anotechs' ability to live up to legend matters little. Keeping them a legend has been our only safeguard for many years. Why do you ask? What has happened?"

"Nothing … yet," Reia said, attempting a smile. A chill sapped her will to put any force behind the smile. "It is just a feeling I have had for a long time, nothing more than a dream really."

"A new dream?" asked Master Niklos. He knew her standard nightmares almost as well as Kiata. "Tell me."

Reia struggled to put her dreams into words.

Understanding that she needed time, Master Niklos excused himself and went to prepare some mintas tea. When he returned a few minutes later, he served the tea and returned to his seat, waiting patiently.

"Drink your tea, Sela," said Master Niklos. "It is good for easing troubled minds."

Reia was surprised to see the steaming cup. She murmured thanks and absently took a sip. The sharp, spicy taste of wuzle roots nipped at her tongue. She swallowed slowly and willed herself to relax.

"It must have been quite a dream," commented Master Niklos.

"Yes," said Reia, letting the word hang in the air. "I asked about the anotechs before because I feel the dream is somehow related to them, but I cannot fathom how."

Master Niklos frowned.

"There are not many accounts of people's dreams being affected by anotechs." A pensive look came over him. "There were rumors that Ranger Gedroo suffered terrible dreams before he lost his mind, but the accounts were too conflicting to be believed."

Reia smiled faintly.

"That's good to know. I would hate to follow in Ranger Gedroo's footsteps or share his fate." She took another small bit of the mintas and wuzle root tea and let the mixture sit on her tongue, causing it to tingle pleasantly.

"There's no chance of that," Master Niklos assured her.

"Thank you for saying so, but if I continue having dreams like this, I may yet want to lose my mind," Reia said. She drew a slow, deep breath and began, "I was completely submerged in cold, clear blue water. I wanted to fight to the surface, but some unseen force held me fast. Panic rose in my chest and my muscles ached. I held my breath as long as I could, but when I could hold it no longer, I let the sea flood my mouth and nose. Everything stung. The sea water scraped my throat raw, but I could breathe the water."

"Do you think the anotechs could accomplish such a thing? Is that what makes you think of them?" asked Master Niklos.

"No, it was more than that," said Reia. "I saw sharp rocks lying below a steep cliff, great waves crashing onto a shore, and a man dressed in dark clothes standing over a cliff cradling something in his arms. He felt familiar. Then, I was back under the water feeling myself drown and yet living. The cycle repeated at least three times."

"You certainly have vivid dreams," said Master Niklos.

"I don't know what it means," said Reia, letting frustration seep into her tone.

"Must it have a meaning?"

Reia began to nod but then turned her head thoughtfully.

"Everything about the dream seemed so real ... so desperate. It's the same creepy feeling I get when I try to think of the future. I feel like I'm being watched."

Master Niklos burst into laughter.

"My dear Sela, you are the queen. Everybody will always be watching."

***

Kest (October) 17, 1538
Same Day
Governor Lord's Estate, City of Resh

Lacking a better way to deal with his restless energy, Terosh paced back and forth in the small space separating the heavy armchairs from Governor Darmon Zelene's massive desk. Since it only took about three steps to go from one end to the other, Terosh constantly had to turn around. Finally, he forced himself to sit down and look at the woman stiffly perched on the camrood leather chair behind the desk.

"Is there nothing I can say to convince you?" he asked, knowing the answer that would come.

"Not one thing, Your Grace," replied Lady Akia Zelene. She tried to smile, but it flickered and faded almost as soon as it started. "I am not my father. I have not his gift for finding the best compromise or willing others to accept my ways. I know these people, and they know my heart has long belonged to the people of Ritand."

"Will you return there?" asked Terosh as heaviness settle on him.

Nodding and attempting a smile with slightly better results, Lady Akia said, "As soon as my father's affairs are in order, I shall return. The skills the queen taught me are much appreciated there."

"Is there anything I can do?" Terosh asked, desperate to be of some use. He was tired of feeling impotent when it came to dealing with the Governors Council. There were too many careful balances to maintain.

"We can always use more aid, Highness," said Lady Akia. She kept her tone even like she dared not let her hopes rise, but her dark eyes added a heartfelt plea.

Terosh nodded absently several times.

"I will do what I can, Lady Zelene," he promised.

A look of mild alarm mixed with complex pain crossed Lady Akia's features.

"Do not trouble yourself on my account, Highness," she said softly. "The Ritand—"

"Are still my responsibility," Terosh cut in. An idea struck him. "It's time we improved relations with them." He cleared his throat to transition into a more formal tone. "Lady Zelene, would you consider accepting an official commission to attend the needs of the Ritand people?"

"What manner of position?" Hope and caution struggled on Lady Akia's face.

"Ambassador from the Royal House," Terosh said.

"They will oppose it," Lady Akia said, referring to the Governors Council and the Senate.

"Not if we present it right," Terosh argued. "With your permission, I will frame the position as a memorial to your father."

"Why would you need my permission?"

Terosh nearly winced at the question.

"Technically, I don't, but I'm trying to be fair. Your father did much to improve opinions concerning the Ritand. You have devoted yourself to their cause. An official ambassador is the next logical step. Will you accept?"

Lady Akia leveled a measuring gaze at Terosh.

"The Ritand will no doubt protest government involvement, but I think a few will see the advantages."

Terosh knew it was not a clear commitment, but it allowed him to turn the conversation to the details.

Chapter 20:
Investigations

Kest (October) 18, 1538
Site of the Attack on Lady Akia Zelene, City of Resh

"Todd, it's been more than ten days since the attack," Kiata Wellum said, doing a poor job of masking her impatience. "A couple of thousand people have trampled over this site." She matched Todd step-for-step for another ten paces. "*We've* trampled over this site at least three times."

"I'm going to try something," Todd announced, abruptly sitting down in the middle of the intersection where Lady Akia Zelene had been attacked. He arranged his legs in a crossed position and let his hands hover just above the ground in front of each knee.

A few passersby watched curiously. A young mother snatched up the arms of her two small children and hustled them away. A drunk waved and saluted them with his half-empty bottle of dark ale. Paying no attention to their reactions, Todd uncrossed and straightened his legs, closed his eyes, and eased back until his head rested on the ground.

Kiata blew out an annoyed breath.

"You look like a corpse, and you're going to get us arrested for erratic behavior. Again."

"Almost arrested," Todd corrected cheerfully. He released some anotechs from his hands, arms, and feet and told them to search the area for clues. Sometimes, if he concentrated hard enough, he could connect to anotechs present at the time a specific event occurred. Occasionally, these anotechs let him witness these events as they had seen it. He hoped this might be one such case. Before fully committing to the search, Todd said, "Besides, that was ages ago, and this time we're officially sanctioned by the Royal House."

"Hurry up and finish before a merchant hov makes you a permanent part of the intersection," Kiata snapped.

"I trust you to watch over me, my love," Todd replied, speaking dreamily. He had committed most of his concentration to the task of directing anotechs.

The tiny machines fanned out away from Todd's prone body. The farther they ranged, the harder Todd had to concentrate to control them. He let himself sink further into a meditative state to facilitate such deep concentration. The anotechs flooded him with sensations.

Kiata had once asked him what it felt like. He had tried to explain, but it was difficult. It felt like drawing each impression across his chest and testing it with his heart. Most impressions flew past leaving Todd with only the faintest echo of a vibration, but strong emotions and significant events touched him deeper somehow. He experienced these like a friendly thump on the chest. When that happened, he stopped the flow and let the current anotech tell its tale.

Several false alarms left Todd weary, but he pressed on, knowing of no other way to get the information he sought. He and Kiata had questioned Lady Akia, Lady Orla Miraz, servants from both estates, Governor Damien Luvak, Master Tyko Tarpon, every officer who had searched the scene, and several witnesses the police had conjured. Nobody could shed much light on who might have attacked Lady Akia. Silent witnesses seemed the best course now. Their evidence would never be accepted in a court, but Todd was more interested in identifying the man who had terrorized Lady Zelene and likely killed her father. He would let the police sort evidence and worry about prosecution.

Todd wished Kiata could help him. This would go much faster with less space to cover, but his wife lacked the patience for the work. Even with only part of his consciousness aware of her, Todd felt Kiata's impatience like a burning torch. If he opened his eyes during this state, he would see an outline of her, glowing orange, red, and yellow. He peeked to confirm this and returned to his work, reassured by the moving blur that told him Kiata paced in front of him.

He watched three hov crashes, several fights between gangs, a few shady meetings, half a dozen robberies, and even a murder.

Popular place for crime, he thought.

Not really. This is a relatively lonely place, but many years have passed, so many things have happened. The voice that spoke in his mind sounded young yet wise.

It took Todd a few seconds to overcome the shock of speaking directly with anotechs.

You can use the common tongue?

Of course, we can, but we usually choose silence. Few understand us. Many fear us. Speaking leads to trouble.

I don't fear you. I seek answers. Who attacked Lady Zelene?

We will show you.

Todd felt the familiar thudding sensation, and his heart skipped a few beats. The short scene unfolded behind his closed eyes as clearly as if he watched a vid. He saw Lady Zelene's hov float into the intersection and stop. The view switched to a different angle, and Todd watched a black-clad figure land on the hov's roof and slap something metallic down. The view switched again, and the whole hov shimmered with energy. The masked man tumbled from the roof and rolled a few times, coming to his feet just as two men holding pistols jumped from the hov. The man in black waved and a disorienting view showed a man's neck approaching at rapid speed. Todd flinched as the

view switched again showing the attacker shoving Lady Akia against the hov and leaning close. He couldn't make out the words, but Lady Zelene had already reported her attacker's words. She slumped, the man retrieved his weapons, and Todd's mind returned to a blank state.

Todd watched the scene a few times to make sure he saw everything. On the fifth time through, Todd saw the hov light up with energy, he noticed the small metallic object fly away from the hov. The police had sent copies of their reports to his infopad. Nobody mentioned finding a small metal device. Perhaps finding it would provide a clue. Todd tracked its flight path and snapped his mind out of the trance.

He tried to open his eyes, felt a stab of pain, and decided to wait a moment. The presence of flingers disturbed Todd. He thought over the matter while his senses slowly recovered. He had recognized the tiny silver throwing weapons on his second time through the anotech memory. Military and police units might spend a few weeks training with them, but the only people who handled the weapons to much effect were Rangers. Kiata, Lucas Telon, and their old master, Kolknir, were the only three people Todd could conceive of making such swift and deadly throws.

"Kiata," Todd called, irritated that his voice sounded so weak. He blinked and squinted up. A few tears squeezed out of his dazzled eyes. He hauled his aching body to a sitting position and immediately regretted it. His felt lightheaded and his stomach rebelled. He shut his eyes and clenched his teeth to will the pain away.

Kiata appeared at his side.

"I'm here. Did you learn anything?" She gripped Todd's arm to hold him steady.

"Flingers—" Todd never finished his sentence.

A gasp from Kiata cut him off as her arm slammed into his chest, driving him to the ground.

***

Kiata Wellum sensed the stun beams move through the air above her back. After flattening her dazed husband, she rolled off him and grabbed her banistick. It snapped open in her hand as another blue beam headed for her. Leaping to her feet, Kiata timed her swing to plow the stun beam harmlessly into the ground.

Seeing no immediate threat in front of her, Kiata whirled to search for threats to her husband. She hoped his recovery was much swifter this time around. Last time, his reactions had been sluggish for at least an hour. She shook off the disturbing thought.

The sudden lull made her very suspicious. She scanned for signs of danger, and unfortunately, found them approaching from multiple sides. Like something out of a nightmare, five men materialized from the shadows.

Furious at not having sensed the danger earlier, Kiata crouched in a ready position, her eyes dared any man to face her in a fair fight.

Each man wore a black RT Alliance uniform and carried a kerlak pistol and a kerlinblade. Two held their kerlinblades in addition to their pistols. The blades were wide and flat, ready to defend the men should Kiata or Todd turn one of the stun beams against them. The other three had only kerlak pistols pointed at the Rangers. Their kerlinblades remained on their belts.

Kiata mentally marked the two with both blade and pistol as the most dangerous and angled her body to face one of these men. The odds did not please Kiata, but neither did they terrify her. She spared a glance at Todd and to her horror, saw him sitting cross-legged in another meditative trance. Sensing Todd needed time to complete a task, Kiata pointed at the nearest man.

"You, state your business," Kiata commanded.

The man's eyes flickered to one of his comrades. A silent message passed between them. Then, the air filled with stun beams.

Panic fueled Kiata as she dodged a few beams. The maneuvers took her about a meter away from Todd, so she fought her way back toward her husband's oddly serene form and slapped at stun beams that came too close to him.

This had better be good, Todd.

Kiata sank into her training and let instinct dictate where her banistick struck. During a brief break, while one of her attackers changed the battery pack on his kerlak pistol, Kiata plucked a flinger from her belt and sent it into the distracted man's head.

It scraped past his left eye, shaving off a bit of his brow. The man had enough time to cry out in surprise before the cormea, radon, and alipo sap combination knocked him out.

Four beams converged on Todd. Kiata had enough time to block two of them but knew the other two would slip past if she didn't do something. So, lacking a better plan, she intercepted the beams with her left leg. It numbed instantly. Kiata hopped on her right leg, trying to maintain her balance and fight. The dead weight of the limb distracted her, and another two stun beams rendered her right arm useless. She briefly wondered why the beams were so weak.

I should be unconscious by now.

The thought was not a complaint, but it did bring up a curious point. Now fighting with right leg and left arm only, Kiata grimly braced for more shots.

None came. It took her a good five seconds to absorb the fact that no one was attacking and identify the reason why. Balanced precariously, Kiata watched as the two attackers in her line of vision groaned and sank to the ground. Two more muffled thumps from behind her said the other two had suffered a similar fate.

"Did I miss anything?" asked Todd, smiling wickedly at her.

"Not much," Kiata responded, torn between laughing and taking a swing at him with her banistick. As adrenaline levels dropped, Kiata's good leg trembled. "But you might want to catch me."

Todd rose gracefully, stepped up close behind her, and pulled her into a tight embrace. Tucking his chin near Kiata's ear, he said, "Nice shot with the flinger."

"You saw that?" Kiata twisted around to peer up at him.

Todd leaned down and kissed her right shoulder.

"I saw everything. Remind me not to anger you while you have a banistick in hand."

"I thought you'd already learned that lesson," Kiata teased.

"I've learned a lot from you, Kiata," Todd said, leaning in for a kiss. Sighing, he added, "Including the need to pack stimulants when I travel with you." He shifted his hold on her, pulled an emergency pack from his belt, and fumbled to open it.

"Let me hold it before you dose yourself," Kiata said.

"Yes, dear," Todd said.

Kiata elbowed him playfully with her good arm and caught the emergency pack as he dropped it. After deftly flipping the pack open, Kiata held it so he could see its contents.

Todd selected two stimulant shots and stuck one in her right arm and one in her left leg. Next, he tucked the spent syringes back in the emergency pack and put it on his belt. Finally, he resumed holding Kiata.

"Reia would have a fit if she knew we used these," Kiata said, as the stimulant brought feeling back into her paralyzed limbs.

Todd shrugged, inadvertently tightening his hold on Kiata.

"She will know," he said softly, in case one of the attackers woke up enough to listen to them. "Her knowledge of anotechs is deeper than ours now, and she's not bound by Council rules. I think I found what we need here, and I've got a lot to tell you about the anotechs."

Sensing faint movement from one of the attackers, Kiata said, "That should be an interesting conversation, but first, we should wake one of these men and question him. I would like to know why Alliance soldiers attacked us in the middle of the day. They usually have more sense than that."

***

Kest (October) 18, 1538
Same Day
Tarpon Estate, City of Kalmata

Brook Tarpon shifted uncomfortably on the camrood leather chair and let his gaze rest on the flickering flames waving hypnotically from the fireplace. He tried closing his eyes but immediately snapped them open again to stave off the nightmarish image of his wife's lifeless face. The dreams had begun the night after her disappearance. Each started out differently, but they always ended the same with his hands around her throat and the intelligence in her pale purple eyes slowly fading to cold blankness.

Knowing only that Brook's sleep was disturbed, Dr. Bartul had recommended relsuma pills, but Brook had only taken them once. The medicine made everything worse by forcing him to sleep and doing nothing to stop the dreams.

The infopad shook in Brook's hands, and he consciously set it down in his lap for fear of breaking it. He looked hard at Nera's image, trying to etch it into his memory. If they had to be apart, this was how he wanted to remember her. The picture showed a close view of her lovely face. She did not smile or frown. Instead, her head tilted thoughtfully, and she stared with a haughty, challenging spark in her eyes.

A strong sense of loss and anger at the forced separation swept over Brook. Nera would return once completing the Lady's task, but he wondered why the mysterious meddler wanted his wife. Surely there were other people she could recruit. What special skill or quality did Nera possess? Guilt and regret hit him. He knew so little about his wife. He certainly admired her beauty and enjoyed her company, but theirs was a slow-growing love planted in the rough soil of business.

Disgusted with the emotional tides, Brook sprang to his feet and nearly knocked the infopad into the fire. It bounced off the low table and landed just short of the flames. A spark sprang free of the fire but died harmlessly a few centimeters above the infopad. He needed to get out and clear his head, maybe pick a fight with someone.

After checking to make sure his miniature kerlak pistol was where it should be, Brook sprang up, dodged the low table, snatched the infopad off the floor, and took another long look at Nera's face. Then, he tossed the infopad onto the chair he had vacated and fled the room. About five steps into the long hallway that would lead him to the front door, something hard slammed into Brook's back.

He tried to tuck into a roll like his defense instructor had taught him, but his exhausted body betrayed him. He landed awkwardly on his left shoulder. Sharp pain radiated from the point of impact, and his head knocked hard into the floor, leaving him stunned. Instinctively, Brook's right hand sought his kerlak pistol, but something smashed into the inside of his forearm, knocking it aside with aching force. He barely registered the new pain before something nestled into his neck just below his chin. He froze and followed the weapon's slender trunk up to a man's hand, arm, and face.

"Cease inquiries into your wife's fate," said the man holding the banistick.

Pain, surprise, and indignation fueled reckless anger within Brook.

"You have no authority over me," he declared, trying to ignore the insistent pressure the banistick placed on his neck.

The man smiled and increased the pressure on Brook's windpipe.

"This is my authority."

"The people I serve—"

"Are the ones who sent me with this gentle warning," finished the man. He lifted the banistick off Brook's neck. "The Lady wearies of your questions. Accept that your wife is performing a vital service and continue handling your Alliance affairs."

"What do you know of the Lady?" demanded Brook, suddenly desperate to know more about the figure his parents had enslaved the Restler-Tarpon Alliance to. "Does she serve Lord Maledek, or does he serve her?"

"It is enough to know that they both serve a free Reshner," the man replied.

Brook chuckled bitterly.

"That rhetoric belongs in the Senate Great Hall. Who are they?"

His question went unanswered. The man double tapped Brook's chest with the banistick and whipped it up toward his face. Brook flinched, and the blow grazed his left check, drawing blood. He soon lost consciousness.

***

Lalri (November) 5, 1538
The Lady's Estate, Kala Mountains

Lady Mavis Altran regretted giving Damien Luvak the ability to contact her. He knew nothing concerning her whereabouts, but the ability to call her private line gave the twit an unfortunate sense of his own importance.

"Would that I could see your face and kiss your hand in thanks, my Lady," said the contemptible little man.

Would that I could kill you and still control Resh, but alas, we must both settle for disappointment.

Instead of sharing these honest sentiments, Mavis double-checked that the voice filtration system was activated, and said, "You have my heartfelt congratulations on your election, governor. The people of Resh have chosen wisely. I trust your commitment to our cause will remain ardent."

"Indeed, my Lady, I know well that I have you to thank for my good fortune." Governor Luvak's chest swelled with pride. His moist eyes beamed delight and his jowls shook with vigorous nodding.

"Is thanks all you called to convey, my friend?" asked Mavis, keeping her voice mild.

If you waste too much of my time, I'll improve someone else's fortunes posthaste.

Horror entered Luvak's pale green eyes.

"Not at all, my Lady, though it be a large part of that which I hope to accomplish through this call." His ability to use many words to say nothing was impressive even for a career politician.

Mavis wanted to reach through the vidscreen and throttle the nuisance.

"Do ease my suspense then, Governor Luvak."

Luvak's gaze darted about nervously.

"My Lady does me great honor by addressing me by title, but I wonder if it is quite safe to do so."

If it were unsafe, it would be far too late to worry.

Mavis pinched the bridge of her nose to relieve a sudden idiot-induced headache.

"We are safe enough," she assured the man. "What knowledge have you to share?"

Luvak leaned closer to the vidrecorder so that his face grew uncomfortably large.

"A Ranger pair was here investigating my predecessor's fate," he said, lowering his voice to a whisper.

I know this! They were there weeks ago as well. What of it?

"Did they find anything?" asked Mavis. She let only mild curiosity into her voice.

"I am not sure, my Lady," said Luvak. He pursed his lips and moved his jaw from side to side. "I am certain they learned nothing about your involvement."

Of all the things he could have said, that statement triggered worry and anger in Mavis.

You told them? Yes, of course, you told them.

After a brief period of near panic, Mavis dismissed her fears. Damien Luvak knew only that the Lady might have something to do with Governor Darmon Zelene's death. Mavis silently thanked whatever providence had prompted her to trust very few people.

Taking her silence for disappointment, Luvak blundered on, "I learned something else, my Lady." He paused, nearly breathless with his news. "The Rangers investigating Zelene's death are related to the queen!"

This man was the better choice for Resh's governor?

Mavis questioned her sanity.

I think I preferred Zelene. He would never deal with me, but at least, he wasn't a complete idiot.

"Is that so? How did you come by this information?" Mavis hated feigning ignorance, especially in the presence of such an abundance of the trait.

"I have many valuable sources, my Lady," said Luvak, bowing his head humbly. The movement brought his greasy face dangerously close to the vidrecorder. "Perhaps I shall one day have the opportunity to lend them to you. As I said, I am much in your debt, and I always pay my debts."

Indeed, you always pay, even if you must murder your neighbors and steal their mines to do so.

The thought opened many delightful possibilities. Should Damien Luvak ever prove more problem than profit, Lady Mavis knew exactly how to deal with him.

"I shall look forward to that day," said Mavis, more to herself than Luvak. Before he could find some way to continue the conversation, she muttered inane pleasantries and severed the connection.

Chapter 21:
Troublesome Request

Lalri (November) 9, 1538
Wellum Home, East Quarter, City of Rammon

Kiata's eyes widened as she recognized the young man standing at her door. Fear lent her speed and strength as she seized hold of the caller and hauled him into the welcome room.

Slapping the door closed, Kiata whirled to face the man.

"What are you doing here?"

"I'm sorry about—I didn't mean—I meant to—" A very pale Talyon Keldor stood stiffly and stammered through several sentence starters.

Instantly contrite, Kiata hugged Taly fiercely.

"You're always welcome here, Taly," she assured the young man, pulling away to study his face. He'd grown so much that he had a few inches of height on her now. "I hope you know that." She squeezed his shoulders and stepped back. "What brings you back to Rammon? Wait, don't answer that yet." Kiata held up a hand to forestall a response then waved toward the sitting room. "Please, sit down. Your expression tells me you bear quite a burden."

Once they were both seated, Kiata waited for Taly to restart the conversation, using the still moments to study him further. The month or so on Terik's farm had done him good. Physically, he appeared stronger and healthier than ever. Taly would never be a brawny man, but he was fit and seemed more comfortable with his body than before. However, the haunted look in his eyes had only deepened, making him appear much older than someone who had lived less than two decades.

Kiata wished she could fix the troubles in his life, as she had healed him from the Porit viper's poison when he was a child. It had been one of the few times in her life she had healed someone else with anotechs and the only time she had succeeded so completely. She longed for such a deep connection with the mysterious machines to be permanent, but even her Nareth Talis bond paled in comparison. Anotechs obeyed certain commands and occasionally whispered words of advice, but nothing came close to the purity of knowledge that told her they would heal Taly that day.

Turning her thoughts away from the unreliable nature of anotech connections, Kiata considered the string of unfortunate events that composed Taly's recent life. His friend Merisia still lived in danger. His RT Alliance superiors likely wanted him captured or killed. His grandfather's trial would officially begin tomorrow. Her mind fastened on the last problem. Though she admittedly knew little about Taly, he struck her as the sort to value family and friends very highly. His commitment to Merisia had proven the point. Kiata believed his claim that nothing but friendship existed between him and Merisia.

Taly stood abruptly and stared at Kiata with anguish in his eyes.

"I shouldn't have come, and I have no right to ask anything of you. But I need to see the queen. Will you help me?"

"That might be difficult," Kiata said, knowing that she could never arrange for an official audience. The Royal Guards would sooner shoot a man bearing the Keldor name than let him within shouting distance of their queen.

"I would never hurt her. I just—" Sudden emotion cut Taly off. He angrily dashed away a few tears. "I need to beg for her mercy."

Kiata didn't know whether to leave him to cry in peace or comfort him. She hoped Todd would return soon with Nils. She settled for something in between. Rising, Kiata slowly approached Taly, placed her hands on his shoulders, and pushed down until he sat. Then, kneeling before him, she gripped both of his hands tightly.

"I honestly don't know how she will respond, Taly, but I believe in your right to seek such an audience. You have my word as a Ranger and as a friend. I will do what I can to convince my sister to hear you out."

***

Lalri (November) 10, 1538
East Servants' Entrance, Royal Palace, City of Rammon

"Majesty, may I have a word with you?" called a man.

Two steps from the freedom and anonymity of a quiet exit from the palace, Reia reluctantly stopped. Resisting the urge to growl, she schooled her features into the slightly aloof, obscenely polite expression Sedir insisted she master and turned to face the speaker.

A tall, thin, dark-skinned man came barreling down the hallway at a pace just short of a run. The tempo of his words matched the crisp, confident stride. He wore a white lab coat and carried an infopad. Skidding to a halt, the man bowed.

As soon as his head snapped back up, he said, "Dr. Kurt Saddic at your service, Highness. We met briefly during your tour of the palace. I am deeply sorry for disturbing you this way. Normally, I would wait until an audience to seek your favor, but I have exciting news. I have made tremendous progress with the project. We are almost ready to proceed with experimental trials, but the king seems reluctant to grant permission for the trials. I thought perhaps if you knew how close we were to discovering a proper defense against comaladon, you could have a word with the king."

Reia's mind raced with questions and implications. Only about half of Dr. Saddic's words made any sense to her. She remembered meeting him and recalled his specialty being poisons, but beyond that, she knew nothing about the man or his project.

Sedir's warning rang in her ears: *Never admit to ignorance. As queen, you must exude confidence and knowledge.*

Reia bought time with a pleasant smile and chose her words carefully.

"I shall certainly do as you suggest, Dr. Saddic. Do you have specific good news I may relay to the king? Perhaps if you give me a copy of your report I can find a favorable time to present it to him."

"Certainly, Majesty, I have my report right here," said Dr. Saddic, holding up his infopad. "I can beam a copy to your infopad or arrange for a paper copy to be delivered to your private chambers." Dr. Saddic's infopad passed from his left hand to his right then back again as he dithered. "The king expects a report tomorrow. If it would not inconvenience you too much, I think it best if you appeal to him before I deliver my report. Do you have a preference for delivery?" An eyebrow spiked and settled as he answered his own question. "Perhaps I shall do both. Yes, both would be good. That way you can read it at your convenience." His fingers flew over his infopad. "I shall also have Mikael pull up the informal report so you can see the full version with my comments. Will that be acceptable to you?"

Reia merely nodded, still reeling from his verbal barrage.

"Excellent! Thank you for your time, Highness. I shall delay you no further. Riden bless the rest of your day. I must return to my lab and continue with the project. There is much to be done!" The scientist's knees trembled with the need to move. As soon as he received another nod, he retreated down the hallway faster than he had arrived.

Torn between going to her sister's house and finding out what Dr. Saddic had been babbling about, Reia pulled her infopad from an inner pocket and looked down at the blank screen. Coming to a decision, she dashed out the door and into the gardens to find a quiet spot to read. Kiata and her sudden invitation to visit would have to wait ten minutes.

***

Lalri (November) 10, 1538
Same Day
Wellum Home, East Quarter, City of Rammon

As soon as the door closed behind Reia, she leaned back against it and blew out a long, slow breath. Escaping from Saddic then encountering a crowd had taxed her energy reserves. She spread her fingers and pressed her palms against the danesque wood, letting the smooth coolness calm her nerves. The effect was so complete that she didn't even sense her eyes falling shut until Kiata's soft laughter made her snap them open again.

"Come in and sit down before you collapse and crack your head open," said Kiata. Her voice commanded but her silver-blue eyes teased. "I would hate to have to clean up the mess or try to explain that to your husband."

Reia released a noise somewhere between a whine and a groan.

"I'm not sure I can move. You must have a few hundred neighbors standing on your doorstep."

Grinning wickedly, Kiata said, "Well, I'm sure I could call upon a few dozen of them to assist you. Shall I summon them?"

"You wouldn't dare," said Reia. A nagging doubt lodged in her mind. She never really knew what her sister might do when that expression crossed her face.

"Wouldn't I?" Kiata asked, raising an eyebrow. A light in her eyes said she sensed a challenge.

"She would," said Todd, stepping up behind Kiata and wrapping his arms around her waist. Then, tipping his head into his wife's he added, "Just to see your reaction." After kissing Kiata's left ear, Todd said, "Dearest, it isn't polite to torment royal guests with threats of unwanted company."

"Killjoy," Kiata complained. She twisted out of Todd's grasp and rushed to Reia. "Come, I'll show you the house."

Before Reia could protest, she found herself on a whirlwind tour of Todd and Kiata's small but comfortable home. The large welcome room led to a tiny sitting room and a short hallway to the kitchen. A washroom, a closet, and a multipurpose room rounded out the rest of the downstairs. Upstairs boasted a master bedroom with its own washroom and a slightly smaller guest chamber.

Gratefully settling onto the couch in the sitting room, Reia leaned back and reveled in the novelty of sitting down.

"You forgot to show me that massive closet you said you could hide a horse in, but it'll have to wait until my legs feel like working again." Reia kept her voice light, but she'd sensed the emotional atmosphere thickening.

"I didn't forget," said Kiata.

Noting her sister's serious tone and Todd's absence, Reia raised her head from where it had fallen back against the couch cushions. "I assume Todd went to retrieve your guest," Reia commented, not quite certain if she should be worried or annoyed.

"Yes, I needed a moment alone with you to explain," Kiata said, sounding sad. A grin flashed and faded. "I know you felt him. You know what he seeks, and you probably already know the answer you're going to give him. Still, I'm asking you to hear his plea with an open mind."

Helplessness crept over Reia in exhausting waves. She hated denying her sister, but now that the formal trial had been ordered for Niktrod Keldor, entertaining requests from his kin felt like betraying Terosh.

"Protecting the boy is one thing, Kiata—you know I'm more than happy to do that—but this is different. I'm not supposed to discuss the trial with *anyone*," Reia said. "Like it or not, my every word needs to be weighed and watched because it's sure to be analyzed from a thousand angles." She hated disagreeing with Kiata while sitting down. It left her at a disadvantage.

"I'm not asking you to publicly broadcast your interview," Kiata said impatiently. "Listen to him."

"I don't want to give him false hope," Reia argued, hearing the subtle shift in tone that said she'd surrendered the verbal battlefield.

Kiata must have heard it too, for she inclined her chin.

"Thank you," she said. "Simply listening will give him much-needed hope. He's still hurting from being cut off from Merisia Restler." Kiata vacated the doorway and went to stand behind the reclining chair, so she could observe the pending exchange better.

Todd entered a moment later with Talyon Keldor, waved the young man over to the chair Kiata stood behind, and left the room.

Taly's tense jaw, stiff shoulders, and clenched fists declared his discomfort. He lowered his eyes, tilted his head forward, and rested his elbows on his knees. His breaths were slightly irregular as he gathered the courage to speak.

Reaching out with the anotechs, Reia sensed his mood and received a flood of impressions. She could not claim to be an expert at interpreting such feelings, but she recognized the heady rush of a racing mind and the tightening across her chest that spoke of pent-up emotion.

"What is it you seek of me, Talyon Keldor?" Reia asked formally.

Taly's eyes flicked up before returning to study the floor near Reia's feet. His head lowered even more.

"If it pleases Your Majesty, grant me this one request." He paused a second to bite his bottom lip, as if afraid to go on. "Spare my grandfather's life. A public trial places him in great danger. The accusation alone of assassinating Her Majesty Queen Kila of House Minstel is enough to condemn him to most people."

"We will do everything in our power to avoid that, Taly," Reia assured. "The trial will be available by infopad and vid broadcasts, but the format has been modified to answer your concerns. None save a committee from the Governors Council and the king even know which justice arena will host the trial. The accused will not appear before the public until the trial concludes. Should your grandfather be found guilty, he …"

Taly's head snapped up so fast his teeth clicked. He locked eyes with Reia, causing her to forget the rest of her statement. His lips pressed tightly together and unshed tears glimmered in his eyes.

"He is guilty, my Queen," said Taly in an agonized whisper.

Kiata's expression darkened, but she showed no other signs of surprise or distress at Taly's announcement.

Reia felt the words like a physical blow. She closed her eyes against the mixture of emotions they unleashed. Soon, however, sorrow defeated the elation of knowing the rigged trial and planned execution would be just.

"I wish you had not said that." She blinked to hold back tears her role forbade.

Alarm crossed Taly's features, and his words flowed like a flashflood.

"The day I joined the RT Alliance, my grandfather warned against following in his—and my father's—footsteps. He said if I traveled their path, my friends and family would be nothing but hostages for the rest of my life."

"That is a fair warning, but not an admission of guilt," Reia said, feeling relief spread through her.

"He also said that the better I got at my job, the more dangerous my allies would become," Taly said, speaking slower now. "To prove his point, he confessed his role in Queen Kila's death and showed me an infopad recording of his instructions. It proves he performed the deed under duress. Against orders, he saved the communication as a guard against his employer."

Reia's spirits rose then crashed. The news of an employer shifted some culpability to another, but any involvement in a murder of this magnitude would carry the death penalty.

"Stop talking, Taly," Kiata ordered, her voice tight. She side-stepped out from behind the reclining chair Taly occupied. "Reia, forget everything you just heard."

"I wish I could," Reia said. Her throat was as raw as if she'd swallowed glass shards.

Kiata rushed to the couch and seized Reia's shoulders. Her silver-blue eyes etched the same message her hoarse voice released.

"I mean it! Forget everything! It was a mistake to bring you here, but that is *my* mistake. He should not pay for it with his life, and if you speak, he will be executed for not confessing sooner."

Every part of Reia wanted to deny it, but Sedir's lessons on the justice system told her Kiata spoke truth. A few tears slipped out.

"What else can I do?" Reia asked, choking back a sob and driving further tears away with anger. She hardly noticed the painful grip her sister maintained on her shoulders. "The law is binding. King Rammon—"

"Was a raving lunatic," Kiata finished, releasing Reia's shoulders. "I'm not surprised that law came about during his reign. If you—"

Taly cut Kiata off by squeezing her shoulder. Then, he dropped to his knees before Reia and looked at her with a mixture of sorrow and guilt.

"I am sorry, my Queen, I should not have come, but if you could convince the king to spare my grandfather, I would count the use of my life worth it."

It took two seconds for his meaning to sink in.

Kiata's gasp halted Reia's thoughts before she could fully comprehend. Kiata looked down at Taly, inclined her head, and clasped her hands behind her back.

"Well-played, Taly," she said with a smile.

The shift in Kiata's manner confused Reia.

"I'm sorry," Taly murmured.

"Why?" Reia asked as nameless dread prickled in her chest. The question was half-addressed to Taly and half-addressed to Kiata and meant something different to each. The answer hit her suddenly, resulting in speechless rage and icy adrenaline. She simultaneously wanted to smack Taly and seize him in a hug.

The Law of Obligatory Revelation dictated that anyone who possessed information on a crime of significant magnitude yet remained silent faced consequences equal to the crime. Thus, Taly's previous silence on his grandfather's guilt doomed him to share in whatever fate awaited his grandfather. By extension, Todd and Kiata, who had harbored Taly, might also be drawn into the legal web. Even if spared from death, they could face serious prosecution. Reia could say nothing and break the law or appeal to her husband for an exception.

Taly must really love his grandfather to take such a risk.

While Reia wrestled with the odd combination of emotions, Todd entered the room like an Ashasten, plucked Taly off the floor, spun him around, and plowed a fist into the younger man's chest. The blow knocked Taly into Kiata who caught him reflexively. Todd drew back his arm for another strike.

"No, Todd!" Kiata cried, stumbling back a few steps and hauling Taly in the wake of her retreat. "Don't you see? This is the only way he could protect himself." She deposited Taly onto the armchair.

The sound of Taly's coughing dominated for a time. Reia tried to absorb the rapid changes. Todd spent the time glaring at Taly. Kiata knelt before young man and checked that nothing had been permanently damaged.

"He used us," Todd said. "He placed our lives in danger and now—"

"And now the king must hear him out," Kiata broke in gently.

With effort, Reia forced herself to think. A plan formed. She steeled her nerves and turned to Taly.

"Do you have the infopad proving the threats against your grandfather?"

Taly shook his head.

More thoughts tumbled around in Reia's head.

"No matter, we can ask him about it later. I doubt it will do much to sway the king or the judge, but I will submit your account and question your grandfather." Reia rose from her seat, swallowing several angry threats that would gain her nothing. "I must return to the palace to fulfill these words," she added, directing the words to Kiata and Todd. Then, facing Taly again, Reia said, "I admire your courage and family devotion, Talyon, but know this: my devotion to my family is equal to yours. Do not test me on this."

Chapter 22:
Threats Within

Lalri (November) 10, 1538
Same Day
King Terosh's Private Chambers, Royal Palace, City of Rammon

"Where have you been?" Terosh regretted the question even as it came out. He managed to suppress further words but had to think them or risk bursting something in his head. He spared a moment to warn the anotechs not to broadcast his thoughts and then launched into his silent tirade.

I almost sent Royal Guards tearing through the city after you. Why would you leave without telling someone? Don't ever do that to me again!

The door to his bedchamber slammed shut, telling him part of his message probably showed on his face. His wife's green eyes looked ready to fire energy beams. She stood inside the door wearing an expression that flickered between collapse-into-tears and kill-something-with-bare-hands. Her flushed cheeks and slightly disheveled hair lent her the air of a beautiful damsel in distress, but Terosh valued his life enough to refrain from commenting.

To give Reia time to respond, he sat on his bed and removed the belt holding his kerlak pistol and kerlinblade. After a brief hesitation, Terosh dropped the weapons belt to the floor next to the bed. He would not need them for this coming battle, though part of him wished they could solve their problems like the Ereni. Natives of Eren IX dueled until one party yielded. The winner won the argument and the loser had to live with it. A nice Dollan duel would go a long way to relieving anger and would certainly be easier than navigating the mysteries of a woman's emotions.

Terosh's unease grew as the silence stretched. Fearing he would start babbling, Terosh studied the pastoral paintings lining the walls. He wasn't enthusiastic about paintings, but his mother had insisted his private quarters be adorned with something other than colored crossblades champions and vid stars. One traumatic day when he was eleven, Sarie had replaced his treasures with wildlife and nature paintings. At the time—and under threat of his mother's wrath—Terosh had left the paintings up, now he was simply used to them. Usually, he paid little attention to them, but he had to admit they were nice scenes.

At last, Reia activated the sound damper and broke the tense silence.

"I had two very interesting conversations today, one with Dr. Saddic and one with Talyon Keldor." The careful way she spoke said she wasn't exactly happy about either conversation. "We need to discuss both. Do you have a preference as to which we attend to first?"

Guilt seized Terosh, and he tried not to wince. He had meant to discuss Dr. Saddic's project with Reia, but the timing never seemed right. In truth, Saddic's research tended to slip Terosh's mind until the bi-monthly reports. Now that Reia mentioned it, Terosh remembered a lengthy infopad message from Saddic saying he was close to a few breakthroughs and would give a full report on Lalri (November) 11, 1538.

"What did Dr. Saddic have to say?"

"His project is nearing the experimental stage. He seeks your permission to proceed with the trials," said Reia. Her curt tone and grim expression declared disapproval. Frowning, she added, "The report I received also included his notes."

Terosh's mind raced, making connections and drawing conclusions. He stood and held both hands out in a placating gesture.

"It's not what you think," he said carefully.

"What exactly do you think I think?" demanded Reia. Her eyes dared him to defend the research.

That's a dangerous question.

"I think *we* think the same thing," Terosh said slowly. "Human trials of this nature are wrong. Science should never have gone there, and it's time to return to a higher moral position or progress to a different level that will avoid such research."

As hoped for, the speech stole some of the raging fire behind Reia's eyes.

"What could possibly have possessed you to commission such research in the first place?" she demanded.

That's a dumb question and you know it!

Terosh fought the urge to rush over and sweep Reia into a crushing hug. Instead, he sent her a long look full of more meaning than words could capture.

"I think you know the answer to that."

Confusion melted into clarity and more fire leeched from her eyes. Reia glided over and threw her arms around Terosh, resting her left cheek against his chest. After several moments, she pulled away and stared up into his eyes.

"I am not going to die that way, Terosh. I promise. The anotechs say any poison they have tasted can be mastered. Your mother's death will protect us and our family for generations. Don't you trust them?"

"Trusting them doesn't mean I shouldn't seek other answers," Terosh replied. "The anotechs will only protect our family and most of the Rangers. If Saddic succeeds, then no one will ever share my mother's fate."

Reia nodded slowly. She released her hold on him and took a small step back, letting her hands drop to her sides. After three seconds of deep thought, she tilted her head and spoke.

"You're right. In that case, I will do it."

Alarm shot through Terosh as her meaning dawned on him.

This is exactly what we're trying to fight against.

"What? No! Reia—"

"We're the only ones truly safe from comaladon," Reia insisted.

"We're also trying to prove that experimenting on people is wrong," Terosh snapped. His head hurt from the sudden shift in the conversation.

"Dr. Saddic's report contains applications for the project," said Reia. Her voice tightened and she looked close to tears. "Several thousand of them in fact."

Terosh groaned.

"He knew that would happen." He wanted to wring Saddic's brilliant neck. "It's going to be impossible to stop him."

"Would you want to?" asked Reia. A faint smile added: *You started this.* "You still believe in his work, just not his methods. So, define his methods. Use the law to regulate the acquisition and treatment of volunteers for scientific research. The existing laws are shifting, useless shadows with no real power."

Terosh shrugged.

"I suppose that would work," he admitted. His hands found hers and clasped them tightly. "But promise me you won't volunteer. I trust the anotechs and Saddic, but I'll feel a whole lot better knowing you avoided that sort of danger."

"Would it be unfair to make it a conditional promise?"

"That depends on the condition," Terosh responded carefully.

"We should probably sit down for this part," Reia warned.

Terosh agreed and they settled onto his bed.

"The second interesting conversion I had today starred Talyon Keldor," said Reia, once she was safely snuggled in his arms. "To make a long story short, he broke the Law of Obligatory Revelation, and by extension, endangered Kiata and Todd. They didn't know he had broken the law until he revealed as much in my presence, but that would be hard to prove. He seeks an audience with you, so that's my condition. Meet with him and forgive his crime."

Terosh let several heartbeats pass while he mulled over the situation.

"No jury would ever convict your sister or her husband of breaking the law based on Talyon Keldor's words, but he could still cause trouble. I will give him his audience and amnesty." Feeling just as manipulated as Reia, he found the last word painful to utter. Terosh had barely met Talyon Keldor, but the young man had always exuded an air of innocence. It pained him to see that image destroyed.

"Thank you," Reia murmured, sounding sleepy.

"What did Talyon say exactly?"

Reia repeated as much of the conversation as she could remember and then let Terosh view the conversation in her mind via anotechs.

"We should speak with the elder Keldor before entertaining Talyon," said Terosh.

"Why?"

"Because I don't want any further nasty surprises to come up in conversation with the young Keldor."

***

Lalri (November) 11, 1538
Niktrod Keldor's Cell, Palace Prison, City of Rammon

The weary guard shifted his weight from foot to foot and looked steadily back at Eldon Altran.

"My apologies, Governor Altran, but my orders are clear. The king, the queen, Master Abner, and the nine members of the select committee from the Governors Council are the only ones permitted to see the prisoner. I can check the list again for you, but it won't change anything."

Eldon Altran struggled against the panic climbing his spine and exploding in his mind. He glared at the guard and wondered if he could overpower the man. A dagger strike might prevail if the guard was distracted enough, but it would have to be across the throat. Soft armorweave protected the rest of the guard's body.

"This is a matter of utmost importance. The prisoner is in grave danger. I demand to see him at once!"

"Appeal to the king or queen for permission," said the guard. "Either one of their Majesties can add you to the list."

Taking a dangerous gamble, Eldon leaned forward and lowered his voice as he said, "I know whom you truly serve. I am trying to protect her. Keldor could reveal some very dangerous information."

The guard's eyes widened in surprise but his cold smile chilled Eldon, and he knew his mother had already spoken with the guard.

"What did she promise you? I will match it if you let me through," said Eldon.

"My deepest apologies, but I cannot help you, Governor." The guard's eyes softened slightly, adding the message: *You don't have her power to make such promises.*

Eldon again wanted to drive a dagger into the guard.

"Please leave, Governor," said the guard, dropping his voice low. "Return to Idonia. Rammon will be a dangerous place for you tonight."

Eldon couldn't believe his ears.

"You dare to—"

"A warning, my Lord, not a threat," said the guard, lowering his head in a bow. "All my instructions were very clear."

The man's meaning wrapped around Eldon like cold fog. Abandoning hope of an easy solution, Eldon spun away from the guard and strode down the long hallway. The prison's white stones seemed to laugh as he fled.

***

Lalri (November) 11, 1538
Same Day
The Lady's Estate, Kala Mountains

Mavis checked and rechecked her security measures. Once certain she would not be disturbed, she retreated to the inner room of her private office, sealed the door, removed her shoes, and sank onto the comfortable cot. She pulled herself back to lean against the cool stones, drew up her knees, rested her elbows upon them, and wept into her hands.

She faced an impossible choice. Eldon's recent actions proved he would interfere. She would have Lucas Telon deliver a final warning, but if her son failed to heed it, he would have to be removed permanently.

The best way to save Eldon from his own foolishness would be to kill Niktrod Keldor. Eldon would undoubtedly feel threatened, but he would simply cut off contact with her, a fine solution and probably the best she could hope for. On the other hand, Mavis needed to deliver Keldor alive to Gardan. If she didn't fulfill the contract, Silvia would die along with any hope of a relationship with Mitrek. While she had long ago accepted that such sacrifices might one day arise, Mavis was not yet ready to estrange all her sons.

As the sobs subsided, the white noise in Mavis's mind coalesced into coherent thought once again.

You can stop this.

One short conversation with King Padric and her plans would crumble but her tenuous family relationships would survive.

Is revenge worth it?

This wasn't true revenge since Padric had failed to ensnare Mavis all those years ago.

It's not only about revenge. I must save Reshner from Gardan's poisonous influence.

Why risk family to save the world that betrayed you? The thought filled her with sharp despair.

Mavis remembered Sedir's long-ago lessons. She frowned, tears spent for the moment.

I was born a princess, my son will rule, and those who dare to enslave this planet will pay dearly.

A surge of purpose entered Mavis. She had triumphed in dangerous games before, though admittedly not with such personal stakes. She vowed to triumph again. Drawing on this strength, Mavis stood and set about composing her clothes, hair, and emotional state.

"Eldon, you fool. You will learn sense, or I will have it knocked into you."

***

Lalri (November) 11, 1538
Same Day
Niktrod Keldor's Cell, Palace Prison, City of Rammon

The condemned man's words came out slowly.

"You are king. You may do as you like, but I warn you that nothing you accomplish here will bring you the peace you seek. For that you need a priest. Your brother found only pain when he looked inside my mind."

"Tate looked inside your mind?" Terosh knew the news shouldn't be surprising, but it released a bevy of odd emotions. After mastering them, Terosh asked, "Did you kill my mother?" He felt Reia's supportive touch via the anotechs.

The Niktrod Keldor's gray eyes locked on Terosh, simultaneously sad and wise.

"That can be a very complicated question, Highness. You have enough evidence to know my part without my lips confirming such. The question then becomes a matter of degree. Who is the ultimate killer, the man who orders a death or the man who achieves the desired end?"

"Both are guilty," answered Reia.

"If you will forgive my saying so, Majesty, I shall tell you that when I was your age I believed as you do." The prisoner looked down at his hands which were cuffed to the heavy table. He slowly flexed his fingers. "Time and circumstances have changed my
view. I make no claim to great wisdom, but I daresay you will understand better when you have more to lose."

The absence of threat in Niktrod Keldor's voice kept Terosh from reaching for where a kerlinblade ought to be on his belt. He had surrendered the weapon upon entering the prison.

"Tell us the story as you see it," Terosh commanded.

"My orders came from someone called the Benefactor. This being convinced me that my son and his family would be very easy targets should I decline the job." Niktrod shrugged. "So, I weighed my options and accepted the job."

Terosh felt devoid of emotion. Then, suddenly his mind and body ached with pain and rage. Conscious thought caught up about the time his fingers closed around Niktrod Keldor's neck. He squeezed hard, pouring his rage and anguish into the task, but he succeeded only in hurting his fingers.

"He will answer for killing your mother, Terosh, but not this way," said Reia.

The strain in her voice touched something inside Terosh. Reluctantly, he released his grip on Keldor's neck. Part of him thanked Reia for protecting Keldor and part of him resented the interference.

"Who is the Benefactor?" Terosh demanded.

Keldor's breaths came in gasps. He swallowed hard several times. When he finally spoke, his voice was just as steady as before.

"My research led to two other names: the Lady and Maledek, but I know nothing more."

"Your grandson said you showed him an infopad containing your orders to kill Queen Kila," said Reia. "Is this true? Did you realize the knowledge would condemn him as well?"

Keldor chuckled bitterly.

"Joining the RT Alliance condemned him a thousand times over. I considered the risk worth it, and I trust the king to decide what is just concerning the boy." His gray eyes sought Terosh's blue ones. "Taly knew nothing about the job until I told him in an attempt to better direct his life. Destroying him for my sake would be almost as contemptible as what I did to protect him."

A wave of sympathy moved through Terosh, making him feel like a traitor to his mother's memory.

"I believe you." His throat tried to close, momentarily preventing words. "I still count you a murderer and believe you deserve to die, but nobody deserves the sentence you will receive if convicted."

"What sentence might that be, Highness?" asked Keldor.

"Extradition to Gardan," Reia answered.

"I see." For the first time, Keldor's eyes widened in fear.

"You see?" Terosh asked. "Say something, man! They want to send you to a place where night and day will melt into one haze of pain!" He slammed his fists down on the metal tabletop. The resulting pain calmed him a little. "Give me a reason to stop this. Help me find the Benefactor, the Lady, and Maledek, be they one person or three. Let me send them to King Padric. He will accept that."

Niktrod closed his eyes and heaved a weary sigh. When he opened his eyes, they held more regret than fear.

"I investigated as best I could. Despite what Taly thinks, I am no closer to the Lady or Maledek or the Benefactor than I was years ago. I will appeal here as long as I can, and if I must go to Gardan then so be it."

Terosh exchanged a desperate look with Reia. She nodded encouragement.

"If—if it comes to that and you wish it, I will give you the means to an easier end," Terosh said quietly.

"I understand," said Keldor. "You have my thanks for the consideration."

Chapter 23:
Questions of Love and Loyalty

Lalri (November) 15, 1538
The Lady's Estate, Kala Mountains
Two huge problems still troubled Lady Mavis Altran. The danger posed to her granddaughter increased as Niktrod Keldor's trial continued. A trial of this nature threatened to linger on and on. Mavis trusted Mitrek's skills, but even he could not exert much control over the speed with which the advocates presented their cases. After listening to more hours of trial recordings than she cared to count, Mavis knew she needed to move Silvia out of danger without Mitrek knowing. Her other problem—that of King Padric Creston's growing impatience for research subjects—would also need to be addressed soon.

Sitting in her office drinking rielberry tea, Mavis closed her eyes and concentrated on breathing. An elusive thought had haunted her night and day since her private breakdown several days before. The harder she pressed her mind for it, the more the thought teased her. Trusting her instincts, Mavis kept her mind as blank as possible, knowing that the thought would be fully realized soon.

As her mind fought the false peace she imposed, she wondered what messages Dennel blocked at this very moment and worried about what Silvia thought of everything. Would the child's sense of innocence survive the experience? The agents had orders to use only minimal force and to keep Silvia distracted where feasible, but by now, the girl had to wonder why they would not let her contact her family.

Solve both problems simultaneously.
But how?
At first, Mavis felt annoyed, but the more she pondered the idea, the more she liked it.
Let the Rangers solve the problem.
Mavis almost dropped her teacup.
Could it really be that simple?
She drained the rest of the rielberry tea in one long gulp and set the cup aside. Then, she rested her elbows on the desk and let her warm fingertips

massage her temples.

How unfortunate that Lucas killed Hiram Alikron.

Mavis had never liked the pompous little Ranger, but if she chose assets based on likes, she would never work with anyone.

The recent, disastrous dealings with the Rangers had burned most of her ties with them, but she still had a camarek spy or two stashed away for desperate times. Players kept only one spy per board, but no rule prohibited several games from being played simultaneously. Multi-board games offered another layer of challenge for serious players. For all their mysterious powers, Rangers possessed common wants and needs. Mavis had devoted many resources to knowing these details, turning her knowledge into power.

Sliding her fingers down her face, Mavis folded her hands when they met at the point of her chin. Her mind raced over the broad details, and she determined to discuss the situation with Dennel later. The man's insights had proven invaluable many times, and moreover, Mavis trusted him.

In theory, the Nareth Talis Rangers numbered in the dozens. In reality, very few showed the sort of power King Padric sought. James and Kelsa Celdin kept busy raising their child and teaching apprentices. Esther Penoi and Adji had good track records, but they avoided using anotechs wherever possible. A self-healing here and a wall scaling there hardly made for grand news. Zed Laverit was not shy about using his powers, but reports spoke of his powers failing at key times. That alone might prove interesting, but certainly not as the first delivery.

Mavis needed Rangers with strong connections to anotechs who didn't fear using them. Kiata and Todd Wellum were certainly candidates. A vid of them rescuing Talyon Keldor had caught King Padric's attention in the first place. Something in Mavis hesitated to involve them, whispering that she should keep them close rather than ship them to Gardan. In the end, practicality triumphed, for few Rangers had the skills to free Silvia.

Mavis stood. Her mind filled with the orders to issue. Lucas and Kolknir could handle the first phase, and hopefully, Kiata and Todd would handle the second phase. She smiled at the irony of twice kidnapping her own granddaughter to save her.

***

Lalri (November) 17, 1538
Ashatan Council Chamber, Riden Mountains

Mentally bracing himself, Todd Wellum bowed to the Ashatan Council, eased onto the nearest cushion, folded his legs into a comfortable position, and silently bid farewell to the rest of his evening.

Sensing Kiata's burning curiosity, Todd shot her a reassuring smile and hoped one of the Council members would speak soon.

Why summon us? Why not just send a comm message?

Their grim countenances told Todd the answer.

To prove a point.

"Thank you for coming so quickly," said Master Jolinda Ekris. "I'm sure you are both eager to know why you were summoned. I will let Master

Deliad explain."

Deliad leaned forward and gazed imperiously at Todd and Kiata.

"About a month ago, we received a report from the Resh police concerning an altercation with some RT Alliance thugs. Why did we not hear the same report from you?"

"With respect, the Council issued no orders to report every incident," Kiata replied.

"You should always report anything that could affect the Order," Deliad snapped.

"Captain Von informed us he was filing a report," Kiata said.

"We read and approved of his findings," Todd added. "A report from us would have been redundant." He suddenly hated sitting on the floor like an apprentice waiting for crumbs of wisdom. "We knew they were Alliance thugs, but they carried no identification cards and had their fines paid by an anonymous source."

"Fines as punishment for an attacking Rangers ought to be a crime," muttered Master Corida.

"Why were you in Resh?" asked Master Deliad, shooting Corida a look that demanded he focus.

"What does your report say?" Kiata asked coldly.

"Mind your tone, Ranger Wellum," Deliad warned.

Todd could feel anger streaming off Kiata in palpable waves.

"The report says that you spent several weeks investigating the death of Governor Darmon Zelene," said Master Corida. "Why?"

"That was not your mandate," Deliad added.

"The Royals requested our help investigating the governor's suicide. He was a personal friend of King Teorn," explained Todd.

"What did your investigation reveal?" inquired Master Ekris.

"Unfortunately, very little," Todd admitted. "Governor Zelene ended his life to ransom his daughter. Lady Akia Zelene was kidnapped the evening before by a very skilled man using flingers."

The three Council members drew in sharp breaths.

"A Ranger?" Master Ekris asked.

"How do you know it was a man?" asked Deliad.

"Kolknir or Lucas," said Corida, frowning deeply. "Their flinger skills were unparalleled. Kiata comes close, but few men certainly."

"We think it was Lucas, but we have no evidence to support the claim," Todd reported.

"He was a good Ranger," Deliad commented.

Corida grunted.

"He was a traitor."

"Masters, please. This isn't helping," said Ekris. She raised her right hand to her forehead like she had a headache. "Kiata, Todd. We want to know that you're sticking to your mission in Rammon."

"Our mission is to protect and obey the Royals," Kiata said shortly.

Todd placed a calming hand on her right knee.

"We understand our mission, Masters," he said.

"Good." Deliad gave them each a long, acidic look as he dragged out the word. "Do be mindful that you obey the Order first, for the good of the Royals, of course."

Kiata stiffened, and Todd fought the urge to seize Deliad and tell him to shut up for his own good.

"Now that we've cleared the air, we have a separate mission for you," said Master Ekris, "a secret mission."

"Nobody can know, not even the Royals," added Master Corida.

"Can you handle that?" asked Deliad, studying them like specimens in a jar.

Todd met Kiata's eyes and saw a reflection of everything he was feeling: curiosity, fear, and excitement. He sat up straighter.

"What is the mission?" he asked.

***

Lalri (November) 21, 1538
Roniak Warehouse, City of Huz Mon

The Lady gets what she wants, Lucas Telon thought wryly, marveling at how well the plan had proceeded. Though not privy to the whole plot, he knew it was wider than him.

The Lady had given him the layout of the Rammon Safe House and a list of agents guarding the child, four RT Alliance agents and two Gardanian Shadow Guards.

The Alliance had become an ungainly beast. Lucas's soldiers had no idea they cut down unfortunate allies. Regret pierced him as he remembered the slaughter. He enjoyed a good kill as much as any man, but sacrificing allies seemed wrong.

His mind locked on one woman's expression when he'd planted his dagger in her chest. Her dark eyes had been pain-filled and curious but not condemning. Lucas cursed those eyes. Why didn't she hate him? The lack of anger only made him condemn himself.

The tap-tap of boots on concrete interrupted Lucas's reverie.

"She's whining about her mother again," complained Alden Tarpon. "What should I do? I'm not here to play nursemaid."

"I'll speak with her," Lucas promised. "Have your men begin preparations. Lord Maledek wants this place to be a fortress."

"I will see to it, Master Telon," Alden said. He partially turned then paused.

"Something else you need?" asked Lucas.

The young man hesitated.

"My brother would like to be involved in the mission." Alden did not sound enthusiastic about the idea, but his tone suggested that alternatives would be worse. "I think he's a bit stir-crazy with his administrative duties, especially with his wife ... occupied with the Lady's business."

"One should avoid speaking of the Lady's business even in passing," Lucas said, staring steadily at Alden. "But I agree. Have Brook help with the

388

warehouse, but tell him nothing of the girl. Tell no one. Those who need to know will hear it from me, understand?"

"Yes, Master Telon," Alden said with a slight bow. "May I send him a message now? It should only take a few minutes."

Lucas nodded permission, wishing Kolknir were still around. Things could get interesting if Brook Tarpon recognized him. While not exactly relishing the meeting, Lucas would not shrink from it. If Brook caused trouble, Lucas would kill him. With his mind humming with various killing methods, Lucas set off to find the child.

Chapter 24:
Unexpected Audience with the King

Lalri (November) 24, 1538
Justice Arena, City of Idonia

Mitrek Altran wanted to drop the Niktrod Keldor case. The presentation of evidence and testimonies seemed pointless. He could hardly believe he'd once enjoyed listening to advocates bicker and shred each other's cases. Under different circumstances, he would have quit the case, the job, and even the planet. He vowed to do precisely that as soon as this case concluded.

Once we get Silvia back, we'll go, but where should we go?

Balar, Riab, Wirsh, and even Gardan were viable options. Balar consisted of three hundred and forty-six separate countries on eight continents with a population close to nine billion people. Blending in would be extremely easy. Having destroyed their natural environment several centuries back, the people of Riab developed self-contained pods to inhabit. Disappearing there would be slightly more challenging, despite the massive influx of tourists. Wild, almost lawless Wirsh would be hard to get used to, especially since it lacked moons. Provided Mitrek could leave his surname behind, Gardan might be a pleasant place to live, and certainly, the transition would be simple since Gardan and Reshner had very similar political structures.

Mitrek did not give much thought to other planets farther away. Long distance space travel required preparations of the sort that would leave a trail for his mother to follow.

"—my client's best interests," concluded Master Isaac Marin.

Mitrek cleared his throat to stall.

"I think it would be in our best interests to take a short recess. When we return, you may continue your presentation, Master Marin." Mitrek typed the appropriate order into his infopad and stood up before anyone could object. Feeling the weight of many eyes, he fled to his private office.

Focus on the case. Every moment you dither, Silvia spends in danger.

These thoughts filled him as he collapsed onto his chair. He let his fingers brush the expensive zalok leather and wondered what stories lay in its history. What life had the beast that once owned the hide lived? What adventurer had illegally poached it, or had it come from one of the rare merchants licensed to scour the mountains for dead zaloks?

A timid knock and a gentle chime both indicated someone's desire to enter his private sanctum.

"Enter," called Mitrek, straightening and trying to look busy.

A tow-headed young man entered and bowed.

"Apologies, Lord Altran. His Highness King Terosh of House Minstel would like a word with you," said the boy.

Mitrek silently cursed in three languages. He could not fathom what Terosh wanted. Normally, he could dodge the conversation under the guise of avoiding a conflict of interest, but one did not lightly cast aside the king's request.

"Send him in, Andel, and extend the recess an extra ten minutes."

"As you wish, my Lord," said Andel with another bow.

About two minutes later, Mitrek rose with all the grace he could muster from his trembling knees. After the customary bow, he stepped away from his chair and gestured toward it.

"Please have a seat, Your Highness. Shall I—"

Terosh waved off the invitation like a man swatting flies.

"I'm not here as your king, Mitrek. I am here as your cousin. What's wrong?"

Mitrek leaned heavily against his desk. His thoughts tripped over each other, but he clenched his teeth to hold them inside.

"What makes you believe something is wrong?" he queried.

"Delia has been at every session with Sullivan and Arabeth, but I've not seen your eldest child for some time," Terosh said slowly. "Given our family's history, I thought it best to inquire. Where is Silvia?"

The question hit Mitrek like a throwing dagger. He stumbled back to his chair and flopped onto it before his knees could completely fail. Avoiding Terosh's gaze, Mitrek said, "She is in my mother's care." The effort to control his emotions left his voice lifeless.

"Where?" asked the king. "Would your mother keep Silvia with her at her private home?"

"I doubt it," Mitrek replied bitterly. "Besides, nobody knows where my mother truly calls home. It's in the Kala Mountains somewhere, but few venture there."

"Should I be concerned, Mitrek? The recordings of Delia say I should. Natural beauty aside, she looks like death warmed over."

Mitrek winced. He'd noticed the terrified look in Delia's eyes, but he had hoped others would see only her brave smile.

"There is nothing you can do, Highness. Pursuing the subject will only complicate matters. I can do my job."

The king frowned.

"I could withdraw the charges and stop the trial."

Mitrek tried to suppress the alarm but knew his countenance betrayed him.

Before Mitrek could respond, Terosh continued, "But stopping the trial is the last thing I want." He fell into moody silence, then changed the subject. "Do you find it odd that nobody knows where in the Kala Mountains Lady Mavis makes her home?"

"If I had a kef for every idealistic reporter who begged for an answer, my fortune would pave a path to our farthest moon," Mitrek said with a dark chuckle. He pressed his fingertips together. "It seems like both of us are in a bit of a bind. Let me finish this trial quickly. He's guilty. Everybody, including him, knows it. The only remaining question is how he will be sentenced."

"You already know the answer to that too, don't you?" asked the king.

"I will weigh every option," Mitrek said carefully. "But the political winds are blowing hard in one direction."

"I want to help, Mitrek," King Terosh said. "Ours is a strange family. If we fail to defend each other, we will fall that much sooner."

Before he could think, Mitrek blurted the first thing that came to mind.

"You can aid my family best by helping us leave." Feeling lightheaded, Mitrek knew blood was draining from his face. If Terosh spoke to the wrong person, Mitrek and his family would die, but the younger man had never struck him as reckless or ruthless. Figuring the damage had already been done, Mitrek forged on. "As soon as this trial ends, I want to leave Reshner. Permanently."

Chapter 25:
More than Simple Smugglers

Lalri (November) 29, 1538
Roniak Warehouse, City of Huz Mon

Despite the discomfort of the white and black mask, Kezem enjoyed the euphoric rush of being Maledek again. It had been a mistake to let Belcross borrow the identity. Kezem had nearly perished from boredom during those long months.

I was meant for this life.

Kezem checked the weapons arrayed on the table, eyeing each like a proud father. Picking up the electrified banistick, he turned it over a few times and reluctantly put it down again. Bringing it to bear against a Ranger would be lovely, but a sentimental part of him wanted to save the banistick for a royal. Shutting his eyes and breathing deeply, Kezem cast his mind back to Deanna's death. He'd not killed her with the banistick, but he had wounded her with it.

After a moment's consideration, Kezem picked up two kerlinblades and clipped them to either side of his belt, tilted at an angle for easy cross-draw. He would leave the shooting to his men. He sensed they were just as eager for a fight after many days dodging the king's soldiers, police, and Rangers. It had been cruel to bait so many traps and not spring them.

You were right again, Mother, he thought, mentally saluting her.

Kezem hated being wrong, but this did not bother him as much as usual. The thought of a challenging fight thrilled him. He still questioned his mother's sanity in having Silvia brought here, but he trusted something significant would happen soon.

***

Ranger Kiata Wellum did not like the odds. If they were detected, she and Todd would have a tough time escaping even with the anotechs' help. Her knees complained and every muscle she owned begged to be uncoiled. She closed her eyes and pressed her back against a large crate, mentally bidding her husband to hurry. She clutched her banistick to her chest and resisted shaking Todd for answers.

Why couldn't I have been born with Reia's patience?

The steady thud of boots announced an approaching guard. Kiata instinctively crouched lower, shifting to a better position in case she had to attack. She prayed her ankles wouldn't crack and give her away. The footsteps stopped for an infuriating moment, and Kiata fought down the suicidal urge to leap over the crate and take out the RT Alliance soldier. As she exhaled the last of a calming breath, Kiata heard the welcomed thud of receding footsteps.

With the danger temporarily gone, Kiata eased one knee to the ground and looked at Todd. He sat exactly as he had the last two dozen times she checked. With his left leg tucked close to his body, right leg stretched out, eyes shut, and head leaning toward his left shoulder, Todd looked far too relaxed for their current situation. Without warning, his head snapped up, his eyes sprang open, his body stiffened, and he moved to rise.

Despite being ready for this, Kiata's heartbeat quickened. She clamped her left hand over Todd's mouth while her right hand braced the back of his head so he wouldn't bang it against the crate.

"Wake up! It's me!" she whispered, leaning close to his ear. She pulled her head back and tilted it enough to come into his line of vision. With a wry smile she added, "Remember me?" She saw only confusion in his hazel eyes. Kiata shrugged. "You will in a moment, but please refrain from loud greetings. We're in a bit of trouble here. The next time the Council has a dangerous secret mission on offer, I say we skip it. We're getting too old to skulk behind crates."

Todd's eyes finally cleared. When Kiata didn't immediately let go, he narrowed his eyes and shook his head impatiently.

Releasing him, Kiata whispered, "Welcome back. What did you find?"

"They're definitely smugglers, but I'm still not sure why the Council sent us," Todd reported. "The crates have everything from firfe spice to zalok scales to kerlak and serlak rifles. They're obviously illegal, but that doesn't explain the number of guards around here or the Ranger interest."

Kiata bobbed her head in agreement.

"They were a little sparse on details. I credited that to their anonymous informant. Now I wonder if there was something more to it."

"Shall I look again?" asked Todd. "I only got through about half the warehouse. We'll probably find more in the offices at the far end anyway."

After helping Todd up, Kiata waited impatiently while he stretched some feeling back into his limbs. Then, they picked their way to a new position closer to the offices. They passed three patrols, but nobody came close to discovering them.

There was no shortage of crates to hide behind. They settled down between a sturdy set marked: Charan wine. A side wall sat within touch to their right and another set of crates blocked their left side. The close fit made Kiata feel both protected and trapped. She hunched her shoulders against an uneasy prickling at the back of her mind and again clutched her banistick for comfort. She almost pitied the first thing to jump her tonight. The tension coiled inside her would not be gentle when unleashed.

***

As soon as he found a comfortable position, Todd Wellum slipped into another anotech trance. His senses heightened to a disconcerting level. The floor felt painfully hard. Faint drafts carried the too-sweet scent of Charan wine, the tangy odor of a few thousand wooden crates, and the musky scent of human apprehension. His ears identified twelve distinct pairs of boots beating different rhythms on the floor. He also heard Kiata's carefully controlled breaths and felt each heartbeat that thundered in his chest.

Pushing past the sensations, Todd sent anotechs to explore the area around his body. They skittered from crate to crate and reported the contents. As before, he found weapons, food, and spices. Telling them to ignore items already noted, Todd sent the anotechs through crate after crate until they reached the wall shared with the warehouse offices. Concentrating so hard his head throbbed, he pressed on, instructing some anotechs to enter the nearest office.

Several minutes passed while the anotechs swept through one office after another. In the fourth office, Todd sensed something different. The anotechs buzzed excitedly in his head. He spent another thirty seconds sorting the impressions they sent back, feeling fear and discomfort. The sound of ragged, shallow breathing and small whimpers filled Todd's mind. He sensed a form lying on a thin carpet. A query identified the individual. Stunned, he recalled the anotechs and told them to wake his body slowly.

Todd waited impatiently for his consciousness to fully return and his senses to revert to normal. He opened his eyes to Kiata's concerned face hovering nearby. Her expression demanded answers. His mouth felt uncomfortably dry.

"There's a child here. Silvia Altran," he whispered. "She must be the reason we're here, but who knew they had her? Why do they have her? Do you think it has to do with the Keldor case?"

"We can theorize later," Kiata said. Her low tone could not mask her tension.

The worry he heard summoned a rush of adrenaline that woke Todd nicely.

Abruptly, every light in the warehouse snapped on to full brilliance. Todd blinked furiously and scrambled for his kerlak pistol. Footsteps made thunderous noise for a few seconds then deafening silence fell. Seconds later, a man shouted orders. Several men responded. A high-pitched yelp rang out from one corner and half a dozen excited barks answered.

This was no ordinary search but a hunt, which meant trap.

Todd's mind cycled through their options. They could elude detection by hiding among the crates, but that would not last long. The trained korvers would find them far sooner than soldiers. A direct fight did not offer favorable odds. They could climb to the highest crates and try to leap out with anotech powers, but that would make them nice targets.

We must save the girl.

No sooner did the thought brush Todd's mind, Kiata said, "Go get Silvia."

Todd opened his mouth to argue but she was gone. Growling in frustration, Todd leapt to his feet.

A triumphant shout told him the men had spotted Kiata.

When we get out of this, we're having a chat about your plans, Todd promised his reckless wife.

Knowing Kiata would be unable to distract all the RT Alliance soldiers, Todd carefully picked his way between crates. Several times, he had to backtrack. Going over the crates would have sped up progress, but it would also nullify the advantage of Kiata's diversion. He only encountered one soldier desperately hanging onto a korver's leash. A command to the anotechs rendered both the soldier and the korver unconscious.

A dizzy feeling gripped Todd. Leaning heavily against the nearest crate, he ordered his feet to carry him forward. He couldn't afford to do that again. As his legs reluctantly obeyed, Todd drew his kerlak pistol and adjusted to medium stun. Normally, he would have left the power on full, but he did not want to accidentally kill the child.

***

Silvia Altran's skin felt alive with unseen things. A scream caught in her throat. A flood of tears was all she could release. Then the korverhide ropes binding her ankles and wrists fell away and a reassuring wave of calmness cradled her. The sobs that tried to form burned hot then disappeared, leaving behind gentle sniffles.

A man appeared and reached for her.

In the darkness, she could not see him, but somehow, she knew him as the source of the calmness.

"Be brave, Silvia. Silent and brave. I'm going to get you out of here, but you need to run to safety." The man lifted her to a sitting position as he spoke. "I need you to stand on my knees and jump as high as you can. Will you do that for me?"

Unable to form words, Silvia nodded.

"Once you're out, you need to be even braver still. Rub some dirt on your face and go where your feet take you. Have Captain Armith contact the palace. Tell him Ranger Todd Wellum told you to speak to no one but the queen or king."

The man spoke so quickly Silvia feared she would forget his instructions, and she really wanted to remember them. The wave of calmness turned to cool confidence that she would remember everything. She nodded again.

"Come then, let's get you out of here," said the Ranger. In one smooth motion, the man lifted Silvia up and turned her around, bracing her feet on his thighs. "When I count to three, I'm going to toss you up. You need to jump then, okay?" He started counting without waiting for a reply.

When he reached three, Silvia jumped as high as she could. Another scream died an unnatural death in her throat, but inside her mind, she screamed with terror and joy. As she thought she ought to start falling, an unseen wind propelled her up with frightening speed. She watched the glass skylight rush up, but before her head could slam into it, the skylight shattered outward.

Silvia squeezed her eyes shut and covered her head with her arms, but not one glass shard touched her. Her stomach lurched as she hovered over the broken skylight. Reassured by that inner calm, Silvia stretched her hands wide and enjoyed floating on the air. Then, she felt very sleepy, but she remembered the man's words. She needed to be on the ground if she wanted to obey them.

As if the wind supporting her body agreed, she floated down to the ground, tumbling head over heels to a standing position. When Silvia's feet touched solid ground, strange energy filled her with an irresistible need to run.

Chapter 26:
Hunted

Lalri (November) 29, 1538
Same Day
Roniak Warehouse, City of Huz Mon

The energy coursing through Kiata Wellum went far beyond the usual adrenaline rush of entering battle. She recognized the anotechs and welcomed their aid. Knocking a man's kerlinblade aside with her banistick, Kiata crashed her right fist into his chin. The man cried out once and toppled into the soldier behind him. The other man had just enough time to catch his friend before Kiata's banistick clobbered him at the base of his neck.

Energy beams flashed toward Kiata. She dropped to the ground, rolled, and scrambled behind the meager cover of the two soldiers she had just felled.

A rat screeched at her for bringing trouble to its home.

Now would be a good time to consider other warehouses, she thought as the rat turned tail and beat a hasty retreat.

"Surrender and save yourselves a lot of pain. Escape is impossible. I have dozens of soldiers guarding every door and window." The synthesized voice boomed from speakers in the ceiling.

Kiata didn't need to see to believe the message. For each of the many RT Alliance soldiers and korvers chasing her through the stacks of crates, she sensed two or three lining the perimeters.

Why don't they kill me?

The thought wasn't exactly a complaint, but she felt unfriendly eyes peering at her through rifle scopes. She crawled behind a crate and hunkered down to catch her breath.

"My orders are to keep you alive, but they were a little vague as to *how* alive." The voice sounded pleasant and cajoling. "Come, face me. I will be at the center where there is a slight clearing. If your fighting skills please me, you will enjoy my protection against the Alliance men."

Who are you? Who gave you those orders? Why are you working with the Alliance? You seem to be in charge, but for how long? Do you mean what you say? She crushed the last question.

Surrender could not be considered. Kolknir had taught her that much a lifetime ago.

Five serlak bullets thudded into the crate Kiata hid behind, tearing a chunk off one corner and raining splinters down on her head. Knowing the shots were meant to rattle her did not prevent the tactic from working. She gripped her banistick tighter, incensed by being toyed with. A tingle creeping down her spine told her a tremendous amount of anotech activity took place very close at hand. Cold fear followed closely on its heels.

"Over here!" shouted a man.

Four excited barks answered.

"We know!" snarled another man. He cursed and one of the korvers whined in pain.

"Have a care with your shots, gentlemen," spoke the voice from the ceiling. "I need them alive."

"If he wants 'em alive so badly, he can haul his backside over here and give us a hand," grumbled a third man.

"I think it's a woman," said the first man. "What should we do?" He sounded uncertain.

"Climb over that crate and drag her out here, or I'll let Alaios have your legs for chew toys," snapped the second man.

His korver rumbled an eager growl.

Hearing the unmistakable sounds of a man climbing, Kiata closed her banistick and attached it to her belt. Still torn between moving toward the increased anotech activity or away from it, Kiata took two steps and jumped toward the crate in front. Her hands gripped the top and held while her knees, legs, and feet struggled for purchase.

More serlak bullets punished the crate for helping her, but she ignored them, reasonably confident that the man in charge would keep a tight rein on his trigger-happy snipers. Kiata's arms ached from bearing her weight and stung from scraping along the rough top edge. Pushing the discomfort aside, she pulled her body up and rolled to a kneeling position.

Banistick back in hand, she lunged to her feet and sprinted across the top of the massive crate. When she reached the far edge, Kiata called on the anotechs to lend strength to her legs and leapt. More shouts and surprised gasps filled the air behind her. At the height of her arc, she tucked into a forward roll that carried her about four meters from where she'd jumped. Bending her knees to absorb the landing shock, Kiata assessed her surroundings.

Stacked crates formed a cage around her. The space was four meters wide and five meters long. A small opening provided the only break in the solid line. Men shouted conflicting orders at each other. A moment later, three scrappy little korvers slipped through the hole and charged at her.

Kiata glared. She'd never liked korvers, and she liked them even less having heard of the attacks during Terosh's Kireshana. A familiar wave of controlled rage blossomed in her chest. Attacking Terosh would have been bad enough, but threatening Reia earned korvers Kiata's eternal ire.

The well-trained beasts surrounded Kiata, moving as she turned so that two constantly flanked her while one pranced about in front. Movement from above and to her right drew Kiata's attention to a soldier peering down from a stack of crates close to the side wall. Four more joined him. She suddenly felt like a spectacle in a pit fight. Her concentration wavered as more soldiers appeared.

Cheers rose from the RT Alliance soldiers. They stood or crouched on the edges, eyes bright with anticipation. Most had kerlak pistols or rifles leveled at her. The few with serlak weapons held them across their chests or left them casually hanging by their sides. This small confirmation that they intended to capture her brought Kiata little comfort. If they all fired upon her simultaneously, the combined stun beams could kill her, but she could not spare the effort to worry.

Sensing her distraction, the korver behind and to her right darted in to snap at her legs.

Kiata swiped at the korver, catching it at a glancing blow across the snout. It yelped and retreated, glaring balefully at her. Too late, she remembered the other korvers. Pain exploded in her lower left leg, at first sharp then dull then indefinable. Tossing her banistick to her left hand, Kiata whipped the weapon down.

A muffled crack and thump preceded a blessed relief to the level of pain in her leg. Warm blood gushed out of the wound. Shifting her weight to her right leg, Kiata paused to instruct the anotechs to staunch the blood flow. Murmurs from above told her the soldiers noticed the healing effort.

Tasting victory in the blood-tinged air, the other two korvers came at her, one aiming for her good leg and the other intent on her throat.

Instinctively, Kiata hopped back and made some adjustments to her banistick. The grip slid to the center, and she twirled the weapon in rapid circles. The instant before the korver's teeth would sink into her right leg, Kiata's banistick slammed into its head. Suddenly, she stopped the twirling and rammed the full length of her weapon up into the korver headed for her throat, pushing off her good leg. Pain and panic lent extra strength and the korver flew away from her into the top of the crate that now lay in front of her.

Three more korvers eased into the space. They moved cautiously, sniffing at their fallen friends and growling at her.

Feeling her strength ebbing, Kiata snatched three flingers from the belt case and sent them flying with deft flicks of her wrist. She could not swing her arm as violently as necessary to give the shots her usual devastating speed for fear of unbalancing herself, but her aim was true. The first two korvers dropped with pitiful cries. A blue energy beam collided with her third flinger, sending it off on a new course where it slammed into a crate.

The third korver stopped short, confused by the sudden light. It danced about excitedly trying to find the new threat.

"Call them off," commanded a toneless, metallic voice from behind Kiata.

"Adean, Endel, heel," called a soldier.

The korver Kiata had thrown and the one that narrowly escaped her flinger froze in place looking disgruntled. One whined a pitiful complaint to its master.

The soldiers fell eerily silent.

Kiata tensed.

"You fared well against the beasts, but I say again: this fight is futile. Do you intend to best a hundred men?" The synthesized voice sounded close.

Wearily, Kiata pivoted to face the speaker and changed her banistick so the handle again rested at one end. Despite everything she had seen and experienced over the years, the sight of the expressionless white and black mask chilled her considerably.

"Who are you?" she asked.

"I have many names and faces, but you may call me Maledek."

She recognized the name, of course, but Kiata could not comprehend why a mysterious figure that generally plagued Idonia, Azhel, and the surrounding areas would show up in Huz Mon.

Her confusion must have shown on her face, for the man spoke again.

"Save your strength for our duel. Questions will keep until later. It's a pity you're injured. I wanted to truly test your reputation."

Kiata's right leg complained about holding most of her weight and her left leg still throbbed from the bite wound. She shuffled back so she could lean against a massive crate as far from the dangerous man as possible.

"Why should I bother fighting you?" she asked, angry enough to be contrary.

The man folded his arms across his chest and tilted his head in an amused nod.

"Would you not do it to satisfy my curiosity, dear lady?" he inquired.

The mechanical words crawled over Kiata's skin.

"Come and claim your duel, and we'll see how satisfied you are afterward." If her wrath could turn into fire, the man would have burned to ashes.

With a mocking bow, the figure hopped down into the makeshift dueling arena, landing lightly. His movements were characterized by a fighter's fluid grace.

"Would you prefer we move to the wider area? The lighting is better, and there will be less korver blood and fewer bodies."

"This will do." Kiata worked frantically to shunt the leg pain to an obscure corner of her mind where it would least inhibit her ability to fight.

"Should we wait for our other honored guest?" Maledek asked, drawing a kerlinblade from either side of his waist.

Kiata gritted her teeth against the pain still radiating up her leg and the knot forming in her stomach. Against her will, she followed Maledek's gaze up to the crate she'd just hurled a korver at.

Soldiers jostled each other, steadily forming a gap. More soldiers filled the gap, dragging something between them.

Todd!

Kiata's heart lurched. Her husband's head hung limply. The agitated flutter of anotechs in Kiata's chest declared him deep in an anotech trance rather than simply unconscious. His features were frozen in an expression of intense concentration.

At a wave from Maledek, the two soldiers holding Todd draped him feet-first over the side of the crate and let him slide to the ground.

Kiata flinched as Todd's body flopped to the floor near the subdued, grumbling korvers. Her fingers longed to cast down her banistick and rush to her husband. Though he looked completely insensible, Kiata still felt the heightened anotech activity. She only hoped he succeeded in getting the girl away.

***

Eager as he was to start the duel, Kezem knew he would gain more satisfaction if more soldiers could watch. He did not relish dodging korver bodies and patches of floor still slick with blood. Besides, the woman looked ready to collapse. The short rest would do her good. Perhaps he would even give her a stimulant to make the fight fairer.

"I'm afraid I must insist on a change of venue," Kezem said. The synthesized voice he used for Maledek sounded too loud, but he enjoyed the vibrations the voice modulator sent through his chest.

The pale woman rested her head against the crate supporting her and shut her eyes. Sweat glistened on her face and arms. A fraying braid of light brown hair curled over her left shoulder. The lower portion of her left trouser hung in strips. The leg itself did not fare much better.

Kezem winced at the sight. Disappointment spread through him. She would require treatment before even attempting a duel. Perhaps her husband would oblige him with the fight he desired.

"You've gone and hurt yourself worse than I thought," Kezem commented. "Be reasonable and surrender or it will go worse for you."

"Worse?" the woman scoffed. "I'm not sure that's possible."

Nodding in a friendly manner, Kezem said, "I could set the korvers on your other leg and let them play with your husband."

Shutting her eyes against a wave of pain, the woman frowned at his words. Opening her eyes, she said, "You're well-informed. What do you want?"

"Answers in time. For now, surrender will suffice."

Their eyes met and measured each other. As Kezem raised his hand to motion the soldier to set Adean and Endel on the woman's husband, she let her banistick slip from her grasp. It clattered to the floor.

"What now?" asked the woman Ranger.

Kezem was pleased to hear defiance in her voice.

"You will be escorted elsewhere," he replied. "Welcome to Huz Mon, Kiata. I'm sorry you won't get to see much of the city."

Chapter 27:
Reflections and Hard Choices

Ferrim (December) 4, 1538
Mount Hakan, Kala Mountains

Ignoring the two Royal Guards hovering nearby, Queen Reia sat down on the cliff's edge and swallowed great gulps of thin, cold mountain air. She wished for Master Niklos's comforting presence. The few comm conversations with him had been nice, but she dared not involve more people she loved while so little was known about why Kiata and Todd never returned from their last mission.

Reia's feet touched nothing but air. The sight of land dropping away so suddenly would unnerve most people, but Reia felt only a flutter of apprehension that could easily be taken for excitement. She had grown up in mountains, and though these were not her mountains, something about the rugged isolation comforted her.

Remembering the awful night she'd been roused from a rare, restful sleep, Reia let her thoughts dwell on Kiata and Todd. The little girl they had rescued ought to be tucked away in the palace, safely in Sarie's care. Reia still didn't know what to think about that situation, but the memory of Silvia Altran's fierce embrace and fantastic story would not release Reia. Lady Mavis had insisted that the child's rescue be kept a secret, but Reia thought the decision cruel to Lord Mitrek. Lady Mavis's reasons made sense, and Reia certainly had no wish to further endanger Silvia. Still, the thought of Mitrek thinking his daughter remained in danger threatened a tide of tears.

Reia pushed past the emotion by appealing to the questions that drove her here.

Is it my fault Kiata and Todd were taken? How do I save them? Are they even alive?

They live, answered the anotechs.

Where are they? How do you know they live? Reia demanded.

Don't know. Just know, you know? Dark Ones guard their plans well. Give many false signals, but their life sense is very real.

What would the Dark Ones gain by holding Todd and Kiata?

Not main plan, we think, but Dark Ones seeking those strong

with Light Ones.

Terosh? Me? Rangers? Who are they after? Who else has the Light Ones in them?

We choose many. Many choose us. Some do not know. Some do.

Ambiguous as always. Can you tell me anything useful? Or shall I return to my worry?

Do not worry, Queen of the Chosen. Probability is very high the Dark Ones do not intend death for them.

No matter how many ways Reia phrased her questions, the answers remained consistently vague. Finally, she cut off communication with the anotechs. As expected, worry crept back in. She tried to focus on the natural beauty around her, but even that cure had its limits.

Reia let her gaze trace a path down the jagged gray cliff to the sprawling valley below where a carpet of kintral trees clothed the mountainside. In the distance, she saw flocks of cannafitch riding gentle wind currents, but she could not hear their screeching cries. For the moment, everything was so completely quiet that her heartbeat echoed in her ears and the ragged breaths of her two guards sounded like the start of a windstorm.

"If it would please Your Majesty, there's a better view from up here," said Captain Ectosh Laocer. He really meant "back here," as in well away from the cliff's edge.

"I'm fine, Captain," Reia said with as much warmth as she could muster. She still felt half-dead inside, but he meant well. "I'm sorry to drag you and Lieutenant Zareb so far from your normal duties."

"No apologies," Zareb scolded gently. "Queen Reia of House Minstel honors us by sharing grief. Elish know grief shared lighter."

Nothing against the two loyal Royal Guards, but Reia longed to share this grief with her husband. A stab of guilt followed the wish, for she knew it was her own fault Terosh stayed away.

He would come if you asked.

The truth shielded her against the cold wind. She remembered the flight they'd shared across part of the Riden Mountains. Her desperate plan had almost killed them, but together, they had made it. The crash landing hurt but facing the subsequent cold with Terosh made the pain bearable.

Before Reia realized exactly what her fingers were doing, she had completely undone the braids holding her hair tightly to her head. She raked her fingers through the hair until the braids unraveled. A gentle breeze picked up the newly liberated strands and sent them flying.

When will Todd and Kiata experience something like this? Are they scared?

Images of Kiata's concerned face came to the forefront of Reia's thoughts, and she understood some of the burden her sister carried over the years. Never before had Reia recognized the full measure of responsibility Kiata had carried since their parents' death. The thought turned Reia's mind to the duties that dictated her own life.

Your life is no longer your own.

Her sister's words had never been truer. Reia could not even worry without involving other people. The Royal Guards flanking her at a respectful distance proved that.

Can I go on like this? Reia shivered against the thought. *What kind of a stupid question is that?*

Life might have been easier had she chosen to stay a Ranger, but for all the annoyances and terrors that came with her new life, Reia knew Terosh and the people were worth it. The spark of anger triggered by the stupid question flooded Reia with determination to forge on. She had things to accomplish. Kiata and Todd would give her an earful if they knew she neglected her duties to worry for them.

***

Ferrim (December) 7, 1538
Prison Level, RT Alliance Safe House, City of Huz Mon

The low-level pain and heavy doses of criessa coursing through his body slowed thinking, but Todd Wellum finally understood why he and his wife still lived. Hundreds of conversations and facts gathered by the anotechs added up to one conclusion. Their captors wished to study the anotechs. He wanted to deny it, but he also knew his duty was clear.

Fighting the chilling numbness of criessa and ignoring the pain, Todd snapped his eyes open and looked to Kiata. She lay on her cot watching him and tapping her left fingers in a regular rhythm. The pain was probably worse for her because of the leg injury. The ugly white gloves and foot covers responsible for the pain looked oddly benign.

For Todd, it felt like sticking his hands and feet into a sonic cleaner set dangerously high. The pain wasn't constant, but it struck whenever their captors' frustration peaked. They pretend to have a purpose besides waiting for transfer orders, but the questions they posed were inconsistent and pointless. Todd did not know where they would be transferred to, but he gathered that it would happen soon, which meant he had little time to consider his moral dilemma.

Noticing his gaze, Kiata tried to grin but it turned into a grimace. She sighed.

"I'm getting really tired of waking up like this." She raised her white-gloved hands and studied them. The muscles in her arms clenched violently then relaxed as another shock charged through.

Todd looked at her and loved her so much that his resolve wavered. He instructed the anotechs to jam the door so they would have more time for discussing their situation.

Recognizing the conflicted expression, Kiata swung her legs over the side of her cot and sat up.

"Out with it," she ordered, swaying gently as her body adjusted to the new position. Her hands gripped the thin mattress. She winced and bit her lower lip, indicating that the shock must have gone through her left leg this time. When the pain faded, Kiata fixed her silver-blue eyes directly on Todd.

"I've been eavesdropping. They're after the anotechs," he

405

announced, sitting up and facing her. "I can't tell who the leaders are because something strange keeps diverting the anotechs away from them." He shrugged and said no more but avoided eye contact.

"It doesn't matter. You know what you have to do," Kiata said. Her voice was steady and commanding, but she swallowed hard and paled.

"It could kill us," Todd argued half-heartedly.

In more ways than one, he added.

Having never experienced decommissioning, Todd had only other Rangers' accounts that the process could be traumatic. The mere thought of being without the heightened senses filled him with dread. History lessons held a tale or two of Nareth Talis Rangers who never recovered from the loss. It would also be hard to hide the change from their captors who could decide they were worthless without the connection.

"Our vows are clear," Kiata said.

An angry, muffled shout from outside the door caught their attention. Kiata's head whipped toward the door then back to Todd. His did pretty much the same thing, and their eyes met.

Kiata spoke quickly, tears pooling in her eyes.

"Todd, listen to me. I'm not strong enough to break our links. They're going to know that. You must be." She paused to brace against another shock. "Promise you'll carry through with it. No matter what threats they breathe or what they do."

Todd felt time grind to a stop along with his ability to breathe or think. The next wave of pain broke the momentary spell. He gasped, feeling something in his heart being squeezed to death. He honestly did not know if he could give her such a promise. There was only one solution. He had to break the connection before his resolve could be tested.

Tears streaming down his face, Todd muttered the ceremonial words and settled in for the fight of his life.

***

Ferrim (December) 9, 1538
Kaypree Springs, Felmon Desert, between Osem and Terab

Terosh Minstel was not in the best of moods. Kiata and Todd Wellum were still missing, and he could do little more than demand the Royal Guards work quickly to find them. He had let himself get trapped arbitrating a dispute for water rights between the Osem Rangers and Terabian water traders.

If Reia had insisted, he would have led a room by room search of Huz Mon to find clues, but she told him their work must continue. While he understood the logic, his heart ached to offer more comfort. He hated that she suffered alone. Reia chose not to join him on the peace mission to avoid provoking the Rangers. He missed her, even though less than a week had passed apart.

The next arbitration case is taking place in the palace, he thought, knowing the promise would be hard to keep.

Outside, the wind made an incessant thumping noise as it pushed hard then let the heavy canvas material spring back with a muffled crack.

Occasionally, the wind would slip a small puff of sand under the tent walls. Terosh watched the new sand slither along like sidewinders and pass through the other side or else form miniature pillars along the edge.

"Both sides have valid points," Terosh muttered, wishing it were not so. He scratched at a bit of stubble he'd missed while shaving and absently bid the anotechs to fix the problem. A cascade of hair fragments rained down onto his dark blue shirt. Even though the hairs were invisible against the dark fabric, Terosh brushed at them anyway.

The Rangers had discovered and maintained the Kaypree Springs for far longer than the Terabian water traders. However, the water traders spoke truth in saying that the Rangers had more options than they did. If they would travel a bit, the Rangers could even draw water off Twin Lake. That would solve the Osem-Terab problem but create a new one between Osem and Azhel. Terosh knew of only one way to completely solve the problem and neither side would be wholly pleased in the end, hence his foul mood.

It's the best option.

"It's the most dangerous option," Terosh said, feeling pathetic for talking to himself.

You know it works. You and the queen pulled water from the Morden Lowlands.

"That was different. We only needed a little water," Terosh said, not even realizing the thought wasn't exactly his own. "We've never tried anything on this scale."

Terosh felt a tingling sensation in his head that indicated the anotechs' amusement.

You pulled water from the air, too. That was much harder than this will be.

Terosh rubbed at his tired eyes.

Now you speak? I've been wrestling with this dumb debate for three days and this is the first time you've deigned to speak to me about it.

We thought you knew. The problem is very simple to solve but warn them of the dangers.

Thanks, I feel so much better. Terosh shook his head, stood up, and walked to the tent entrance. *Might as well get this over with.*

After flinging the heavy flaps aside, Terosh said, "Covin, please fetch the representatives. Tell them I have reached a decision and would like to explain it to them before making a formal announcement."

"Right away, King Terosh of House Minstel. Covin honored to carry message," said the Elish. He bobbed his head three times and hurried off to summon the chief representatives.

In less than ten minutes, Ranger Knight Caius Drake and Master Milo Carlangas sat cross-legged on the floor in front of Terosh's sturdy travel chair.

"Before I render a judgment in this matter, I need answers to a few questions," said Terosh, after the exchange of customary greetings. "Covin will keep a record of my questions and your responses. The first question is obvious but must be stated for the record. Do you agree that the forthcoming judgment will be final and completely binding upon yourselves and the parties you represent? If so, please say 'I do.'"

"I do," chorused the representatives without hesitation.

"Good. Now, this part is important. Ranger Drake, can your Order spare several dozen volunteers with the rank of Knight or Healer to accept special instruction from myself or the queen?" Terosh fixed his gaze upon the young Ranger.

I hope Reia agrees to this, Terosh thought belatedly.

He did not look forward to that conversation but decided to worry about that part later.

"It may take a day, a week, a month, or many months. I have no way of knowing how much time will be required, but each volunteer would need to agree to certain ... security measures."

The Ranger frowned.

"With respect, Highness, I will say that gaining volunteers should not be a problem, even with the security measures. I assume you mean to teach us a new technique. We—especially those sworn to the Nareth Talis—are well acquainted with taking precautions to guard our powers. However, there will be great opposition for accepting instruction from Her Majesty the queen." The man's cheeks reddened.

"That is why I asked," said Terosh. "Will your people let themselves be bound by your word, Ranger Drake?"

After a brief hesitation, the Ranger said, "Yes, Your Grace. I am authorized by the Osem Ashatan Council to seek an end to this dispute. The Rangers are peacekeepers. If attaining peace requires us to swallow our pride, then we will do it."

"Very well, I accept your word," said Terosh. He turned his attention to the other representative. "Master Milo Carlangas, can your people survive on half rations of water until such a time as instruction to the Osem Rangers is complete?"

"Half rations? What is to become of the rest of the water?" cried Carlangas.

"I will explain shortly, but I first need confirmation that your people will accept my proposal," said Terosh.

Master Carlangas drew his shoulders back and spoke quickly.

"My people can survive almost any condition." He hesitated, staring up at Terosh. "I am authorized by Governor Edeline Pallav to accept terms of arbitration on behalf of the city of Terab. We trust House Minstel will do right by the Terabian people."

"I accept your word, Master Carlangas. Then, if we are all in agreement, I shall render judgment." Terosh paused a moment for each man to nod. "Please allow me to finish before protesting a particular point. In the matter of control over the Kaypree Springs, judgment is decided in favor of the Terabian water traders upon several conditions."

The Ranger looked stunned. Master Carlangas looked relieved, triumphant, and then cautious.

Before they could speak, Terosh continued, "The conditions are as follows. The Terabian Water Trading Union is fully responsible for supplying both Osem and Terab with adequate water for the indeterminable time until the Rangers can raise their own supply. The Rangers are obligated to work to master such lessons in a timely manner, as both cities will be operating on half rations until then."

Master Carlangas raised a hand, indicating a wish to speak.

"Forgive me, Highness, but I fail to see the necessity of half rations. Even at the height of this dispute, both cities operated at close to unrestricted water status."

"The half rations are to spare your people from exhaustion, Master Carlangas," Terosh said, trying not to sound patronizing. "With the Rangers devoting several dozen members to the studies I have in mind, they will have no time to retrieve water. In essence, the Water Trading Union is using labor to purchase the Kaypree Springs from the Osem Rangers."

"What if they never master the lessons?" asked Master Carlangas, his voice dangerously close to a whine. "We will be slaves for this indeterminable time!"

Ranger Caius looked insulted.

"I assure you we are quick learners, Water Master. We do not accept charity lightly either. The Rangers will put every effort into returning both our cities to normal. You have my word on that."

"Good. Before you leave, compile a list of contacts for Covin." Terosh rose signaling an end to the matter. It had gone much better than anticipated, though as predicted, neither representative looked entirely pleased.

***

Ferrim (December) 9, 1538
Same Day
Maladek's Private Retreat, City of Idonia
This is bad.

"Why would he take such a risk?" Kezem wondered, working hard to keep his voice steady.

"I do not know, Lord Maledek. I only know this will foster peace between Osem and Terab," said Aster Captain Surd Antar, speaking swiftly and softly.

"What exactly *is* he doing?" Kezem wondered.

"I know nothing more, Lord Maledek," said Captain Antar. "The king promised to teach the Rangers how to form water. He mentioned the queen would help, but I do not think he's raised the matter with her yet."

"Keep watching and update me regularly," Kezem instructed, cutting the link before Antar could utter farewells.

Needing to kill something, Kezem drew a kerlak pistol from his desk, growled, and shot a target dummy seven times. It helped a little. He couldn't believe how quickly things could change. A week ago, he had two perfect Ranger prisoners and a tidy feud between two powerful cities. Now, he had two broken, useless prisoners his mother insisted he keep alive, and Terosh had somehow gotten both cities to back down. Grunting, he shot the dummy in the nose one more time for good measure.

Unbidden, his mind fixed upon the memory of the chaos in the Rangers' cell. The man had been in some sort of trance then racked with seizures. Kezem's men could do nothing but hold the man down and wait. When the strange fit passed, it truly had been over. The man had looked positively triumphant. Lucas Telon had guessed at what transpired, and the man admitted to severing his link to the anotechs. Kezem had ordered proper retribution, but it could not change the fact that the Ranger had ruined his mother's plan. While he might once have been happy about that, this scheme would have greatly aided his cause.

A pleasant chime signaled an incoming call that interrupted his woeful recollections. Stifling a groan, Kezem smacked the accept button and waited for his mother to speak, staying well out of vidrecorder range and leaving the screen blank. He did not need to deal with her condescending looks today.

"I have need of the Ranger prisoners," Lady Mavis said coolly. Her tone conveyed sympathy for his feelings but enough warning to tell him not to argue.

"Why?" Kezem demanded, grimacing at how childish he sounded.

"I am returning them to the queen to foster goodwill," said his mother.

"You're buying trust?" Kezem asked incredulously, not sure if he wanted to laugh or shoot something. He flicked the kerlak pistol's safety on and off several times.

"I am," his mother confirmed.

"How will you do it?" Kezem demanded, lacking the good cheer for a verbal duel.

"Dennel will send you the details," said Lady Mavis. "This is why we keep our resources separate. I wanted to keep you informed since you complain I don't tell you enough."

Kezem bristled at her last statement. He certainly never complained to her, which confirmed that her spies were literally everywhere.

"How did King Padric take the news?" he asked, redirecting the conversation.

"Not well, of course, but I shipped him some intriguing commoners to pacify him."

That news surprised Kezem. His mother usually shied away from involving commoners.

"He hopes I'll send him the queen one day," Lady Mavis continued. "I need to keep that hope alive for the time being."

"Will you send him the queen someday?" Kezem asked innocently. It seemed his mother changed her mind every other day with regards to keeping Terosh and Reia alive. He wondered which side she leaned toward today.

"If necessary," said his mother.

Kezem shook his head and cursed under his breath. He knew she lied, but he had entertained hopes of recording something he could turn against her one day, even if it meant dealing with King Padric Creston.

Chapter 28:
Aunt Mavis's Gift

Ferrim (December) 18, 1538
Prison Level, RT Alliance Safe House, City of Huz Mon

Life went on without the anotechs. It felt strangely quiet, but slowly, Kiata Wellum had adjusted to normal senses. Retraining her thoughts took longer, for she had not realized how much she anticipated receiving anotech answers to the simplest questions. She pitied Todd and wished she could ease his suffering. His stronger connection to the microscopic machines made the loss of them many times more painful. In addition, their captors' wrath fell twice as heavily upon him.

"I wish there was some information we could betray," Kiata whispered.

She cradled her husband's head in her lap, gently brushing at his fiery hair and tracing his face with her fingertips. She kept her touch light and slow so the stuncuffs engulfing her forearms would not consider it a threat and shock her. While annoying, she found the stuncuffs an improvement over the gloves and foot covers that had inflicted pain at their captors' whims.

Todd's cracked lips spread in a faint smile.

"You would never do it. Too stubborn."

The weariness in his hoarse voice slipped tendrils around Kiata's heart and pulled tight. She blinked back frustrated tears. A noise consisting of one part choking sob and two parts bitter laughter escaped her constricted throat.

"Yes, but perhaps you would show enough sense to give them what they want and save us."

He rocked his head back and forth once as a substitute for shaking his head.

"Want nothing. Just angry." Todd breathed the explanation so softly Kiata's ears strained to catch the words.

"Even if we still had the anotechs, what could they gain by studying us?" Kiata wondered, not really asking Todd. Feeling his lips part to offer an answer, she shifted three fingers across them. "Hush, that was rhetorical. Rest."

His lips spread in a grin beneath her fingers then pushed up in a gentle kiss.

Kiata pulled her fingers away and chuckled.

"You get romantic at odd times, my love."

"Prisoners can't be picky," Todd mumbled.

"In that case, I'm glad it's me you're stuck with," Kiata said, flicking some stray hairs off his forehead. She meant it in a light-hearted manner, but felt tears forming anyway. She wanted to throw her arms around this man and hold him forever. "I love you, Todd Wellum." Her fingers found the stubble along his cheeks and chin. "Scruffy beard and all."

Todd peered up at her with first one warm hazel eye then with both.

"Love you, too. No beard. Good thing."

Kiata's laughter held genuine warmth this time.

"I would look terrible with a beard."

"Neviasuakayleen," Todd said solemnly.

Never. You're beautiful forever.

The words wrapped themselves around Kiata's spirit and cradled it gently, sinking in and lending a new kind of strength. Kiata's cheeks flushed and her eyes stung.

"Stop that or I'll cry all over you," she said.

"Please do," he whispered with a long look.

Direct communication through anotechs had never worked consistently well for Kiata and Todd, but she needed nothing to translate his look. It meant: *I want to know every part of who you are. I vowed to love you. Let me prove it.*

Before Kiata could respond, the sound of the locks cycling open made her flinch. She drew her hand away from Todd's face in case the temperamental stuncuffs decided the sudden movement warranted a shock.

Four people rushed in wearing black from head to toe. Two paused at the door, kerlak pistols ready to challenge anyone daring to follow them. The other two converged on the trussed-up Rangers.

Kiata immediately started calculating which looked easiest to take out. Her eyes darted between the two but fixed on the one aiming a pistol at her forehead. Her pulse quickened. She had been in many bad situations before, but this one ranked high in hopelessness. Usually, she had a weapon or at least the energy to think straight. Two and a half weeks of mistreatment and inactivity severely taxed her energy reserves. She felt Todd trying sit up, but out of the corner of her eye, she saw a figure pressed a palm firmly into Todd's chest.

"Just listen. I'm here to deliver you to the palace," spoke a woman's voice from beneath the black mask.

"They're releasing us?" Kiata asked, uncertain whether to be overjoyed or worried sick. The scene didn't exactly have the markings of a rescue, especially the eye-level pistol.

"Not exactly," the woman said dryly. "But my people will handle any resistance."

"Who hired you?" Todd croaked, sounding short on breath.

"Questions must wait," said the leader. "For now, we must render you unconscious and move you to a hov sled. Please don't struggle."

The words "render you unconscious" did not sit well with Kiata. She stiffened, ready to spring.

"You can accept the sedative or take a stun beam," snapped the woman. "Your choice, but the sedative shouldn't hit your head as hard as the beam will. I highly recommend it."

Kiata willed her shoulders to relax and leaned back to prove her reluctant compliance. She watched the woman's companion unfold a second pair of arms and pull out a small black object. Instinctively, she shut her eyes and leaned back against the wall as the Elish figure stepped forward.

With two hands gripping Kiata's head just below her ears, the Elish used a third hand to place the device close to her neck and activated it while a fourth hand kept the pistol trained on her.

She was unconscious before the object's pleasant beeping sound faded.

***

Ferrim (December) 18, 1538
Same Day
Royal Gardens, City of Rammon

Despite Lady Mavis's assurance that everything would be fine, Nera Tarpon really hated this part of the plan. She knew at least four different plans that would accomplish her goals without this ridiculous risk.

It's like she wants me to be discovered.

She dismissed the thought. Why would Lady Mavis wish her unmasked after spending so much time and effort on training?

"Halt!" shouted a young Royal Guard. "Who trespasses on the king's land?"

Nera's soul tried to leave her body through the top of her skull and got stuck in her throat, making her teeth tingle. It took tremendous effort not to clasp a hand over her heart.

"Speak quickly!" yapped the young guard, striding into view with another man close on his heels.

"Dillain," drawled the man behind the young guard. "It is usually best to quietly confront intruders so as to not wake the entire Market District." He placed a calming hand on the younger man's shoulder and gave a gentle squeeze. The gesture said: *let me handle this.* Stepping around Dillain, the other guard bowed to Nera, and said, "Welcome, Lady Nera, I have informed the queen of your arrival. She will meet you by the Fountain of Nouvirn shortly. This way please."

I'm expected?

The shock overrode the disturbing news that the man knew her name. Knowing she had little choice in the matter, Nera followed the two guards through a maze of paths meandering through the palace gardens. Evenly spaced sticks topped with something soft and gooey looking lined the path and attracted hordes of flitnits and shiners to light the way. If a display required brighter light, glowcrystals were artfully arranged in intricate patterns that made them appear alive.

Nera longed to rip off her mask and gaze around in wonder. They passed dozens of plants, trees, and creatures she had never dreamed of seeing in person. Fireblooms from the Ash Plains surrounded cormeth trees from the Talmeth Mountains. The path turned and dayde flowers from the Felmon Forest lit the way, their glowing heads slowly turning to face her as if they felt her presence. A colana bird whistled a warning then darted into a hole in a cormeth tree.

The path turned again and sloped gently down to Nera's destination. She paused and took a moment to admire the sight. Light from the three moons—Marishaz, Corid, and Gemuln—streamed down and blessed the Fountain of Nouvirn. Though only half-full, the moons shone down from different angles, throwing light about in such a way that the colorful Nedis crystals winked back. The combined effect created the impression that the entire fountain shimmered with inner magic.

"This was my favorite fountain," said a female voice to Nera's right.

Nera gasped and jumped. Her hands flew to her waist where a kerlinblade would have rested had she brought one.

The Royal Guards whirled and leveled kerlak pistols at the woman stepping up next to Nera. The lady drew back her hood, and the guards immediately put their weapons away.

"My apologies, Lady Mavis," said the older man. He bowed deeply. "We were only informed that the queen would come here tonight."

"There is nothing to apologize for, Lieutenant Brycen," Lady Mavis said graciously. "I had not intended to come in person, but these matters are much too important to be delegated."

Nera felt the statement like a well-placed shot to her pride. She shrugged off the feeling in favor of paying attention to the conversation. She longed to demand a reason for Lady Mavis's presence.

"Shall we attend you, my Lady?" asked Lieutenant Brycen.

"Thank you, but that will not be necessary," Lady Mavis said, sweeping past the two guards and approaching the fountain. She dipped one hand and skimmed it along the water's surface before turning back to Nera and the two guards. With a gentle smile, Mavis said, "You may return to your patrol. The queen should be along in a moment. We will be fine until then."

"As you wish," chorused the guards. They clapped right fists to left shoulders and tucked their chins as a salute.

Then, much to Nera's relief, they left.

Irritation and curiosity buzzed within her. Nera slowly approached the fountain. Her heartbeats slowed, and she noticed more about the famed Fountain of Nouvirn.

A statue rose out of the center featuring two men with fierce expressions brandishing swords at one another. Each man grasped one side of a golden chalice, lifting it high above the stone pedestal it had once rested upon. Water flowed out of the chalice and arced over the two combatants, providing an underlying, urgent splashing noise. More water trickled down the sides of the stone pedestal and spewed out of spouts around the fountain's gently curving sides. Each smaller stream added a different nuance to the rush of water. Nera could easily imagine how this fountain became Lady Mavis's favorite.

"I spent most of my childhood beside this fountain," Lady Mavis said. She sat primly on the wide edge and let one of the side spouts spit water up into her palm.

Nera watched Lady Mavis thoughtfully study the water. An odd feeling sputtered to life in her chest. She had never seen Lady Mavis appear so open and vulnerable, and she couldn't decide why she found this image of her patroness frightening.

Sensing her attention, Lady Mavis peered at Nera and offered a small, knowing smile.

"So, at last you see the princess who was, and you don't know what to make of her."

Nera's voice failed.

Lady Mavis's smile brightened, and she laughed.

"I did not always exile myself beneath a mountain, my dear." Her smile dimmed. "I was once young and carefree." The smile completely melted away. "And now I have returned, somewhat heavier of heart." She looked down at her right hand which was still wet and slowly curled the fingers in, forming a loose fist. After a moment, she dropped the fist into her lap and cleared her throat. "But enough of these pointless reflections. Take off your mask."

Nera hesitated for half a second then ripped the mask off and breathed deeply. The cool night air filled her, pleasantly chilling her lungs. Sweet and sharp flower scents converged on her. The choirs of night insects sounded louder. She nearly wept with relief at regaining such freedom.

"The queen must know you and trust you. This will go a long way in earning her favor." Lady Mavis's voice contained no trace of uncertainty or vulnerability now. "Ah, here she comes. Rely on your training, my dear. Keep to the script I gave you. This is the true test."

***

The beauty surrounding her meant nothing to Reia as she ran full tilt down path after path. Her bare feet slapped against the cool stones, nimbly navigating each turn. The sound of her breath rasped in her ears, but not from the run. The message had said to meet at the Fountain of Nouvirn for news of Kiata and Todd.

Thudding footsteps behind her warned of Terosh's pursuit.

"Wait! Reia, this could be a trap!"

"In our own gardens?" She tossed the question over her shoulder as she plunged on.

"Anywhere!" Terosh shouted in exasperation.

"Let us check the area first, Majesty," called Aster Captain Surd

Antar.

"You will find no trap tonight, Captain," said Lady Mavis.

Sheer surprise succeeded where shouting had failed. Reia came to a jarring stop as the path entered the clearing surrounding the fountain. Terosh bumped into her and they stumbled forward a few steps, his arms firmly around her waist.

"Aunt Mavis? This is quite a surprise," said Terosh.

"A pleasant one I hope," replied Mavis.

"Where are they?" Reia demanded, desperation making her voice waver. Suddenly grateful to have Terosh close, Reia folded her arms across his.

Mavis rose gracefully from her seat on the fountain's ledge.

"They are safe, Your Majesty. My agents found them in a compound beneath a Restler-Tarpon Alliance warehouse."

"Antar, draw up some warrants," Terosh ordered. "I want every high-ranking Tarpon and Restler brought in for questioning."

Lady Mavis held up a hand to catch their attention.

"Wait, there's more, but I will let my agent explain." She nodded to her left and waved a figure forward.

Reia's attention riveted upon the young woman dressed completely in black. She could not see much of her features until the woman cautiously stepped into the pool of warm light cast by the portable lightbars carried by Antar's men.

Blinking rapidly, the woman knelt on one knee and endured the collective stare for several long seconds.

"I am Nera Tarpon, daughter of Arista and Tobias Restler and wife of Brook Tarpon." At a wave from Terosh, Nera rose and clasped her hands in front of her body. "The men who attacked the Rangers were traitors to the Alliance, villains who wore the uniform without the honor behind it."

"You're connected to the Alliance?" Terosh asked. His arms tightened around Reia as his body went rigid.

The question confused Reia until Lady Mavis answered.

"My agents come from many backgrounds. Any connection to the Alliance is coincidence. I typically deal in information, but this mission required a more direct approach. So, I activated my best."

"We tried to take the traitors alive, but they fought to the end," Nera said slowly. Her hands unclasped and fell to her sides. "Our priority as per Lady Mavis's instructions was, of course, the safe recovery of the Rangers." She looked directly at Reia. "To that end, we succeeded. They are convalescing in their home tonight. My people can watch over them the rest of this night, or if you wish, I will have them stand down in favor of Royal Guards."

Reia felt her knees weaken with relief, but she willed them to continue holding her upright.

"Thank you, Lady Tarpon, Lady Altran. I am greatly in your debt," said Reia.

Terosh issued a series of orders that sent Royal Guards scurrying.

Mavis and Nera bowed and took their leave.

Reia let Terosh lead her over to the fountain and settle her on its edge. The next thing she felt was Terosh's hands warm upon hers.

After a few moments, his concerned voice finally pierced the fog in her mind.

"Reia, they're all right. I called for a hov to be prepped. You'll be with them soon."

Chapter 29:
Keldor Conclusion

Ferrim (December) 19, 1538
Fountain of Nouvirn, Royal Gardens, City of Rammon

"Sit down, Taly," said Queen Reia Minstel. She sat on the fountain's wide shelf and patted the space to her left.

Talyon Keldor mutely obeyed. His stiff legs carried him forward with the grace of a wooden soldier with gummed up joints. Her weary tone and sympathetic expression ripped his heart out and crushed it. Hands clamped tight to the shelf he sat upon, Taly braced for her next words.

"Common sense speaks against this conversation," the queen began, speaking swiftly yet softly. She paused to take a deep breath. "But Kiata insisted I say something to prevent you from getting yourself killed. I believe her concern is warranted, so here I am. However, I will only continue this conversation on one condition. You must not attend the sentencing hearing tomorrow."

Despite bracing, the pain brought about by the condition left Taly short of air. Fountain mist chilled him. He trembled under the strain of reining in his emotions.

"Why?" he managed to croak at last.

"Do you agree to this condition?" inquired the queen. "If not, then you may go your way. If so, as soon as we finish here Royal Guards will escort you to your grandfather's cell. You may stay with him as long as you like, even until the hearing tomorrow if you wish."

The chance at a protracted farewell seemed a better choice than seeing his grandfather at the hearing, but Taly wasn't sure how much time passed before he finally spoke.

"I agree."

"I trust you understand the enormity of what I am about to say, but promise you will never speak of it," Queen Reia pleaded. "I have ways to ensure your compliance, but I would rather have your word."

"You have my word," Taly responded automatically, unsure whether he meant it.

"You know the sentence that will be handed down," said the queen.

"What you do not know is that the king and I will not abide it."

Taly's head snapped right with painful force.

"What do you mean?"

Queen Reia gravely met his gaze.

"Your grandfather will be sentenced to death according to Gardanian custom to be carried out on that planet."

"But you said—"

"We said he would not suffer, and we will honor that word," the queen replied, not waiting for him to finish his protest.

"Gardanian law condones executions by torture," Taly spat.

"And Reshner's laws do not," said the queen, before Taly could work himself into a frantic state. "Nor do moral and natural laws, and those three dictate our actions. For reasons you need not know, we must appease Gardan's king, so your grandfather will be sent there."

"How will he die?" asked Taly with a sinking heart. "Can you call for mercy? There must be something you can do!" Taly leapt to his feet and turned to fully face the queen.

Queen Reia glanced into the shadows behind Taly, held up a hand, and shook her head.

Taly figured a dozen weapons were leveled at him, but he didn't care.

"Sit down before you unbalance one of my guards," Queen Reia ordered. She waited until Taly reluctantly complied before continuing, "I wish I could do more, Taly, but the truth is that justice too must be met. Under duress or not, your grandfather murdered my husband's mother and your former queen." Tears pooled in the queen's sea green eyes, but she held them in. "He is rightly sentenced to die, but no man deserves the end Gardan would give him." She drew a shuddering breath, like the forming words sickened her. "In fulfillment of our promise, we will give him the means to choose his end. I pray you will one day understand."

Wild thoughts thrashed about in Taly's mind. He imagined lashing out and striking the queen then sprinting into the surrounding gardens as fast as his legs would carry him. He wanted to throw his head back and scream himself hoarse.

He did none of these.

Instead, he sank to his knees and surrendered to the sobs clogging his chest. The next thing he felt was the queen's arms gathering him close.

***

Ferrim (December) 20, 1538
Justice Arena, City of Idonia

Silence covered the arena. The faint hum of vidrecorders and lightbars loomed loud.

Every eye fixed upon the judge.

Governor Judge Mitrek Altran stared grimly at the condemned man. Niktrod Keldor returned the gaze with resigned weariness etched into his features. As expected, the evidence had left no shred of doubt that Keldor had poisoned Queen Kila Minstel. Pleas for leniency based on circumstances might have persuaded a jury in some cases but not this one. The discussions took longer than Mitrek wanted, but finally, he could hand down the sentence and have his daughter returned. Knowing the crowd expected a grand speech, Mitrek gathered his notes and courage and stood.

"Master Niktrod Keldor, you stand convicted of the gravest sort of crime. The people of two planets have cried out for your blood. It falls to me to decide which of them has a greater right to it, but first, I will ask you to state your preference. For the record, please say your name then indicate which planet you would rather carry out your execution."

"I, Niktrod Keldor, choose to die on the planet of my birth. If I must die for my actions, then let it be at the hands of my people."

Mitrek nodded slowly in acknowledgement of Keldor's choice. Fervently hoping his mother had spoken with his cousin, Mitrek addressed the king.

"Highness, you have heard the doomed man's wish. As the one most wronged and as Reshner's voice, I ask what say you in response to his request?"

"I object!" shouted Ambassador Valad Neldro of Gardan. "King Padric lost a daughter. You have no right to claim that King Terosh's loss is any greater than that suffered by my king."

Anticipating the outburst did nothing to stop anger from burning hot within Mitrek.

"We are not here to debate degrees of loss, Ambassador Neldro. I will appeal for your opinion in a moment, but until that time, I shall ignore your objection." Returning his attention to Terosh, Mitrek asked, "What will you do, Your Grace?"

King Terosh stood, looking paler than usual.

"Were I free of responsibility, I would grant his wish, but the good of my people must come first. King Padric Creston of Gardan has claimed my mother's killer since before we knew his name, face, or story. Therefore, Reshner forfeits her right to the life of Queen Kila's murderer."

The announcement released cries of outrage and rumblings of agreement. Mitrek had to call for order four times before it could be restored.

After waiting out the expected outburst, Terosh continued, "Some will cry foul for sacrificing one life on the altar of peace, but perhaps a few will understand that I do not make this decision lightly."

Mitrek's stomach clenched and twisted with distaste as he spoke the next line expected of him.

"Are you aware of the execution protocols employed on Gardan?" he asked.

"I am aware of them, yes." Terosh shivered like a cold wind swept through the room.

"Are you also aware that by submitting to Gardan on this issue, you may set a dangerous precedent?" asked Mitrek, battling to keep the strain from his voice.

"I am," the king intoned again.

"Furthermore, do you acknowledge that your actions seen in light of your foreknowledge come perilously close to violating our laws against cruel deaths?" Even as he asked the question, Mitrek prayed Terosh had prepared a very good answer.

"Governor Judge, I am perilously close to violating the moral law of my own conscience, but I will not allow anything to jeopardize the safety of this people," declared the king.

"How do the two have anything to do with one another?" Mitrek asked. The question flew out before he could think about it.

"You don't need to know," King Terosh insisted. "Nobody here needs to know the mechanisms behind the measures keeping them safe. Such knowledge would be a burden to them. It is part of the price I must pay for the privilege of my birth."

"Thank you, Highness. Your words have been recorded and will be afforded due consideration." Heaving a mental sigh of relief, Mitrek addressed a stunned Ambassador Neldro. "You have heard my king forfeit his right to the prisoner's blood in favor of King Padric Creston's claim. How do you respond?"

Drawing himself up to his full height, the blustery little man sucked in a giant breath before launching into his speech.

"Gardan gladly accepts the responsibility for carrying out the execution. We do not fear to give criminals exactly what they deserve. My king shall be most pleased. May the relationship between our two great planets continue many thousands of generations."

Eager to be done with the matter, Mitrek looked to Keldor.

"It was never really a question of guilt, but more a question of what to do because of that guilt. You have heard the exchange that took place here in your presence. I will now make it official. Niktrod Keldor, you are hereby sentenced to death by execution through methods deemed appropriate by King Padric Creston of Gardan. Your execution will proceed with all due haste as soon as you arrive on that planet. May Riden have mercy upon your soul, for the king shall surely have none."

***

Ferrim (December) 21, 1538
House Minstel Private Hangar, Spaceport, City of Rammon
"May I have a private word with him?" Terosh asked.

Ambassador Valad Neldro wore a harried expression.

"As you wish, Highness," said the ambassador. "I will discuss final details with the pilot." He motioned for the two Shadow Guards flanking the prisoner to follow him.

Once they were relatively alone, Terosh activated his personal sound damper and stepped close to Niktrod Keldor.

"I did not forget my promise, Keldor," he said, ducking his head in case some vidrecorders escaped his initial sweep.

"Nor did I think you would, Your Grace," replied the prisoner, likewise addressing the ground between them. "But while I have your ear, I will make one last request. Watch over my grandson. Talyon is a good but troubled lad. Politics mean so little to him. For my part, I understand the mercy you offer. It is a cold mercy but better than none."

Carefully keeping his hands at his sides, Terosh sent some anotechs to Niktrod Keldor.

"The queen's sister has already taken an interest in Taly's well-being. We will as well. As long as he will stand for it, he will be welcomed at the palace. Taly already knows this. As for you, I can ask no more but that you wait until you reach Gardan."

"Have you more to say?" inquired Keldor, after waiting several long seconds through silence.

Their eyes met.

Terosh's mouth felt like it had never touched a sweet drop of water. His lips moved slowly as he forced them to shape words.

"I have spent too much time hating you, Keldor. It has made me miserable. My mother is still gone. Riden knows I wish things were different between us. This justice feels hollow."

"You'll get no argument from me," said Keldor. "I have made peace with my choices. Horrible as it sounds—and Riden as my witness—I stand by my decisions. Hate me as you will, but I face my death knowing I did what I could for my family. When your end comes, may you be able to say the same."

Feeling cold disquiet creep over his heart, Terosh nodded solemn farewell to his mother's killer.

***

Ferrim (December) 27, 1538
The Lady's Estate, Kala Mountains

Lady Mavis Altran shook her head and groaned. Several blissful months had slipped by with only scant communication with King Padric Creston. The timing concerned her. Niktrod Keldor probably just arrived on Gardan. The trial and sentencing had taken place much as expected, yet Mavis found her thoughts disturbed by the nagging notion that Terosh would somehow ruin her plan. With a sinking feeling, Mavis activated the interplanetary communications unit.

"He's dead!" roared King Padric, glaring into the vidrecorders. He flushed crimson from the tips of his white hair down through where his neck disappeared into his shirt collar. "I will not stand for this treachery!"

"Was not killing Keldor the point?" asked Mavis. She wrapped her arms close around her body partly to aid the image of disdain and partly to hide her shaking hands.

Terosh has done something, but what?

"He was to die on my terms!" cried the enraged king. He leaned forward and lowered his voice to a hoarse, menacing whisper. "What have you done?"

"Everything I said I would," Mavis said evenly. "I arranged for Keldor to be sent to you. Anything that transpired once he reached Gardan is not my responsibility." She narrowed her eyes, deciding to go on the offensive. "And speaking of treachery, reports have arisen of citizens disappearing again. Have you an answer for such reports?"

"Your deliveries have been sparse, my scientists grow impatient," grumbled King Padric. "I sent agents to your planet and some of them got ambitious. I am still restraining most of them, but I also figured you could use the motivation."

"My word is motivation enough," Mavis said slowly. "In time, I will send all the subjects you need, including the queen herself if necessary, but do not question my timing."

A battle of will ensued as each stared deep into the other's eyes. Finally, Mavis flicked her eyes down in well-calculated submission.

"You have my condolences on the justice denied you this day. Let us have no more of these petty disagreements. Keep your agents in line, and I shall move my plans forward. To prove my utmost commitment to our cause, I will allow you to study my son while you attend that part of our bargain."

"I could do with him as I liked," Padric said darkly. "What makes you think I would not?"

"You are very powerful. Such power does not come through foolishness," Mavis explained. "You know that I am the best means to the ends you seek and that I did not gain my position through letting myself be manipulated by emotions."

"What makes you believe I would even wish to study him?" Padric persisted peevishly.

Mavis let a faint grin touch her lips.

"You are obsessed with this planet, desperate to discover our secrets. You would study a wallay so long as it came from here. Shall I send you one with my compliments?"

King Padric considered that with a stony stare then grunted. With visible effort, he shook off the dark mood gripping him.

"Were we operating on the same planet, one or the other would be dead. You would make a formidable enemy, Lady Mavis. Tell me, in your opinion, is that insolent boy, my grandson, responsible for robbing me of my prize?"

Most definitely, yes.

Mavis did not respond immediately. Her mind raced ahead to what he might say to the various responses she could give.

Why do you wish to know?

"I think it very likely Terosh would interfere any way he could, but I could not tell you how," said Mavis. "I know he had a private conversation with Keldor before the ship left, but he did not even touch the man."

Padric pressed his fingertips together and leaned forward, a gleam in his eyes.

"What would you say if I told you I wanted my grandson removed from the throne?"

Get in line.

"I would first inquire as to your reasons," Mavis said, again speaking slowly to give her mind a chance to cope with the twist. She peered curiously at the vidrecorder, letting her confusion show. "I must admit you baffle me, King Padric. You spent a great deal time, effort, and resources to extradite your daughter's killer and now you request my response to harming her son. What am I missing?"

"Who would inherit the throne?" demanded Padric, ignoring her question.

"Queen Reia, of course," Mavis said.

Padric waved his hand dismissively.

"Yes, yes, suppose she is gone as well."

Taytron's daughter, Mavis answered silently.

Kezem thought himself quite clever keeping the girl alive, but he had yet to master the art of keeping his people loyal.

"If they had a child before such misfortune befell them, the child would inherit the throne, but a regent would rule until his or her sixteenth birthday. If no such child existed, the Senate would conduct a search for the nearest living relative. My father's line would be spent but he had a brother."

"What about you, my lady. Do you not still possess Minstel blood?" asked Padric with affected gentility.

Mavis gave him a tight smile.

"You know my history well enough to understand the impossibility of ever claiming the throne for myself, so I wonder where your questions are going. I have much to do, King Padric, as I am certain you do as well. Please ask what you wish to know."

"Your history does not taint your progeny. One of your sons stands to inherit Reshner's throne should some accident befall my grandson and his wife before they bear a child. Why have you not moved against them?"

His tone brought Mavis the image of a little boy cocking his head in innocent curiosity.

I am not rid of you yet.

"So far, my nephew has proven himself a capable if somewhat idealistic ruler and my sons have their own lives to lead. I see no immediate reason to change the situation."

Afraid she might say too much, Mavis closed the conversation as quickly as possible.

Chapter 30:
Safe Service Act

Ferrim (December) 29, 1538
Queen Lissa's Ballroom, Royal Palace, City of Rammon

Terosh Minstel cast a furtive glance at his wife. She sat beside him watching the Terabian Dance Troupe throw their bodies about in rhythmic waves. The lively, percussion-heavy beat reverberated in his chest, but nothing could shake the disquiet shrouding his heart.

Over a week and a half had passed since Kiata and Todd Wellum's miraculous rescue by Aunt Mavis's agents. The drama surrounding the end of Keldor's trial had occupied Terosh much of the week, but now that he could think, he admitted that something about the rescue bothered him. Despite this, he worked hard to hide his misgivings from Reia. Right now, Lady Mavis Altran could do no wrong in the queen's eyes, but Terosh knew his aunt never did anything without a convincing reason.

Just how compelling are her reasons?

Terosh worried how much this rescue would cost them in the end. It also disturbed him that neither the anotechs nor his own agents could say much about the whole Ranger capture-and-release saga. The former told him they knew not where or how to conduct such a search for truth and the latter returned with only baffling pieces of conflicting accounts.

What if Aunt Mavis set them up in the first place? Her resources are adequate to the task.

Terosh braced against the thoughts and shook with denial. Aunt Mavis could be both sneaky and self-serving, but part of her soul still carried the Minstel name. She loved the people with a fierce passion unique to those born royal.

Love for the people does not equate to love for you. She still resents the family for casting her out. Could it be that simple?

Terosh's grandfather, King Salen, had cast Aunt Mavis out, officially disowning her in every legal and emotional sense. Terosh's father, King Teorn, had cautiously welcomed her back emotionally, but the legal distance remained. Terosh could, in theory, rescind some of the legal ramifications.

It would be dangerous, whispered the anotechs.

How so?

She has many secrets.

As the music ended, Reia's hand landed on Terosh's forearm and squeezed gently. She leaned close.

"Something bothers you. Shall I press you for it now or later?" Her expression stayed true to the aloofness Sedir had drilled into her for formal entertainment occasions, but her cool green eyes promised unwavering support and love.

"Later," Terosh murmured. His voice sounded painfully loud in the relative silence caused by the cessation of drumbeats.

"I shall hold you to that," Reia whispered, releasing his arm.

Terosh silently hoped she enjoyed the next song.

Master Wesley Roth loudly thanked the performers and announced the next phase of entertainment.

"Royal Highnesses, honored guests, it is my pleasure to present Lady Gianna LeCross. Tune your ears and prepare to be swept along by musical talent the likes of which have not graced the palace in many years."

The ballroom doors opened to reveal a young woman with flowing black hair. Head held high and soulful, dark eyes full, she glided in with grace enough to make any princess jealous. She stopped short of the dais and curtsied. The crowd fell silent as she smiled and drew a deep breath. She held it a long moment, letting the air fill with anticipation. When she finally sang, it was the crowd's turn to let breath linger long. Her voice needed no musical accompaniment, but soft, heartfelt, stringed notes played in the background anyway. Terosh and every soul present listened as Lady Gianna sang:

> "Love shall find whom it will.
> Dear father mine, need I remind?
> You taught me what a man should be.
> Strong, brave, kind, and truly free
> To love, honor, serve, and save.
> What matters his lowborn birth?
>
> Love shall find whom it will.
> Flee not, my love. Stand with me.
> I hear their words and care not.
> They hold no power over me.
> Should they call for my crown
> I would pay that price for you.
>
> Love shall find whom it will.
> Let learned men say otherwise.
> From the way my heart cries
> I know this love will pass
> Test of time, trial of birth,
> All reasons declaring it foolishness.

Love shall find whom it will.
I should know. It found me
When I wanted nothing more
Than to flee this strange new pain.
For the world I stand to gain
I choose you and our love."

Midway through the song, Terosh's eyes slid away from the singer to his wife.

I would pay any price for you.

His fingers found hers and intertwined.

***

Though she could not hear Terosh's thoughts, Reia felt their meaning when he picked up her right hand and folded his fingers through hers. Lady Gianna's song filled the room at first pleading, then reflective, and finally declarative. The story belonged as much to Reia and Terosh as to Princess Sora Ann and her Royal Guard lover, Quinard. Knowing Terosh had chosen the song for her touched Reia deeply.

I guess I'm lousy at hiding my insecurities.

She sent her husband a small rush of anotechs to deliver her approval.

Terosh responded with the mental equivalent of a relieved sigh.

Turning her attention back to Lady Gianna LeCross, Reia was struck by the woman's youth and something else, something indefinable in her eyes. Curious, Reia reached over with her left hand and patted Terosh's arm affectionately before extricating her right hand. Then, she tilted her head down and pretended to examine a nonexistent spot on her purple shimmersilk gown. While doing so, Reia sent a stream of anotechs to the young singer.

When the first anotechs returned, a few hundred impressions bombarded Reia's senses. She felt the weight of deep concentration and heard the traces of passionate anger under the songs. Dozens of words beat at her as different anotechs tried to describe the singer: desperate, hurt, weary, and scared seemed to dominate. Out of the confusion flew a new name: Carla Segore.

Reia's eyes flew open and she flinched. She swiftly wiped her expression of all traces of surprise, but she noticed a few curious glances from the crowd.

Check again, she ordered, sending them back to the girl.

No mistake.

There must be some mistake! What do I do?

The easiest answer would be nothing, but Reia knew that was no answer. The girl radiated terror. Reia happened to possess the attuned senses necessary to pick up on it. Ignoring Carla now would be a crime only slightly less repulsive than whatever first put the fear in her.

Save her.

That's easy for you to say. You're not the ones the senators and governors are going to verbally slaughter.

Reia's mind skipped ahead to other possibilities. The harder answer would be confrontation, but the situation demanded tact. If done improperly, she might heap greater harm upon the girl rather than help her.

Then save her here.

The anotechs spoke so confidently that Reia could not help but feel her courage rally. She did not bother asking them how. She had worked with them long enough to know they rarely answered "how" questions. Reia contemplated the problem so hard that she barely heard a word of Lady Gianna's last two songs. When the final note faded, she joined the polite applause as the performer curtsied again.

Master Roth stepped forward to announce the next act.

Before he could speak, Reia shocked everybody by standing. The crowd drew a collective breath and fell strangely quiet. With heart thudding in her ears and cheeks burning, Reia mustered a brilliant smile and leveled it at the people.

Praying her voice didn't fail, she said, "I find myself deeply moved by that wonderful performance. Would you count me selfish if I begged for a few moments alone with the young woman?"

Conversations burst out over the ballroom as guests discussed the odd request, attempting to divine the queen's meaning. A few people started to move toward the exit.

"That won't be necessary," Terosh called after them, appearing at Reia's side.

The conversations died as abruptly as they had started as people strained to hear Terosh's next words.

He did not disappoint them.

"Please, stay and enjoy yourselves. The queen and I shall retire to the Central Library. Master Roth, please send in the next performers. Lady Gianna, would you grace us with your company?"

The young woman's eyes darted to a man in the crowd, but she nodded.

"I would be honored, Your Grace," she murmured.

Reia calmly grasped Terosh's elbow and sent him silent thanks for trusting her. They exited the ballroom at a painfully slow pace, but she managed to look unconcerned. What she really wanted to do was tear out of the room at a full sprint. When they reached the hallway, the urge to run intensified, but Reia forced herself to maintain the regal pace all the way to the Central Library.

As the doors swung shut behind them and their bewildered guest, Reia stepped to the sound damper controls and activated the security measures.

Terosh quirked a curious eyebrow at her and waited for Reia to explain.

"What is your name?" Reia asked. She kept her tone as kind as possible, but the girl looked ready to flee right through the doors.

Terosh's eyes shut as he sent anotechs to investigate the strangely terrified young lady.

"We're not here to hurt you," he assured the girl. "We will help you if you wish."

The girl backed into the door looking ready to burst into tears.

"Let me return. You can't help me. He would know."

"We *can* help you, Carla, but you need to trust us," Reia said, wagering that hearing her own name might rattle the girl just right.

Carla drew a shuddering breath. A soft whine escaped, and she sank to the floor and gripped her knees. She clenched her eyes shut but a tear slipped out. One tear turned into two, three, and a flood. Within seconds, her shoulders shook with suppressed sobs.

"How did you know something was wrong?" Terosh asked Reia in a whisper.

"Her eyes," Reia answered. She slowly approached Carla and knelt beside her.

After a brief inner debate, Reia laid her hands on Carla's right shoulder and bid the anotechs to encourage the girl to share her burdens.

Carla needed this chance to cry.

Eventually, the suppressed sobs morphed into unsuppressed sobs then subsided to gentle weeping. Terosh paced the room impatiently, and Reia stayed by the girl.

"How old are you?" Reia asked. The anotechs had already told her, but she wanted to hear the girl's response.

"Fourteen," Carla admitted at last.

Terosh's pacing came to a violent stop.

"Where are your parents? How did you end up with Master Nazhu?" he asked.

"My parents are dead," said the girl.

"Dead how?" Reia wondered.

"My mother died when I was ten. Father borrowed money from a man in Meritel to buy some hovs for his delivery business. Somebody robbed him before he could make the purchase. The man he borrowed from killed him when he could not repay the debt and sold me to recover some of the loss."

"How did you come to sing, Carla?" Terosh asked gently, trying to distract the girl from her pain. He sat on the floor where he was, so he would not tower over her.

"My mother taught me." Carla's gaze turned distant. "She died of Candela Fever. Near the end she said the best legacy she could leave me was the gift of song. She said I could heal any hurt if I found the right song for each type of pain. Master Nazhu discovered my gift when I used it to help another servant."

The conversation stretched several hours. In the end, Reia knew more than she wanted to and less than she needed to about indentured servitude and the slack regulation thereof.

***

Idela (January) 10, 1539
Senate Great Hall, City of Rammon

Terosh struggled not to smile and wondered why he had worried about Reia facing the senators and governors today.

It's natural to worry when your wife enters a korver's den.

Despite obvious animosity from certain parties, the discussion remained remarkably civil. Even Senator Gabriel Luvak and his oafish brother, Governor Damien, had stayed miraculously quiet thus far.

Only Sedir's advice kept Terosh from showing his support more openly. Politically speaking, Reia needed this cause to strengthen her position. Should the unthinkable ever happen to him, she would need a strong base of supporters from both governing bodies. The people needed to understand her as a compassionate, capable queen in her own right, rather than merely an accessory to Terosh's power.

Understanding the reasoning did not make it easier to calmly play moderator. Terosh's control panel blinked and flashed in a riot of colors as governors, senators, and reporters vied for speaking rights. His head ached from thinking so hard about the balance of speakers. Few would be completely satisfied and favoritism complaints would air anyway, but Terosh's sense of honor required he let a wide variety of people have their say.

Idonia's senatorial light blinked blue. Intrigued, Terosh entered his approval code and all lights returned to white except the one belonging to the person to whom he'd granted speaking rights.

His mind wandered to how he would spend the evening. Perhaps he would ask Reia to walk the gardens with him. He couldn't remember the last time they had spent an entire evening together. Meetings had dominated the last couple of weeks, and before that, Reia's attention rested with Todd and Kiata's recovery.

Senator Victoria Turrel's bold voice rang forth.

"Royal Highnesses, fellow Senators, Honored Governors, I think we can agree the queen's ideas are noble, but how shall our great cities continue to function without the indentured workforce? What shall become of those unfortunates who find themselves in great debt? And how shall we integrate these non-citizens back to citizen status? Will these steps not plant seeds of rebellion?"

Murmurs of agreement rose around them. Terosh sat up straighter and silently thanked Senator Turrel. At last, someone had raised the right questions. Many others had come tantalizingly close, but so far, none had worded it just the way Reia wanted.

The faint, thoughtful smile on Reia's face said this might be the turning point where the governors and senators quit posturing and finally declared sides. Terosh waited a few heartbeats in case Senator Turrel had more to say. When the senator ceded the speaking rights by sitting down,

Terosh simply ignored the blinking lights and waited for Reia to respond. As the one to call for this joint session, she had full speaking rights throughout.

"Senator Turrel raises many interesting questions, which I shall address soon," Reia said with an acknowledging nod toward the senator. "Before I get there, however, I think we can agree that the seeds of rebellion already exist. Were we to offer free food, water, shelter, and medicine, people would still complain."

Several heads nodded reluctant agreement.

Reia shifted to address a different section of the crowd.

"Contrary to popular belief, I am an ardent supporter of maintaining tradition. However, I do not approve of indentured servitude as an institution because it is vastly unsupervised and impossible to regulate under the current guidelines. Something dies within a sentient being robbed of freedom. We as rulers of this people are responsible for their well-being in body, spirit, and mind. Indentured servitude seeks only care of body at the cost of spirit and mind. We can change this."

Despite not possessing speaking rights, several spectators raised the obvious question.

"How?"

"It will take time to explain my plan in detail, but I shall summarize," said Reia, turning to yet a new section of people. "What we require is a Safe Service Act, a comprehensive series of laws regulating an alternative to indentured servitude as it stands now. In essence, those seeking aid for a debt will hire their services to the cities. Contracts will dictate what sort of work each is qualified to do and how long a term is necessary to absolve their debts."

"That will never work," scoffed Governor Holum. "You're adding a complicated layer of bureaucracy to the very institution you claim to despise."

"The forms and files will no doubt land on the governor's desk," grumbled Governor Naverick.

Reia gave Holum and Naverick each a sympathetic look and a gentle smile.

"You might have more work for a while, but I am certain adequate help could be found. In any case, it would be work done to directly aid others. What better way to fulfill our vows?" Reia's smile turned a touch ironic. "Besides, if set up properly, the programs will soon be self-sufficient. Funds will be generated two ways. First, businesses and private estates wishing to hire temporary servants can still do so through the cities, and second, anyone wishing to deal directly with a particular person may also do so for a price. Yes, my friends, I realize it comes down to money in the end."

The unexpected admission drew a warm chuckle from the crowd.

Reia's expression became earnest.

"Minus necessary administration costs, the vast majority of kefs generated will be funneled into programs for ensuring the safety of each servant." She paused to stare at each section. "Some people will not like the changes, and if we accidentally put the wrong people in positions of power over these services, we may do more harm than good. Unfettered slavery will probably always exist, but none of these facts ought to dissuade us from trying to save at least some from the tyranny of indentured servitude as it exists today!"

Terosh wanted to cheer along with most of the onlookers, but he settled for a small smile.

She had won.

The discussion would likely continue for days, but a glance around confirmed that Reia would have plenty of support in the detail battles ahead.

***

Idela (January) 11, 1539
The Lady's Estate, Kala Mountains

"How would you suggest handling this situation?" asked Kezem, his tone curious.

Mavis allowed one eyebrow to climb a little higher. Her youngest son must be extremely baffled to seek her opinion. Usually, she had to wring reports from him or pay off his agents. She had devoted much thought to the situation, but thus far, taken no real interest in it. The queen's grand plan to ease people's suffering struck Mavis as highly naïve but ultimately harmless. The thought of having missed something crucial bothered Mavis.

"Opposing our dear queen on this issue will leave you in a morally weak position." Mavis stopped to consider her feelings. "However, this may prove useful. Do you know where everyone stands with regards to the Safe Service Act?"

"So, I should support the queen?" asked Kezem, avoiding her question. "Would that not work against my ultimate designs?"

"Quite the opposite, I believe. Outwardly support the queen. In fact, secretly support measures that inconvenience the governors and senators. I must emphasize the secret part because you must also subtly let those governors and senators know that you sympathize with their causes, whatever they may be."

"It is a slow plan," Kezem complained.

Laughing, Mavis said, "It is not even the main plan, darling, but only fools risk everything on single strategies. Consider that the next time you send an assassin blundering about my mountains."

Kezem shrugged.

"He had too high an opinion of his skills. I had to humble him. Did your people leave him whole?"

"Unfortunately for him they did, but I deemed him too great a threat to keep around," said Mavis.

"What a waste," Kezem murmured.

"Were I in your position, I might show such signs of impatience, but you still need me, Kezem. Suspend this nonsense between us at least until the Gardan campaign ends."

"Speaking of Gardan, I received some new reports of people vanishing. I assume you are aware of such. What are you going to do about it?" Kezem's cobalt eyes flashed with indignation.

Your people should be shot for slowness.

"I have spoken with King Padric, and naturally, he claims the responsibility belongs to a few rogue agents. I told him to control his people, but I do not know how long that will work. Patience is not a strength for him. The Rangers were supposed to appease him, but we both know how that ended," Mavis said with a small frown. "I am taking certain measures to ensure no one important vanishes, but hopefully, this too will work to our advantage. We shall simply have to choose targets for the Shadow Guards."

A new thought struck her, and she smiled broadly.

"What does that look mean?" Kezem demanded.

"Perhaps nothing, perhaps everything," Mavis whispered. She ended the call with Kezem and stared into empty space.

I wonder how closely King Padric keeps watch over his Shadow Guards.

Chapter 31:
Ambassadors

Idela (January) 17, 1539
Restler-Tarpon Safe House, City of Meritel

Kolknir raised a hand to stop his protégé from punching their prisoner.

A rebellious look crossed Lucas Telon's face, but he straightened and reluctantly stepped back.

"We want to turn him," Kolknir reminded the younger man.

The man hanging from the wall glared but said nothing.

Lucas touched the sore spot on his jaw where the prisoner had clouted him during the take down.

"I am sorry for the restraints," said Kolknir. "We have an offer for you and wish to deliver it in peace."

"If the Lady did not find you useful, I would kill you," Lucas added. He folded his arms across his chest and leaned against the far wall.

"My friend would enjoy persuading you to our cause the traditional way, but I would like to try words first," Kolknir explained. "What is your name? Surely you can tell me that."

He knew the name but wanted to see what the man would tell them.

The prisoner studied the floor.

"I can be a very patient man, but I would like to let you down from that uncomfortable position," said Kolknir. "The sooner our conversation progresses, the sooner we can release you."

The man grunted, managing to convey derision and bitter amusement.

"It is in your best interest to cooperate with us," Lucas said, fiddling with a dagger retrieved from an arm sheath. He flipped the dagger several times before slowly slashing it through the air in front of the man.

"You are well-trained and suspicious; I respect you for both. Allow me to lay out the Lady's proposal, and then you may make your decision." Kolknir tapped a command into the control panel and a metal footrest slid under the prisoner's feet. "Be comfortable for a moment so you can concentrate on my words."

The prisoner's contemptuous look carried several curses.

"Relax," Kolknir advised. "You'll hurt yourself hating so hard."

"This is pointless," Lucas muttered, attention still fixed on his dagger.

"As I am sure you can guess, my patroness would like to buy your services as an informant and agent," Kolknir said, pausing in case the man decided to respond.

The man barked a short, humorless laugh.

"Her sources are already good. You would make them better, Nolan," Kolknir said. He said the name lightly like it was a known fact, not a piece of information dearly bought.

Surprise flickered across the prisoner's face, but his training slapped it away almost instantly.

"Join us. Why let your precious sister toil long days in a field in some sun-cursed part of Gardan, when she could join you here and live like royalty?" Kolknir spoke slowly to let the words stoke the fires inside the prisoner.

The man jerked against his restraints and clenched his teeth.

"I have no sister," he lied.

Kolknir's sympathetic look meant little for the man would not meet his eyes.

"There's no use denying it. She may not believe she still has a brother, but you know you still have a sister. Your parents and grandparents are dead. You have chosen no wife. You have sired no children, and you keep few enough friends. Your unmarried sister, Kara Demilak, is really all you have left. Did you know she's pregnant by her master?"

"Do not involve her," said the prisoner.

"Do you hear what I'm telling you, man?" Kolknir snapped. "Not involving your sister is the worst thing I could do. I am offering to help her— to rescue her from the terrible situation in which *you* left her." His voice struck at the man like a banistick.

The man glared at him.

"If you're so well-informed, then you know I did not simply leave her."

Kolknir smiled and nodded. They had reached the turning point.

"Indeed. You were taken from her, sold as a soldier while still just a boy. You owe Gardan nothing, save your training. You owe your king nothing. Your only loyalty ought to be to your elder sister who protected you the best way she knew how. She who sold herself—body and soul—to save you from horrors that would have crushed your innocence to dust."

The Shadow Guard's cautious expression, now devoid of the anger, told Kolknir they had won. The conversation would naturally go around and around, for one does not switch loyalties on a whim. Nolan would take some time to fully convince, but he would accept the Lady's offer and become her spy.

***

Idela (January) 28, 1539
Docking Bay 17, Spaceport, City of Rammon

Reia halted the hov bike about twenty meters from the shabby-looking ship and dismounted, absorbing the entire scene in a glance. The ship rested serenely at the hangar's center, looking prepared to endure a siege. Royal Guards formed a loose perimeter around the ship, kerlak rifles in hand but not quite pointed at the ship. Several mechanics gawked.

A grim-faced Captain Donald Garahad strode toward her.

"You should not be here, Your Majesty. It might not be safe. My men can handle this."

"I was informed the ambassador requested an audience with a royal. The king will be in a Senate hearing for another few hours, so I am here to welcome our guests," Reia explained, affecting calmness she did not quite feel.

"That ship hails from Rorge II," Captain Garahad said, as if that were a condemning fact.

"All the more reason to attempt peaceful overtures, Captain," said Reia. "Have your communications officer inform the pilot of my arrival."

A soft metallic whine sounded, and a ramp descended like a mouth slowly opening in a yawn.

"They are aware, Your Majesty," Garahad said tightly. He turned to face the ship and shifted to a better position to defend Reia from any danger that might come down that ramp.

Having chosen the Healer's path early in her Ranger training, Reia had not been sent on many missions to protect people, but Kiata and Todd had shared many of their experiences. Needless to say, the people being protected did not always welcome the help. Part of her had always wondered why, until now. Too much protection could be a nuisance.

Reia took stock of the situation. A Rorgen stood with all four limbs flush against the deck and had his head lowered in a defensive posture. Dark eyes darted around, measuring the various threats. He presented no sign of weapons but wore pride like a personal shield. His movements were the slow, measured steps of a natural predator exploring a new place. Black fur covered much of his body, and three streaks of silky, golden hair sprouted from his head and ran down his back.

Stopping at the bottom, the Rorgen bowed low then sat down as if unimpressed by the significant number of Royal Guards surrounding his ship.

"You must be the dominant female. I am called Nirrolik Tul. I am sent of my people to request aid. The star that warms our planet will die a violent death." His smooth, strong voice rumbled from deep in his chest.

Dominant female? I've never thought about it quite so literally, but I suppose it fits. Well, at least they don't mince words. That's refreshing.

Reia eased past a very tense Captain Garahad.

"Greetings, Nirrolik Tul. I am Queen Reia. Welcome to Reshner. I hope this may be the restful place you seek for your people, but for now, all I can offer is an introduction to my husband, King Terosh of House Minstel, and our ruling bodies. I will call for a special session to take place tomorrow. In the meantime, Captain Garahad can escort you and any of your people to the palace to await an audience with the king."

"There is only me. Two dozen of my kin went forth to other life spheres. Some are captives. Some are dead. Many returned home with no good news. People fear. Few want to stand against our masters. The masters say my people are not worth saving." The rolling cadence marking the Rorgen's speech softened the terrible meaning of his words.

"Who are your masters?" Reia asked, still trying to wrap her mind around telling any people that they were not worth saving.

"Masters are many. They are of the Galactic Alliance of Populated Planets," answered Nirrolik Tul. "They come many years ago and say our resources are theirs in exchange for care. Resources gone now. Taken to other life spheres. We say to masters take us to other life spheres. Masters say find new minerals, new technologies, new slaves, and maybe we save you."

"I do not wish to give you false hope, Ambassador," said Reia. "My people have long sought to avoid entanglements with GAPP."

"You are dominant female. Make them listen," said Nirrolik Tul.

"As I said, I will call the governing bodies to order and let you present your case, but I do not know if we can help you. Rest now, we can deal with these heavy issues later." Reia could picture how the Senate Great Hall would look on the morrow and tried not to wince.

***

Idela (January) 29, 1539
Senate Great Hall, City of Rammon

Terosh sympathized with Rorge II's plight, but he also knew his first duty must be to his people. The GAPP ambassador had conveniently arrived an hour after Nirrolik Tul. Terosh found the ambassador and her timing unsettling.

Senator Gabriel Luvak held speaking rights for the moment.

"Your Highnesses are suggesting we risk the lives of our citizens to help strangers!" He said the last word in a tone that added: *they're a race of overgrown korvers.*

"We are suggesting you hear the ambassador's request and evaluate it in light of moral and natural laws, Senator Luvak," Terosh said. "We are asking you to decide whether we have an obligation to help the people of Rorge II, and if so, how we can best acquit ourselves in that regard."

The lights for both guests blinked. Terosh swallowed some of the tightness creeping across his throat and pressed the button to transfer speaking rights to the GAPP representative. Sabrina Raquel stood and immediately drew every eye. Terosh noticed most of the males straightening in their seats. With his own pulse quickening, he couldn't really blame them.

The ambassador wore a deep red gown more suited for a ballroom. Her wide eyes shifted shades from a warm, friendly gray to a mysterious, murky green. Her seductive smile said she knew how to wield her natural beauty well. Sabrina Raquel swept her gaze slowly over the crowd.

"Honorable people of Reshner, we are each committed to averting a tragedy. The solution is simple. We are not your enemy. I do not blame Ambassador Tul for painting us in such a light, but I do mourn the miscommunication that has tainted our reputation." Her voice gushed forth with a breathy softness that caressed every ear.

"If you have a solution, Ambassador Raquel, please share it," Terosh said, though he knew full well what her suggestion would entail.

"Join us. Add Reshner's voice to the largest power base in this galaxy. With your strength and resolve, we can address the terrible fate looming over the Rorge system." Sabrina Raquel somehow managed to make it sound absolutely foolish to consider any other option.

"Why don't you address it anyway?" asked Senator Victoria Turrel.

Several others—mostly females—echoed the question.

Sabrina Raquel tipped her head toward Senator Turrel and smiled in a self-deprecating manner.

"With great power comes great responsibility. We are handling delicate situations that span the galaxy. We lack the physical resources and people to address every concern. The Rorge II settlements are sparsely populated compared to places like the Olic Cluster. Our choices may seem heartless, but we must deal with the stark reality of sacrificing a few billion to save hundreds of billions elsewhere."

"Ambassador, I am not certain I follow your reasoning," Reia admitted. "How exactly does Reshner factor in? Whether we join you or not, you still face the same resource deficit."

"That is an excellent question, Your Majesty," Sabrina Raquel crooned. "In this case, I am happy to inform you that we are not immune to politics. What the honorable Nirrolik Tul has said about recruiting holds true. I can divert evacuation ships to Rorge II if I offer your joining our cause as justification."

Murmurs arose, and lights danced across Terosh's control panel. He selected Senator Byron Price to summarize the people's sentiments.

"I believe I speak for my colleagues when I say that you have given us very interesting insight into GAPP politics," said Senator Price. "We will discuss the matter at length before rendering a decision. Unless either of their Royal Highnesses objects, I move to break down into regional discussion groups."

***

Lanolin (February) 8, 1539
Senate Great Hall, City of Rammon

Reia steeled her heart against the words she must speak. The discussions over Rorge II's plight had dragged on for days. The governors had polled the people. Then more discussions took place. Finally, a decision was rendered, and while opinions still varied, most senators and governors believed the decision embodied the will of the people.

Reia did not hear a word of Terosh's introduction, but she felt the crowd shift attention from him to her. Standing, she belatedly hoped her voice still worked.

"Ambassador Nirrolik Tul, it is with deepest regrets that I must inform you that Reshner will decline to join the Galactic Alliance of Populated Planets. However, six cities have offered to accept up to ten thousand refugees and seven more believe they can harbor five thousand each. The Rangers will take an additional thousand people into their care in the Riden Mountains. Finally, House Minstel will accept responsibility for fifty thousand people to be sheltered in new settlements in the Frozen North, the Kevloth Plains, and the Felmon Desert."

Both ambassadors leapt to their feet.

Terosh granted speaking rights to Nirrolik Tul first.

The Rorgen ambassador slid to the room's center with stealthy movements. Once exactly in the center, the Rorgen walked a tight circle and sat directly facing Reia and Terosh.

"There is only me. My kin return home. This place was our last hope. Five years is long time. Life star not explode for five years. Keep talking about Rorge II. Remember us."

"We will commission a subcommittee to annually revisit this issue," Terosh promised. "You will not be forgotten. As the queen has said, we offer refuge to some of your people. We do not have many large ships, but we will put out contracts to hire a few freighters. Working steadily, we should be able to complete the evacuation in time."

Ambassador Sabrina Raquel stabbed an impeccably painted fingertip at the button to request speaking rights. Her pale gray-green eyes looked almost feral. When granted the floor, she put on a frosty smile that immediately bothered Reia.

"Honorable people of Reshner, I humbly urge you to reconsider," said Ambassador Raquel. "While we may lack the resources to implement an effective evacuation of Rorge II's entire population, we will certainly safeguard our remaining interests there."

"Speak plainly, Ambassador," Reia said. "What interests can GAPP be keeping on a planet with a dying star? Do you mean to say you will interfere with an evacuation?"

"Rorge II is still considered a colony, and several teams of scientists maintain research outposts there. Some of them have military contracts." Her smile grew colder still. "Speaking plainly, Your Majesty, Rorge II belongs to us. I fear the commanders stationed there may misinterpret your philanthropic efforts."

Dead silence reigned for several seconds as Ambassador Raquel's words crystallized in everyone's mind. Reia could not have been more stunned if the sleek ambassador had whipped out a kerlinblade and brandished it at her.

Chapter 32:
Lull

Lanolin (February) 9, 1539-Temen (July) 30, 1539
Tour of Reshner: Cities of Rammon, Chara, Kalmata, Ritten, Meritab, Meritel, Calsola, Idonia, and Azhel

After the stresses of the first four months as Reshner's rulers, Reia and Terosh threw themselves into the task of exploring the various cities. In addition to keeping up with Senate and Governors Council meetings, they attended banquets and balls, entertained ambassadors, held court to arbitrate disputes, studied galactic and local politics, and visited with countless people. While touring, Reia often spoke to generate support for her Safe Service Act. She especially enjoyed talking with indentured servants benefiting from the programs.

While in Chara, they visited the surrounding vineyards, fruit farms, and traditional farms. They saw how hovs could be turned into water hovs and spent a few days on various fishing boats. Reia had her first real experience with a beach and stepped into the cool waters of the South Asrien Sea. Students from the University of Chara impressed them with a beautiful fireworks display and a play about the miraculous rescue of Princess Lystran from her father, King Rammon. Terosh discussed new irrigation plans with Chara's governor while Reia continued her lessons with Sedir.

Before moving on to Kalmata, they escaped their duties for four whole days at a private house along the Glass Coast. Royal Guards maintained a perimeter but kept well away from Reia and Terosh. The royals threw their efforts into swimming, exploring, and foraging. Each meal became an adventure to share, enjoy, and mutually conquer. Each day as the sun set and the moons rose, they spent precious moments in blessed silence, watching the waves roll in and enjoying each other's presence.

On the way to Kalmata they stopped at the Imberg Tosh Mines where Reia sensed something familiar. They toured the mines and used the anotechs to ascertain some of its history. Imagine the queen's surprise when she realized her parents had once owned part of the mines and died for it. The discovery set off a legal battle which resulted in Kiata Wellum owning part of the mines and signing the shares over to Reia for the benefit of indentured servants with mining skills.

Finally, in Kalmata, Reia and Terosh saw how workers reclaimed salt from the West Remon Sea. On a visit to Fort Tiree, they talked with many of the Royal Guards stationed there. Reia noted that most soldiers were human, so she added diversification of the armed forces to her list of causes. At the Kalmata orphanage, they discovered an overworked, underpaid, and generally worn out staff. Naturally, the king ordered immediate changes and set Master Roth to the task of improving things. Lady Akia Zelene offered her expertise, and soon, the orphanage stood in much better stead. Though the aid recipients could only pay in smiles, the royals considered it more than enough.

The factories in Ritten turned raw materials from the Riden Mountains and Imberg Tosh Mines into everything from comms to hovs to ground vehicles to small starships. Reia and Terosh both enjoyed learning to fly klipper fighters, but their enthusiasm paled in comparison to the young lieutenant instructing them. Soon thereafter, Reia also learned how to drive a hov. While she liked the experience, she still felt more comfortable with the natural rolling gait of a horse.

The people of Meritab and Meritel hosted a huge festival in honor of Reia and Terosh's visit to their fair cities. Games and contests abounded. Reia politely declined to participate but encouraged Terosh to do so. He entered a serlak pistol shooting contest and fared well, though he did not win top prize. Todd and Kiata Wellum both entered several competitions. Although they had rejoined with the anotechs, both avoided enhancing any senses or reflexes during the competition. Nevertheless, Todd won top honors in kerlinblade combat and several kerlak shooting contests. Kiata soundly defeated her challengers in banistick and unarmed combat and earned great recognition for her skills with flingers. Each evening in Meritab or Meritel featured a new play or dance demonstration, sometimes both.

Although they found the twin cities enthralling, Reia and Terosh tore themselves away in early Enis (April) to return to Rammon and oversee the Festival of Future Fighters, sending the next wave of Kireshana travelers on their way.

Next, the horse lords and ladies in Calsola proudly displayed their steeds. Reia marveled at how much she had missed the previous year by rushing through Calsola in hot pursuit of Prince Terosh and his Royal Guard entourage. Practically every man, woman, and child they met in Calsola could competently ride a horse. Most could even race them, a fact proven time and again in both official and unofficial races. Reia found the wild spirit of Calsola's citizens infectious. They reminded her of Rangers. Though that thought brought pain, she loved being around the unpretentious people who taught her to love racing of any sort. Before her time in Calsola, Reia viewed hovs, hov bikes, and horses simply as means of transportation, but afterward, she appreciated the joy that drove people to pit their skills against one another.

On the way down to Idonia, Reia and Terosh camped a few days in the Clear Mountains and then again in the Ash Mountains. While the two mountains invoked vastly different feelings within her, Reia was thrilled at being fully immersed in wild lands and breathing free air. They narrowly escaped a windstorm, but the experience challenged them to continually defy the weather. A large korver pack took mild interest in them as well, but the Royal Guards used kerlak stun bolts to good effect. Despite chilling memories of the korver attack in the zalok cave, neither Reia nor Terosh were eager to slaughter korvers outright.

The weeks in Idonia returned the king and queen to refined culture. On separate occasions, they visited with Governor Lord Eldon Altran and his family and Governor General Kezem. With their help, Governor Judge Mitrek took his family to Balar the week after Keldor's trial ended. Being in Idonia caused them to think of Mitrek, but they dared not speak of him for fear of somehow betraying him. They had routed the family through several pods on Riab due to Mitrek's insistence that no one—especially his mother—be able to trace them. Lady Mavis surprised Reia and Terosh by seeking them out one afternoon.

Around the family visits, the king and queen toured crystal factories and the Nedis Crystal Mines. The mine owner admired them so much that he readily accepted Reia's proposal for having former indentured servants work some of the packing lines. An assassination attempt dampened their experience a bit, but they found most Idonians pleasant people. Senator Victoria Turrel bestowed a lovely pair of glass swords upon the young royals and arranged for a demonstration of their use by Idonia's colored crossblades team.

The last stop before the long-awaited Colored Crossblades Tournament in Korch was Azhel. There they met Father Morgivesh Niktol and communed with the man who had presided over their marriage. He admitted a desire to see them as motivation for his current spiritual journey and guided them around the a few of the temples. Naturally, a serene, deep spirituality marked the people of Azhel. Reia found the time among them very relaxing. Their music seemed to mean more whether provided by the Azhel Grand Percussion Band, the Children's Choir, or the Gentle String Quartet. This last portion of their trip around Reshner left Reia feeling refreshed and confident that she could face most anything. She would need that feeling in the months and years to come.

Chapter 33:
Colored Crossblades Tournament

Allei (August) 1, 1539
Colored Crossblades Arena, City of Korch

Queen Reia Minstel braced against the thunderous noise crashing down upon her from the frantic crowds. She marveled that so much of her life could pass without hearing of colored crossblades, a series of sporting events that dominated a good portion of the culture. Master Colander had immediately rectified the sad deficiency in her education, but she had all but forgotten the games until Sedir reminded her of this duty to grace the events with her presence.

Although almost a year had passed since inheriting her role as queen, Reia still found crowds unnerving, especially crowds as large and enthusiastic as this one. A wall of harried Royal Guards kept the people at bay, but she still felt closed in by the sheer number of people. Upon reaching her designated area, Reia resisted the urge to fling herself into the nearest seat. Instead, she steadied herself on a railing and scanned the crowds.

As she soaked in the sight of rank upon rank of colorfully attired people, inexplicable pride filled her. One could tell which section belonged to each city by the banners and flags and blinking arrangements of coordinated infopads.

Korch's dark green and black banners with the image of a goritor dominated because of the location. Reia was surprised goritors did not represent Meritab or Meritel since those cities were closest to the Lotrian Fields, the place made famous for its goritor infestation. Green and brown banners bearing the emblem of a horse represented Calsola, and green and yellow banners bearing the likeness of a cannafitch represented Osem.

It took Reia a moment to find the purple and green, zalok-bearing banners representing the Royal House and the red and gold, korver-bearing banners from the city of Rammon. Master Sedir and Master Colander had both warned her against favoritism, but the majestic images of her new home and family secretly held her loyalty. It amused her to think of a korver as a noble symbol for once. In obedience to good advice, Reia bestowed her smile and attention as equally as possible.

The section claimed by people from Azhel shimmered with orange and red flames. One of their signs read: FLAMES BURN ON. The Idonians held their banner of a helmeted soldier aloft and rhythmically chanted a warrior's cry. A large number of those from Estra wore dark blue outfits studded with white pieces of glass that reflected the sun sharply. The people of Kalmata were a riot of colors in tribute to their mascot the kyrie bird. They contrasted with the black and silver worn by Meritab natives whose symbol of a sharp dagger hardly needed the garish trappings of multiple colors. The Charans roared with the challenging battle cry of a mythical dalagon.

Exceedingly glad not to have to speak at the opening ceremonies, Reia thoroughly enjoyed the team parade and the show that followed. The songs and traditional dances from the various cities were expertly performed, but they could not match the splendor of the portion put on by the city of Korch. Reia especially liked the part where two teams of five hov riders performed a series of acrobatic maneuvers, often flipping from one bike to another high above the crowd. The welcoming speeches were far less exciting but mercifully short.

Her favorite part did not come until the very end. Though it consisted of nothing more than a simple recitation of the vow to fight for the honor and glory of each home city, the sight of nearly a thousand kerlinblades raised over the players' heads could not fail to inspire awe. Reia wished Terosh could have joined her. He had promised to watch a recording, but no vid could adequately capture such a moment.

***

Allei (August) 7, 1539
Colored Crossblades Arena, City of Korch

King Terosh watched the Kamarachi Duel with interest. It wasn't his favorite duel to participate in, but he admired the skill it took the four teams of five to fight in a hundred-meter-long, half-gravity field. This match featured teams from Meritab, Meritel, Azhel, and Osem. As expected, the Meritab Blades and Meritel Vipers were allied at the moment, which left the Azhel Flames and Osem Cannafitches to either unite or lose.

Terosh couldn't help but compare the teams to their respective governors. Beady-eyed, suspicious Governor Holum of Meritab and silent, somber Governor Naverick of Meritel were practically inseparable. Azhel's venerable Governor Westis tended to keep to himself, and Osem's good-natured Governor Ella Price kept her affairs neat and unobtrusive. Terosh spared a wish that Governors Council meetings could be solved like colored crossblades duels.

"Stop that," Reia scolded, slipping her left hand into Terosh's right.

"How do you always know what I'm thinking?" Terosh wondered, giving her a guilty grin.

"You're wearing that special, slightly sickened expression you reserve for the Governors Council," Reia said. "No more politics. Enjoy your one month of complete freedom from councils and meetings. It only comes once every three years."

"I'll try," Terosh promised, tightening his grip on her hand.

On the field, two Meritel players had the Osem current flag bearer trapped against a barrier that had materialized on the seventy-meter marker. Before the barrier could form a roof and complete the trap, the Osem player executed a backflip onto the barrier's frame and used it as a launching point to spring over his attackers. While still in the air, he casually tossed the flag to a teammate. Despite its name, the "flag" was really a lightweight glowbar a little smaller than a standard kerlinblade handle. The throw was a little wide and the other Osem player lunged to catch it before it touched the ground. The Osem fans drew a horrified collective breath then let it out in a rush once they realized the flag was safe.

"They make it look so easy," Reia commented. "There's so much to keep track of. How do they do it?"

"Long hours of intense training for a start," Terosh said, watching a Meritab player bat aside strikes from Azhel and Osem duelists. "It's meant to be chaotic. Kamarachi Duels began as war games to train soldiers to fight in space."

"The inventor must have been quite a commander."

"Don't say that to Master Sedir unless you want to suffer through his three-hour lecture on the history of colored crossblades duels," Terosh warned. He took the opportunity to lift his wife's hand and gently traced her fingers. His interest in the duel waned as he enjoyed the simple pleasure of being near her.

"Only three-hours? You must have gotten the short version," said Reia, pulling her hand free of Terosh's loose grip to clap politely. "I thought he would talk on straight through the evening meal, but Master Colander rescued me."

Feeling bereft, Terosh returned his attention to the field where the Meritab team was celebrating the successful capture of the flag. The bar changed from green and yellow to silver. Seven separate duels still raged around the field.

One brave Azhel player fended off three opponents at once. Despite her obvious skill, the Azhel player slowly found herself corralled toward a barrier. She tried to leap free, but two Meritab Blades blocked her efforts. A moment later, a Meritel player knocked the Azhel woman into the barrier and it held her fast.

Terosh flicked his eyes to the scoreboard. Meritab led by a mere ten points with a score of two hundred and twelve, followed by Osem at two hundred and two, Meritel at one hundred and seventy-eight, and Azhel at one hundred and sixty-two. Three minutes remained in the second round.

Although he did not really care who won the game, he silently cheered for the Azhel team just because they were so behind. He wasn't worried. Leads changed almost by the second in this type of duel. Captured flags were worth twenty-five points, strikes against opponent players were worth one point, and captured opponent players were worth five points for the first up to twenty-five points for the last.

"Is there a limit to how many times the flag can be passed within a team?" Reia asked.

"Not under these rules," Terosh answered. "There are several very similar games where passes matter, but here players can hold the flag the whole time or continually pass countless times."

The round ended, and Terosh and Reia rose to stretch.

The barriers released their prisoners, and the players retreated to their respective corners to regroup.

Two more rounds, Terosh thought, suddenly anxious to be done with the match. Then, he could spend some quality time with his wife.

"Patience, love," Reia whispered, leaning over and wrapping him in a friendly, one-armed hug. "The world is watching."

Four giant vidscreens displaying their image to every eye in the arena emphasized her words. Terosh forced himself to smile and wave, but inside, he cringed at the attention.

***

Allei (August) 30, 1539
Colored Crossblades Arena, City of Korch

Ariman Keldor eagerly anticipated the coming duel. It would change everything. The king would finally receive his due for that mock trial and the subsequent death of Ariman's father. He knew it was dangerous to be here, but he had to see the plan unfold. He shook his head, trying to shake off a sudden chill. A year ago, he would have never even considered assassination, but the year had changed him.

As soon as he witnessed the king's death, he would keep his promise to Dr. Nabern, an old, brilliant friend.

***

Lord Kezem Altran dutifully waved to his cheering supporters. Inside, he battled rising resentment. His patience with his mother's endless schemes was all but spent. He could not shake the uneasy feeling that this plan would fail. Trying to predict the people's reaction to the pending accident left him cold.

He marched over to his starting area and let the officials inspect the sensors built into his black dueling suit. He did not have to look to know Terosh was also submitting to a similar inspection. He listened with half an ear while one official dutifully listed the rules he had memorized since childhood.

"This is a Dollan duel to an Ideal Fifty. Three ground strikes may be used to change the blade color, but additional ground strikes will incur a five-point penalty. If the officials determine you are using additional ground strikes to purposefully lower your score, you will be disqualified, and your opponent will be declared the victor. Do you understand?"

Kezem grunted and glared at the man.

The official hurried on with his recitation.

"Blade colors will follow the standard rainbow from red to violet through white and back to red. Red strikes are worth seven points, orange

447

six, yellow five, green—"

"Get on with it!" Kezem demanded.

"Apologies, my Lord Kezem, but I am bound by the rules of my office," said the stuffy little man.

Kezem gritted his teeth and endured the rest of the man's speech.

"Green strikes are worth four points, blue three, indigo two, violet one, and white ten. Score panels to the sides will show the current scores as the duel progresses. You may refer to these at your own risk. Sensors in your suit will register valid body strikes. Please avoid blows to the head, neck, and other vital areas as they carry no point value and may result in disqualification. Also, please respect the boundaries of the dueling circle. Violation of these boundaries will result in disqualification."

"What colors will we start with?" asked Kezem. He could not remember whether Dollan duels started with red or randomly. It had been quite some time since he had indulged in an officially regulated match.

"You are the challenger, my Lord Kezem; therefore, the choice rests with the challenged, His Majesty, King Terosh."

"I know this," Kezem snapped. "What did he choose?"

"Random, my Lord Kezem," answered the official, blinking slowly like a sunning sand lizard.

Once the tiresome official was finished with Kezem, the babbling announcer picked up the cause to annoy him. The man introduced Kezem and the king and spewed facts everybody knew about them. He tried to emphasize the deep rivalry between the cousins. Though he spoke truth, Kezem wished the fool would get on with the duel.

At last, the match moderator stepped into the center of the dueling circle and beckoned to Kezem and the king. Kezem pulled on sensor-lined cloth gauntlets and tightened the straps. Then, snatching the modified kerlinblade from the boy holding it out, Kezem entered the circle and saluted his young cousin with his unlit weapon. Terosh returned the gesture. They bowed to each other, and the match began.

Kezem activated his kerlinblade, and it blazed into orange life. Terosh's blade lit green. Their blades crashed several times as each tested the other's defenses. The rapidly changing colors dazzled Kezem's vision enough to allow Terosh first strike, a red glancing blow off Kezem's left forearm. It did not hurt, but the tingling sensation from the sensors further distracted him. He retreated several steps, blocking eager strikes from Terosh as he went.

As the duel continued, Kezem relaxed into the rhythm of the fight. Anticipating Terosh's strikes grew easier. The color changes ceased to bother Kezem, though he did have to pay close attention to them to plan his strikes. Dollan duels were especially useful exercises for they forced the combatants to constantly think several moves ahead.

After using a particularly hard over-the-head blow to unbalance Terosh, Kezem scored twice, once with a violet blade and once with a white blade. Terosh answered a moment later with a yellow hit.

From time to time, Kezem switched his grip from right hand to left hand to a two-handed hold on his kerlinblade. Each new hold allowed him to attack Terosh from a slightly different angle. The duel ebbed and flowed as they further provoked each other by changing the speed of their attacks. Slashes met parries. Their kerlinblades locked together and pressed close, draining each man's strength. Kezem disengaged but attacked right away, lest anyone think him the weaker party.

Suddenly every joint in Kezem's dueling suit stiffened. When Terosh's blade next connected with Kezem's, both weapons emitted a bright flash of light followed by the sizzling crackle of raw electricity. Kezem saw Terosh fly backward just before pain crashed in on his senses from head to foot.

He barely had time to wonder why his mother would betray him before consciousness deserted him.

***

Reia watched in horror as the spirited duel between Terosh and his cousin turned deadly. A sharp crack like a danesque tree trunk snapping in half preceded a series of lesser pops. Twin whips of energy, one white and one green, flew between Terosh and Kezem. The charge lifted both men bodily, cradled them for a second, and flung them away from each other with the force of a windstorm.

Kezem landed on the boy who had given him the kerlinblade, killing the child instantly. Reia felt the loss of his life like a cold wave of water across her whole body. Still glowing green from energy pouring out of his kerlinblade, Terosh's body hurtled through a small cluster of officials judging the match. Their pained cries were immediately lost in the cacophony of confused shouts.

Reia's skin tingled, practically buzzing as agitated anotechs flooded her senses with information. Memory took her back to the korver attack on the zalok cave. A sickening sense of helplessness flooded her. She reverted to Ranger training to continue to analyze the situation when she really wanted to collapse in despair.

A feeling of dread seized her stomach. Kezem's body bounced off the crushed boy like a stone skipping across a calm lake then skidded another five meters. Another four unfortunate bystanders were knocked aside. Terosh's body finally set down hard against the ground. Both men still instinctively clutched the smoking handles of their destroyed weapons.

The dread multiplied, driving Reia to her feet with sudden clarity burning through her skull. Terosh and his cousin still lived, but something else was about to happen. Sedir's dire warnings against using anotech powers were banished by the panic that fueled Reia to action. Clenching her hands around the metal bar in front of her, Reia closed her eyes and slumped forward as if in a dead faint.

Reaching out with the anotechs, she pried the weapons from the two stunned men now lying on the arena floor far below her. She had two choices. She could have the anotechs carry the hazardous handles high into the air, risking an explosion over the frantic crowd, or she could try to contain them while still on the ground, risking her husband and his cousin. Much as it sickened her, she chose the second option, frantically bidding the anotechs to diffuse whatever danger still lay inside the kerlinblade handles.

Not knowing what else to do and having very little time to do anything, Reia wrapped each weapon in a shield of anotechs and braced for pain. An agonizing second passed in terrifying anticipation. Then, Reia felt two sensations. The first was like a thousand glass shards trying to rip through her, and the second sensation was like being bathed in firebloom extract. Her whole body convulsed as the twin torments punished her for saving the two men and the crowd.

As suddenly as it had started, the pain cut off. She moaned as her body began falling. Warm hands caught her and held on tightly.

"Don't worry. I've got you!" declared Captain Ectosh Laocer.

Welcomed blackness slipped over Reia's vision. She had just enough time to command the anotechs to protect her husband and his cousin before truly fainting.

Chapter 34:
Aftermath

Allei (August) 30, 1539
Same Day
The Lady's Estate, Kala Mountains

Mavis Altran relished the fresh air that met her as she stepped out onto the carefully hidden balcony she had ordered built into Mount Corith's side. The extensive airflow system kept her underground estate supplied with fresh air and even a passable imitation of cool breezes from time to time, but it could not replicate the wild spirit of natural wind. She breathed deeply several times, trying to force the tension from her body.

Though well-acquainted with fear and anger, Mavis was not used to experiencing them in such toxic quantities. Her cheeks flamed and her head pounded with the force of her boiling blood. She wanted to kill the man who had failed her. She would kill him, but she needed to calm down enough to deal with him properly. If she faced him now, she would probably riddle his body with serlak bullets, and that would be a terrible waste. Proper punishment always took time. She had already issued the necessary orders and now had only to wait.

A cannafitch screeched a hunting cry as it soared past Mavis's balcony. She admired the impressive wingspan of the leathery creature, a male with a splash of white across the crest of his forehead. Then, she shot its skinny head off its slender neck and felt a little better. She watched the body float along on the wind current for several meters before twisting awkwardly and tumbling out of the air stream. It then plummeted toward the rocky valley below. Some korver or mountain lion would feast without having to work tonight.

Mavis returned the small, sleek kerlak pistol to its holster hidden beneath her heart. Dennel would not question her, but he would frown that deep, disapproving frown if he knew. Mavis smiled at the thought of the faithful old servant's reaction. For a second, she almost wished he would scold as he had done during her childhood. He had long since abandoned scolding aloud, but Mavis read him well enough to know when one of her actions displeased him. It bothered her that she cared so much for his good opinion, but she accepted the weakness.

In addition to dealing with the failed scientist, she had vid recordings to watch, a protégé to check on, false sympathies to prepare, and a wounded son to ship to Gardan. Thinking about the list of tasks made her weary, so she let her thoughts brush the recent near disaster. The resulting spike of anger woke her muscles, and Mavis found herself wishing another cannafitch would fly by.

Kezem almost died.

The resulting rush of helplessness turned her anger cold. A sudden, fierce wind whipped strands of her graying black hair painfully across her face. She closed her eyes and leaned into the wind, letting it rake its cold claws along her cheeks.

Reia saved him.

That set some mixed emotions loose in her. She silently thanked the young woman and experienced an odd guilt that they could never be friends. She opened her eyes and fixed them directly on the sun, squinting against the glare. It bothered Mavis to not know exactly what the young queen had done to save Kezem, but she had seen enough recordings to recognize when anotechs were at work.

She saved them both.

The reminder that her nephew also still lived gave her a confusing twinge of disappointment and relief. It had not been her design, but she could have easily adjusted plans to accommodate Terosh's unfortunate demise. Her nephew and his wife had thankfully not produced an heir yet. Kezem might have inherited the woman as well as the throne. Mavis shook her head at the ridiculous notion.

They should not have needed saving.

The thought brought Mavis full circle back to her anger. She nursed it this time, letting it wash through her and enjoying the safe emotional ground it offered.

***

Allei (August) 30, 1539
Same Day
Royal Palace, City of Rammon

Reia awoke mere moments after losing consciousness and forced herself to action, issuing dozens of instructions to see order restored.

Terosh, his cousin, and the other wounded people received immediate care. The dead were covered. The stunned crowds were calmed and ushered out of the arena by police and soldiers. Bolstering what little courage existed in the crowd to prevent panic took every scrap of reserve energy and concentration Reia had left. When she finally collapsed in exhaustion, Todd and Kiata took care of the remaining details.

Reia spent the hov ride back to Rammon in fitful sleep by Terosh's side.

Kiata and Todd parted from the company as soon as it reached the palace, informing the queen they would issue public statements in her stead.

Reia nodded absently and followed the four Royal Guards surrounding her husband's hov sled. She quickly fell behind their rapid steps. Several other Royal Guards, including Captain Laocer, hovered at her side and kept pace with her, ready to catch her should the day's events prove overwhelming.

No one dared utter a word, so the somber procession proceeded through the palace hallways in silence.

Head and heart pounding, Reia feared she wouldn't make it to Terosh's private quarters. The gentle rocking motion of the elevator almost made her sick. Somehow, she held herself upright until the guards had placed Terosh's still form on his bed. Then, she ordered everybody out and sank to the ground beside the bed. Only then did she allow the aching sobs to collapse her emotional defenses.

She woke up with her head resting in her arms and the right side of her face creased from the sheets. Her eyes swept over Terosh's body, seeking a sign of life. He lay on his back with his hands folded neatly across his stomach, appearing so much like the peaceful dead that Reia's heartbeat quickened with dread. She levered herself to a standing position and tenderly laid her hand on his chest. The brief moment before she felt the gentle rise of his chest was one of the longest in her experience.

Her headache returned as a tight band around the top of her skull. It was tolerable as far as headaches go. Reia shut her eyes and directed anotechs to explain the damage done to Terosh's body. Before they could report, the outer door slammed open with a solid crash.

Reia's eyes flew open, but she left her hand hovering over Terosh as she lifted her head to face the intruder.

"What are you doing?" demanded Ezzai Dentelich, rushing into the room. His face flickered between anger and astonishment.

"Trying to see what's wrong with him," Reia replied, lacking the energy to be irritated with the doctor.

"That is my job, Your Majesty," said Dr. Dentelich, recovering a bit from his shock. "Please allow me to do it," he added, stepping around the bed and motioning her to move aside.

Reia was not sure she could safely move at all. Her legs refused to respond to the first few impulses she sent them. Finally, she managed to stumble back and nearly fell over. Only Dentelich's strong grip on her upper right arm kept her upright.

Dentelich shouted for a Royal Guard to help him, and said, "Tell me what you're feeling."

"Tired," Reia mumbled, as her knees buckled.

Dentelich slipped his left arm around her waist and draped her right arm over his shoulders so he could support her. He grunted with the effort and shouted for the guard again.

"You are more than merely tired, my Queen."

Reia didn't hear if he said more, but she felt strong arms pick her up like a child, carry her around to the other side of Terosh's bed, and lay her gently next to him. Letting her eyes close, she reached out to grip Terosh's right hand. Her hand found his wrist instead, and the steady beat of his pulse sent waves of comfort through her.

***

Pirua (September) 1, 1539
Central Communications Room, Royal Palace, City of Rammon

Kiata Wellum stood to the side, out of range of the vidrecorders and hologram projectors, wishing she could do something to help her sister. It pained her to watch Reia's slow, stiff movements. She seemed to be holding herself together through stubborn will alone. While this did not surprise Kiata, it did frustrate her.

"How fares the king, Your Grace?" asked Lady Mavis Altran, her elegant face lined with worry.

"He has not regained consciousness yet, but Dr. Dentelich believes he will," Reia answered without much inflection.

"You are a healer of the finest degree," Lady Mavis gently reminded her. "What do you believe?"

Kiata could not see her sister's face, but she heard the uncertainty and desperation in her voice.

"I have never seen anything like this," said Reia. She gripped the back of the chair in front of her for support. Her voice dropped to a whisper. "I don't know what to do."

An emotion Kiata could not identify flashed across Lady Mavis's face and was gone in an instant. Genuine compassion took its place.

"You will know what to do when the time comes," said Lady Mavis. "You will save our beloved king."

"Thank you for the kind words, Lady Mavis," said Reia, reluctantly releasing her grip on the chair and standing slightly straighter. "How is Lord Kezem?"

Kiata could tell Reia wanted to assure the older woman that she had done everything she could to protect Lord Kezem. To Kiata's great relief, Reia had the sense to contain any statements that would lead to awkward questions.

"I suspect he fares exactly as our king." Lady Mavis's words were heavy with sadness. "I am sending him to some specialists on Gardan."

"What do these specialists do?" asked Reia. Her tone finally had some life to it.

"I am not quite sure," said Lady Mavis. "I only know their practices are dangerous yet have near miraculous results. If you like, I shall keep you apprised of their progress. Should their methods work with my son, perhaps we can risk them with our king."

Reia's shoulders slumped slightly.

"I see. Will Lord Kezem be all right?"

"We can only hope and pray it is so," replied Lady Mavis.

"Is his situation really so desperate as to warrant such risks?" Reia pressed.

"Unfortunately, I fear he was struck by something more than simple electricity," Lady Mavis announced.

What makes you say that? Kiata wondered, thinking it an odd observation.

Dr. Dentelich said the samples taken from King Terosh would require a full day to analyze, even with several top scientists devoting their full efforts to the task.

Reia tensed.

"What causes such fear in you?" she asked, echoing Kiata's sentiment.

The lady responded with a small, self-deprecating smile.

"Your Grace, I have lived long enough to know that things are never quite as simple as they seem. So, when I see my son fall in a flash of light, I know to expect a complicated explanation."

"What more do you expect? A poison?" asked Reia, horrified.

"We will not know until the results are in, and I think it best we not worry until then," Lady Mavis advised. "Now, if you'll excuse me, I must see my son off personally."

"Certainly," Reia said with a nod. "Thank you for taking the time to call."

"It was my pleasure, Highness," responded Lady Mavis.

A moment passed while the two women silently regarded each other, waiting for someone to end the call. When the connection had been cut and the machines stopped humming, Reia finally turned around and leaned wearily against the chair she had been gripping for support.

"What is it?" she asked, probably in response to Kiata's expression.

What is it? Kiata silently repeated. Something bothered her, but she could not fathom what.

"I'm worried," she admitted, lacking words to better define her feeling.

"Well, that's specific," said Reia.

"Something's not right here," Kiata said, frantically trying to make the scattered feelings give her answers.

"Not much is right," Reia answered, leaning her head back and shutting her eyes. "My husband's in a coma, the councils are outraged, the people are worried, and I'm not ready to do anything about any of it."

Kiata's helpless feeling returned, but she stepped forward and swept her sister into a firm embrace.

"You will do fine," she whispered.

***

Pirua (September) 1, 1539
Same Day
The Lady's Estate, Kala Mountains

After changing out of the drab outfit she had put on to contact the queen, Mavis found herself back in the communications room once again. She ran her hands down the front of her bright red shimmersilk gown and idly wondered how many more times she would be burdened with talking to Gardan's king. Though she doubted anything would impress King Padric, Mavis favored the dress because of how well it worked with her light skin and dark hair. She tapped in the proper commands and waited.

As usual, King Padric made Mavis wait to prove his importance. When he finally answered, he eyed her critically and skipped the pleasantries.

"I am told your plan has gone somewhat awry. Is this true?"

That's an understatement.

"Not at all. My plan has proceeded quite well," Mavis answered.

"I always knew you to be an ambitious woman, Lady Mavis, but nearly killing your own son is a dedicated step indeed," said Padric with a rare smile. "I commend your strategy, and I take it you are ready to proceed to the next phase."

"Almost ready," Mavis corrected. "I believe I have underestimated the length of time it will take for you to properly repair my son. His wounds will have to be answered for before the improvements can be implemented, and I am told those alone can take a year or two to complete."

The smile melted into the usual scowl.

"That is unfortunate. This partnership seems plagued with delays. What added incentive will you offer in exchange for the extra time and effort I must waste on behalf of your son?"

Mavis smiled carefully, trying not to seem too eager. Having Padric believe the suggestion a concession rather than something she deeply desired was crucial.

"I have had my people do some research on our young queen, and I believe she would provide your scientists with some fascinating results."

Despite the scowl, Padric looked intrigued.

"I have thought as much for a long time, but how will you deliver her without bringing our respective peoples to war?"

"It will not be easy, but I believe I will soon be in possession of the proper leverage," said Mavis.

"The sister?" asked Padric. "Did you not try and fail at that before?"

"The incident you refer to was some of my men trying to acquire a target-of-opportunity, and yes, they failed at it," said Mavis. "However, I do not have to force the queen to do anything. If I can convince her to learn some special healing techniques found only on Gardan, she will come to you."

"You possess a very dangerous mind. Take care to not bring harm to yourself or your own in the process," Padric warned with a hard stare.

"That is sound advice, King Padric," Mavis said evenly. "I shall heed it. I only called to inform you that my son should arrive in a little over a week and advise you that I may be unreachable for a time. Dennel will be here to receive any reports your people send."

Padric blustered for a time, but Mavis calmly nodded at the right times and ignored the childish rants. After a few minutes, she concluded the conversation and signed off.

She had some frustration to work off, and she knew the perfect cure for it. A few instructions to the right people set things in motion nicely. Mavis decided to grab some fresh mountain air to clear her mind while she waited for Kellen to make the necessary preparations. He had indicated there might be some delay. She hoped not, but she trusted his judgment.

Chapter 35:
Anotech Assessment

Pirua (September) 1, 1539
Same Day
King Terosh's Private Chambers, Royal Palace, City of Rammon

"Are you sure there is nothing more I can do, Majesty?" asked Captain Ectosh Laocer.

"I am certain, Captain," answered Reia. "Ensure that the guards around this chamber are refreshed every few hours."

"It will be done," said Laocer solemnly.

Reia returned her full attention to her husband. She folded Terosh's hands neatly across his stomach, tucked her knees up to her chest, and wrapped her arms around them. Her forehead hovered over her knees. She held the position for a few seconds as the anotechs' disturbing words floated through her mind.

We sense much poison in him. Very powerful poison, but also very familiar.

What does that mean? Reia demanded.

We know this poison. We can fight it.

What aren't you telling me? Reia asked, feeling their hesitation as a fluttering in her stomach.

It is a form of comaladon. It changes structure to prevent eradication.

Reia's throat constricted, jamming her breath inside her chest.

Not again! Her mind protested the possibility that Terosh would die by the same poison that had claimed his mother. *Can you heal him?*

Not alone, but you can.

How? Her breath escaped in a rush, ending in a strangled sob.

The anotechs explained the task they required of her. They needed Reia to direct complete transfusions of anotechs so they could continually remove the poison from Terosh's system. The reality could not easily be explained with words. They could not tell her how many times she would have to lay her hands on her husband's burning hot chest and feed fresh anotechs through one hand while ones saturated with poison entered her through the other. To be fair, they did warn her about the discomfort she could experience during the process.

Reia accepted the role with grim determination and a sense of elation. She would not have to sit idly by while her husband's fate rested in others' hands. Worry about all that could go wrong tried to press in, but she crushed the half-formed thoughts and concentrated on directing the anotechs.

***

Pirua (September) 4, 1539
King Terosh's Private Chambers, Royal Palace, City of Rammon

A cool hand brushed Reia's forehead. She opened her eyes to find Dr. Dentelich leaning over her.

"How do you feel, Highness?" asked Dr. Dentelich. "Well rested, I hope. You've slept for more than two days."

Slept more than two days ... Terosh! The thoughts jolted her wide awake and she struggled to sit up.

Dr. Dentelich quickly straightened to avoid a collision.

I didn't dream, Reia realized, before pain engulfed her head. She knew she was falling back but could do nothing about it.

The doctor reached out, caught her, and eased her back to a prone position.

"Lie still. Your fever's gone, but you need to eat and drink," said the doctor.

"How is Terosh?" Reia asked, ignoring the reproving tone but obeying the good advice. With much effort, she turned her head to look at her husband.

He wore a simple pair of black pants and a loose white shirt. It surprised her that he wasn't tucked tightly under the covers.

"No change," Dr. Dentelich admitted. "We will need to discuss treatment options, but first, you must take care of your own needs."

"What options do we have?" Reia asked, turning back to Dentelich.

Before the doctor could answer, Sarie Verituse appeared in the threshold.

"May I enter, Your Majesty?"

"Yes, of course," said Reia, wishing she were not lying flat on her back.

"Thank you, I would hate to return to Lady Wellum with nothing to report," said Sarie. She bustled in carrying a large tray with fresh fruit and a glass of water.

"Kiata's here?" Reia asked, surprised. She tried sitting up again, slower this time.

After asking for and receiving permission, Dr. Dentelich helped Reia to a sitting position and tucked three pillows behind her.

Sarie shook her head.

"She said she or Master Todd would return this evening for a report, but I planned to tell her sooner." Sarie walked over to the table beside Reia.

Dr. Dentelich ducked out of the way and retreated to the foot of the bed.

Sarie reached with her left hand and tapped a few commands into the control panel near Reia's head. The table extended and a pair of slender stands descended to the floor. Sarie expertly swung the tray around and placed it on the table.

"Thank you," Reia said, not really interested in the food.

Dr. Dentelich opened his mouth to bluster more orders to eat, but Sarie stopped him with a gesture.

"Lady Kiata also said that she would give you a rather large piece of her mind if you refused to eat," said Sarie. "She added that if need be she would break into the palace and spoon feed you. It may not be my place to say anything, but I believe she would keep her word."

Reia rubbed at her temple to fight the weariness.

"I agree, and I surrender to your good will." Reia picked up a grape and rolled it between her thumb and forefinger. Her eyes flickered between Dr. Dentelich and Sarie who watched her intently. She raised the grape in a small salute before eating it. "You may tell my sister her persuasion skills have not waned."

"I will do so, Your Majesty," said Sarie, as a bright smile lit up her dark face. "I shall leave you to finish your meal in peace, and I believe Doctor Dentelich would like to speak to you alone."

One look at Dentelich's expression confirmed as much. Reia continued to pick at the fruit array and waited for the doctor to share his thoughts.

"You may speak your mind, doctor," said Reia, once it was clear he would not speak first.

Dentelich straightened.

"Your Grace, I have been a physician for the Royal House for more than thirty years," he said gravely. "I watched Queen Kila fall to comaladon mixed with poison from a gully fish." As he spoke, his expression melted from inscrutable to stricken. "I have never seen a poison like this. It is comaladon, but it has been modified." He stopped speaking when he noticed Reia nodding.

"I know. It changes form, so it's hard to treat," Reia said, repeating what the anotechs had told her. "But I can help him."

From Dr. Dentelich's distant expression, she doubted he had heard the last part.

"There are certain methods practiced on Gardan we could try," Dr. Dentelich offered. His hesitant tone conveyed deep reservations.

"Lady Mavis mentioned them in passing," said Reia. "She is sending Lord Kezem to Gardan for treatment. I assume it is for the methods you speak of, but you sound uncertain about them."

"They require sacrifice," Dr. Dentelich informed her.

Reia's hand froze midway to the fruit tray.

"What manner of sacrifice?" She let her hand flop down and rest in her lap.

Dr. Dentelich reluctantly explained the process of transferring blood from one person to another.

"It would kill Terosh to know someone died for him," said Reia.

Dentelich nodded wearily.

"I expected as much, which is why I hesitated to tell you about it. I can keep him sedated to let his body rest as much as possible, but it won't cure him."

"I can help him," Reia said again.

"How?" asked Dr. Dentelich.

Sedir's warnings against sharing about the anotechs came to the forefront of her mind.

"I cannot tell you how," said Reia. "It would break a vow I have made."

The doctor flushed with a fresh tide of anger.

"We are talking about your husband's life! I am his physician. I must know every treatment he receives!"

His tone provoked some anger in Reia, but she had not the energy to indulge it.

"I am aware of the topic," she said slowly, coming to a decision about how much to tell him. "As I am sure you are aware, members of the Royal House have access to power most people do not. I can help Terosh through this power, but no one can know the details of it, not even you."

"Saving him would be a miracle. The medical implications would be—"

"Doctor, no one can know," Reia repeated. "I don't know if I can save him. I think I can, but it won't be easy. It must remain a secret because if it were known everyone would expect a miracle and chaos would ensue upon any sign of failure."

They exchanged long, solemn looks.

"I will do what I can to help you," Dentelich promised. With the assurance hanging in the air like a blessing, he bowed to Reia and departed.

Chapter 36:
Retribution

Pirua (September) 4, 1539
Same Day
The Lady's Estate, Kala Mountains

"I want you to tell me exactly how you failed me." Mavis had not liked the idea of waiting, but now that it was over, she did not mind half as much.

Sweat beaded on the man's brow and glistened in the bright light. He smelled powerfully of sour fear. Dr. Edwin Nabern ran his tongue across cracked lips.

"The charge was too strong," he whispered.

"Exactly." Mavis knew everything worth knowing about him, but she preferred to think of him in the detached sense. She mopped sweat from his face with a clean white cloth. Each gentle pat resulted in a muffled whimper. She contemplated offering him water but remembered the unfortunate incident where he had spit at her and decided against the small comfort. "And what else?"

"And I added a comaladon derivative I stole from Dr. Saddic," the man reluctantly admitted.

Mavis shut her eyes and swallowed the sudden rage that threatened to boil over and kill the man. When she spoke, her voice was almost lifeless.

"Why would you do such a thing?" Her eyes opened and stabbed into the man. "Why would you alter one of my plans?" The two questions unfolded in slow, rhythmic waves.

The man's lips trembled as he tried to keep a confession in. A few more seconds baking under her withering glare crashed his defenses and words poured forth.

"I was afraid of what you might do to them. When he contacted me, he said he knew exactly how you worked and that if I wanted to save my family I would do as he said."

"Who contacted you?" Mavis asked. Her tone cracked like a serlak rifle.

The man flinched.

"Keldor," he said.

462

"Which one?" Mavis asked, though she knew precisely which one.

"Ariman Keldor," answered the man.

He has finally chosen a side. Too bad. I had high hopes for him.

She was getting answers at last. They had been over this many times in the last couple of days. At first, the man had protested any wrongdoing and even defended his faulty calculations with scientific theories and experiments. Mavis had let Kellen and Lash explain the error of trying to justify mistakes and outright lying. They had clearly done well. She nodded appreciatively at the two who stood respectfully out of the way.

Lash, a lovely young Terabian woman with an unhealthy attachment to a plain, korverhide whip, lowered her eyes shyly. Kellen crossed his right arm across his chest in a salute and executed an elegant half bow to acknowledge Mavis's unspoken praise.

"Do you remember what I promised when I hired you?" asked Mavis. She took one more swipe at fresh sweat on the man's forehead and tossed the sullied cloth to the ground by his feet.

The man nodded miserably, but Mavis was pleased to see a touch of anger glitter behind his watery blue eyes. Stepping back, she lifted her right hand like someone lifting praise, then twisted her wrist with a flourish, and held her thumb and pointer finger about a centimeter apart. Lash's whip cracked into the wall by the man's left ear.

He yelped as if the blow had struck him. His hairless chest heaved, displaying the scars where some of Lash's other lessons had landed. The muscles in his arms and legs tensed instinctively, straining against the restraints securing him to the wall. He twisted his head as far to the right as it would go, inadvertently exposing his neck.

Feeling Lash's eagerness to strike, Mavis shook her head, sorry she had to disappoint the young woman.

"Do try to remember how much I loath unresponsiveness," said Mavis with a small sigh.

"Yes, I remember. You said you had a job where the rewards and risks would be extraordinary." The man's eyes darted about the room not daring to meet hers.

"And my promise?" she prompted.

He swallowed hard. The little color left to him drained from his face.

"Continuous work for me and protection for my family, pr-provided I succeeded."

"But you did not succeed," Mavis said slowly.

The man met her eyes as the statement yanked him out of the discomfort-induced stupor.

"Don't hurt them," he pleaded.

Mavis was impressed by the weight of will the man put behind his words.

"I'm going to let your work speak for itself." She pulled a controller from a pocket and tapped in a few instructions.

A vidscreen slid out of the ceiling behind her head to the left. She did not have to turn to see what it would show. Her instructions had been quite explicit. The man's wife and two children would be bound. Dressed in colored crossblades suits, they would each be seated with knees tucked up to their chests and hands and feet secured to one of the man's inventions.

The man renewed his attack against his unyielding restraints.

"No! They're innocent! You can't—"

Kellen's fist slammed into the man's gut, cutting off the rest of his protest.

"Speak civilly to the Lady," muttered Kellen.

The man sucked in great gasps, trying to catch his breath. Tears flowed freely down his face.

"Please, please, let them go. They are nothing to you."

"If they survive, I will set them free," Mavis promised. Then, she tapped in a few more commands to activate each device.

***

Pirua (September) 5, 1539
Village of Kerimia

Lucas Telon kept his senses alert for trouble as he walked through the deserted village streets. Boards covered most of the windows and shifting shadows covered the rest. Lucas felt nervous eyes follow his progress down the street. A faint breeze kicked up puffs of dust and brushed against Lucas's pants. He breathed deeply, enjoying the thrill of the hunt.

"These people are accustomed to fighting," said Kolknir, "but we are not here to destroy the village."

Lucas cast an annoyed glance at his mentor.

"I read the orders," he said.

"Yet you're still trying to provoke them," Kolknir pointed out. "We do not have time to indulge—"

"You want to kill them as much as I do," Lucas said. "Don't bother denying it. We're too much alike."

"If you were less brash, humbler, and better looking, I'd agree."

Lucas stopped, stunned by Kolknir's uncharacteristic flash of humor. "Where—"

A red kerlak bolt slammed into the ground in front of Lucas, cutting off the rest of his question. His serlak pistols were in his hands an instant later, but by that time, Kolknir had drawn his serlak rifle from the holster across his back, aimed up, and fired into the inky blackness of a window.

A man's cry of pain sounded just before a satisfying clatter and thud. Then, relative silence fell again. A distant korver howl punctuated the eerie feeling that struck Lucas in the gut.

"You knew," Lucas said, torn between anger and relief. "How did you know the man was there? How did you know I'd stop?"

"Keep your senses alert," Kolknir advised. He started forward again, still gripping his rifle.

"My senses are alert," Lucas muttered, holstering his pistols and falling into step beside his mentor.

"You're distracted," said Kolknir. "If it continues, you will die. The Lady has little patience for repeated failure." He spoke almost pleasantly.

"This time, if I fail, you fail," said Lucas, noting that they were nearing their destination. He wished they could have ridden hov bikes to Keldor's door.

"Which is why you will not fail this time," Kolknir assured him. "But I cannot hold your hand on every mission. You had better shake off whatever has wrapped around your mind."

"It's nothing," Lucas insisted. A search of his feelings proved him a liar, but he forced the irritation aside.

You're pathetic. She's moved on.

His thoughts froze on the last three words. He wondered at his inability to do the same. His love for Reia Antellio had never even been fully realized.

"Focus," Kolknir snapped.

Lucas shivered and forced himself to concentrate. Channeling his frustration, he kicked the door. It flew open and banged against the wall.

"Try the handle next time," Kolknir said.

Lucas ignored him and stepped into the cozy front hallway. Signs of a female presence were everywhere. Wildflowers arranged in simple vases added bright spots of color. Scented candles filled the air with the pointed, yet pleasant, fragrance of kintral trees. Baskets of varying sizes were stashed in nearly every conceivable space, holding everything from clothes to wood to drying ira petals. Lucas wondered what the rest of the house looked like if all that was packed into the first hall.

He was just about to ask which direction they should search when a female voice spoke from the darkness beyond the candlelight.

"Leave my home." Her voice held enough command that Lucas suspected she had something to emphasize her order.

"Where is Ariman?" asked Kolknir, shifting his rifle toward the voice.

"I haven't seen him for months," said the woman with enough bitterness to lend credence to her statement. "I've barely seen him since the Alliance formed. What makes you think he'd come back now?"

To protect you, Lucas thought as his danger senses flared.

He snatched up one of his pistols and threw his body toward the left wall just as Kolknir fired several shots into the darkness above the woman's head.

She screamed.

Something heavy dropped to the ground. Light flooded the hall from glowpanels built into the walls and ceiling.

Lucas squinted into the glare.

The woman screamed again, a cry of anguish and disbelief this time. She knelt beside Ariman Keldor and threw herself across his chest, sobbing.

Kolknir reached over and plucked a kerlak pistol from the holster tucked in the small of Lucas's back. Then, he calmly shot the weeping woman twice. Both blue stun beams slammed into her right shoulder. A sharp cry from the woman was answered by a groan from the man on the floor. Kolknir returned Lucas's pistol and walked to where the woman still lay atop her husband. He rolled her off, gripped the man by the shoulders, and hauled him into the hallway.

Each of Kolknir's moves tonight had been marked by swiftness and decisiveness. Lucas sighed, feeling silly with his serlak pistol raised in the air.

I guess I do have a lot to learn yet.

Kolknir knelt beside the man and checked his wounds.

Meanwhile, Lucas searched the small house to make sure they were truly alone. He returned as Kolknir administered a stimulant shot. The man gasped as the stimulant temporarily held off death. A visual assessment said it would not work for long.

Most men would be dead already.

Two holes in the man's chest, one near his left shoulder and the other a little lower but on the right side, formed pools of blood steadily working their way toward each other.

"Your … mission done," the man said haltingly. "Don't … hurt—"

"We're not here to kill your wife, Ariman," Kolknir assured him. "The Lady sends her regrets and asks why you betrayed her."

The man shook his head.

Kolknir looked up at Lucas and nodded toward the woman's still form.

Understanding his meaning and eager to be of some use, Lucas contemplated the best way to accomplish his new task. Though short, the woman looked solidly built. Lucas collected a stimulant shot from the case Kolknir had left open on the floor and stuck it in the top part of the woman's right arm. He returned the spent dispenser to the case and closed it. Then, he stepped over the groggy woman, knelt behind her, and pulled her up to a kneeling position so her husband could see her face. He considered adding a dagger to the picture but both his hands were occupied propping the woman up.

"Give me an answer, or we will have to question your wife," Kolknir said.

"She … doesn't know," Ariman protested. His voice sounded weaker than before.

"For his father," answered the woman.

Ariman grunted but nodded.

"Revenge," he confirmed, his voice fading even further.

Kolknir glared down in disgust.

"You are a fool, Ariman Keldor, and you deserve your fate. I should kill your wife here in front of you just to make your last moments as miserable as possible."

Lucas agreed. He didn't know the details, but he knew Keldor had endangered one of the Lady's recent plans. It had something to do with the Colored Crossblades Tournament accident, but Lucas had not been privy to the original plan. Therefore, he remained uncertain as to how Keldor had caused the plan to go awry.

"Kezem ... is ... Mal—" Death cut off the rest of Ariman Keldor's words.

"Ah," said Kolknir, as if Keldor's last words explained everything.

The woman's soft sobs held off the silence that tried to fall.

"What did he mean?" Lucas studied his mentor intently.

"He knew," answered Kolknir. "I wonder that the Lady did not tell us he knew."

Knew what? Lucas glared the question at Kolknir.

The woman fought his grasp suddenly.

Lucas held on for a few seconds, but eventually, he let the woman struggle free and stood up.

"He knew Maledek's real identity. He also knew the Lady," explained Kolknir.

"Why does that matter?" Lucas asked. "I know. You know. I'm sure a lot of people know."

Kolknir shook his head.

"Only a privileged few had access to that knowledge. It matters because it explains the Lady's anger."

A sniffling noise drew Lucas's attention to the floor where the woman clutched at her husband's bloody shirt and wept.

Lucas cocked a questioning eyebrow at Kolknir.

His mentor spared only a glance at the woman before he picked up his case of stimulant shots.

"Leave her," he said.

Chapter 37:
Healer's Return

Pirua (September) 5, 1539
Same Day
King Terosh's Private Chambers, Royal Palace, City of Rammon

Dr. Ezzai Dentelich finished his examination of King Terosh Minstel. The burns, bruises, and cuts decorating the king's body had largely disappeared. Though it pained Ezzai to admit it, he knew nothing he had done could account for the rapid healing.

The queen's words sounded in Dentelich's mind.

Members of the Royal House have access to power most people do not.

Her words troubled Dentelich for several reasons. Needing to think, he sat down on the chair he had set up to keep vigil beside the king. His scientific mind was simultaneously intrigued and vexed by not knowing how she intended to heal the king. If he could convince her to let him understand, perhaps he could find a way to utilize the power without compromising the secrets. He shook his head, amazed to find himself accepting the queen's strange healing powers as legitimate science. Not long ago, he would have fought fiercely to defend the purity of conventional medicine.

A thought struck him, and he gasped. Sitting bolt upright, Dentelich pressed his fingertips to the sides of his temple to concentrate. Besides Queen Kila and now Terosh, Dentelich rarely ever treated members of the royal family. Years ago, when he had been young and eager to impress his mentor, Dentelich had pored over the palace's medical records. With close to a thousand regular staff and about half that number in Royal Guards and security officers plus any current guests, Dentelich and his staff kept very busy.

He searched his mind for actual encounters with the royals and recalled about half a dozen occurrences throughout his term as head physician. One of them was a birth. He frowned, remembering the scandal surrounding Prince Taytron's birth. As per Gardanian custom, the queen had confined herself to quarters throughout her term, refusing all medical aid except that rendered by her personal maidens.

King Teorn had protested so strongly that the queen had acquiesced to Reshner customs by Terosh's birth. Besides that, Taytron broke his left arm and right leg on separate occasions, Terosh punched through a glass window, Kila had been poisoned, and Teorn had been depressed when she died. Dentelich did not count the last incident as his case because he had turned it over to Dr. Briella Ender.

Taytron walked on that leg far too soon, and there wasn't enough blood around Terosh and the broken window. Both realizations made Dentelich's stomach lurch. *What else have I missed?*

Before his thoughts could spin toward panic, the sound of the inner door opening interrupted Dentelich. He dropped his hands to his sides and stood hastily as the queen entered the room trailed by her sister. The Ranger wore simple black pants, black boots, a white blouse, and a blue and black travel cloak that fell to her waist. Something about her looked different. She was halfway across the room before Dentelich realized she wore no weapon. A Ranger without a banistick seemed as awkward as a cook with no food.

The queen wore a black cloak that engulfed her body from the neck down. The cowl framed her face as she entered, but she threw it off as she approached Terosh's bed. Then, slowly, her left hand appeared from under the cloak, reached up, and unfastened the clasp holding the cloak together beneath her chin. With practiced ease, she swung the cloak off, rolled it into a bundle, and placed it on the foot of the bed. The cloak's removal revealed a simple purple night dress.

Dentelich's cheeks flamed as his breath caught in his throat. Before the king's accident, he had hardly seen the queen in anything but an elegant gown or a combat training outfit. During the two days she had slept straight through, the servants had clothed her in loose pants and a long-sleeved nightshirt. He had never seen her like this. The thin straps revealed gentle, sloping shoulders connected to thin, toned arms which bore a few faint scars.

"I thought it best to save someone the trouble of changing me should this healing venture have similar results to the last time," said Queen Reia. Her eyes lowered. "I apologize if I'm making you uncomfortable, Doctor."

Her words brought Dentelich back to his senses. He drew his shoulders back like a soldier coming to attention.

"No apology necessary, Your Majesty. I am thankful for the opportunity to witness this … momentous event." He searched for the proper term.

"Healing," supplied the Ranger.

Dentelich flinched, wondering how he had not noticed her standing right next to him. He cast a questioning look her way.

"I am here to translate for you, Doctor," said the Ranger, looking at King Terosh's still form. Her voice was low and calm. "You may call me Kiata. I have no need for titles. Tonight, I am not here as a Ranger, merely a guide."

Ah, that is why she bears no weapons.

"If you are to be my guide, then please call me Ezzai," said Dr. Dentelich. "Tonight, I am not a doctor, merely an observer."

Kiata smiled as he mimicked her phrasing. She turned her attention back to the bed and nodded.

"She is almost ready to begin. We should retreat to avoid disturbing her."

When they reached the windows, Kiata motioned for Dentelich to be seated then settled onto the wide cushion nestled beneath the window with the clearest view of the bed.

Dentelich watched as the queen climbed up onto the bed and crawled over to the king's still form. Kneeling beside the king, she leaned over and ran her left hand down the side of his cheek twice. The glowlamp set beside King Terosh's head presented her somber expression in stark detail.

"To honor tradition, she prepared a song for him," Kiata whispered. "Healing is a gift given to very few. No matter what our Council says, she will always be a Healer and a Ranger."

Dentelich's heart lurched as the queen's voice floated to him.

"Shelsuoresfet abriesepalasu," sang the queen. (Shell-soo-ore-ez-fet ah-bri-eh-say-pal-la-soo)

"Should your ears fail to bear these words to you," said Kiata.

The song continued with the queen singing a line and pausing while her sister translated.

Queen: "Sansemasuspira." (Sahn-say-mah-soo-spy-ear-ah)

Ranger: "Feel them with your spirit."

Queen: "Peremscritonsuelstom." (Pear-rehm-screet-on-soo-el-stowm)

Ranger: "Let them write upon your heart."

Queen: "Peremlevesusalua alieucongrasi." (Pear-rehm-lev-eh-soos-ah-loo-ah ah-lie-oo-con-grah-see)

Ranger: "Let them carry your soul to a place of safety."

The queen shifted her knees to one side so she could sit closer to the king and face him. She picked up his left hand, clasped it tightly for two seconds, drew it to her lips, and kissed it. Then, resting her left cheek on the back of his hand, she continued, "Idesuon mekeroesus." (Ee-day-soo-on may-care-oh-ee-soos)

Ranger: "I told you once my love is yours."

Queen: "Prasuoramantomoa." (Prah-soo-ore-ah-man-toh-moh-ah)

Ranger: "May you hear it many more."

Queen: "Difetesasehsuliese." (Dee-fet-ez-ah-say-soo-lie-esse)

Ranger: "Hard as it is to see you like this."

Queen: "Cremploraidesicry." (Crem-plore-ray-day-see-cry)

Ranger: "Please believe me when I say."

Queen: "Kerosimsusninqwirmessecam." (Care-oh-seem-soos-nen-qwhere-eh-say-cam)

Ranger: "A love like ours cannot be conquered this way."

The queen lifted her head off her husband's hand. Next, she returned the hand to its resting place across his stomach. Then, she maneuvered her knees close to her chest and folded her hands around the left one, so she could hold the position. Her head slumped down in a gesture of grief, and when she sang again, Dentelich had to strain to hear her.

Queen: "Selvafelshelsupertosovali." (Sell-va-fell-shell-soo-pear-toe-so-val-ee)

Ranger: "Part of me feels, should you perish so would I."

Queen: "Efnonencorponamin." (Ef-noh-nen-corp-oh-nah-min)

Ranger: "If not in body then in mind."

Queen: "Etoiknoivalirencresonta." (Et-toe-ee-know-ee-valley-rain-cray-son-tah)

Ranger: "Yet I know I would go on living."

Queen: "Jusalevteparosucompleame." (Joo-sah-lev-tay-par-oh-soo-com-play-ah-meh)

Ranger: "Just to carry the part of you at one with me."

The queen's voice subtly changed, becoming stronger and more determined.

Queen: "Ehvikerohatotpuntier." (Eh-vie-care-oh-ha-tot-poon-tie-eh)

Ranger: "If ever love had any power."

Queen: "Praetonsufietahiasu." (Pray-ton-soo-fie-et-ah-ee-ah-soo)

Ranger: "May it be enough to heal you."

Queen: "Idesuon mekeroesus." (Ee-day-soo-on may-care-oh-ee-soos)

Ranger: "I told you once my love is yours."

Queen: "Prasuoramantomoa." (Prah-soo-ore-ah-man-toh-moh-ah)

Ranger: "May you hear it many more."

The queen held the last note until her sister's quiet translation had finished. Then, she repeated the song in the common tongue.

Dentelich had found it touching the first time through, even with the translation pauses, but the second time made his eyes sting. It presented the desire to heal and strengthened it with the underlying promise to go to great lengths to succeed.

"Now, she will draw the poison out of him," Kiata explained.

"How long will it take?" asked Dentelich, watching with interest as the queen climbed off the end of the bed and walked around to the chair set up next to the bed.

Pulling the chair closer, Queen Reia sat down and placed her left hand high on the king's chest and her right hand on his stomach, just above his folded hands. Body tense, the queen leaned forward and bowed her head as if resisting the urge to pull her hands away.

Dentelich took two swift steps forward before the Ranger pulled him to a halt.

"I don't know how long it will take," Kiata said, speaking rapidly. Her clipped tone and strong grip said she was holding a lot of emotion at bay. "It could be minutes; it could be hours. We will know when she's done." She released her hold on Dentelich's shoulder but looked ready to stop him again if he moved to interrupt the healing.

"How? What is she doing?" The need to do something helpful made Dentelich's questions come out harsher than intended.

"She said she will rest when she finishes," Kiata answered, appearing equally as frustrated. She spun away from him. "As for what she is doing, you know about as much as I, Doctor. Our role is to tend to her when she finally rests."

The bitterness in her voice stunned Dentelich.

"You disapprove," he said when the ability to speak returned.

"I disapprove," Kiata agreed with a nod. She took a position beside the chair where the queen sat and knelt. "I hate seeing her like this, and I hate waiting and wondering whether or not a healing like this will kill her."

"Surely, it cannot be that dangerous," Dentelich protested. He waited for her to agree. When no agreement was forthcoming, he stepped forward again. "We should stop her at once! We cannot lose them both!"

Kiata intercepted him again, this time by stepping into his path.

"We will not lose them both," she promised.

"How can—"

"She is taking the poison out of him. If anything, I worry more for her than him. She knows exactly what he means to the people." The Ranger looked very near tears.

Words twisted around in Dentelich's stomach.

Would she trade her life for his?

Dentelich did not know much about the queen, but what little he had observed told him she would.

They watched in silent agony as Queen Reia held her position. When Dentelich could stand it no more he paced the wide bed chamber. He lost count of the times he crossed and re-crossed the room. His legs ached as much from the tension as from the unexpected exercise. Watching the Ranger woman stand vigil to the right of and a little behind the queen did not help Dentelich's nerves.

How can she stand to stay still so long?

Dentelich quickened his pace unconsciously trying to balance the Ranger's inactivity.

"It is done for the day," Kiata declared at last.

Dentelich turned so fast he nearly pulled something in his back. His eyes immediately fell upon the queen who lay draped over the king's body with her head resting between her hands. The sight touched him. They looked so terribly young.

Our hopes rest on them.

Dentelich might have wept if he knew how many days he would witness a healing battle fought for his king's life. He could have delegated the duty of watching, but he learned much by seeing the queen work and listening to her address the king's still form. It did not take long for his admiration to morph into genuine affection.

When the king finally shed his unnatural sleep a few months later, Dentelich had more to do to get his charge fully healed. Even with the queen's faithful ministrations and Dentelich's finest work, King Terosh's health remained fragile for several years.

Chapter 38:
Save the Queen

Pirua (September) 6, 1539
The Lady's Estate, Kala Mountains

"Welcome back," said a rich, female voice from behind.

Nera Tarpon stiffened and reached for her kerlinblade. She stopped just short of drawing the blade but let her hand rest a second upon the hilt.

"Lord Kezem said you had studies of a different sort for me to attend to," said Nera, turning to face Lady Mavis.

"To succeed in your mission, you must study the queen," said Lady Mavis.

"To what end?" asked Nera. Her heart fluttered. After all this time, she still could not fathom why Lady Mavis had chosen to train her.

"To become her for a short time," answered Lady Mavis. "Come with me, and I shall explain."

The flutter in Nera's heart turned to a frantic pounding as she followed Lady Mavis out of the waiting room and through several long halls in the labyrinth that was the Lady's lair. Nera resisted the urge to skip with girlish delight. She had always loved exploring new places. As a child, she had driven her mother and the servants mad looking for her.

As Nera began wondering when they would reach their destination, Lady Mavis stopped and ushered her into a room filled with three wide vidscreens, a few hologram projectors, two vidrecorders, several comfortable chairs, and a very strange floor. The far side of the room had simple, smooth wooden floorboards, but the rest of the room was a patchwork of small squares featuring every sort of walking surface from loose sand to hard-packed dirt to fresh grass. Nera took two cautious steps into the room and stopped.

"Here, you will learn to walk as the queen does," said Lady Mavis. "There's a control panel that will allow you to simulate nearly any terrain. Dennel will instruct you in its use later. The vidscreens can show you many hours of the queen walking to or from some function. Eventually, you will record your work and compare your gait to the queen's."

"Why is it so important to master how she walks, my Lady?" asked

Nera.

"It is of no greater or lesser importance than learning how she speaks or dines, but success depends on mastering everything," said Lady Mavis.

"But why must I pretend to be the queen?" asked Nera.

Lady Mavis glided past Nera to the desk holding a lot of the recording equipment. There she reached down and pressed some buttons Nera could not see. The door swung shut with a click of heavy-sounding locks.

"You must pretend to be the queen to save her," said Lady Mavis without turning.

"What threatens her? Why did you choose me? What can I do?" Nera was about to spew more questions, but Lady Mavis halted her with a delicate gesture. Strange anxiety made Nera's fingers twitch to hold her kerlinblade.

"You are perfectly safe here," said Lady Mavis, sounding slightly weary. She turned and swept her eyes over Nera from head to foot. "My reasons for choosing you are many and varied, not the least of them is that I believe you can accomplish the ends I seek. Your physical build is a close match for our queen, and you possess a spirit conducive to learning new skills."

Nera still felt lost.

"What are we fighting for, my Lady? You keep saying we shall save the queen, but I know your heart is not truly committed to that end." Nera paused as thoughts coalesced in her mind. "I do not believe saving her is your end at all, so when does the end come? When may I return home?" The last question surprised her for it conjured a mixture of strong emotions. She missed her husband, but she enjoyed the challenge of this new life. Having seen and done so many terrible and wonderful things, she could never simply return to her life as Lady Tarpon, wife of Brook.

"Rescuing the queen from this current threat may not be my ultimate end, but that is indeed your end. Once you finish, you may go with my blessing," said Lady Mavis. "Like my reasons for choosing you for this task, my motivations concerning the queen's welfare vary. You know what you need to know and must trust me on the rest. For now, I bid you study well and lay other thoughts aside." She executed a graceful turn and again pressed some buttons.

Nera heard the locks snap open and felt her heart jump with more inexplicable fear.

Chapter 39:
Awakening

Lanolin (February) 13, 1540
King Terosh's Private Chambers, Royal Palace, City of Rammon
The darkness lightened.

A familiar voice reached down through the remaining darkness.

"Terosh, I know you're awake," said Reia. "The anotechs told me as much. Please open your eyes and drink. I want to hear your voice. I'm getting tired of talking to myself."

It took tremendous effort, but Terosh finally gathered enough strength to force his eyes open. The sight of Reia leaning over him took some of the meager breath left to him. Her soft hands brushed his cheeks, chin, and neck. Her left hand settled over his heart and fresh anotechs flooded into him, restoring a sense of energy and vitality. Relieved tears streaked her face, but a brilliant smile lent her a beauty that no tears could diminish.

"Don't even think about rising," said Reia. She dashed some tears away. "A newborn kyrie chick could knock you flat with a look. You've slept over five months."

Five months?

Her hand left his chest, and soon, he found a waterbag spout between his lips. Cool water poured slowly down his throat. He gulped it down as quickly as possible.

"Take it slowly," Reia said, easing the bag back so the water gently trickled. "The anotechs kept you in good repair, but you've had nothing but Dr. Dentelich's nutrient injections for a long time."

Terosh drank his fill and rested his head back against the pillow. His body tried to drag him down to sleep again, but his mind fought for consciousness. The effort left him short of breath. He closed his eyes.

"What did I miss?" he asked.

Reia's gentle laughter wrapped around his sinking consciousness and held him fast. She picked up his left arm and moved it aside then curled into the space created.

"You do realize this is going to take a long time, right?"

"Hope so," Terosh murmured. Despite the high energy cost, Terosh

476

curled his left arm up to draw his wife closer. He had missed feeling her for five whole months and come close to never laying eyes on her again. He wasn't about to let another moment be wasted.

Once settled, Reia sighed.

"Let's see. While you slept, Fort Savad suffered some structural damage from a windstorm. We received enough sympathetic messages to nearly crash the network. The Huz Mon salt mines had a riot. A maw was reported on the Kevloth Plains, but thankfully, no one was hurt. The Morden Lowlands flooded. Mount Kelleth had a minor eruption, covering Korch and its surrounding villages with ash. GAPP delivered a few more sweetly worded threats not to interfere in the Rorge System. Kiata and Todd left a couple of days ago to undergo a ceremony so they can have a child. Oh, and I politely declined at least three marriage invitations."

Terosh stiffened.

"Marriage invitations?"

Reia's laughter vibrate pleasantly against his side as she tightened her one-armed embrace.

"Yes, it seems if you were conveniently gone, Reshner could forge strong alliances with Benata, Riab, or Praxitti VII," Reia said matter-of-factly. She nestled her head to a slightly different position on Terosh's shoulder. Her voice softened. "I could have had an emperor, a sultan, or a high king. Call me selfish, but I think I'll keep the king I've got."

***

Lanolin (February) 14, 1540-Jira (March) 1, 1542
Royal Palace, City of Rammon

One would think the healing process would have sped up once King Terosh regained consciousness, but it took over a year to fully purge the poison. About that time, he took to reading Senate and Governors Council reports and making some of the decisions necessary to run the government. Over the next year or so, his body slowly regained most of the strength lost during the months of inactivity.

Terosh could not know how fierce the battle would be inside his body as the Linonos and Dalonos—light and dark anotechs—fought for him. Although the Dark Ones knew they could not kill him, they kept him weak.

For her part, Lady Mavis Altran spent the anxious months of Kezem's recovery, arranging things for the final stages of her grand plan. As Terosh slowly mended, countless days passed while Mavis struggled to stick to her plans. It would have been simplicity itself to assassinate Reia and Terosh, especially with the anotechs subduing him, but the king and queen had a key role to play in other plans.

Chapter 40:
Return of the Restler Raiders

Jira (March) 2, 1542
The Lady's Estate, Kala Mountains

Shadow Guard Nolan Demilak had proven himself invaluable time and again. Mavis replayed his message twice to let the good news settle fully upon her. In the privacy of her office, she indulged in a gesture of profound relief by placing her hands over her heart. Her fingertips brushed the pendant bearing the symbol of her father's house. She tipped it up to examine. Its smooth metal soothed her by reminding her why she had spent most of her life planning to destroy the Minstel name.

Kezem will leave Gardan within the week.

The message repeated countless times in her mind and heart. To her dismay, she felt tears prickling her eyes. The depths of her relief surprised her. She had not realized how much she longed for Kezem's return. Mitrek's cowardly flight to an unknown planet hurt more than she wanted to admit. Eldon and his family still resided in Idonia, but as expected, he had withdrawn emotionally, hiding behind his work.

It is time.

The three small words thrilled her. Mavis snatched up her comm and called Dennel. They had a lot of calls to make. The next phase needed to be executed with precise timing to provide a diversion.

Within minutes, Kolknir's hologram appeared before Mavis.

"Is Lucas with you?" Mavis asked, before Kolknir could bother with greetings.

"I am," said Lucas, stepping into view.

"What are your orders?" queried Kolknir.

"It is time to move against the Restler-Tarpon Alliance," Mavis announced. "Dennel will send you instructions. Kolknir, you will strike at the Tarpons while Lucas harries the Restlers. Remember, I want them scattered and broken, but no names must be released until the time is right! Many of the key people will need to be eliminated, but leave the lower ranks alone. My son will have need of them one day. Turn those you can and kill whomever you must, except Brook Tarpon and Merisia Restler. I have further need of them."

"As you wish," said Lucas.

"Yes, my Lady," said Kolknir a half-second later.

Mavis ended the communication.

Now, we shall see if all those visits to Terosh's bedside were worth it.

With a giddiness she'd not felt in years, Mavis went to find Nera Tarpon. The young woman would need to be put in isolation. Despite her orders, Mavis did not trust that no names would be leaked. If necessary, Brook Tarpon and his sister, Merisia, would persuade Nera to continue with the plan, but Mavis really wanted to avoid that kind of persuasion. Her plan would work best if Nera Tarpon believed in the cause.

***

Jira (March) 4, 1542
Restler Estate, City of Meritab

Life had not been particularly kind to Merisia Restler. Even as she gazed upon the peaceful face of her infant son, she wondered what her unborn daughter would have been like had she survived the fight at the Deegan Estate. The familiar ache of guilt wormed its way through Merisia's chest.

I'm sorry, her mind cried to both children.

She longed to turn back time. Had she known the cost, she would never have run away. She also wished her scarred heart knew how to truly love this little life before her.

What sort of man will you be, Daniel Restler?

Her thoughts flooded with terrifying images. She imagined Daniel as a boy catching frogs and mice as she once had with Talyon Keldor. The image smiled sweetly and lifted up a squirming frog. The scene gave her peace until the boy tripped and fell headlong into the shallow stream. Pure, impotent fear and rage nearly burst her heart as she watched him slowly drown. Next, she saw him as a young man wounded through the side with a kerlinblade, slowing bleeding to death. Finally, he was a grown man, looking just like Gareth, glaring down at her in arrogant disapproval.

She could almost hear him say, *"You let my sister die!"*

Merisia burst into tears and dropped to her knees by Daniel's crib. The noise woke him, and he cried. Standing, Merisia leaned over the crib.

"I'm sorry!" she said, rubbing a trembling hand across the baby's chest and stomach. Tears poured out of her and rained down on Daniel. He fussed some more. "I'm sorry," she whispered again, trying to turn her head away and let the tears fall elsewhere.

"Don't be," said a male voice behind her.

Too stunned to scream and almost too tired to care, Merisia slowly turned to face the man. Daniel wailed but her heart numbed to the plaintive cry. Feeling faint, she braced herself against her son's crib. Strangely, the kerlak pistol leveled at her chest had a calming effect on her. She sniffled and wiped at some tears, wishing she could conjure enough emotion to be upset.

"My apologies, Lady Restler. Please make no sudden moves," said the man. "I did not bring a pair of stuncuffs for you, and I have business to conduct with your husband. He should be along in a moment."

"Kill me," Merisia dared. It took three seconds to recognize the hoarse, desperate voice as her own. She remembered saying the very same thing to Talyon Keldor and prayed he was somewhere safe. Gareth and his henchmen could tell her a hundred times that he died, but she knew Taly was alive.

Before the man could respond, a commotion in the hallway caught Merisia's attention. A few muffled curses and a thump sounded. Then the door flew open and three men burst into the baby's room. Gareth stood between two men with thick stuncuffs covering his forearms. To Merisia's surprise, her heart lurched with sympathy.

"I demand to know—" Gareth began. His protest turned to a pained grunt when the men holding him each kicked a knee and put pressure on his shoulders.

Merisia glared at the two men and received a second shock. The man holding Gareth's right shoulder refused to meet her eyes, but she knew him. Merisia gasped and stared, dumbfounded.

Nobody spoke.

"Hello, Meri," greeted the familiar man.

She drew short breaths, but none of them gave her enough air to speak.

"It's not what you think," said the lead man kindly.

If he'd not pointed a gun at her, Merisia might even have believed he cared.

"What should I think?" she asked.

The man on Gareth's right snapped his head up, finally meeting her gaze.

"I'm here to protect you," said her brother.

"You can imagine why I'm having some trouble believing you, Alden, a lot of trouble actually," said Merisia.

"I can vouch for him," said the leader. He braced the gun against the crib's railing. "The RT Alliance is failing. Alden chose the right side and wanted to make certain you do as well, Lady Merisia."

"We are an alliance of legitimate businesses," Gareth said.

"You are an alliance of thieves and thugs," responded the lead intruder.

Gareth laughed sharply.

"That's interesting from a man threatening my wife and son! Who are you? Who sent you? What do they want?"

The attacker laughed mirthlessly.

"We want justice, Master Restler," said the attacker. His kerlak pistol darted away from Merisia's chest and sent a brilliant red beam toward the child.

"No!" cried Merisia and Gareth.

Unaware of her actions, Merisia threw herself at the man, pushing him back a few steps. Her limbs flailed and her fingers sought blood from any part of the man she could reach. One nail caught the vile man just below his left eye. He screamed. The sound of shattering glass struck Merisia at the same time burning pain engulfed her stomach and sharp pain exploded from her head. Neither pain could match that gushing from her heart. She welcomed darkness.

***

Jira (March) 4, 1542
Same Day
Tarpon Estate, City of Kalmata

Kolknir hoped Lucas finished his mission well. The man had sounded truly distraught when he checked in, but at least he'd included adequate vid footage to convince Brook Tarpon not to be an idiot.

"Good evening, Master Tarpon," Kolknir greeted entering Brook's office.

"Who are you?" Brook demanded, right hand sliding under his desk.

"I am a servant of the Lady. She requires your presence and sent me to fetch you. Will you come peaceably?"

"What does she want with me?" asked Brook. "She already has my wife."

"It is not my place to question the Lady's will, neither is it yours. I ask again, will you come peaceably?"

"No," answered Brook, his features hardening.

Kolknir waited, wishing the man would hurry up and use that pathetic gun under his desk. With a shrug, Kolknir tossed his infopad onto Brook's desk.

"You're welcomed to verify those images if you like."

Brook reluctantly picked up the infopad and flipped through the images. His lips pressed tightly together, and his eyes flashed with anger.

"What makes you think I care?" he spat. "The brat probably deserves whatever you have in store for her."

Kolknir raised both eyebrows. He had never known the Lady to misjudge a situation, but if Brook truly did not care about his little sister then Kolknir would have to deal with him the hard way. Kolknir met Brook's glare until the man looked away, and in that moment, Kolknir understood. Brook truly cared. He just did not wish to let Kolknir hold the knowledge over him.

"That's not a very brotherly thing to say," Kolknir scolded. "And I can tell you care because you look queasy. Don't worry; she's perfectly safe with my men. Your brother is watching over her."

"Why would Alden help you?" Brook asked.

"He helps for the same reason you will—to save your dear sister from something worse than death." Kolknir didn't know what that would be, but he figured Brook would fill in the gaps as he liked. He couldn't permanently harm Merisia if he wanted to since the Lady wanted her alive, but Brook did not know that. Seeing Brook consider going for the gun, Kolknir added, "Leave it. You don't want to test me."

Brook leaned back in his chair looking resigned.

"Where are we going?"

***

Jira (March) 4, 1542
Same Day
City of Meritab

Gareth Restler wandered the dark streets. Several shady beings started to approach him, but one look at his expression made them back away. He should be dead. His wife and son were dead. Things had not always been smooth with Merisia, but they had grown closer in the last few years. She might not have been perfect, but their son certainly did not deserve to be shot in his crib. Gareth wanted to fight something; perhaps killing would assuage his grief.

He had sought refuge in a friend's tavern where he watched story after story of strange attacks unfold. Reporters glowed with excitement as one RT Alliance safe house and estate after another fell under attack.

Gareth did not know which stories told whole truths, which told half-truths, and which contained no truth, but he knew for certain the Alliance was no more. His heart shattered to little sharp shards. He melted them in the fires of his anger, knowing eventually they would crystallize into something unbreakable.

Chapter 41:
Subdue and Switch

Jira (March) 6, 1542
Upper East Library to King Terosh's Private Chambers, Royal Palace, City of Rammon

"Pardon me, Your Majesty," said Aster Captain Surd Antar. "Lady Mavis Altran has arrived to visit with the king. She is with him now."

The usual mixed feelings fluttered through Reia as she put down *To Conquer the Sea: A History of Osem*. While grateful Terosh's eccentric aunt visited him often, she could not help feeling some resentment. Some warning would have been nice so Reia could arrange a proper welcome and give the impression she knew what transpired in her own home.

Thanking Captain Antar, Reia dashed from the room, her bare feet slapping the polished floors. Midway to her destination, Reia halted and considered whether or not she should change. Since no important meeting or audience had been scheduled, Reia wore only plain white pants and a light blue shirt with silver patches artfully arranged across the neck and down both sleeves. In an effort to remove herself from the palace trappings, she had left both weapons and jewelry in her room.

Antar would throw a fit if he knew her loose sleeves held neither the miniature kerlak pistol nor a tiny dagger in a sheath. Her training had been too thorough for her to simply forget them, but she felt reasonably secure in the palace. She paused to consider what Lady Mavis would think of her casual attire and lack of queenly accoutrements. Reia soon decided she didn't really care. Her pride minded a great deal, but since she tried not to indulge that less-than-admirable emotion, she would leave the judgment up to Lady Mavis.

Inner equilibrium restored, Reia finished her journey to Terosh's private chambers at a respectable pace. She quietly greeted the two Royal Guards flanking the door. They saluted her in unison and the one nearest the control panel immediately pressed the button to open the door. Reia hesitated the necessary second for the door to finish swinging aside.

They looked awfully serious, almost grim, Reia thought once she was three steps into the outer room.

Dismissing the thought, she strode toward the main bedchamber. Upon entering the middle room, Reia heard the sound dampers activating. She crossed the room in a few quick steps and reached for the door's control panel. The door opened before she touched the panel.

At first, she saw nothing unusual. Terosh sat up with a pillow propped behind him and the covers tucked neatly around him. A figure Reia assumed must be Lady Mavis stood next to the bed. A heavy maroon cloak with a deep cowl hid most of the figure's body. One look at Terosh's pale face and furious expression stopped Reia cold with one foot across the threshold. She had expected the pale part, but the fury surprised her. Terosh ranked among the most even tempered, affable men she knew. She had never seen him this angry. The dark emotion thickened the air.

"Welcome, Your Grace. I trust you know my companions," said Lady Mavis. She waved gracefully at the space to Reia's right.

Heart nearly freezing in her chest, Reia stumbled forward two steps. When her heart started beating again, it pounded on her ribs painfully. Her throat constricted and her hands instinctively searched her waist for a banistick. Even after a few years, her fingers ached to hold a Ranger weapon. Conflicting impulses warred for control. One impulse told her to whirl and flee while the other bid her to comfort Terosh. She did neither. Instead, she looked where the woman indicated.

"You'll have to forgive me for the theatrics," Lady Mavis said, affecting a humble tone. She removed her hood, revealing the intensity in her blue eyes.

Three figures lined the wall. They wore black cloaks with deep hoods. The two farthest away moved to where Reia could see them better. After a two-second pause, the figures reached up and removed their hoods.

"This is not right!" Terosh protested. "What use is it to bring up her past?"

"That is not my intent," Mavis said. Her silky voice slid over Reia's senses.

Feeling cold and dizzy, Reia regarded the three figures. Her mind numbly spoke the names as if that would make them less like a living nightmare.

Kolknir, Lucas, Nera.

The first two fit the role of haunting specter very well. Both had entered her life as trusted instructors. Kolknir had quickly destroyed that image, but she had once counted Lucas a friend. Once upon a time, they had even been on the cusp of becoming something more, until Reia realized Lucas's possessive nature would only cause her grief. She wondered how he had come by the angry-looking scratch beneath his left eye. No matter how hard she tried, Reia could not comprehend what Nera's role would be.

Finding her voice at last, Reia whipped her attention back to Lady Mavis.

"I know them." Her eyes searched Mavis's face. "But *why* are they here?"

"Lucas and Kolknir are present to ensure you and Terosh remain cooperative. Nera is here to replace you," Mavis explained casually.

"Aunt Mavis, this is madness. What do you hope to accomplish by it?" Terosh wondered.

Reia hated how tired he sounded.

"Explanations shortly, Terosh dear," Mavis said, patting him lightly on the shoulder. "Do not spend your energy worrying. You have my word that she will not be needlessly harmed."

Needlessly harmed? As in, you might have a legitimate reason to hurt me?

Reia's mind was too busy racing to prompt her to breathe. When something touched her right arm, she gasped and jerked her arm away. Something caught her wrist and pinned it to her left shoulder. Drawing breath to scream, Reia looked at the "something" which turned out to be Lucas. He dropped her hand and stepped away, but a strong arm encircled her throat and a hand slammed against her mouth hard enough to hurt her teeth. Her head snapped back, resting partly on Kolknir's shoulder and partly on his neck.

Helpless but not yet hopeless, Reia jerked forward and screamed. The scream died a muffled death in Kolknir's palm, and the effort to break free only strained her neck. Desperate, Reia bent both knees so Kolknir suddenly bore her full weight, trying to throw him off balance. He must have expected the move because he released her suddenly, planted his hands on her shoulders, and pushed down until she landed hard on her knees.

Next instant, Reia lay flat on the floor with Kolknir's knee digging into her lower back and tingling, fiery pain shooting from her right shoulder. Ignoring the pain, Reia gathered energy to spring free at the first opportunity.

A hand landed gently on her left shoulder and gave a friendly squeeze.

"Stop struggling before you kill him," hissed Lucas.

Against her will, Reia tuned her senses to the things happening around her. She felt Mavis's frustration, Nera's helplessness, and impatience from both Lucas and Kolknir. The impression she received from Terosh combined rage, panic, and intense pain.

She froze. Angry tears slipped out as Reia gritted her teeth, stilled her body, and said two painful words.

"All right."

***

Seeing Terosh's violent reaction to Reia's captivity, Mavis Altran feared she might have miscalculated. The stupid boy was likely to break something vital in his head if he didn't calm down. While her plans might eventually call for his death, the timing mattered a great deal, and right now, she needed him alive. Even with Nera leaning across his shoulders, the wretched boy thrashed violently enough to almost roll free.

This was not how the scene should have panned out. Growling low, Mavis clamped both hands on Terosh's right shoulder and leaned forward.

"Calm down before you kill yourself," she ordered. "So help me, Terosh, if you die now, I will inflict unimaginable horrors on your precious wife!"

Nera gasped and withdrew her hands like she'd been scalded.

Mavis glared a warning at her then returned to staring absolute sincerity into Terosh's eyes.

"I truly intend no harm to you or Reia, but I have plans much grander than both of you," said Mavis, softening her tone. "I will not take kindly to interference."

Terosh sagged, gasping for breath. His fit had carried him halfway down the bed where he lay on his back.

"What do you want with her?" he asked, staring up at Mavis like a wounded puppy.

Mavis sighed as she released his shoulder. She had seen her nephew stoically endure battle after battle against the poison, yet one tiny threat against his wife reduced him to a state just shy of blubbering idiocy.

This sort of sentiment will undo you one day, Terosh, Mavis thought as a pang of sympathy touched her.

She wished things could be different. He reminded her so much of his father, her baby brother. Like Teorn, Terosh had a heart that could abide no pain in others.

"My Lady, the queen is yours to command," Kolknir called.

"Or at least try to control," Lucas said dryly.

Mavis turned, shaking off her reverie.

"Thank you, gentlemen. Bring her here so I may avoid shouting." She waved to the foot of the bed and waited for Kolknir and Lucas to guide Reia to the indicated spot.

Besides casting death glares, the queen seemed to accept her new lot. She wore the stuncuffs with an ease that indicated familiarity. For some reason, Mavis found that upsetting. Aside from having the poor judgment to marry Terosh, the girl struck her as intelligent and innocent, the sort of person easy to love.

Kolknir and Lucas gently lifted Reia and deposited her on the edge next to Terosh's left leg.

Mavis noticed they had bound her ankles as well. The short chain linking the two cuffs allowed for slow walking but would stop her if she tried to run. While the measure seemed excessive, she trusted Kolknir and Lucas knew their business. If she remembered correctly, both men had briefly instructed Reia in Ranger ways. If anyone could predict her capabilities, they could.

"Nera, please have Captain Antar send the message to Gardan," Mavis instructed.

"Captain Antar works for you?" Terosh asked, sounding horrified.

Reia looked equally shocked.

"Many people work for me," Mavis replied. "And you must understand that I can say no more on the matter. What I will explain is that I need you both to remain here for about a week."

"Why?" inquired Reia.

Terosh said nothing, but Mavis could sense his mind frantically working. His breath hitched, and he shut his eyes as if he could not bear the thought.

"No," he said miserably.

"You have piqued my curiosity, Terosh," Mavis admitted. Teorn had often touted Taytron as the swift thinker, but Mavis suspected Terosh was quite capable of solving this little puzzle. "What precisely do you think my plan entails?"

"Grandfather," Terosh said.

Mavis smiled down at him.

"He has ruled Gardan far too long," she said.

"If King Padric Creston is your true target, why bother with us?" Reia wondered.

"My grandfather has wanted you as a captive for years," Terosh explained, shaking his head slowly. "Aunt Mavis intends to give him Nera in your place."

Turning to the young queen, Mavis said, "Do not worry; your part is easy. I need you to stay here within Terosh's chambers until the deed is done."

***

Jira (March) 12, 1542
King Terosh's Private Chambers, Royal Palace, City of Rammon

Terosh wept quietly when Kolknir showed him the vids covering his grandfather's death, trying not to wake Reia. He had feared King Padric and even hated most of what the man stood for, but the burden of foreknowledge weighed heavily upon him.

I could have stopped it!

The anotechs could have warned enough people to get a message to Gardan in time, but Mavis had anticipated such a possibility and issued appropriate threats. Tarnished honor or not, Terosh refused to risk his wife's life. The assassination's success meant that Reia too had believed Mavis's threat and done nothing as well.

The week had been tremendously stressful. They barely ate enough to keep themselves alive. Days passed in quiet conversation or strained silence. Occasionally, one or the other or both would struggle to stand and pace the room for a while. Nights passed side by side yet chained to the bed frame while Lucas or Kolknir grimly stood guard.

Aunt Mavis entered the room, and Terosh wondered if she would kill them now. His expression must have explained his fear.

She gave him the sympathetic smile he'd come to expect.

"And now we will take our leave, Terosh," said his aunt. "How you handle the fallout that will surely come is up to you, but a word of warning before I go: say nothing."

He shot her an incredulous look.

"Telling everybody on this world and the next how vulnerable you are would be extremely foolhardy," Aunt Mavis said earnestly. "You will have aspiring assassins clogging your hallways. You are more than welcome to search for me. Try to bring me to justice if you must, but by all that is holy, do it quietly."

She actually made sense.

Terosh's head ached. He looked to Reia who slumbered beside him then back to his aunt. Relatively assured at last that Mavis truly meant to leave them alive, Terosh cleared his dry throat.

"Before you leave, tell me why. You must have planned this for years. Was it worth it? What did you gain from his death?"

"We are all pieces of a greater camarek game being played, Terosh. That might sound stupid, but one day, you—or perhaps a descendant—will understand." Her expression changed becoming reflective before returning to neutral. "My part is finished for now ... perhaps forever. This is likely the last time we will speak, so I will leave you with these lessons. Never love so much that you cannot lose and live. You are a king. Like it or not, even family must bow before duty."

Terosh felt a needle bite into his arm. He barely had time to groan before a warm darkness descended upon his head and drew him to restful sleep.

Chapter 42:
Records

Jira (March) 22, 1542
The Lady's Estate, Kala Mountains
Back in her lair, Lady Mavis Altran stared down at the report her spies had compiled for her concerning her son and his treatment on Gardan. She'd not moved against King Padric until certain Kezem was finished with the planet.

Pirua (September) 9, 1539: Unconscious male subject arrives from unspecified location off planet. Landing permission granted to automated ship by authority of King Padric Creston. Security clearance level nine required to access any information concerning this case. Subject checked into Panosh Facility under identification #195183. Blood, bone, hair, and muscle samples taken from the subject. Head physician: Dr. Ian Noir. Head scientist: Dr. Tasha Amie.

Pirua (September) 16, 1539: Dr. Noir orders three blood transfusions. Immune suppression necessary. Donors 154322 and 154324 expire; notifications prepared for next of kin. Dr. Amie works with samples acquired from subject to build a stock of friendly blood to work with.

Pirua (September) 23, 1539: Dr. Amie reports adequate stock of subject's blood to attempt first friendly transfusion. Subject responds well but remains unconscious. Dr. Amie adjusts medium subject's blood is grown on.

Lalri (November) 5, 1539: Subject regains consciousness. As per instructions, King Padric informed immediately.

Lalri (November) 19, 1539: Dr. Noir reports subject has

adequate strength to attempt height modification. Surgery delayed. Dr. Amie reports bone growth from subject's samples proceeding slower than projected.

Ferrim (December) 10, 1539: Subject's upper and lower leg bones replaced. Additional sections of enhanced synthetic muscle woven into existing muscle matrix. Height gain upon standing estimated to be 12.64 centimeters.

Ferrim (December) 17, 1539: Subject indicates readiness for additional modifications. Dr. Noir argues that subject needs to recover further first. Dr. Amie reports additional time needed to grow more synthetic muscles.

Idela (January) 1, 1540: Dr. Noir is pleased with subject's physical therapy and agrees to perform arm surgeries if subject can walk down to Dr. Amie's office and back. Subject succeeds but exertion proves too much for his body.

Idela (January) 8, 1540: Subject's right and left arm bones replaced. Additional sections of enhanced synthetic muscle woven into existing muscle matrix. Reach gains estimated to be 6.85 centimeters.

Idela (January) 15, 1540: Subject's left arm develops infection. Dr. Amie takes sample and reports simple bacterial problem. Subject treated with standard antibacterial agents.

Lanolin (February) 13, 1540: Subject's right and left hands injected with bone growth serum.

Jira (March) 4, 1540: Dr. Noir performs surgery to lengthen subject's trunk and broaden subject's shoulders. Dr. Amie reports improvement in bonding time between synthetic and natural muscle.

Jira (March) 11, 1540: Subject still very weak from modifications to trunk and shoulders. Subject reports aching pains throughout modified areas. Dr. Amie takes samples for further study.

Jira (March) 25, 1540: Dr. Amie finds new bacterial strand in subject's sample and treats with modified antibiotic agent.

Enis (April) 9, 1540: Subject begins coordination training.

Enis (April) 16, 1540: Subject begins endurance training.

Retsi (May) 14, 1540: Subject begins building muscle mass. Dr. Amie supervises cautious use of chemical aids.

Zeri (June) 12, 1540: Subject begins training with Shadow Guard Captain Jonas Ri.

Lalri (November) 15, 1540: Subject injured during training exercise. Dr. Noir treats wounds.

Lanolin (February) 28, 1542: Subject indicates desire to return to home planet. Dr. Amie protests. Subject appeals to king.

Jira (March) 5, 1542: Subject checks out of Panosh Facility. Subject returns to single passenger ship. Exit clearance granted by authority of King Padric Creston.

Welcome home, my son. I am eager to see what you have become.

Chapter 43:
Final Gift

Lalri (November) 16, 1542
Karanak Falls, Kala Mountains

Confused and angry, Kezem Altran bellowed a question into the comm clenched tightly in his hand.

"Why?" He could have left the comm on his belt and still carried on the conversation, but he needed to feel its slender casing straining in his strong grip.

Cold wind tore at his dark clothes, ripping through them as if they did not exist. It clawed at his eyes like a cold-hearted beast, freezing tears to death before they could fully form. His modified bones ached which registered as sharp pain in his head. The roaring rumble of rushing water crashed into Kezem's senses, trying to sweep his courage down into the Kala River. Traitorous legs trembled. He knelt beside a large boulder, seeking shelter behind its bulk and peered out at the heavily shrouded figure poised on the cliff's edge.

Not more than ten meters separated them, but Kezem knew he would never reach her in time. He didn't even know if he wanted to reach her. The conflicting emotions left his mind battered. This woman had controlled his life since before he was a thought. Every scrap of knowledge he possessed about manipulating situations and people he owed to her. He'd also tried to kill her several times, and each time, she had survived and turned it into a life lesson. His love and hate roiled about so strongly that they became inextricably linked.

"Why now? Why this way?" Kezem whispered hoarsely.

The figure turned to face him, smiling one of her knowing smiles.

"You have always known the answer to those questions, Kezem." His mother's voice entered the receiver fastened just below her chin, flew through the space separating them, and crawled up through the comm he clutched. "All creatures are simplistic, humans in particular. What makes any human heart beat?" She paused to let him answer. When he said nothing, she said, "Love." Her tone held amusement, irony, and a hint of bitterness.

Love.

The word seared Kezem, burning through his heart.

"You called me here!" he shouted, concentrating hard on forming words. "What do you want of me? Am I not the son you wanted? Have I not learned enough?" The questions surprised and shamed Kezem. They sprang forth from the wounded child within, and he despised them.

Mavis shook her head slowly. She stood taller and lifted her chin imperiously, seemingly oblivious to the wind hurling itself at her. Loose strands of hair and clothing writhed and thrashed under the assault, but Mavis stood rooted to a broad rock that jutted out over the Karanak Falls.

"I want you to accept your destiny."

"Destiny?" Kezem asked, genuinely confused. His shallow breaths sounded loud in his ears.

His mother's proud features softened a trifle.

"You were always the best and brightest of my boys, Kezem." She removed her infopad from an inner pocket. "Mitrek has chosen his path, and I wish him well. He is a selfish fool, but alive and hopefully prospering. If you reject my plea, I will force Eldon to act, but he would be a poor substitute for the sort of leader you could be. If I have raised you right, then you will want this as much as I do."

"You want me to rule." It was more the echo of a shell-shocked heart than a question or a statement. A spark of anger flared. "How? You destroyed most of my informants before I returned."

"Not destroyed, only purged of weakness as your body had to be," answered Mavis. "Complete instructions are here and with Dennel should you lose this." She waved her infopad and flung it at him. "He will find you if necessary."

Kezem instinctively snatched the infopad out of the air before it could crash into his face. It clattered against the comm in his right hand, nearly causing him to drop both.

"That's it? You're just going to leave me some instructions and quit life?"

"Not exactly how I would have phrased it, but yes," said his mother. "I have given you everything. You are finally ready, and the last steps must be taken completely alone." She started to turn away, but hesitated and glanced back at him. "When you finally achieve our goals, find a good woman and settle down." Then, with one more smile, Mavis reached up and unclasped the heavy pendant she had always worn around her neck. Finally, she wrapped it in the chain, kissed it, and threw it at Kezem.

He caught it as she turned her back on him and dove off the cliff.

***

Mavis Altran heard only the first note of her son's anguished cry. It warmed her even as mist off the falls soaked her. Tucking her arms across her chest, she tried to quiet her screaming mind. She hoped the anotechs did their part well, for despite the impression she wished to leave with Kezem, she really wanted to live. Her entire life was wrapped up in that man. She'd finally given him the last gift she could: freedom. Dying before seeing what he would do with it did not fit her plans.

The anotech shield around her made her skin shimmer but did nothing to ward off the terrible cold. Her body sliced through the air like a living scythe. Most of the way, she hurtled headfirst, but a split second before impact, the anotechs managed to flip her. When Mavis's feet struck the water, it felt like she had landed on concrete. Sharp pain shot from both legs up through her stomach and slashed through her brain in an instant.

She gasped a great lungful of icy water and experienced all the horror of drowning. Then, peace descended on her mind, and she felt nothing of the cold or pain. She floated deep below the Karanak Falls at the foot of the Kala Mountains. Mavis had just enough time to realize her plan had succeeded before darkness claimed her senses.

***

Lalri (November) 16, 1542
King Terosh's Private Chambers, City of Rammon

Every anotech in Terosh stilled at once, and he knew something drastic had changed. His entire body felt somehow lighter and less conflicted. He considered the possibilities but could think of no reason for the change.

Two days later, when Kezem grimly recounted his mother's death, Terosh thought of the lightening of his spirit. Careful reflection upon the timing convinced him. Profound relief and sadness pulled his aching heart in different directions. He tried to cling to righteous anger birthed during the brief captivity many months before, but pity proved stronger.

Chapter 44:
Beautiful Forever

Lanolin (February) 3, 1543
Wellum Home, Riden Mountains
The unforgiving wooden floor outside the Wellum's private quarters made Todd's legs and backside sore, but a small part of him welcomed the discomfort. It would feel completely wrong to be comfortable while Kiata suffered so intensely. Master Jolinda Ekris had gently, yet firmly, tossed Todd from the bedroom into the antechamber soon after her arrival with Master Niklos some four hours prior. Todd had been allowed to hold Kiata's hand until a complication had arisen.

Do they not understand my terror?

For the thousandth time, Todd wished they had not undergone the ceremony to temporarily relinquish control over the anotechs. At least then he could have comforted Kiata and perhaps even eased her pain. Tradition older than the banning of relationships with royals dictated that Nareth Talis Rangers take measures to avoid passing anotechs on to their offspring. Todd understood the logic, but he disliked the implication that anotechs were a heritable disease.

Todd forced himself to stand and started pacing. A moment later, he grunted as he slammed into one wall in the tiny front room. Muttering to himself, Todd turned around and stared around his temporary prison. Normally, the dwelling's front room held only a collection of spare cloaks and dirty boots.

At Reia's suggestion, Kiata had brightened it with sprigs of fragrant mintas and dried ira petals. Todd had no idea where the apprentice sent to fetch the flowers managed to get the ira petals. Though abundant on the Riden Flats and Kesler Plains, flowers of any sort were rare this high and deep in the mountains. Even the lower hills, which played host to many tretling herds, could only boast scattered patches of flowers.

Unlike most of the Ranger dwellings, this temporary-quarter cabin sat above ground, rather than in a converted cave. The Ashatan Council likely wanted to keep the Wellums as far from others as possible.

A pain-filled moan sliced through the closed door and pierced Todd's heart. Terrifying helplessness gripped him, almost as bad as those first seconds after losing his connection to the anotechs. It wasn't a normal feeling for him, and he hated how much it reminded him of the dark days as an Alliance prisoner. His knees felt weak, and cold sweat broke out over his body.

What's taking so long?

His muscles coiled and uncoiled every time he heard his wife's muffled moans. Occasionally, a sharp cry would break the steady groans. Then, the worst would come: silence. Each time silence fell, Todd felt like the universe stopped. His breath caught in his throat, choking him with fear.

She can't die. She can't die.

A sense of uselessness replaced some of the fear with frustration. Todd had sent a young apprentice to notify the queen, but that left nothing for him to do. Master Niklos had traveled in from Resh two days ago to share this time but even he had agreed with Master Ekris's decision to exile Todd.

The inner door swung open and crashed into the wall with a bang like a discharging serlak gun. Todd spun to face Master Niklos.

"What's wrong?" Todd barely refrained from clasping the older man's finely stitched tunic and shaking him.

Retired from the Rangers or not, the man would always be Master Niklos to Todd.

Smiling wearily, Master Niklos reached out a calming hand toward Todd and gripped his shoulder.

"Nothing's wrong. This is all quite normal. It could be seconds or hours though. Why don't you inform the palace that everything is fine before Reia dispatches Royal Guards?"

That's normal?

Todd's ears burned, turning almost the same fiery color as his hair. He recognized the dismissal. His feet responded by planting themselves more firmly.

"I sent Addin to contact her a few hours ago. I want—"

Master Niklos's grip on his shoulder tightened.

"You're distraught; you'll only upset her."

A long scream sent chills through Todd. Then, eerie silence fell again. Todd couldn't take it anymore. He shouldered Master Niklos out of the way and rushed to his wife's side. Master Jolinda Ekris gave him a disapproving look but didn't interfere as he fell to his knees beside Kiata.

She lay on a mountain of coarse blankets and quava feather pillows with her knees drawn up and her night dress draped down to mid-calf. Her eyes opened as soon as Todd took her slick right hand between his own and kissed the knuckles.

"Hi," she greeted with a weary grin. "I missed you."

Todd leaned forward and said he had missed her too with a long, insistent kiss. A small part of his mind remembered that others were in the room, but he didn't care. The woman he loved was here and safe, nothing else mattered. After the kiss, he settled on the bed beside Kiata and clutched her hand again.

"You're just in time," said Master Ekris.

Suddenly, another cry split the air. Todd's head whipped up and around with wonder and alarm. He squeezed Kiata's hand out of pure reflex. This cry was different: younger, newer, and thoroughly annoyed. Todd's lips formed a silly grin. He twisted further for a better look and nearly fell off the bed.

Master Ekris stood in the corner by the wash basin cradling a freshly cleaned and wrapped infant.

"She's beautiful," she murmured, slowly approaching Todd and Kiata. With infinite care, the older woman deposited the baby into Kiata's waiting arms.

She's beautiful, Todd's mind repeated numbly.

He took in the sight of his daughter's wrinkled, bright red face and fell in love instantly. Wisps of soft damp, red hair crowned the baby's head. Her eyes were still screwed shut. The loose fabric Master Ekris had tucked around the child writhed as she squirmed. The infant's cries lessened in intensity, then subsided when a tiny thumb found its way into her mouth. Kiata tucked her close, and the child promptly fell asleep.

"What's her name?" Master Ekris asked in a whisper.

Todd and Kiata exchanged a deep look. No words could recreate its entire meaning, but in essence, it meant: *our love is pure and whole and perfected in her; it will last forever through everything she comes to love and cherish.*

They had prepared both boy and girl names, but right now, none of them seemed right for their first child.

Kiata nodded and smiled, reading his thoughts. After gazing at her newborn child for a long, tender moment, she said, "Kayleen."

Beautiful forever. That fits her perfectly.

"Well, don't just sit there, boy. Tell everybody!" Master Niklos ordered.

Todd needed no more encouragement. He dashed out the door and down the mountainside hollering for all to hear. He sprinted so fast that one slip would have broken his neck, but nothing could touch him today. He had a daughter.

Chapter 45:
Treasured Eternally

Enis (April) 8, 1543
Royal Gardens, City of Rammon

If Reia wanted proof of his health, Terosh would give her proof. He stood below the balcony leading to his wife's private chambers. He could not blame her for the fear. After all, he had almost died countless times during the last few years.

Carefully tucking a fresh rose into his belt, Terosh smiled and remembered the last time he'd performed this feat, minus the rose, of course. That time, romance had been the last thing on his mind. Proving a point to Tate was closer to the mark. Terosh mentally calculated the time it would take and privately promised to beat that time.

Are you with me tonight, friends? He felt a little stupid for not realizing they had helped him up the wall the first time.

She is going to yell, they replied.

She will understand, he assured, hoping it was true.

We liked you better deathly ill, more sensible, they complained.

He chuckled.

Just have her come out to the balcony when I tell you to.

As you wish, King of the Chosen.

With the anotechs strengthening his limbs and increasing the grip on the smooth palace walls, Terosh made good time climbing the seven floors to his wife's balcony. As he reached the top, Reia's voice floated out from the shadows next to the light streaming from her bedroom.

"You know very well that this is not what I meant."

"Permission to board the balcony, Your Majesty?" Terosh asked cheerfully.

Reia sighed.

"You're idiot enough to climb back down the way you came if I refused you, so come on in," she said imperiously.

Terosh wasted no time scrambling onto the wide balcony and closing the distance between them. He pulled her close as if he'd not seen her in ages.

"I missed you."

Her arms encircled his waist then flew wide.

"Ow!"

He released her suddenly and groped behind his back for the rose he had stashed there.

"Sorry. That wasn't exactly the surprise it was meant to be. They're beautiful, but they can be painful." He opened his mouth to say more then cleared his throat awkwardly. "Well, that was smooth as a mountain range." He sighed. "Here, this is for you." He shut his mouth with an audible click of teeth, thrust the rose forward with two hands like a sword being surrendered, and sucked in a deep, bracing breath. "I need more practice talking intelligently. Can I still claim the 'recently ill excuse'?"

Reia laughed and graciously accepted the rose with two hands, being careful to avoid the thorns this time.

Seeing the faint scratches marking her forearms, Terosh ran his palms over them and used anotechs to soothe the skin. The healing took only a few seconds; then Terosh awkwardly removed his hands to let her admire the gift.

Twirling the rose once and raising it to her nose to inhale the rich scent, Reia smiled and gracefully swept back into her room. A few seconds later, her voice floated back to Terosh.

"You can claim whatever you want."

Terosh stood on her balcony puzzling through possible double meanings when Reia returned.

"You're not angry? The anotechs thought you might yell."

Reia sighed again, hooked a finger into the collar of his shirt, and tugged gently.

"Why can't men take hints?"

"Why can't women speak clearly?" Terosh asked, rising to the defense of his gender.

Reia lifted herself up on tiptoes and encircled Terosh's neck with her arms.

"Focus, dear," she said, once they were eye to eye. "There was a reason you climbed seven levels of the Rammon palace tonight. Do you remember what that could be?"

His arms fell into place around her, and he answered her question with an ardent kiss that made his heart soar and ache. During his long recovery they had been close many times, but not like this. His senses filled with awareness of everything about her.

When the kiss finally ended, Terosh rested his forehead on hers.

"This balcony is feeling far too public."

"I completely agree." Reia chuckled, kissed him shortly, and pulled him further into the room.

***

Idela (January) 13, 1544
Reia and Terosh's Private Chambers, Royal Palace, City of Rammon

A cool cloth brushed Reia's forehead and cheeks. With eyes shut, she enjoyed the novelty of not being in pain.

"Imagine doing that without the blessing of anotechs," Kiata said.

Reia's eyes shot open and she groaned in sympathy as her mind did as bid.

"Sorry I was not there for you. We could have cheated the pain a little."

Laughing, Kiata shrugged and perched on the bed beside Reia. Her left leg rested on the bed and her right leg braced against the floor.

"I understand. You had other things occupying your mind, like a husband to heal and a planet to run."

"No, really, I should have been there," Reia said.

Kiata picked up her left hand and held it in her lap.

"Reia, I long ago gave up the notion that I could always save you from every danger you might face. Now, I'm going to have to ask you to do the same."

Reia shook her head, feeling like a silly child.

"Why?" she asked, not caring how petulant she sounded.

Scooting closer, Kiata tapped Reia on the nose with the side of her index finger.

"Because your family is growing now," said Kiata. "Besides, birth order still dictates that it's my job to worry about you, not the other way around. How are you sleeping these days anyway?"

A wan smile tugged at the corners of Reia's mouth.

"I will say one thing for pregnancy. The anotechs worried for the child, so they taught me some useful lessons in controlling the nightmares. Guess my own struggles for sanity mattered less to them."

"They have their own brand of logic," Kiata said. "It doesn't always make sense."

"How is your connection with them?" asked Reia.

"Mine is still unpredictable, but Todd's connection seems to be stronger, at least stronger than it was after the first separation."

They fell silent as both thought back to that horrible time when Kiata and Todd had been captives and needed to cut ties with the anotechs. Kiata's grip on Reia's hand loosened as her distraction increased.

"I … can help with that," Reia offered tentatively.

Kiata's expression said *I wish it were that easy.*

"The Council would have a conniption. While I wouldn't mind watching Master Deliad's reaction, I'm still kind of fond of Master Ekris and Master Corida. I'll just have to prove I can do my job without relying so heavily upon anotechs. It's not impossible, only harder. Speaking of harder, enjoy every peaceful moment you can. Kayleen just started sleeping well, which means *we* just started sleeping well again."

"I shall keep that in mind," Reia promised. "Given that first wail, I believe Teven will be very vocal."

Kiata futzed around with Reia's sheet, neatly tucking it along her left side.

"What made you call him Teven?"

Sadness wound cool fingers around Reia's heart.

"He was the youngest McNoughten child, the one who did not survive the Heskrin attack." As usual, she felt the ache of that failure despite knowing she and Terosh had done absolutely everything they could to save him.

It had been Terosh's idea, but Reia still had mixed feelings over the whole situation. On the one hand, it was a good, strong name with solid meaning. On the other side, it could not change the past, nor replace the life lost.

Kira McNoughten had shed quiet tears when Reia asked permission to name her son Teven. The older woman seemed to understand the need and feigned deep honor, but Reia knew the wound caused by losing her Teven still bled.

Kiata gently tipped Reia's chin up.

"It is a fitting name for any prince." She leaned forward and kissed Reia's forehead. "No more second thoughts tonight. Your life has changed forever."

***

Idela (January) 24, 1544
Chamber of Wisdom, Loresh Cave System, Frozen North

Queen Reia Minstel marveled at how very young and innocent her first—and only—Loresh recording sounded. So much had happened since then; she could not decide where to start. She could easily have stayed hours describing each event that had transpired, but in the end, she decided to focus on her reason for coming.

Instructing the anotechs to keep her first message safe, she tried recording a new message. Several failed attempts later, she stopped and spent several minutes thinking about Terosh and Teven and how much they meant to her. Other concerns tried to rise, but she pushed them back.

Finally, with Teven's sweet little face firmly fixed in her mind's eye, Reia let every scrap of joy shine through her smile.

"We have a son!" There, her news stood delivered, planted like a joyous banner. What more should she say? Her enthusiasm dimmed a little, but she forged on. "Terosh could not come with me this time because one of us had to stay to receive the representatives from the Galactic Alliance of Populated Planets. But I had to come." She spared the mental energy to protest the lousy timing, then pictured her son's face again. Her spirits recovered. "Teven is beautiful. He has his father's black hair, my green eyes, and a scream that can penetrate every corner of the palace! I know I am supposed to be recording bits of wisdom here, so here is my lesson for future generations: enjoy every moment you can basking in the love of family."

Reia silently bid the anotechs to stop recording then dashed out of Loresh. She loved being here among the pillars of Terosh's family, but the satisfaction paled before the prospect of spending time with her family. She would just have to collect Aster Captain Laocer and Captain Zareb, and they could be back in Rammon in half a day. She thought about the former

Captain of the Royal Guard. Reia had liked Surd Antar, but his obvious betrayal left them little choice but to imprison him. Unable to help it, Reia wondered how many more betrayals would assail them and what sort of damage it would cause. She determined to be ever vigilant to protect her growing family.

Terosh and Reia would spend most of the evening entertaining their GAPP guests, but then, they could spend a few precious moments watching Teven sleep. She faintly dreaded the day when that simple act failed to tug her heart so strongly.

Chapter 46:
Contested Refuge

Idela (January) 25, 1544
Upper East Library, Royal Palace, City of Rammon

King Terosh usually relished quiet moments in the library sipping wine with a beautiful woman, but this time, several factors marred the experience. First, the woman was not Reia, and second, the woman was a GAPP agent. Third, she made decent arguments. Fourth, she had a companion with all the personality of a granite statue.

As if summoned by Terosh's desperation, Reia swept into the room wearing a gorgeous gown of green shimmersilk that skimmed along the ground. She even wore matching heels. A deep purple wrap caressed her shoulders then wove down and around her otherwise bare arms. Her green eyes sparkled with sympathy, amusement, understanding, and love.

Terosh and his guests hurried to their feet. He could not have wished for a more fitting or beautiful guardian angel to watch over his sinking spirits. Terosh swiftly handled the pleasantries.

Once they resumed their seats, Terosh said, "Ambassador Raquel, would you kindly repeat your new proposal for my wife?"

"Certainly, Your Grace. I would be delighted," answered Sabrina Raquel in her smooth, measured voice. "During the years since my last visit to your lovely planet, the Galactic Alliance of Populated Planets has added a new kind of member state. As an Associate Member State, Reshner would have no voting rights in our ruling councils, but would otherwise receive full membership rights. This would, of course, allow your agents to move freely about on GAPP worlds, which should aid your cause in rescuing the Rorgen people."

"There is the small matter of the fee, but I am certain we can work out a mutually beneficial deal," said Barlo Elaird.

"I am certain," Terosh echoed.

"What sorts of membership rights exist?" asked Reia.

"The obvious right members receive is the safety of the name," responded Barlo. "We live in dangerous times. Pirate nations exploit lonely worlds, but they usually think twice once they know the united might of

503

GAPP stands ready to defend a planet."

"We have gone more than four centuries without a serious threat from the galaxy at large," Terosh pointed out.

"All the more reason to fear such a possibility now," Sabrina Raquel reasoned. "Members also receive free trading privileges. Safeguarding the trade of information and resources is a vastly expensive undertaking. By sharing the costs among GAPP worlds, the burden is made lighter for everybody." Raquel's perceptive eyes traveled from Terosh to Reia and then back again. "However, I can see that these arguments hold little appeal for you, so I will reiterate my earlier statement. By joining GAPP you would be free to offer aid to planets in the Rorge System."

"Our people have already answered the question about joining GAPP," Terosh said. "However, in light of this new possibility, we will bring it up in the next session." He rose, effectively ending the conversation. "In the meantime, please enjoy your stay in the palace. If you would like to visit any particular city, I can have Master Roth make the arrangements for you."

***

Enis (April) 27, 1544
Prince Teven's Private Chambers, Royal Palace, City of Rammon

"I feel like a coward," Reia admitted, gently rocking her son.

"That is utter rubbish," Kiata said.

"Rubb-eesh!" declared Kayleen.

Both women looked down at the toddler who looked perplexed but delighted. The child had her right index finger stuffed into her mouth and had clapped a hand to her left cheek.

"Rubb-eesh!" Kayleen repeated, enjoying the sound of her own voice.

Bothered by the noise, Teven whined and wiggled in Reia's arms.

"Don't mind her, Tev, she means well," said Reia, redoubling her rocking efforts.

"Hush, Kayleen, your baby cousin is trying to sleep," Kiata gently scolded.

"Why?" asked the child. She grinned from ear to ear at getting to use her favorite new word.

Reia tried to hide a smile as Kiata winced. She failed at it rather handily but sobered enough to share a long-suffering look with her sister.

"We're going to regret teaching her that word, aren't we?" Kiata asked.

"Probably," Reia answered.

"Why?" Kayleen wondered again. She made a strange noise that did not really qualify as a word, but it was loud and she loved it. She made the noise again and threw herself sideways stretching her arms wide, flopping about like a fish out of water and reveling in peels of laughter.

"I'm getting tired just watching her," Reia said. She walked the four steps to the bed and rested Teven on her knees to relieve her aching arms.

"Wait until he's Kayleen's age," Kiata said. "Our neighbors have three children, one girl and two boys. They said their boys were much more active than their girl."

Reia studied her sleepy son. His black hair stuck out in multiple directions. Green eyes blinked at her slowly. Chubby little cheeks flushed as he flailed his arms about and did an odd dance on her legs.

"Did you hear Aunt Kiata, Teven? In this one regard, you have my permission to be more like a girl," Reia told him.

He drooled in her lap.

"I think that's an ambiguous response at best," Kiata said, chuckling.

Kayleen screeched, impatient at not receiving answers.

Teven leaned back and twisted, trying to find the source of the racket.

Reia grunted.

"I don't think we're going to be allowed a civilized conversation in their presence. Here, take him for a moment." She handed Teven off to Kiata and went to summon Sarie, grateful the woman had a plan for such an occasion.

The Melian Maiden bustled in a few minutes later and immediately took charge of Kayleen.

"Come, Lady Kayleen, we shall explore your aunt's fine collection of clothes while she and your mother speak." She held out her hand and waited for the toddler to stagger to her feet. Then, she scooped her up. "Shall I take the other little one on our tour as well?"

Reia raised a questioning glance at Kiata who still held Teven.

"We'll be fine. Thank you, Sarie. Kayleen, you mind what Lady Sarie says," Kiata said.

Kayleen bobbed her head vigorously.

"Okay!" She raised both hands to her mouth, kissed them noisily, and flung her arms wide, almost falling out of Sarie's arms in the process. "Bye!"

"Who taught her to blow kisses?" Reia wondered.

"Three guesses," Kiata said dryly.

They settled down facing each other on the window seat and sat in comfortable silence for a while. Teven slept in Kiata's arms.

Finally, Kiata nudged Reia with the foot that hung off the seat.

"So, back to the coward comment uttered ages ago," Kiata prompted. "I'll give you one minute to explain it before I tell you each and every reason why it's rubbish. Fair enough?"

"Since when were you ever interested in fair when it comes to proving a point?" Reia asked.

Kiata shot her a grin.

"Since you became queen, and I discovered the usefulness of letting you think you can get your way."

"That's the supportive sister I remember," Reia said. "You had me worried."

"And you *have* me worried," Kiata admitted. "You usually don't avoid a subject so long."

"I should be with Terosh," Reia said, hating how much it sounded like a whine. "He's fighting this GAPP thing by himself, while I hide here. Truth is, I don't even think he really wants to join GAPP even under their new provisions."

"Why would he raise it in the Senate and Governors Council if he did not support it?" Kiata inquired.

Reia stared into the seat's cushions and traced some of the flower pattern before answering.

"Duty. He—we feel it's our duty to aid those thrown into need by the destruction of the Colza Star."

"Do you trust GAPP?" Kiata asked, striking the heart of the matter.

"It depends on what you mean by trust," said Reia. "If by 'trust' you mean 'place hope in,' then, no, we do not trust them. If by 'trust' you mean 'depend upon them to reliably act in the same predictable pattern,' then, yes, we trust them."

"I see you have given this deep thought," Kiata commented.

Still tracing the flower, Reia tried to decide how much to tell her sister.

"I know that expression, Reia," said Kiata. "You might as well tell me the rest now. Todd and I will probably find out whatever it is anyway."

"It's ... nothing really," Reia hedged.

Kiata narrowed her silver-blue eyes.

"'Nothing' has never put that look on your face."

Reia winced, hoping she wasn't that readable in public.

"I am concerned with how much opposition we are getting to this GAPP question and where it centers. Lord Kezem seems to be turning the issue into a political storm. That places us in the awkward position of possibly having to pick the opposite side just to keep the discussion alive. Moral reasons alone dictate that this should not be an issue dealt with as lightly as Kezem would have it treated. Then again, by default, the position opposite the one Kezem holds is as GAPP proponent."

"I gather from your tone that you're not pleased with that," Kiata noted.

Reia rested her head in her hands.

"We trust GAPP to act dishonestly in its dealings, but they are still a bureaucracy. If we deal with them cautiously enough, their own words and laws should prevent them from harming us."

"Is it worth it?" asked Kiata.

"I do not know," Reia said, picking up her head and letting her hands drop into her lap.

"Do you think you could ease the situation by standing at Terosh's side?" Kiata asked, tuning her tone to contain more tenderness.

A helpless shrug was all Reia could conjure.

"Then, you're not a coward," Kiata concluded. "You're just unsure which arena would best serve your husband. My advice is: do both. It sounds like Kezem wants an image battle. If you think you can handle it, then give him one. Take Teven along on good days, not that you want to subject an innocent child to senators and governors for very long, but let the reporters see him. Let them see the royal family united in raising a question about compassion. Do not commit to one side or the other; simply raise the question as you did five years ago. The people will eventually return a definitive answer for you."

Chapter 47:
Restful One and Restless One

Enis (April) 21, 1545
Reia and Terosh's Private Chambers, Royal Palace, City of Rammon
"Are you comfortable, Your Majesty?" asked Dr. Ezzai Dentelich.

The tender tone coming from the usually gruff man caused Reia to look up at him and smile.

"Yes, Ezzai, I am much better than an hour ago. You can go rest your ears now." She remembered a time when she thought the doctor nothing more than an arrogant fool, but the years nursing Terosh back to health after the kerlinblade accident had formed a bond of respect and even affection between them. "At least this little one was less stubborn about coming out than Teven."

The doctor returned her grin and glanced down once more at the sleeping newborn.

"She's as well mannered as any princess born in the palace in the last few decades," he pointed out.

"I suppose it helps that she's the only princess born in this palace in the last few decades, but thank you anyway."

"I should go rescue your poor Melian Maidens from our dear king," said Dr. Dentelich. "Shall I retrieve the young prince as well?"

After careful consideration, Reia shook her head.

"Have Sarie bring him by in an hour or so. I'd like a few moments with Terosh and my daughter. We still have an important decision to make."

"I understand your wishes completely, Your Majesty, and as your doctor, I completely concur with your desire for rest." Ezzai bowed and left to inform the king of the happy news.

A few minutes later, Terosh sprinted into the room with Teven clutched to his chest.

Reia stared at him in alarm but had to laugh when two pairs of wide eyes stared right back at her, one pair brilliant blue and the other pair deep green.

"Terosh, you'll shake his head right from his little body," she scolded, ruining the effect with a smile.

"Mommy!" Teven pointed at Reia, turned in Terosh's arms, and began fussing.

Dr. Dentelich entered the room, breathing hard.

"My deepest apologies, Majesty, he would not wait for me to explain your wishes," said the doctor.

Reia sighed and leaned back against the pillows.

"It's quite understandable, Ezzai. We both know he can be hard to reason with," she said, giving her husband a look of mild reproof.

"Are you all right?" Terosh asked, breathing hard.

Just then, Sarie Verituse rushed in with the skirts of her heavy, dark green Melian Maiden robes clutched in her hands to facilitate running. Most of the younger maidens favored the simpler tunic and pants uniform or the flowing green shimmersilk dress as they proved much easier to fight in, but Sarie liked the formal robes.

"What do you need me to do?" asked Sarie.

Teven's whining woke the baby who added her scream to the racket. Reia shifted her hold on the baby and gently rocked. Then, tucking her into the crook of her right arm, Reia reached with her left arm for Teven.

"Are you sure it's safe?" asked Terosh, holding Teven back as the boy lunged for his mother.

"Pass him to Sarie. Then, you can take the little one, and I can safely take Teven," Reia instructed.

The child swapping proceeded as smoothly as can be expected, which means it got more chaotic before relative peace returned. Teven screamed and squirmed in Sarie's grasp, nearly breaking free twice, but she recovered him both times.

"Stop that squirming, child," Sarie admonished. "You'll knock your poor mother senseless, if you keep up that nonsense."

As Sarie spoke, Terosh tentatively stepped close to the bed, leaned over, and slipped his left arm gently underneath the bundle nestled against Reia. When the infant's head rested in his palm, Terosh straightened and brought the bundle to his chest. His face shone with the solemn wonder of a man holding a new child for the first time. His eyes stayed transfixed on the infant's face.

"Watch me!" shouted Teven, tired of being ignored.

Reia pried her gaze from Terosh's face to smile at her son. She held up her empty arms and beckoned to Sarie.

"We didn't forget you, love," said Reia.

Sarie gratefully surrendered Teven.

He immediately threw his arms as wide around Reia as he could and rested his head against her heart.

Reia returned the embrace, relishing the warmth of his body and the tugging sensation where he gripped her shirt.

"Would you like to be alone, Highnesses?" asked Dr. Dentelich.

Terosh appeared not to have heard the question.

"Please wait a moment, Dr. Dentelich," said Reia. "Teven will be asleep soon."

"No sleep!" cried Teven, lifting his head and reaching for Reia's mouth. He pressed his small palm over her mouth and giggled.

Twisting her head to free her mouth, Reia used her left hand to capture Teven's hand.

"You keep that up and I might just decide to eat your hand," Reia said, her eyes twinkling as she teased her son. She pulled his hand close to her mouth, slid her grip downward, and planted a small kiss on each tiny finger.

Teven squealed and tried to pull his hand away.

Reia let his hand go but raised her knees under the loose sheets and penned him in with her arms.

"Where do you think you're going?" she asked.

The boy didn't answer. Instead, he leaned back on her knees and looked to his father.

"What's that?" he asked, pointing to the small bundle in Terosh's arms.

"Your sister," Reia answered, feeling sleepy but perfectly peaceful.

"Have you named her yet?" asked Sarie.

"I'm not sure," Reia murmured, casting a curious glance at her husband. "We spoke of many names."

As soon as their eyes connected, Reia felt a hundred wordless messages pass between them.

Terosh looked down at their daughter and whispered, "Rela."

"What does it mean?" asked Sarie. "It's a lovely name."

Rela. Rela.

Reia tested the name with her mind several times before explaining.

"It has several meanings, but the most common meaning is 'restful one.'"

We certainly need more of that sentiment, Reia thought, as thoughts of the GAPP debates rose.

"I'd say that fits the princess rather well," said Dr. Dentelich.

Reia agreed.

***

Zeri (June) 3, 1545
Spaceside Inn, City of Rammon

It is treason, whispered an inner voice.

"It is necessary," Aster Captain Ectosh Laocer muttered into his ale tankard. His gaze darted around the room even though he had already swept for listening devices and had a personal sound damper activated.

It is madness.

"It is the only way," he argued.

You'll never do it. You're a coward.

"I am here," Laocer said.

"I must admit I did not think you would come," said a man.

Laocer's head snapped up, and his kerlak pistol centered on the speaker's chest in less than a second. He recognized the man as one of the Lady's agents, a former Ranger called Kolknir. His mind locked on the long list of crimes laid at Kolknir's feet. For an instant, he wanted to pull the trigger.

Kolknir chuckled.

"Very good reflexes, Captain, but you can put your weapon away. I see that you recognize me, but remember, you called for this meeting. I am merely the response. Lord Maledek was very surprised about your proposal and sent me to test your sincerity."

"It is no trap," Laocer assured. "I desire the king's removal, and I have heard rumors that your master possesses the resources to see to it. My reasons are my own."

The man took the seat to Laocer's left and ordered a drink through the control panel built into the table.

"Your reasons are as clear as the Crystal Lake, but I am not here to critique them," said Kolknir. "For what it is worth, this is no trap on our end either. Lord Maledek understands and even sympathizes with your cause."

"Queen Reia must not be harmed," Laocer said, clutching his ale tankard tightly.

A buzzing noise indicated that Kolknir's ale was ready. Laocer turned to his right and slid the hidden panel aside to reveal the drink.

"I will get that if you don't mind," Kolknir said, reaching across the table and plucking the drink out of the delivery window. He took a long pull of his ale then resumed his seat. "As for not harming the queen, my master wishes to know what you propose to do with her. He cannot come to power if she lives. Upon the king's death, she alone will inherit the throne—at least until the children come of age."

"Fake the queen's death, and I will take her away. Count her part of my fee if you must," Laocer said, eager to move on.

"And the children?" Kolknir asked.

I don't care about the children!

Laocer drank some ale to steady his nerves. If he answered this question wrong the whole deal would fall through. He suspected Lord Maledek wished the heirs gone as well, but the thought of assassinating toddlers and infants naturally unsettled him.

"Kill them," he answered hoarsely.

"You do not sound very certain on that point," said Kolknir.

Laocer let cold anger enter his eyes and voice.

"I believe Lord Maledek would be a better ruler for Reshner. I don't have to pretend to enjoy the idea of destroying the royal family. Necessity does not make it any less distasteful."

"Why not fake their deaths as well?" Kolknir asked with a knowing grin.

Laocer longed to punch the grin off Kolknir's face.

"It will be hard enough to fake one death and smuggle the queen off the planet."

Kolknir drank part of his ale then set his jaw and stared hard at Laocer.

"How far would you go to get her?"

Glowering, Laocer said, "You know exactly how far I would go." His teeth clenched so hard his head hurt. "I am here offering my services and my access codes to Lord Maledek. I have already admitted a desire that my king and his heirs die. This conversation is enough to condemn me to death. *That* is how far I will go."

"No, that is how far you *think* you will go and even that may be fortified by the ale," Kolknir said rising. "If that is all, I think our time together is at an end."

"Wait!" Laocer said, holding up his left hand.

"How deep is your commitment to this cause?" Kolknir asked again.

Laocer felt sharp emotion tear through his chest.

"I have loved the queen since the day I laid eyes on her. The king and his brats are a burden to her. I hate how she has suffered these long years. I want to take her away from the danger and the pain that comes with the position. But for the light that would cast me in her eyes, I would kill the king with my own hands. That is why I sought your master. I need him, and I can ease his path to the throne."

"Better answer," Kolknir acknowledged. "Please continue."

Chapter 48:
Traveling Fire

Lalri (November) 15, 1546
Prince Teven's Private Chambers, Royal Palace, City of Rammon

Two shrieks cut straight through Terosh's ears and into his head. The shrieks morphed into triumphant screams then challenging yells then dissolved into giggles. Little feet frantically pounded past him first one way and then the other as Rela chased Teven around the room. From his seat on the foot of Teven's bed, Terosh felt like a spectator at a piroball match.

Teven stopped suddenly in front of Terosh. Rela howled victoriously and slammed into him. Both children tumbled to the soft carpet and rolled until they crashed into their father's legs.

Bending down and gathering them in his arms, Terosh asked, "What sort of strange beasts have I captured?"

"Daddy!" Screaming, Rela wriggled around until her arms were free before throwing them around Terosh's neck.

Teven heaved his whole body back and slammed himself full force up into Terosh's chest, trying to knock him back. Laughing, Terosh fell back on the bed.

"Yield, villain!" cried Teven, pushing himself off Terosh's shoulder.

"Never!" declared Terosh. He slipped his right arm up under his son's body, hooked his hand around, and lifted him up with an exaggerated roar. With Teven clinging to his arm like a burr, Terosh slammed it onto the bed at his side, effectively pinning the boy.

Teven giggled.

"Me too, Daddy," Rela pleaded.

Terosh hesitated, not wanting to hurt his daughter. He smiled.

"Princesses are not made for tackling," he said, pulling her further onto his chest. Before she could cry, he added, "They fly." Saying such, Terosh grasped under her armpits and lifted her high, sliding his palms closer together so they formed a sling to support her tiny body. Spurred on by her laughter, he hummed and made sputtering engine noises while waving her back and forth, up and down above his head. When his arms started aching, he lowered her back to his chest.

"My turn!" Teven declared.

Terosh groaned.

"Ride's over. Machine's broken."

"Where's Mommy?" Rela asked, sliding off his chest and landing on her knees next to him. She swatted his stomach when he didn't answer immediately.

Terosh's mind went painfully blank for an awful second. He propped himself up on his elbows and tried to think of a delicate explanation.

"Mommy's busy," he answered lamely, looking from one child to the other.

Teven blinked at him with expressive green eyes that were pure Reia.

"Mommy's baby coming?" asked the boy.

"That's right," Terosh confirmed. He finished sitting up. "The baby's coming today."

"Wanna see!" said Rela.

"Soon," Terosh said, praying it would be so. He hated the thought of Reia in so much pain. Absently, he hugged Rela close with one arm and drew Teven in with the other.

I should be with her.

No, you belong—

Teven squirmed free, scrambled to his feet, and leapt from the bed.

"Where are you going?" Terosh asked, trying to untangle his legs enough to stand.

"Find Mommy," Teven answered.

"Wait! You can't see her right now," Terosh said. He clutched Rela to his chest like a shield and formed a ledge with his right arm for her to sit on.

Seemingly oblivious, Teven ran to the door and looked up at the control panel. Finding it out of reach, he pressed his palm to the button near the floor. The door promptly opened revealing a Royal Guard in resplendent dark blue uniform.

"Sorry, Seth, false alarm," Terosh told the guard. "He's not allowed where he wants to go right now."

Noticing the guard's distraction, Teven slipped through his legs and headed for the last door before the hallway.

Seth started to pursue him but then hesitated.

"Stop him," Terosh said, hoping to clear up the debate apparent on the young guard's face.

Seth caught hold of Teven just before the prince could touch the button that would summon another Royal Guard to open the door.

"Hold there, Young Prince. You're not allowed out there yet."

Teven screeched a wordless protest and threw himself to the floor, kicking and screaming his way into a full-fledged tantrum.

Seeing her brother crying, Rela started fussing too.

The nervous expression on Seth Rolik's face made Terosh laugh.

"Perhaps it might be best if you summoned one of the Melian

Maidens, it seems you and I are outmatched here." Terosh shifted his hold on Rela, turning her so she faced him. "Chin up, lass," he said affecting the accent one might expect to hear around Ritten or the Kevloth Plains. "There's no sense crying over nothing."

"Tev cry," Rela pointed out.

Terosh couldn't argue with her logic.

"Well, we'll just have to cheer him up. How should we do that?"

"Kiss?" Rela suggested. She wriggled to get down.

Instead of lowering her to the ground, Terosh tightened his grip. Teven's fit was subsiding, but Terosh didn't want his daughter getting accidentally clobbered by the last vestiges of tantrum.

"That would be nice, but this probably isn't the right moment for that approach," said Terosh.

"What shall I do, Highness?" asked Lieutenant Rolik.

"Wait until he's done thrashing. Then pick him up and bring him here," Terosh ordered.

A few minutes later, a red-faced, exhausted Prince Teven stood sullenly before Terosh.

Although he sympathized with his son, Terosh knew something needed to be said about the fit or there would be many more. Kneeling, Terosh looked his son directly in the eyes.

"Bad Tev!" Rela shouted.

Nearly choking on suppressed laughter, Terosh instinctively clapped his hand lightly over her mouth.

"Not helpful, Rela."

She mumbled something into his hand.

"Hush, I need to have a word with your brother," said Terosh.

Rela huffed but leaned back and eyed the accused.

"Teven, I know you want your mother, but she cannot be disturbed right now," Terosh said, wishing Reia was there to explain better.

"Why?" Teven asked.

Terosh groaned inwardly. He should have expected that question. His mind scrambled but came up with nothing. The sound of the door opening rescued him.

"Sarie!" Rela announced. She broke free of Terosh's loose grip, hopped down, and raced to the Melian Maiden.

Teven whipped his head around and stared up at Sarie.

"Where's Mommy?" demanded Teven.

Terosh felt his heartbeat quicken.

"Is she all right?" he asked, standing.

A brilliant smile spread across Sarie's dark face as she stooped, gathered Rela into her arms, and straightened.

"She is more than all right, Your Highness. You should go see her and the new prince," said Sarie.

The anotechs could have told them the child's gender, but Terosh and Reia felt it was more fun to simply pick names for either.

A boy!

That meant his name would be Tavel, meaning "traveling fire" in Kalastan.

Feeling as if he would burst if he didn't move, Terosh scooped Teven off the floor and dashed for the door.

Chapter 49:
Fiery Trap

Ferrim (December) 27, 1546
Upper East Library, Royal Palace, City of Rammon
Terosh frowned and entered the code to repeat the message.

A frightened female voice surged forth again.

"Your Highness, I have information concerning Maledek and his long reign of terror. He is someone close to you! I dare not trust any more than that to technology such as this. Meet me in Estra between Cartan and Hiver an hour before moonrise tomorrow. I can tell you more then."

A meeting tomorrow could be arranged, but Terosh questioned the wisdom of it. The obvious questions swirled around his head, leaving him frustrated. He supposed the woman could have faked the fear, but he doubted it.

In the end, the chance to know more about Maladek proved too tempting. Terosh summoned Zareb and Laocer to plan his trip. The attack on the way to Fort Savad last month left him wary enough to take travel precautions.

***

Ferrim (December) 28, 1546
Reia and Terosh's Private Chambers, Royal Palace, City of Rammon
Reia did her best to fight the sorrow and weariness making a mess of her emotions. She frowned down at the baby in her arms surprised to find herself crying again.

"It's not your fault, little love," she assured Tavel, swallowing a sob. She forced a dim smile. "Women are complicated."

"I wholeheartedly agree," Terosh murmured in her left ear. As he spoke, his arms wrapped around her waist and pulled her close. "But they are also soft." He kissed her neck. "And smooth." He ran his fingers over her forearms which still cradled Tavel. "And intelligent, compassionate, and beautiful."

"Terosh!" Reia said unable to keep the surprise out of her voice. She twisted her head left.

"Were you expecting some other man to sneak up on you in our

517

private quarters?" he teased, catching her lips with a tender kiss before she could respond. Then, he loosened his grip so she could turn and face him fully. He kissed her again, leaning forward so as not to smother their son in the process.

"I thought you had left already," Reia said hastily between kisses.

"Officially, I did," Terosh replied, trading passion and length of kiss for frequency and the ability to talk. "Unofficially, I could not bear to leave without a proper farewell."

A fit of laughter welled up in Reia.

"I—am—glad." She gave up speaking and leaned into his next kiss. Tavel whined.

Reia broke the kiss off with a soft groan and leaned back.

"Let me just put him down."

"May I?" Terosh held his arms out for the child.

Reia eased the baby into his arms, feeling suddenly cold without the tiny bundle.

Terosh cradled Tavel for a few minutes, pacing the room until the baby fell asleep. Then, he kissed the soft cheek, murmured a goodbye, and laid the infant in his crib.

"He'll probably grow three inches by the time I return tomorrow," said Terosh.

"I thought you'd be back tonight." A pang of dismay shot through Reia.

"Night crossings can be tricky," Terosh said with a shrug. "We'll be safer spending the night in Estra and crossing to Chara in the morning."

While Reia could not argue with the logic, she dreaded spending the night alone. She gazed bleakly down at Tavel.

"It's only one night, my queen," Terosh promised, pulling her into a tight embrace. He kissed the top of her head.

"Let me come with you," she urged.

For a moment she thought he would consent, but he said, "It's too dangerous."

Reia leaned back, straining against the circle of his arms.

"If you suspect danger, then send someone else!" she said, feeling tears rise again. "Why go if you expect a trap?"

Terosh moved his hands to her shoulders and held her at arm's length so he could meet her eyes.

"I suspect no more danger than usual, especially since Todd's traveling with me. I should be safe enough. I meant only that it is dangerous for us to travel together." He squeezed her shoulders. "Reia, we have more to live for than ever. I want to know you are here and safe with the children."

Feeling her heart might crack under the strain, Reia fought off a tide of bitterness, stepped up to Terosh, and nearly crushed him with the force of her affection.

"Alosoolsusonana, my love," she whispered, pulling his head down for a long kiss. (To success on your journey.)

***

Ferrim (December) 28, 1546
City of Estra

Memories of holding Reia provided Terosh with bittersweet company during the long trip down to the city of Estra in the Frozen North. Illness had cheated him of approximately half the years spent with her. Every moment apart felt like a cruelty.

Terosh generally distrusted anonymous contacts, but he understood the necessity of such given the soaring political tensions. The Colza Star explosion had been but a tiny flare in Reshner's sky, but Terosh suspected the true extent of the ramifications would be acutely felt for years. The more he learned about GAPP the less he felt inclined to champion their cause, but at the same time, he truly believed in the absolute rightness of aiding Rorge II. If GAPP proved the easiest means of lending aid, then they still warranted consideration. The debate had waxed hot and cold for years now. Terosh couldn't decide whether he should hope for heated discussion or cold indifference. He only knew that something would need to change soon or the Senate and Governors Council would splinter into ineffective messes.

The anotechs warned Terosh of danger two seconds before a massive explosion launched his hov many meters into the air. He immediately encased himself and his guards in thick anotech shields. A desperate scream merged with the explosion's roar, and Terosh knew that the driver's shield had failed. The hov flipped several times as it rose then hurtled nose-down toward the ground again.

Feeling like his chest and head would split open, Terosh threw his awareness outside of the hov. Once he saw where the hov was headed, he seized it in a mighty anotech grip and slowed the descent enough to avoid fatal impact. The crash bent metal and broke glass. The hov's interior filled with smoke and dust. Terosh's ears rang. The anotechs filtered the air going into his lungs, but his guards were not so lucky. Even though he could not hear them, he saw their bodies convulse with violent coughs. Dazed, Terosh instructed the anotechs to filter air for his two living guards.

Sensing danger approaching from several directions, Terosh bid the anotechs to find him a quick exit and grabbed hold of his two semi-conscious guards. Part of the hov's roof peeled away above his head. Relying on adrenaline and anotechs, Terosh clutched the guards one under each arm, clenched his eyes shut, and imagined rising. Much as he had done to escape the maw ages ago, Terosh continued lifting all three of their bodies until they cleared the hole in the hov's roof. Then, he released the guards and let them tumble to the ground.

Hoping his energy reserves held, Terosh aimed his body forward and landed on his hands and knees. Two kerlak shots warned him the danger had not passed. Terosh flinched as the anotech shields still encasing his two guards shuddered under the influx of energy. His gaze flickered toward them, and he allowed his dismay and worry to shine clearly in his expression.

Todd!

The Ranger lay unconscious beside Zareb. Terosh tore his attention away from them but demanded a report from the anotechs. Both had been shocked unconscious by the first explosion. The additional kerlak shots would have killed them, but the anotech shields held. Terosh entertained a brief debate with himself before issuing his order.

Keep them unconscious until it is safe. Convince everyone they're dead, and then send them home.

Unfortunately, the plan could not work for him. The fact that no kerlak beams or serlak bullets riddled his body meant the figures he sensed approaching intended capture, a contradiction considering the force of the initial explosion.

"I see you have survived," said Kezem.

"Kezem?" Terosh asked, whipping his head up to look at the dark figure that stood before him. His cousin's physique had grown quite impressive during his time on Gardan. Questions crowded Terosh's head.

"Welcome, Terosh," Kezem greeted. "We never did complete our duel all those years ago. I believe it is time we finished the matter." He pulled two kerlinblades from his belt and activated them simultaneously. A green blade with a yellow core and a blue blade with a red core sprang into existence.

"Doesn't this strike you as a tad unfair?" Terosh muttered. He staggered to his feet and took out his kerlinblade. After brief contemplation, he left the blade unlit.

"I couldn't decide whether I wanted you to die in the explosion or kill you myself. Now that the explosion has failed, I am grateful," said Kezem.

Glad I could make you happy.

Terosh gingerly shook each limb to make sure they worked properly.

"What happened to the woman in the message?" he inquired, trying to stretch out the moments before the inevitable duel so the anotechs could conduct emergency repairs on his battered body. "Was she real?"

Next time, avoid explosions! the anotechs scolded.

Just make sure there is a next time, Terosh answered.

"Oh, she is quite real," Kezem said darkly, waving to his left with the blue and red kerlinblade. "I present Lady Merisia Restler, to whom I owe great thanks for setting these events in motion."

A door hissed open, and three figures emerged. Two men supported a woman bound hand and foot with stuncuffs. Terosh recognized the man on the woman's right as former Ranger Lucas Telon. A faint scar marked the space below his left eye. The woman's dark hair hung limply around her shoulders. A red, black, and blue welt decorated her left cheek. Her purple eyes glittered with tears, bleakness marring their beauty. She would not meet the king's gaze. Her expression declared both helplessness and hopelessness.

Some of Terosh's weariness vanished beneath a tide of anger. Whether she had willingly or unwillingly participated in this trap, he hated to see her as Kezem's prisoner.

"The trap worked fine. Let her go," he commanded.

Kezem's smile filled with paradoxes. It contained aspects of ice and fire, kindness and cruelty, love and hatred, sympathy and contempt.

"I always knew your compassion would kill you. I just did not know how. Now I have my answer." Kezem motioned toward Merisia again with his lit kerlinblade. "For what it's worth, she did not betray you. She betrayed me, and for that she will die here and now."

The men flanking Merisia Restler shoved her onto her knees.

Knowing he could stall no longer, Terosh activated his kerlinblade and turned his body to face the woman and her captors. He thrust an open palm toward them and made a fist, all the while issuing frantic orders.

The anotechs answered his commands with relish. Lucas Telon cried out in terror as his body hurtled toward Terosh's blazing white blade. Terror turned to pain as blade met and triumphed over flesh. Meanwhile, Lucas's partner hurtled backward through the open doorway they had emerged from and crashed into something hard somewhere beyond.

Merisia dove to the ground, but not before several kerlak beams converged on her, struck the anotech shield surrounding her, and reflected back to their startled sources. Three unlucky men fell to the ground with pain-filled cries. A fourth man caught the reflected beam in his left arm and dropped to the ground with a stream of curses. Merisia ran dazed eyes over the chaotic scene.

With another thought, Terosh released the stuncuffs binding her wrists and ankles and imbued her with the urge to flee.

Several of Kezem's men started to pursue Merisia, but Terosh hauled them back with invisible anotech tethers. They started to rise only to be cut down by a hail of kerlak beams.

"Merisia!" called a young man. He waved frantically and shot at a few more of Kezem's soldiers.

"Taly!" shouted Merisia Restler. The cry was two parts a plea for help and one part stunned greeting.

"Get gone!" Terosh ordered. He drew his kerlak pistol and covered their retreat long enough to see them disappear into a hov and speed off.

Good luck, my friends.

An inarticulate roar warned Terosh as Kezem's blades descended toward his head. Hoping Taly and Merisia would make it, Terosh yanked his concentration back to the moment and raised his kerlinblade to parry the blows. The force of them shuddered through Terosh's tired arms. He successfully blocked three more swift strikes, but each drained a little more of his precious energy.

Kezem's remaining men formed a loose circle around them. The duel proceeded in an abrupt, desperate manner. Terosh and Kezem lashed mercilessly at each other with blades, fists, and feet.

As the moons rose, a kick from Kezem knocked Terosh into the crowd. Many hands fell upon him. A desperate swipe with his kerlinblade separated several of those hands from their respective owners, but more hands took their place.

Terosh screamed his frustration as his kerlinblade was plucked from his grasp. His eyes caught a flash of metal arcing toward his face. He threw his head right but a kerlinblade handle slammed into his jaw anyway. He tasted blood. His head ached. Something knocked hard into his chest, driving breath from his burning lungs. Another head blow set off a storm of lights behind his eyes. The anotechs cried out for orders, but he could not think straight. Images of his children filled his mind as he lost consciousness.

Chapter 50:
Sweet Servant

Ferrim (December) 29, 1546
Maledek's Private Retreat, City of Idonia

King Terosh Minstel's return to consciousness was not a pleasant experience. Despite the anotechs' best efforts, most of his body hurt. Everything ached. His head throbbed so badly his teeth tingled. He tasted blood. Every breath felt like swallowing a dagger. The few parts of him that didn't ache stung horribly.

His mind jumped back to the explosion and the fight that followed. *Zareb. Todd.*

He hoped both friends still lived. They would be understandably furious with him, but he did not regret his actions.

I'm sorry, Reia.

A wave of sadness brought an ache to his chest that almost drowned out the physical pain coursing throughout his body. He beat back the tide of self-pity by focusing on anger. Very few people knew about the meeting in Estra. Fewer people still had the contacts to bait such a simple, almost elegant trap.

Kezem.

The dungeon's heavy door swung open before he could fully follow his thoughts to completion. He gathered his strength to face his cousin. To his surprise, a girl about nine or ten years old entered hauling a bucket and carrying a sponge. She said nothing as she gently washed his wounds, and she kept her expression neutral. She could have been anybody, but Terosh recognized the icy blue eyes and gentle, innocent features.

Elia! Oh, Tate, if only you knew. She's alive!

He wanted to speak to her but could not work up enough energy. His efforts went into sucking in one more fiery breath and forming useless tears. He wept for his long-dead brother, his niece—this child tending his wounds—himself, his children, his wife, and his unsuspecting people.

When the girl leaned over to clean the blood off his neck, she whispered, "I'm not supposed to talk to you, but I like you. I hope you fight well."

Terosh longed to tell her about her father, but she was almost done cleaning him. Pouring his will into the gesture, he lifted his hand. Instinctively, the child took hold of the hand. Terosh closed his fist around her tiny hand and willed some anotechs to leave him. When the time was right, they would explain the child's heritage to her. He could do no more, and the effort drained him.

He released a few anotechs into his surroundings and felt the hard stone floor in a new way. This was no modern prison. It was a dungeon, carefully preserved throughout the centuries to crush the hopes of its occupants. Terosh idly wondered how many people's blood had filled the cracks between the stones digging into his back. When the scouts returned, they told him news that broke his heart anew.

Lord Kezem killed Princess Deanna Koffrin Minstel here. The stones still echo with her presence.

But why kill her?

Dark man, First Maladek, likes power and pain.

There must be something more to warrant such lengths of cruelty, Terosh argued.

He has promised to destroy House Minstel.

But he's a part of it. His mother once carried the name. Why hate us so much?

The anotechs remained strangely quiet, but Terosh knew the answer. He had known the answer for most of his life. Knowing in his mind and being here—feeling the traces of Deanna's despair—were completely different matters. His father's sister, Princess Mavis Altran, had been disowned by her father. Her hatred had obviously been cultivated in her sons.

Terosh would have laughed at such petty hatred, but two thoughts sobered him. He lay atop the very place his brother's wife had been murdered, and his own family would likely be consumed by the same hatred that had killed her so many years ago.

The threat to his family caused Terosh to rally some strength, organizing the anotechs to maximize their healing efforts. He wished for his wife's presence then immediately regretted the thought. He would never wish such danger upon her. She had been through too much already.

He closed his eyes to rest while the anotechs began their healing works on him.

Chapter 51:
Ralose Charm

Lanolin (February) 30, 1547
Princess Rela's Private Chamber, Royal Palace, City of Rammon

"I want to put the Ralose Charm on Rela," Reia announced calmly from where she sat on the edge of the large bed. She cradled the sword Terosh had given her years ago. Her left hand rested atop the scabbard and her right hand cupped the hilt from underneath.

Kiata Antellio Wellum closed the inner room's door and stared hard at her little sister. Her instincts had warned that the early morning summons did not bode well, but nothing could have prepared her for that proposal. She opened her mouth to speak but could not find words to respond. She settled for several long, slow breaths as she organized her thoughts.

"I know the plan is dangerous," Reia said, not daring to meet Kiata's eyes. "That is why I need your help. I need you to live." The last statement came out almost painfully slow, yet it bore an edge of conviction.

And everybody needs you to live, so why can't you listen to reason?

"Reia, you're talking crazy," Kiata snapped. "Even if the Ralose Charm works exactly as it is supposed to, what do you hope to accomplish by it?"

"Should the palace fall, my daughter will survive," said Reia, raising her chin defiantly.

Should? Of course, it's going to fall if you keep sending its defenders to all corners of the planet!

Kiata glared the message at her stubborn sister.

"She would survive if you abdicated. Kezem wants the throne and—"

"And he cannot have it while even one of Terosh's children draws breath," Reia finished, rising from her perch on the bed. She clipped the sword onto her belt, walked past Kiata to the cradle tucked into the corner, and gripped its edge. "If I surrender, he will kill them. If I escape, he will tear apart many lives in the pursuit of them." She lingered a moment longer staring at the child, and then, she shifted her gaze back to her sister. "This way, perhaps part of his bloodlust will be sated, and he will be thwarted

525

by the inability to harm Rela."

You're still talking crazy.

"The last two people to be connected by the Ralose Charm died the same day," said Kiata harshly, trying to shock her sister back to sense. "How can you be certain Kezem won't kill her before he even realizes the connection?"

Reia flinched.

"I … cannot be certain of anything, but I believe Sarie will agree to warn him." She leaned back against the sturdy cradle.

Hearing the bewildered then slightly hopeful words crushed some of Kiata's will to resist.

"And what is my part in this scheme?" asked Kiata, though she knew what her sister would ask. "Please say, go kill Lord Kezem."

"You must sever the connection when the time comes," said Reia.

"How will I know when the time comes?" Kiata asked, trying valiantly to keep her tone gentle.

And how exactly does one sever a Ralose Charm?

"You will know," Reia said cryptically.

Kiata simultaneously feared and respected the tone.

You do not even know if I will live long enough to be of use in this.

Pushing the sobering thought aside, Kiata sighed.

"When do we begin?" Before she knew what was happening, Kiata was caught up in a fierce embrace. The hilt of Reia's sword bumped into Kiata's left thigh.

"I knew you would help," Reia whispered, arms still locked around Kiata.

I always did have trouble denying you.

A tingling sensation emanated from where Reia's hands and arms touched her back. Kiata knew she ought to recognize the feeling, but the impression eluded her attempt to identify it. Deciding to worry about the feeling later, Kiata returned her sister's hug.

"You always did get your way, even before you were queen," said Kiata with forced levity. "There's no sense breaking with tradition now."

Reia tightened her grip even more before suddenly releasing her hold on Kiata and pulling away.

"Thank you," she said. Her voice trembled with suppressed emotion.

"You can thank me better by letting me help you escape," Kiata said wearily. She fought the impulse to knock her sister out cold and cart her away to somewhere safe. She put a half-step between them, drew in a fortifying breath, and concentrated on releasing it slowly. The last bit flew out in a frustrated rush. "But since you seem bent on this path, I will help you any way I can. What provisions have you made for the boys?"

"Teven will go with the McKnights, and the Osem Rangers have agreed to shelter Tavel," said Reia, her voice recovering some of its strength for having something to report. "Todd sent the news yesterday. He said he had a few more things to take care of in Osem, but he hopes to return tomorrow. He also sends you his love." Her lips formed a sad smile.

Kiata's expression darkened. She mentally railed against her insensitive husband for inadvertently reminding her sister of what she had lost.

Reading Kiata's annoyance in her narrowed eyes, Reia's smile broadened.

"Don't hold it against him. It is good to know love still exists."

Kiata grunted, still miffed at Todd.

"Do you trust the McKnights?" she asked, needing to redirect the conversation.

"I trust them less than I would you, but you and Todd have Kayleen to think of," said Reia. "Surrounding my son with soldiers would only catch Kezem's attention. Pria and Nathan have the best chance of moving about anonymously, and they are good people besides. I will send Laocer and a few others to guard them from a distance."

"The captain will not take kindly to that order," Kiata pointed out.

"But he will obey it," Reia said confidently.

Seems to be the only thing to do around here, Kiata thought darkly.

She leaned over her niece's cradle and envied the girl's peaceful repose.

"Should we wake her for the ritual?" asked Kiata.

"No, let her sleep," said Reia. "She would not remember it anyway."

A chill climbed Kiata's spine at those words, but once again, the exact reason for the worry eluded her.

***

Reia's emotions threatened to spill over and send her into a sobbing fit. Each heartbeat pounded painfully in her chest. Knowing if she hesitated any longer she might fail to do what was necessary, Reia pressed a code into the cradle's railing and watched it slide down. Then, she drew the thin sword and placed it next to her daughter. Not satisfied with the layout, Reia scooped up the child, adjusted the sword so it lay diagonally across the cradle mattress, and gently laid Rela on top of the sword's flat edge.

The child stirred and almost woke up, Reia touched her daughter's right shoulder and sent some anotechs with soothing thoughts.

"That was close," Reia said. She glanced at her sister. "Please repeat the words in Kalastan."

Kiata gave her a strange look but nodded.

Reia closed her eyes and placed her left palm on Rela's chest and the tips of her right fingers on the sword.

"Bind the intended souls together." She stopped so Kiata could speak.

Clearing her throat, Kiata said, "Tinetonenkalaensem." (Tin-et-on-en-kal-la-en-sem)

"May their bodies reflect any harm," Reia said. As she spoke, she instructed anotechs to enter both the sword and her daughter. Then, she bid them each to divide and send the new copy to the other form.

"Praesucorpraltonmal," Kiata repeated. (Prah-eh-soo-corp-ral-ton-mahl)

"Where one bleeds, so shall the other," Reia intoned. Her arms, shoulders, and neck tingled as anotechs flowed up one arm and down the other in both directions. Some of the anotechs argued about leaving her, but she willed them to obey.

"Quelunsans cosaletotre," said Kiata. (Kel-lun-sans co-sal-et-oat-ray)

"May this preserve them both," Reia finished. She waited for the anotechs to finish moving. Then, she slowly removed her hands from Rela and the sword.

"Praeseprimalosamb," Kiata translated, sounding relieved to finish. (Prah-esse-pre-mahl-los-am-be)

Remembering she needed to instruct the anotechs on which code to listen for, Reia returned her hands to Rela's chest and the sword. The anotechs stopped their flurry of activity to listen as she sent them the proper phrases to end the Ralose Charm. When she finished, she again removed her hands and told her sister the same phrases.

"Prietal? Why that dialect?" Kiata asked, surprised.

Reia shrugged.

"It sounds better than regular Kalastan. It's also easier to memorize." She winced. She had not meant to mention that last part. She braced for the question Kiata would inevitably ask.

"Why should that matter?" Kiata's voice was saturated with suspicion.

Reia ignored the question, using the careful extraction of her sword from beneath her slumbering daughter as an excuse to do so. Her emotions once more threatened to sweep away her senses. She frantically searched for something reasonable to say. Unfortunately, by the time she had the sword safely sheathed, she had still come up with nothing to allay Kiata's suspicions. Reia stared at her daughter, trying to buy a few extra seconds to think.

Kiata grabbed her right shoulder and turned her so they stood face to face.

"Reia, what aren't you telling me?"

The tide of Reia's inner battle shifted, and her vision suddenly clouded with tears. A sob caught in her throat and burned.

I love you too much to lose you!

She squeezed her eyes shut so they would not send that message, but it was too late.

"No!" Kiata's voice was a fierce whisper, and she held her sister by both shoulders. "Whatever you've done, Reia, undo it right now. Don't you dare waste any effort trying to protect me!"

The admonishment shattered the barriers Reia had carefully erected around her heart.

It's too late.

Her knees went weak, and she dissolved into tears. She would have fallen, but Kiata wrapped her in a tight hug.

As the need to sob slowly drained away, Reia debated how much to tell Kiata. She could barely explain it to herself, let alone anyone else. Losing Terosh had been the single most painful experience of her life. She almost wished Kezem had not sent her his body. Then, at least she would have some irrational hope he still lived. She could not bear the thought of Kiata dying as well.

Or Todd or Kayleen or any of my children.

The next time she saw them she would do for them what she had done for Kiata, but she could not tell her sister anything about those plans. She would not risk provoking her Kiata's anger in what could be their last moments together.

Finally pulling out of the hug, Kiata said, "Reia, please. You have enough to worry about without adding me to that list." Unshed tears made her eyes shiny. "Concentrate on saving yourself."

Can't. I have to save you from you.

Reia couldn't help but smile as she used her knuckles to dash a few late tears from her eyes.

"I love you. Remember that," she whispered.

"You're not going to tell me, are you?" Kiata asked with an exasperated yet resigned expression. "May I ask why?"

Reia shook her head.

No, if I tried to explain, you might talk me out of it.

"Trust me," Reia said, not quite keeping traces of pleading from her tone. "The most important thing now is that you live long enough to free Rela from the burden we just placed on her. Whatever happens, please free her."

Chapter 52:
One True Failing

Jira (March) 2, 1547
Wellum Home, City of Rammon

Kiata Wellum futilely wished she could access the anotechs like she had a few years back, but the first and second decommissioning ceremonies had severed her connection and left some disturbing blanks in her memory. Her third joining ceremony had restored some of her memories and occasionally allowed her to call upon the anotechs. Master Niklos assured her that such a thing was normal and that the full connection should return in a few years. The knowledge had set her mind at ease at the time, but she knew now that she could not wait a moment longer.

She wished Nils Clavon luck and speed on his quest to see Kayleen to the safety of the Riden Mountains. Kiata's grip on her banistick tightened painfully as her thoughts brushed against the hasty parting with her daughter. A large part of her wanted to leave Todd an encrypted message and chase after Nils and Kayleen.

Torn between waiting here and retreating to the palace, Kiata paced and took a few practice swipes with her banistick. Reia would need her. Kiata hated not being with her sister during this desperate time, but she knew Kezem would send someone to seek her and Todd. She dashed off another futile wish, urging Todd to hurry home from his mission. If Kezem's men did not find anyone in the Wellum home, they might search for Nils and Kayleen. Kiata would not let that happen.

While her thoughts still tumbled about in a flurry of wishes and partial plans, a simple knock sounded at the door. Kiata froze as trepidation and curiosity mingled in her gut. As she stepped close to the front door, she traded her banistick for a kerlak pistol and set it to high stun. She doubted the caller was friendly, but it would be terribly bad form to kill a neighbor, even in these stressful times.

A second knock sounded, and then came the terrifying sound of the locks clicking open. No sooner had the sound registered with Kiata, the door swung out and a flood of burgandy uniforms crashed into her front room. Three shots dropped a trio of eager soldiers before a fourth, fifth, and sixth tackled her to the floor.

As she fell backward, Kiata managed to smack one of her assailants aside. Landing on her back, she squeezed off another stun beam into one of the soldiers and jerked her head violently right to avoid a devastating blow. She lost her grip on the kerlak pistol and heard it clatter away.

The soldier's hand met the floor with an audible crack where her head had been a second before. His howl ripped at Kiata's nerves. Her shoulders hurt where the remaining soldier—the one she had temporarily knocked aside—used his weight to pin her to the floor. Kiata reached for the pressure points in his upper arms and squeezed hard. The young man recoiled, giving Kiata enough room to bring her knees up into his chest and heave him off balance.

Momentarily free, Kiata rolled to her right. Something heavy landed on her, forcing her back to the ground. It was a man. His left arm slipped around her neck. Pressing off the floor, Kiata brought her left elbow up and drove it back as hard as she could where she hoped the man's head might be. The blow connected with a satisfying impact, but she paid for it with sharp pain in her elbow. The man behind her went limp, but she lacked proper time to revel in the small triumph.

Two men reached for her arms. Kiata let them each get a grip before grasping their shirts and yanking them toward each other. They bumped heads but not with enough force to do any real damage. Kiata snapped to her feet, thrusting her arms forward to push the two men away. She drew her banistick and sent it hard into the two dazed men in front of her before whipping it downward and back to deal with the man who had tried to strangle her.

"Well done," said a mocking male voice from the threshold.

Kiata raised her banistick to a guard position and eyed the speaker warily. He stood calmly in the doorway flanked by four men, two kneeling and two standing. All held kerlak rifles pointed her way. Her breath caught. Deflecting or dodging one energy beam at this range would be very difficult. The possibility of facing four at once filled her with icy fear. Her eyes darted about the room, making sure no more surprises waited to make her day worse.

"Have you no words of greeting for a former master?" Kolknir asked. His dark blue uniform was laden with pins and tiny ribbons. He took a small step into the room. "You should congratulate me on my new rank. I am now a sublord."

"Your men haven't exactly given me much time to talk," Kiata said, again scanning for further signs of trouble.

"You'll have to forgive them for being so eager. I promised a reward for the first to subdue you," said Kolknir.

"You always were an inspiring instructor," Kiata said dryly.

Kolknir tipped his head in a small bow.

"And you were one of my finest students. You have no idea how long I pleaded with Lord Kezem to let me spare your life. I told him that I believed

I could turn you to our cause." His voice tried too hard to sound refined.

"Really? What did he say?" Kiata quirked an eyebrow at Kolknir and carefully stepped over one of the fallen soldiers. If she was about to die, she wanted a lot of room to take as many of them with her as possible.

"Unfortunately, he did not believe me," said Kolknir. "I told him everything comes down to motivation." His slow words chilled Kiata. He chuckled at the alarm in her eyes. "I am certain your little girl would make fine motivation."

Kiata's whole body tensed, but she willed her muscles to uncoil.

Neelyak is safe. Nils got her away.

"You don't have her," she said, shaking her head and praying she was right. She longed to kiss her daughter one more time.

"What makes you believe that?" asked Kolknir, affecting innocent curiosity.

"Because you're twisted enough to flaunt her if you did have her," Kiata explained.

Kolknir's chuckle deepened into gentle, rolling laughter.

"You are correct, for now, though more of my men are seeking her than those I have here. It simply gives you more time to contemplate the moral dilemma."

As Kolknir spoke, he took another small step forward, giving his men enough room to file in. Some bent to tend their comrades, but most fanned out along the walls. Soon, Kiata would be surrounded.

"You would risk Lord Kezem's favor to prove a point? That's either brave or stupid, possibly both," said Kiata, trying to fight off the sinking despair that threatened to sap her energy.

After his soldiers completed the loose circle around her, Kolknir said, "I'm sure he would forgive me for the novelty of seeing the queen's own sister raise a weapon against her. What do you say, Kiata? Will you help me prove my point?" Kolknir's cold smile sucked warmth from the air.

Kiata fought the urge to speak, but her response slipped out anyway.

"No." Her voice sounded weak to her ears, and she could only imagine how pathetic it sounded to Kolknir and his men.

He gave her a puzzled, almost wounded, look.

"Not even to save your own daughter?"

"What would it gain to save her, only to leave her in your hands?" Kiata fired back.

"Not even to save her from pain?" Kolknir pressed.

Despite knowing Kolknir wielded the words as empty threats, Kiata felt the pain of them. She couldn't believe she was having such a conversation with this vile man. "Anyone who fashions such a threat against a child has tarnished honor," she said, blinking away tears. "Your promises are only true as far as they suit you." The declaration came out stronger than her first statement, thanks to the anger coursing freely through her. When it ebbed, she added, "Should my poor daughter ever find herself in such a position, she would already be beyond hope."

"Good logic, Kiata, but I wonder if your reasoning would hold during the real test. Could you listen and watch as—"

"Could your men?" Kiata interrupted. "Could they listen and watch you harm a child?" She glared at the soldiers surrounding her.

Most of them had the grace to look down.

"Ranner, shoot her. Stun only, please," said Kolknir.

The soldier to Kolknir's left jerked in surprise, giving Kiata enough time to move her banistick into line as he shot three blue stun beams in quick succession.

Kiata ducked under the first two and deflected the third into one of the men standing to her left. The soldier uttered a surprised cry as the beam plowed him into a wall.

"Stop!" Kolknir shouted.

Everybody froze.

Sighing, Kolknir said, "Wesley, Collins, Abrams, the backup plan. We have need of it."

Three men chorused, "It will be done," and hurried from the room.

Kiata felt relief at their parting, but it was followed by worry for whatever ills composed the backup plan. Tense moments passed in painful semi-silence. Only the sound of ragged breaths and a few moans from soldiers regaining consciousness stirred the tension. As Kiata decided not to wait for the backup plan to be implemented, Kolknir's voice seized her attention again.

"I am testing my theory, but if this goes poorly, I will kill them," Kolknir promised.

"Who?" Kiata asked, her banistick half-raised to take a swing at the nearest soldier.

She didn't have long to wait. Wesley, Collins, and Abrams returned with a small herd of terrified neighbors. They shuffled past Kolknir with lowered gazes. From their tight-lipped expressions, they had obviously been warned not to speak. Master Ullier's face boasted a puffy, black and blue left eye which leaked slow tears of blood and bore the marks of a rifle stock.

Groaning, Kiata fought the impulse to fling her banistick to the ground in frustration.

"That's your backup plan?" She poured contempt into the question. "It's a fine example of what Kezem's order offers the people." She tried to make eye contact with her neighbors, but they studiously considered the ground.

"Drop your weapon," Kolknir ordered. His voice held none of the levity it had possessed before.

Kiata hesitated.

Kolknir moved so fast he was a blur, snatching a small child out of the line and pressing a dagger to her throat. Kiata couldn't even be certain where he'd drawn the dagger from. The girl whimpered. Kiata's breath hitched. The child, Ishella Ullier, was only a few months older than Kayleen.

"No! Leave her!" shouted Adam Ullier, the girl's father. He took a step toward Kolknir only to be stopped by several rifles leveled at his chest and three pairs of hands grasping his arms. His frightened eyes roamed the room, settling on Kiata. "Do something, Ranger!"

"What do you really want of me?" Kiata demanded, glaring at Kolknir. "Surely it must be more than trying to prove to Kezem you can bend someone to your will. I will not harm my sister for anything." She prepared to attack Kolknir. It wouldn't save the child, but the one casualty was the best Kiata could hope for at this point.

Grabbing a handful of Ishella's golden hair, Kolknir pulled the child's head back, exposing her neck. The girl's jaw trembled and tears streamed freely down her face. Kolknir's right hand swept the dagger close enough to draw a thin line of blood. A whimper escaped the child before she remembered to keep silent. Her tears dropped onto Kolknir's hand.

"Look into her eyes, Ranger," Kolknir challenged. "Can you really make that move?"

She couldn't or she wouldn't. Kiata's mind flashed to a training exercise many years ago where Kolknir tried to teach her that sacrificing one life or even two might be necessary. She had hated the lesson and her inability to dispassionately fulfill her duties.

"Let them go," Kiata said. Her voice sounded hollow. She let her banistick drop to her side.

"They will be free as soon as I have your complete surrender," Kolknir promised.

Kiata's thoughts raced. Other than threatening her, Kolknir had no use for her neighbors. He probably wouldn't kill them out of spite. Kezem wanted to conquer Rammon, not kill its inhabitants. Too much bloodshed would force the people to choose a side. Heart thudding in her ears, Kiata concluded Kolknir would keep his word. She straightened out of her combat stance and let her banistick tumble from her fingers.

Kolknir's eyes lit with feral triumph, and he laughed again.

"Now kneel," he ordered.

"Release them," Kiata countered, standing her ground.

Kolknir nodded to his three hand-picked henchmen who hustled the prisoners out the door. He maintained his firm grip on Ishella.

"I will not repeat the order," he warned.

"She has suffered enough," Kiata said, slowly dropping to one knee and then the other. "Let her return to her father. You gain nothing by forcing her to watch what comes."

"As you wish," said Kolknir, releasing his hold on the girl.

She wisely scampered away.

Before Kiata could regain her feet, Kolknir tucked his dagger behind his back. When his hand returned, it held two flingers. He threw them with quick snaps of his wrist.

The first raked along Kiata's left cheek and the second struck her high in the right shoulder. She cried out at the sudden pain and found herself falling backward. Many hands caught her and forced her back to the kneeling position. One hand pressed against the back of her head, pushing downward. Instinctively, she tried to wrest her body free of the grasping hands. Her right shoulder protested every movement.

"Up," said Kolknir.

The hands pulled Kiata to her feet and bound her forearms and wrists together with rope. The man who had pushed her head down now reversed direction until she faced Kolknir again. Most of the hands let go, but two tall men each had firm grips on her upper arms.

Stepping close, Kolknir plucked his flinger from her right shoulder. Absently flipping the flinger with his left hand, Kolknir tenderly traced the tips of his right fingers over the wound on Kiata's face.

"You never learned that lesson about sacrificing others. I think it was your one true failing." He had said as much all those years ago.

Kiata's response from the past echoed in her mind and strengthened her heart.

If this is failure, Master, then I am glad to fail.

Kolknir let his hand drop and studied the damage done to her shoulder.

"Such a tiny wound," he said. The next instant, his dagger was back in his hand and then lodged in Kiata's shoulder.

She had braced for something like this, so only a groan and a stream of tears told him she felt the dagger.

As Kolknir slowly pulled the blade out, he tugged down, smiling when it earned a small cry from her.

"Better," he said, admiring his handiwork. He flicked his eyes at the soldier standing to her right.

The man tightened his left hand but released his right hand. A second later, his right hand found the wound on her shoulder and squeezed.

The increased pain darkened Kiata's vision. She thought she would welcome unconsciousness.

I'm sorry, Reia. I love you, Todd. Be safe, Kayleen.

Epilogue:

Retsi (May) 28, 1547
Priest's Quarters, Temple of Marishaz, City of Chara
A faint knock tore Father Morgivesh Niktol's concentration away from his half-finished sermon. He sighed.

If you wanted an uninterrupted life, you should have joined Tormi at sea.

A second, more insistent, knock prompted him to speak.

"Hold, friend. I hear you."

"Are you Father Niktol?" inquired a woman. Her words, despite being muffled by the door, possessed urgent energy.

The queen's cryptic message suddenly made sense. Niktol's heart lurched. He hurried to the door, flung it open, and hauled the startled woman inside.

The woman threw off his hands, spun away from him, and assumed a fighter's stance in the center of the small welcome room, fierceness and confusion equally present on her face. The cloak that had previously hidden her features hung from her shoulders.

Niktol shut the door then turned and spread his hands in a non-threatening manner.

How did you escape? How did you get here? How much do you remember? Those questions and a hundred like them crowded Niktol's head.

"Welcome, friend. You are safe here. I am Father Niktol."

The woman straightened slowly and stared down at her hands in confusion. Frustrated tears glittered in her eyes as she looked to Niktol.

"I can't remember who I am," she said in a hoarse whisper, "but I felt drawn here. Can you help me?"

I will do whatever it takes to keep those I love from harm.

Niktol remembered the queen's declaration. He had not exactly dismissed it, but he had never imagined Queen Reia possessing the power or the will to do what she had done.

Trust that time will restore all to right. Protect my treasures until the proper time.

"Can you help me?" repeated the woman. Her haunted eyes scanned his welcome room for signs of danger.

Niktol wondered what sort of burden he had agreed to bear, but he could see the prolonged silence weighing on the woman.

"Dear lady, I do not know how much I can help you, but I do know your name. You are called Kiata."

The End

(The story continues in *Reshner's Royal Guard*.)

Anotech Chronicles Book 3:
Reshner's Royal Guard

By Julie C. Gilbert

Table of Contents:

Cast of Characters:
(Spoiler Alert)

Royals:
King Terosh Minstel – ruler of Reshner
Queen Reia Antellio Minstel – ruler of Reshner
Prince Teven McKnight – Crown Prince of Reshner
Princess Rela Minstel – Princess of Reshner
Prince Tavel Minstel – Second Prince of Reshner

Rangers:
Kiata Antellio Wellum – Nareth Talis Ranger, Reia's sister
Todd Wellum – Nareth Talis Ranger, Kiata's husband
Kayleen Wellum – Todd and Kiata's daughter

Other:
Sarie Verituse – Melian Maiden, caretaker of Princess Rela
Ectosh Laocer – Captain of the Royal Guard
Talyon Keldor – former RT Alliance operative
Jalna Seltan – daughter of the anotech creator

Villains:
Lord Kezem Altran – usurper; Terosh's cousin
Merek – Kezem's advisor

Prologue:

Ferrim (December) 29, 1546
Kezem's Private Retreat, City of Idonia

"Get up," Lord Kezem Altran's voice commanded from above.

King Terosh Minstel blinked up at his cousin. The stone floor dug into his back, but his head, which rested in the groove between two stones, felt oddly comfortable for the first time since he woke up a few hours ago. He lifted his head slowly, relieved to feel no new pain.

Terosh's poor vantage point made his cousin seem taller and more menacing than usual. Kezem's features hardened into a mask of hatred, disgust, and sadistic pleasure. The Gardanian enhancements had given him new height and breadth. His body trembled with energy as he kicked Terosh's left side, just below the battered ribs.

Terosh grunted and instinctively curled to protect his side, breathing slowly to minimize the pain. Anotechs rushed to the abused area and started repairing the damage.

With an annoyed grunt, Kezem stooped down and hauled Terosh off the floor as if he weighed no more than a small child.

Terosh whipped his arms up under Kezem's arms and slammed the flat of his hands into the crook of Kezem's elbows.

Kezem dropped him and laughed.

"Fight all you want. It won't save you or your family."

Terosh kept silent. He would not beg Kezem for mercy. The man had none. Terosh's heart ached to hold his wife and kiss his children, but he let nothing show on his face. Killing Kezem might be the only way to protect his family, so Terosh gathered the anotechs for a final attack.

"You can't win," said Kezem, pulling a small device off his belt. "Even if you seized this, my men have a different set of controls to subdue you. Do not let the crude stones fool you. This room is fully equipped to deal with a royal prisoner. My mother designed it, thinking it might one day hold her siblings, but other plans prevailed first. Would you like to see what it does?"

Despite his determination not to play games with Kezem, Terosh shook his head.

"Experience can be so educational," Kezem commented. He pressed something on the small, gray device.

Terosh shouted as his arm and leg muscles suddenly clenched, dumping him to the floor in a mass of quivering muscles.

Kezem plucked Terosh off the floor again and pinned him to the wall with his left forearm across Terosh's throat.

Air rushed out of Terosh. Soon, his arms and legs were bound to the wall.

Kezem stood back to take in the scene.

"My mother also left me several interesting people," he said pleasantly. "I think I'll introduce you to Kellen and Lash. With your self-healing abilities, I'm sure you could entertain them for days. Should I arrange for your wife to join us? Look, she could even stand near you." He gestured to the wall to Terosh's left where a similar set of bindings awaited another prisoner.

Anger brought a flush to Terosh. He hated that Kezem could get a rise out of him so easily.

"Is that what they taught you on Gardan?" Terosh asked. He didn't have to work for the tone of contempt. "How to torture people chained to walls?"

"These walls have hosted many distinguished guests over the years," said Kezem. "Spice traders, informants, spies, ambassadors, minor nobles, but you might be the first king, Your Grace."

"Princesses," Terosh added.

"Indeed." Kezem looked mildly impressed. "Your brother's wife spent some time here, but alas, she did not last long."

"Deanna," said Terosh. "Her name was Deanna."

"Was it?" asked Kezem. "Good to know. I had forgotten. So much has happened these past nine years."

"Does Elia know?" Terosh asked. He tried to stop the question, not wishing to remind Kezem of the girl's royal blood.

"Who?" inquired Kezem. His feral smile contradicted the question.

Terosh waited out the moment.

Kezem's expression said he really wanted to gloat.

"You must be referring to Taytron's daughter. I am keeping her alive for now. Luckily for her, she has no idea the trouble built into her lineage." Kezem shrugged like he didn't care, but his expression darkened. "Should she ever discover her past, I will have to kill her. Do we understand each other?"

"We do," said Terosh.

Silence would keep Elia alive and safe, but no such solutions existed for Terosh's children while they stayed on Reshner. As his hopes for peace slowly crumbled, he abandoned his stance on not reasoning with Kezem. A crazy thought struck his heart with equal parts pain and hope.

"Let me annul my marriage." The words turned sour as they left his mouth. He forged on anyway. "Reia will have no claim to the throne, and you can seize control as you like once I'm dead."

"Her death will void the claim quite nicely," Kezem responded.

"Besides, your plan has three tiny flaws."

The reference to his children hit Terosh harder than any blow.

"Reia could take them away," said Terosh. "Help me arrange transport. There must be a thousand of planets suitable for—"

"The trouble with exiles is that they tend to resurface at inconvenient times," said Kezem, cutting him off. "No, cousin, they must die."

Guilt tore at Terosh. If he had never entered Reia's life, she might have married some Ranger or merchant or farmer and lived in relative peace. He wished with every scrap of will left that he could protect his children.

We will watch over them, King of the Chosen, the anotechs promised.

With that assurance warming his spirit, Terosh snapped the bindings holding him and used anotechs to rip the controller from Kezem's hand. He would not wait to be slowly tortured to death. If Kezem wanted his throne, he would have to earn it.

***

Ferrim (December) 30, 1546
Kezem's Private Retreat, City of Idonia
No turning back.

Cold exhilaration filled Lord Kezem as he watched recordings of the queen's reaction to Terosh's homecoming. Laocer had delivered the body mere minutes ago, and the timing could not have been better. The three moons set, and the sun reached out cheerful beams to caress the palace as it claimed the planet for day. Kezem could not help seeing it as a metaphor for the events he had set into motion.

"You will not mourn for long, Your Majesty," Kezem murmured as he replayed his favorite short scene.

Queen Reia Minstel hurtled into the vidrecorder's range. Pain and irrational hope battled in her expression. Spotting the body, the pain proved victorious, and Reia froze in the hallway and swayed slightly. Her muscles tensed and her eyes clenched. She tilted her head and leaned forward like a woman bracing against strong wind. Then, she staggered forward and fell beside the hov sled holding Terosh.

Hope rekindled for a second as Reia reached out and touched Terosh's chest with her palms. Her eyes bore into the king's tranquil, pale face with a fierceness bordering on anger. Whatever magic she used to snatch him from death by poison all those years ago failed. In a second stretched over an eternity, her features changed as the reality tore through her and dashed her hopes in a flood of pain. Several long seconds passed, dominated by mute horror. Then, the queen gasped and surrendered to sobs.

A sympathetic pang stabbed Kezem in the chest. Startled, he crushed the feeling with anger. He could not afford such weak feelings. Determination flared in him. He needed to move quickly. If the queen's grief could shake him this much, he could only imagine what it would do to the ignorant masses.

Chapter 1:
Dark Days Come

Idela (January) 2, 1547
Royal Palace, City of Rammon

An enormous crowd waited in the courtyard for her to speak. Reia's mind flew back to the time eight years before when she stood here with Terosh. Now only Sarie Verituse and Aster Captain Ectosh Laocer filled the balcony space that ought to hold her husband. Reia froze the emotions so she could think long enough to form words. When this was over, she would return to her grief, but for now, she needed to be much more than a heart-broken widow and terrified single mother.

She needed to be queen.

Drawing desperate breath and praying for strength, Reia turned her stinging eyes to the crowd.

"My people, I find myself hard-pressed to find words to comfort you." She tried to steady her voice. "My husband, my best friend, my children's father, your guide and king, is gone, and we mourn a mighty loss."

Hope lives, whispered the anotechs.

Reia swiped a hand across her eyes to catch some tears. The cool night breeze offered little respite from the hot despair clinging to her.

"I come before you today to ask your aid. Let Terosh live on in your hearts. Remember King Terosh of House Minstel as a man who stepped into his role with equal parts strength and compassion."

House Minstel is not yet broken, Queen of the Chosen.

The anotechs' reminder restored some peace to Reia. She forced herself to look over the gathered people and meet as many gazes as possible. She briefly wrestled with the idea of sharing the insight with the people. It might ease their pain, but Terosh's murderer might take it as a challenge. She couldn't think about him or the depths of his betrayal.

"Some of you may be frightened by so many changes in such a short time," said Reia. "Some may also claim me unfit to rule because I came by the Minstel name by marriage rather than birth. I have not the strength to argue with you, but I assure you my life belongs to you. There are three strong reasons you should not despair. Their names are Prince Teven, Princess Rela, and Prince Tavel." The palest ghost of a smile brushed her lips. "Come what may, this Royal House will not bow to a tyrant."

Chapter 2:
Chaos in the Palace

Jira (March) 2, 1547
Throne Room, Royal Palace, City of Rammon
Death comes not-so-softly in the night.

Queen Reia Minstel felt this truth reverberate in her chest as she recalled Aster Captain Laocer's painful report. The East Quarter had fallen to Lord Kezem. Only five hours into the attack, Reia knew that Kezem's forces would breach the palace by daybreak. Then, she would be dead, he would be Reshner's ruler, and her people would be plunged into civil war.

War is anything but civil.

Sweeping aside some unruly strands of wavy light brown hair escaping the braid, Reia turned sharply and smashed the polished floor with her right boot.

"For what?" she demanded, wincing at the hoarse voice she barely recognized. Hours spent arguing with servants and soldiers bent on standing with her to the bitter end drained her. She had been thinking of years ruling with Terosh, searching her heart for something they had done wrong, something they could have done better, something that would justify Kezem's bold coup.

"For greed, hate, revenge; does it matter, Your Grace?" asked a grave voice, loud only because of the previous silence.

Reaching for her sword, Reia stiffened as adrenaline banished the weary shoulder droop. Then, she recognized the voice.

"Have you something to report, Captain?" Her hands released the weapon, and she drew herself up regally.

"The fortifications are complete," reported the Captain of the Royal Guard with a bow. He paused to consider his next words and lowered his voice. "But they will not hold." Concern etched deeply across his strong, square face, which carried a fair number of scars.

"I know, Captain Laocer," Reia assured him, eyeing the man with something akin to pity. She took in his sweat-matted, black hair, and tired eyes. Nothing in his posture or appearance betrayed fear, but she felt it rolling off him anyway.

What do you fear?

"Lord Kezem really wants my job," the queen added with a sad grin. A bit of humor sparkled to life behind her green eyes and vanished just as quickly. She sighed, like she was exhaling the weight of the universe. "I will not last this night."

"We will—"

"Are the arrangements made?" Reia asked, interrupting his predictable protestations of her fatalistic views. There are times to dream and times to be pragmatic. Since dreams would not save her, Reia figured she might as well accept it. After much thought, she concluded she had done everything possible for her people. The future would be played out by others. Her mind flashed a series of faces, family and friends she had finally convinced to flee. She sent a prayer after Kiata, Todd, Kayleen, the McKnights, the Etans, and Dr. Dentelich.

"They are, Your Grace," Laocer reported with a stiff nod.

"Good. Then, let them come." Reia spun on her heel, glad for the microgrips built into her boots. The highly polished throne room floors would be good for thwarting the enemy for a while. The battle's outcome was certain, but nothing said she had to forfeit her life peaceably.

"We will be ready," Laocer promised, saluting out of habit. He turned away then hesitated. "Your Majesty, may I speak as a friend?"

Reia nodded permission. Her thoughts turned to the last conversation with her sister. The memory of Kiata's desperation haunted her. It was strange how fate had reversed their roles. During their early years, Kiata had been the protector and Reia the one protected. Now, it fell to Reia to save both her sister and her people.

If only I could have preserved our parents as well. I'm sorry, Kiata.

Laocer's words interrupted her dark thoughts.

"Flee into the Riden Mountains! Accept exile. Gather the Rangers and the people will rise with you. Overthrow Lord Kezem when your forces are strong again."

"I cannot do that, Captain. Lord Kezem's wrath will cease once he claims the throne. Ruling is not as easy as he thinks it will be. If I escape he will feel threatened. I will not give him reason to pursue my children." Her tone left no mistake that the line of conversation was over. She knew the words consisted more of wishful thinking than facts, but she also needed Laocer as far from the palace as possible. "I have one last order for you."

"Anything," he said instantly.

She faced him again, and her expression said he wasn't going to like the order. Weariness, worry, and fear fled her face and stance. She studied Laocer carefully, then spoke with conviction.

"Aster Captain Ectosh Laocer, you are to quit this battlefield. You—"

"No!" Laocer dropped to his knees. "Please, let me serve! I can defend you. I—and every soldier here—swore by the three moons that my last breath would be spent in your service."

Like any good diplomat, Reia waited until Laocer finished. Then, she covered the five paces that separated them and knelt in front of him.

"You *are* serving me. My children matter most. Their survival is all that matters now. I know their fate is tied to yours. You must escape. The servant guardians are loyal, but they are no soldiers. Teach my children to defend and serve the people. If they cannot learn that, Reshner will surely suffer. Will you do this?"

Laocer nodded.

Reia could tell that it took much effort for him to meet her gaze. She was glad to see that he braced himself like a soldier.

"Thank you," she whispered, regaining her feet. "Come, there is much to be done before chaos enters the palace."

***

Jira (March) 2, 1547
Same Day
Princess Rela's Private Chambers, Royal Palace, City of Rammon
The haunting quiet in Princess Rela's nursery contrasted sharply with the muttered curses and loud commands filling the rest of the palace. Soldiers hurried to their stations. Servants who defied the evacuation orders rushed to quarters for weapons then reported to the throne room. Those who found no serlak or kerlak guns borrowed steel blades from the historic displays. Some even raided the kitchens for meat cleavers and mallets.

The princess's nursery remained calm only because Sarie Verituse refused to let anyone upset her charge. Her beady, dark eyes darted from one rushing servant to another. Her dark skin would have allowed her to blend in with the shadows had her cloak not already done so. She stood outside the nursery's heavy doors using a hard stare to threaten those who might disturb the princess. She refused to carry a weapon, clinging to the belief that even Kezem's brutes wouldn't cut down an unarmed woman.

"May I see her?" asked a soft voice from under a green cowl usually worn by the Melian Maidens. The female servants sworn to serve the queen for life were named in honor of their founder, Aster Captain Aria Melian.

Sarie flinched with surprise, yet she knew there was nothing unusual about Queen Reia wanting to see her daughter. Willing her heart not to break, Sarie immediately granted the queen access to the haven.

"Will you place the Ralose Charm upon her, Your Majesty?"

"I already have. It will preserve her life for a time," said Queen Reia, throwing off the hood and gently caressing her daughter's cheek. "Sarie, warn Lord Kezem about the charm and watch over my daughter. She will be safe in body but not in mind. Promise me you will guide her. Teach her to be loving, honest, and fair. When Kezem discovers her, he will try to twist her to his ways. That would be a fate worse than death."

"I promise, my Queen," Sarie whispered. Unable to say more, Sarie struggled to keep her sobs silent as she watched Queen Reia gently cup the slumbering toddler's chin. The expression on the young queen's face was hard to decipher. Sarie had not seen her this relaxed or vulnerable since before King Terosh's assassination two months before. She stared openly at the queen's profile, swiping at hot tears trying to blur her vision, determined not to miss one moment of the queen's farewell. Her efforts started to succeed until the queen spoke again.

"Sarie, see that Rela receives this when she is old enough to understand," said Queen Reia, pressing a small object into Sarie's right hand and embracing her tightly.

The gesture broke Sarie's resolve to not cry. Her hand clenched around the ring tight enough to make the emerald stone dig into her palm. She did not need to see the ring to imagine its elegant beauty.

"She and her brothers are Reshner's future," the queen reminded Sarie softly.

The queen continued whispering encouragements, but Sarie heard none of them. Instead, she concentrated on studying the queen. The hood was back on again, framing Reia's smooth, cream-colored skin. Her long, braided hair draped over her right shoulder. Her green eyes glistened with the emotions of the night. Her lips, though devoid of their usual smile, still appeared kind and gentle. Sarie memorized every graceful line of the queen's face then bowed and took her leave, knowing the queen needed time alone with the princess.

***

Reia gazed down at her daughter and thought about the Ralose Charm. Knowing that only she, her sister, and perhaps a high-ranking Ranger could break the charm tightened her throat with worry. She remembered whispering the ceremonial words and willing the anotechs to accept Rela as mistress.

What's done is done.

Reia concentrated on planting messages in her daughter's mind, messages that would not activate for years. Infopads could have been left with trusted servants, but these thoughts were meant for no one else.

"Always be sweet, my love. Never be bitter of the fate that befalls you," murmured Reia. A tear fell and the little one stirred. Reia resisted the urge to pick the child up, knowing she might crush her with the fierceness of goodbye. Instead, she drew two ragged breaths, leaned over, and kissed the tiny face. Her lips barely brushed the soft skin. More tears escaped and rained down upon the child, resulting in a scrunched up nose and a piercing whine.

Sleep, little one, thought Reia, soothing her daughter with anotechs.

Once certain the child again slept, Reia leaned back, laughed softly, and wiped the tears from her daughter's face. She wondered how much Rela would resemble her one day and how many features would come from Terosh. The toddler already had her father's piercing, deep blue eyes.

The servants would save Teven, the Rangers would save Tavel, and the Ralose Charm would save Rela, but no one could bring back Terosh or save the people from what would surely be long, dark years.

"Ensueltsom icretton, mef sela," she murmured.

In your heart, I will dwell, my daughter.

An alarm programmed into her infopad drove her from the room. She paused to encourage Sarie Verituse one last time. The servant's intense stare spoke of her strong loyalty. Reia lent her what strength of will and courage she could, before leaving to continue her heartbreaking farewells.

After seeing her eldest child into the secret tunnel below the old prison level in the care of the McKnights, Reia tucked her younger son into the life capsule that would protect him until he reached Osem. This third and final goodbye brought her so many mixed feelings that she feared she would burst open and spare Lord Kezem the trouble of killing her. The other farewells were said with some certainty that the children would end up where she intended. But as she clicked the life capsule locks into place, she felt a great distance between herself and her son. Doubt lingered.

The Rangers will care for him well.

She did not like the idea of shipping her son out of the palace like a crate of sweet nuts. If only Terosh could wrap warm arms around her, the pain might be more bearable. Having finished her task, Reia returned to the throne room to prepare for the last stand. At least she could join her husband knowing the children would be safe.

As she waited, Reia fingered the anotech-laden steel blade gently bouncing at her side. She could have drenched the blade with poison, but that would have been dishonorable and dangerous to her daughter. The tiny machines had been reluctant to obey her, but she had convinced them of the necessity of this long, strenuous mission where they would have to endure silently for years.

The few hundred servants, Melian Maidens, Palace Security, and Royal Guards arrayed before Reia held their shoulders back defiantly, serious gazes fixed upon her.

Rolling thunder crashed, causing everyone to flinch. It was as if the planet itself protested the political unrest. Reia smiled, putting every ounce of strength she possessed into maintaining the illusion of calm. They would feed off her emotions because she was their queen. She wished upon all the good left in the universe that she could order them to escape as she had Captain Laocer, but they would not listen. They had pledged their lives in defense of hers, and she could no more steal that honor than she could escape as an exile.

When she stood upon the dais and held up her hands, the surrounding murmur ceased.

"Lord Kezem will come soon to capture, conquer, kill, and destroy. This is a dark day for Reshner, but hope remains. Let us make sure he never forgets this night!"

Chapter 3:
Shipment to Osem

Jira (March) 2, 1547
Same Day
Spaceside Inn, City of Rammon

Reshner's not bad. If this moody Edge planet could kick its habit of forming acid storms every three months it would be downright pleasant.

As a former freight hauler captain, Trina Kiren liked the semi-metallic tinge left in the air around the spaceport.

Love's worth some sacrifices, and we could have fled somewhere horrible, like Moza.

The thought of that evil little ball of dirt where earthquakes were a daily occurrence and only the nobility ate regularly put a sour taste in Trina's mouth. She forced her thoughts back to the current situation.

On the other hand, Lord Kezem's violent bid for the throne makes Moza sound like a vacation hot spot right now.

Spending time with her man was one thing. Being trapped in an apartment half the size of her cockpit with her incessantly pacing husband was quite another. Queen Reia's version of martial law had been bearable. But now that Lord Kezem controlled Rammon's only spaceport, the situation had taken a turn for the worse. It seemed every two-bit, grouchy bounty hunter, mercenary, and other flavor of scumbag had chosen to join Kezem's rebel army.

Trina loved Kel, despite his unfortunate tendency to out think himself.

Safer closer to danger—humph.

Trina mentally cursed herself for letting Kel win the stay-or-go argument with idiotic logic.

Never again. My kerlak pistol—set for stun, of course—is doing the talking at the next family discussion.

She moved to stare listlessly out the grimy window and absently noted the click as Kel turned off the thought monitor.

"Hate to interrupt your mental bashing of me, dearest, but we're leaving," said Kel.

Trina's head snapped up and met her husband's cool blue eyes. His serlak pistol and kerlinblade were already donned. Although they'd been married four months, she still hadn't gotten used to him reading her moods, expressions, and thoughts.

"And where exactly are we going?" she asked, cocking an eyebrow.

"Away from here," Kel responded. "I doubt we'll have a chance to interview Queen Reia about me being a distant cousin of her late husband. So, anywhere away from that psychotic man who wants to be king will do." Kel handed her the weapon belt he had been adjusting.

With a slight frown, she took the belt, slung it around her slim waist, and clicked it snuggly into position. The move, made with grace earned through nineteen years of space lane travel, marked the shift from restless fugitive to self-confident captain.

"Do you think we could convince the queen to leave with us?" Trina inquired.

"We won't even get an audience with her now, but we should keep that meeting with Ranger Wellum," Kel said.

For someone in hiding, Kel did a lousy job of keeping a low profile. A mere two days after landing, they had received an encrypted infopad from Ranger Todd Wellum informing them of an urgent job. Today—day seven of their visit to Reshner—Trina checked the charge on her weapon and grunted at the thought of fleeing yet again.

We need to find a nice, out-of-the-way planet where the rest of the galaxy will ignore us.

"When, where, and how many do we have to take out to get there?" Trina asked, pushing the thought aside.

"That's why I love you," Kel said. His tender tone threw Trina off balance as much as the sudden kiss-embrace combo that followed. "Forty minutes, Rinten Tavern, and unknown but no more than four or five bounty hunters and the odd Kezem lackey too drunk to recognize humble fugitives like us." He flashed her that blasted smile that rarely failed to turn her heart into mush.

Trina agreed with his assessment of the opposition. This section of Rammon, the Southern Quarter, had fallen first, and the assault on the palace had most of Kezem's troops thoroughly occupied.

Precisely forty minutes later, Kel and Trina sat facing each other in a private booth and stared into miniature tankards of local ale that smelled strong enough to take off space-grade paint. After one whiff, Trina poured the offensive liquid onto the fuzzy, plant-like thing that was creeping too close to her arm for comfort. A high-pitched, ecstatic yelp startled her.

Kel's laughter at her expression morphed into a cough followed by muffled cry of pain when her steel-tipped boot brushed his shin.

"I forgot to warn you that bovas like Reshner ale. They'll tickle your arm until you either surrender your drink or smack them," he informed, swatting the bova that had been steadily approaching his drink.

Somehow, Trina doubted he'd forgotten, but she let it go because his eyes narrowed, telling her their contact had arrived.

Kel cautiously took a sip of ale, coughed, and gladly surrendered the remainder to the bova.

"The ale is an acquired taste," said a synthesized voice.

Trina watched Kel as he shifted to have easier access to his pistol. Engulfed in oversized robes that hid species, gender, age, and weapons, the being seemed harmless but Kel's wary expression made her cautious. The timeless, tense moment of first contact grated on her patience.

"Please, join us," Kel said cordially, gesturing to the empty chair next to their table.

The voice volume dropped, and Trina had to lean forward to hear.

"I am Nils Clavon. I give you my name as a sign of trust. My time is short. My master apologizes for his absence. He had urgent personal business to attend to, as do I."

"Lord Kezem moved much quicker than anyone anticipated, right?" Kel guessed.

"Your reputation precedes you, Master Kiren. My master heard of your inquiries and informed the queen. She conducted her own investigation and now asks that you prove your loyalty by accepting a dangerous mission. Here is the information. Please consider the job. Many lives hinge upon your decision." The being dropped an infopad onto the table and left.

Trina watched Kel snatch up the infopad and rise to leave. She settled the ale account while Kel searched the infopad for tracers or malicious traps. She feared they would be accosted, but they exited the tavern without incident.

The only place private enough to view an important message was their Glaborn pleasure craft: *Zipper*. They met only one patrol on the way to the ship. The short confrontation went down like a great harvest celebration including lots of flashes, curses, and crashes. It ended with more than half the participants unconscious.

Three of the foes fell before Kel's flashing kerlinblade. One opponent, a particularly pungent Tedgmian, absorbed four energy blasts from Trina who then resorted to a more hands-on approach. She leapt onto the short man's back, rung his filthy neck, and held on for dear life.

When the Tedgmian finally lost consciousness, Trina tossed him aside with a disgusted grunt.

"I thought only Bozme could smell that bad," she commented, fondly recalling the elderly furball of a first mate.

"Well, I doubt this fellow's captain is quite as emphatic about personal hygiene as you were," Kel said, while relieving the unfortunate mercenaries of their various weapons.

Old pirate habit, Trina thought at her husband.

"You know those die the hardest, my love."

She shot him a read-this look and proceeded to mentally call him everything from an Asher tree toad to a Julip banker and worse.

"Such language is unbecoming of a lady," Kel said, smirking.

A kiss stamped a satisfactory end to the brush with death. They hastened on toward their ship. Although *Zipper* was greatly modified with illegal weapons and defense systems, Trina futilely wished for Kel's old Driden cruiser *Kel's Swift Hand.*

That beauty was a flying fortress.

Kel had been torn between his lucrative plundering business and her, but he had made the right choice. She would even have settled for her old cruiser, *Sassy One*, which had been rechristened as *Pride of Zopha*. The new name had come from the Driden god of fortune, a fitting name for the moderately armed cruiser that had survived several bounty hunter poundings. But wishes would get her nowhere so she pushed them aside.

Trina warmed the engines while Kel locked down the loading bay and swept for tracers. She was surprised and grateful that the engines worked. Kel found three tracers in the usual spots and two more in creative spots like the lavatory door handle. They worked swiftly and silently. Lord Kezem's nosy lackeys were no match for professionals.

Once secured in the cockpit, Kel activated the sound damper and flipped the infopad's active switch. The face that appeared on the screen was far younger than Trina had expected.

The man's fiery, rust-colored hair was balanced by his deep, concerned hazel eyes.

"Greetings, Master and Lady Kiren, I am Ranger Todd Wellum, and my faith in you rests upon your distant relation to the Royal House Minstel. By carrying out my mission you will greatly aid the queen. She is concerned. The informants in Osem report that Lord Kezem's forces have bombed the water reserve, set fire to the fields, and cut off aid to outlying villages. The death toll is rising. There is a special shipment at Ranger Corida's house in the West Quarter of Rammon. The shipment must reach Osem safely. I trust no one else. Fly safe."

Kel slapped the active switch again, and his brows furrowed in concentration.

"Well, I guess that solves the personal mission here," he mused. "What's so important about Osem?"

"He's hiding something," Trina said, not bothering to speculate on Osem's significance.

"But what? And why trust strangers, even related strangers?" asked Kel.

"Being the king's fourth cousin six times removed counts for something," Trina said deadpan. "Seriously, look at how his eyes shift when he speaks of the shipment," Trina urged.

Kel did so and his eyes softened ever so slightly.

"This is a dangerous time for the royal family," he said.

Trina's mind replayed clips from conversations overheard in the past few days. Her fingers lightly massaged her temple while she sifted through the rumors, double speak, and outright lies. Then, she stopped and muttered an imprecation.

"These people are crazy. How the flipping horn bats do they expect to smuggle anyone out of the palace?" The objective half of her recognized that the ranting meant she had committed herself to the task.

"That's not our problem," Kel reminded. "We only have to see the passenger or passengers and other supplies safely to Osem." He unlocked further instructions, flew to the site, and maneuvered the ship into the narrow alley without lights.

The Rangers had the supplies ready for transfer to *Zipper*'s cargo hold. *They're well organized; I'll give them that.*

The moment the cargo was stowed, Kel shot the tiny ship straight into the air, hoping to surprise any anti-spacecraft guns Kezem might have on hand looking for a good target. As soon as he'd cleared the city limits, Kel made the ship dive until they were traveling mere meters above the ground. Twelve minutes later, Kel sat straighter in the pilot seat and relaxed a micron.

"We should be at Osem in fi—"

"It's gone." Silent tears crept down Trina's pale face as she pointed to the screen.

"Gone," he echoed. "The entire city? That's not possible!"

They set the security vidrecorder to look at Osem and zoomed in. Smoke rose from the city, spiraling upward and disappearing into the moonlit sky. Dark storm clouds followed closely behind *Zipper*. The pending rain would drown the fire and smoke, but the port city would be nothing more than a collection of craters for a long time.

"What will we do with the cargo?" Trina asked.

"We'll take it with us when I run the pathetic little blockade," Kel declared, throwing switches and pressing buttons. He gathered every scrap of energy he could temporarily borrow and added it to the engine reserves.

Trina worried about the dozen ships set up as a blockade around the planet. Lord Kezem didn't need to have a massive blockade to hinder travel around Reshner because its three tiny moons created unstable gravity wells which made many exit vectors unsafe. Trina nodded and sent some of the power Kel had gathered to the weapons systems. They had been hugging the planet's surface and powered down many systems to avoid sensors, but with the decision to run the blockade, subtlety could be ditched.

"Correction: you punch a hole in Kezem's blockade, and *I'll* run it," Trina said. As soon as Kel surrendered the pilot's chair, Trina slipped in, adjusted the safety restraints, and moved the chair forward to compensate for the height disparity between herself and her husband. She flew by instinct, veering sharply left to avoid the first shots. Belatedly, she hoped Kel had had time to strap in. A dull thud, yelp, and incoherent stream of angry words told her he hadn't.

Seconds later his voice came over the ship's communications system. "Maybe I should fly."

"Since I want to live and I'm realistic about my shooting abilities, we stick to this plan," Trina said. She threw the ship into a thrilling series of spirals, partly to avoid the bullets and energy blasts trying to turn them into scrap and partially for fun.

"Dearest, unless you want to be scraping Reshner ale and the crackers we had for the midday meal off the walls, I suggest you stick to the less exciting evasive maneuvers!" Kel shouted.

Trina grunted but acquiesced to his request. Forgoing further fun, she skipped through the blockade in the most efficient manner possible. She tried to count the explosions but lost count around five. Then, they were out of range, and the ship's guns quieted. Kel joined her in the cockpit again. After setting the autopilot, she looked up, met his faint smile, and held out her hand. He took it and squeezed. For a moment, they didn't move. The short space battle had provided the perfect outlet for energy and emotion, but the effort was also draining.

Trina glanced over her left shoulder and checked the charts. They were safely en route to the edge of the galaxy.

"You picked a lovely escape vector," she commented, facing Kel again.

"You said you wanted to find a nice, out-of-the-way planet where we could be ignored," Kel reminded her. "Besides, a few of the nearby Wild planets look habitable."

"I *thought* I wanted that, but now I'm not so sure. And you'd better be right about habitability or this cockpit's gonna get real small, real quick." She leveled a finger at him.

He smiled roguishly, captured the accusing finger, pulled her to her feet, and kissed her.

"Let's hope so," he murmured when the kiss finally ended.

"We'd better go check on that cargo," Trina said somewhat reluctantly.

Hand-in-hand, they wandered back to the cargo hold where the Rangers had hastily stowed the supplies. Immediately spotting one container marked: fragile, this end up, Trina knelt and pulled the tab at the top. The outer container retracted, revealing a life capsule. Kel quickly disengaged the locks. A flat screen slid out of the top, and soon, Kel and Trina found themselves staring into the cool, pain-filled green eyes of Queen Reia Minstel. A long pause indicated the young queen's struggle to find proper words with which to instruct her son's guardians.

"Greetings. Thank you for coming to our aid. My troubles with our Order notwithstanding, the Rangers have long been guardians and friends to House Minstel. I had hoped to see Reshner through the darkness, but I expect I shall soon join my beloved Terosh in death. Servants have charge of Teven and Rela, but I think it best my children not stay together. As guardians, you have every right to add a surname of your own choosing, but he will always be my youngest child, Tavel, Dulad Prince, third in line to rule Reshner.

"When the time is right, the anotechs will convey my messages to him. They will activate suddenly and most likely distress my son. Hopefully by then, he may return to Rammon to help his brother and sister restore peace. Should he have no desire to rule, I hereby release him from royal duties, provided Reshner has a king or queen either from the Minstel line or duly elected by the Governors Council and the Senate. I would send a Royal Guard with him, but I suspect treachery from somewhere in those ranks. Guard him well, my friends. Queen Reia Minstel, second day of the month of Jira (March), 1547."

The message ended and looped around to the beginning, ready to repeat if necessary.

For several minutes, Trina and Kel clung to each other and stared at the tiny prince.

What do we do?

Despite the panicked thought repeatedly charging through her head, Trina felt herself falling in love with the boy. They had planned to put off parenting for several years, perhaps indefinitely, but it seems the Fates had different plans for them.

"Well, Prince Tavel, looks like you're stuck with us," said Kel.

Chapter 4:
Rough Welcome

Jira (March) 2, 1547
Same Day
East Quarter, Streets of Rammon, City of Rammon

Weary, Todd Wellum shivered with anticipation and dread. His mission had been a complete waste of time. They should have been mounting a rescue. Queen or not, Kiata's sister needed to leave the palace soon. He hoped Kiata had sent Nils to meet Kel and Trina Kiren in his stead.

His head hurt from lack of food, and his heart hurt with despair and anger. He growled, remembering the Ashatans' verdict concerning Queen Reia's plight.

It's nothing short of sanctioned murder!

The Ranger High Council had agreed to raise one of the children but immediately quelled discussion of a more direct intervention because the dispute for the throne involved two members with ties to the Minstel line, Reia by marriage and Kezem by maternal blood. Todd suspected Master Liam Deliad wanted Kezem to replace Reia because she'd chosen to marry Terosh against the Ranger code. Todd had arranged for the youngest child, Prince Tavel, to reside in Osem, but without the full support of the Rangers, Lord Kezem would soon rule. If that happened, the young Minstel heirs would be vulnerable to destruction for many years.

This will not end well.

Todd furtively picked his way through the darkened streets. Malevolent eyes followed his every move from the shadows. Being a Ranger taught him about courage and handling fear but being the father of a four-year-old girl taught him a new kind of fear, one resulting in a stabbing sensation that tightened his chest.

His recent travels confirmed Lord Kezem's firm grip on the planet. Despite the dangers, Todd focused on little else besides completing his new mission of getting his family far away from Rammon. The need to hold his wife and child warred with his judgment and urged his legs to carry him home swiftly. Nearing his house in the East Quarter, Todd traded stealth for speed.

One pace from home, safety, and Kiata, the door swung out abruptly.

Finely tuned reflexes saved Todd's nose from a beating, but the head blow would have hurt less than the sight before him. Ceiling lightbars brightened the grim scene. Kiata lay on her left side facing the doorway. The mass of bruises, gashes, and blade marks covering her face represented only a portion of the punishment inflicted upon her body. Todd rushed to her not caring that there were others in the room. Her lifeless eyes pierced Todd's heart, killing the hope he had held for the future. Moaning, he sank to his knees, sick in heart and body. His stomach held nothing to surrender so he choked and retched and sobbed until his strength was gone.

Where's Kayleen? The thought burst through the walls of mental anguish.

Todd's head snapped up.

Kiata must have sent her with Nils, he thought, wishing Ridenspeed to the servant. The hope returned some of his strength.

"Lord Kezem sends his greetings," a familiar male voice announced. "I'm sorry your wife expired before you could see her. Pity. I would have liked to see that reunion."

Todd's body moved before consulting his mind. Screaming, he spun and kicked. His left foot connected with flesh and bone. The satisfying impact brought a smile to his face, but it was short lived. A fist landed on his left cheek and smashed into his nose, releasing a flood of blood. Oblivious to pain, Todd fought with the strength of a man bent on revenge and the courage of someone with nothing left to lose. Strong arms gripped him from behind, but he threw them off, spun, and battered the man's face and neck. More hands grasped him from all sides. He traded punches and kicks with half a dozen young soldiers.

"Enough!" snapped the first man.

Suddenly, the hands let go and everybody backed away, leaving Todd standing near his dead wife. Still dripping blood from his nose, he glared at the speaker who wore a blood-spattered blue uniform filled with fancy rank pins. The man was plain except for his shiny, dark hair which was as well-tended as his ego.

"Kolknir." Todd spat the name like a curse. "What are you doing here? Murdering Royalists seems a bit below your new station. This is Kezem's big night. Have you forgotten everything you learned as a Ranger?"

If the sarcasm irritated the man, he hid it well. Shaking his head, Kolknir glanced down in dismay at his bloody uniform.

"The Rangers are nothing to me. Haven't been for quite some time. You and Kiata were always my favorite students though, so fierce, so competitive," said Kolknir. "You would have been fine allies. Too bad Lord Kezem believed Kiata would never betray her sister, even if they weren't truly sisters."

Blood doesn't make family. Love does.

This second reference to Kiata snapped something inside Todd. With an enraged scream, he launched himself at Kolknir again. Before anyone could draw a breath, Todd's fingers gripped Kolknir's neck and squeezed hard.

To their credit, Kolknir's men reacted in the next instant. Some tore at Todd's iron-like fingers, while others kicked, punched, and cursed him. After much effort, they finally freed Kolknir.

"Do not kill him!" Kolknir shouted.

His men eyed him carefully, clearly confused.

"Don't kill him, my Lord?" a young soldier asked cautiously. His arm was cocked awkwardly above his head ready to deal another blow to their prisoner.

"You heard me!" Kolknir brushed at his sullied uniform, which would forever carry a mixture of his and Todd's blood. "Lord Kezem wishes him to experience the palace prisons."

"Lord Kolknir?" Todd asked contemptuously.

"Yes, Todd, Lord Kezem has made me a sublord," said Kolknir. "You should show me more respect than Kiata did."

Todd had heard of Kezem's sublords. Soldiers, traders, merchants, and even Rangers who supported Kezem's cause through funds, favors, and other traitorous activities were rewarded with high positions in the new government. Todd could tell Kolknir expected a response, so he spat blood at the man's feet. At this point, he cared only about the hope of seeing his daughter again.

***

Jira (March) 2, 1547
Same Day
Merchant Quarter, City of Rammon

She's not dead. She's not dead.

Talyon Keldor silently chanted the phrase, but his eyes argued with him.

This is crazy.

Kiata Wellum certainly looked dead. She lay on a hov sled surrounded by six of Kezem's men dressed in the muddy red uniform of his poorly named Reshner Liberation Army. She was the strongest woman he knew. It pained him to see her so still, pale, and fragile looking. One of the soldiers had the decency to close her eyes. Taly breathed a sigh of relief that Kolknir hadn't bid his men to remove Kiata's head or anything like that.

The queen's plan to rescue her sister was pure insanity, but so far, it seemed to be working as predicted. If anyone else had been asking Taly to go on this strange mission for any other reason than saving Kiata, he would have laughed in their faces, but he owed her his life. He also owed the queen for her treatment of his grandfather. Taly forced down the storm of emotions as he thought of the king's assassination, the queen's danger, her orders, Lord Kezem's hunt for the royal children, the rebellion, and the rest of this mess.

He wished the queen would let him kill Lord Kezem. Taly was realistic enough about his chances of successfully completing that task, but somehow dying in a blaze of glory seemed easier than this shadowy stalking that could go on for years.

The soldiers' steady march brought them in range. Taly eyed them through the scope of his rifle, sent up a prayer for steady hands and clean shots, and fired. The first two dropped before the rest could draw weapons.

Suddenly, the air around Taly and the soldiers lit with energy beams. Some were blue stun beams, but most were the brilliant red color of full-energy, kill shots. Reacting by instinct, Taly fired wildly and dove for cover. The scene before him unfolded in his mind again. As much as he had faith in his own shooting abilities, he could never have released so many beams simultaneously. That left only one explanation: another shooter.

Merisia!

Taly cursed under his breath. He had told her to stay in hiding. He ran to another window two away from the one he'd originally attacked from and cautiously peeked out. Sure enough, a steady stream of beams flooded from a window a few stories up from his current position. A glance down amused and horrified Taly.

The shots from the window were so wild that the remaining four soldiers were firing in several directions, trying to pin down the origin point. They would find it soon, but for now, Merisia's lack of shooting skills gave Taly an advantage. Seizing the opportunity, he shot two more soldiers.

Frustration built in Taly. He needed to get to Kiata soon or one of Merisia's wild shots would kill her. Even as he thought it, one of Merisia's beams struck Kiata in the center of her chest. For an instant, she glowed red as the energy beam washed over a wide area like it had struck a personal shield. Taly blinked but couldn't fathom what was protecting her. The soldiers would have no reason to equip a body with a Personal Shielding Device. Torn between going up to get Merisia and going down to get Kiata, Taly grunted and scanned the area again with his scope.

A fresh squad of soldiers arrived. Their commander pointed up at Taly's building.

Taly shot the commander and then abandoned his rifle and went to find Merisia. He wished he could take the weapon with him, but it wasn't exactly designed as a close-quarter weapon. He and Merisia would be in for the fight of their lives, but perhaps searching the building would slow the soldiers down enough to let them sneak out and rescue Kiata.

"Merisia!" Taly shouted. He had to call her name twice more and put a hand on her shoulder before she dropped the kerlak pistol, turned, and practically tackled him with a fierce embrace.

"I'm sorry, Taly, so sorry. I had to come, had to!" Merisia babbled.

"We've got to go," said Taly, returning her hug. "Kezem's soldiers have entered the building."

A determined look crossed Merisia's face. She scooped up the handgun and held it out to Taly.

"I'll stall them. Go get the Ranger, Taly. Go."

"They'll kill you," Taly argued. "Come with me."

"You don't know that; you can't know that," said Merisia, grinning faintly. "You'd make a terrible damsel in distress, Taly, but they might buy it from me, just might."

Although he hated to admit it, Taly saw that her plan offered him a faint chance. Emotion choked him.

"Merisia, I—"

"You have your mission, Taly, and I have mine," said Merisia, placing a hand over his mouth. "Save the queen's sister." With tears streaming down her face, Merisia fled the room.

Taly wanted to sit down and think about Merisia's words and the million messages in her eyes, but instead, he locked his emotions away, tucked her pistol next to his own, and climbed out the window. The building would be crawling with soldiers by now, so Taly would do the unexpected.

Chapter 5:
The Royal House Falls

Jira (March) 2, 1547
Same Day
Royal Palace, City of Rammon

Governor General Third Lord of Idonia, Kezem Altran—known as Lord Kezem—strode into the Rammon palace at last. He finished clearing the first floor and grunted at the thought of clearing four more floors before reaching the throne room. He'd already passed more guard posts than he could count and each new one irritated him more than the last. Thankfully, many posts were empty, having been abandoned by those enlightened to join the right side before the palace fell.

By the time he reached the two Royal Guards stationed outside the throne room, Kezem's anger overflowed, lending strength to his body. He moved with grace for such a large man. He enjoyed towering over lesser men, and almost laughed at the memory of his scrawny self only a few years prior. Surprisingly, he also missed his mother. After all, tonight was the culmination of her hopes, dreams, ambitions, and years of planning. His movements were quick, decisive, and deadly. He might have let one of his eager soldiers gut the hapless guards, but he figured it would be healthier to vent some anger before reaching Queen Reia. It would be a pity if he skewered the young woman without at least gloating.

Despite their vaunted training, the Royal Guards were no match for Kezem. He wasted little time dispatching them with his electrified banistick and kerlinblade. Although banistick modifications could be as simple or complex as one desired, Kezem had chosen shocks because of the delightful ability to torture people while fighting them. He attacked both guards simultaneously. The banistick in his left hand caught one man in the armpit, resulting in a loud shriek as every nerve fired at once. The thin edge of Kezem's yellow kerlinblade slammed into the other guard's neck, instantly removing his head.

As the guard on the left breathed his last, Kezem casually punched in the code for the throne room door. Ironically, the traitor had rigged the king's hov with explosives for next to nothing but demanded six hundred thousand kefs for the simple code. When nothing happened, Kezem cursed in Resh, Hintle, and Borner.

"I will kill him," he vowed, forgetting that he had already planned on killing the traitorous Captain of the Royal Guard. "I will rip him apart piece by piece! No one betrays me!"

The tone and volume caused his nearby minions to cringe. The soldier stupid enough to be within striking distance paid dearly for it. The banistick slap left him unconscious.

"Deven, get me a prisoner!"

No one moved.

Dark blue eyes blazing, Kezem turned to his soldiers. His high emotional state caused a yellow streak shaped like lightning to slash through either side of his irises. Being one sixteenth Bornovan, Kezem's eye color shifted shades of blue in accordance with his mood. His chiseled face twisted into a fierce expression.

"You struck him, Lord Kezem," a brave soul murmured.

"Then *you* get me a servant!"

The lieutenant bowed and left as fast as his stubby legs would carry him. Luckily, he found a prisoner being led down the hall to the meeting chamber where Kezem's forces were storing servants who surrendered without too much trouble.

Kezem preferred to keep prisoners alive until he was certain he wished them dead. He could always kill them later. He watched with amusement as his youthful lieutenant struggled to subdue the servant girl. Thin but wiry, the servant used her lower center of gravity to spin Kezem's man into the wall.

"Enough! Jorg, Makil, relieve Lieutenant Toft of his burden," said Kezem, recalling that he had a queen to kill.

The twins shared a grin.

"It will be done, Lord Kezem," they answered, moving to follow his order. What they lacked in intelligence, the twins made up for in blind loyalty and delightful cruelty.

Soon, the pale servant was on her knees before Lord Kezem.

"Give me the door code," he ordered.

Fear made the girl's eyes glaze, and Kezem suspected she might pass out.

He deactivated his banistick and returned it to his belt. Then, he changed the kerlinblade settings so that the blade was long and thin before pointing it at her neck.

"Do not faint, or you will never wake."

"Let Atellia go, Kezem. She does not know the code. I had it changed an hour ago," said a calm voice.

Kezem spun on his right heel and stared up at the vidscreen showing Queen Reia's image. She sat erect on her oversized throne, dressed in green and purple ceremonial robes. The hood of the outer cloak touched her forehead, framing her face. Her expression was sad and strained, as if she concentrated very hard on something.

"There has been enough death tonight," said the queen.

"I should slaughter everyone in this palace," Kezem said.

Her expression relaxed ever so slightly.

"But you will not," Reia said with confidence that irked him. She appeared weary, but the coolness of her green eyes helped her maintain the indomitable illusion. "You live by terror, but not even your coldest allies would stand for a complete massacre of the palace staff."

"You believe that? Perhaps this will change your mind." Kezem thrust his kerlinblade at the servant's neck. A scream and curse escaped him as a sharp pain in his blade hand caused him to jerk violently. The blade veered to the left of its target, leaving only a mild burn on the servant's neck.

The girl looked as surprised as he was that she still lived.

Kezem dropped his kerlinblade which suddenly burned in his hand.

"What have you done? Your tricks will not save you! I knew my cousin was insane to marry a Ranger!"

"Why you think me such a threat, I shall never know," Reia commented. "I could never protect so many …" A flicker of amusement entered her eyes, and the right corner of her mouth crept upward slowly. "Perhaps Terosh protects this place."

"It's not possible!" Kezem hated that her mockery could provoke him so easily.

The queen sighed.

"I claim little by way of goodness, but you are evil, Kezem. The easy paths, fleeting wealth, and power promises may sway people for now, but Reshner will come to its senses." Her eyes bore into him. "I promise you. My people will not suffer your rule for long."

He seethed that she momentarily lay beyond his grasp. Snatching his kerlinblade from the floor, Kezem clenched his fists around the weapon and imagined it was her neck. He considered killing the servant for spite but dismissed the thought.

She's not worth the effort.

"Take her away," Kezem ordered. "Jorg, Makil, Toft, break down those doors!" He whirled right to face different soldiers. "The rest of you finish clearing the palace. I want every child, soldier, servant, and other being within these walls rounded up immediately!"

His soldiers rushed to do his bidding, but the battle for the palace raged for two more hours. Eventually, Kezem's soldiers battered through the throne room doors.

Inside, more Royal Guards, Palace Security, and Melian Maidens tangled with his men. Kezem slashed his way through the crowd but only got halfway across the throne room before a dark-skinned Melian Maiden leapt into his path, halting his progress. His red kerlinblade locked with her banistick. He shoved forward, using his superior size and strength to knock her back a few steps. They traded strikes. He added his banistick to the fight. Finally, he smashed the modified banistick under her chin. The blow stunned her and his kerlinblade finished her. Gritting his teeth at the delay, Kezem stepped over the body and continued towards the throne.

Head tilted forward and arms resting at her sides, Queen Reia stood at the edge of the meter-high platform holding the throne. From a distance, she appeared immune to the death and destruction around her. But up close, a steady stream of silent tears spoke her pain at watching good people die in her defense.

Their eyes met and Kezem felt shame, guilt, and grief shoot through him. Her youthful beauty struck him dumb. He despised her for having that effect on him, and the anger drove the feeling away. Kezem wished to possess her, but the people of Reshner would never stand for such dishonor to royalty.

Realizing he had halted, Kezem gathered his courage and marched up to the queen. A triumphant grin spread across his face.

"I am surprised that you have chosen to face honorable death, Your Majesty."

"There is little honor in this, Kezem," said Queen Reia, waving around them. "I stayed because my people needed me here."

"Your people abandoned you, Reia. You lost them long ago when you considered GAPP for an ally." Kezem shook his head in mock sadness. "When will you learn that people are selfish? They want a strong ruler. They seek money and comfort, and I have promised them both. Their greed makes them easy to manipulate for someone with power, ambition, and—"

"Little respect for life," Reia finished. "You may seize the throne today, but years of war will follow. Are you prepared to fight for it?"

"Do not concern yourself with my well-being, Your Grace. My men will handle the pathetic peasants sympathetic to you," Kezem assured her. "And your children will never reach their destinations. Osem is being destroyed as we speak."

The statement caused a momentary crack in Queen Reia's sad, solemn expression. She closed her eyes to ward off the pain.

"So, the betrayal runs that deep," Reia murmured, blinking back tears.

Kezem's kerlinblade blazed red in his right hand. He contemplated it then made a slight adjustment so that the blade flattened and shone bright green on both sides of a thin, purple center.

"I respect you, Your Grace. Were circumstances different, we might have even been friends. See, I shall even kill you in the colors of your chosen House." A flick of his wrist brought the blade tip to the point of Reia's chin.

She tipped her chin up but did not retreat.

Kezem secretly admired her nerve.

"You know who your betrayer is, don't you? He had hoped to woo you, but your death fits better with my plans. Do not worry. My men will kill him soon enough."

"I do not wish his death. Too much of that has already touched this people," said the queen.

"Well spoken, Your Majesty," Kezem sneered. "Fitting words before you die." He drew his arm back for a killing thrust.

"My death will come but not that easily." Queen Reia twisted to her right and released the clasp securing the outer cloak and robes to her neck. The ceremonial robes flew away from her like living things. Underneath, she wore a comfortable white shirt and plain brown trousers which allowed free movement, clothing more befitting of a Ranger than a queen.

Her clothes reminded Kezem of her humble roots. Without the ceremonial robes, her appearance matched that of any woman, but she was no ordinary woman. A delicate, deadly looking silver blade appeared in her right hand. She saluted, grasping the smooth handle and turning the blade sideways.

One of Kezem's eager men leapt onto the dais ready to strike.

"No!" Kezem roared, fearing his underling might kill the queen.

He need not have feared.

Reia spun away from the clumsy strike, using natural momentum and the flat edge of her sword to beam Kezem's man upside the head.

"I will kill her! All who interfere will die!" Kezem snatched his banistick from his belt and launched his first attack. He struck hard but avoided killing blows, determined to savor the moment.

Their duel lasted untold minutes. Kezem forgot the stress of taking over Rammon. Only this battle mattered. They fought from one end of the throne room to the other and back again several times, dancing over bodies and screaming wounded. His men scrambled out of the way of the desperate duel. The clash of steel on crackling energy mingled with shuffling feet and labored breath. Their weapons met, locked, released, and crashed in a dizzying display of lights and sparks.

Queen Reia drew first blood, catching Kezem's right forearm with the tip of her blade. She smiled radiantly as if that single touch could win back the world he was so bent on taking from her. One of his banistick slashes glanced off her shoulder, but she fought on. Kezem was surprised she could still hold a blade after the shock that must have gone through her. He then poured all his energy into jarring strikes. Her smile disappeared as she concentrated on catching the blows.

Eventually, his brute strength prevailed. He smacked her blade down with the banistick and swept the kerlinblade at her neck. Kezem might as well have struck rock. He pulled his blade back revealing a faint line of blood. His eyes widened.

That blow should have beheaded her!

Queen Reia smiled faintly.

"My friends don't seem to want to let me go."

Though baffled, Kezem redoubled his efforts striking wildly and with more force. Finally, he disengaged and took two steps back.

"Shoot her!" he ordered.

A dozen shots flew toward them.

Kezem jumped aside as one came too close.

For several seconds, Reia did well dodging the energy beams and serlak bullets, but the sheer number proved too much. Three beams struck her in the back, knocking her forward, and a bullet bounced off her head, leaving her dazed.

"Cease fire!" Kezem shouted.

A few steps brought her within striking distance. He thrust the kerlinblade forward and his blade met real flesh and pierced her heart. She winced but uttered only a sigh. Sinking to her knees, Queen Reia breathed her last.

It was over.

As he watched the light of life fade from her eyes, Kezem waited for the sense of joyful victory to come, but he only felt tired.

Chapter 6:
Linked Fate

Jira (March) 2, 1547
Same Day
Throne Room, Royal Palace, City of Rammon

"Do you like my new accommodations, Sublord Kolknir?" Lord Kezem asked. Having changed into a crisp black uniform and donned a silver cloak, Kezem looked every bit the victorious king he wished to be.

He smiled and gestured expansively. Majestic crimson banners hung from the walls and ceilings approximately every four meters, spanning the throne room's seventy meters length and forty meters width. Each banner featured the silhouette of a man locked in combat with a zalok. The zalok's claws held the man in a bone-crushing grip, but the man's sword was buried in the beast's chest right where the largest heart would be.

"How did your mission go?" Kezem inquired, before Kolknir could answer his first question.

"My mission was a great success," Kolknir said, bowing stiffly, a gesture suggesting familiarity as well as respect.

A big bruise on the left side of Kolknir's face said differently, but Lord Kezem refrained from commenting. After all, the healing wrap on his arm proved even successful missions had their hard edges.

"We cleared the Merchant Quarter an hour ago. The North Quarter will take more time, but I am confident Rammon will fully submit to your rule by tomorrow."

"And what of the young royals?" asked Kezem, pleased that Kolknir sounded suitably humble. Kezem was not fool enough to believe the heirs would always remain helpless babes. If they survived, Royalist hope would survive, and he would never have a moment's peace.

Kezem had purchased control of the Senate and the Governors Council, but many people clung to the notion that only the Minstel bloodline ought to rule. Technically, Kezem was in line for the throne, but his claim was far less solid than the three, knee-high royals. His mother, Lady Mavis, had been disowned by her father when she'd married his father, Dravid Altran.

Crushing Royalist hopes was why he had struck Osem—stronghold of the Rangers—so hard. Most other Royalists were merchants and peasants, not soldiers, but Rangers could fight rather well and tended to take their vows to protect House Minstel far too seriously.

"No, my Lord," Kolknir said with a frown, "but we are tracking down every Ranger. Despite personal tensions, the queen would seek their aid first. Kiata Wellum is dead, her husband is in our custody, and their child is missing."

Kezem's cobalt eyes narrowed dangerously. A flash of yellow entered his eyes but faded as he clamped down on his anger.

"Where is the queen, my Lord?"

"My plans have changed," Kezem said, rising from the throne and walking to the platform's edge. "She had too many supporters to be spared. Kill the traitor. His loyalty is far too fickle."

"It will be done, my Lord," Kolknir promised. He stepped aside to issue the proper orders.

Kezem nodded absently and paced the dais lost in thought.

What of the girl?

His spies had spoken of plans to smuggle the princes out of the palace, but there had been no mention of moving the princess.

What would Reia do to protect her daughter?

Kezem's cloak swirled as he turned. He fiddled with his banistick and the ceremonial dagger he had taken from a vanquished Melian Maiden. To his knowledge, he had no children, but if he did, the palace would be the last place to leave them. With Rammon's central location, "far away" could mean anywhere.

"The princess must be near." Kezem quit pacing and narrowed his eyes. "Kolknir, seal off Rammon. No one gets in or out until every human child less than four has been killed. Children of other species are irrelevant. Deal with them as you see fit."

"Forgive me, Lord Kezem, but wouldn't it be better to spare the children?" Kolknir inquired. He hastened on before Kezem could object. "Create a camp to sift the youth. The weak will die, and you will be left with strong, impressionable youths to mold into a loyal fighting force."

"Go on."

"It will serve a double purpose, my Lord. The children will become soldiers and their parents will work the weapons factories ... for free."

"How would I ensure loyalty?" Kezem wondered, liking the plan. He found it interesting that the people he disliked intensely often proved most useful.

"Fear, power, and rewards. Hold their families hostage. You have done it before, just not on this scale," said Kolknir.

"True," Kezem admitted.

"Turn the Festival of Future Fighters to your own purposes. Compel able-bodied youths to participate in the contests. The top ones could be commissioned as Royal Guards or Melian Maidens and be sent on the

Kireshana as usual, and the rest would be given rank and file positions in Reshner's Liberation Army."

"I see. It is a slow plan, but it has promise," Kezem said. Understanding came upon him. Although Kolknir had command of Kezem's invasion force, the power of the rank would soon disappear. "Of course, the Royal Guard would need a new commander," Kezem mused.

"Would you consider me for the honor, my Lord?" asked Kolknir.

"I thought you wished to be Governor of Idonia," said Kezem.

"This sounds more suited to my talents," Kolknir replied. "I have taught many students over the years."

Kezem's deep chuckle filled the space between them.

"That you have. Very well, kneel." When Kolknir followed the direction, Kezem drew his banistick and touched it to the man's shoulders. Even at low power, the electric shocks made Kolknir's shoulders tremble. "I hereby grant you full command of Reshner's armed forces, including the Royal Guard and the RLA. Rise, Supreme Commander Kolknir. Summon Captain Linel so I can promote her to Aster Captain. She will serve directly under you and conduct business pertaining to a new order of the Melian Maidens."

"It will be done, my Lord," Kolknir said.

It never ceased to amuse Kezem to hear the former Ranger address him so respectfully, but he watched the man closely, expecting betrayal someday. "Accept only human candidates of the finest appearance and abilities, Commander," Kezem instructed. "Turn the aliens and the inferior over to Commander Tigert and the factories. I expect your first report in a month."

"As you will, Lord Kezem, so be it," said Kolknir. The new commander saluted sharply and left in a hurry.

Despite the late hour, Lord Kezem ordered the cooks to prepare a celebration feast. The silence in the throne room struck him full force, making him frown. Something was missing. Such a momentous occasion required female company.

"Guards!"

Two of his ever-present, unobtrusive shadows appeared at his side.

"Have the prison guards select some pretty companions. Have them properly attired and send them to the dining hall."

The junior guard nodded, saluted, and stepped back to deliver the order. Kezem looked critically at his outfit and concluded that the military look suited the night. Smoothing back his graying dark hair, Kezem settled back onto the throne and let his mind wander over the glorious evening.

The hard part was over. With Terosh and Reia dead and the Rangers scattered, Reshner was his to rule. Tonight, Kezem would have the political prisoners interrogated and then invite them to join him in building a better, stronger, richer Reshner. He would spare what palace staff he could and have his agents ferret out disloyal subjects. Taking the planet had been a challenge but keeping it would truly test him.

***

Jira (March) 3, 1547
Throne Room, Royal Palace, City of Rammon

Lord Kezem had a splendid night and rose late in the morning, feeling the effects of too much ale. To make matters worse, he received several awful reports as soon as he stepped into the throne room. The squad he had sent after the traitor had returned empty-handed, and pockets of resistance still burned around Rammon.

In a surly mood, Kezem summoned Kolknir for his report, praying it would be good. He could hardly bear more bad news. If things failed to favor him soon, his reign would be extraordinarily short.

"Have the interrogators finished questioning the palace staff?" asked Kezem.

"They have, my Lord," Commander Kolknir replied.

"And?" Kezem prompted, slamming a fist against the throne.

"Queen Reia smuggled the princes out of the palace. One went west with some servants, and one was put in a life capsule and shipped east, most likely to Osem."

"I destroyed Osem," Kezem said. That was an understatement. In hindsight, he admitted the complete bombing had been excessive as well as expensive. The three klipper fighters dropping the bombs had gotten too close and blown themselves to smoky little pieces. "What of the child sent to Osem?"

"No word on that, my Lord. Most of the servants know only rumors. One—"

"You're telling me not one of the royal brats has been found?" Kezem interrupted.

"Most servants claim the princess is still here in the palace," said Kolknir.

Kezem had expected the princess to be within the city limits, but he had not expected her to be that close.

"Bold, even for her," he mused, thinking of the queen. He laughed sharply. "No doubt she believed her Ranger magic would save the child." He chuckled again before issuing his next order. A gleam entered his eyes. "Assemble the palace staff. Seize every female child the princess's age and line them up on the dais facing the crowd. Gather the other children as well."

Within half an hour, Kezem's soldiers had stuffed the exhausted palace staff into the throne room. A couple hundred soldiers had been summoned to guard them and witness the momentous occasion. Kezem would begin his reign by killing Reia's brat. He just had to choose the correct one.

"Welcome to the new order," Kezem announced. A wave of weariness washed over him.

His soldiers laughed nervously, and the palace staff stared silently.

"The princes have been eliminated," he lied, trying to stave off weariness. This was to be a fine moment, and he would enjoy it.

Several people gasped, a few wailed, and most cried.

"I'm told the princess is here. Tell me which girl has royal blood or I shall kill them all," said Kezem.

The large throne room doors swung in slowly, and six soldiers entered carrying sedated toddlers. Another twenty soldiers entered, escorting the remaining children belonging to the palace staff. An outraged cry rippled through the crowd. The lines wavered as Kezem's men held the crowd back. The servants' pleas, threats, curses, and shouts made Kezem smile.

"A hundred and nine children, including six girls the princess's age, were found, my Lord," a young captain reported, saluting.

Receiving Kezem's acknowledging nod, the soldier motioned, and the six toddlers were placed on air cushions. The older children huddled together behind the air cushions, trying to stay as far away from Kezem as possible. Lights ensured that the audience had a clear view of the slumbering children's peaceful expressions.

"There is no reason for these children—your children—to die today," said Kezem. "I will do what I must to protect my people." He stopped speaking and reflected on the Reia-like comment. He dismissed the disturbing thought. "I consider myself a fair man. If someone tells me which child belongs to House Minstel, the others will be spared." Kezem could feel the hatred emanating from the staff and wondered if he had overstepped a fine line. If the staff rioted, he would lose men he could ill-afford to lose. As the silence stretched, his patience waned. Drawing a dagger, Kezem approached the nearest infant.

"Wait!" a defiant voice commanded from within the throng. The sea of people parted, revealing a straight-backed, grim-faced woman with dark skin. Her black eyes pierced Lord Kezem. "You cannot harm her!"

"Bring that woman here," Kezem ordered. The large woman was hustled up to him. "What is your name? Explain your statements."

The woman's glare never wavered.

"I am Sarie Verituse, maiden of Queen Reia Minstel and caretaker of the one you wish to destroy. If you cut her, they will heal her. If you poison her, they will cure her. If you—"

"I get the point. Who?"

"You are powerless against her guardians. Her parents' legacy will preserve her life until you are no more." Her booming voice filled the throne room.

"Her parents are dead!" Kezem shouted. "I cut them down myself. Her mother died just yesterday. Reia believed herself invincible, but she bled and died, same as the child will!" He circled the air cushion as he spoke and raised the knife over the nearest toddler.

"That is not the right child!" Sarie declared.

Kezem whirled on the woman and lifted her chin with the dagger's tip. The blade drew blood even at the slightest pressure.

"Then, perhaps you'd be kind enough to point out the correct child," he said, dragging the dagger two inches to the left.

"The first child is Princess Rela Minstel," Sarie informed with unsettling calm, despite the warm trickle of blood running down her neck. She locked eyes with Kezem almost daring him to kill her. "Do not harm her, for her pain will be your pain until events transpire to set you both free," she intoned.

Fear and anger shot through Kezem. He had to dispel this Ranger-inspired madness before it spread.

"She is not immortal!" he cried.

"Wound her then, but I tell you now, if she dies this day, so do you," Sarie said.

Without hesitation, Kezem went over to the princess and slit the toddler's left arm. She awoke with a cry, but Kezem's own surprised scream prevailed. He jerked back, dropped the dagger, and gripped his arm tightly, surprised to find blood on his right hand. His arm stung fiercely for several seconds. Then, the pain eased, as the cut on the child's arm closed itself. Kezem retrieved the ceremonial dagger from the floor and sliced off a portion of his black uniform sleeve. The bloody cloth fluttered to the ground. Kezem gaped at his arm which appeared perfectly normal.

"You would do well to keep her from harm," Sarie said.

Kezem ordered the throne room cleared and the servant seized for further questioning. He assigned two guards to protect the child. This turn of events greatly disturbed him. As much as he wished to destroy Reia and Terosh's daughter, he would have to make other arrangements.

This is Reia's fault. Even in death she haunts me!

Chapter 7:
Dark Years

Zeri (June) 3, 1547-Temen (July) 25, 1554
Royal Palace, City of Rammon

Three months passed, and still Royalist rebels harried Lord Kezem's troops. How could they not embrace his vision for Reshner? He had attacked Rammon first, knowing the capital controlled the other cities. Calsola, the nearest city northwest of Rammon, had also fallen quickly, but since then, there had been no clear victories.

At least Supreme Commander Kolknir and Aster Captain Leena Linel's joint recruiting report held good news. Youths from most major cities jumped at Kezem's offer of adventure, fortune, and glory. Unfortunately, they were no match for roaming Rangers and stubborn Royalists.

Rammon had once been famous for its hospitality. A high wall had surrounded the city for centuries, but citizens could boast that the four gilded gates never truly closed to strangers. Friendly gate guards always waited to welcome merchant and traveler alike. Thinking the policy irresponsible, Kezem had soldiers question everyone entering or leaving the city.

The Rammon spaceport was also jealously guarded, and soon, only the foolish and the criminally inclined used it. Kezem welcomed anyone willing to help him maintain power and preferred the cheap, expendable, unsavory types.

Four months into Lord Kezem's reign, the first good news came in. New secret passages had been found in Loresh. The discoverers had looked forward to early retirements, but the payment had come in the form of bullets.

By the first anniversary of Lord Kezem's ascension to the throne, Meritab, Meritel, and Ritten had submitted. Korch stubbornly clung to its independence, despite a lengthy siege. Kezem didn't have the manpower to block each of the underground passages. It irked him that bleeding Royalist hearts in other cities kept supplying Korch, despite their own troubles. He cared not where Ritand stood, for its poor inhabitants could not help him. Supposedly, Huz Mon and Resh were also conquered, but with the pesky Rangers entrenched in and around the Riden Mountains, that assessment was debatable.

Kezem held court for four hours at the end of every week. The ridiculous requests usually amused him, but today, the food shortage complaints, land disputes, and petty disagreements grated upon his nerves. His mind wandered back to his successful sacking of the palace. He was about to cancel the last hour of court when one more peasant slipped into the throne room.

"My Lord, I seek an audience," said the diminutive man. With head tipped forward respectfully, the ragged stranger cautiously approached the throne, not daring to meet Kezem's gaze.

"Speak," he commanded.

"I am Merek, a humble servant. I have traveled far from Terab. Word has spread that you have captured one of House Minstel's heirs. Legends say they possess the power to heal grave wounds and diseases. I seek your blessing to study the child." The stranger held his hands palm-out and slightly in front of him so the guards would know he was unarmed.

"And what would you do with such knowledge?" Kezem asked. He knew of the rumors and had even experienced that odd healing when he'd wounded Princess Rela.

"Sell it," the stranger answered promptly. "I have contacts that would pay a premium for such knowledge."

Kezem burst into laughter. He liked this materialistic stranger. He'd been about to dismiss the little man outright, but the promise of money intrigued him. Planetwide war was frightfully expensive.

"How do you plan on gaining such knowledge?"

"Observation mostly, though when the child is older, more in depth experiments may be performed." Merek's words flowed off his tongue. "A sterile blade could—"

"I forbid harming her. I already know she can heal herself," Kezem broke in.

"You have seen this, my Lord?" Merek asked excitedly, meeting his eyes for the first time. "Remarkable. I had only rumors to fuel my dreams, but you have given me true hope."

When the man fully facing him, Kezem noticed his unusually sharp ears, a sign of non-human blood. Revulsion shot through him, but he determined to hear the being out.

"I will give you access to the princess. She is under guard in the nursery ..." Kezem trailed off, noting that Merek wasn't listening.

The small man returned his gaze to the floor and tilted his head thoughtfully.

"A thought, my Lord," Merek began slowly. "Is there one close to the princess?"

"One of the queen's maidens refuses to leave her side," Kezem answered. "Her presence seems to calm the child." He shrugged, wondering where the stranger was taking the conversation.

"The child is still young, my Lord. May I suggest—"

"Do you presume to speak to me as an advisor?" Kezem asked, smiling at the man's boldness. He could use more advisors like this wretch. Keen intelligence could be quite useful; it could also be dangerous. Kezem preferred keeping dangerous people close.

"Raise her like she was your own, and you will gain a powerful ally in your quest to rule Reshner. Mold her mind and control her and those around her."

The wisdom in Merek's words struck a favorable chord within Kezem. His plans for the girl had gone no further than keeping her locked away until he could undo Reia's curse. If Merek could discover her secrets, Kezem might profit. Merek was already correct about Kezem needing more leverage against the young princess. He would give her a few friends to grow close to. Then, when the time came, she would obey him for their sakes. He had a few candidates in mind, including Prince Taytron's brat and the young Meetcher girl. He imagined the rivers of money that would flow if the princess's healing powers could be controlled. Rulers and wealthy people would come from afar just to see her. Suddenly, ruling one planet seemed so insignificant.

Two more years passed. Slowly, the remaining cities recognized Lord Kezem as their ruler. But the fighting continued. Every year a new class of RLA soldiers, Royal Guards and Melian Maidens entered Lord Kezem's service, but despite their enthusiasm, he could not help but compare them to those who had served the king and queen.

Merek's observations of Rela had proven useless, so Kezem's interest in the child waned.

Another four long years slipped painfully by. The annual Festival of Future Fighters replenished the supply of eager young fighters, but the war's length wore on Kezem. He grew weary of putting down rebellions. An uprising in Terab would be quelled just in time for trouble to spring up in Kalmata on the other side of the planet. The joy of vanquishing enemies had long since faded.

One morning, Lord Kezem wandered the throne room feeling trapped. He had known major sections of Reshner would not accept his rule peaceably. He had been prepared to put down several revolts, but he had not been prepared for seven years of civil war. It also irked him that the Royalist influence denied him the title of king.

His thoughts turned to the princess. Anger flowed freely in him, and his eyes turned deep blue with haphazard yellow streaks. He longed to seize Rela's fragile neck and squeeze the breath from her body, but Queen Reia's curse remained upon him. Every captured Ranger, Azhel priest, and dabbling magician had been thoroughly interrogated, yet no one could tell him when his life would cease being connected to that pathetic last link to a vanquished royal line.

Normally, he enjoyed the daily duties of ruling: observing the Melian Maidens and Royal Guards practice, sentencing and executing captured rebel leaders, and watching underlings squirm. However, the times he needed to be alone to think, meditate, and curse the galaxy that clearly hated him were becoming more frequent.

The rage burned within him so hot he shook. A long, loud, and thoroughly satisfying scream escaped him. The mournful, primeval cry echoed in the empty chamber, rattling statues of himself.

"Where did I go wrong?" he roared the question.

Chapter 8:
Harmless Defiance, Hidden Heroes

Jira (March) 3, 1547-Temen (July) 25, 1554
Same Years
Royal Palace, City of Rammon

The standing death sentence for anyone who harmed the princess made it so that no hand was ever raised against Princess Rela Minstel. The situation made the young princess bold. Her every whim was answered with pampering and patience. The turnover in the palace staff charged with caring for her was quite high. Eventually, she outgrew tantrums and began perfecting the art of manipulation. Even Kezem's toughest RLA officers could not hide an occasional smile while in her presence.

Although Sarie worked hard to instill a sweet disposition in Princess Rela, the task seemed nearly impossible. Since no hand could discipline the princess, Sarie received ample practice in diplomacy. Though Sarie sometimes felt Rela's sole goal in life was to make her miserable, she deeply loved the child. It fascinated Sarie to watch her young mistress grow, revealing admirable traits her parents had possessed and wild tendencies that were uniquely Rela.

Lorian Petole, a dark-haired, brown-eyed servant child with golden brown skin who was orphaned by the palace invasion grew up with Princess Rela. Even tempered and two years older than Rela, Lorian was a great blessing to Sarie. Sensible and quiet, Lorian had handled weapons from before she could walk. Her parents had even given her a dull dagger to play with, hoping she would join the Melian Maidens when she got old enough.

Lord Kezem encouraged the palace staff to become proficient with weapons. Most children were trained in camps, but Lorian received training at the palace. Anabel and Marc Spitzer, Elia Koffrin, and Kia Meetcher were also encouraged to grow close to the princess, the first two as friends and the second two as guardians.

Lord Kezem forbade everyone from teaching Rela anything beyond rudimentary self-defense skills, but he insisted she learn the basics for his own sake because his few experiences feeling her pain were not pleasant. The annual tradition of letting Merek cut Rela's arm to test healing time was about all he could tolerate. When a glass snake Rela rescued from the food refrigeration chamber bit the princess on the ankle, Kezem felt the bite clear across the palace. Since Lord Kezem had his hands full trying to subdue the planet, Sarie secretly arranged for Captain Peter Estan to give Lorian and Rela shooting lessons.

The young captain pretended to enjoy the small chance at harmless defiance while still serving Lord Kezem, but secretly, his heart always belonged with the princess.

Sarie didn't know whether to be pleased or mortified that by the age of five her charge knew how to hit targets with kerlak guns, serlak guns, crossbows, darts, shootavs, and all manner of other weapons. She feared Rela would one day need such skills.

Merek's constant presence weighed heavily upon Sarie's heart, for she could see what was happening. One day Merek's notes would reach Lord Kezem. Then, she, Lorian, Elia, Kia, Anabel, and Marc would become camarek game pieces. Sarie knew not how exactly Kezem would use them against Princess Rela, so she decided not to worry about the future and devoted her attention to raising the child.

***

Temen (July) 26, 1554
West Detention Block, Prison Level, Royal Palace, City of Rammon

Deep within the palace, a labyrinth of passages hid horrors from the peace lovers still dominating much of Reshner. Supreme Commander Kolknir stood in an observation room on sublevel two looking down on the West Detention Block's combat arena, absently checking his reflection to see if every dark hair was in place. Ever since his Ranger days had ended, he'd become a fanatic about neatness. This was his peaceful spot.

After a hard day's work critiquing Royal Guard hopefuls and handling administrative drudgery, Kolknir liked to come here and listen to riffraff interact. Sometimes he would arrange for the door between two or more chambers to release, mixing volatile occupants. Despite his many duties, Kolknir always made time for selecting someone to fight Lord Kezem.

The prisoners were a filthy, underfed, pathetic lot, but Kolknir made certain they had enough strength to put up a good fight. A delicate balance had to be maintained. Lord Kezem insisted on being tested physically, so Kolknir occasionally gave the combatants stimulant shots to make them more aggressive. He contemplated such a move for tonight's duel. The lucky combatant was none other than his former student, Ranger Todd Wellum.

"Can I help you, sir?" asked a tentative voice.

Startled, Kolknir clamped down on a tide of anger and glared at the young lieutenant. Everyone else knew disturbing Kolknir's thinking time was very dangerous.

"I trust you have a good reason for disturbing me," Kolknir said softly. He considered changing tonight's combatants. Lord Kezem had mentioned that he might not be able to partake in the daily exercise anyway due to an important meeting with Azhel's ambassador. The outlying city was the most recent to sue for peace. "What is the first rule we teach here?"

The young man's eyes widened, but he had the sense to swallow any defensive statements. His pale, thin cheeks flushed as he ducked his head.

"Never disturb a superior officer," said the soldier.

Kolknir enjoyed the game.

"Correct, marksman," he said, a predatory smile forming on his lips. He remembered this soldier. The weakling had barely passed his test to be posted to this prison. He eyed the man contemptuously, recalling how he had trembled after doing his sworn duty in the service of Lord Kezem.

"Lieutenant second class," the man corrected. Realizing his second blunder, the soldier lowered his eyes.

Kolknir glared.

"No, there is nothing you can help me with. Mind your place or join the ranks of the weak below." Kolknir gestured out the window that overlooked the massive empty sandpit filled with gray volcanic ash. The color was just dark enough to be grim and cause bloodstains to blend in. The man nodded vigorously but dared not speak. Kolknir waited to see if he would be foolish enough to leave without permission. He could sense the soldier's stress level rising. "Is the prisoner ready?" he asked, after letting the lieutenant sweat a while.

The boy straightened.

"Yes, Supreme Commander, but I haven't administered the stimulants yet."

"Bring him to me," Kolknir ordered.

The soldier saluted and hurried off to fetch the prisoner.

Kolknir shook his head, amazed that Wellum still lived after seven years in captivity.

The prisoner filed in obediently, wrists bound in front, head down, and eyes fixed on the floor. His thin yet muscular arms held traces of the strength that had once coursed through them. Todd's face bore a dozen marks from shaving with dull prison razors. Kolknir was only mildly surprised that his former student hadn't slit his wrists or attacked a guard.

Kolknir preferred standard cord bindings over stuncuffs because of the marks they left. He half-expected Todd to snap the bindings as Kolknir had taught him to do so many years before. Much had changed since then.

"I don't think this one's up for a fight tonight," said the soldier.

"You're dismissed," Kolknir said. He waited until the soldier was out of hearing range before addressing the prisoner. "Look at me."

Slowly, Todd's head came up.

Kolknir studied him.

The prisoner stared back with intelligent hazel eyes.

Considering their history, Kolknir was surprised to find no hatred in Todd's eyes. He opened his mouth to taunt Todd by mentioning Kiata but changed his mind.

"Can you fight?" asked Kolknir.

"Yes." The answer was clipped but polite.

"Do you need stimulants?"

"No."

"Lord Kezem has an important meeting tonight so you will fight Lieutenant Tayce. Kill him."

That got Wellum's attention, but his only reaction was a clenched jaw.

"What'd the boy do?" he asked.

"He's too weak to be a Royal Guard," said Kolknir. "I despise weakness. There's a good meal in this if you make him suffer before killing him."

***

Todd Wellum worked hard to hold his contempt in check. Not trusting himself to speak, he nodded at the grim order and returned his gaze to the floor. Inwardly, he cringed. He would have to give the boy the dead-man liquor tablet he had saved for so long. The young man's life meant more than a few more months in this wretched place, though not by much.

The fight that evening was swift and brutal. Todd carefully struck the boy in places that would bleed a lot without causing too much damage. He put on a good show, and to his credit, Lieutenant Ethan Tayce proved to be tougher than his boyish features, soft golden hair, and slight frame indicated. Supreme Commander Kolknir enjoyed the bout. As Todd wrestled Tayce to the ground, he slipped the dead-man tablet down the boy's throat and held him in a chokehold until the man went limp.

True to his word, Kolknir had a tretling steak and real fertia wine waiting for Todd back in the two-by-three-meter cell. Todd sighed wearily and sat down on the hard cot. As he ate, he closed his eyes and concentrated on the happier moments of his life. Most featured Kiata and the adventures they had shared while growing up in the Riden Mountains then later as part of the Nareth Talis. The small group of specialized Rangers, whose Kalastan name means Night Torch, dedicated their lives to keeping peace across Reshner. The rest featured Kayleen's birth and the few precious years he had known her.

I will find you, Kayleen. This prison cannot hold me forever.

Chapter 9:
Beautiful Prison

Temen (July) 27, 1554
Princess Rela's Private Chambers, Royal Palace, City of Rammon

The Rammon palace Princess Rela Minstel grew up in differed mightily from the palace her parents ruled. After his invasion, Lord Kezem fortified the walls with guard towers and inlaid glass. Rela's seventh-floor suite of chambers overlooked the east wall, which she privately named Maran, after the Arthuri god of oppression and pain. One of her many tutors had drilled Rela on the three thousand gods of Arthuri before Lord Kezem deemed such knowledge useless and had the man replaced with a historian who specialized in magic and myths.

That one didn't last long either.

When the sun rose, it winked off the glass pieces imbedded in Maran. Rela imagined that each glass piece contained a tiny bit of magic which she could collect if she looked at it a fraction of a second after the sun winked off it. When she collected a hundred, she could make a wish. Soon, the wishes became one wish: to pass beyond the wall.

As the years passed, the game got old. Nevertheless, sunrise was a special time for Rela. Sometimes, like today, Sarie would join her. This morning, seven years into Lord Kezem's reign, Princess Rela sat in her usual spot by the large middle window which offered a generous view of the palace gardens below.

On a clear day, she could see some of the farms scattered about the Kevil Plains. If she used a rifle scope, she could watch the people in the Market District going about their business buying food, selling craft items, or looking enviously at those who could buy or sell. On a really good day, someone would try to steal something, and Rela could watch the soldiers chase the scoundrel. Occasionally, she wondered what became of those criminals, but her innocent mind couldn't yet fathom the horrors that awaited them.

"What's it like out there?" Rela wondered, resting her head against the cool glass.

"Full of dangers," Sarie replied.

Unsatisfied with the answer, Rela sighed. With each passing week, she felt the beautiful palace walls closing in on her. Turning toward her caretaker, Rela looked past the woman to the designs etched into the dansque wood doorframes and let her mind wander.

Who made the carvings? How long did they take? Why did they choose mean creatures like zaloks and goritors? Why not pretty things like wisil, colana, or kyrie birds or strong, noble things like dalagons?

The mental image of the great beasts as tall and wide as hundred-year-old cal trees with three heads, four arms, and a tail strong enough to break through two meters of solid concrete made Rela smile.

Although her tutors showed her countless images of exotic creatures and places, Rela had yet to see most of them, even ones native to Reshner. In fact, the only creatures she saw were those crafty enough to slip into the palace gardens. The glass snake she had freed from the refrigeration chamber didn't really count since it had never been covered in the lessons. Doctor Graven had explained about glass snakes while removing the mild toxins from Rela's left ankle.

"Here, eat something," Sarie instructed, breaking into Rela's thoughts. She gave Rela a riellberry muffin and let her hand rest on her wrist. A gentle squeeze conveyed understanding and sympathy.

The princess took two unenthusiastic bites of muffin before tossing it back onto the tray Sarie had taken it from. She eyed the variety of delectable breakfast treats with disinterest.

Riellberry muffins, blueberry tarts, appola pastries, wheat cakes with fertia jam, and mintas tea, just like always. I bet they don't have to eat the same thing every day out there.

Princess Rela was unaware that most people would attack such a meal like starved korvers. Her thoughts returned to her plight.

"I want to go to the Market District or take a trip outside of Rammon. Can I go, Sarie? Please."

Sarie's compassionate expression disappointed the princess as did her words.

"I am sorry, love. Not today. Lord Kezem has forbidden it."

"I could have some Melian Maidens escort me," Rela pointed out. A desperate note flavored her speech. "They would protect me. Besides, Lord Kezem leaves the palace all the time, and Lorian, Marc, and Anabel have been out lots of times too. Even Elia and Kia come and go as they please. Why not me?" By this time, Rela had abandoned efforts to sound mature. Her whine was pure nine-year-old frustration.

"You will get your chance for adventure, Princess," Sarie assured her.

"When?" Rela demanded. She looked at Sarie with a penetrating gaze, barely noticing the long scar on the right side of Sarie's chin. It had been always been there as far as she knew.

Ignorant of the problems people faced just beyond the palace walls, Rela couldn't understand Sarie's gloomy mood or the undercurrent of anger. Across Reshner, citizens lived in fear for their lives. Lord Kezem's soldiers patrolled the cities and villages with unsettling power. Anyone could be stopped, searched, interrogated, robbed, beaten, or killed any time for any reason. Since the anger wasn't directed at her, Rela shrugged and accepted that Sarie would tell her in her own time.

"We will speak more later," Sarie promised. "Let's walk in the garden."

A thrill rushed through Rela. The gardens were a special place where Sarie often shared stories of a brave, good king and a queen who fought evil beings and creatures to save their people. The stories usually ended happily, but sometimes, the good king and queen had to suffer to defeat the evil.

Rela scrambled out of her silky night dress and into the beige leggings and brilliant blue shimmersilk shirt with golden threads woven throughout that Sarie had chosen for the day. A thin, black goritor leather belt and matching boots completed the ensemble.

Soon, Rela skipped through familiar corridors, down six flights of stairs, and through the main kitchen to the servants' entrance to the royal gardens. The plants and flowers suffered from neglect, but it was easy to picture the stunning place the gardens had once been. Rela raced ahead to her favorite spot, a remote stone fountain with a statue of some unknown ancestor covered in ivy. She climbed onto the outstretched stone arm and hung off by her legs.

"What's the story today, Sarie?"

"You can start the story, Princess. It always begins the same." Sarie sat on a soft bench near the statue.

"'There once lived a good king and his queen. They were brave and kind and fair,'" Rela recited.

Sarie picked up the story neatly.

"Before the good king became king, he was a prince, and before the good queen became queen, she was a Ranger."

Having never heard this story, Rela's eyes sparkled with excitement.

"Daria said the Rangers are the most troublesome group of terrorists to ever plague Reshner, but Lord Kezem defeated them during the last rebellion."

"Daria is wrong," Sarie replied. "The Rangers are a noble order who stabilize villages and protect important people, including members of House Minstel."

Princess Rela's mouth flew open at Sarie's treasonous words. Lord Kezem hated when people spoke of House Minstel.

"One day, the young prince was sent away on a journey to test his strength. The noble order of Rangers sent a young healer apprentice to safeguard the prince on his journey, for they knew he would encounter many dangers. On the morning of our tale, the young prince awoke surrounded by enemy soldiers from the Restler-Tarpon Alliance."

Rela gasped.

"The Kireshana!" she exclaimed. "Rivira told me all about the Kireshana, but she said it was only for soldiers. Will I ever get to go on it,

Sarie?" Excitement and terror mixed in Rela's expression.

Sarie chuckled.

"No, Princess, you are not destined to be a soldier. The prince went because it was a family tradition. His older brother, his father, and all his uncles and aunts—save one—completed their own Kireshana journeys. At this time, his elder brother and father still lived, and everyone expected the older prince to one day be king."

"What happened to the older prince?" Rela wondered. Her head tilted to get a better look at Sarie.

"That is a tale for another day, Princess," Sarie answered. "This is the story of how the younger prince met his bride-to-be. As I said, she was a Ranger."

"Merek said Rangers are bad. Mikel, Plarit, and Wes Vik Iven all said it too," Rela informed. "How could she be a Ranger and be good?" Rela thought she saw pain cross Sarie's face, but it was gone so quickly that she couldn't be certain.

"Do you know why I tell you these stories, Princess?" Sarie asked gravely.

Rela considered the question carefully. Something indefinable whispered the answer into her mind.

"You speak of my parents," said Rela, surprised she had never realized the truth before. "But Merek said they died in the rebellion. He said the people turned against them, but Lord Kezem saved me. How could they be the good king and queen? There were no evil creatures in the rebellion, just people afraid of GAPP."

Frowning deeply, Sarie folded her hands in her lap.

"What else did Merek tell you?" Her voice trembled with an emotion Rela could not identify.

"Lord Kezem is my father's cousin. He stopped the rebels from killing me, but my parents and two brothers died in the attack," Rela answered.

Sarie's hands flew to her face and she started sobbing.

The outburst shocked Rela. She nearly fell off the stone arm but managed to lower herself safely to the ground. She went to Sarie, slipped under her arms for an embrace, and cried, not knowing why her caretaker wept.

"I'm sorry! I'm sorry! What did I say wrong? I'll take it back, honest," she babbled.

With great effort, Sarie composed herself and drew Rela further into a warm embrace. Eventually, she calmed enough to speak.

"The fate of your brothers is unknown, Princess. You mother had them sent away from the palace that dark night. You may not wish to hear—"

"Lord Kezem didn't kill them," Rela protested, knowing exactly what Sarie was thinking. She wriggled out of the hug. "It's a rebel lie meant to undermine Lord Kezem's good work."

Sarie closed her eyes and drew in a deep breath.

"He is smart to have told you his lies early," she admitted. "I am only sorry I had not thought to enlighten you first."

"Who should I believe?" asked Rela.

"At this point, Princess, you must make that decision yourself. But know that your parents were the good king and queen, and that not all evil creatures are enchanted monsters."

Rela disliked it when Sarie got philosophical on her.

"What should I do?" Rela inquired.

"Take this and keep it safe. It belonged to your mother," said Sarie. She opened her right fist to reveal a gold ring with a sizable emerald stone set in purple Nedis crystal. "Search out your past," Sarie encouraged, placing the ring in Rela's palm and curling the child's hand over it. "This palace may be a beautiful prison for you, but your friends are not as confined. Use them wisely and you will discover all you need and much more. The future will come soon enough, and I hope by then your heart will be prepared for the weighty truths."

Sarie steered the conversation away, and Rela quietly listened with half an ear, wishing she could sort out the conflicting stories. As Merek often said, Lord Kezem had been kind to her, how could she think ill of him? On the other hand, Merek was sort of creepy, and Rela felt more inclined to believe Sarie over any of her tutors.

Rela determined to follow Sarie's advice and enlisted her friends' help. They made a game of discovering the facts about her family and keeping her abreast of the current news. Part of her understood that the truth might never shine through the tangled web of lies, but she knew the knowledge would determine her fate someday.

***

Temen (July) 29, 1554
Throne Room, Royal Palace, City of Rammon

Lord Kezem was not in the mood for Merek's complaints, but he listened anyway. It had been a very bad day. A bomb in Kalmata had killed three of his most loyal servants, the settlements near the Crystal Lake reported death from foul water, and a massive fire raged through the Ash Mountains. He didn't care how many people died, but the stream of bad news gave him a sizable headache.

"My Lord, the woman is poisoning the child against you," Merek insisted for the third time in four minutes.

"I do not have time for your petty jealousies, Merek," Lord Kezem said.

"Please, my Lord, it is vital to keep in the girl's good graces!" Merek insisted.

Kezem couldn't fathom what this spineless idiot driveled about, but it taxed his nerves.

"Deal with the woman as you see fit," Kezem instructed, deciding to preserve his sanity.

"Thank you, my Lord, I shall do so at once," Merek prattled.

"If you kill her, make sure it is far from the palace, or Rela will never trust you again," Kezem advised, wishing the man would just go away.

Why do I keep him around?

***

Temen (July) 29, 1554
Same Day
Streets of Rammon, City of Rammon

Sarie Verituse left the Rammon palace with a broken heart. The gutless worm had been quite clear: leave or die. He had been tactful and formal about the whole affair, coming personally to deliver the message supposedly from Lord Kezem. She gritted her teeth. Sarie was no coward, but she could not help Rela if she died. So, she left.

Chapter 10:
Escape from the Mines

Temen (July) 29, 1554
Same Day
Imberg Tosh Mine, Morden Lowlands

Half a planet away, young Teven McKnight struggled to carry a load of tosh out of the dim, claustrophobic mining tunnel. Though only in his fourth month here, he could hardly remember a time when he wasn't stooped over scraping the dingy tunnels of the Imberg Tosh Mines. His thoughts ranged far and wide but did not touch political realms. All the hand carts had been claimed by the time he arrived at work today, despite his extra effort to arrive an hour before his shift started. He tripped on the uneven ground, pitching his load away so he wouldn't land on the bucket. A cloud of tosh dust rose, making his eyes water.

"I can't stay here," he said, choking from the dust.

"No, you can't. It is time you moved on," commented a man.

"Who are you?" Teven demanded, eyeing the man and beginning to scoop tosh back into the bucket.

The plain clothes could not hide the man's powerful presence, and there was something familiar about him. He moved with ease, smooth and balanced, as if ready to dance or fight. His black hair and eyes added to the mysterious air surrounding him. The man hunched to hide his height, but the breadth of his muscles and the strength in his voice told Teven that this man was no miner.

"Leave it. You won't need it, and we cannot stay."

The urgency in the stranger's voice intrigued Teven as much as the promise of escaping the tosh mines.

"Watch it! That wall's coming down!" a man shouted.

A thunderous crash followed as another unsteady tunnel succumbed to Reshner's restless shifting. Teven dashed forward to aid the people inevitably trapped beneath several tons of rock and tosh.

The stranger caught his arm.

"Come with me!"

"I have to help them!" Teven argued, tugging futilely against the stranger's grip.

"You can help them more by escaping," the man said, pinning the boy in place. "Some sacrifices must be made for the greater good. You will understand one day. Now, come!" He picked up one of Teven's arms and tugged.

"Why should I go with you?" asked Teven.

"Because I am a Ranger, and I promised your mother I would train you."

"Why didn't she tell me?" Teven asked, planting his feet.

"I speak of your real mother not your guardian," the stranger replied.

"Why would my mother want me to be a Ranger?" asked Teven, allowing himself to follow the stranger.

How does he know I had a different mother?

"You will be something far greater than a Ranger, Teven."

They emerged from a side tunnel tucked behind some rocks, conveniently out of sight of the mine master's tent. After they'd gone three steps, Teven stopped suddenly.

"I forgot my pay! I should collect—"

"You will not need the money." Sensing Teven's hesitation, the stranger continued, "Your guardian and her son are coming with us to a Ranger camp in the Riden Mountains."

Without further discussion they hurried toward Teven's home.

Teven's head whirled with the rapid changes.

The ten-minute walk to the McKnight ramshackle dwelling turned into a five-minute sprint to beat the rain. They were still a few hundred meters away from safety when the skies opened. Knowing that if too much rain touched his skin he'd get acid poisoning and die, Teven pumped his legs hard. Still, he fell behind the stranger. Teven started falling.

"I have searched too long to lose you now," the stranger muttered.

Teven experienced a brief floating sensation before passing out.

***

Temen (July) 29, 1554
Same Day
McKnight House, Outskirts of City of Huz Mon

Pria McKnight peered out of the shack's only window and idly watched the rain pound the dirt road. She had just finished sweeping and needed to rest. She caught sight of a cloaked man rushing her way carrying a bundle. She frowned. The man's burden looked suspiciously like Teven.

For a heartbeat, she imagined the man was her husband, but that was impossible. Ormek's men had killed him four months ago. She shoved the bad memories aside.

"Nate, get the door!" she shouted to her son who was playing with the wooden animals Teven had carved for him.

"Tev!" the boy shouted, rushing to the door. He flung the door back enthusiastically and some raindrops fell on him. "Owwie! Hot!" he yelped, shaking his small arm about to make the stinging go away.

"Be careful, Nate, that rain could hurt you," Pria warned belatedly, starting a fire to boil water.

While Nate held the flimsy door open, the stranger entered carrying Teven.

"Tev okay?" Nate asked, closing the door and leaning against it.

"It's been a long time, Pria," said the stranger.

Pria turned so fast she nearly knocked the hot pot over.

The man stepped forward and steadied her.

"First things first, let's get the acid off him." His voice carried an edge of command.

As he placed his burden on the bare wooden table, Pria stared at him like he was an apparition. Teven stirred. Nate rushed over to help but only managed to get stepped on and ordered to the corner. He sniffled but obeyed.

"What happened, Captain?" Pria asked.

"He had a rough day in the tosh mines," answered Ectosh Laocer, former Captain of the Royal Guard. "He'll be fine."

Pria flinched when she saw the healed burn marks on his arm but decided not to probe until they finished cleaning Teven. The wooden table over which Pria and Laocer worked creaked and popped in protest. Laocer stood ready to snatch Teven up if the table collapsed. They finished wiping the acid off Teven, who woke up just long enough to swallow some thin broth.

"It's good to see you, Captain," said Pria, once certain Teven would live. "How goes the war?"

"It has been a long time since I was in command," said Laocer.

"Somehow, I highly doubt that," Pria replied, regaining some of her composure.

So much has happened. She glanced around her sparse surroundings. *It's a far cry from the palace.*

One lightbar bravely lit the room but wasn't nearly enough to drive off the gloom. She spotted Nate rubbing his rain-stung arm and watching everything dispassionately.

My brave little sentinel.

Pria waved her younger son over to wipe the acid rain off his arms. The tiny, one-room dwelling perfectly summed up the last few years.

"I have avoided entanglements with Kezem's forces waiting for this day," said Laocer.

A chill shot through Pria, but she ignored it.

"He's too young for the responsibility," said Pria, not bothering to hide the sadness. She shut her eyes in a vain attempt to block everything out. She had trouble reconciling her hopes that Teven would one day save them and her need to protect him and preserve what little childhood he had left. Nate's gentle touch brought her back. She picked the boy up, feeling Laocer's gaze follow her movements.

The captain's expression was unreadable as he gathered Teven up and deposited him on the room's sole sleep pallet.

He seems bitter. Pria knew too well what service to King Terosh and Queen Reia could cost. *What have you lost, Captain?*

"Where do we begin?" Laocer inquired, meeting Pria's cautious stare.

"Should we wake him?" Pria asked, obviously reluctant to do so. She set Nate down to play. Finding her arms suddenly empty, Pria hugged herself.

Laocer looked like he was suppressing the impulse to comfort her with an embrace.

"Not yet. How did you end up here?" asked Laocer.

Grateful he didn't ask about her husband, Pria turned to boil more water for tea.

"A lot has happened since the night we fled." She stopped speaking, not sure how to explain without ripping open deep wounds. "Nathan insisted we stay to defend the palace." Pria smiled even as tears formed. "We had quite a fight over that, but I finally won by reminding him of our vow to the queen. The night was a game of hide-and-seek with Kezem's soldiers, but we made it. We had thought we made it cleanly, but someone must have connected us to the palace because we ended up with a black mark."

"Ah, that explains this," Laocer said, gesturing around at the four close walls.

Pria nodded and sat down at the table, motioning for Laocer to sit as well.

"We couldn't work anywhere but the mines, and the kefs the queen entrusted to us for the care of her son only lasted so long. We did fine for five years, but it got tougher when the money ran out. Even though the mine never paid enough, Nate worked hard to put on a good front for the boys. Then, things got really bad," she said with a thoughtful expression. At the mention of his name, little Nate abandoned his wooden figures and crawled into his mother's lap.

"Who hurt you?" Ectosh demanded. His voice crackled with anger.

You always were perceptive.

"I used to bring food to the mines for my husband and a few of his friends," Pria explained. "Nothing much, just whatever scraps I could gather. The shift master, Ormek, took an unwanted interest in me."

Laocer rose from the chair.

Pria reached over and patted his arm.

Startled, he sat down again.

"What happened?"

Where do I begin?

Pria let her gaze linger on her boys. Nate grew tired of sitting and jumped onto the table and then into Laocer's ready arms. The water finished boiling so Pria got up and made wuzle root tea. She set a cup in front of Laocer, but he only looked at her expectantly.

Knowing she could stall no longer, Pria returned to her seat and fingered her cup of tea.

"The attention grew worse, until I finally stopped going to the mines. I thought that would be the end of it, but one day, about four and a half months ago, Ormek came here with several men."

Laocer tensed again, obviously longing to pound some manners into Ormek's skull.

"Nathan saw them slip off and confronted Ormek." Pria squeezed her eyes shut but a few tears slipped through anyway. Her right fist crashed onto the table and her left hand desperately clutched her cup of tea. "I will not cry!"

Despite the words, she wept.

"It's okay, take your time," Laocer said quietly. He held little Nate and waited.

Eventually, Pria dried her eyes.

"Ormek backed off that day, but he returned the next day and the next. Each time, Nathan was here, until Ormek's men dragged him outside and killed him."

"Did you see who killed Nathan?"

"I—I don't remember! I was so afraid. I gathered the boys and bolted the door, refusing to come out for three days. If it had only been me, I might have given in or tried some of those defensive moves you taught us." A faint grin flickered and faded. Pria cleared her throat. "By the time Ormek's wife put an end to her husband's harassment, it was too late to save my husband."

"Has anyone else given you trouble?" Laocer's tone said woe to that man.

Pria released her teacup and burst into a fresh round of tears.

"It's okay," he said again, sounding suddenly nervous.

"I'm sorry." Pria smiled through the tears. "You must think I'm—"

"You have nothing to apologize for," Laocer said.

"Yes, I do, Captain. I'm a coward," said Pria. "I let a young boy take on a man's job in a dangerous mine to protect myself. What would Queen Reia think?"

"She would understand," Laocer murmured with an odd expression. *What are you thinking?*

Pria didn't know he was thinking of the last seven years preparing for this meeting. He'd dreamed of teaching a tall, strong, vibrant adolescent not a boy traumatized by the tosh mines.

"He's so young," Laocer commented.

"He will grow into a fine man, like his father," Pria said. "I have cared for him like I promised. You will train him like you promised, and somehow, this planet will be set right." She was on a roll now. The words flowed from the deep place where she had hidden hope under years of worry and hardship. "It is more than a promise made to our beloved queen. Riden has placed you here at this time for this time."

Nate slipped away. Laocer folded his hands on the table and stared at Pria.

As she watched his shoulders straighten and his posture adjust to exude confidence, Pria realized he could only be here for one reason.

"I'm coming with you," said Pria.

"Where are we going?" asked Teven. Black hair tousled, sleepy-eyed, and still looking exhausted the boy staggered to his feet.

"Some place safe," said Laocer.

Pria felt him watching her but paid no attention. She was too busy packing. Fortunately, the diminutive dwelling didn't hold many possessions. Pria stripped the coverings off the sleep pallet and used them to wrap up the few food stuffs left in the house.

"We're ready," she announced.

Food bundle tucked under her left arm, Nate strapped to her back, an ancient dagger clipped to her waist, and a bewildered Teven in tow, Pria left the shack she had called home for seven years and never looked back.

Chapter 11:
Ambush

Allei (August) 2, 1554
Restler Campsite Near Riden Mountains

In a desolate part of the planet west of Rammon, some mercenaries sat around a dying fire.

"Remember, under no circumstances are the boys to be harmed. We are getting paid good money to take them alive," Gareth Restler warned his men.

"Are we going to keep the woman?" Coleth Timmer asked. His gaze stayed fixed on his infopad which bore images of their targets. The Chermesh's long ears wiggled with suppressed hope.

Gareth shook his head and thought about how much he hated lengthy stakeouts.

"I tried to bargain for her, but the client wants her dead so that's the way it goes." Internally, he wondered if he should have pressed the issue of the woman's life harder.

"What's so special about these mine rats?" Tyron Hither asked, looking up from the blade he was sharpening. His fangs glinted in the bright moonlight. "The fee's generous, but you've got to admit the request's very unusual."

"I don't question orders," Gareth replied.

The others nodded and continued to clean their weapons. Most of his people were still at Base Camp near Kalmata, but Gareth had chosen four of his best to handle the Riden Mountains job. The job was typical for these days. Sometimes they would be hired to rescue rich brats that wandered off. Other days they would carry out an assassination for one side or the other.

The Restler Raiders had existed long before the ill-fated Restler-Tarpon Alliance, even before Lord Kezem set his heart on Reshner's throne. Gareth fully intended to carry on the family tradition. He hired professionals, but occasionally, he had to remind his people of the top three mercenary rules: get paid, never question, and remain emotionally detached. He had once broken the third rule and paid for it dearly.

As the sun began its descent, Gareth stretched to prepare his muscles for the coming hike and subsequent fight.

"Let's go," he said.

**

Allei (August) 3, 1554
Riden Mountains

The McKnight family and their guide traveled for four days bundled up in rain cloaks provided by Ectosh Laocer. By sunset the fourth day, the storms had passed, but the air still hung in a thick layer over the Riden Mountains. Despite this, Teven McKnight felt lighter with every step he took toward the nearest peak, Mount Palean.

I'll never have to step in a tosh mine again.

"Tired, Momma," Nate complained.

"You're tired?" Teven asked incredulously. "Who's been lugging you around the past week?"

"Tev tired too, Momma," Nate added.

Teven smiled down at his little brother. Nate could be annoying, but he had a heart of gold.

"Be brave, boys, when we reach the mountains we can stop to rest," his mother encouraged.

"Here, let me take him," Laocer offered.

Teven gratefully surrendered his burden and continued to follow Captain Laocer. They traveled with this arrangement for several kilometers. When they came within twenty meters of the mountains, Nate got a second wind and challenged Teven to a race.

"I beat you to big rock," Nate stated, squirming from Laocer's grasp and taking off.

"Oh, no you don't. I'll catch you running backward!" Teven jogged along behind his brother, letting the younger boy have a solid head start. The thrill of the race brought a broad smile to his face.

"You boys be careful," Pria admonished.

For several meters, Teven concentrated on the race.

"I win!" Nate shouted, triumphantly jumping on a flat rock in front of Mount Palean. The mountain walls rose up sharply on either side of the rock.

Teven didn't see the well-muscled, furry being rise from behind the rock Nate had claimed, but his mother's scream said something was amiss.

The attacker's responding shriek slammed into Teven's back.

Teven whirled. His feet tangled, and he landed flat on his face. He coughed, sputtered, and spat dirt. Looking up, Teven saw a cargo sack swallow his brother. Fear drove Teven to his knees, but the travel cloak hindered his efforts to rise.

Four more shadowy figures separated from the nearby rock walls. One man pointed a heavy serlak gun over Teven's head and fired.

More screams followed.

The crack of the serlak gun crashed across Teven's senses as a bullet tore through the air and struck Pria full in the chest. The impact threw her back almost a meter before her body collapsed.

Teven's breath fled as shock claimed his mind. He stared at his fallen mother, waiting for a bullet to strike him and end the burning ache twisting inside his stomach.

It never came.

Suddenly, Laocer filled Teven's vision. He was everywhere at once, driving the attackers back with swift, sure blows from a flat yellow blade of energy. Teven had heard the miners speak of kerlinblades and dreamed of holding one, but no fantasy—or nightmare—could have prepared him for this fight. Laocer's blade meted out justice to one attacker after another so fiercely that the three left alive fled.

A whistle from the leader signaled the retreat.

For a moment, Teven could imagine his mind had conjured the attack, but Laocer's grim expression and torn clothes convinced him this was real. Struggling to his feet, Teven teetered and focused again on his mother's crumpled form. He rushed to her and would have embraced her lifeless form had Laocer not grabbed his shoulder and held him fast.

Rage and despair rose in Teven. He knew people died every day, but there had always been a distinction between danger and safety. Home was always safe. Four months ago, that illusion had been severely assaulted. Now that both guardians he loved and regarded as parents were gone, the illusion shattered.

"We should leave," Laocer said, releasing Teven's shoulder.

Teven didn't say a word. Instead, he fought off his grief long enough to gather brush for a fire to burn his mother's body. He would not let either beast or acid rain lay further claim to her.

His eyes fell upon the broken pieces of the two dead attackers. He consciously turned his gaze away.

Scavengers can have the murderers. They deserve no better.

***

Allei (August) 3, 1554
Same Day
Eastern Edge of the Riden Mountains

Tired, hungry, and frightened, three-year-old Nathan McKnight bawled inside the sack. Had he lain still, the bag would have seemed much less confining because it was designed to allow air to flow freely. But fear drove him to thrash until utter exhaustion overtook him. The frantic rocking motion of someone carrying him made his stomach hurt. Nate threw up inside the sack. The combination of sudden stench and burning throat made him scream, cry, and thrash with new energy.

"What's that smell?" a male voice asked. He followed the statement with a long stream of angry words.

The sack carrying Nate sailed through the air and crashed into something hard and bony. Vomit splattered all over this second being, eliciting more curses. With the mission a solid failure, tempers were short.

The Restler Raiders had not expected any opposition, so the fierce counterattack surprised them. The big man who fought back certainly knew how to handle a kerlinblade.

Nate tumbled from the sack and landed in a dusty heap. He caught a brief glimpse of his captors before passing out.

"Coleth, dump the boy in that stream we passed a few minutes ago," Gareth instructed. He glared at the filthy wretch, but he could not afford to kill him. They had already lost too much on this mission. "We'll take him to the slave market in Fort Riden."

"We won't get much for him," Coleth commented, hating his current assignment.

"We'll get something. Supreme Commander Kolknir always wants children for the production lines," said Gareth.

Nate heard none of this conversation that would greatly alter his life.

True to their word, the mercenaries took him to Fort Riden's slave market where Captain Glaiser of the Reshner Liberation Army bought him. Glaiser, a widower with no children, determined to raise Nate as a son.

Chapter 12:
New Recruit

Allei (August) 7, 1554
Ranger Camp, Riden Mountains

Sky watching, as much a survival technique as a hobby, helped Aveni pass the time. Patrol duty bored him.

Roughly every three months the Talmeth Volcanoes, located on the southwestern coast of the main continent, spewed molten metal and chemicals most life forms found toxic. Soon thereafter, the acid storms would begin. Only the first would be potent enough to melt spaceship paint. The next two would sting, and the last few would only cause harm on rare occasions. Most of the days between these cycles would be sunny and fair, but sometimes, the planet got moody. That's what sky watching was all about, seeing the subtle signs of Reshner preparing to make life interesting for her inhabitants.

At such times, it was best to find a hole or a tavern and hide until things calmed down again. Despite the instinct to dig, Aveni preferred taverns. The chairs and benches usually adjusted to accommodate his bulk. With two arms and two legs as thick as dansque tree trunks, Wirshers made remarkable fighters but lousy scouts. Still, when a Wirsher could be convinced to play guard for a while, one could rest easy.

As the sun plunged behind the mountains farther to the west, Aveni noticed the white clouds multiplying rapidly.

"Uh oh, we in for it now," he wheezed. "Oy, Bova!"

"What?" snapped the surly Ranger. A day night sneaking around enemy posts had put the Rorgen in an especially foul mood. Bova—whose real name no one seemed to remember—crashed onto the planet seven years ago, just in time to run afoul of Lord Kezem. His nickname came from those first days when frequent trips to the tavern usually ended with him being locked up for lifting kefs from other patrons or fighting.

"Storm coming," Aveni said cheerfully. "Gonna be nasty."

Bova grunted then trudged off into the labyrinth of tunnels and caves where he knew food awaited. Had this been Rorge II, Bova could have hunted stelberg rats all night. This was not Rorge II, nor would he ever see the beautiful caves of his youth again. The exploding sun had made certain of that. When his home had disappeared in one terrible instant, Bova had lost his sense of humor. The thought of each perished loved one was like a thousand paralyzing bites from voracerflies, ironically one of the few life forms Rorge II and Reshner shared. These thoughts shadowed Bova, wrapping so closely around him that he didn't hear Aveni's frantic, lumbering steps until the cave vibrated behind him. He whirled, preparing a scathing response to the brute's intrusion on his thoughts.

"Visitors," Aveni announced.

Bova narrowed his eyes, somehow managing to look down his nose at the two-and-a-half-meter-high Wirsher filling the tunnel behind him.

"Who?" he asked.

"Don't know. Not dangerous, I think," said Aveni.

"I'll judge that," Ranger Knight Bova muttered. "Go meet them and see what they want. If they're friends feed them. If not, try to take them alive but don't let them escape. Think you can handle that?"

Aveni squeezed himself around and went back to the main entrance. Wirshers made excellent interrogators due to their natural ability to measure a being's intent. Countless centuries hunting brizer panthers at night on moonless Wirsh had taught them to feel which way their prey would leap. It also produced excellent night vision. Aveni saw a figure he recognized.

"Captain? Captain! Wayward lost Captain Laocer back!" he bellowed.

"I see you're still faithfully guarding the last stronghold of the Rangers," Laocer commented. Catching Aveni's questioning glance, he started on introductions. "This is—"

"The one," Aveni finished. The Wirsher's calculating gaze swept over the young shell of a human more thoroughly than any sensor.

The dark-haired ten-year-old wore a vacant expression.

Aveni sensed that Captain Laocer had yet to explain things to the boy.

"Apologies. Apologies. I mean not say too soon," said Aveni.

"Everything will be explained in time," Laocer assured him. "We were ambushed near Mount Palean. His family did not survive. We didn't stop for much rest along the way. I'm going to make arrangements for the boy now."

"Food do good," Aveni agreed. "Go see Bova or he yell."

"Long day?" Laocer asked, knowing the surly knight's moods well.

"Very long. Very grumpy," Aveni said, bobbing his head left and right in the Wirsher version of agreement.

***

Kayleen Wellum slumped against a tunnel wall by an air vent listening to a storm beat the mountains. With one leg propped against the opposite wall and the other tucked under in a position most would consider extremely uncomfortable, Kayleen idly sucked a mintas drop while counting the seconds between claps of thunder. She thought of the day's training. The duels had gone well until she faced Cloat, and then, as usual, she lost. With eyes open and head bowed so that her shoulder length, wavy, red-gold hair hung in her face, she let her mind replay every move of that last hand-to-hand duel. She frowned at the memory.

"I thought I might find you here," said a voice she recognized.

"Captain!" Kayleen cried, dropping to her feet. She waited in a glowlamp's tiny pool of light for Ectosh Laocer to reveal himself. Excitement coursed through her, making her come alive. Laocer filled a void in the orphan's heart. The unpredictable times between his visits were always too long for her.

"Hello, Kayleen. Agile as ever I see. Good. You're going to need that when we start giving you real assignments," Laocer said. Although he held no official rank among the Rangers, Laocer had lent a stabilizing authority during the war. Most Rangers below the rank of knight would follow his orders without question.

"I'm ready. I'm always ready. Can I go on a mission with you?" Kayleen knew the answer would be negative, but the tradition of asking had to be maintained.

"You get bigger every time I see you," Laocer commented, sidestepping the question. "Have you beaten Cloat in a duel yet?"

"Almost," she muttered. A frown crossed her face. Her silvery-blue eyes gazed into empty space as she recalled the duel again.

"Uh oh, what happened?"

"I had him, Captain! I had him in a chokehold, and then, I lost the will to fight. He slipped away wearing that stupid grin of his," Kayleen complained. "Before I knew it, I was staring up from the ground trying to catch my breath."

"Ah. I thought as much," Laocer said. "Cloat's mildly telepathic; it's not unusual in his species."

"His species?" Kayleen repeated. She braced her arms against both walls and pushed until she could move her legs into position to help her climb. "I thought he was human," she added, once she'd reached a satisfactory height. Kayleen placed one foot on an air vent's narrow ledge and the other on the opposite tunnel wall. Exercise always helped her think.

"He's actually Danatesh," said Laocer. "They age in spurts and live to be four or five hundred years old. Cloat may look thirteen, but he's probably seventy."

"Seventy? I want to be Danatesh too," Kayleen said with an easy smile. "That telepathic power could come in handy."

"There are other ways to gain power," Laocer reminded her.

"Practice and hard work," she recited, her voice muffled by the height. Having done this hundreds of times, she conquered the wall easily. Kayleen possessed her own powers, pure grit being one of the most potent. Higher up where the distance was greater, Kayleen performed a few flips. She kicked off one wall, somersaulted in the air, and kicked off the other wall. Finally, she caught the right wall and clung to it.

"I'd sap Cloat's will, throw him to the mat, and squash him like the dung beetle he is," she declared.

Her voice floated down in a dainty way that made Laocer chuckle.

"I have an assignment for you, Kayleen," Laocer said casually.

Next instant, she stood before him, still as a statue, waiting for him to continue.

"I thought that might grab your attention," Laocer said with a laugh, "but don't get too excited until you've heard what I want you to do."

"I'm ready for anything," Kayleen said, echoing her earlier sentiments. "Walk ready, stand ready, and live through the fight." The words proved she had paid attention in her survival classes. Even if she didn't enjoy the task, she would do it to please him. It was the least she could do for her mentor and friend.

"I've brought a boy about a year younger than you. He's as a guest, and he's going to need a friend."

Her excitement changed to a mixture of curiosity and disappointment.

"He will train here with you, but eventually, I'd like to send you both to the palace for a very special mission."

"Really? When can we go?" The girl bounced up on her toes, brimming with energy.

"When the time comes," Laocer promised, telling her nothing.

***

Allei (August) 7, 1554 – Allei (August) 11, 1554
Ranger Camp, Riden Mountains

The Ranger cave system in the Riden Mountains reminded Teven too much of the Imberg Tosh Mines for him to feel comfortable. Luminescent rock and scattered lightbars could only brighten the area so much, and the effect was quite eerie. Despair ate at him. Then, anger flared bright and hot, making his eyes sting with unshed tears. He growled and clenched his teeth until his jaw ached. His posture was such that a slight nudge would have laid him out flat.

Somewhere on the road between the ambush site and the Ranger camp a wall had formed between Teven and his mysterious companion. He didn't want to live anymore, not without his mother and Nate. He dug his fingernails into the flesh of his palm. It hurt and that was good. Physical pain could be controlled. The emotions flowing through him made him queasy and lightheaded. His knees started to buckle so he leaned heavily against the nearest wall. His anger spiked again for no other reason than his body and spirit were both tired of fighting numbing emotional pain.

A breeze from a vent column coursed through the dim tunnel carrying shiners. The bugs created their own light, rode the wind current, and twirled around Teven's legs. He reached for them instinctively. Several dozen perched on his hand. Had the last few days not transpired, he might have been charmed by their peaceful glowing.

Several minutes later, Teven forced himself to stumble to a large, semi-deserted cavern where he picked at a flavorless meal.

Captain Laocer showed up as he finished eating.

"I have acquired quarters for you," Laocer announced.

The small room Teven shared with two other boys made him feel lonelier than ever. Laocer left him there to unpack and grieve in peace. Teven curled up on the assigned bed and cried. By this time, four days after the attack, the salty taste of tears was familiar to him.

Teven spent two days mourning while conversations with his mother played over and over in his mind. He remembered the day she had spoken to him about his real parents. The conversation had started simply enough with him saying, *"I love you, Momma."*

Pria McKnight had finished tucking baby Nate into his makeshift crib. Then, she turned and leveled a warm, serious gaze at him that sent a shock of fear through him. Kneeling before him and gathering him into a comforting embrace, she had whispered, *"Teven, I could not love you more than I do. You will always be my son, but once upon a time, you had a different mother. One who gave you life and breath and loved you just as much as I do."*

"Who was she? Why didn't she keep me, if she loved me?" he had asked.

Her answer played in his mind like soothing music.

"She was someone I greatly admired: beautiful, brave, kind, and selfless to a fault. Evil people killed your father and then threatened her, but she did not fear to face violence or death, only that these might befall you. She gave you to me, so you would be safe from her enemies."

"Who was my father?"

"An honorable man, noble and brave," his mother had answered. Her eyes had twinkled with amusement. *"Both your parents possessed such strong personalities, it's a wonder they didn't kill each other over a petty disagreement."*

Teven had laughed with her even though he didn't really understand. Then, he turned the conversation serious again.

"Who killed them? Why would someone kill them?" he had asked.

Recalling those questions released new waves of hurt, pain, and anger.

"The reasons are complicated, but part of it was that they possessed great power and used it to help the weak. Some people despised their benevolence."

Subsequent conversations had slowly revealed more about his parents, but Teven knew there was much more to be learned. The McKnights spoke well of them but would tell him nothing about what sort of power they wielded.

Teven slept the third day straight through and awoke on the fourth morning with a ravenous appetite. Sick of fighting despair, Teven determined to fight back. He would let the Rangers train him, but he would never truly be one. He would learn enough to exact revenge for his murdered parents—all of them. In due time, he would find the murderers, and they would pay for their deeds in full.

Chapter 13:
Trainers and Teachers

Allei (August) 11, 1554
Ranger Camp, Riden Mountains

Before the sun rose, the Rangers attended to various chores. Morning guards hastily finished meals and trudged to their posts, expecting boredom but ready for excitement. Night guards retreated to their quarters for much needed naps before afternoon training sessions. The Ashatan Council members prepared for a day of making weighty decisions and issuing orders. Masters put finishing touches on lectures and knights—including Talyon Keldor—prepared for missions. Healers scrambled about on various errands. Older apprentices began lessons or corralled young recruits.

Teven McKnight found himself in the Grand Assembly Chamber with a group of apprentices. Feeling the stares of his peers, he hoped no one would try to talk to him. He wasn't in the mood. He kept his stance slightly hostile, but something brushed his left sleeve anyway. Looking up, Teven found himself staring into silver-blue eyes tucked in a youthful face with friendly challenge written all over it.

The girl leaned closer, further invading his space.

"Captain Laocer sent me to fetch you. It's not time to train you with the group yet," she whispered.

Teven liked her gentle, vibrant voice. The girl wore a tan tunic over dark trousers. A leather belt held a variety of pouches whose contents Teven could only guess at. An empty belt loop marked the place where a banistick would hang one day.

"Follow me." Without waiting for a response, the girl turned and walked swiftly through the small crowd.

Teven made a split-second decision and followed the girl, admiring the way the tunnel lights highlighted her reddish-blond hair. He jogged to match her rapid pace.

"Where are we going?" he asked.

She turned a corner and either didn't hear him or refused to answer.

Teven rounded the corner and stopped abruptly. Four tunnels converged at this point. He had come from one, another curved sharply left, one stretched out in front and a fourth branched right. Lost and feeling silly, Teven muttered something he had heard miners say and turned to return the way he had come. Two steps back toward the familiar, he stopped again.

She's down the middle path.

The knowledge entered his head like a whispered thought. It seemed like a crazy stab in the dark, but every instinct drew him down the center tunnel. Taking a deep breath and preparing a few questions for the girl, he stalked down the tunnel after her.

"You're walking like a herd of Terabian elephants," the girl's pleasant voice scolded from behind him. "We're going to have to fix that if you're going to be a Ranger."

"Who said I wanted to be a Ranger?" Teven demanded, whirling on her. "I didn't want to come! I want to go home! I want my mother and brother!"

"You're not the only one who's lost family. Deal with it," snapped the girl.

Her voice cut deep into Teven's strung out emotions. Tears formed, but he refused to let them fall. His teeth clenched so hard his head hurt. He wanted to punch something, even her—especially her—but he could do nothing more than stand there helpless and miserable.

"Your brother is probably still alive," said the girl, placing a hand on his tense forearm. "Kezem pays mercenaries for children he can brainwash and turn into soldiers or factory workers. Only the Rangers stand between him and more kids like you … and me."

"Who are you?" Teven asked, jerking his arm away. He didn't want to think about his family.

Instead of replying right away, the girl jumped, placing one foot on each tunnel wall and climbed higher.

"Kayleen Wellum," she said finally. "Nils, the man who brought me here, was murdered at the start of the war. I should have died with him that day. Master Ekris said she didn't know how I survived my wounds. I must have been about four, but I don't remember anything about that or my parents, except that they sent me away." The girl paused to let the words sink in. "So, you see, Teven, we have more in common than you might think."

"Like what?" he demanded.

"Losing family," Kayleen replied softly.

"What does it matter?" asked Teven.

"I don't know," Kayleen answered, "but Captain Laocer has special plans for you. He came here at the start of the war too, but he left four years ago to go on a personal mission. Since then, he's come and gone every few months. This time, he returned with you."

Teven's neck hurt from peering up into the darkness where Kayleen had disappeared. Then, she appeared before him, face to face, only upside down.

He retreated a step, eyes wide.

"Why would he look for me?" Teven inquired, curiosity replacing frustration.

"Does it matter? You're here," Kayleen answered. "Captain Laocer asked me to train you." She disappeared again into the unknown heights, reappeared directly behind him, and struck the center of his back.

The blow drove Teven forward. He clumsily dropped into a defensive position.

Kayleen serenely observed him, crossing her arms.

"We have a lot of work to do," said Kayleen.

"He'll learn," said Captain Laocer from behind Kayleen. If Laocer's presence surprised her, she hid it well.

Teven guessed her casual, almost bored, stance could be changed to combat readiness in a heartbeat.

"What's going on, Captain?" asked Teven.

"Your home is here now," said Laocer. "The Rangers will teach you to fight, and when you are ready, you will be given a mission which will answer questions you have yet to ask."

"Why should I do anything you say? You got my mother and brother killed!" Teven shouted.

"You will one day have the power to overthrow Lord Kezem," Laocer said quietly. "He destroyed everything I held precious. That makes for a rather large score to settle. Kayleen is right. Your brother is alive, but you must learn to fight if you want to rescue him."

"Glad to know I have a say in my future," Teven said, glaring.

"Deep down, we want the same thing," said Laocer. "Listen to me. Learn from me. Join the Rangers and then the Royal Guard. From there you can destroy Lord Kezem."

"Why me?" Teven asked. "What makes you think I want to destroy Lord Kezem?"

Teven expected a vague, unhelpful answer. Instead, Laocer met his eyes and spoke in an unexpectedly tender tone.

"It's in your blood. You are Crown Prince Teven of House Minstel, son of Queen Reia and King Terosh, and for your mother's sake, I will help you reclaim the throne."

The title landed on Teven like a crashing spaceship.

"He's the lost prince?" Kayleen's words mixed question and statement.

"What happens if I don't want to take the throne?" Teven asked, crossing his arms defiantly.

"Then, we had better hope your brother and sister still live," said Laocer, "because a royal from House Minstel must take the throne or this planet is doomed."

"Doomed. Right," Teven muttered. "Well, I guess training beats mourning forever."

Teven sensed a deep, almost ominous, sense of satisfaction rolling off Laocer. He dismissed the observation and let Kayleen lead him back to the chamber they had started in. The silence between them was deep but not necessarily uncomfortable. Teven spent the rest of the day idly watching hand-to-hand duels. His mind kept repeating the conversation with Kayleen and Laocer.

If that's normal Ranger recruiting, they're pretty lousy at it.
***

Allei (August) 12, 1554
Ranger Camp, Riden Mountains

On the fifth day at the camp, Teven McKnight dragged himself to the morning training session. It certainly beat working in a tosh mine, but he felt out of place. Most of the other apprentices had been born to this life or trained from a very young age. They possessed faster reflexes and stronger muscles than he did. They could quote Ranger codes, tell a hundred legends, and survive for weeks in the Riden Mountains with nothing but a banistick and a travel cloak. He wasn't sure whether to envy or pity them. Most were war orphans.

"Relax. You're tenser than a coiled Porit viper," Kayleen said.

"That's what happens when one might get hit," Teven said with a scowl.

"It wasn't personal," said Kayleen. Her tone lacked apology. "I had to check your reflexes. You did rather well."

One of the largest beings Teven had ever seen lumbered in and conversation ceased. Lightweight armor protected the figure's broad chest while a chitin carapace protected his back. His two arms waved about madly, but Teven attributed this to excitement rather than psychosis. He looked familiar. Teven eventually remembered the guard who had spoken briefly with Captain Laocer when they first arrived.

The being's voice boomed across the chamber.

"Good. Good. Young ones learn fast. Aveni teach weak points. Pressure weak point and opponent fall. First, I teach Rorgen weak points. Young ones greet volunteer Ranger Knight Bova!"

The class clapped politely. Teven craned his neck to see a lithe, muscular being sidle into the chamber. The being walked upright but each limb looked the same, indicating that all four could be used to run. Golden fur covered his arms, legs, and lean, shrewd face. Sharp yellow eyes glared at the bumbling giant who had summoned him.

The short lecture fascinated Teven. Aveni methodically walked the apprentices through each of Bova's weak points, occasionally jabbing the Rorgen. Finally, as expected, Bova leapt at Aveni, aiming for the throat, giving the latter a chance to demonstrate firsthand how weak points worked. Two well-placed punches drove Bova to the ground, quivering.

"Brilliant, Aveni, but you'll be the first guest for my lesson." The irritation in the yellow eyes melted into glee.

Next, they covered human, Elish, and Danatesh weak points. After a quick review, the youths paired off. As Teven had suspected, Kayleen pulled him aside. She repeated the key points before inviting him to strike her. His hand shot out but not swift enough to overcome her finely tuned reflexes.

After five fruitless tries, he grunted, eliciting a smile from his self-appointed trainer.

"Quicker," Kayleen urged. "Anticipate my moves. Make feints, pretend, catch your opponent off guard. Distract them."

"What do you mean?" Teven asked, straightening out of his defensive position.

Automatically, she followed suit.

Then, one quick step forward brought him in range.

"I mean—" A split second later, her right arm was twisted behind her back with both his thumbs digging into her elbow. "You did it! Excellent!"

Teven had never heard someone so happy about having an elbow tweaked. For the first time since his arrival, he genuinely smiled.

"You're ready for a match," said Kayleen.

His smile disappeared.

***

Masquerading as one of the recruits, Jalna Seltan worked hard not to hurt her opponents. Carefully orchestrating convincing falls and clumsy maneuvers took some serious concentration. Still, centuries-worth of practice had taught her something about judging beings. In addition, the anotechs fed her information on heart rate, brain capacity, pulse, temperature, and temperament. Most of the adolescents were human and thus easy for her anotechs to read.

Everyone except the newest boy had normal readouts, but a few spikes in his brainwave activity intrigued her. The anotechs acted as if they had found old friends within the boy. This warranted further investigation. He fought well enough to tell Jalna that one day he would be a great fighter, but his troubled green eyes spoke of deep, distracting pain. He was pale with a round young face, lean build, and curly, jet black hair that needed cutting. Jalna watched him duel a red-haired girl. His movements were stiff but swift, yet there was no doubt about the duel's outcome. Within a minute, the girl threw the boy to the training mat and then helped him up again. Jalna brushed some brown hair off her forehead and approached the pair.

"Greetings. I am Jalna. Would you like to duel?" she asked the boy.

"No," the girl replied. "He's not ready yet."

Jalna smiled politely and focused on the girl.

The anotechs reported: **Kayleen Wellum, possessive of subject.**

"Sure," the boy said, ignoring Kayleen. "I'm Teven, by the way," he added, offering his right hand to shake.

As soon as their hands touched, information flooded into Jalna's brain. Chemical composition, percentage sweat, firmness of grip, and other signs became character clues.

"You don't like it here," Jalna commented, brows knit together. "Why do you stay?"

"I have no choice." Teven looked away.

"There's always a choice!" Jalna said, tempted to emphasize the statement with a smack upside the head. Too many times had she uttered that admonishment to deaf ears.

"What would you know about it?" Kayleen demanded.

Jalna detected an undercurrent of strong emotion in Kayleen's question. She eyed the pair with renewed interest. Something, besides rumors, had led her to this camp, and she got the impression that the boy might have something to do with that.

"The lesson is over," Jalna said. "I suggest we continue this conversation in private."

The youths exchanged surprised glances at her sudden authoritative tone.

"No way," Kayleen declared. "You can't order us around, and none of this is your business anyway." With that, Kayleen seized the boy's arm and hauled him out of the chamber.

Jalna considered following them. They had absolutely no chance of avoiding her if she chose to pursue. The girl walked softly, but the anotechs would sense the boy's footfalls practically anywhere, even in a crowd.

She let them go. Nothing would be gained by pushing them today. If anything, Jalna Seltan knew how to wait well.

***

Allei (August) 19, 1554
Royal Palace Roof, City of Rammon

Heart aching within, Ranger Knight Talyon Keldor crouched on the palace roof and considered his next move. He had spent years as Captain Peter Estan searching for news of Merisia. Officially, he was in Rammon to observe Lord Kezem and protect the princess, but personally, he needed to know what happened to his friend. To search so long and so hard and learn that he had missed rescuing her by mere months caused crushing pain that stole his breath.

As he silently mourned his friend, Taly thought of everything that brought him to this roof tonight.

Who am I? What am I doing?

His career had started in the Tarpon organization because his father worked for them. When the Restler-Tarpon Alliance formed partly through the marriage of Merisia Tarpon to Gareth Restler, he had traveled with them as an Alliance agent. Then, when Merisia had gotten pregnant with Gareth's child, she'd talked Taly into helping her flee her husband, so the child would not become an Alliance hostage.

That didn't end well.

Honestly, Taly had never expected it to end well. Jumping to a logical but completely inaccurate conclusion, Gareth Restler had sent RT Alliance agents after Taly and Merisia. The pursuit had started in Meritab and ended in Terab where they had both been captured. Taly almost wished to go back to that time and face Gareth's misplaced retribution, for at least then Merisia had been alive.

A pair of Rangers, Kiata and Todd Wellum, had rescued Taly from the Deegan Estate in Terab, placing him in Kiata's debt a second time. The first time Kiata had rescued Taly from a Porit viper's poison when he was just a child, despite his father's mistreatment of her over some firfe spice. The Rangers had smuggled Taly into Rammon then out to a farm on the Kesler Plains owned by Todd's older brother, Terik.

I owe them so much.

After about a month, Taly learned his grandfather was about to be put on trial for murdering the last queen, so he snuck back into Rammon and sought help from Todd and Kiata again. They had arranged for him to meet with Queen Reia so he could plead for his grandfather's life.

The trial was a horrible, nerve-racking time for Taly who knew that Niktrod Keldor had indeed poisoned King Terosh's mother, Queen Kila. At first, Taly had merely feared his grandfather might be assassinated by a citizen too eager for justice, but he'd soon learned the danger was greater still because King Padric Creston of Gardan—Queen Kila's father—had claimed the right of execution. The best King Terosh and Queen Reia could do for Taly's grandfather had been to offer him a peaceful end before King Padric could torture him to death.

After the colored crossblades disaster that left the king half-dead, Taly had begun to repay his debt to the queen by escorting Lady Akia Zelene on an herb gathering mission through the Riden Mountains. That was the first time he'd experienced what life as a Ranger might be like. After that, he spent some time helping Lady Zelene with her duties as royal ambassador for King Terosh to the people of Ritand.

From time to time, Taly had discretely inquired after Merisia Restler. When Lord Kezem had the Restler-Tarpon Alliance destroyed, Taly feared for Merisia's life once again. With Lady Akia's blessing, he left her service to seek his old friend. For years, Lord Kezem kept her in prisons Taly couldn't hope to breach, so he watched, waited, and honed his fighting skills. Finally, the day came when Kezem used Merisia to bait a trap for King Terosh. Taly hadn't realized what was happening until the only thing he could do was take Merisia and run.

Not a day went by without him questioning whether he should have gone back to rescue the king.

He ordered us to go.

The reminder did nothing for Taly's sense of guilt. Right or wrong, they had fled, hiding in Estra for a few days then slipped across the Asrien Sea to Chara where they waited out the beginnings of Lord Kezem's rebellion. Soon after the king's death, the queen had contacted Taly about saving her sister. At the time, the instructions seemed cryptic and crazy, but then Kezem's forces moved in precisely the manner Queen Reia predicted. It was eerie.

Merisia, why couldn't you listen to me?

Despite Taly's pleading, Merisia had followed him in search of Kiata Wellum. Once again, Taly had been faced with an impossible choice: complete his mission or stand with his friend. He completed his mission and safely stole Kiata from Kezem's lackeys, but the price had been very high.

Merisia's crazy plan failed because one of the soldiers recognized her. Had Taly stayed with Merisia, they would likely have both been killed and Kezem would have tormented the queen by showing her Kiata's body. Still, Taly wished things could have gone differently for Merisia.

What good are the gods if all they grant good people is a life of captivity, heartache, and pain? Taly knew the question was inherently unfair, but he hurt too much to care.

After reviving Kiata and delivering her to Father Morgivesh Niktol in the Temple of Marishaz in Chara, Taly had returned to Rammon to seek Merisia. The gate guards had been showing people infopads with his description, so instead, he went into the Calsol Forest until things calmed down. Wandering aimlessly worked for a few days, but somehow, he'd ended up in the Riden Mountains seeking the Rangers.

Life goes in strange circles.

If anyone had told his childhood self he would one day be a Ranger, he would have thought them the worst sort of insane. Now as a Ranger, his orders to keep an eye on Lord Kezem's plans and guard the princess from afar were very vague. He enjoyed his work with Princess Rela, but every time he became Captain Peter Estan, he took a grave risk. He wasn't egotistical enough to think nobody else capable of teaching the princess to shoot, but few else would dare.

Do I stay or do I go?

Chapter 14:
Farm Country

Allei (August) 26, 1554
Ranger Camp, Riden Mountains

Two weeks later, Jalna spotted her quarry right where she had arranged for him to be. Anotechs could be quite persuasive when they wanted to be. At her bidding, they had suggested the boy explore this side tunnel. He looked uncertain, but then, his brows knit together, and his jaw tightened with determination. He clearly braced for a surprise. When he drew near, Jalna used anotechs to light the path leading to a dead-end chamber.

"Where is your lovely bodyguard?" asked Jalna from the shadows. On a whim, she modified the tone to reflect both age and wisdom. Even as the words left her mouth, she molded her features to match that of an elderly woman she had met more than two centuries ago.

"She's not my bodyguard. She's a friend," said Teven.

"Whether either of you intended it, she has tasked herself with guarding you," said Jalna. "Surely you have noticed she hardly leaves your side."

"Who are you and what do you want?" Teven asked, rubbing his temple.

"You sound weary, which I find worrisome at this stage."

"Stop!" Teven's shout bounced around the chamber.

Jalna silently thanked the anotechs for dampening the sound.

"I'm sick of it! No one speaks to me normally. I'm not blind! I see how they watch me. I can feel their hope, but no one tells me what I'm supposed to do! All I ever get is riddles. What am I training for? What am I fighting for?" He sounded decades older than his ten standard years.

Jalna smiled. Her previous observations had revealed only an eager student. Today, she heard the boy's determination and knew he needed her direction.

"My name is Jalna Seltan. We met some time ago, though I was much different then," Jalna said, flashing him a memory of the occasion.

"You're the girl—the one who wanted to duel," Teven said.

"Correct, and you are Teven McKnight, prince and scion of a fallen

Royal House. I confess to knowing little more than you concerning your past, but I offer my services as a teacher. Such a thing will require much trust, so I will tell you and your companion about my past when the time comes."

"What could you teach me?" Teven's question was laced with suspicion. "And what will it cost me? I have nothing."

"You are marked for greatness, and many will suffer under—or be saved by—your hand," said Jalna. "Since you have that fate and power, I wish to guide you to good purposes."

"Why?" Teven stood with his hands at his side, feet slightly apart, chin lifted defiantly.

"Because I could not save my planet," Jalna said softly. "I spent decades fighting greed and corruption before being banished. Now, I take up the causes of people I come across."

"How do you decide which side is right?" Teven wondered.

"Everyone knows what is right. As thinking beings, we respond to stimuli, such as pleasure and pain, and take steps to achieve or avoid these. But it is deeper than that. We know kindness, compassion, and love are good, but they constantly war with malice, cruelty, and hatred. Though we know what is right and good, we fulfill selfish desires first, often to the detriment of weaker beings."

"Great, another philosopher, as if Aveni wasn't enough," Teven muttered.

"Enough talk. It is time for lessons." Jalna instructed the anotechs to fully light the chamber.

The sudden bright light did not faze Teven.

"First lesson, do not trust your eyes or ears, for they are easily fooled," Jalna said, switching to her youthful voice. She modified her features to match the voice.

Teven's lips parted, but he said nothing for several seconds.

"What can I trust?" he asked finally.

Jalna's face and voice melted back to the elderly woman.

"Instinct. You were born with strong will, which shall serve you well. Strengthen your mind. Learn everything you can, even your enemies have much to teach you."

"I don't have any enemies," said Teven.

"You will," Jalna promised. Sadness clung to both words.

"Oh … okay. Anything else?" Teven wondered.

"The second lesson for today is confidence."

"Confidence?" Teven repeated. "Confidence in what?"

"Your walk is heavy because you seek to please the universe, but the core of you doubts your ability to accomplish such. Drive doubts from your mind and your heart, soul, and body will be lighter." Teven's mouth opened to protest, but Jalna held up a hand and continued, "That is the chain one way, but let us work the other way. Walk with me and concentrate on placing your feet instead of letting them punish the earth you tread. Don't speak. Just walk."

Rolling his eyes, Teven attempted to walk as she described.

Jalna suppressed a chuckle at his enthusiastic but very clumsy gait which reminded her of one of Porit's bow-legged stilt birds.

"Relax and glide," she suggested.

"I feel like an idiot."

"That will pass with time. Try turning it into a dance."

"I don't know how to dance," Teven objected.

That is apparent.

"Place your feet, as if stepping too hard would break some barrier separating you from a pit. Good. Slower now. Left foot lift; left foot place. Right foot lift; right foot place. Just like that. Repeat that same process slightly faster now ... and faster still. Good. Now try side to side. It's the same smooth motion in a different direction. See, you can dance. You may rest now. We will continue later, and someday your footfalls will be graceful and sure."

***

Elsewhere in the compound, Kayleen spent the afternoon beating wooden dummies to burn off the unexplained anxiety caused by Teven's absence. For some reason, she kept picturing the pretty girl who had tried to duel Teven a few weeks back. The girl's face had been flawless. That perfection irked her.

By the time she finished with the dummies, the time for the evening meal had long since passed. She headed to the dining chamber and found Teven contemplating a half-finished bowl of stew.

Tretling stew again.

She tried not to wince. Mountain herders traded tretlings for protection from korvers, panthers, bears, and zaloks. The late hour explained the lack of others but not Teven's presence and unfocused gaze. She glared at the top of his head and took a seat opposite him.

"Hello," he greeted.

"Where have you been?" they asked simultaneously.

"You first," Teven said, politely deferring.

"Stop that!" Kayleen ordered.

"What?"

"That—that *noble* thing," Kayleen sputtered.

"If my manners offend thee, fair lady, I do apologize," Teven quipped. His green eyes teased her.

Kayleen threw a playful punch at him.

Teven ducked right into his bowl of thick brown stew. At first, he looked annoyed, but seeing Kayleen's face contort with suppressed laughter made him laugh. Then, she too lost her battle, and their laughter filled the empty room.

"You deserved that." Kayleen said, handing him a cloth to clean his nose.

"Agreed," Teven replied, just to bother her.

She threw another punch which he caught easily.

"You've been working on that," said Kayleen.

"It beats getting hit every day," said Teven with an infectious grin.

Kayleen blushed. She couldn't understand him or herself when it came to him. Teven's boyish charm and compassionate spirit intrigued her.

"So, where have you been?" Teven asked again.

"Training," Kayleen answered. "Speaking of which, I have a special training mission for you, but it requires a six-day commitment. Want to take a trip with me?"

"Where are we going?" Teven asked.

"I'm not telling you until we get there," answered Kayleen. "That way, you can't
back out on me."

***

Allei (August) 27, 1554
Riden Mountains to Riden Flats

The next day, Teven and Kayleen set out early. They started with a shortcut through a series of tunnels snaking under much of the central Riden Mountains. Ranger Knight Bova escorted them for much of the way. Then, they hiked alone over the remaining mountains, reaching the last by late morning.

Teven gasped for breath.

"Don't die on me yet," Kayleen called over her shoulder.

Teven didn't have the breath for a comeback, and Kayleen wouldn't have heard him anyway for she jumped the last three meters of the perilous descent. She landed lightly and smiled a challenge up to Teven.

He narrowed his eyes and leapt, landing with a loud grunt.

"We'll rest, eat, and then hike the last distance," said Kayleen.

Teven groaned.

"You said six-day commitment, not tunnel trekking, mountain climbing, endless hiking, feet hurting, six-day commitment."

"No whining. Besides, it'll be good for you."

After a brief rest and some food, Teven had enough strength to plod on.

"We're going to help some relatives of mine with the harvest," said Kayleen, once they'd gone too far to turn back.

"Meaning ..."

"Meaning I'm going to hand you a long stick with a really sharp blade attached and teach you how to use it on wheat, barley, and polata plants," Kayleen said cheerfully. "Besides providing much needed help for my aunt and uncle, it should strengthen your arms and teach you to control heavy weapons. Just don't cut your hand or head off. They're hard to reattach."

"I'll try to remember that, but I thought you said you didn't know much about your parents."

"I don't," Kayleen said. "Uncle Terik is my father's brother. Both he and Aunt Nala refuse to talk about my parents. All I ever get is 'Too dangerous to discuss, lass' or 'You'll know everything when you need to know, dear.'" Kayleen's voice dropped then rose in pitch as she imitated first her uncle and then her aunt.

They continued their journey through the Kesler Plains toward the Riden Flats, passing many bright, golden grain fields, stretches of rich, green grass, and patches of countless wildflowers. Here and there tiny fossa trees and scruffy looking pora bushes broke the utter flatness of the plains. Near the end of the day, they arrived at their destination.

"Kayleen!" cried a voice.

Teven felt the air move as a small girl flew past him and crashed into Kayleen.

"Owww. Watch the ribs, Chloe," Kayleen said, returning the hug. "Teven McKnight meet my cousin, Chloe Marie Wellum. Chloe, this is Teven."

"Hello, Chloe," said Teven.

The child's return greeting got muffled against Kayleen. When the girl finally released Kayleen, she turned and studied Teven.

"He's handsome, Kaylee," she whispered loudly, causing Teven and Kayleen to blush. "I have to show him to Momma." With that declaration, Chloe grabbed Teven's hand and hauled him into the tiny farmhouse.

Soon, Teven found himself the center of attention, but eventually, things settled down. Fresh bread and appola juice were set before the guests. As the family exchanged greetings and news, a brief pang of jealousy pierced Teven. Kayleen's young cousins chattered incessantly. Their craziness reminded Teven of Nate, causing a dull ache in his chest. Nevertheless, he forced himself to smile and answer the questions flung his way.

That night, Teven shared a tiny bed with two of Kayleen's cousins. The younger boys didn't seem to mind, and Teven was too tired to care. He slept soundly until somebody shook him awake. His eyes snapped open. Kayleen stood at the foot of the bed grinning sympathetically. Chloe knelt on the bed beside Teven, leaning forward so that her face hovered a few centimeters away.

"Up!" Chloe bellowed into his face. "Sun's been out for a half-hour. You're late. Momma left biscuits for you, so get dressed while I go get your food." With that, Chloe scrambled backward on her knees and leapt off the bed.

After consuming the delicious biscuits, Teven and Kayleen set out for the fields. It didn't take Teven long to get a feel for the heavy staff with its built-in blade. Following Kayleen's instructions, he methodically swung the scythe back and forth across the ripe fields. His arms became tired and his breath grew labored, but he continued swinging. Small insects buzzed and chattered near his ears, adding their voices to the laughter bubbling forth from Kayleen's cousins. Their carefree attitude made Teven feel ancient inside, but he chose not to worry. Instead, he relaxed into the rhythm of the work. A gentle breeze cooled the sweat on his brow, as he breathed deeply of the fresh, earthy scent of the he Kesler Plains.

"Let me see your hands," Kayleen said, after about an hour.

Glad for the rest, Teven complied. He liked the feel of her rough hands on his.

"No blisters, that's odd," said Kayleen.

"Some of the miners had blisters, but I've never gotten one." Teven shrugged and hefted the scythe. "I want one of these. It'd probably go through those nasty mountain creatures pretty easily."

Kayleen nodded and returned to binding the loose stalks of grain Teven felled. She didn't speak for a full minute.

Teven watched her work, admiring the smoothness of her movements.

"When I'm here, I almost forget about the war," she said softly.

Teven nodded, understanding the feeling.

"Me too. I could stay here forever." Teven continued working but stole glances at Kayleen.

The sun bounced off her hair, making the red sections flicker like flames.

The next three days passed quickly, and as promised, they undertook the return journey on the sixth day. Much of the harvest still lay in the fields, but a good portion had been brought in and bound. Part of Teven didn't want to return to the Ranger compound or continue his training. This simple life felt right to him, but cruel reality would not be put off.

Chapter 15:
Daughter of the Maker

Pirua (September) 3, 1554
Ranger Compound, Riden Mountains

After listening to Teven and Kayleen explain their farming adventure, Jalna took advantage of their exhausted state to share her story with them. She brought them to the same obscure cave where she had first taught Teven how to walk softly and bid the anotechs to seal off the chamber and direct others away.

The anotechs native to Reshner had finally shared some of the recent past. She figured the young prince and his sister ought to know the whole story someday, but for now, she would ease the prince and his Ranger companion into knowledge of the anotechs' history. They also told her of the severe restrictions concerning everything related to the anotechs.

That needs to change.

Jalna had waged quite the word war with the Reshner anotechs. They still weren't fully persuaded, but at least they were being civil about the disagreement.

"What do you want from us?" asked Kayleen.

"Nothing yet, dear child. For now, I wish only to give you a proper introduction to me," said Jalna. Once again, she adjusted her features to match those of a thirteen-year-old girl.

Kayleen's eyes widened in surprise, but she only nodded, waiting for Jalna to explain. Teven had already seen this transformation, so his expression remained passive.

"Would you like me to tell you the story or shall I let the anotechs show you?" asked Jalna.

"What are anotechs?" asked Teven.

Suppressing a sigh, Jalna explained that anotechs were microscopic machines that could adapt, learn, change, and grow like living beings. Certain protocols kept them dependent upon humanoid species, but a subset of anotechs called Dalonos, literally "Dark Ones," had been trying to sow seeds of chaos across the galaxy for many centuries.

"The best way for you to understand anotechs is to experience them," said Jalna. "Are you ready for this?"

Both children nodded eagerly and exchanged nervous smiles. Impulsively, Teven reached out and held Kayleen's hand. Jalna held her left hand out to Teven and her right hand out to Kayleen. Once their hands were connected, Jalna guided them to a sitting position and instructed the anotechs to start the scene.

The children fell into a trance-like state.

Jalna didn't need to see the scene. She had experienced it hundreds of times over the years and lived it once upon a time.

*****

Enis (April) 19, 730
Over Eight Hundred Years Ago ...
Headquarters of InGeneus Designs, Planet of Kalast
Once I leave here, I'm never coming back. Ever. I will infect your precious system and turn the mockeries of humanity against you.

The words filled the air then left a heavy silence in their wake.

Dodging a small metal table, Jalna's father, Sebastian Seltan, approached the unconscious form strapped to the wall. He was an undisputed genius, but also a madman. Hate or revere him, everybody feared the man who, through decades of careful engineering, had perfected the anotechs. Through these tiny machines, he controlled the mysteries of life. Those he wished dead suddenly died. Those he wished alive miraculously recovered from deadly wounds or illnesses.

"Come now, Jalna, be reasonable," said Sebastian, as if he could control her through will alone. Normally, he would use anotechs for such a task, but she was currently using hers to protect her mind against such assaults. "I'm your father. You know I only want what's best for you."

"You're my father. You should have seen this coming," Jalna said, from behind him.

Sebastian whirled and saw a full-sized, translucent representation of his thirteen-year-old daughter. His glance flitted back to her still form then back again to the hologram.

"I didn't teach them that," said Sebastian. "Interesting."

The near-perfect representation of Jalna studied the body fixed to the wall. Life support machines kept the heart beating, blood flowing, and lungs breathing. Despite the wicked-looking straps, the living corpse wore a peaceful expression.

The child's translucent essence walked through the small table, stepped around Sebastian, and stood protectively in front of the physical girl. She regarded Sebastian coldly.

"Best for me, best for Kalast, call it what you will, Father." Bitterness dripped from the girl's words. "For years, I deluded myself into believing you truly had good intentions, but one can only believe fabricated dreams for so long."

"You're like your mother: beautiful, brilliant, and stubborn," Sebastian said in an even, reflective tone. He ran his left hand through his light brown hair. His synthetic skin looked as fresh and clean as it had decades ago when Proyles, a nasty skin disease, prompted his anotech research.

"I have decided I am more like mother than you, which is why I trust myself with the anotechs." The corners of Jalna's mouth quirked upward.

"You cannot win," said Sebastian. "There are thirteen billion people waiting to be healed of their problems. Would you deny them that?"

"Healing I don't mind, for its own sake. But at what cost? Would you have them sell you their souls?" Jalna asked. Her voice flowed with passion. "I know the masses wait for your delusions, but I also know they mean less than nothing to you … like me." A note of real pain crept into her voice. "They think you're a god, but I know better. You don't care what—"

"I *do* care. Don't you see? Godhood is finally within our grasp. We must seize perfection and superiority, to end disease, crime, poverty, and—"

"And everything that makes life worth living besides," Jalna finished. "Being alive isn't about the winning or losing. It's about fighting. Population control failed years ago, Father. Imperfection, rising above bad circumstances; these things are at the core of life."

"Where do you get your crazy ideas?" Sebastian wondered, shaking his head. "I'll have to modify the genes next time."

"There will not be a next time," said Jalna. "I destroyed your samples of my genes."

"What's to stop me from taking new samples?" Sebastian asked.

"Everything that can be created can be destroyed. The anotechs you gave me as a baby are only machines. They obey their masters. In this case, me."

Sebastian growled and cursed Jalna's long-dead mother.

"I knew she would rig the anotechs!"

"Of course, I did, Bastian, no one in their right mind would let you completely control anything," replied a mature female voice from Jalna's young holoform.

Sebastian nearly jumped out of his synthetic skin.

"Meria!" He tried to back up but bumped into the table.

The holographic figure stepped forward. With a seductive expression totally unbefitting of a teenager, Jalna's translucent form gently caressed Sebastian's left cheek. The skin there tingled.

He shivered.

"Hello, darling, I won't ask if you've missed me since you wouldn't have murdered me if you were planning on feeling bereft," Meria Seltan said through Jalna. "Do not worry. Our daughter is safe, despite your best efforts to perfect her into oblivion."

"Meria," Sebastian repeated, dazed. "How—"

"Since you cannot stop the changes now, I shall explain things. This insane affair with perfection must cease," said Meria. "When reasoning with you failed, I took matters into my own hands."

"But you're dead!" Sebastian protested.

"Anotechs are wonderful things, aren't they? You're not very good at hiding murderous intentions, Bastian," said Meria. "I knew you would succeed in destroying my body, so I transferred to Jalna in a dormant program. She is still here and quite fine, but it seems both of us might be out of bodies if you have your way. I have learned to live without, but I will not let you harm our daughter. I'm going to reprogram your anotech files."

"That's impossible." Sebastian wanted to shout, but the protest came out weak and raspy.

"You keep telling yourself that. It might help you sleep."

"Wha—"

"Shhhhhhh. Let the anotechs take over."

Following orders from Meria, the anotechs flowed from Jalna's fingertips into Sebastian. They conquered the brain first then the body by systematically surrounding and rupturing each cell. Sebastian collapsed, writhing as his cells exploded. Aware that she doomed herself as surely as she had her husband, Meria, through Jalna, spent the next three days destroying the rest of Sebastian's dangerous technology. Then, she broke the cruel bonds binding her daughter and set the child free to live in the chaotic universe.

*****

Enis (April) 19, 730-Allei (August) 8, 1554
Kalast and many other Planets

At least that's how the anotechs portrayed the story. Jalna

herself had been unconscious. Her mother had not been completely successful in confining the problem. Although Meria debugged the system, destroyed the anotech makers, and obliterated every file pertaining to the malevolent technology, several ships piloted by thieves and idealists alike had already left Kalast carrying anotechs.

After the confrontation with her father, Jalna tried to save her world but not even the anotechs could save Kalast from the damage her father had inflicted. She spent seven decades working tirelessly to establish a strong government, but greedy politicians thwarted her efforts. Finally, she lost heart and went into exile.

In a rickety old ship, Jalna left her home planet to follow the anotech trail. She felt burdened to control the rogues among them. Her anotechs allowed her to mimic nearly any humanoid feature, even horns if necessary, but Jalna preferred the face she had once possessed as a young woman.

She needed little sustenance, but natural curiosity often propelled her to local taverns and other common meeting places. She could have done anything. The anotechs could regenerate themselves. They made her impervious to disease, untouched by age, practically immortal. But she could still be harmed. She learned the hard way that anotechs didn't react well to bullets or energy blasts. One or two holes could be repaired in time, but she could bleed to death if she sustained too many wounds at once.

At any time, she could command the anotechs to shut down and let Fate have her body, but something drove her on. She spent seven centuries traveling the galaxy. Eventually, hope of finding the other anotechs faded, but Jalna found solace in aiding people she came across. Some welcomed her help, others scorned it, but everybody feared her. As much as people fight to gain power, they fear it in others. They also fear things they do not understand, and few understand the anotechs. Inevitably, Jalna's secret always came out. Then, no matter how much people revered her, she became an outcast.

On the remote planet of Porit, the guardians of the semi-sentient vipers had once suffered greatly because they stood between crystal hunters and untold fortunes. Although viper crystals could be safely extracted through careful surgery, few hunters considered that option. Many hunters fell to toxins, but the triumph of a few ensured a steady stream of adventurers.

Upon landing, Jalna was attacked with poisoned darts. Although she avoided most darts, a few struck her, and when the poison failed to kill her, she became like a goddess to them. She organized the viper guardians, called the Gedenia, under a respected leader and helped beat back the invaders and establish profitable trade agreements with nearby planets.

Porit had been a success, but like all successes, it came to an end. Jalna considered staying there permanently until the Gedenia tried to build her a temple. Then, she left in a hurry. Exhausted, Jalna chose nearby Reshner as her next home.

*****

Pirua (September) 3, 1554
Same Day
Ranger Compound, Riden Mountains

"Upon arrival, I took a job in a tavern to gather information," said Jalna as the scene ended. "Eventually, the anotechs led me here, to the two of you."

"Why to me?" Kayleen wondered. "I get why Teven. He's a prince, but I'm just a Ranger orphan."

"The anotechs from this planet have yet to share everything with me, but they are never wrong," said Jalna. "They tell me you're very important, so I have decided to invest myself in your training. Is that acceptable to you?"

Kayleen and Teven exchanged puzzled yet excited glances before accepting the aid.

Chapter 16:
Strike Hard

Kest (October) 23, 1559
Ranger Camp, Riden Mountains

Five years passed like nothing to Jalna Seltan, but Teven McKnight and Kayleen Wellum changed significantly. Kayleen slowly blossomed into a young woman, losing none of her agility yet gaining more strength and grace. The wisdom burning behind her silvery-blue eyes further enhanced her pretty features.

Teven transformed from boy to young man seemingly overnight. He flourished in the crisp mountain air, which liked to toss his wavy black hair around. His nose sloped gently downward toward the wide, mischievous grin that often brightened his face, and his intense green eyes glittered from beneath the neat, dark strips of his eyebrows. Teven's thin, wiry frame gave way to confident muscles, but he hesitated to use this newfound strength.

"Blast it, Teven. There's nothing gentle about combat!" Kayleen scolded. "You know the moves, and you have the strength to hurt your opponent. Use it!"

"I'm trying!" Teven snapped.

"She is right," Jalna said. She was in her elderly woman form today, a persona she was growing attached to because it aptly portrayed her feelings about Reshner. In short, the whole planet seemed aged by the constant fighting. "Strike harder. She is trained for this."

"If you don't hit me harder, I *will* hurt you," Kayleen said. Her petite nose flared, and her lips pressed firmly together, causing her jaw to slide forward in a downright stubborn expression. Her long, red-gold braid whipped over her left shoulder as she swung a strike that would have seriously hurt Teven's right shoulder had he not twisted out of the way.

"Fine." Teven circled Kayleen, waiting for an opening.

As she had done for years, Jalna studied the combatants. She wished Teven would get over his fear of hurting Kayleen. Their fighting styles, though different, complimented each other. Teven measured his movements, flowing back and forth, dancing in to strike swiftly, and then fading out of reach. Whenever he could, Teven would dodge a strike rather than meet it.

Kayleen was more direct. Though just as light on her feet, she was efficient about her movements, choosing to let Teven draw near, catching his strikes, and then unleashing a series of lightning swift strikes to drive him back.

Jalna expected the match to go on for some time. Teven had greater size and strength, but Kayleen had more experience. Furthermore, Teven failed to press his advantages, a weakness both Jalna and Kayleen tried to correct. Kayleen repeatedly knocked Teven down but his energy seemed limitless. Each time he leapt to his feet and continued the match. Their banisticks met with loud satisfying cracks but neither was willing to land a finishing blow.

"Would you prefer to fight me?" Jalna asked, silently berating herself for not thinking of this solution sooner. "I can't be seriously hurt," she reminded them. The statement stretched the truth, but they didn't have to know that part.

Kayleen and Teven stopped sparring.

"Sounds good to me, but lose the old lady look," Kayleen said, walking to the combat ring's edge.

Jalna smiled and complied, stepping into the ring as the girl they had first met.

"Better?"

"Much. Thanks," Kayleen replied with a satisfied smile. She tossed Jalna her banistick. "Fighters begin when ready," Kayleen instructed, taking over as match moderator.

Teven shook his head in amused exasperation.

Jalna bowed to Teven, feet together and arms held at her sides. The bow showed that trust existed between the combatants. Opening ritual over, Jalna and Teven assumed ready stances and began the bout. Again, Teven dashed in and out with surprising fluidity. At first, Jalna simply deflected his blows. Her eyes followed his movements carefully, waiting for the right moment to strike. The fight continued in this manner for several minutes. Then, Teven launched a right-to-left slash at Jalna's knees. Instead of jumping away, Jalna jumped toward him and thrust her weapon at his left shoulder.

Caught off guard, Teven stopped his attack mid-swing, stumbled back a step, twisted his upper body to the left, and whipped his banistick up to meet hers. The force of the weapons crashing together sent Teven spinning further left. He used the twisting motion to his advantage by spinning and kicking simultaneously. His foot grazed Jalna's side. The small hit was inconsequential but bolstered Teven's confidence. He intensified his attacks. Blows rained from every side, and Jalna was hard-pressed to catch them.

After several minutes, Jalna disengaged and bowed again, ending the match.

"Well fought. Your strike quality is much improved," she said.

"See, you can fight hard." Kayleen glared at Teven. "You were holding out on me."

"Am I interrupting?" a familiar voice asked from the entrance to their little dead-end cave.

"Captain!" Kayleen exclaimed, stepping forward and embracing Captain Ectosh Laocer. "You're late. You said you'd be back by the tenth of the month. That was thirteen days ago!"

"Good to see you, too, kid," Laocer said, returning Kayleen's embrace.

Jalna watched an amusing flash of jealousy flashed through Teven's eyes. No doubt the boy would deny it. Jalna had paused a moment so Kayleen could greet her old friend, but now she stepped forward.

"Greetings, Captain Laocer. It has been quite some time," she said.

"Jalna Seltan, I don't know how you do it, but I like the young look."

Jalna felt the intensity of Laocer's gaze, and something in his eyes said he felt differently. The look faded in a heartbeat, and Jalna didn't dwell on it.

"But that's not why I came. The Festival of Future Fighters approaches, and I think it's time these two joined the Royal Guard and Melian Maidens," Laocer announced.

"Are we ready?" Teven wondered. He idly flipped his banistick from hand to hand.

"Of course, we're ready," Kayleen said. "Some derringers go on the Kireshana as young as eight or nine, at least they used to. Wait. You don't think we're ready?"

"I didn't say that. It's just—" Teven began.

"We must intensify our training, if you are to do well," Jalna commented, cutting off the rest of Teven's defense. "The Kireshana has killed many a candidate before you."

The anotechs had been very detailed in their reports of Kireshana deaths from the recent and ancient past.

"We'll be fine," Kayleen assured her. "It's probably no more difficult than a level seven apprentice trial."

"We've not been on our level seven yet," Teven pointed out. "As I recall, we had a bit of trouble on last month's level five trial."

"Trouble we handled nicely, as I recall," Kayleen replied, crossing her arms smugly.

"Trouble we *could* have avoided," Teven said.

"Hey, they were holding out on us," said Kayleen. "I just called them on it. We rescued the hostages, didn't we?"

Teven snorted but ruined the effect with a smile.

"Two on seven are not good odds," he pointed out. "Next time, we should try something less confrontational first."

"I am curious as to what lies ahead," Jalna said before Kayleen could continue the argument. "I too may try this Kireshana. Besides, someone has to watch your back while you two argue." Jalna shifted her facial features, arranging them into that of a young man about Kayleen's age of sixteen.

"That is so creepy," said Kayleen.

Jalna could feel the girl's eyes travel over every millimeter of her new body. The anotechs shivered under the scrutiny, causing a tickling sensation.

Calm down! she commanded the tiny machines.

Captain Laocer nodded with approval.

"A male persona will allow you to stay closer to Teven," said Laocer.

"That and it'll give me a chance to exercise my powers," Jalna said, placing her right fist into her open left palm. "No offense to my gender, but when it comes to cracking heads, males certainly have more fun."

Despite freely demonstrating a few anotech tricks and letting them see pieces of her past, Jalna had never fully explained her father's invention to Teven or Kayleen. She wasn't about to do so in front of Captain Laocer. Something about the man made her cautious.

"What will we call you?" Kayleen asked. "We certainly can't call you Jalna. It means 'delicate flower' in Kalastan. Though that certainly would earn you the fights you're looking for, that kind of attention could be bad."

"How do you know that?" Teven asked. "They didn't teach that in the code class."

"Oh, I know many things," Kayleen said, lifting her chin imperiously. "To be honest, I don't know how I know. I just do. I guess it's just one of the odd facts floating about in my head," she continued with a shrug.

Jalna added a note to her mental log on Kayleen.

Memory flashes.

The mental list of intriguing details concerning Kayleen was growing quite long. Beyond the surface beauty, too often hidden by dirt, Kayleen had proven herself to be thoughtful, impulsive, athletic, intelligent, loyal, and dangerously fearless.

"You are correct. Call me Jal then," Jalna said, after a moment's thought. "It means 'wanderer,' a fitting title for our purposes."

***

Kest (October) 24, 1559
Wellum Farm, Kesler Plains

Captain Jairis Selok locked gazes with the defiant farmer.

"Terik Wellum, you have fallen behind with taxes and contributions to the cause. We are here to collect them." He resisted the urge to sigh and kept his voice stiff and even.

He lost count of the number of farmers who had died protecting their pathetic pieces of property. Still, he admitted this land was remarkably beautiful. Golden fields of wheat stretched for kilometers around, interrupted by green and red rows of polata plants.

I wouldn't mind owning this, he thought, though knew it would ultimately go to one of Lord Kezem's pet governors or senators.

"I refuse to be robbed any longer!" the prisoner declared, interrupting Captain Selok's thoughts. "I cannot meet the quotas without starving my fam—"

A muffled crash and a sharp female scream came from inside the house.

The farmer's face drained of blood.

"Nala!" He turned to enter his home again, but two soldiers each caught an arm and held him firmly while a third applied stuncuffs. The man flinched as a shock coursed through his arms.

Captain Selok glanced sideways at his aide.

"Lieutenant Surin, help Dobbin retrieve the family."

Within five minutes, Terik Wellum, his wife, two sons, and daughter were lined up outside of their tiny home. There was no need for this much ceremony, but Selok enjoyed exercising army authority. He rotated the men performing executions, and it was currently Lieutenant Surin's turn. Captain Selok watched dispassionately as Surin positioned himself and the men.

The farmer and his wife wore expressions that wavered between outrage and fear, with fear having a distinct edge. The boys, Jacob and Jared, twelve and thirteen respectively, stood to either side of their younger sister. Each young man had his body angled to intercept any threats to Chloe. For her part, the ten-year-old child glared at Lieutenant Surin.

"Leave us alone!" Chloe said, stamping a foot.

Jared's hand shot out and covered Chloe's mouth. A brief but distinct shake of the head further stressed the need for silence. The movement also placed Jared firmly in front of Chloe so that any retribution would fall to him.

The child's outburst caused most of the soldiers to tense. Selok casually held up a hand, signaling his men to relax. Lieutenant Erid Surin and Lieutenant Aaron Kaelo—on loan from the Coridian Assassins—were the only two, besides Captain Selok, who didn't flinch.

Twenty seconds passed, then Surin spoke.

"Terik and Nala Wellum, you are charged with failure to pay taxes, supporting subversive causes, and—"

"That's a lie!" Terik shouted.

Kaelo slammed a fist into Terik's face. The blow drove the man against the house and unleashed a steady stream of blood from his nose. Nala screamed and tried to go to her husband, but the sharp prick of Kaelo's kamad dagger halted her. Most soldiers preferred energy weapons, but Kaelo preferred the traditional weapon of Coridian Assassins. The boys protested the rough treatment but fell silent as the blade moved from Nala's shoulder to her throat.

"Steady, boys," Kaelo murmured, keeping his gaze on Nala.

Selok wondered if he would have to step in.

"Be silent while the charges are listed," Surin instructed, staring each of them down before returning his attention to Terik. "Your relation to Rangers casts doubts on your loyalty. The decrease in crop production proves your guilt. You have also failed to register your children for service to Lord Kezem."

"My production rates remain steady, but the quotas keep rising," Terik said bitterly. "What do you want me to do? I cannot keep up with unreasonable demands!"

"Take us to Rammon," Nala said suddenly. "Let us appeal to Lord Kezem. There must be something we can do to—"

"There is," Kaelo assured her. With a swift flick of the wrist his dagger opened the right side of her neck.

The woman's husband and children screamed. Her body stayed upright for one long second before slowly sinking to the ground.

Lieutenant Surin shot an angry glare at Kaelo but didn't dare reprimand the Coridian Assassin.

Captain Selok cleared his throat, breaking the stunned silence that had fallen thickly over prisoners and soldiers alike.

"That was … unconventional, but the penalty for these crimes is indeed death. Terik, you have been informed of the charges against you. Lieutenant Kaelo will now carry out your execution. Do you have any last words?"

Terik's eyes riveted upon his wife's body. Tears mingled with the blood on his face, but his features hardened.

"Riden bless House Minstel."

The treasonous words sealed his fate. At a nod from Selok, Lieutenant Surin drew his serlak pistol and shot Terik in the face. The three children collapsed together in a sobbing mass. Selok ordered them separated and bound so they could await transportation to a manufacturing plant.

When it was over, Selok retired to his private tent and took notes on the incident. He wasn't one to play favorites, but both Kaelo and Surin would bear watching.

***

Ferrim (December) 26, 1559
Ranger Camp, Riden Mountains

Another two months slipped by as Teven threw himself into his training. He would soon need endurance, strength, and courage in abundance. First, there would be the Festival of Future Fighters, which would determine his place in the Kireshana. Then, he would face the long journey itself. If he survived the race's seven trials he would be commissioned as a Royal Guard. High Commander Torent expected perfection from those undertaking the Kireshana. At least, Teven wouldn't have to go through the trials alone. Kayleen would be there trying to impress Melian Maiden High Commander Leena Linel.

"You're not listening to me," Kayleen said, clearly annoyed.

They sat facing each other in a narrow hallway practicing the honor codes.

Teven shrugged and nodded agreement, earning a playful swat on the shoulder.

"Ouch! All right, I'll listen but this is so boring," said Teven.

"You'll thank me later, when you know the Royal Guard code of honor backwards and forwards," Kayleen said.

"I know," Teven said. "But is it really going to help?" The question hung in the air. He didn't want to admit that he already knew the code because learning it had almost been too easy.

"It is time," Jalna answered in her Jal tone.

Teven and Kayleen were on their feet in an instant. Teven rocked back on his heels to avoid smacking heads with Kayleen who turned her head so fast that he caught a mouthful of her long hair. She had given up on shoulder length hair a few years back because long hair could be braided easier.

"Why are you dressed like that?" Kayleen demanded, gathering and re-braiding strands of escaped hair.

Jal wore beige slacks with brown boots and a dark shirt. The ensemble was cinched with a bright red belt, which declared the wearer a hopeful in the Festival of Future Fighters. When they made it to the Kireshana, they would trade the red belt for a more functional brown leather one.

"It is time," Jal repeated. She had made a conscious decision to speak as little as possible while being Jal. Listening would provide many more learning opportunities. She still felt something dangerous lurking in the shadows surrounding this planet. Before long, he, she, or they would reveal themselves.

The trio withdrew into their own thoughts.

First to stir, Jal said, "Don't let me interrupt. I'm just here to listen."

"This boring exercise is going to be the death of me," said Teven.

"Quit complaining and recite the seven Royal Guard codes of honor and the pledge to Reshner's Slimy Sovereign Ruler." With an attractive smile, Kayleen eased herself to the ground with natural grace.

"The abuse I take," Teven said. He grinned and reclaimed his patch of dusty ground.

Jal watched the two friends with lazy interest.

Teven cleared his throat grandly.

"From the top, if you please," Kayleen prompted.

Clearing his throat, Teven launched into the pledge first.

"This day, I pledge my service to Reshner's Sovereign Ruler, Lord Kezem of Idonia. I will serve, protect, and honor him all my days, forfeiting life if necessary to fulfill this duty." He paused.

"Code of Duty," Kayleen encouraged.

He made a face at her but started reciting the code.

"The Code of Duty—serve, protect, and honor Reshner's Sovereign Ruler, Royal Guards, and Melian Maidens. This requires strength. The Code of Strength—mind, heart, and spirit must be strong enough to carry the burden of truth. Strength comes in many forms; to overcome one must persevere. The Code of Perseverance—should someone threaten Lord Kezem, infinite space cannot hide him from me, yet I shall employ wisdom when seeking my foes."

He paused thinking, *I'd rather just lock Kezem in a korver den.* The thought's vehemence surprised him.

As if she had heard the thought, Kayleen's grin widened.

"The Code of Wisdom—to possess great wisdom is a rare gift," said Teven. "I will share my knowledge with Lord Kezem and his agents. Courage, the companion of wisdom, will walk with me always. The Code of Courage—

I fear neither battles of word nor sword nor blazing blade. My enemies will flee or fall. While courage strengthens my heart, my feet will swiftly pursue justice. The Code of Swiftness—justice must be swift, yet stillness may best catch my enemies. The Code of Stillness—silent, vigilant, and alert, I await evil, so I can strike it down with word or sword. If I fall in this service, my life will have been well spent."

By the end of Teven's impassioned recital, Kayleen's mouth hung slightly agape.

"You read that once. How did you do that?" asked Kayleen.

"I'm just that good." Teven shrugged and smirked.

Kayleen threw the code book at him.

He laughed and caught the projectile.

"Is that any way to treat a genius?" he wondered.

"Only if he deserves it," Kayleen replied. "We'd better hurry up and get you into the Royal Guard. Maybe they can knock some humility into you."

"Yeah, Kezem's men are always good for violence," Teven agreed.

Immediately, a chill settled over the threesome.

"Sorry," Teven whispered.

Tears welled up in Kayleen's eyes, but she held them back.

"Not your fault." Kayleen's tone held all the weariness and frustration they had both felt since hearing of the attack on the Wellum farm. She wiped at her eyes, even as her left hand formed a fist at her side.

"I know, but that's why we must join the Royal Guard and the Melian Maidens," Teven said. "They were once noble orders dedicated to protection and peace. Something's gone terribly wrong at the highest levels of government." He picked up Kayleen's left hand and squeezed. "We're going to set things right. I promise."

Chapter 17:
Dangerous Good Deeds

Ferrim (December) 26, 1559
Same Day
Princess Rela's Private Chambers, Royal Palace, City of Rammon

Princess Rela Minstel sensed her companions' unease. She endured almost a quarter hour of strained chatter and half-hearted banter before she had to know what bothered them.

"What's wrong?" Rela's eyes scanned slowly from left to right, studying Lorian, Marc, and Anabel in turn.

No one said anything, but their faces spoke volumes.

"We're leaving tomorrow," Marc said at last.

"The Festival of Future Fighters begins in a couple of weeks," Anabel explained.

"Captain Titus is running a pre-festival camp out on the Balor Plains for the candidates from the palace," Lorian added, seeing no change in Rela's perplexed expression.

"Why was I not made aware of this?" Rela asked, irritated.

"Tell her," Anabel said, elbowing her brother in the ribs.

"What good would it do anyway?" Marc Spitzer frowned and glared at Anabel.

"She deserves to know," Anabel insisted.

"Tell me what?" Rela's attention flickered between her two friends, but she settled her attention on Marc.

He lowered his eyes and swallowed hard.

"If you won't tell her, I will," said Anabel.

"We discovered that your uncle is locked in the prison below the palace," said Lorian. She placed a calming hand on Anabel's arm.

A few hundred questions vied for Rela's attention. She could voice none of them, but her friends knew most of them and tried to give her answers. At first, they spoke as one and nothing made sense, but finally, they agreed to let Marc be the speaker.

"His name is Todd Wellum," said Marc. "I found his name when I was poking around the prison records. It meant nothing to me until I broke into the vid logs for Lord Kezem's daily fights. I was testing a new program to—"

"Get to the point," Anabel snapped.

"My program filters out background noise, so I can focus on one conversation at a time," Marc explained.

"What did you hear?" Rela asked, folding her hands to remove the temptation of throttling her friend. A thought struck her. "And does Lord Kezem know about your program?"

"I don't know if Lord Kezem knows about it, but if he knows, he hasn't done anything about it," Marc said shrugging. "Anyway, I heard Supreme Commander Kolknir boasting to Ambassador Ilidan that the entertainment would be provided by Ranger Todd Wellum, husband of the late queen's sister. Since you're—"

"She gets it. You can shut up now," Anabel said. She nodded to Rela who was lost in thought.

Marc reached out and gently touched Rela's hand.

Unused to being touched, Rela stiffened, but before Marc could pull his hand back, she clasped it with both her own and squeezed desperately.

"We didn't want to tell you because there's not much we can do," Lorian said, keeping her voice cool. "The Kireshana can take a year or more to finish."

"There's always something to do," Rela murmured, releasing Marc's hand. She didn't know what she would do, but the challenge lit the first flickering flame of rebellion within her. She would free her uncle.

"What are you thinking?" Marc asked.

Rela's mind raced. She needed help, new friends to be her eyes, ears, and voice.

"What do you know of the new kitchen boy?"

"Nicholas Riggs? Nothing special," Lorian said, shrugging. "His parents are Governor Nolan and Senator Katarina Riggs of Ritten."

"He wants to join the Royal Guard, but he's too young," Marc added.

"No, he's not. His mother forbade him from entering the Kireshana," Anabel clarified.

An idea came to Rela, causing her to smile.

"Before you go, I have one last task for you," said the princess.

***

Ferrim (December) 30, 1559
Palace Gardens, City of Rammon

Princess Rela reached out and touched the statue, remembering the last time she had come here with Sarie. She smiled at the memory of hanging upside down from the statue's strong arm. She wondered what had become of Sarie.

Even Lord Kezem wouldn't dare harm her, Rela thought, knowing it was more wish than declaration.

The sound of footsteps interrupted her thoughts.

"You summoned me, Princess," said the servant boy, bowing respectfully. "How may I serve you?" His warm brown eyes and slight frame gave him an air of innocence.

Doubts crowded Rela's mind. The temptation to send him away and forget the whole thing tormented her, but the memory of her uncle's plight gave her courage. Straightening her shoulders, she studied the boy. He shifted uncomfortably, and Rela realized she should say something.

"I have a task for you." She paused. If she had misjudged Nicholas Riggs, the consequences for her uncle would be dire.

You must do this!

"I will do my best to please you, Highness," the boy promised. The reserve in his tone told her next to nothing, but he leaned forward eagerly.

"It will be dangerous," Rela said, staring into Nicholas's eyes. "Can I trust you?"

"What must I do?" Although he controlled his emotions admirably, Nicholas's eyes gleamed with a craving for purpose.

"Deliver this infopad to RLA Captain Tayce, former Royal Guard, assigned to Fort Vik," Rela instructed.

The light in Nicholas's eyes dimmed.

"No one else must know of the correspondence. Your parents are visiting your brother at Fort Vik in a few days, are they not?" Urgency drove Rela's words out with speed.

"They are, Highness," said Nicholas.

"I have encrypted the infopad such that Captain Tayce should be the only one able to access the data, but the RLA possesses resources I do not. You must deliver it into his hands directly without anyone else knowing." Rela considered adding a vague threat about what Lord Kezem would do if Nicholas got caught. Seeing she had the boy's full attention, she rejected the idea. He was idealistic, but the threat of actual danger might harm her cause more than help.

***

Idela (January) 10, 1560
Captain Tayce's Office, Fort Vik

Lieutenant Ethan Tayce survived the surprise duel thanks to Todd Wellum's dead-man pill. He deserted the Royal Guard that night and fled to his sister's house in Meritel. Two weeks later, after three hours convincing both of his sisters he was still sane, Tayce enlisted in the RLA. Hard work brought Tayce up the ranks from derringer to marksman to lieutenant to ventor to paladin and finally, captain of Fort Vik. As captain, he finally had time to think. The more he thought; the more he frowned.

What do I have to show for my life?

His uniform finally fit well around the upper arms and his boyish features had hardened. Unfortunately, he had no time for romance, and he certainly wasn't out to impress his men, or the political prisoners housed at the fort. He frequented taverns for the rumors soldiers spread freely, but his position and an aversion to burning brain cells left him few friends there. His younger sister, Elena, a mother of three, also kept him abreast of the current news.

The years of ignoring injustices weighed heavily on Tayce.

Lord Kezem's a madman and I've spent years serving him!

He didn't know when seditious thoughts first entered his mind, but once they did, he could not shake them. Shortly thereafter, he received his first encrypted letter from Princess Rela.

The depths of her knowledge initially frightened him. If she wanted to get him killed, she had only to breathe a few words to Supreme Commander Kolknir. Her first letter explained what she knew and why she was contacting him. Since then, he had done

his best to fulfill her orders. Most were small deeds, but sometimes, he altered lives for the better in more significant ways. Rescuing slaves, feeding refugees, and conducting prison breaks paid only part of the debt he had built up over the years.

Tayce's thoughts turned to his darkest memory. After completing his Kireshana, he'd been so fired up with patriotic pride that he had immediately transferred to the Rammon palace prison. He had no idea his commanders expected him to beat a woman to death to prove his loyalty. His hands shook as he remembered the political prisoners being marched into the combat arena. All had been terrified women. Their hands were bound in front with chains connected to their waists and ankles. They wore only minimal clothing, but they appeared clean and groomed. Only later did Tayce realize they'd been kept in such pristine condition so that the horrors of the night would be clearer.

The five new recruits had each been given a number corresponding to a prisoner. Supreme Commander Kolknir had relished introducing each woman and her crimes. Tayce didn't remember much about the others, but his prisoner was Merisia Restler. Her crime was aiding enemies of Lord Kezem and escaping lawful custody. The sentence, of course, was death. The longer Tayce could make her execution last, the more bonus pay he would receive.

Phantom screams echoed in Tayce's mind. When he had refused to torture the woman, Kolknir brushed him aside, telling him to learn well. Defiantly, Tayce had killed the woman as soon as possible, but he felt nothing but shame for the whole incident.

A knock startled Tayce back to the present. Grateful, he pushed the memories away, stood, and squared his shoulders as the door swung slowly in.

"Marksman Cory Tiridan reporting, sir," said the soldier.

"Tiridan, good to see you. Please, have a seat," Tayce said, gesturing to the chair.

The marksman hesitated briefly before lowering himself onto the chair.

"What would you say to a transfer to the Royal Guard, marksman?" Tayce inquired, choosing his words carefully. He hoped he had judged the young man correctly. If not, he probably wouldn't be around long enough to fully realize the consequences.

Surprise and resentment flashed across Tiridan's features.

"As you wish, sir," Tiridan said, starting to rise.

Tayce waved for the younger man to remain seated. To avoid appearing imposing, Tayce took his own seat.

"You are a conscript, correct?" he asked.

"I am," Tiridan said. His mouth pursed, as if holding back more words.

"I have watched you for some time, and I think I can trust you," Tayce said, trying to gauge which way Tiridan's anger would blow. "By speaking this way, I place my life in your hands. One word to the wrong person will land me in prison or worse. You see, I owe a great debt to someone, and I'm far behind with payment."

"I'm sorry, sir, but I don't see what that has to do with me," Cory said.

"The man I am indebted to is a prisoner in the Rammon palace. Supreme Commander Kolknir had me fight Ranger Todd Wellum, thinking he would kill me, but the Ranger helped me fake my death. I fled here, so you see my predicament. Honor dictates that I help Ranger Wellum, but I cannot return to the palace."

Tiridan straightened.

"How can I help, sir?"

"I can transfer you to the palace prison's third watch," Tayce explained. "It would be your job to deliver a packet of stimulants, an infopad containing instructions, and food to Ranger Wellum. My sister, Elena, will give you the supplies upon request. Here is her Rammon address," Tayce said, holding out a small scrap of paper.

The marksman stared at the paper then slowly reached for it.

"She will give you some last-minute instructions and two hundred kefs for your troubles," Tayce added.

Tiridan tucked the paper into his pocket.

"Thank you, sir. The money will help my family. They've been having a rough time of it since I got conscripted. My pa's health is failing, and the Kala Mountains show no mercy to the weak."

Standing face-to-face with a young man concerned about his family moved something inside Tayce. He walked to the safe tucked behind the large, ugly painting of Lord Kezem and retrieved the hundred and fifty kefs he'd been saving for a new kerlinblade.

I despise that painting!

His old trusty blade would have to do for another month.

"Take this for your family. It's not much, but I hope it will go to better use than my ale fund. I will write the transfer orders effective tomorrow." As he handed Cory the money, his heart felt lighter.

Cory Tiridan bowed, saluted, and retreated to pack his bags.

"Ridenspeed to you, marksman," Tayce murmured.

Chapter 18:
Anotech Upgrade

Idela (January) 12, 1560
Path to Festival of Future Fighter's Camp, Kesler Plains

Gazing back at the long stretch of road behind them, Kayleen Wellum let a faint grin cross her weary face. She leaned back against a rock, tired but happy to be outside. Having spent much of her life in tunnels and caves, Kayleen had developed a deep appreciation for fresh air, even if it was occasionally tinged with metals or ash.

After traveling thirteen days on borrowed horses and three more on foot, Kayleen eagerly anticipated their pending arrival in Rammon. A hov could have covered the distance in a few hours, but these days, most vehicles were RLA controlled.

Only scattered farmlands on the Kesler Plains, Balor Plains, Resh Grasslands, Riden Flats, Kevloth Plains, and Kevil Plains could boast safe grasslands. Besides these, a few poor villages, the ruins of Osem, and some cities composed the rest of inhabited Reshner. It amused Kayleen to know that maps show the inhabited section of Reshner in grand detail and relegate the rest to a narrow strip, when in fact most of the planet is solid ice.

Kayleen had studied the major cities of Rammon, Korch, Azhel, Ritand, Ritten, Korch, Huz Mon, Kalmata, Meritab, Meritel, Terab, Chara, Estra, and Idonia, but she had never visited any of them. Each city had a governor and at least five senators, but most cities had many more senators, depending on how closely they ingratiated themselves with Lord Kezem.

As they passed more open land, Kayleen enjoyed the peaceful beauty. She knew the peace was an illusion, but she grasped it anyway. She silently thanked Master Kelsa Celdin for teaching her to recognize various wildflowers and other plants vital to the healing arts. Kayleen wondered if she possessed the mental endurance to become a healer master. She dreamed of living out under the stars and walking past seemingly endless fields.

She winced. Thoughts of beautiful fields reminded her of Uncle Terik and Aunt Nala's execution. Their fields and house belonged to Senator Elosh of Meritab now, and her young cousins belonged to the RLA Manufacturing Corps.

I doubt I'll ever see them again. The depressing thought weighed on her and turned her musings to the parents she couldn't remember.

Nils, a good friend and caretaker, had been killed bringing her to the Rangers.

Love is dangerous.

Kayleen steered her thoughts away from that black hole of despair. It would never work anyway. She loved helping people too much to withdraw. She also had an important mission to complete.

The weather the past few days had been unusually pleasant, but that was about to change.

Kayleen watched the sun steadily lose ground in its valiant battle against dark clouds.

"We should hurry," she murmured, regaining her feet. She looked at Teven who merely nodded, not bothering to rise. "We need to get there before the acid rain catches us."

Jal nodded.

Teven rose, picked up his pack, and mechanically walked past his companions wearing a vacant stare.

"Is he okay? What's wrong with him?" asked Kayleen, drawing Jal close.

"He is feeling the collective pain for the first time," Jal explained, studying Kayleen for a long moment. "Remember the special machines I spoke of before? The ones my father invented many years ago? Teven already has access to the anotechs because he is royal. They give him great empathy, but he cannot control them right now."

"Why would he need to control them?" Kayleen asked.

"Anotechs have many uses," Jal said. "Some uses can be learned through experience, and others may be taught. But I had not expected them to keep him quite so in tune with this world."

"What do you mean?" Kayleen asked, alarmed. "Will they hurt him?"

"It's complicated," Jal said.

Kayleen glared.

Jal made a placating gesture.

"They are as much a burden as they are a blessing. And they are in you as well, though not to the extent they are in him."

"What?" Kayleen let her frustration come through the question.

"Do you truly wish to help Teven?" asked Jal.

"Of course," Kayleen answered.

"Then hold this." A small, glowing orange orb materialized in Jal's hand.

Kayleen accepted the orb with her left hand.

"What—ouch!" Kayleen released the ball and shook her hand but small spikes held it tightly against her palm. Instinctively, she used her right hand to try and free her left. Spikes sprang out of the other side, snagging her hand. Against her wishes, both hands closed, driving the spikes further in. She bit back a cry. A wave of something like acid and fire rushed through her, spreading up from her hands and traveling every millimeter of her body. Too busy fighting the anotechs to scream, Kayleen groaned. Slowly, the orb disappeared, as the anotechs flowed into her.

"Do not fight them," Jal said with maddening calm. "Be strong, Kayleen. The pain will pass soon. The anotechs must create the passages through which they will travel in you."

Kayleen's eyes sparkled with a mixture of shock, anger, and pain.

"I will explain further shortly," Jal promised.

Kayleen desperately cast her gaze upon Teven who had stopped ten paces in front of them. His back was to her; his shoulders slumped. Though paralyzed, every fiber of her cried out for help. Contrary to Jal's order, Kayleen fought the invaders. Her face flushed with fever. Though her eyes remained open, her concentration stayed focused on the strange entities traveling through her body.

***

Teven's pack slipped from his shoulders and hit the ground with a thud. He had started the trip feeling excited, but now, he felt strangely drained. His limbs refused to move. A hot pain shot through him and disappeared in an instant. Then, he heard Kayleen's cry echo within his mind. Anger welled up and rushed out of him like a breath held too long, snapping him from the lethargic state. He whirled, drawing his banistick.

"Wait," Jal commanded. "She will control them."

"This isn't right," Teven said through clenched teeth. His heart beat so fast it pressed painfully against his ribs. "She didn't choose this, and neither did I. I—"

"You are stuck," Jal said, with a sad, knowing expression. "And now, so is she. The anotechs have chosen her, as they chose you. They will help you save this planet, but they only help the worthy. You have broken their hold over you, gaining their respect. They will serve you forever."

"I don't want them! I want to be left alone!" Tears of self-pity slipped down his face. "I can't do this!"

"You must, Teven. The people need a strong prince," Kayleen stated. "Lord Kezem's reign has been far too long as it is."

Teven whipped his head left to look at her. Kayleen stood serenely, as if nothing had happened.

Seeing her unharmed, Teven willed himself into a calmer state. He returned the banistick to his belt, rushed to Kayleen, and picked up her left hand.

"Do you trust them?" asked Teven.

"I'm fine. See, they're already repairing the damage," Kayleen answered. She held out her right hand palm up and wiggled her fingers as proof.

He turned her left hand over and watched the wounds close. Then, he gazed into her eyes.

"You didn't answer my question."

"Yes, I trust them," said Kayleen with a wry smile. "We've come to an understanding about who gets to run my life."

Kayleen's smile melted the icy anxiety around his heart, so Teven reluctantly released her hand.

"Now I know where you get your I-am-invincible-and-have-a-death-wish attitude," said Kayleen. "I have half a mind to bust down the palace doors and have it out with that usurper right now."

"Kezem is a petty tyrant, but even petty tyrants have the nasty habit of drawing unsavory people to their sides. We must be cautious," Jal said.

Chapter 19:
Festival of Future Fighters

Idela (January) 13, 1560-Idela (January) 16, 1560
Linderberg Inn, West Quarter, City of Rammon

Teven's churning thoughts kept him awake that night. He felt strangely free. Since his mother's death, a cloud of despair had clung to him like a suffocating blanket, even during the happy times with Kayleen and Jalna. Everything changed in the brief, agonizing moment of feeling Kayleen's pain through the anotechs.

Eventually, he slipped into an uneasy sleep. Sometime during the night, a beautiful woman filled his mind. Other thoughts fled. She wore flowing, deep purple robes which had generous green swatches around the sleeves and sides. He knew her.

"If you hear these words, my son, then I am gone." The woman smiled faintly, tipped her head forward, and slowly shut her striking green eyes. *"I can picture you looking just like your father. You are sixteen today, a man by custom and tradition, but I remember the first moment your father held you. Terosh was so proud to have a son."* Her smile faltered, and her eyes opened, glistening with unshed tears. *"You are my eldest child, Teven, and as such, it falls to you to save this people from Lord Kezem. Listen to Pria and Nathan, but never forget you are the Crown Prince of House Minstel. Your sister, Rela, will stay in the Rammon palace. I fear for her. The Ralose Charm will preserve her life but do little to protect her mind. Your brother, Tavel, should be with the Rangers in Osem. Seek him out. He will help you reclaim the throne."*

Then, just as suddenly as she had appeared, his mother vanished.

Despite the disturbed sleep, Teven rose ready to begin his trials. He dressed in dark brown pants, a beige shirt, and the red belt of a Kireshana hopeful. Anyone with the twenty-kef entry fee was a hopeful, but most candidates wore a red belt to signify their status anyway. Anyone who made it to the Kireshana earned the right to be considered a derringer, the lowest rank of Royal Guard or Melian Maiden, even though technically you had to pass the trial to join either order. The rank only existed for the Kireshana though since survivors gained a rank upon completion.

The vision of his mother returned, making Teven pensive.

How will I reclaim the throne? Do I even want to?

He considered discussing the dream with Kayleen or Jal. Both would certainly have something to say, but Teven wasn't ready to invite advice. With effort, he pushed the thoughts aside and descended the stairs to the common area where he found Kayleen and Jal waiting.

The innkeeper served a morning meal of wheat cakes and lila juice. The food barely touched their tongues for the haste with which they ate. Thirty kefs passed into the innkeeper's hands to settle their account. Then, they were off to the Balor Plains where the Festival of Future Fighters would give the high commanders a good idea of who would make it in the Royal Guard and Melian Maidens.

Teven divided his attention between navigating the crowded Rammon streets and thinking of what lay ahead. He thought he could win three of his first five duels and become a first-class derringer. There would be twenty each of first, second, third, and forth class derringers. The Royal Guard and Melian Maiden hopefuls competed within their orders, but overall rank was scored against every candidate. Those not earning a rank could still compete in the Kireshana, but they had to wait two days to start. That was a change from the past.

Rising to marksman status required surviving the Kireshana. The journey started in the Balor Plains, ran through the perilous Calsol Forest, into the Huz Mon salt mines, and over most of the Riden Mountains before dumping candidates at the coastal city of Resh. From Resh, roughly the halfway point, one would turn south to Fort Riden for return supplies.

Before Teven knew it, the tournament grounds stretched before him. Excited shouts of hopefuls mingled with merchant cries and drunken laughter, forming a festive atmosphere. The scent of cooking meat, strong perfumes, and the sweat of thousands of beings assaulted Teven's senses. The merchants remained confined to a few neat rows on the southeastern corner. Ten dueling squares dominated the northern half, and tents for the combatants decorated the southwestern corner. The city of Rammon provided the southeastern border while other borders were marked with fences.

"Snap out of it," Kayleen said. "You're going to have your head bashed in if you daydream during a duel."

"I'll be fine," said Teven. "You worry about beating your opponent without breaking something on her."

"But I am such a gentle spirit," Kayleen protested. She flashed him an innocent grin.

"We should split up for now," Jal said, before slipping off into the crowd.

Teven exchanged a weary glance with Kayleen, nodded, and walked toward the registration tables.

"Quit now while you're still alive," said the corpulent man behind a rickety wooden table. He rumbled with laughter.

Teven ignored him and placed the entry fee on the table.

"Don't mind Rither here, lad, he's just sore his boy couldn't cut it in last year's duels," said the man next to the one who had spoken.

"It's your blood to be lost, boy. Have at it," Rither commented taking the money and putting it in the collection bin. "Now, I just need your name."

Teven gave the man his name, watched him punch it into an infopad, and wandered through the merchant stalls pretending to study the wares. He let his ears investigate the competition.

"Lorian Petole will win in the Melian Maiden contests hands down. I've never seen anyone move that fast," a woman insisted. "She may even win overall!"

"Aww swiftness won't save her out there," replied the woman's companion. "Darien Torrington will do fine though. That boy could take on a Driden lion with his bare hands."

The woman scoffed.

"Slow as a night creeper, he is. Some unknown's bound to beat him."

Teven scooted to the next stall.

"I heard they're changing the rules this year," a young man commented to a merchant man selling healing packs and herbs. The boy's voice was high with excitement. "The top female and male duelists receive a weapon of their choice from any merchant, a hundred kefs, and a two-day head start on the Kireshana! Two days, and that's on top of the two days the no-ranks have to wait!"

"Only if they survive," said the merchant, waving a healing pack in the youth's face.

"The prize money for the other first-class derringers ain't bad neither," piped up a boy, obviously related to the other young man. "They'll get something between twenty-five and ninety kefs. That could buy a whole lot of kertcha jelly or blaze bug taffy." The child sounded wistful.

"They ain't gonna spend it on no bug taffy," the brother scoffed. "They need to buy weapons to kill the wild korvers and other creatures they're gonna face."

"More important, they also get an extra one-day head start on the rest of the hopefuls," the merchant added. "A day behind the top two, but three days in front of the pack. My money's on those first-class derringers to win it."

Teven had heard enough. He and his companions would have to be in the top twenty to gain good position. He wanted to refrain from getting too much attention though, so winning the tournament was out of the question, even if he thought he could do it. The head start would help, but really, all that mattered was surviving the Kireshana with enough points to earn the rank of marksman. Only the high commanders, supreme commander, and respective councils for the Royal Guards and Melian Maidens knew exactly how points would be granted, but Teven had a basic idea of how the system worked.

A series of trumpet blasts announced the opening of the Festival of Future Fighters. After a small parade and a few long speeches, High Commander Torent directed the candidates to check the screens scattered about to see when they were scheduled to fight.

Teven's name appeared next to challenger, Treve Baringer, challenged, square two, and duel six. It took him ten minutes to locate the correct box. Excitement filled him as he watched two young men engage in hand-to-hand combat. As challenger, Teven could choose a weapon to fight with or declare the match a weaponless one. Despite the added risk of injury by using banisticks, Teven decided it would be best to fight with the weapons. There would be very few hand-to-hand duels during the Kireshana itself. He reported his decision to the announcer's assistant and turned back to the current duel.

One young man finally triumphed. The combatants bowed, the victor was announced, and two young women took their places.

"Lorian Petole, challenger, will face Anabel Spitzer, challenged, in weaponless combat. Hopefuls step forward," said the announcer who doubled as match moderator.

One girl had light brown skin that reminded Teven of a plains rabbit. The other girl's complexion ranged closer to creamed tretling milk. From the looks the combatants exchanged, he figured they knew each other. The duel that followed seemed to be a vicious battle, but Teven saw the fleeting smiles the girls exchanged.

They must be friends.

Each girl anticipated the other's moves, and for a time, it seemed neither would win. Finally, Lorian landed hard on her right side. Anabel moved close to deliver one final blow, but Lorian whipped her legs around and back so fast they blurred before sweeping Anabel's feet. Teven didn't even see Lorian get up, but suddenly, she had Anabel pinned to the ground.

The next three duels were sorely mismatched and ended within the first minute. Then, it was Teven's turn.

"The challenger, Teven McKnight has opted to face the challenged, Treve Baringer, with a banistick," said the announcer. "Stand back, people, this could get violent."

An excited murmur rippled through the small crowd around box two.

Teven felt like he'd spent every day of the last five years preparing to step into this dueling square. Kayleen, Captain Laocer, Jalna, and many Rangers had personally invested hours in him. Nothing would stop him from earning a place in the Royal Guard and coming one step closer to Lord Kezem. Not much thought had been given to what he would do once he made it into the palace, but that didn't matter now.

Only this duel matters.

Teven bowed, saluted, and opened the banistick. He did nothing, daring his opponent to attack. Through force of will, Teven waited a hair longer than he should have to block Treve's strike. The blunder gave Treve a false sense of security, which fueled the fires of overconfidence. Mindful of his footwork, Teven led his opponent around the dueling square. The area provided for the duel was more than adequate for hand-to-hand matches, but the introduction of banisticks quickly cut down the space. Teven conserved his energy by letting Treve hack away. Then, when he sensed his opponent tiring, Teven maneuvered the other boy into the corner and out of bounds.

"Penalty! The challenged has violated the arena bounds. The challenger is declared victor!" shouted the match moderator.

Teven stepped back and grinned at his stunned opponent. Treve glared murderously at him. As Teven tipped his head forward to bow, Treve's banistick snapped up. Only well-tuned reflexes saved Teven's chin from the devastating blow. Still, the banistick's rough tip grazed Teven's right cheek, drawing blood. The two young men locked gazes. Teven shook his head, sighed, and left the dueling square. He felt the anotechs begin knitting the torn flesh back together but stopped them. It would not be wise to let anyone know the anotechs could heal wounds.

The competition passed quickly. Teven fought four more duels over the course of several days, two with banisticks and two hand-to-hand. He won them but made certain that the fifth win was on a technicality like the first, resulting in him getting sixth place overall and third place for Royal Guard hopefuls.

Kayleen scored high enough to earn third place overall and second place for the Melian Maiden hopefuls. Kayleen and Lorian Petole initially tied, so the officials arranged one more duel between the two young women. After four rounds, Lorian prevailed, earning first place both overall and for the Melian Maiden candidates.

The closing ceremonies consisted of more speeches and a recitation of the codes of honor, first the Melian Maidens and then the Royal Guards. Teven, Kayleen, and Jal stood on stage, interspersed among the other top candidates. The prize money was determined by place, and in addition, all twenty winners received a ceremonial dagger that marked them as first-class derringers. After the ceremony, the commoners left and derringers of every class gathered for debriefing.

High Commander Leena Linel's voice boomed through the crowded tent. Teven noted that her mouth barely moved when she spoke. She spoke very fast, but he had no problem following her.

"Welcome ladies of the Melian Maidens and gentlemen of the Royal Guard. You have surmounted the first phase of integration into these fine orders. Soon, each of you will begin the Kireshana, a true test of character and strength. If you pass the seven trials laid out for you on the journey, you will earn the ranks given to you today. If you fail any test, you will be stripped of the rank. You can then try again next year or accept a post in Reshner's Liberation Army. Supreme Commander Kolknir could not come today so High Commander Torent will explain further." She stepped back and surrendered her spot in front of the voice amplifiers.

A powerfully built, swarthy man strode to center stage.

"Hand in 1000 kefs at the Kireshana's end and quote the honor codes to fulfill your duties. Obtain the kefs any way you wish."

Teven worked hard not to shake his head in disgust.

"Get a purple scale from a queen zalok to prove you have courage.

Show your strength and endurance by scaling Mount Palean in a day. Guides waiting at the foot of the mountain will monitor your progress. Outwit, outmaneuver, and otherwise thwart those who come behind you, but do not kill them. And be patient when you reach the Lotrian Fields. If you rush through them you will die." With that, High Commander Torent stepped away from the voice amplifiers, and High Commander Linel took his place.

"Remember, loners travel faster but also die sooner. Expect to take anywhere from six months to a year to finish the Kireshana. In fact, a few derringers from two years ago reported in last week. This is rare but not unheard of. And one more thing … be mindful of the fact that other elements of our orders train during this time. Good luck. You are dismissed."

Teven felt the commander's sharp gray eyes upon him. The noise level in the room rose, but Teven pondered High Commander Linel's last warning.

Kayleen will know what she meant.

He went in search of his friend.

"Teven! Over here!" came Kayleen's voice through the babble of the crowd.

He waded against the press of people.

"Let's get out of here!" she shouted into his ear.

Once outside, Teven drew a sweet breath of cool evening air. A mild wind whispered of coming rain, but for now, the night was peaceful. He walked silently beside Kayleen for several minutes, enjoying the sense of calm streaming off her.

"What do you think High Commander Linel meant about other elements training?" asked Teven.

"There are rumors that Coridian Assassins hunt derringers," replied Kayleen. "I don't know if it's true, but I wouldn't put it past them. We can debate that point later."

Teven accepted this. He didn't know much about Coridian Assassins, but he could bet Jal would have quite a bit to say about them. Pushing the issue from mind, he wandered the tournament grounds with Kayleen conversing about everything and nothing. Neither wished to end the night.

Chapter 20:
Head Start

Idela (January) 17, 1560
Kireshana Starting Point, Balor Plains

Next morning, dark storm clouds hung over the Calsol forest, northeast of the Balor Plains and right along the path of the Kireshana. Nevertheless, the mood remained festive. The crowd cheered the top two duelists who had earned the right to start today. The rest of the derringers took a short break from their final preparations to watch Lorian Petole and Bari Aleron step up to the starting line.

"So long, suckers," Bari Aleron muttered, idly slapping dust from his dark blue travel cloak.

"Good luck," Lorian Petole offered with a thin smile.

"Don't need it, but thanks," Bari replied, looking at Lorian for the first time and scrapping his plan to sprint ahead. He imagined her light brown skin touching his own, warm and inviting.

Her dark brown eyes held a depth and sincerity not found in many. The bulky rain gear could not hide her feminine figure, a fact he fully appreciated.

Her smile broadened slightly.

"See you at the finish," said Lorian.

At that moment, High Commander Linel's sidearm spit a green flash of energy across the starting line into the padded target put there for that purpose, signaling the start of the race.

Lorian shot forward, kicking up some dirt which landed on Bari's immaculate black boots.

"Hey!" Bari protested, smiling despite himself. He hitched up his heavy pack and trotted after her, thinking he liked the view fine from here.

She won't be able to keep that pace long, Bari thought.

Nevertheless, Lorian's figure kept getting smaller and smaller in the distance. When she disappeared into the Calsol forest and Bari was still a kilometer behind, he realized his error. Tightening his pack straps, Bari sprinted full tilt toward the forest.

***

Back at the starting line, Teven and Kayleen walked slowly to Kayleen's tent to check on their supplies.

"That girl sure can run," Teven commented.

"Yup," Kayleen agreed. "One of the girls I fought yesterday, Vania something or other, said Lorian came from the palace where she does nothing but run and train."

"Sounds like someone I know," Teven said, turning and staring down at her. He straightened his shoulders which had broadened nicely. He liked the way the stiff wind played with Kayleen's hair.

The cool humidity caused her reddish-gold hair to curl more than usual.

"Look who's talking," Kayleen said, meeting his critical gaze.

"Did I imply something?" Teven asked innocently.

"It is way too early to jump on my nerves, boy," Kayleen said. She had more to say but a mouthful of hair delayed her long enough for Teven to speak.

"Must you say it like that?" he asked, wincing. "What's wrong with my name?"

"Say what?" Kayleen asked. "Would you prefer something more endearing, like Tevvie?"

"Point taken."

"I kind of like 'Tevvie,'" Kayleen continued with an evil grin.

"I shall say no more. Round one goes to the fair lady," Teven said, reaching past her and flinging the tent flap aside with a flourish. Bowing from the waist, Teven waved Kayleen in.

It took them all morning to gather various supplies. In addition to weapons, they would need camping, climbing, swimming, and emergency gear. Flashfloods, korver clans, windstorms, and graveground were just four of the life-threatening challenges they could face. Despite the danger, Teven sort of wanted to see a wallay.

The tiny creatures responsible for graveground had the nasty habit of digging their tunnels dangerously near the surface. When they moved to a different area, nothing was there to put fresh cradul onto the tunnel walls. Eventually, the walls grew brittle and collapsed. The depressions—depending on size—could do anything from twist an ankle to swallow a herd of tretlings.

Jal stopped by early afternoon and invited them to share the midday meal. Their conversation was guarded, but Teven gathered that Jal had some interesting information to share. After the simple meal of peri juice and tretling meat in wheat wraps with lettuce and tomatoes, the trio continued with Kireshana preparations.

Throughout the morning, the storm clouds had thickened. The wind picked up, buffeting the tents.

After lunch, Teven and his companions rushed back to Kayleen's tent. A steady rain fell. The howling wind and the rain's enthusiastic cadence eased their fear of being overheard.

"I had forgotten how crude young men could be," Jal commented, referring to the rowdy group in the mess tent.

Teven shrugged.

"Manners aside, did you learn anything?" he asked.

"A little about our competition." Though still speaking as the youth, Jal's tone slipped into teacher mode. "Bari Aleron hails from Idonia. His parents are Senator David and Lady Anna Aleron. He's strong, hardy, and knows how to handle a banistick and a kerlinblade. Lorian Petole is an orphan raised as a servant in the Rammon palace. I imagine she knows how to use any weapon."

"She's got a nasty right uppercut, too," Kayleen added, gently touching her chin.

"Oh, and Lord Kezem has standing bounties on information leading to anyone connected to House Minstel," Jal added.

"It's been more than a decade since he took over," Kayleen commented. "The man sure knows how to hold a grudge."

"In any case, it will make our trip more interesting," said Jal.

Teven didn't say anything because the vision of his mother sprang to mind. He thought so hard he became lightheaded. As he began falling, Kayleen caught his left arm and steadied him.

"Are you all right, Tev? Teven, answer me," Kayleen said, squeezing his left arm.

"No, wait. The anotechs are working," Jal said.

Teven heard the conversation faintly, as though it took place across a great distance. He felt himself being lowered to the ground.

Once he was down, his mother appeared again.

Do not fear, my son. This strangeness will pass. Let the anotechs work, but also, learn to divide your attention between them and the world around you. She vanished.

Teven found himself staring up at Jal and Kayleen who were kneeling over him.

"You'll be fine in a few seconds," Jal promised.

"I saw her," Teven whispered. "Twice now."

"Saw who?" Kayleen asked.

"My mother. The first time was in a dream I had a few nights ago."

"Why didn't you share this dream with us?" asked Jal. "I might have been able to explain sooner and prevented this. You're lucky it didn't happen in public. That would take some explaining."

"You *do* have some explaining to do, a lot of it. What are the anotechs? Besides tiny machines. What do they do? Why do I keep seeing my dead mother?" Teven's voice rose until he practically shouted the last three words.

"The anotechs are guides and guardians," Jal explained. "My father invented them before losing his mind to some of the nastier personality twists of rogue anotechs. They call themselves Dalonos, which means Dark Ones in Kalastan. Although I hunt these dark anotechs, most are neither good nor evil, only what you make of them. Someone like Lord Kezem is not to be trusted with anotechs."

"Will the visions continue?" Teven wondered.

"Will I have dreams, too?" Kayleen inquired at the same time.

Jal thought a moment.

"Teven, I think the dream is a start to more detailed messages your mother gave you before she died. If so, I can teach you techniques to streamline them. They are probably triggered by certain phrases or events. And no, Kayleen. You need not worry. I doubt you will have dreams of this nature. Most of your anotechs came from me, and I certainly didn't plant any messages in them."

"That's a relief. Well, I think you two have some anotech controlling to discuss, so I'll finish packing our supplies," Kayleen said, climbing to her feet. "I also wanted to do a little browsing at the merchant stalls."

With a short break for an evening meal, the lessons continued long into the night. From time to time, Kayleen would join them. Teven listened with rapt attention as Jal described the various advantages that came with anotechs.

Jal cautioned Teven against becoming too dependent upon the machines. If used properly, they could provide protection from acid rain, various insects, and even some diseases. Most of the benefits were limited to the anotech's current master, but a few of the generalized healing benefits could be bestowed upon others.

"Why didn't they protect me from the acid rain before?" Teven asked, having stuck his hand outside the tent at Jal's bidding. The water flowed off his hand easily without leaving red, irritated marks.

"They probably did protect you from most of the poison, but they rely on you for direction as much as you depend upon their aid. Like small children, they only perform complicated tasks when instructed how to do so. Tell me, have you been sick much?"

"No," Teven admitted. "Never really."

"I thought not. They must have general instructions to guard your life. Once you learn to wield them yourself, you will be able to stand against anything the Kireshana can throw at you. Now, I think it is time we retire. It is nearly morning, and we will need the rest."

"Goodnight then," Teven said. He hauled his weary, stiff self off Kayleen's bedroll and staggered from the tent.

That night, he had no trouble sleeping.

Chapter 21:
Danger in the Calsol Forest

Idela (January) 17, 1560
Calsol Forest

Tryse steadied his breath with two different calming techniques. Almost ten when Lord Kezem came to power, Tryse had been raised in the RLA youth camp based in Korch. When his aptitude for hand-to-hand combat caught his commander's attention, he found himself transferred to the Royal Guard camp at Azhel.

Now, more than twelve years later, Tryse frowned into the semi-darkness created by the thick canopy of cal and dansque trees. His thoughts tried to wander, but he forced them back to the mission, mentally reviewing the list of twenty targets that would start the Kireshana ahead of the others. His assignment was simple: kill three derringers.

Tryse cocked his head to the side, wondering how he felt about the mission.

It is a great honor to get the Kireshana trial.

So far, he had performed admirably. Despite starting a half-hour behind the first two derringers, he had surpassed them. Anxious to test them, he decided to swoop down upon them like a bird of prey and attack with his kamad dagger. As a trainee, his blade was not poisoned, so his blows would have to have force behind them.

The sound of heavy footfalls echoed in the quiet forest. He concentrated and picked out two different pairs of feet approaching him with all the subtlety of the Azhel Grand Percussion Band. Tryse shook his head with disgust.

You'll have to do better than that if you want to survive.

Pity touched him. Perhaps their steps faltered from weariness.

Fatigue is no excuse for faulty technique! The remembered admonishment came fully charged with Kelp's voice. Tryse almost flinched, expecting to feel the sting of a whip.

The derringers were suddenly below him. Tryse waited for them to pass and dropped to the ground with a muffled thump. He covered the two steps to the female derringer and thrust the dagger at the back of her neck.

At the last second, she threw herself forward and spun to face him. "Bari!" the girl cried.

In that instant, Tryse saw her raw fear, and it shook him. Having missed his first target, Tryse switched direction and propelled his kamad dagger toward the second derringer. The boy twisted aside and caught Tryse's weapon hand. Grunting, Tryse dropped the weapon to his other hand and threw it at the female derringer. By this time, she had a banistick in hand and used it to swat the dagger away. His dagger lodged in a cal tree with a loud thump.

Suitably convinced these two were worthy enough to continue, Tryse shoved the young man into the girl, straightened, and bowed. They watched him warily. Instead of renewing his attack, Tryse retrieved his dagger and used a low branch to haul himself higher. Within seconds, the bewildered derringers were far behind, and Tryse began planning his next attack.

Knowing the others would not be along for a day or so, Tryse settled down in a tree to sleep. The battle rush faded, and his emotional state calmed. He pictured the recent fight and noted several places where a different move could have altered the battle.

I won't make those mistakes again.

As often happened during quiet moments, Tryse wondered what killing someone would feel like. His friends from the first camp had probably already shed blood, but Coridian Assassins trained significantly longer than others. The Kireshana trial was the last test. Those who passed gained power and honor, and those who failed never bothered returning.

My dagger was a centimeter from a living being!

The thought thrilled and frightened him. Part of him knew he should not be so pleased to kill. Eventually, he forced his mind to his old life in Korch with his parents and two brothers. It gave him enough peace to fall asleep.

***

Idela (January) 18, 1560
Kireshana Starting Point, Balor Plains

The next morning, as they stood amid controlled chaos, Kayleen practiced using anotechs to glean information from her surroundings. At first, the information overflow left her disoriented, but slowly, her mind accepted the influx of information. She stiffened when a hand touched her shoulder and relaxed again upon realizing the hand belonged to Teven.

"It's about to begin," Teven warned in a whisper.

Kayleen shut off the sensory anotechs.

"That is definitely going to take some getting used to," she murmured.

Teven answered with an understanding nod.

"Where's Jal?" asked Kayleen.

"Back there somewhere," Teven said, waving a hand toward the back of the small group.

Soon, eighteen first-class derringers, including Kayleen, Teven, and

Jal, would begin the Kireshana. They would not see Rammon for months. Some would never see it again. Everyone would be changed by the trials ahead.

A wave of sadness touched Kayleen as she studied the faces around her. Most were around her age of sixteen, almost seventeen, but a few appeared as young as nine or ten. Their faces radiated excitement, but she could easily picture those same faces twisted in pain or still in death. A powerful desire to protect them came to her.

Kayleen categorized them by needs. Each had proven he or she could handle single opponents and direct attacks, but the enemies on the Kireshana would include fatigue, hunger, and cold. Growing up in a Ranger camp in the Riden Mountains gave Kayleen a slight advantage, but she knew this journey would greatly tax her reserves.

There are no rules out there.

The living enemies would not strike one by one. Before the end, teeth, guns, banisticks, daggers, and kerlinblades would draw more than their share of blood from the young derringers.

High Commander Linel fired her pistol. Again, a flash of green zipped past the derringers, tracing the starting line before slamming into the padded target. Under less pressure to start the race strongly, most derringers began with a steady trot. Kayleen set off at a gentle pace, enjoying the coolness of the morning. Her thoughts turned to Teven who jogged beside her. A few kilometers down the path, well out of sight of the cheering crowds, everyone slowed to a brisk hike. Steps waxed increasingly cautious as they approached the Calsol Forest.

If everything went well, it would take a few weeks to traverse the Calsol Forest. They could walk or rent horses in Calsola for three hundred kefs each. For those, like them, who could not afford a horse, the benevolent masters of the Huz Mon salt mines had a credit system set up with the Calsola stables. On horse, it would take a week to cross the Riden Flats. Kayleen fully intended on renting horses so she counted a few extra days to pay off the debt. Three more weeks would see them through the northern Riden Mountains. A month or two after that they should be past Fort Riden and to the foot of Mount Palean. These were rough estimates based upon educated guesses on how fast their group could travel.

"Planning ahead?" Teven asked. They had dropped behind the main derringer pack, so it was safe to talk.

"This is going to be one long trip," Kayleen said.

"Just think, in another year we'll be inside the palace ready to bring justice to Lord Kezem," said Teven.

"How will we bring justice to him?" Kayleen asked, genuinely curious.

"Kill him, I suppose," Teven answered. His tone betrayed doubts.

"What do we really know about him? Does he deserve death?" It surprised Kayleen that this conversation hadn't come up earlier. They had never questioned Captain Laocer's orders. "Besides usurping the throne …

and killing your mother … and condoning the murder of my aunt and uncle … and stealing their farm and shipping my cousins to manufacturing plants and starving half the people. Okay, I'm convinced; he's got to go."

"Life in the mountains has left us a little naïve," Teven admitted. "The people at the Festival of Future Fighters seemed happy enough, but … there was fear there, too."

"The thought of starving will do that to you," Kayleen said dryly.

"Maybe it's Lord Kezem's fault, maybe not," said Teven. "He can't control everything, right? He's only one man, but he is the man in control. This is confusing! I just don't want to create more problems if Reshner's in good hands."

"You wouldn't want your throne back?" Kayleen asked, shocked. "I haven't known many royals, but I know enough to know that that's definitely odd."

Teven smiled and adjusted his pack.

"Thanks." He shook his head, struggling to explain. "I've never tasted the power attached to the throne, so I don't miss it, but from what little I know of my parents, they would have risked everything to right Reshner. There are enough problems to warrant righting. I can do no less."

Kayleen turned her head to hide a smile. She kind of liked this philosophical Teven who argued himself in circles.

***

Idela (January) 18, 1560
Calsol Forest

Midmorning the next day, Tryse resumed his stakeout refreshed and ready for anything. He heard the next group of derringers crash through the forest three minutes before he saw them. Tension wound his muscles tight. Adrenaline pulsed through him, giving him the euphoric rush that could only be experienced before and during combat.

Like the day before, Tryse fell upon his unsuspecting victims like a windstorm. They screamed and scrambled for weapons, but it was too late. Tryse's kamad dagger found a target. He felt the blade sink into a boy's chest and watched blood bubble from the wound.

Cerulean eyes widened, then deadened.

The picture burned into Tryse's mind. Had his body not been aware that death awaited him if he stayed, Tryse would have stared at the body for ages.

He couldn't remember the fight after that. He came back to himself shivering in a cal tree. A dark stain on his left sleeve reminded him of the spilled blood. A shudder coursed through him.

This isn't right! It's not supposed to feel like this!

Before he knew it, Tryse sobbed, not caring if anyone or anything heard.

The bloodstain mocked him. With a frustrated cry Tryse attacked his sleeve with his clean dagger. Even distraught, he had remembered to clean his weapon after the battle. The offending portion tore free and fluttered to the ground. Gripped by a strong sense of futility, he stared hard at his dagger and pondered slicing his wrists.

I can end this pain.

A strange, slippery memory stopped him. When he was a boy, his father, a representative for Korch farmers and merchants, had taken him to Rammon to request royal aid for recent crop failures. Tryse had not been allowed into the meeting, but later, his father had presented him to King Terosh and Queen Reia. Their faces returned to him clearly. He relaxed into the memory. Both had been elegantly attired in green and purple ceremonial robes.

Tryse couldn't recall much of the conversation, but he remembered the queen's words.

"Your father speaks very highly of you, Tryse. I hope you will one day exceed his expectations."

Tryse gritted his teeth.

Father would be ashamed of a murderer. I will never serve Lord Kezem again.

"I'll start again," Tryse vowed. Then, reality crashed on his head. He could not give the boy his life back, but he would not return to his masters. That left him halfway to nowhere.

I can't go back.

Tryse spent the rest of the day and much of the night planning his next move. He worried about the other two Coridian Assassin candidates. Plian, an ill-tempered coward, favored poisoned flingers stolen from the armory. He would probably sit in a tree and rain death from above. Stealing the flingers would stop Plian. Gia preferred to become friends with her targets, but she wouldn't have that luxury on the Kireshana. Most likely, she would strike at night while the derringers camped. Tryse could claim a camp for himself, but that would only force her to change targets. Maybe he could talk to her. A chill settled on him. Gia's reputation for manipulation was well founded. If Tryse didn't watch it, her dagger would one day be lodged in his chest.

***

When they reached the edge of the Calsol Forest, Kayleen set up the tents, Jal prepared a meal, and Teven gathered some fire fixings. Afterward, Teven sat on his bedroll and fiddled with the used kerlinblade he had bought with his winnings. The handle was old and worn, but the blade worked well.

"Have you practiced with it yet?" Kayleen inquired.

"Nope. You up for a sparing match?" asked Teven.

"Sure."

It took them two minutes to reach the Balor Plains again. Even after the long day of walking, new energy coursed through Teven as he squared off against Kayleen. They set the blades to the lowest shock setting to avoid killing each other. Kayleen saluted. Teven returned the gesture, stepped forward, and threw himself into the duel. When their blades crashed together, his blade turned from yellow to green, and her blade changed from red to orange.

"That's odd," he muttered.

"I think it's meant for a colored crossblades game," Kayleen said, swinging at his head.

"It's distracting," Teven grunted, catching her blade. They fought for several minutes with the colors changing until Teven called a halt. "Bothersome color changes," he muttered, inspecting the handle. After a few seconds, he finally noticed a series of tiny black panels lining the bottom and sides of his kerlinblade handle. He fiddled with the panels, having Kayleen test the changes by knocking her blade into his.

Within five minutes, they figured out how to keep the blade a steady color. Teven chose a blue blade, and Kayleen chose a purple one. Then, their duel resumed.

Kayleen faked an overhead strike. The violet blade descended but stopped short of Teven's raised guard. A turn of her wrist slipped the blade under the guard to the point of his chin.

"I win," she said.

"Draw," he challenged, raising his blade slightly so she could see it in her peripheral vision.

She sighed.

"Draw it is. Time to eat?"

"Always," said Teven.

They held the blades at each other's throat for a second longer, neither wanting to back down first. By mutual agreement, they lowered and deactivated their weapons at the same time. An awkward silence and stillness settled between them, as they stood at arm's length regarding each other. Teven wasn't certain where their relationship stood. He cared for her deeply but feared revealing his feelings might destroy the five-year friendship. If it was true friendship, it could withstand the blow, but he hated to take the risk. He caught her eye.

"Good match," she said, boldly stepping forward.

Something fired in his brain, telling him to make a move. Wildly clutching his fleeing courage, Teven attached his kerlinblade to his belt and wrapped his arms around her. The warm embrace felt right. Had she hesitated, he would have backed off, but he felt the strength of her affection compressing his ribs. He was about to follow the embrace with a kiss when a keen sense of danger took control of his body. Pushing away from Kayleen, Teven stumbled back and twisted, narrowly missing a silver flinger.

The sharp little weapon would not have done much damage had it struck him, unless it was poisoned, but Teven didn't want to take a chance. Kayleen's kerlinblade flared to life. Teven followed suit. A zinging sound alerted him to more flingers. He crouched, holding the blade across his body to provide the most protection. A flinger sailed past his left ear. Another flew at the center of his chest. He raised his blade and made a slight adjustment so that it was wider and flatter than normal. Suddenly, there were two blades for Kayleen had crossed hers with his. The flinger hit dead center of their blades and dropped harmlessly at their feet.

They braced for more, but none came. The usual music of early evening resumed as if nothing had happened. They stood ready for a tense minute longer.

Finally, Teven took a cloth from his pocket and wrapped the weapon inside.

"We should get back to Jal," he said.

Returning to the campsite, Teven and Kayleen reported the incident to Jal.

"Judging by the traces of gully fish poison on the tips, it's probably from a Coridian Assassin," Jal commented, examining the weapon's sharp points. "They're earlier than I had anticipated."

"What will we do?" Teven asked.

"Stay alive," Jal replied.

Teven couldn't argue with the logic, but he had been hoping for more detail to the plan.

"We should take turns watching the camp," Kayleen suggested.

"We should pick up more traveling companions," Jal offered.

Teven nodded to both suggestions.

"I'll take first watch tonight. I'll wake Kayleen in three hours, and she can wake you in six."

During his watch, Teven practiced accessing his mother's messages and letting the anotechs do most of the watch work. He had finally been able to shut the dreams out, but then, he had not been able to find them. After following several convoluted mental trails, Teven imagined a plain, bare room with only a table and a chair. In the chair sat his mother, wearing a purple shimmersilk gown and her usual smile.

"It might surprise you to see me as I was the day I died. I hope you will continue to listen to me long after you are older than I." Her smile dimmed. *"As I ponder my impending death, I find myself at a loss to share wisdom with you. Terosh always was the better thinker. I wish you could have known him better. Never be afraid to love, Teven. To lose is a part of life, but to love is to gain the universe. Despite the pain, you will be a better man for the experience."*

The woman and the room faded.

Teven's watch passed, but he continued to think. He became aware of eyes watching him but received no anotech warnings. Eventually, he woke up Kayleen. The anotechs could keep watch while they slept, but for the sake of appearances, they would have to get used to watches.

Chapter 22:
A Quiet Escape

Idela (January) 23, 1560
Todd Wellum's Cell, Prison Level, Royal Palace, City of Rammon
The unmistakable sound of the lock disengaging roused Todd Wellum from his peaceful slumber. More than a decade in this hole had taught him to sleep lightly. One could never tell when the locks might suddenly release, allowing the prisoners to roam freely and abuse one another. Todd knew better than most people that changes could happen in a heartbeat. It was always best to be prepared. Kezem's prisons below the Rammon palace were extensive.

Todd rose and dropped into a defensive position ready to defend his meager possessions. The crude comb, a pack of cards, and other trinkets were probably worth less than a few kefs, but they were amenities that eased the painful boredom between carefully regulated exercise sessions. His neck popped, reminding him of the unkind years that had passed.

"What do you want?" he whispered in a tone somewhere between curiosity and hostility.

"I am here to set you free," a young guard announced quietly.

It took a moment for Todd to recognize the newest addition to the prison regiment, a conscript if prison gossip could be trusted. The young man spoke softly and swiftly, but Todd heard every word.

"Your benefactor arranged for a sick form saying you've contracted yellow fever. I'm supposed to give you these and escort you out of the prison." The man slipped a small pouch around Todd's neck. It bulged slightly. "Maybe you should turn it the other way."

Todd nodded and twisted the string so that the pouch hung over his back.

"Do you have bindings?" he asked.

The young man nodded and slipped stuncuffs onto Todd's arms, activating the energy bindings.

"Once we're outside, you're free to go, but you have to attack me first. The infopad has further instructions. Go to the house indicated and wait for the manhunt to end." Saying such, the soldier turned around and strode out of the cell.

Todd followed with a mixture of elation and trepidation that made his head spin, but each step he took toward freedom strengthened his limbs. His initial clumsy steps became more graceful until he glided along behind his escort. Hope of seeing his daughter further spurred him on and his instincts slowly came to life again.

She will be a woman by now.

As they neared the first checkpoint, the young man straightened his shoulders and marched confidently up to the two guards.

Remembering the cover story, Todd stumbled and leaned heavily against the wall, keeping his head bowed so the guard couldn't see his alert eyes.

"This man has yellow fever. I have his quarantine orders here," said his escort, thrusting some papers forward.

"Sure, whatever," said one guard.

"Rookie," muttered the other with disgust.

They were through.

The second checkpoint proved a bit more harrowing.

"Look at me," demanded the gate guard.

Todd lolled his head to the side and rambled something unintelligible.

"He can't understand you, ma'am," Todd's guard explained.

Todd felt the woman's eyes heat the top of his head. He silently prayed to Riden, Kala, and Resh that the explanation would satisfy her.

"Get him out of here," she finally ordered.

"Yes, ma'am."

As he stepped outside, Todd glanced up; the sight froze him in place.

"Beautiful!" he said, referring to the millions of twinkling stars. Some were far off worlds with problems of their own, some were balls of hot gas lending life to those worlds, and others were reflective rocks hurtling toward those worlds bent on destruction, but all possessed a majestic beauty Todd had not seen for untold nights. He smiled up at the three moons, Gemuln, Corid, and Marishaz, each present only in partial glory but adding a gentle glow to the night.

"This is no time to stargaze!" the guard hissed, drawing Todd back to the present situation.

"You're right," Todd replied, prying his eyes away from the night splendor.

They hurried in the direction of the quarantine cells.

The guard stopped suddenly.

"Here's good enough. I'll release the bindings now. How will you incapacitate me?"

"I'll put you in a chokehold. It will be quick and painless," said Todd.

To his surprise, the guard shook his head.

"It's got to leave a mark."

"What's your name?" Todd asked.

"Marksman Cory Tiri—"

Todd swept his hand out and brought it down on the young man's neck. The guard's surprised scream was muffled but loud enough to convince any possible witnesses that an attack had taken place.

"Thank you, Cory," Todd whispered to the fallen soldier. He slipped away from the prison to view his new instructions, anxious to meet his benefactor.

***

Idela (January) 23, 1560
Elena Carpan's Home, Merchant Quarter, City of Rammon

Aware of the late hour, Captain Ethan Tayce slipped into his sister's home, feeling like an intruder. His stomach twisted.

"Ranger Wellum?" he called softly.

A search of the first floor turned up nothing. A thousand thoughts of the plan going wrong flooded his mind as he climbed the stairs to the second floor. Instinctively, he clutched the weapons he had brought for his guest.

"Right here, Captain," Todd said from behind Tayce.

Ethan whipped, pistol coming to bear on the unseen voice. Flicking on a lightbar to banish the oppressive dark, Tayce saw the man who had saved him years ago.

The men regarded each other.

Relief and worry silenced Tayce for several seconds.

Despite the smile, the former prisoner was a shell of a man. The prison rags hung from his lean frame. The regular exercise regime kept him in shape, but poor diet and abysmal sanitary conditions had left their marks. His light brown eyes bore the haunted look of having seen hope rise and die too many times. The small spark found in those eyes could easily be lost or mistaken for insanity.

"I'm glad you made it," Tayce offered awkwardly.

"Thank you. Your aid means more to me than I could ever express or repay," Todd said.

"It is a small thing compared to what I've done in Kezem's name," Tayce said.

"Kezem's will is far reaching," said Todd. "You cannot undo everything but standing against him now should help."

"I wish I could do more for you," Tayce said.

"I will be fine. Return to your post, wherever that may be. I do not wish to know it. Todd assured him. "You have endangered yourself enough on my account. I will return to my Order with all possible speed."

A cautious look crossed Tayce's countenance.

"The Rangers may not be the noble peacekeepers you remember."

"What happened?" Todd demanded.

Tayce motioned for Todd to sit, buying time to choose his words.

"Rangers still inhabit camps in the Riden Mountains, but they have new leaders, including some who condone terrorist activities." He held up a hand to ward off Todd's protests. "Hear me out. The Captain of the Royal

Guard gave Kezem access to the throne room then disappeared shortly before the invasion. One of my older brother's first missions was to hunt down the queen's betrayer, but his men lost the fugitive in the Riden Mountains."

"Laocer," Todd breathed the name like a curse. Prison whispers suddenly made sense. "He always regarded Reia strangely."

"You knew the queen?" Tayce asked, clearly shocked.

"She was once a Ranger, a friend, and my wife's younger sister as well," Todd said, chuckling at Tayce's expression. "But please continue. I must know everything."

"A man like Aster Captain Laocer does not simply disappear forever," Tayce said. Every few months, I hear of him leading a raid or showing up in a village where a bomb explodes. It could be that the captain is long dead and merely a convenient excuse, but that doesn't change the fact that many of the attacks are senseless. It seems the noble Order has sadly declined."

"Your concern is noted and much appreciated, Captain Tayce, but I must seek them out anyway."

A thought occurred to Tayce.

"The Kireshana began a couple of days ago. The Coridian Assassins also train during this time. They will pick off the weaker derringers. I have always detested the practice. Why don't you protect them like the Rangers of old? It will help you hone your skills and give you time to gather information on the new Rangers. If the rumors are unfounded, rejoin them, but if they are true, be cautious."

"Your plan is wise, and I will consider it," Todd promised.

Tayce remembered the weapons meant for the Ranger.

"These items no longer exist as far as the army is concerned," he said, handing Ranger Wellum a serlak pistol, an outdated kerlinblade, a personal communications unit, and a handful of flingers. "The comm links directly to my own, but it's possible for listeners to gain the frequency. Use it when you need me most. I may only be a captain, but I have some useful connections in other branches of the military and government." As an afterthought, he added his own kerlak pistol to the pile.

"I couldn't take that," Todd protested.

"You will need every advantage possible," Tayce said. "Now go, I will return to my post and look for more ways to help your cause."

"Then it is your cause, too."

"Yes, but I have little time to devote to it," said Tayce. "I'm concerned for Princess Rela's safety."

"Do what you can, and I shall do what I can. Riden willing, we will meet again, Captain."

The men shook hands. Then, Tayce supplied Todd with a tent, bedroll, blanket, some kefs, and food enough to see him on his way.

As dawn lightened the streets, Tayce watched the Ranger slip into the early morning shadows.

Chapter 23:
Huz Mon Salt Mines

Idela (January) 19, 1560-Lanolin (February) 21, 1560
Kireshana Path, Calsol Forest to the Huz Mon Salt Mines
Kayleen pondered Teven's tale of someone watching them. They broke camp and continued their trek. Late afternoon, they stumbled across the body of a young derringer. A deep gash in his chest marked a blade's trail. It struck her heart to see a child so violently dead.

"We should bury him," she whispered.

It took them several hours to burn the body and bury the ashes. The young derringer's traveling companions had stripped his body of supplies except the clothes he wore and the small derringer dagger. Kayleen watched Teven finger the handsome blade handle. After laying one final handful of dirt over the remains, he reverently placed the dagger over the grave.

The small group was exceptionally quiet that night. It is one thing to know danger exists around every tree and quite another to touch flesh recently rendered lifeless. Kayleen had seen bodies before, even ones that met violent ends, but this was different. Those bodies had been carefully prepared by someone else. This time, she had prepared the body, touched fire to the sticks beneath it, and helped dig the small hole for the ashes.

The encounter did much to dispel Kayleen's remaining romantic notions about the Kireshana. As the days slipped by, she too became aware of the watcher. Sometimes she would feel malevolent eyes but then the sensation would fade and calm would take its place.

Kayleen's seventeenth birthday on Lanolin (February) 3, 1560 dawned bright and clear. Teven surprised her by giving her a simple necklace made with sturdy wistril weed wound through the tiny carved figure of an astera flower.

Upon reaching Calsola several weeks later, Teven and Kayleen watched Jal skillfully barter with the horse master. Finally, the grumpy old man rented them three horses for five hundred kefs. One hundred was paid up front and the other four hundred would be worked off in the Huz Mon salt mines. The Riden Flats flew past in seven days. Kayleen was pleased with their progress. On foot, the same journey could have taken a month.

Conditions in the mines were horrendous. Kayleen worked hard to control her rising anger at the poor treatment of the workers. The outrage burned hotter still, knowing she was powerless to change things. They steadily scraped salt off the mine walls for five days. To gather their quota faster, Teven and Kayleen climbed the rock walls to reach untouched salt reserves.

Word spread and soon the mine master dragged his corpulent self down to where they worked.

"Fine work! Fine work! And who might you young ones be?" he asked.

"Teven McKnight, Kayleen Wellum, and Jal Seltan," Teven said succinctly. A small tick above his left eye betrayed deep irritation.

Kayleen silently willed him to hold his temper. She swiftly descended and stood by his side, resisting the urge to physically hold him back.

"I am the master of this humble mine, Gavrie Jeriton, and I hope I can convince you to stay on. There's good money to be made."

"I'm afraid that is impossible, sir," Kayleen said.

"Your debt is almost paid off, but I could offer you four hundred more for half a week's work," Gavrie said a bit too eagerly. His shifting eyes declared him a liar. If they agreed, they would never leave the salt mine.

Reading the thought process happening inside his thick skull, Kayleen removed the heavy salt pouch from around her neck and thrust it at him. "That should settle our account, Master Jeriton," she said in a frosty tone.

Panic entered the man's black eyes.

"But see how much good you can do? These poor workers could use the break."

"Then give them one," said Teven.

Gavrie had them on his playing field now and Kayleen knew it. Her dislike for the man increased tenfold.

"We all do what we can, young sir, but there are quotas to meet," said Gavrie.

His cold attitude grated on Kayleen's nerves. She briefly considered offering their services in exchange for a day of rest for the workers. It would be a small price to pay if they could momentarily ease the despair. The idea came and went in a flash, as Gavrie opened his cavernous mouth again.

"I find you too valuable to let go," Gavrie said apologetically. His massive hand clamped around Kayleen's right forearm.

"That was dumb," noted Teven.

Gavrie apparently didn't hear him.

"Why don't you two gentlemen get a couple of pouches and gather some of that precious salt? Your lady friend and I will wait for you in my office."

As soon as Kayleen felt the slightest tug, she threw her arms into Gavrie's ample gut, eliciting a rush of foul breath. She would have choked, but the smell vanished almost as soon as it began. Kayleen grabbed her assailant's right hand and bent the fingers back until she felt them about to snap.

Meanwhile, Teven's arm swept out and pressed Gavrie's sweaty neck against the wall. It pleased Kayleen to see Teven could hit hard when it counted. Jal stood out of the way.

"First of all, Jal doesn't climb mine shafts," Teven began. "Second, never threaten a lady or a derringer and especially not a lady who *is* a derringer. Third, learn some manners. Our debt is paid so we will take our leave now. Do *not* follow us." A bit more pressure caused Gavrie to gurgle and fall unconscious. Teven let him slip down the wall, looking entirely too pleased with himself.

Uncomfortably aware of the audience forming around them, Kayleen started toward the exit. A desperate voice stopped her cold.

"Take us with you!" called a young female voice.

Turning, Kayleen saw a girl with skin a few shades darker than her own pale complexion.

The child's expressive blue eyes pleaded her case.

"I am Jenell, and this is Karric," said the girl, gesturing to a stout youth at her side.

"We're derringers, too," the boy insisted. "Take us with you. We can help," he offered. His dark face made his white, toothy smile that much more brilliant. "We got here a few days ago. We had enough kefs to pay off our debt yesterday, but Gavrie wouldn't let us go."

"We were afraid to fight him," Jenell admitted.

"Come on then," Teven said.

"Me too!" shouted a boy. "I've got to get out of here!"

"We can't take everyone," Kayleen said. More shouts and requests followed as they fled up the tunnel to the surface. Kayleen figured anyone bold enough to follow deserved to come. She would not encourage it, but she didn't have the heart to turn anyone away either. As surely as she knew her own feelings, she knew Teven felt the same way.

"We should not make a habit of this," Jal commented, jogging along beside Kayleen.

"Which part? The fleeing for our lives or picking up strangers?" Kayleen fired the questions and stole a glance over her shoulder at the three mine urchins they had acquired. They grabbed their packs, and then, ran for four kilometers without stopping. Slightly winded, Kayleen took a good look at their younger companions who gasped for breath. "Tev, hold up a minute, or we're going to lose our new friends!"

Teven stopped running, looking none too pleased with the delay.

"Can we ditch them in Huz Mon?" he asked.

"Not likely," said Kayleen. "They'll just end up back in the salt mines or worse."

"I don't like taking responsibility for them," Teven complained.

"Oh, a fine, princely attitude that is," Kayleen teased, trying to lighten the grim mood. "I don't like it either, but they're safer with us than without.

No one ever said right things were nice things."

They whispered so the others, who stood a respectful distance away, would not be able to hear.

Just then, Jal and the last salt mine clinger arrived.

"This, my fleet-footed friends, is Quasim. He has quite a tale to tell," said Jal.

"I want to go home," Quasim declared, holding his chin high and pressing his trembling lips together. He looked no more than seven years old. "My family lives in Ritand. Bad men stole me and sold me to the soldiers in Fort Riden. A Ranger bought me."

Kayleen's mouth gaped. As far as she knew, the Ranger policy stood firmly against slavery.

Hiding his shock better than Kayleen, Teven shot her a look that said they should hear Quasim out before responding.

"The Ranger sold me to Master Jeriton," said the boy.

"What did this Ranger look like?" Kayleen asked, dreading the answer.

"He was sort of tall with dark brown hair, dark eyes, and skin a little lighter than his," said the boy, pointing to Karric. "I don't know much more. He didn't speak much."

Kayleen suppressed a groan.

Lots of men answer that description.

Teven looked like he wanted to continue the conversation, but Kayleen didn't want to pursue the thought any further.

"We should continue," she said. To Quasim, she added, "We'll take you to Resh at least. That's not far from Ritand."

No one argued with her. The weather darkened to match their mood. Each trudged on lost in thought. The torrential downpours of acid rain stuck to a regular pattern, but one could never quite predict Reshner. Surprise storms were also common.

"We need to hurry," Jal urged, spurring the group forward.

Hurry to where? Kayleen thought, quickening her steps. The wind caught her travel cloak and slammed her to a halt.

"Get the tents out!" Teven ordered. He threw his rain cloak over Quasim's shoulders. "Stay down!"

"What about you?" the boy shouted.

Kayleen didn't hear him but read the message on his lips. She whipped off her travel cloak and draped it over Quasim's head. Then, she ran to help Teven unpack the tents. They couldn't set up the tent beams for fear the wind would turn the poles into skewers, but the hardy fabric would protect them. Once the rain hit the ground, the dirt would neutralize the acid, but if it landed directly on skin it would feel like a million ravenous **voracerflies** having a feast. She futilely wished the younger derringers had their equipment packs. There had been no time to retrieve them during the hasty retreat from the salt mines.

Teven's tent was thrown over the two derringers. Next, Kayleen's tent was opened. Before they could get under its protection, the gray skies loosed their arsenal. They dove under the cover but not before getting soaked. Kayleen groaned and leaned over to Teven.

"We're going to have to explain this!" she shouted.

He shrugged, settled onto the quickly soaking ground, and motioned for her to join him.

Hoping Jal had Quasim safely tucked under the third tent, Kayleen sat down next to Teven and rested her head on his shoulder. His left arm wrapped protectively around her. Content to listen to the rain pound on the tent, she didn't speak. Teven was a little soggy but comfortable.

I could get used to this.

The hectic day slowly faded from mind. Kayleen let her thoughts wander to the trials ahead. The first pass through the Riden Mountains would begin in a day or two followed closely by stops in Resh and Fort Riden where most derringers earned kefs doing odd jobs. Then, they would scale Mount Palean.

"We'll make it," Teven said, surprising Kayleen. The rain had slowed to a gentle flow, allowing them to speak. "The anotechs said you were agitated," he explained. "It doesn't take much to read into 'agitated' on the Kireshana."

"I suppose not. How are we even going to find a zalok queen, let alone get close enough to take a souvenir?" Kayleen asked.

"You're the Ranger; you figure it out," he teased.

"Most Rangers have enough sense to avoid zaloks they aren't assigned to protect," she shot back.

"Well, derringers don't, so we'll find out soon enough," said Teven.

When the rain ceased, they continued their hike toward the mountains. Many hours later, they finally set the tents up properly and prepared to spend the night. It was a little tight, but Kayleen shared her tent with Jenell and Teven squeezed in with Jal, having surrendered his tent to Quasim and Karric.

We'll need to pick up more supplies when we get to Resh.

Chapter 24:
Lair of the Zalok Queen

Lanolin (February) 23, 1560-Jira (March) 14, 1560
Entrance to Zalok Cave, Northern Riden Mountains

Staring down the gaping, teeth-lined mouth of a four-and-a-half-meter-long young zalok, Teven McKnight almost wished he hadn't known exactly where to find the beasts. After two uneventful days of travel, it was time things got interesting again. He just wished there was such a thing as interesting without involving death.

"Watch the tail!" Quasim cried, staying well behind Teven and Kayleen.

Teven was grateful that Jal had a firm grip on the boy's shoulder.

"Do you have a plan?" Kayleen asked tersely. Her kerlinblade was raised in a guarded position that would do very little if the zalok's swinging tail connected with her.

"Not getting smacked with that spiked tail," Teven replied.

The young zalok reared back on its hind legs and loosed a shriek that cut through Teven, rattling his bones.

"And shutting that thing up."

"A serlak rifle would come in handy right about now," Kayleen said wistfully. She danced away as the flailing tail came her way.

"How's your aim?" Teven inquired.

"What am I shooting at?"

"The zalok's left eye," Teven responded. "It's got a heat sensor right above it. An energy blast there should blind it long enough to let us slip past." As he had no intention of further involving Kayleen, so by *us* he really meant *me*. If he died in the cave beyond somebody had to live to see the younger derringers through the rest of the Kireshana.

"Should?" Kayleen's voice was incredulous, but she traded her blade for their only energy pistol, an ancient-looking thing that hadn't been worth the scrap metal it was made of until Jal's technical genius and a fresh energy pack breathed new life into it. It took Kayleen three shots to hit the eye sensor, a fact the zalok did not appreciate. Louder, longer shrieks came from the depths of the massive creature. Its black bulky body shivered with pain and rage. The tail swung faster and harder. "Go!"

Teven scrambled under the creature's legs and into the short tunnel that led to the zalok queen's lair. The tunnel was plenty wide for him but would be a tight squeeze for a zalok. The anotechs had been right so far. It didn't take him long to find the queen. Slightly larger than the zalok Kayleen had temporarily blinded, the queen had a black, leathery face, a back covered by row after row of purple scales, and a broad powerful tail. Teven paused to consider how to extract the prize. He had no desire to kill the beautiful creature.

"Let me talk to her," Kayleen suggested.

"What are you doing here? Who's going to let us out of here?" His heart beat faster. He didn't like her being so near to danger, a ridiculous notion considering their mission.

"Relax, Jal has the pistol," said Kayleen, holding out her empty hands as proof. "Besides, the anotechs say the warrior zalok should be disoriented for another twenty minutes or so."

"Just stay back," said Teven. "If you fail, she's going to brain you with that tail."

"Thanks for the vote of confidence," said Kayleen.

Teven crept to the left wall and waited. His movements gave him a good look at Kayleen who, to his horror, sat cross-legged right in front of the zalok queen. The creature eyed Kayleen carefully then suddenly snapped her head in Teven's direction.

"Kayleen, what are you telling her?" asked Teven, feeling the full weight of the queen's stare.

"He does not intend you harm. We seek scales to give to our masters," Kayleen explained to the zalok. She fell silent, but the expression of fierce concentration said the communication continued.

She's crazy.

Several long minutes later, Kayleen climbed to her feet and bowed to the zalok.

"Thank you. With your permission, we would like to collect more scales than we need so we can leave some for the many others who come behind. Then, they will have no reason to disturb you."

Teven shifted his concentration to the zalok. He sensed her reluctant approval. The zalok settled to the ground and tucked all six legs beneath her large body. He approached cautiously.

"Hurry, Teven, she has eggs to lay and young to feed," Kayleen said.

Teven shook his head in bewilderment but did as requested. Four swift steps brought him close enough to touch the zalok. He hesitated. Warmth radiated from her body.

"Take as many as you can carry but not all from the same spot, and she requests that we seal the entrance when we leave."

"Don't they need to get out?" Teven asked. He carefully began pulling scales from the creature's body. The scales pulled off easily with muffled pops. Teven selected an even distribution of deep purple scales and slipped them into a soft pouch at his waist.

"The half-year hibernation approaches," Kayleen explained. "Besides, zalok claws are especially well-suited for carving through rock. Whatever barrier we can erect won't be a problem for them."

Ten minutes later, Teven and Kayleen stepped back into the fresh mountain air. A sharp bark from the queen's cave caused Teven to jump. The zalok warrior they had wounded to gain entry glared balefully at them but made no move to harm them. More barks followed and the young zalok trundled toward the opening.

"How are we going to seal that?" Teven wondered.

"With a charm," Kayleen said.

"What charm? You don't know any charms."

"They don't know that," she murmured with a grin. "We're going to sacrifice a tent, and you're going to write about the horrible death that awaits those who enter the cave unbidden."

Teven grunted but understood the direction of her thoughts.

"Why am I doing the writing?" Teven didn't really mind; he just wanted to argue with her.

"Because you have such pretty handwriting," Kayleen answered. "Besides, this is my brainchild so you get to do the grunt work." The silly grin came back, making her appear younger than her seventeen years. She unpacked her tent, and together, they attacked it with their daggers.

"What are you doing?" asked Quasim, voicing the question written in every eye.

The corner of Jal's mouth twitched up. No doubt the anotechs were telling Jal quite a tale.

"Placing a curse on this cave," Teven replied.

"A curse," Quasim repeated. Doubt filled the two words.

"Help or stand aside," Kayleen said.

"Stand aside," Teven amended. "In fact, go get some stones to make a container."

Quasim, Karric, Jal, and Jenell gathered small stones and fashioned a small container out of them. By the time they had finished, Teven and Kayleen had the tent cut in roughly the right shape with several strips and poles to use as anchors. The broadest, cleanest side was placed face up on the ground. Teven ground up some soft rocks and a few purple scales. Then, he added water to make a paste and wrote his message.

Death beyond to the mortal who dares breach this portal.

"Lovely," Kayleen commented. "Please don't become a poet."

"Is it that dangerous in there?" Jenell wondered. Her crystal-blue eyes widened, and her chin length black hair framed her face, despite the mountain breeze.

"How are we going to get our scales?" Karric demanded, scratching his short, dark, fuzzy head hair.

"I have enough for all of us," Teven said, removing the pouch from his belt and dumping the contents into the stone box. "Take whichever one you want. We're going to need a few more stones to make this a little higher. I don't want the wind to catch any of the scales." He reached in and selected a scale for himself and Kayleen.

"Thanks," Kayleen said, tucking the purple scale into a pouch on her belt.

Teven put his scale back into the bag he had upended and refastened the pouch to his waist. His knees cracked as he stood.

"You'll sleep well tonight," said Kayleen.

"Are we camping here?" Quasim wondered.

"That would be wise," Jal said. "Night will fall within the hour. We have the favor of this zalok queen, but the others may not be so kind to strangers. We will need to seek shelter in the cave if rain comes."

Teven shot Jal a warning look, catching Quasim and the others looking curiously at him. Jal shrugged as if to say that at this point the charade hardly mattered. Teven wasn't so sure but said nothing.

Quasim and Kayleen wandered off to forage for mountain herbs. Jenell and Karric tackled the task of making one big tent out of the two remaining ones. Jal built and attended a small fire. Teven perfected the stone box, shoring up the sides with more layers. He also put several slits in the tent blocking the cave so fresh air could enter and fierce winds could blow through without ripping the cover away.

The herb-seeking expedition yielded a bit of mintas, corlia, and yelcha to add to the three ration packs they could afford to use for the evening meal. They still had a week or two of mountains to traverse and another two weeks or so to Resh. Teven reasoned there must be a small village or farmhouse along the way where they could seek aid, but conserving food was still necessary.

The evening passed pleasantly. Kayleen sang an old ballad about Kolpec Rinn, a Ranger who fell in love with the daughter of a sea captain. Not approving of Ranger Rinn, the girl's father took her with him as he sailed on the North Asrien Sea. Kolpec swam twenty-one days through icy waters until he caught the ship. His devotion won the hearts of father and daughter, but Ranger Rinn died the next day from an illness brought on by the Asrien Sea. The distraught woman vanished into the air the same night her lover died. Although she was never seen again, it is said twenty-one stars were born that night.

Jenell and Karric shared a local dance from their small village of Kerimia. Jal weaved several tales of adventure on far-off planets. Though Teven had never heard of any of the planets, he detected a ring of truth to the tales. Quasim described how to properly gut a gully fish to avoid the poison glands. He explained that bones became utensils, poison was sold, normal oil became fuel, and most other parts became food. No part went to waste. Teven showed off a few of the minor anotechs powers under the guise of silly magic tricks. He stacked rocks, made his skin light up from within, and created a small dust devil.

The six travelers squeezed into the makeshift double tent to sleep.

They rose when the sun's first rays shined over the mountains to the east. The morning and afternoon hikes went smoothly. Kayleen shot a cannafitch to supplement their supplies. The tough meat was bland but provided a passable midday meal. The evening meal once again came from ration packs and random herbs.

The days slipped by much the same: eat, walk, eat, and walk some more. With the slightly larger group, they could only travel as fast as the slowest member, Quasim. Teven didn't mind much, until supplies dropped to a dangerously low level. On the other hand, his feet had ceased to ache, and his lungs again adjusted to the thin mountain air.

Despite still feeling someone watching them, Teven began to enjoy the Kireshana. Since they had come across very few dangerous predators, Teven concluded the watcher must be friendly.

Occasionally, they stumbled across a korver or panther shot cleanly through the neck, no doubt gifts from their mysterious protector. They had one close encounter with a small korver clan but escaped without a fight. The bloodlust and excitement in the korver shrieks fascinated Teven as much as his first encounter with them so many years ago.

Nine days after collecting the scales from the zalok queen, Teven led his small band down the last mountain onto the Resh Grasslands.

"We'll reach Resh in a couple of weeks. Perhaps someone there will be able to escort you home, Quasim."

"I don't want to go home," Quasim stated.

Teven said no more but spent the rest of the afternoon thinking of ways to convince Quasim to stay in Resh. The frail boy had held his own on the trip through the Riden Mountains, but Teven had enough to worry about protecting Karric and Jenell. Jal and Kayleen could defend themselves, but he still felt responsible for them.

"We'll figure something out," Kayleen said.

Teven felt better knowing that someone understood him. Jal did most of the corralling and prodding of the younger derringers and Quasim. The length of the Kireshana wore on Karric and Jenell. Nevertheless, Teven and Kayleen pushed the group to keep a steady pace. The longer they stayed out on Resh Grasslands, the more time they would spend vulnerable to Coridian Assassins. They had no idea how many assassins roamed, but a bone here and a body there kept the sense of danger powerful.

Chapter 25:
Priest's Good News

Lanolin (February) 27, 1560
Laocer's Safe House, City of Ritten

Ectosh Laocer had spent many hours coaching Benali in Azhel priest mannerisms. The actor knew the script solidly. A few wrong gestures might be lost on Lord Kezem, but too many mistakes would lead to failure.

As Captain of the Royal Guard, Laocer had been to Loresh several times, but only royalty were allowed into certain sections.

Such secrecy must hide treasure!

If Lord Kezem could be lured to Loresh, Laocer would kill him and force the princess to open the forbidden chambers, winning both the treasure and the throne. The legends were ambiguous about what age the royal must be to open the chamber, but even if the princess was too young, Laocer could still send for Teven. Terosh and Reia's eldest child was sixteen now and legally considered a man.

Timing was crucial. Laocer had paid his mercenaries only a quarter of the amount promised, relying on Loresh's treasures to make up the difference. They would go to Loresh according to a very specific timetable, but if Benali messed up, the timetable would burn.

Deep worry lines covered Laocer's face, as he paced the small dwelling. He had lived here ever since betraying the main Ranger compound several months back. Most Rangers had escaped, but hopefully, they would be too distracted to care much when he launched his bid for the throne. He hated depending so much upon others, but he needed the mercenaries. The strain of passing years had begun to tell on his body, showing up mostly in his dark expression.

Laocer threw himself into a series of training moves, imagining his opponent was Lord Kezem. The sweet sensation of approaching revenge made his movements frantic. The wooden dummy shuddered under several devastating blows. By the time Laocer had finished, the dummy's head hung sadly to the side and one arm lay on the floor. Laocer silently swore that one day Kezem would resemble the broken dummy.

***

Lanolin (February) 27, 1560
Streets of Rammon to Royal Palace, City of Rammon

Benali practiced his lines and priestly gestures during the hov ride from his employer's safe house to Rammon. It had been no small feat to gain a pass into the palace, but even Lord Kezem was loath to snub an Azhel priest.

Benali had only been to Rammon twice, but he noticed the difference in the atmosphere. Part of him missed the majesty and beauty of the old Rammon. While the old city had many buildings with beautiful, rounded architecture, this new Rammon boasted block after block of ugly, square, gray monstrosities.

There had always been poor people walking about in drab clothes, but they had always been balanced by a sea of bright colors representing the middle and upper classes. What Benali saw today definitely favored somber tones, except where the dark red uniforms of army soldiers dominated. The soldiers roamed the streets at will, collecting protection fees and generally causing more trouble than they prevented.

Benali instructed his driver to go near the Merchant Quarter. Maybe his mind was being selective, but he could clearly recall the beaming faces of children and merchants from the old Rammon. Today, the market hummed with activity, but a desperate air hung over the crowd. The shouts sounded angrier and the bartering sounded cutthroat.

"My heart aches for these lost souls," Benali said, trying to stay in character.

The driver laughed; it was not a pleasant sound.

Benali had the driver stop three blocks from the palace so he could jog the rest and appear suitably exhausted. The strictest Azhel priests abhor technology. Benali personally thought the belief ridiculous, but he didn't have to agree with the cult, just pass for one of the wackos. Rounding the final corner before the block leading to the palace, Benali slowed to a walk. Although slightly late for his noon appointment with Lord Kezem, Benali wasn't worried. Such would be expected of a man who had supposedly crossed the Kala River, climbed the Ash Mountains, ridden many days on horseback, and walked the length of Rammon. He grew tired thinking of the trip.

The Royal Guards at the palace gates waved Benali by with hardly a glance at his pass, which was good because he could barely breathe let alone talk to them.

Must exercise more.

He wandered down several wrong passages before asking a servant girl for directions to the throne room. He figured a servant would be the least dangerous person to ask. She gave him a strange look but kindly pointed him in the right direction.

On the way up to the fifth-floor throne room, Benali passed statue after statue bearing Lord Kezem's likeness. He snorted with disgust. Noticing several guards lining the walls, Benali turned the snort into a hacking cough. Now approaching eyes and ears that mattered, he began his routine of priestly movements, waving his arms about slowly and muttering blessings.

The stoic throne room guards were a bit more cautious than the other guards. They stopped him and studied his pass carefully while an automatic sensor scanned him for weapons. Once he was cleared, they signaled someone inside who disengaged the dozen locks keeping the throne room door shut.

Someone's a bit paranoid.

The heavy doors swung slowly inward powered by two identical young men throwing their whole bodies into the task.

Lord Kezem sat perched on Reshner's throne, staring down his nose at Benali.

Been practicing the look, have we?

The expression made Kezem appear simultaneously powerful, important, and omnipotent.

And idiotic.

Benali approached with a careful limp and briefly nodded. Azhel high priests did not fully bow to any man, even the planetary ruler.

"Greetings, Lord Kezem, keeper of Riden's flock," Benali said, being mindful to move his mouth slowly. He kept his tone wavy and inserted convincing cracks here and there to keep Kezem concentrating on the voice instead of the actor.

"State your business," Kezem snapped. "I haven't the time or patience for word games."

"Reshner's three moons align with the Lady's favor four months hence. Riden's consort, the goddess Zaria, knows you seek her treasures deep in Loresh but takes pity on your mortal soul. In exactly four months, take the young princess there, and she will unlock the hidden chambers."

With his heart trying to escape his chest, Benali struggled to keep his voice slow and grave. Kezem's expression was hard to read, but Benali saw a gleam at the mention of Loresh. He wasn't quite sure where he stood with regards to the ancient tale, but obviously, two very powerful and ambitious men believed it to be true.

"Why do you not seek the treasures yourself and donate the money to the poor?"

Benali knew he was being mocked. For someone who claimed to not like word games, Kezem did a fine job of throwing words around. Benali clamped down on an un-priest-like retort.

"The servants of the gods merely worship and deliver messages, Favored One. I was bid to tell you what I have; my part is finished." At this point, Benali figured less was more.

Lord Kezem would form his own plans, which were hopefully in line with Benali's employer.

"And what if I command you to tell me again?" Kezem challenged. He spoke with the cool confidence of a man used to getting his way.

Benali grew tired of Kezem's pettiness, but he let none of his impatience reach his expression.

"Then, I would repeat myself, Favored One," he answered with all the graciousness he could muster. "In four months, Princess Rela of House Minstel will be able to unlock the secret halls of Loresh."

"How will she find the door or doors to unlock?"

"The gods know all, but they do not always tell mortals every secret, Favored One." Benali enjoyed placing the imaginary ball back on Kezem's side of the playing field.

"Is her presence enough or are the rumors true, will the gods require her blood at Loresh's hidden gates?" Kezem asked the question with a straight face, but Benali knew he must be quaking at the thought of having to hurt Princess Rela. More specifically, Kezem feared the pain he might have to endure to reach the treasure. It was common knowledge that Queen Reia had somehow linked her daughter's life to Lord Kezem.

Benali thought very carefully about his answer. Upsetting Lord Kezem would not be wise, but not encouraging him enough would also be bad.

"Sacrifice may be required, but with the Lady's favor, the power of the moons should augment any power the princess lacks. Assuming, of course, she is willing to help."

"What do you mean by *willing*?" Kezem demanded.

How should I know? I just made that up!

"If the princess does not wish to find the secrets, the treasure will not call to her," said Benali, struggling to keep his voice steady. "Without the call, her steps could forever wander Loresh." Benali knew he was rambling, so he consciously stopped talking.

One look at Lord Kezem convinced him he had succeeded in his mission. Then, everything went wrong.

"Thank you for your time, Father Benali. You have been very helpful. In fact, I'm going to invite you to stay with us until we see your vision come true."

Kezem's tone was benevolent, but Benali sensed two Royal Guards flanking him.

"Jorg and Makil will escort you to your quarters," said Kezem.

Benali's head spun. He nodded dumbly as the Royal Guards led him from the throne room. He ran the conversation over and over in his head. Not once had he messed up. Every inflection and word had been perfect. Then, it hit him; he'd been too good. Never, in all his life, had a flawless performance been a negative thing. He had no choice but to continue with the charade. Worse still, Azhel priests shun strong drinks, so he couldn't even drown his misery in a tall tankard of ale.

***

Lord Kezem slumped on the throne, rubbing his temple with both hands. The priest's words about Rela's willingness to find the secret chambers disturbed him. He had ways to make her willing, but it would be difficult.

The child had an exasperating stubbornness about her.

Probably from her mother.

Equally disturbing was the part about wandering Loresh forever and never finding anything, for it had proven true so far. His men had been up and down Loresh's tunnels hundreds of times to no avail.

Rela was his key to the treasure. He grew more certain of this every day. He had been nothing but benevolent toward her for years, yet she snuck around behind his back trying to aid dissident fools! Fine gratitude indeed. It was high time she started paying back the debt she owed him. Leading him to the treasure would be a good start.

Chapter 26:
Princess Rela's Near Escape

Lanolin (February) 29, 1560
Princess Rela's Private Chambers, Royal Palace, City of Rammon
Life for Princess Rela Minstel was not unduly hard, but her frustration at being confined to the palace grew as the years passed. She only ever felt real pain during the annual ritual of letting that fool, Merek, slice her left arm with a dagger, but she gradually became aware of Lord Kezem's crueler side. She spent much time studying history and politics, practicing shooting, exploring the palace, and aiding marked people. For a while, she had Sarie Verituse and her friends to tell her how the commoners fared.

Oppression and corruption ruled, and she was powerless to stop it. Lorian Petole and Anabel and Marc Spitzer went to train in the Kireshana, leaving only a bitter Nicholas Riggs behind. The instructors said Nicholas wasn't ready for the Kireshana, but Rela knew the truth had more to do with his mother's wishes than his readiness. Since having him deliver the infopad to Captain Tayce, Rela had sent Nicholas on a few errands, but she couldn't really confide in him. Still, she knew enough to suspect Nicholas would be in danger if he stayed after helping her escape.

Several years back, Rela realized she barely had two kefs to her name. It had started with Lorian selling some trinkets they had found in storage rooms and morphed into a tidy network of business contacts and private trade deals. Slowly, the pile of kefs grew. The money meant little to her except that it would pay off some corrupt guards.

After agonizing over where to flee, Rela chose Idonia because her favorite geography tutor, Dasel, had described it as the place where the richest land met the matchless beauty of the South Asrien Sea. In truth, Rela wished to visit every part of Reshner, even the Felmon Desert and the Frozen North, but she would go to Idonia first.

"Princess? Are you in there?" called Nicholas.

She hesitated then remembered she had sent him on an errand. Rushing to the door, she threw it open.

Nicholas stepped past her holding a tightly wrapped bundle.

"Thank you, Nicholas, set it on the chair over there. Did you get everything?"

"Are you still going through with this crazy scheme?" asked Nicholas.

"We've been through this," Rela said with infinite patience. "I can't spend the rest of my life trapped in—"

"A palace," Nicholas interrupted. "You're in a palace, Princess. Half the planet's crammed into community housing and you're complaining about being trapped!" He threw her package onto the chair with disgust, a flush breaking out over his pale cheeks. His servant's robes had a few dirt smudges from his recent errand.

Rela marveled at how much Nicholas had matured in the last few months. Part of her knew he had a point, but it didn't change her mind. Feeling very weary, she sank onto the edge of a fancy chair and sighed.

"I'm sorry, Nicholas. I wish I could do more for the people, but I must escape. I have to break this link to Lord Kezem, and I cannot learn how to do that from here."

"I know," said Nicholas. "That's why I'm helping you. It'll probably be the death of me."

His joke fell flat, hitting solidly upon her fears.

"Don't say that!" Rela cried. "That's why you have to come with me."

"I can't. Lord Kezem will never let me be a Royal Guard if I run away," said Nicholas.

"Forget the Royal Guard. This is your life we're talking about!"

"No," Nicholas said, dragging the word out. "We're talking about your plan to leave the nicest place on this planet."

Rela snorted and wondered how dense her friend could be.

"Lord Kezem can't harm me, but he has placed good people around me so I'd remember how much I have to lose." Rela had never realized how much she cared for Nicholas.

"What could Lord Kezem possibly want with you?" asked Nicholas.

"I have heard my family has special powers, but those who tell me that already know more than I do," Rela said with a self-deprecating grin. She thought of her mother. Several dreams had brought messages of encouragement and love, but so far, none had explained what Rela could do for Kezem. Perhaps she was only alive because of the curse linking her to the man. Sarie used to speak of the Ralose Charm as a blessing, but after hearing Lord Kezem refer to it as a curse, Rela had come to consider it a curse as well.

"I've heard only royals can unlock the secrets of Loresh." Nicholas said, surprising Rela. "But it's just a fable. No one in their right mind believes the story."

"What story?" Rela demanded, wondering why Sarie and her tutors had never mentioned Loresh. "Tell me."

"As you wish," said Nicholas. "Loresh is a series of caves in the Frozen North, southeast of Estra. The legend says that the first cave system has an enchanted door to another series of caves. Supposedly, only members of House Minstel can unlock the door and reach the treasures beyond."

"What treasures?" Rela wondered.

"No one knows," Nicholas answered, making his voice extra mysterious. "Some say room after room of gold and gems, but I doubt that's true. House Minstel would never have fallen if it possessed that kind of wealth."

"Why do you say that?" asked Rela.

"If even half of what the legends say is true about the Loresh treasures your parents could have surrounded the palace with a wall of mercenaries for fifty years!"

"They wouldn't do that," Rela argued, shaking her head. "Besides, it's pointless to speculate about what they should have done. What I *am* going to do is get out of here, and you're going to help me."

Nicholas bowed deeply.

"Yes, Princess, I will help. I have paid the guard half of his fee, and the rest is still in the pouch. In one hour, you will be walking the filthy streets of Rammon in glorious freedom."

"You're coming too, remember?" Rela's sharp blue eyes dared him to disagree.

"No one is leaving," said a chilling voice from doorway.

Both youths gasped. Rela glanced at Nicholas and knew some of his surprise was feigned. Her heart stopped beating, and her breath caught in her throat. Her thoughts slowed. Rela could only stare at Lord Kezem with dumbfounded horror.

"Greetings, Lord Kezem." Nicholas bowed from the waist.

"You are lucky to have such good friends, Princess," said Lord Kezem, ignoring the boy.

"Am I?" Rela whispered, tasting the bitter betrayal. She sucked in sharply, trying to hold back frustrated tears.

Princesses never let people see them cry!

"I see you've been busy," Lord Kezem commented, waving at the bundle on the chair. He strode up to her, flanked by a dozen Royal Guards in splendid dark blue uniforms.

Her spacious front room suddenly felt crowded.

Kezem's hand shot out and caught her neck, spilling the tears that had formed. His hand tightened enough to make breathing difficult.

"My Lord, the Ralose Charm!" cried Nicholas.

Rela couldn't tell if the warning was meant to protect her or Kezem. The hand at her throat loosened. Her hands hung at her sides, rendered useless as much by emotion as physical predicament.

"I will deal with you later, Lieutenant. Get in uniform and go arrest that greedy fool," Kezem ordered. "You're on watch tonight."

The mention of Nicholas's new rank shot anger through Rela and gave her back her voice. She twisted her head enough to look at her former friend.

"Congratulations on your commission, Lieutenant Riggs." Rela squeezed each word through clenched teeth.

Avoiding her piercing gaze, Nicholas hastily exited the room.

"The sooner you understand you cannot escape, the sooner your life will be easier, Princess," Kezem lectured, releasing her. "You may think you hate the boy, but his life is still in your hands, as are the lives of those on the Kireshana. Since you cannot be trusted to behave, I am assigning some Melian Maidens to watch over you."

Rela stared at the doorway, wishing the floor would swallow her and end the misery. Silent tears continued falling as she listened to Kezem. With effort, she choked down sobs.

"What do you want from me?" she asked at last.

"You will know when I wish it so," replied Kezem. "Until then, consider my words concerning your friends." He left the threat hanging in the air and marched out with the Royal Guards on his heels.

Rela collapsed onto the plush carpet and sobbed, letting her emotions run their course. After several minutes, she calmed down enough to notice the others. A woman knelt in front of Rela, flanked by five more spread in a semi-circle at her back. Rela sat up and wiped away the tears.

"We are the Melian Maidens assigned to protect you, Princess," spoke the woman closest to Rela. She had a pleasant face with smooth features and a lithe body that spoke equally of grace and strength. Her voice calmed Rela's frazzled nerves. "I am Kia Meetcher. With me are Linnea Price, Jola Westin, Clara Argnon, Elia Koffrin, and Nalana Vastel. Lord Kezem bids us watch you constantly, but you have nothing to fear from us."

Rela regarded each woman carefully. The leader appeared to be in her mid-twenties, and the others looked in their late teens or early twenties.

"Can you teach me to fight?" asked Rela.

A flicker of amusement crossed the head maiden's face.

"You wish to challenge him one day," she stated.

Rela nodded.

"The charm works both ways," Kia gently reminded her. "If you harm him, you will feel the pain you cause, and his ability to sense your injuries will make practice difficult."

"Lord Kezem has trained for years and sustained many injuries I have shared," Rela argued. "It's time I returned the favor."

"Hand-to-hand combat should be fine, but we're going to have to be very careful with kerlinblades," said Kia, thinking aloud.

"There is a way," Jola offered.

"Explain," Kia ordered.

"Train when he does," Jola said.

"It will take some coordination, but it should work." Kia nodded approval of the plan.

"I have had a little training but not nearly enough. The instructors have taught me all they are willing to, but I fear I must one day confront Lord Kezem," said Rela, mostly talking to herself. "If I kill him and die in the process, I will count it a fair price for freeing this people."

The speech came easily to Rela. Though she was trapped in the palace, she understood that the situation outside was grim. Perhaps the maidens would be willing to act as her emissaries to the marked people in her friends' stead. The prison could certainly use more of the medical supplies Lorian had smuggled in. Rela would take them to the prison herself if necessary, but there were many other tasks to be done outside the palace.

The head Melian Maiden looked deep into her eyes, searching for something. Rela endured the pointed stare and gave the maiden one of her own.

"We will teach you what we can," Kia promised.

Relief rushed through Rela. Perhaps this constant guard would be a good thing.

Chapter 27:
Rescue Mission

Jira (March) 15, 1560
City of Resh

After weeks traveling through mountains, fields, and forests, Resh's hard structures seemed strange and foreboding to Teven, Kayleen, and their companions. The city, highlighted by a series of centuries-old elegant spires, possessed an austere beauty. Used to the annual influx of Kireshana travelers, many merchants gathered in the main square to sell them anything, legal or otherwise. Some people offered legitimate work for the derringers, but just as many sought to take advantage of them.

The first day in Resh, Teven tracked down suitable living quarters. The overpriced small housing unit in a rough section placed them in close quarters, but Teven clung to the optimistic notion that they would not be there long.

Each day, the group went out in pairs to query the locals about work. There was never a shortage of menial labor opportunities, but more often than not, such opportunities merely taxed the body, numbed the mind, and paid pathetically.

A week passed, then two. Among the six of them, they made enough to continue renting the small housing unit and eat decently, but the point of staying in Resh was to earn the kefs to pay the price required to rise from derringer status. As he watched their resources dwindle, Teven gained a new sympathy for mine workers and tenant farmers. Preoccupied with worry, Teven barely registered the agitated conversations taking place around him.

"We've got to do something!" a distinguished elderly man shouted. That statement alone would not have caught Teven's attention but the next one did. "Kezem's men are becoming bolder by the second!" The man gestured angrily with a walking stick.

Teven slowed his steps, and Kayleen followed suit.

"It's Lord Kezem, Father. Show some respect, or the RLA will cart you off to prison!" admonished a younger man. The man's shiny tunic and gold lined trousers spoke of money.

Teven paused. They had nowhere pressing to be anyway.

"Pretty soon there will be no one left to work the fields," a woman lamented, possessively clutching the younger man's arm. "How will Brana make me sweet frolers if all the farmers get conscripted or killed?" Her tone indicated more distress over the loss of the treat than the farmers' plight.

"It's all right, my dear. Lord Kezem's army will crush the rebellion soon," said the man, patting the woman's arm.

"Don't think you've escaped this thing, Gavin," the father warned, shaking the walking stick in his son's face.

The younger man leaned back to save his nose.

"Abiel may be too young for them now but in a year or two they'll come to claim him. Mark my words!"

Teven exchanged a glance with Kayleen. He didn't care if the family knew they'd been eavesdropping.

"Excuse me. Is there some trouble, sir?" he asked.

"Mind your own business," Gavin snapped.

The older man drew himself up. He was not dressed nearly as finely as the young couple, but he wore his plain attire with dignity. Fire burned brightly in his eyes.

"Trouble! I'll say there's trouble, and it's got Kezem written all over its ugly self!" said the man.

"Father!"

"Hush, Master Niklos, that's treason!" cried the woman. "Hurry now or we'll be late for the performance." She detached herself from her husband and placed a placating hand on the older man's arm.

Master Niklos softened his tone but not the resolve in his steely gray eyes.

"You two go on ahead, my dear. I'll only slow you down."

"But you're the one who wanted to see the Kalmata String Quartet," the woman protested.

"Old men and women of all ages have a right to change their minds," said the man.

Shaking their heads, the man and woman continued down the busy street. Teven watched them walk away then looked back at the older man and found himself pinned in place by a probing stare.

"Etoni eva alaeris!" Master Niklos exclaimed under his breath.

Teven recognized the exclamation as Kalastan, but the man spoke too swiftly for him to guess at its meaning until the anotechs provided a translation: *By the stars, there is hope.*

"Come with me!" The man took off down the street in the opposite direction from the young couple. His steps suddenly had a youthful spring to them.

Teven and Kayleen struggled to match his pace.

"What's this about?" Kayleen demanded, when they finally halted three blocks from the start of their frantic dash.

Teven suppressed a grin. He could always count on Kayleen to not mince words. He took stock of his surroundings. They were in a nicer section of Resh. The streets were clean but cold and devoid of joy. The neighborhood boasted single family housing units packed tight enough for plains sparrows to spread their wings and touch two walls.

Master Niklos waved his hand in front of a security sensor on a door midway down the street. A triumphant chime announced success. The lock disengaged, and their
host waved them in.

Teven hesitated briefly but sensed no danger. He strode through the door into a receiving room which favored the colors green and purple. Master Niklos motioned for them to continue into a comfortable side room to the left of the receiving room. Teven walked into the room and tensed when Niklos touched a button at his belt. An energy field buzzed to life across the doorway.

"Do not be alarmed," said Master Niklos. "That is a sound damper which will allow us to converse freely."

"About what?" Kayleen demanded. As usual, she beat Teven to the question by a fraction of a second. Her hands crept toward the inside of her cloak where she had stashed her kerlinblade.

Teven twitched his head negatively and willed her to be patient.

"We're listening," he prompted, taking a seat.

Kayleen remained standing.

For a while Master Niklos just stared at Teven. He opened his mouth several times but always closed it again.

"I knew my feelings were not wrong," he finally said in a rush. "They said to go to the square during the Kireshana, and I have for the past five years."

"Who are you?" Kayleen asked.

"I am a former Ranger turned tosh merchant. My name is Niklos Mikhail McGreven." The man's tone told Teven he did not like the direction his life had taken. "When I was a Ranger, I taught many students and had many apprentices. Though I grew close to most of them, two orphans, sisters in name but not in blood, became like daughters to me. You are are the son of the younger one." He spoke the words with deep emotion that rang true.

"You knew my mother?" Teven asked, torn between caution and the need to know more.

"Queen Reia Minstel was not always queen," Niklos said tenderly. "She was once a Ranger and my student, one of the best. Young, idealistic, headstrong, impulsive." He smiled as he said it. His gaze turned from Teven to the floor, deep and unseeing as he stared into the past.

"Please go on," Teven begged, hardly daring to breath. The few scraps of information he had heard about his past only whet a ravenous appetite to know more. Although the Kireshana consumed his energy and ability to puzzle out his past, that did not remove the desire to know.

Niklos's cloudy gaze cleared a little.

"Your parents met on your father's Kireshana, as he battled Restler-Tarpon Alliance soldiers. At the time, Prince Terosh fully believed the Royal

Guard was all life could ever offer him, so he spent happy months traveling with Reia Antellio. The Blood Harvest changed everything. Your grandmother, Queen Kila, had been dead for ages by this time, but King Teorn and Prince Taytron went to Mitra to secure a wife for the crown prince. They were assassinated along with the Mitran royals."

"And suddenly my father was king," Teven said sadly.

"Soon thereafter, yes, but Prince Terosh was away from the palace when the news about King Teorn arrived. RT Alliance soldiers had lured your mother into a trap to draw out the prince, and it worked."

"How did they escape?" Teven wondered.

"I do not know for sure. However, I do know that they married soon after being reunited, before receiving news about the king and elder prince. See—"

"She wasn't supposed to marry him," Kayleen finished.

"What? Why not?" Teven asked, surprised that Kayleen knew some obscure Ranger rule he did not.

"Reia was forced to choose between her love and her life as a Ranger," said Master Niklos. "The prohibition against marrying into the royal family has existed for centuries, but it is not something all Rangers believe in."

"How come I never heard of this?" Teven asked, feeling left out.

Kayleen shot him a *think-about-it* look.

"You're the prince. The only royal you'd be eligible to marry is you sister."

"Oh."

Lost in thought, Master Niklos winced.

"The situation was sorely mishandled."

Silence stretched and Teven feared he would never go on, but Kayleen came to the rescue with a timely prompt.

"Mishandled, Master Niklos?"

"Yes, gravely. Reia chose to love her prince, and the Ashatan Council stripped her of her rank as a healer and banished her. It broke her heart and split the order. Many prominent Rangers thought the council unjust. I did not know what to think. She had spurned our codes, which forbade loving a royal, but should ignoring an unjust rule have earned her our ire?"

Another long pause ensued. Teven waited this one out.

"I left the Rangers soon thereafter but stayed in touch with Reia during her time as queen. From time to time, she would seek my counsel. Your parents faced many a crisis with wisdom and boldness. Then, your father was murdered, and this business with Kezem began."

"How did you know I'm her son?"

"I have eyes and ears, boy," Niklos said. "I have heard the whispers surrounding Reshner's lost princes. So many stories swirl I no longer know what is true, but I see you here and know there is hope. Lord Kezem's fist has been hard on this people for far too long. Join the rebellion. Fight for your throne!"

"It is not yet time," Teven murmured, surprised at how calm he sounded.

"Then at least right some wrongs," Niklos insisted. "You are a derringer. You seek jobs, do you not?"

Teven and Kayleen nodded, but Niklos paid no attention to them.

"Of course, you do. Yesterday, a troop from Fort Riden came to collect the young as they do annually. The salt mines, the weapons plants, and the RLA training camps await the captured. Did you not feel the pain of the bereaved mothers in Resh? My own wretched son and his fool wife think themselves immune from the suffering, even after seeing the soldiers seize my daughter's son. But their son will soon be old enough for the mines. Then, they will know. Save my daughter's son and as many of the others as you can. Five thousand kefs are all I can spare, but they're yours if you can rescue those doomed souls."

Teven's jaw dropped. He had never seen that much money, but he knew they desperately needed it. The only remaining question was how five derringers and a salt mine survivor were going to find and defeat a detachment of RLA soldiers.

Before he could voice his question, Kayleen spouted off a stream of questions.

"How far ahead are they? How many are there? How well-armed are they?"

"They are headed back to Fort Riden. The troop is twenty-three strong including officers, and they should be moderately armed. But they are also unsuspecting and lazy. I followed them once, but I could never fight so many by myself. They took about thirty captives. The boy you will be looking for is Garrett Rimton. He is about a head shorter than you with blond hair and brown eyes."

Teven's heart sank.

A quarter of the planet answers to that description!

"Won't the soldiers just return and take the children again?" asked Kayleen.

"Leave that to me," said Niklos. He gave them a thousand kef advance and some tamitin powder to knock out the soldiers.

After a few final instructions, Teven and Kayleen returned to the tiny housing unit and convinced Jal to stay behind to look after the others. They needed to move swiftly and silently to succeed in a rescue. They packed a few supplies, picked their way through Resh to the outskirts, and followed the road south and slightly west.

***

Two days later, they caught up to their quarry. The first sighting was midmorning. They spent the rest of the day shadowing and carefully observing. Thankfully, Niklos had been right about the sloppy soldiering. Twice they spotted prime opportunities for the captives to slip off unnoticed. Throughout the day, Teven and Kayleen bounced possible rescue plans off each other.

When night fell, Kayleen slipped close to the camp. Teven waited thirty seconds for her to get into position before using the anotechs to imitate a korver's hunting call. At the same time, he took a thick stick and beat the nearby bushes. He repeated the eerie call, catching the attention of the two guards closest to the prisoner tent.

"Should we tell the captain?" asked one guard.

"He's got ears. It's just a bunch of mangy korvers; nothing to worry about," replied the second guard.

Teven changed tactics. Taking the sturdy stick, he stepped on one end and hauled up with all his might. As the satisfying snap filled the air, he cried, "Ahhhhh! Help! They're everywhere! Help!"

That worked, perhaps too well.

Sputtering curses, the guards grabbed their rifles and charged toward Teven. He didn't stick around to see how many followed.

***

Jira (March) 17, 1560
Temporary Camp, Morden Lowlands, Path to Fort Riden

Teven's cry for help froze Kayleen's heart, but the anotechs assured her he was fine. It was not part of the plan, but it made a weird sort of sense and worked well. Most of the guards rushed toward the disturbance. Shaking her head, she poured tamitin powder into any container she thought the guards might use. She smiled when one jug marked water emitted the sharp stench of ale. A generous portion of powder found its way into the jug. She had to be careful not to knock out the prisoners, but she doubted they would be treated to the ale.

When the last of the powder had been poured, Kayleen considered slipping away to wait. Then, she had a better idea. Quickly, she found the supply tent and started searching. She found some nice blankets and spare tents. She thought about donning a spare uniform but dismissed the idea. Kezem's armies weren't big on assigning female soldiers escort details. After dumping a sack of potatoes, Kayleen filled the bag with several tents, kerlinblades, kerlak pistols, and serlak pistols. She forwent the bulky blankets.

Finding a bunch of ration packs, Kayleen threw the whole stack into her bag of purloined goodies. On second thought, she opened a grain bar and ate it as she waited for Teven. They would have to wait until most of the guards were neutralized before looking for Garrett Rimton. She finished the bar and tossed the wrapper into the corner. To her surprise, she felt some of the anotechs leave her and move toward the wrapper. She watched it disintegrate then felt the anotechs re-enter her right hand.

That was weird. Point taken. No more littering.

Part of Kayleen felt guilty for stealing, but she reasoned that the supplies had probably been stolen from good people already. She was merely redeeming what had already been lost. The more she thought about the mines, taxes, raids, fear, graft, and thousands of other wrongs with their roots in Kezem's government, the less guilt she felt.

Something rustled behind her. Kayleen whipped her head around but not before a hand covered her mouth and nose. She stiffened. Her heart slammed into her throat.

"It's me! Don't scream. It's okay. It's only me!" Teven spoke into her ear.

Anger replaced her fear, but relief overpowered both emotions. Kayleen relaxed, leaning back against him. Slowly, his hand released her mouth and nose. He continued to hold her.

"Teven, you scared a year off my life!" she scolded in a loud whisper.

"I'm sorry. I couldn't think of a better way to quietly get your attention."

The deed was done so she let it drop. They sat in silence, enjoying each other's company and waiting for the grumbling soldiers to go to sleep.

An hour later, a strange silence settled over the camp.

"Naptime for all the good soldier boys," Kayleen whispered. She struggled to her feet and rubbed her legs to regain some feeling.

Lacking a better plan, they resorted to direct interrogation. They settled into a pattern. Kayleen would poke a prisoner, while Teven held his hand over their mouth.

"Are you Garrett Rimton?" Kayleen would ask. At a negative head shake, she would ask her second question. "Do you know who is?"

Teven would cautiously lift his hand to hear the answer. The interrogations were not as quiet as they had hoped, but the fourth prisoner questioned shook his head yes and looked at her with wide eyes.

"Your grandfather sent us to fetch you," Kayleen quietly informed. "Let's go."

"I can't!" Garrett said, visibly upset. "They've got us chained together."

Kayleen hissed in frustration. That would hinder things.

"Teven—"

"I'm on it. One key coming up."

While Teven searched for the key, Kayleen roused the other sleepy prisoners. A confused babble rose, threatening to grow exponentially.

"Quiet!" she ordered. "We're getting out of here. Anyone who wants to go home is welcome to come along." She cocked her head to the side and listened hard. The anotechs were trying to tell her something.

"I'm not going!" one boy announced, breaking her train of thought. "I'm going to be a Royal Guard and protect Lord Kezem from those Ranger terrorists." Superiority dripped from every word.

"Then you're headed for the wrong camp," Kayleen retorted. "The Royal Guard is based in Rammon and Azhel. Anyone who wants a career in or near the palace must compete in the Festival of Future Fighters and finish the Kireshana. Fort Riden recruits go to the Huz Mon salt mines, Azhel energy plants, Idonian glass factories, or some obscure army post. Trust me. It won't be the glorious life you're picturing." She didn't know why she was arguing with the child. He seemed like a nice fit for the RLA.

"I'll scream," the boy threatened. "Then, they'll capture you and take *you* to the salt mines!"

Scream and I hit you, Kayleen silently promised. *On second thought, why wait?*

Holding out her hand out in a non-threatening manner, Kayleen said, "Hey, take it easy. Not everyone wants to join the RLA. They at least deserve the chance to choose." With each soft word, Kayleen stepped closer to the troublemaker. Her movements were fluid and graceful. The swift crack of her right hand across the side of his neck barely rustled the air.

The kid dropped unconscious.

No one spoke.

Teven returned and surveyed the scene with grim amusement.

"Well, that ends that discussion," he said cheerfully. "I'll just release you all and you can choose. Except you, Garrett, your grandfather made your choice. Your mother's worried sick."

The last statement convinced Garrett it was for the best. Kayleen was grateful for that. She didn't think her nerves could take much more excitement. As Teven unlocked the chains holding the last prisoner, Kayleen finally heard what the anotechs were trying to tell her: **Touch chains to unlock.**

"Oh!" Kayleen exclaimed. Everyone looked at her confused. "No keys next time, Teven."

He nodded.

Twenty-eight of the thirty-one children left with Teven and Kayleen. They stopped by the supply tent for the pack she had readied. The sheer number of escapees forced them to grab extra food and tents. They split the group in half to increase the chance some would make it back to Resh. The tamitin powder would work for several hours, but that was a small window to rely upon, especially since their pursuers knew their destination.

Chapter 28:
Ritand Refugees

Jira (March) 20, 1560-Jira (March) 21, 1560
City of Resh

Fear prompted them to move quickly. By some miracle, both Teven and Kayleen safely guided their charges back to Resh within three days. Returning them to proper families proved a bit chaotic, but it was a task Niklos Mikhail McGreven undertook happily. He explained that the children would be sent to safe houses scattered around the western half of Reshner where they would be shielded from Lord Kezem's wrath. Teven wasn't surprised when the former Ranger announced he had another job for them.

Tired but still experiencing intoxicating success, Teven listened to Master Niklos.

"I have gathered more funds from the parents of those you rescued," Master Niklos began. "By all rights, the money should be yours, but please, hear me out. The Ritand Quarter on the west side of Resh is sorely in need of help. Twelve more community shelters need to be built soon. Winter is coming. The government has dragged its feet for months. Governor Zelene would have set it right promptly. Governor Luvak speaks of freeing funds, but he doesn't care. There's no food and scarcely any medicine."

"And you want to use the money to help them," Teven concluded, nodding his head.

"And you want us to build the shelters," Kayleen added. She sounded less than ecstatic about the idea but that was most likely the exhaustion showing. Dark circles and bloodshot eyes attested to the fact that she had had little rest on the return journey to Resh.

Niklos nodded, looking guilty. He frowned.

"Here are the four thousand kefs I owe you for rescuing Garrett plus the five hundred from his parents. The other families put forth another three thousand. I will give you the money if you ask it." His eyes begged them not to ask, and his hand hovered protectively over the pile of kef notes.

Teven looked to Kayleen for support. Her approving nod was almost imperceptible.

"Keep the money, Master Niklos," said Teven. "We will help as long as we can, but I want to reach Mount Palean before the winter storms."

"Thank you." Master Niklos solemnly bowed his head.

"There's just one catch," Teven added. "One of our companions, Quasim, is from Ritand. Help us search for information on his family or a family willing to take him in."

"You ask much, Prince Teven, but you give much as well," Niklos said, bowing from the waist. The title flowed easily from his tongue.

"You might want to be careful about saying that name," Kayleen cautioned. "I know, you know, and Teven knows, but if Lord Kezem finds out there's going to be big trouble."

"Your words are wise, Kayleen." He looked like he wanted to say more but stopped himself. "I pray the day hastens when such caution will be unnecessary. Until then, I will be careful. Now, if you will excuse me, I will go order concrete and wood for the shelters."

Thus dismissed, Teven and Kayleen stumbled to their rented unit. A wonderful shower and a few hundred questions later, Teven collapsed onto his bedroll and fell into a deep sleep.

He opened his eyes the next morning to a vision of his mother. She wore the same exquisite robes of purple and green he had seen her in the first time.

"Greetings, Teven, I apologize for placing such responsibility upon you. House Minstel has been granted great power. With that power comes the duty to care for the people. They are stubborn and foolish at times but good at heart. Misused power leads to tragedy. The truth of the anotechs awaits you in Loresh. Go there if you need a more thorough lesson on abuse of power." She smiled that sad smile he had come to expect. *"Lord Kezem seems bent on reliving the past. I am tired now and must go face my destiny. May Riden watch over you, my son."*

The vision disappeared, leaving Teven feeling empty. The finality of his mother's message tore at his heart. He could replay the message, of course, but that would only twist a blade through the pain. His emotions ran the usual course of anger, despair, resolve, and pain. Silent tears fell, and he mentally railed against the universe that left him alone in so many ways.

Kayleen sat down beside him. Along their Kireshana, a vision would come to him with some word of wisdom. Before, she had let him deal with the pain as he saw fit, but this time, she drew near and embraced him.

"Another dream?" she whispered into his dark hair.

A wave of embarrassment washed over Teven. Tears were unbecoming. He drew in several ragged breaths and willed the stream to a stop. There must be some unwritten rule that princes shouldn't cry, especially in front of their friends.

"A vision, of my mother … just before she left to face Kezem," he said.

Kayleen nodded.

"A last message," she said, sensing his fear and embarrassment. "Don't be afraid, Teven. Tears are natural; don't fight them."

"I want to do what she expects of me, but I don't know what that is!"

"What did she say?" asked Kayleen.

Teven repeated his mother's message word for word.

"That's it; her last words to me," he finished.

"Savor them, Tev," Kayleen encouraged. "They're gifts. Not many mothers get to say goodbye."

He knew she was right but couldn't shake the grief. Then, it hit him that she might mean more by that statement.

"Did your mother or father say goodbye?" he wondered.

"No, my earliest memories are of the Ranger camp." Kayleen gave him a weak smile. "But sometimes I dream they're still alive somewhere, searching for me. It's a foolish notion, but it gives me something to cling to."

"It could be true. We both know what happened to my parents, but not knowing about yours leaves room to hope," Teven said.

"Speaking of hope, we have some to bring to the Ritand refugees," Kayleen said.

Her words spurred him to action.

Within ten minutes, Teven was dressed in dark brown pants and a beige shirt. Suddenly, it dawned on him that he and Kayleen were alone. Jal must have taken the others out to the site early. He hesitated before adding his belt with the banistick and resisted the urge to take one of the kerlinblades. He didn't want the refugees to feel threatened. Kayleen wore her travel cloak so she could take a kerlinblade and a pistol. Teven preferred the banistick anyway.

As they left, Kayleen handed him a large chunk of wheat bread and a small flask of appola juice. He swallowed the bread whole and poured the juice down his throat with such speed he almost choked. Kayleen just shook her head at him. They hurried down block after block until they came to the grim gates surrounding the refugee section.

A grumpy man dressed in a rumpled, rusty brown RLA uniform stood stiffly at his post. He sniffed with disgust.

"Turn back or be prepared to smell like filth for a week!" he warned. "Gotta keep watch or these wretches will pollute the whole city."

Teven didn't trust himself to speak properly, so he said nothing. As if the high fence was not enough of a change, the concrete stopped and the dwellings turned to rickety shacks at best, tarps thrown over half-rotted sticks at worst. It was like stepping into another world. Their steps automatically slowed.

"I don't smell anything strange," Teven whispered, as they hurried further into the dismal wreckage of broken lives.

He felt eyes watching them and let his gaze wander from one shack to another. Dressed in rags, a few of the younger children played with the dirt. The older ones stared blankly, having lost interest in that small joy. Several children coughed. Many of the refugees were short, bipedal creatures with flat ears, three large black eyes spaced evenly across their faces, and smooth olive skin. A fair number were human of varying skin tones.

Teven cast a glance at Kayleen's troubled expression. Her walk stiffened as she concentrated on something. Then, she stopped walking altogether, drew in a breath, and paled.

"Wait," she said, reaching for Teven's arm. "Tell the anotechs to stop filtering your sense of smell for just a moment."

He did so. The stench of a thousand rotting things hit him at once. He let the anotechs continue their wonderful work.

"I see what he means," said Teven.

"I don't think there's a good sanitation system here," Kayleen noted. It was an understatement. Rotten cores of unidentifiable things lay in the streets covered with flitnits and the grubs of many other insects.

"Can we do anything?" Teven asked.

"We'll find out," Kayleen said, continuing down the street. "Let's find Master Niklos and the others."

At Niklos's name, an older boy looked up.

"He's down Hope Street planning the new shelter project." The boy struggled to his feet. "I'll take you there." He swayed a moment, and Teven thought he might fall over.

"Are you okay? When was the last time you ate anything?" Kayleen asked, stepping to the boy's side and reaching out to steady him.

"There are six others in my house," the boy responded, glaring at Kayleen. He raised his head defiantly and removed his elbow from her grip.

She gave Teven a bewildered, pained look. He shrugged and followed the boy.

"Ah, Crispin, I see you bring the young benefactors," greeted Master Niklos. "Come, come, I am eager to show you the plans."

Crispin said nothing but looked at Teven and Kayleen with a little more respect.

Niklos put them to work pounding nails into boards arranged to form walls. It was early afternoon before Jal and the others made an appearance.

Karric and Jenell bowed in greeting.

"The midday meal will be ready soon. Master Niklos says you can stop now," Karric announced.

"I'm glad we have his approval," Kayleen said with a grin.

"Come outside," Jenell said. Her excitement seemed a bit much for a simple meal.

Teven hefted the wall section they had just completed. Stepping outside, he was surprised to see a large crowd. He froze, holding the wall in front like a shield.

"Don't just stand there," Niklos snapped, eyes twinkling. "Greet the grateful people."

Teven tried to retreat into the doorway but was blocked by Kayleen.

"Wrong way, hero." Kayleen pointed the other way.

"Traitor," Teven shot back, setting the wall section down.

After the morning of hard work, the midday meal led into a celebration of thanks for the much-needed supplies. Teven and his friends were stuffed with many Ritand treats. Part of him felt guilty for eating their food, even if he did help buy it, but he had enough sense to know the cultural affront it would be to refuse. He vowed to work harder for these people. Winter was coming, and many would perish if the shelters were not finished in time.

***

Jira (March) 22, 1560-Zeri (June) 1, 1560
City of Resh

Despite Teven's wish to reach the mountains before winter, the small band returned to the refugee section of Resh every day through the rest of Jira (March) and through the months of Enis (April) and Retsi (May) until the beginning of Zeri (June). The shelters hastily erected before the first snowfalls in the middle of Enis (April) proved to be just the beginning of a long list of projects that needed doing. The labor kept their muscles toned, and daily practice duels and shooting contests kept their fighting skills sharp. It also entertained the refugees, especially the children.

In the few spare hours, everyone but Kayleen performed a variety of tasks to scrape together kefs to continue their journey. Kayleen spent her time planning and directing a waste management system. By their fourth week of work, the air around the refugee section smelled much cleaner. She had wrestled funds for proper pipes and contractors from the stingy governor and the city council. The trick had been to keep pushing the idea that the sections which bordered the refugee sector would be less prone to disease and free of the awful stench.

Master Niklos kept his promise to seek information on Quasim's family. Eventually, he tracked down an older sister who agreed to care for the boy, despite a growing family of her own. Quasim was harder to convince, but the weeks among his people had endeared their simple life to him.

As Teven walked Quasim to the sister's shack in the southern portion of the refugee sector, he noticed the boy was unusually quiet.

"What's wrong?" asked Teven.

"You don't want me to travel with you!" Quasim complained.

Teven stopped and looked down into the boy's hurt eyes.

"It's not that, Quasim. We enjoy your company. You're a great help, but we want you to be happy. The rest of the Kireshana will be rough. I don't want to put you through that."

"I would be a burden," said Quasim sadly.

Teven said nothing; he struggled to sort the swirling feelings inside him. A sense of foreboding had been on his heart for several weeks now.

"You are a fine traveling companion, Quasim, but there is danger ahead," said Teven. "Danger I must face alone."

"You're leaving the others?" Quasim asked, sounding part pleased and part upset.

"I don't know," Teven answered honestly. "Jenell and Karric aren't ready to go on yet."

"You'll come back, right?" Quasim asked with some concern.

"If I can," said Teven.

They came to Quasim's new home and said goodbye. A lump rose in Teven's throat. He swallowed hard.

The simple conversation weighed upon him until he returned to the small rental unit. He didn't bother greeting his friends.

"We have to leave," he announced.

"Jenell has a cold," Jal commented with a frown. "She shouldn't travel right now."

A deep, wracking cough came from the back corner as if to confirm Jal's words.

"I know," Teven said calmly. He hadn't really known Jenell's cold had worsened, but it confirmed his guess that he and Kayleen would travel alone. If it got any worse Jal
might have to use the anotechs. "Stay here with Jenell and Karric. Master Niklos insisted on giving us four thousand kefs for our labor. That should be enough to pay the rent for another few months. Kayleen and I will take some weapons and supplies. Follow whenever you can."

Loud protests answered his plan from everyone slated to stay behind.

"I'm fine!" the half-delirious Jenell insisted.

Karric's firm hand on her shoulder kept her in the bedroll.

"No, you're not," Karric said. "But I am; I'm going."

"Something's not right. Our friends are nervous," Jal said cautiously. They had never explained the anotechs to the younger derringers and now did not seem like the best time to start. "Karric, stay with Jenell. I must talk some sense into Teven and Kayleen." That seemed to mollify Karric and the sick one.

"Jal, you know we travel faster alone," Teven began, once they were outside.

Jal raised a hand to wave off more reasons.

"I don't like it," said Jal. "Lord Kezem's plans will reveal themselves soon, and you are walking into a trap."

"He doesn't even know about me," Teven protested.

"Doesn't matter—" Jal began.

"They need you," Kayleen interrupted. "You have trained us well, but Jenell and Karric will not survive the Kireshana alone."

"I suppose not," Jal admitted, letting Kayleen switch the subject.

"Trap or not, Jal, we've got to go," Teven said.

The argument continued in circles for an hour. Eventually, Kayleen slipped away to pack. Finally, Jal insisted they take three thousand kefs with them and gave them some last-minute instructions on handling the anotechs.

Karric reluctantly helped them finish packing. Teven took him aside and spoke words of encouragement, reminding him to take care of Jenell and Jal. Kayleen slipped over to Jenell's bedroll and whispered similar encouragements. The hardest farewell was to Jal. Knowing the separation would only be temporary did not lessen the pain of parting with their friend.

Teven and Kayleen left Resh a little after dawn. They traveled down the familiar road south toward Fort Riden.

Chapter 29:
Trouble in Fort Riden

Zeri (June) 8, 1560
Entrance to Fort Riden, Morden Lowlands

After about a week, Teven McKnight and Kayleen Wellum finally reached Fort Riden, Lord Kezem's northwest stronghold. The fort was a city unto itself, complete with a small theater, barracks for up to four thousand soldiers, four taverns, and a prison capable of holding a few hundred captives.

As soon as they arrived, a gate guard directed them to an imposing set of heavy doors to their left. There, they checked in with the marksman manning the desk.

"What brings you to Fort Riden?" he asked, attempting to be friendly but coming off as bored. He didn't even bother looking up. A series of random circles across the paper in front of him also attested to boredom.

"We're derringers," Kayleen offered, stepping in front of Teven. They had agreed that the less people knew about him, the better.

Hearing a female voice, the marksman's head snapped up, and he shoved his drawings under a stack of official looking documents.

"You're late," he commented with a frown. "Most of the derringers were through here weeks ago."

"Our business in Resh kept us longer than expected," Kayleen explained, carefully telling him nothing. She gave the man a coy grin and leaned close as if to whisper a secret. "We've never been here. Where's the best inn? Is there anything we should know? Who's in charge?"

"That'd be Commander Arnold Glaiser, ma'am. You probably won't see him while you're here though. How long are you going to be here anyway?"

"A few days," Kayleen said vaguely, standing up straight. "Enough to rest up for the finish."

"Perry's Palace has the best rooms, and the tavern attached to it serves the best ale and wine," he informed, glancing about furtively. "And twenty kefs gets you a detailed tour of everything Fort Riden has to offer. Most derringers find the tour *very* interesting." His dark eyes lit up as he mentioned the tour.

Kayleen got the impression the man had a side business going on. She queried her anotechs for Teven's feelings on the matter and got a warm sense of approval.

"We'll take the tour, marksman …." Kayleen trailed off as she placed twenty kefs on the desk in front of the man.

"Weldon. Clive Weldon."

Kayleen worked hard to keep a straight face.

"And the tour is twenty kefs *each*," Weldon added.

"You'll get the other twenty when we get our tour," Kayleen assured him.

"Fine. Meet me outside this tower in an hour. That's when my shift ends."

They went to Perry's Palace and arranged for a room. There wasn't much to unpack so they spent the remaining time in the tavern listening to the off-duty soldiers chat. They wanted to learn the latest news from the palace but welcomed rumors as well.

"The commander's too easy on that boy of his," complained a mostly drunk lieutenant.

"I heard he tried to run away with one of them derringer dames that came through here last month," his drinking companion added.

"Aww, he didn't really want her," said the lieutenant. "The kid's not even ten! He just wants out of this blasted fort. Not that I blame the boy."

The conversation seemed mundane to Kayleen, so she focused on another. She only caught part of the conversation because the soldier and his two buddies were on their way out the door.

"—tried to put a hov engine fire out with water from Crystal Lake last week. Blew 'imself to bits."

Kayleen tuned in to a third conversation.

"I heard Lord Kezem's closing in on Gordon's band of misfits," a short, fuzzy creature commented.

Kayleen did not recognize the species, but that was nothing unusual considering her lack of experience with the wider universe. Most Rangers were humans, and Kayleen had grown up interacting with less than a half-dozen species.

"Alexi Gordon's a fine soldier. He could have had a great career," the being's drinking companion lamented. "Now, he'll just be another corpse on the Kesler Plains."

Kayleen continued scanning conversations. Her gaze fell upon a woman serving drinks to a surly looking man who sported a colorful left eye.

"I warned you to keep those paws to yourself," the woman chided. "Prisoner or not, that girl can pack a punch. Don't fret, dearie, Lord Kezem's personal guards will be here late tomorrow to pick her up."

Kayleen's ears perked up at the mention of Kezem's guards. Teven's expression also reflected interest.

"Shut up, Maybel," the man muttered, staring into the black ale swirling in the clear container he had clenched in his fists.

The woman shrugged and went away. She drew up to the table Teven and Kayleen had chosen.

"What can I get you dearies?" she asked in a syrupy voice.

"Do you have appola juice?" Teven asked.

"Ah, a good boy, very rare these days. She's got you whipped, don't she, love?" she said, winking.

"I'll have the same." Kayleen raised an eyebrow and gave the woman a cool stare.

Maybel bustled off to get their drinks. At this early hour, the tavern was sparsely populated. She returned in a moment with their order.

"What's got him down?" Teven jerked his head at the customer with the black eye.

"Who Jake? That's nothing. He'd been bothering a pretty derringer for a while. Then, last night, Commander Glaiser sent him in here to arrest her and her friends. She didn't take kindly to the arrest or his wandering hands and walloped him good."

"What were they arrested for?" Kayleen asked, trying not to sound too interested.

"Now, I don't like to tell no tales," Maybel hedged. She slid into the booth next to Teven and spoke in a whisper loud enough to be heard clear across the room. "But rumor has it the orders came from the top—the way top—as in Lord Kezem himself. The Commander's orders to arrest the derringers even say Royal Guards are coming to collect 'em."

"What did they do?" Kayleen pressed.

Maybel shrugged and waved her hand across her face like the question was a bad smell.

"It could have been anything, dearie. Lord Kezem's word is law. I don't ask no nosy questions. It's much safer that way."

"That's smart," Teven agreed.

Kayleen had the sudden urge to kick him but resisted when she realized he was trying to squeeze more information out of Maybel.

Suitably encouraged, Maybel continued to jabber.

"Some say these derringers hail from the palace. The one that gave Jake what he had coming arrived a few weeks ago but waited for the others. She obviously knew them. Criminals usually stick together, don't they? They probably killed someone or some such."

Subsequent theories were only more outlandish.

Kayleen sipped her drink. The tingling sensation on her tongue said there was more than appola juice in her glass, but the distraction it provided helped her control her tongue. Besides, it didn't taste too bad, just a little strange.

When the time for their tour approached, Kayleen rose.

"Excuse us. We have a meeting to attend now. You've been very kind." She tossed a few kefs onto the table, not waiting for a response.

Teven slipped out the other side of the booth to avoid Maybel.

"What do you think?" Teven asked quietly, once they had exited and were striding toward the tower where they would meet Clive Weldon.

"I think the prison just became part of our tour," Kayleen replied.

An extra sixty kefs added the prison to the Fort Riden tour. The first half-hour consisted of Clive Weldon listing off troop strengths and showing them the barracks and the supply rooms. In the armory, Clive hinted he might be able to sell them some fine weapons. Their last stop was the prison, which was in the same building as the armory.

What idiot planned that? Kayleen wondered.

She charmed Clive into letting them walk by the cell she sensed the derringers in. Fortunately, Clive was conceited enough to have several days' worth of good things to say about himself. All she had to do was get him started and fake interest. Their conversation allowed Teven to talk to some of the prisoners.

***

Zeri (June) 8, 1560
Same Day
Prison Block and Armory, Fort Riden, Morden Lowlands

Since they were conveniently in the same cell, Teven quickly located Lorian Petole and her companions. He remembered seeing the other two at the Festival of Future Fighters, but their names escaped him.

"Do you stand with those against Lord Kezem?" whispered Teven.

Lorian's dark brown eyes searched his. She got to her feet, approached the bars keeping her from freedom, and gripped them firmly.

"My loyalty will always be with Princess Rela Minstel," said Lorian evenly.

Teven gasped.

"You know her! She's alive?" His mother had said the Ralose Charm would protect Rela, but he had hardly expected the thing to work. Besides, knowing she should be alive and hearing as much from someone who knew her were two very different things.

"Of course, she's alive. Lord Kezem's life is linked to hers. He wouldn't dare harm her," said Lorian. "Hence our predicament," she added, gesturing to her friends. "We were raised with the princess to be hostages whenever Lord Kezem decided he wanted something from her. I guess that time approaches."

"Then you are my friends," Teven said, pushing down his anger and raising a hand to touch the lock. The lock obediently clicked open. He swung the heavy gate out.

Clive Weldon spun at the noise. Kayleen's eyes widened, but she reacted with characteristic swiftness. Before Marksman Weldon could utter a word, her right fist crashed into the back of his neck. He sank to the ground with a groan.

Kayleen peered down at him, hoping she hadn't caused permanent damage.

"Teven, tell me why I just knocked out our guide," said Kayleen.

"Because we're causing a small prison break," he replied, rushing up to Weldon and relieving the man of his kerlak pistol and their kefs. Then, setting the kerlak pistol for high stun, Teven systematically put the four prisoners he wasn't interested in down for naps. "Here," he said, tossing the pistol to Lorian. A plan formed as he spoke, "Try not to use it. We want to leave without having half the RLA after us."

"That's going to happen anyway," said Kayleen.

"Where are we going?" Lorian inquired, checking the pistol.

"You two are crazy," the other young woman remarked.

The anotechs identified her as Anabel Spitzer.

"I'll take crazy if it gets us out of here," the young man pointed out. **Marc Spitzer.**

"We'll continue with the Kireshana until we get to the Kesler Plains. Then, we can head south to Meritab. We should be able to get a hov there to take us back to Rammon," Kayleen said.

"What will we do in Rammon?" Lorian asked, growing more skeptical by the second.

"We'll figure that out when we get there," Teven said, forcing confidence into his voice.

"Shouldn't we be moving *away* from the palace?" Marc asked. "Just a thought, but isn't the point of escaping to deprive Kezem of hostages to use against Princess Rela?"

"We have to help her, Marc," Lorian insisted.

"Argue on the road," Kayleen hissed.

"Sorry. Oh, this is Marc and Anabel Spitzer. Who are you?"

"Kayleen Wellum. That's Teven McKnight. Now, if we're done with introductions, we should be on our way."

"We should wait until evening," Teven suggested.

They had a brief argument via the anotechs.

Kayleen looked at him impatiently but finally agreed.

***

Not wanting to risk going back to any of their rooms, they raided the armory and a supply room for new weapons and equipment. While the others packed supplies, Kayleen poked around the armory, hoping to find the special weapons Marksman Weldon had alluded to. She concentrated hard and let the anotechs search. They found nothing from a preliminary scan but admitted there was too much metal to get an accurate reading.

Practicing some of Jal's last-minute instructions, Kayleen stretched out her fingertips and gently touched the wall. Then, she imagined the anotechs flowing from her fingers. When she pushed too fast her right index finger began bleeding. The anotechs immediately repaired the small tear, but from then on, Kayleen proceeded with more caution.

Fifteen minutes later, Kayleen crouched on her haunches browsing the selection of special weapons. She took the few dozen flingers, ten shock nullifiers, two flash grenades, and several kerlinblade upgrade packs. The shock nullifiers would clamp onto the ends of banisticks and counter any energy influx.

After distributing the new toys, Kayleen made everyone eat a ration pack. They would have to run most of the night to put distance between themselves and the Fort Riden troops. She didn't want anyone fainting from hunger along the way.

Soon after they finished eating, a pair of guards entered with the evening meal. Lorian stunned them with the kerlak pistol and took their weapon belts. Then, she locked them in the cell she and her friends had vacated. The group forced themselves to eat the prison fare, in addition to the ration packs, knowing it might be their last warm meal for a while. They spent two more tense hours waiting for Fort Riden to settle down for the night.

Kayleen used the time to modify the banisticks and update the newly acquired kerlinblades. The chores provided a pleasant distraction.

A glance out the window revealed the sun's dying rays.

Patrols are still wandering around, but if we don't do something stupid, we should be able to stroll out the back checkpoint.

***

As Teven rounded the last corner before leaving the prison, he crashed into a boy who looked strangely familiar.

"Nate!" he said with wonder, elation, and fear.

"Teven? Is it really you?"

"What are you doing here?"

"I live here," his brother replied, grinning. "I came to see Marksman Weldon. One of the guards said he saw him going this way."

After a brief hesitation, the brothers awkwardly embraced. The rest of the group hung back to watch the exchange. Teven pulled back to study Nate. The six years had made quite a difference, but Nate was still just a boy. Teven's heart ached to see the hard look that came so easily to his little brother.

"What are you buying from Weldon?" asked Teven, protective instincts on high alert.

"Just a little Nespin spice." Nate's posture stiffened with defiance.

"Nate! That stuff will kill you," said Teven.

"No, boredom will kill me," Nate responded. It was then that Teven noticed Nate's pretty maroon uniform. It was obviously custom made for him. Feeling Teven's scrutiny, Nate pulled at a rank insignia. "Instant lieutenant, who'd have thought? It's the privilege of being Commander Glaiser's son."

"Don't rush it, Nate," Teven said gently.

You're nine!

"But I'm missing so many adventures!"

"Teven, we need to leave," Kayleen said. She moved to a position behind Nate.

"I'd drink to that if my father would let me drink. What's your hurry?" Nate asked, casually leaning against a cold wall and crossing his arms.

A torrent of emotions threatened Teven's ability to function. He forced himself to breathe regularly.

"Nate, promise me you'll forget you saw us." He didn't want to hurt his little brother, but they couldn't afford to be caught.

For the first time, Nate noticed the others.

"Hey! You're those derringers they arrested yesterday!"

Kayleen didn't wait for him to shout a warning. She grabbed his mouth and neck and applied pressure until he passed out.

Teven watched with horror, unable to move.

Gently lowering Nate's unconscious form to the ground, Kayleen apologized with her eyes.

"He'll be fine, but we should go," she said.

The small group dragged Teven out of the prison where the cold night air slammed into them and brought him back to his senses. They strolled casually toward the back entrance to Fort Riden, which would place them on a southeast road to Mount Palean.

Once out of sight, they broke into a swift trot. They needed to place as much distance between themselves and the fort as possible. Their initial pace was slower than Teven would have liked due to the need to conceal their trail. He felt hunted.

Less than a day from Fort Riden, the small band of fugitives began dodging search patrols. Teven had not expected the commander to be happy with the escape, but he hadn't expected him to empty Fort Riden either. News must have reached Lord Kezem that his prisoners had escaped. Occasionally, Teven felt their mysterious guardian watching.

Even Lorian sensed it.

"Someone's watching us," said Lorian.

"We know," said Kayleen.

"We don't know who it is, but someone's been protecting us for months," Teven clarified.

"That's odd," Marc commented. "Same thing happened to us."

"I don't care who he is as long as he's not shooting at us," said Kayleen.

Twice, they got caught by small patrols, and twice, they fought their way free.

Teven learned to appreciate Lorian's kerlinblade skills. He was also relieved to know that the fair-haired siblings could hold their own in a fight. It gave him a keen sense of satisfaction to know that Lord Kezem's finest instructors had taught his new companions how to fight. The third patrol they came across were dead, victims of their own explosives. Teven shuddered to think of Kayleen or one of his other friends stepping on a mine.

Once they were two days away from Fort Riden, Teven began to breathe easier. On that second evening, they risked a small fire to have a warm meal. Exhausted, Lorian, Marc, and Anabel went to sleep immediately after the three plains rabbits were devoured. Teven and Kayleen sat by the fire and listened to the chatter of various insects and small creatures that populated the Morden Lowlands.

"Listen," Kayleen whispered.

"To what?" Teven's hand automatically reached for a weapon.

"Life," she said softly.

He did as instructed and found it beautiful. The twittering, clacking, buzzing, and screeching created a lovely natural symphony. Teven's hands stopped searching for his weapons and found Kayleen's left hand. He gave it a reassuring squeeze, before leaning back against his pack. He closed his eyes and concentrated on identifying the creatures.

Chapter 30:
Conquering Mount Palean

Zeri (June) 17, 1560
Morden Lowlands

For more than a week, they struck a convoluted path to throw off pursuit. Finally, they arrived at the foot of Mount Palean. Lorian Petole stared up at the steep slopes.

A long, low groan came from Kayleen.

"My feelings precisely," Lorian remarked.

Sunlight bounced off the white mountains, causing Lorian to shade her eyes, but Kayleen seemed unaffected.

"One day's not a very long time," Lorian said.

"At least we have good motivation," Kayleen replied, waving toward the long road behind them. Distant smoke announced patrols preparing their morning meal.

"Agreed," Lorian whispered.

They checked in with the man living at the foot of the mountains.

He warned them to watch for falling ice and other dangers, urging them to reconsider attempting the climb.

"This is a very bad time of year to be doing this," said the guide.

"It's more exciting this way." Lorian flashed him a tight smile.

The man grunted and proceeded to supply them with spike strips for their boots and thick gloves to aid their climb.

"You'll have to climb straight up on three different occasions. I suggest you choose a leader wisely. There should be a row of small flags on the top, but if there aren't any left, hand this cloth to Kladder when you get to the other side." The man gave Anabel a blue and green handkerchief.

They tied themselves to each other with ropes through their belts. Kayleen was chosen to lead, since she was the only one with significant climbing experience. Teven had been dragged out to climb short cliffs several times, but Mount Palean was on a completely different level. If they had had three days to do it, the climb would have been simple, even enjoyable, but a one-day deadline called for unsafe haste. The challenge was designed to conquer those who had the strength for the Kireshana but lacked cunning, endurance, or courage.

The first hour of ascent was easy, the second grew arduous, and Lorian found herself gasping by the third hour.

Kayleen called for a short break.

"I can't ... feel ... my feet," Anabel complained. She began to remove her left boot.

"Keep those on," Kayleen instructed.

Lorian felt there was something odd about the way she said it. After a few seconds, it occurred to her that Kayleen sounded completely normal.

"But my feet hurt!" said Anabel.

Kayleen concentrated, weighing the consequences of an unmentioned plan.

"Give me your hand," she commanded Anabel.

"What?" asked Anabel, looking baffled.

Instead of repeating herself, Kayleen reached out and touched Anabel's gloved hand.

"Ouch! What was that?" asked Anabel.

"They're called anotechs, and they'll help your blood circulate better. Be nice to them; I want them back later," Kayleen said with a teasing grin.

Lorian opened her mouth to request a more thorough explanation.

"It's a long story," Teven warned. "We should continue. I'll tell you on the way." With that, he reached out and touched her arm.

She felt a sharp prick. Then, she felt a rush of warmth spread through her body.

"Whoa! No, no, no. None of that for me thanks," Marc protested, as Teven reached over to touch his arm.

"It's okay, Marc; it really works," Lorian assured her friend, amazed at how good she felt.

They began climbing again. As they did, Teven explained what he knew about anotechs, which wasn't much.

Marc held out for another twenty minutes, but as they approached the first vertical climb, he broke down and let Teven give him some anotechs.

"I can barely feel my arms," he said.

"Serves you right for refusing help," Lorian said unsympathetically.

Kayleen started the vertical climb. Marc followed then Anabel, Lorian, and Teven.

Lorian felt her arms tremble when she was a third of the way to the top. The supply pack strapped to her back grew heavier every second. She reached carefully for a more suitable handhold so she could rest a moment. A cry from above drew her attention.

"Look out!" called Kayleen.

A rock the size of Lorian's head came barreling down the mountain. Without thinking, Lorian threw her body to the left and scrambled for a new handhold. Just as her hand closed around a sturdy rock, Lorian felt Anabel's full weight on her belt. A surprised cry escaped her. More confused shouts came from above, but Lorian's eyes were clenched shut as she concentrated on gripping her rock. She fervently hoped her belt wouldn't break or pull her pants off. The few seconds it took Anabel to get a new hold on the mountain seemed like a lifetime to Lorian. When the danger passed, she willed her hands to release the rock. Ten minutes later, she gratefully took Marc's hand and let him haul her up onto the small plateau.

"Let's not do that again," Lorian said, when her breathing returned to a semi-normal rate.

"Sorry, we've got to do it twice more," Kayleen said, "but I vote we eat before taking on this next stretch." She placed a gloved hand on the rock wall rising straight up into a cloud in front of her.

Over ration bars, Lorian, Marc, and Anabel talked about their life in the palace.

"It's got its hardships but we poor, humble servants survive," Marc concluded.

"What's Princess Rela like?" asked Teven.

Lorian detected more than mild interest in his tone, and his deep green eyes looked hungry for information. There was also a buried pain that Lorian could not explain. She pushed these observations aside to answer him.

"She's frustrated."

"Has been for years," Marc added.

"What does she look like?" Kayleen asked, though Lorian got the impression the question would have come from Teven sooner or later.

"She's pretty—"

"Oh, Lorian, you do our princess a great injustice!" Anabel exclaimed. She spoke directly to Teven. "She's gorgeous. Her crystal blue eyes are like rare jewels redeemed from the depths of the South Asrien Sea. Her light brown hair's so soft that—"

"I'm sorry," Marc interrupted. "My sister reads too much romantic sappy stuff."

"You know I'm right, Marc. I've seen the way you look at the princess," Anabel teased.

Marc shrugged and nodded agreeably.

"How does he look at the princess, Anabel?" Teven asked slowly. A muscle in his right arm twitched.

Detecting a shift in Teven's demeanor, Lorian defended Marc.

"Like any man with eyes. Princess Rela is indeed beautiful like her mother." Lorian could swear Teven flinched at mention of the former queen. "I was only a child when Lord Kezem claimed the throne, but I saw Queen Reia once or twice. Her image is forever etched in my mind."

"I know the feeling," Teven replied dryly.

The shadow of a grin touched Kayleen's face.

Teven rose, and everyone took that as a sign to move on.

There were no more mishaps on the next vertical climb, but it was a good fifteen meters more than the last one and left everyone short of breath. It also contained fewer handholds. At one spot near the top, Lorian couldn't find any place to hold. The wind picked up, whipping through her clothes and touching her with its cold breath. She clung to the rock surface and endured a barrage of tiny ice flakes. A few tears escaped and froze, further adding to her misery.

The next segment consisted of a slippery slope at a forty-five degree angle. Teven and Kayleen both took the lead, practically dragging the others along by the rope. Lorian held her own during this part, but her legs shook with fatigue.

"We've got four hours of daylight left!" Teven shouted. "We've got to move faster!"

It was not pleasant news. Thinking of the constant danger Princess Rela faced, Lorian found the strength to push on. Being confined to the palace had made Rela naïve but not stupid. Lorian admired her friend's easy affection. For as long as Lorian could remember, Sarie had charged her with keeping Rela safe and informed. She had done her best so far, and she would not let the princess down now.

Were Lord Kezem's fate not linked to the princess, my blade would have been buried in him long ago.

Lorian was pulled away from her thoughts by the third and final wall standing between them and Mount Palean's peak. With her resolve fortified by warm memories, Lorian scaled the wall like she had been climbing her whole life. She knew exactly where to place her hands and feet. This time, she was a half-step behind Anabel in reaching the plateau.

They ate the next meal while climbing to the peak. At the top, they took a moment to enjoy the view. The Riden Mountains stretched out to the north as far as the eye could see. Behind them, to the west, Fort Riden looked like it could fit in an infant's palm. Smoke rose from the southwest where the Imberg Tosh Mines and processing plants belched smoke into the air. To the south, the city of Ritten appeared as an ungainly bump on the vast flatness of the Kevloth Plains. To the east and northeast, the gorgeous, colorful Kesler Plains and Riden Flats seemed to go on forever. In between, Lake Ceree showed up as a glittering strip of blue.

Lorian found no words to capture the beauty.

"I've got one!" Marc exclaimed triumphantly. He held up a frozen stick with a piece of red cloth tied to it.

"Great, Marc, great. Make me deaf while you're announcing your wonderful discovery," Anabel said, rubbing her left ear. The move brushed some frost crystals from her short, blond hair. "Besides, we don't need it since we have the blue and green cloth."

The descent was more harrowing than the ascent. Several times, one or more of the group slipped, pulling everyone down the slope at unsafe speeds. The most terrifying moment for Lorian came when Marc slipped and fell sideways into Kayleen and Anabel, tossing both young women from the mountain. Their surprised screams were drowned out by Lorian's own scream as she, Marc, and Teven followed them headfirst. Fortunately, they landed in a snowbank five meters below the cliff they had tumbled from. Despite the danger, they remained tethered together.

The sun had weakened the ice on this side of the mountain. As they neared the bottom, a solid crack split the air. Lorian's heart stopped and she looked up to see a wall of ice and snow headed their way.

"Run!" Kayleen, Marc, and Teven cried simultaneously.

They took off, but Anabel tripped on the rope, slowing progress. By the time everyone had regained their feet, the wall of snow slammed into them. The five friends flew a good six meters before landing one by one. Anabel landed hard on her left arm, which responded with an audible crack. Tears flowed freely as she clutched her left arm and opened her mouth in a silent scream. Everyone gathered around her.

"Oh, no, now we're in for it," Marc commented. "She doesn't do pain well."

Anabel gritted her teeth and glared daggers at her brother. Blood started seeping through Anabel's sleeve and dripped onto the snow. The shock of seeing blood brought on bone-wracking sobs that shook the wounded arm, which increased the pain and resulted in more sobs.

Lorian felt helpless. She could set a simple fracture, but this one was far from simple.

"Calm down, Anabel," Kayleen commanded. She removed her gloves, touched Anabel's right arm, and closed her eyes to concentrate.

Anabel passed out.

"What did you do to her?" Marc grabbed Kayleen's right shoulder.

"I put her to sleep so she wouldn't feel the pain," Kayleen answered, shrugging off his grip.

"Get me a thermal blanket," Teven ordered, already loosening Anabel's travel cloak and slicing the sleeve of her shirt away. "Lorian, see if you can set up a tent around us. It's going to be dark soon, and the wind will pick up."

Marc ripped into his pack trying to find a thermal blanket. It took him a moment to find one and tear it open.

Teven took the blanket and wrapped it tightly around Anabel.

"Marc, take the flag to the cabin and tell Kladder we're going to be here for a while. See if he has a bed he can spare for her," Kayleen ordered, knowing they needed to get Marc away from the sight of Anabel's injury.

Lorian built a tent around Teven, Kayleen, and Anabel. It was difficult because she had to work without moving them. With her task done, Lorian entered the tent to watch Teven and Kayleen work. Kayleen had started a small fire by the door and was filling a pot with snow to make water. While the water warmed, she added a packet of sterilizing chemicals.

"Can I help?" Lorian inquired.

"Hold her still. I think she's waking," Teven answered.

Lorian rushed to Anabel's side and held her shoulders down. She watched Kayleen dip a cloth in the sterile water and toss it to Teven. He braced himself, used the cloth to cleanse the wound, and slid a bone back beneath Anabel's skin. The sight of blood seeping out of the wound turned Lorian's stomach. She tried to look away but couldn't. A muffled cry came from Anabel who suddenly fought Lorian's grip. Kayleen lent her weight to Anabel's legs so she wouldn't kick Teven while he worked. Lorian looked down and noticed the makeshift gag for the first time. Poor Anabel was as pale as the snow around her.

"Ssshhhh, it's okay; it's over," Lorian murmured, stroking Anabel's sweaty hair. She moved her head so tears wouldn't fall on her friend.

"Kayleen, are the bandages ready?" Teven asked hoarsely. He looked pale as well.

"Yes, but they're still hot," Kayleen replied.

"Well, cool them down fast," said Teven. "The anotechs are slowing the blood flow, but they can't stop it. She's bleeding all over the place here."

Lorian watched fascinated as Kayleen gathered several strips of a former shirt that lay on the snow beside the pot in which they had been sterilized. A minute later, she handed the strips to Teven who wrapped Anabel's wound tightly. Then, Teven and Kayleen placed their hands on Anabel, bowed their heads, and closed their eyes. Lorian remembered how the anotechs had helped her climb Mount Palean. She peered down at her poor friend through tear-filled eyes. Anabel's face flushed a bright pink then turned a deeper, frightening shade of red.

Lorian's alarmed cry brought Teven and Kayleen back to the present. "She's burning up!"

"Let the anotechs fight for her," Kayleen said.

"Will she die?" A lump of fear lodged in Lorian's throat.

"Hard to say, but I don't think so," said Teven, shrugging wearily. "The anotechs are helping her fight the infection. She should be okay in the morning."

"How is she?" Marc asked, entering the tent.

Teven repeated his prediction. Kladder did have a bed to offer Anabel, but at this point, no one wanted to move her. Instead, all five weary travelers crammed into the tiny tent and huddled for warmth. Marc fell asleep holding Anabel's good hand. Lorian settled herself on Anabel's other side. Teven slept in front of the tent's entrance, and Kayleen squeezed in between Lorian and the tent wall. Aside from Anabel, nobody slept well that night.

Chapter 31:
Terrible Truth

Zeri (June) 18, 1560-Zeri (June) 25, 1560
Kesler Plains

Next morning, Teven and Kayleen collected some of their anotechs.

Anabel awoke looking pale but much better.

"What happened?" she asked, lifting her bandaged arm and studying it curiously.

"You don't remember flying through the air, landing on your arm, snapping it like a twig, bleeding all over the place, and scaring me half to death?" Marc stared at his sister incredulously.

She shook her head.

"Was it bad?" asked Anabel.

Lorian chuckled first, then Marc, then everyone.

"Yeah, it was bad," Marc answered, rubbing his stiff neck.

"Squeeze," Teven ordered, taking Anabel's left hand in his.

She grimaced but managed a weak squeeze.

"Good; it's healing," said Teven. "The anotechs have reinforced the bone, but it'll take some time to completely heal. I suggest you use your other arm as a landing pad for a while."

"Thank you, Doctor Teven. I'll try to remember that," said Anabel.

They ate a hearty morning meal of fried eggs and korver jerky, courtesy of Kladder and his wife Nora. Then, they packed their tent and continued their journey into the Kesler Plains. The weather on this side of the Riden Mountains was much nicer. Winter on the Kesler Plains could be very brutal but was usually mercifully short.

A week later and well into the Kesler Plains, Kayleen grew weary of seeing one gorgeous field of grain after another. A sea of fresh purple flowers made her recall something her father had said. She frowned and concentrated. Since when was she able to remember anything about her father?

Kayleen could almost hear his voice saying, *"When in come the iras, out goes the winter."*

"Iras," Kayleen murmured at the memory.

"Did you say something?" asked Teven.

"My father used to talk about iras," Kayleen said, gesturing to the pretty purple flowers. More of the memory returned to her. "We used to take a hov from Rammon to my uncle's farm on the Kesler Plains. Sometimes we would stop to watch small animals hop in and out of the iras."

"I thought you couldn't remember your father," Teven said.

"I couldn't but now I can. Strange," Kayleen said with a one-shoulder shrug.

"Very strange," echoed Teven.

"Where are you from?" Lorian asked.

The anotechs unlocked new information every second, and a deep longing to know her parents swept over Kayleen.

"Rammon, I think. My parents had connections to the palace, strong connections."

"What kind of connections?" Teven wondered.

A phrase popped into Kayleen's mind and wouldn't go away.

"Enuli asanti rimnula," she murmured.

"Which means, what exactly?" asked Marc.

"I don't know. It just came to mind. I think my mother said it once," Kayleen said, shutting her eyes. "It was important to her." She concentrated so hard that she broke out in a sweat. A cool breeze sprang up and gave her a chill.

"Easy now. Don't think about it. It'll come to you when you need to know," Teven said.

Ignoring him, Kayleen opened her eyes.

"The words sound vaguely Kalastan, but I've never heard of them before."

"What language is that?" inquired Anabel.

"An old language used by the Rangers," Kayleen replied. "They're the ones who raised—"

"Not to be rude but those clouds look odd to me," Marc interrupted, waving a hand behind Teven and Kayleen.

Kayleen whirled and saw a long line of fluffy white clouds hurtling toward them. Her heart picked up its pace.

"He's right. This is not going to be pleasant. We should head for that farmhouse," she said, pointing to their right. About four hundred meters away, a small house shuddered against the swiftly rising wind.

"I don't know about that house. It looks like it wants to swallow us, shake us around, and spit us out again," Marc commented.

Everyone ignored him.

"What's wrong? It's just a storm," Anabel said. "We have equipment to handle rain courtesy of the Fort Riden troops."

"Don't bother with rain gear. It won't protect us from that," Kayleen said, shaking her head. "And there's never just a storm out on the plains!" she added over her shoulder as she dashed for the tiny house.

They sprinted as fast as they could with their heavy packs. Teven caught up to Kayleen but stumbled to his knees because he was off balance from the added weight of Anabel's pack.

Kayleen paused to heave him to his feet again.

"Leave the packs!" she shouted, whipping off the shoulder straps of her own pack. "We'll get them later!"

Seeing she was serious, Teven, Lorian, and Marc dropped their packs.

Anabel ran with her left arm tucked across her chest, trying to keep the recently broken bone from moving. The anotechs had done wonders with it so far, but it still had a long way to go for complete healing. Each jarring step sent a stab of pain shooting through it.

"I can't! It hurts!" she cried, halting suddenly.

Kayleen ran back to Anabel.

"I'm sorry, but you can't stay here!" She shouted to be heard above the rising wind. "This is a windstorm!"

"Please, just leave me!" Anabel begged.

The others stumbled on with Marc in the lead.

Kayleen shook her head.

"These fields are going to be alive with flying debris soon! We need shelter now!" She grabbed Anabel's good arm and dragged her along in her wake.

As they approached the house, they heard a piercing woman's wail above the wind.

"Mika!"

The shriek of the wind grew louder in response.

Kayleen spotted a woman running back and forth in front of the house wringing her hands and shouting. Next instant, Kayleen's sharp eyes picked out a boy about forty meters beyond the left side of the house.

"Get that woman to shelter!" she ordered.

Teven and Marc ran for the woman.

"Get her inside!" Kayleen screamed. She shoved Anabel at Lorian and didn't wait to see if Lorian obeyed.

Kayleen analyzed the situation as she ran toward the boy standing in a sand patch kicking his legs and screaming as particles pelted him from every direction. Small stones cut into his bare legs. A branch snapped off a nearby tree. Controlled by the massive, unseen hand of the wind, the branch bucked first one way then the other before hurtling at the child. Kayleen urged her legs to pump faster. With a desperate cry, she flung herself at the boy, caught his waist in her arms, and yanked him along her flight path.

The branch struck her back with enough force to beat the breath from her body. Midair, she twisted to land on her back, biting her lower lip in the process. Another branch ripped a hole in the shirt sleeve protecting her left forearm and a stone scraped along the exposed skin. Feeling the sting of flying dirt, Kayleen launched to her feet again, still cradling the boy. Running with Mika in her arms was awkward but desperation strengthened her legs. Kayleen ran harder than ever. The wind buffeted her left then right then from above, trying to rip the boy away. She fought it, determined not to lose him. Twenty seconds later, she pounded on the door to the basement shelter. The doors swung open, and Kayleen allowed a dozen hands to ease her and her burden to safety.

"Nice job," Teven greeted cheerfully.

Kayleen looked up. He was upside down from her perspective. The hands lowered her to the floor.

"Ugh, I feel awful," moaned Kayleen.

"Complain; complain. Well, this time you have a right to," Teven said. His smile didn't quite mask his worry. "Next time, warn me when you're going to do something like take on a windstorm."

Teven's face was replaced by the boy's mother.

"Thank you! Thank you for saving Mika! He's my only child! I'd be lost if I didn't have him!"

Kayleen sat up. The sudden shift in position made her lightheaded. Tiny sparkles of light danced around her vision.

"Glad I could help," Kayleen mumbled, speaking slowly so as not to further upset her stomach which was already fully prepared to rebel. She wiped blood from her bottom lip. "Where's Anabel?"

"I'm here," Anabel said, not sounding happy about being alive.

"How's the arm?" asked Kayleen.

"Still there," Anabel replied. Her tone spoke of incredible pain.

The wind howled above them, drawing every eye to the rattling shelter door.

Teven knelt beside Kayleen and used his derringer dagger to cut away the tattered lower half of her left sleeve. A thin line of blood marked the path the rock had taken.

"Don't worry. It's just a small cut," Kayleen said.

Teven frowned, but she silently reassured him that the anotechs had everything under control.

It struck Kayleen that there was no father with the family. She pondered ways to bring up the question, but the woman saved her the trouble.

"I'm sure my husband would thank you if he could, but he was conscripted into the RLA last year." The woman's voice trembled with a mixture of sadness and anger.

Kayleen's heart went out to her.

"Have all the farmers in the region been taken?" Teven wondered. He settled into a more comfortable position on the floor.

"They have. My husband, Marcus, was among the last to be taken to serve that beast!" the woman spat. She yelped, realizing the consequences her words might have. "Oh, please don't tell anyone I said that!"

"We're not exactly in the good graces of His Excellency," said Teven.

"Who are you?" Mika asked with childlike innocence. He sat on the dirt floor in between Teven and Kayleen.

Introductions went around. Everyone who was still standing sat down, resigned to the fact that it could be a very long night. Outside, something heavy smashed into the shelter doors, startling everyone.

"How long's it going to last?" Marc questioned.

"Hard to say when it comes to windstorms," said Kayleen. "They can last minutes, hours, or days, but most commonly they're only a few hours in length."

"I wonder why we never heard of windstorms in the palace," Anabel said. "One would think the tutors would mention something like that."

"You work in the Rammon palace?" Carla Etan asked. "Marcus and I did as well. He was a cook, and I was a serving maid. Before that, I was an indentured servant who
sang under the stage name of Lady Gianna LeCross. The queen's Safe Service Act rescued me from my abusive master."

"How long ago was that?" Kayleen queried.

"Oh, years ago," Carla said with a dismissive wave of her hand. "We left about a year before Lord Kezem took the throne. We didn't agree with King Terosh and Queen Reia's move to align Reshner with the Galactic Alliance of Populated Planets. It's nothing but a tax burden and a headache." Her tone turned thoughtful. "Still, I wonder what would have happened if the king and queen had not been murdered."

She lies, said the anotechs.

What do you mean? Kayleen kept her expression neutral even as she grilled the tiny machines.

This woman was among those the queen urged to flee just before the palace invasion.

Why would she lie to us?

The anotechs stayed silent for several minutes while they subtly searched for the answer. Finally, they returned to Kayleen.

She does not mean to lie, but this is the story she has told for years. Those who fled as the palace fell were the closest allies of House Minstel. The lie is all that has saved her family for years. She believes it now.

"Can you tell us what happened? When the palace fell, I mean," Teven said eagerly.

"Where have you been, young man?" asked Carla.

"We've been away a long time," said Kayleen.

Teven shot her a grateful smile.

"I will tell you what I know," Carla promised. "King Terosh was lured into a trap and assassinated. The Captain of the Royal Guard delivered his body to the palace a couple of days later. The queen did not take the news well. Most of Reshner spent months in mourning while Lord Kezem urged rebellion. Finally, he moved against the palace."

"Who was the Captain of the Royal Guard?" Teven's tone indicated he could guess but dreaded being right.

That got Kayleen's attention, and she waited anxiously for Carla's answer.

"A fine soldier who disappeared about the same time as the palace changed hands," said Carla. "He was probably killed."

"What was his name?" Teven asked.

"Captain Laocer, of course. You must have hidden in a box for the last thirteen years not to know that," said Carla.

Traitor, whispered the anotechs.

What do you mean? Kayleen demanded, dazed.

Aster Captain Ectosh Laocer conspired to kill King Terosh and betrayed the throne room codes so Kezem could capture the queen.

Why? Every instinct in Kayleen argued with the anotechs.

He loved the queen and wanted to marry her, but Lord Kezem betrayed him.

Kayleen's mind reeled. From Teven's expression, she could tell a similar conversation was taking place in him.

"I heard he escaped that night," Lorian said helpfully.

"I *know* he escaped," said Kayleen hoarsely.

"What's wrong?" Anabel asked. She placed her good hand on Kayleen's arm. "You look like you've seen a ghost."

"Not just any ghost, *that* ghost," Teven said, confusing everyone but Kayleen.

She felt ill.

"He's alive!" Anabel exclaimed, still not understanding. "We should find him. He can help us fight Lord Kezem."

"He would help us, but we're *not* seeking his help," Teven declared.

Every eye turned to him.

Mika inched away from Teven and closer to Kayleen.

"Captain Laocer betrayed the queen," Kayleen explained in a whisper. She knew the words in her heart, but saying them aloud drove the emotional dagger deeper. The image of the man who had been a father figure to her shattered, destroying a treasured piece of her childhood.

"How can you know that?" Carla demanded.

Because I believe the anotechs, thought Kayleen. She searched her mind for a logical explanation to give the curious crowd without betraying the anotechs' full powers.

"Because Laocer is very much alive." One look at Teven's deep green eyes said things were swiftly clicking into place.

"I guess that makes sense," said Lorian, understanding slowing entering her eyes. "Everyone knows he was in love with Queen Reia."

Teven stiffened, and Kayleen placed a calming hand on his arm.

"He also conveniently found King Terosh's body," said Lorian, either ignoring or not noticing Teven's reaction. "If he was truly protecting the king during the assassination, he would be dead. His survival must mean something, and he disappeared the night the palace fell."

"He arrived in a Ranger camp in the Riden Mountains with several wounds. He gained their respect and made many friends." Kayleen was surprised at the depths of bitterness rising inside of her. "He searched many years until he found the lost prince."

"He murdered the prince's guardian and trained him to fight Lord Kezem," Teven added, spitting the words out like poison.

"You speak of yourself," Lorian said with awe.

Anabel and Marc gasped.

Teven looked away.

"Couldn't the captain have earned his wounds defending the queen?" Carla asked.

"He could, but he'd be dead," Lorian answered. "No one of significance who stayed survived that night. Only servants and children lived to become Kezem's slaves. He must have run. At the very least, he's a traitor by cowardice."

"I still don't believe it," Carla argued. "That doesn't sound like the man I knew."

It didn't really matter what she believed. They still lacked many pieces to the past, but this one terrible truth about Laocer's betrayal created a new bond among the five fugitives.

The tiny cellar fell silent save for the distant sound of rushing wind beating the fields and trees. Kayleen sat surrounded by her friends, wondering what she would say to Captain Laocer when she saw him. There would certainly be angry words, but what did she seek from him?

An apology? A confession?

What did she wish upon him?

Retribution? Revenge?

Until now, he had never done anything to hurt her, but this pain tore deep. She became aware of Teven's smoldering presence. She needed to speak with him alone but worried that the others would misunderstand such a request. The more she wondered, the less she knew, and the larger that ball of frustration grew within her.

Chapter 32:
New Perspective

Zeri (June) 26, 1560
Etan Wind Shelter, Kesler Plains

The windstorm carried on throughout the night. They shared a meal of dried tretling meat and grape juice. The conversation was kept purposefully light and meaningless, but the weight of the first conversation left Teven McKnight tossing and turning, tormented by bitter feelings. A small part of him questioned the conclusion he had drawn. He wished that his mentor was a righteous man, but his instincts told him otherwise. The anotechs, with their endless logic, calculated the odds of other scenarios and always came back to the first, most painful one.

When sunlight finally blazed through the tiny crack between the double doors of the shelter, Teven got up. He cast a brief, jealous glance at Mika who had fallen asleep in Kayleen's arms. His friend seemed so peaceful that he hated to wake her.

Anabel began to stir and moaned.

Teven crept over to her and squeezed her right shoulder gently.

"Wake up, Anabel. We need to change the bandages," Teven whispered, trying not to wake everyone.

The jostling during the windstorm had caused Anabel's wounded arm to bleed.

"I have some sterile wrap around here somewhere," Carla offered, already wide awake.

"Thanks. That would help," said Teven.

Carla searched the small shelter and finally found the sterile wrap.

Teven wasted no time in changing the bandages around Anabel's arm. The wound looked fairly clean. A thin layer of anotechs formed a protective barrier over the place where the bone had pierced the skin, but most of the anotech efforts concentrated on knitting the bone fragments back together or fighting off infection. The frantic flight for shelter had undone some of the previous healing efforts. The anotechs cut down on some of the aching pain, but they could do nothing for the sharp pains which struck whenever the arm was moved.

Everyone worked to lift Anabel's flagging spirits. Then, they hastily ate a meal of preserved ira petals and bid farewell to Carla Etan and little Mika. Pushing the shelter doors open took a lot of effort because a heavy branch had fallen across them.

Outside, the sun shone brightly, but fallen trees and disheveled ira fields testified to the windstorm's destructive power. Teven surveyed the damage as they retrieved their packs. As they continued along the correct path, Teven and Kayleen fell behind the others.

Lorian hesitated a moment and then nodded when Teven waved her on. She ushered Anabel and Marc along at a slightly faster pace.

Kayleen said nothing, giving Teven time to gather his thoughts.

"I've thought about the discussion last night, and I've gained a new perspective on the matter," Teven began.

"Which one?" Kayleen asked. "The war, Lord Kezem, Captain Laocer, us?"

Teven was surprised she had included them in that list, but he had pondered their relationship too.

"All of it," he said, tipping his right shoulder up in a half-shrug. "I began my training because Laocer told me to, and I had nothing else to do. But then Jalna showed up and introduced the anotechs, and I met you and learned practically everything else." He halted suddenly and placed a hand on her right forearm. "I've come to realize, I have more than Laocer's dream to fight for. It's become *my* dream, Kayleen. A dream of taking down Kezem, righting every wrong he's done to the people, and spending the rest of my days with you."

"You dream big." Kayleen smiled broadly but sadly.

"What's wrong?" Teven asked, taking her left forearm and tenderly tracing the cut she had earned during yesterday's rescue. At his touch, the anotechs in his fingers healed the wound.

Kayleen stood still with her head bent forward and her eyes closed for the few seconds it took to fix the cut. Then, she looked up with tears in her eyes.

"Teven, I—" she broke off and drew in a shaky breath. "I can't love you!" The words broke the dam holding back the tears.

"But you could love me!" Teven protested, mistaking her meaning. Confused, he stepped closer and wrapped his arms around her.

She answered the embrace willingly. Her voice was muffled because her head was buried against his chest.

"I don't know what it is! It's just something inside me that says we can love each other but not be *in* love! And I do love you and want to be in love with you. That's what hurts so bad!"

She wasn't making much sense, but he didn't feel right telling her that while she was so distraught.

"It's okay. We can take it slow. We're still good friends," Teven said, wishing he had a better rebuttal. He held her tightly to prevent himself from leaning down to kiss away her distress. He feared saying the words aloud, but his mind shouted *I love you!* After a few moments he reluctantly said, "We'd better catch up with the others before they get themselves into trouble."

Kayleen sniffled and stepped away, wiping tears.

Teven's arms felt empty.

"I'm sorry," Kayleen whispered, as they slowly began walking after their friends.

Me too, Teven thought.

After half a minute of silence, Kayleen cleared her throat.

"I really don't know what it is … it's just a cold feeling that says any commitment of love we make will shatter before it's realized."

"We're both confused right now, that's all." Teven didn't want to think about what she'd just said.

Kayleen attempted a weak smile.

"More memories returned to me last night. The anotechs can tell me many things but not how to react to their information overload. I asked about my parents and they answered, but I'm not sure I trust them."

"Why not?" asked Teven.

"They said my parents were Rangers. It makes sense, but there's something more—some fact I'm missing—and it's driving me crazy!"

Teven happily noted that she sounded more like the fiery Kayleen he loved. A smile started forming but froze at a man's harsh voice.

"Whom do you serve? Are you friend or foe?" the stranger demanded. He emerged from the tall grain to their left and pointed a kerlak pistol at the side of Teven's head.

Teven weighed the odds of answering the question and attacking the man. They were at a slight disadvantage because their opponent already had his weapon out. He concluded answering the question would be the best start.

"The answer to the first is reserved for friends, and the answer to the second depends on whom you serve," said Kayleen.

"Do you serve Kezem?" demanded the man.

"No," Teven answered instantly, noticing the absence of title. He waited for an energy beam to burn his head open.

It never came.

Instead, the man lowered his weapon.

"Then, you are friends, and we are in sore need of friends right now," said the stranger.

Teven studied the man who had the careworn look of someone who had lost much. A hard glint in the man's black eyes promised he would fight until death claimed him. His brown hair was shaggy, but his beard was neatly trimmed.

"Kezem's forces gather around us," said the stranger. "I think it best if you join us. We can offer you some protection."

Teven held in a laugh but could not suppress a smile.

"You have a strange way of asking for help," Kayleen said, voicing Teven's thoughts.

"I do not ask for aid," said the man, drawing himself up proudly. "I offer it."

The weight of the man's gaze settled squarely on Teven's shoulders.

"What did you do to get on Kezem's bad side?" asked Teven.

"I was an RLA captain who found his conscience," the man replied. "And you?"

"I was born," Teven answered.

The intensity of the man's scrutiny increased tenfold.

Teven offered the man his right hand in a gesture of friendship. He didn't know whether he could trust the man or not but figured the truth would be the best course of action.

"I am Teven McKnight, and my friend is Kayleen Wellum. We travel in the company of several derringers from the palace, people Lord Kezem would like to reclaim."

"My people should have spoken to them already," said the stranger.

"You must be Captain Alexi Gordon," Kayleen said.

Gordon nodded stiffly.

"Fort Riden rings with tales of your impending destruction," said Kayleen. "When will Kezem's forces arrive?"

"We don't know for sure, but my scouts reported Commander Perit's troops gathering near the Lotrian Fields yesterday. They have hovs and could be on top of us at any moment."

"How many strong are you?" Teven questioned.

"Forty-seven, counting you," said Captain Gordon.

"It is a hopeless battle then," said Kayleen.

Gordon flexed his jaw.

"I do not enter hopeless battles! We will drive them off!"

Teven had no doubt Alexi Gordon believed the words, but he personally agreed with Kayleen. Commander Perit would easily commit a thousand soldiers to the battle. This small band of rebels would probably be wiped out, but Teven refused to abandon them to such a bleak fate.

"Well, Captain Gordon, we are at your service," Teven said, tipping his head respectfully. "Take us to your camp so we can talk strategy."

On the dash to the tiny rebel camp, Captain Gordon explained the situation.

"We've been lucky so far. Commander Perit split his division into four sections and spread them out over the Kesler Plains. Unfortunately, my forces are also scattered to draw Perit away from our main force. Perit's a fool I had the misfortune to serve under once upon a time. He prefers overkill."

"Is that why you left?" Teven asked. Months of conditioning and mild anotech augmentation allowed him to keep up the conversation while they ran.

"Yes, we stumbled on a group of seven Rangers while on a recruiting mission. Perit ordered my entire command to attack them. My men killed more of each other than the Rangers. The man may be a fool, but he commands many soldiers. What's worse is that I don't want to kill those wretches. They're children, farmers, and miners, not killers."

Teven let the man rant before steering the conversation back to the current situation.

"How many soldiers will Perit commit here?" he wondered.

"Best estimates say four hundred, but it could be more," said Captain Gordon. "Perit's an idiot, but I'm worried that Captain Renith and Aster Captain Selok may have formed their own plans. They are definitely not fools."

"Are they friends of yours? Would they let you slip away?" Kayleen inquired.

"No. They may have been my friends long ago, but they've gained too much under Kezem to let friendship get in the way," Gordon replied. "Selok's men especially worry me. Some of them have a reputation for being unpredictable, hot-headed, and cruel."

They arrived at the small camp hidden in a collapsed graveground depression. For as much as the position protected them from sight, Teven could easily picture it as a death trap. Most of the tents and supplies were packed. No one spoke but adults nervously fingered weapons or frantically rounded up children.

"I thought you said there were only forty-seven of us," Teven said.

"Forty-seven fighters," Gordon clarified. "Most of the children are too young to hold a gun."

"We cannot fight here!" Teven declared.

"We don't have a choice," Kayleen announced. As she spoke, her kerlinblade came to life in her left hand, and her right hand pointed a pistol over Teven's left shoulder.

A danger sense told Teven to move. He dove to the right as an energy beam sizzled through the space he'd just vacated.

Chapter 33:
Battle on the Kesler Plains

Zeri (June) 26, 1560
Alexi Gordon's Rebel Camp, Kesler Plains
The pitched battle on the Kesler Plains raged out of control. The red-clad enemy separated from the surrounding fields and swept into the depression like a flashflood.

Kayleen Wellum twisted away from a young soldier's lunge. His kerlinblade sailed past her so close she felt its heat. Dropping her kerlinblade and pistol, she grabbed the soldier's right wrist and squeezed until he dropped his blade. Then, she wrenched his right arm up behind his back and buckled his left knee by stomping on it. They hit the ground as three energy beams flew over their heads. The soldier threw her off and tried to roll away, but her right foot lashed out and caught his chin, ending the fight.

Kayleen scooped up her weapons, scrambled to her feet, and frantically looked for Teven. Another soldier slashed at her with a steel sword. There was something simultaneously cruel, crazy, and cocky in his expression, but she had no time to ponder what it could mean. She caught the strike with her kerlinblade and disarmed the man with a deft flick of her left wrist. He stumbled to one knee. Her blade hovered near his neck, but she hesitated to land a killing blow, wanting him to yield and live. A child ran past, and before she could react, the man whipped a dagger from his boot and grabbed the boy.

"No!" Kayleen cried, knowing it was already too late.

The man's dagger struck the child above his right hip. Kayleen didn't hesitate this time. Her blade bit deep into the soldier's neck. She didn't enjoy killing, but there was no way to prevent that now. She tried to block out the screams, curses, cries of pain, and sickening thuds of serlak bullets slamming into flesh. Holstering her kerlak pistol, Kayleen rushed over to the screaming boy.

"Mommy! I want my mommy!" the child wailed, clutching his bleeding side.

"Calm down! Hold still!" Kayleen instructed.

An energy beam zipped toward them, and Kayleen knocked it out of the air with her kerlinblade. She debated herself briefly before shutting the blade off and tucking it back on to her belt. More beams came at them. Kayleen yanked the child aside, letting the beams pass harmlessly and find other victims in the crowd around them. She wrapped both arms around the boy's split side and willed the anotechs to stitch the gaping wound closed.

The boy fainted.

A nearby rebel screamed as one of Perit's men thrust a kerlinblade into his chest.

The stench of charred flesh struck Kayleen's senses until the anotechs took over. Horrified, she grabbed her kerlak pistol from its holster and put a hole in the soldier's back. She hated to leave the wounded boy, but she was attracting too much attention to adequately protect him. She shot two soldiers advancing on her from the left, ran five steps, and shot another three.

Several beams and bullets came her way. Kayleen back flipped to avoid some of them and retrieved her kerlinblade from her belt to deal with the others. Suddenly, something slammed hard across her shoulder blades, throwing her forward. Kayleen tossed her weapons away so she could land without killing herself. As she hit the ground, she rolled to face her attacker. A banistick beat the dirt next to her head. She lashed out with her feet, catching the assailant across the knees, dropping him. Propelling herself to her feet, Kayleen planted a fist in the man's face.

Flexing her painful right hand and squinting against the dust clouds being raised by the battle, Kayleen rolled twice and reached for her kerlinblade. Her shoulders throbbed, but adrenaline gave her the strength to regain her feet and swing the violet blade up in time to block a blade closing in on a little girl.

The man behind the blade rocked back on his heels and eyed her with amusement. His biceps nearly burst from the strained uniform shirt, and he towered over her by a good half-meter.

They locked gazes.

A few other soldiers looked like they wanted to enter the duel, but Kayleen's opponent stared coldly at them until they chose different targets.

Kayleen gently pushed the girl aside and behind her.

"Put down your blade, and I'll kill you quickly," promised the massive soldier.

"Sorry, but I like my chances with the blade better," Kayleen retorted, sucking in some deep breaths. A bullet whistled past her right ear. She half turned to check on the child.

The man struck at her head quicker than she thought possible.

Kayleen ducked and took two stumbling steps backward to keep her head.

"Come, let me kill you," the man taunted. He took a few casual swipes at her. His swings rapidly got harder and faster. Then, he took a small step forward. "If we capture you, Lord Kezem will crush every bone in your rebel body."

"That's reassuring," Kayleen replied, backing up, reluctant to have her arms snapped in two by the force of his blows. A massive swing struck the ground where she had been standing.

"Stand still!" roared the solider.

"Not likely!" Kayleen danced out of the way of three more thrusts, suddenly glad for Teven's example on the importance of dodging. She pivoted on her left foot and nearly tripped over the child she was trying to save. "Get out of here!"

The girl turned to run, but a wall of fighting soldiers blocked her way. Kayleen jumped back to avoid a slash. She backpedaled, whirled, and cut a hole in the line so the girl could scramble away. A young soldier yelped with pain as Kayleen's blade batted him aside to make way for the child. She paused to watch the girl slip through.

"How noble!" mocked the large soldier directly into her left ear.

Shock coursed through Kayleen, and she expected to feel a blade burning through her chest. Instead, a hand slammed into her back, flinging her into the wall of soldiers. She bounced off someone and sprawled on her back in the dirt. Somehow, she managed to keep a grip on her kerlinblade without taking her legs off.

"Get up so I can skewer you properly!" said the soldier, standing to her right. His dusty boots were even with her waist, and his white blade blazed inches from her neck. His dark eyes widened with the unholy gleam of battle lust.

"Kayleen!" called Teven.

She looked out of the corner of her right eye and caught a glimpse of Teven rushing her way, fighting through a crowd of soldiers. Suddenly, she realized a line of maroon uniforms encompassed her.

"No, Guidan! Lord Kezem wants them alive!" someone shouted from the crowd.

The man blinked, confused by the interruption. He frowned with disappointment but pulled his weapon back slightly.

"Get up!" he snarled. "You're now a prisoner. Your unconditional surrender begins now, or pain will pave your way to the palace. Do you understand?"

There's no way I'm surrendering! Kayleen's mind screamed even as she nodded slowly and climbed to her feet, glad that the child had made it though the line. She stared up into the soldier's face.

Dirt and blood showed up as dark splotches on his pale face, lending to his ruthless appearance.

"Let's get this over with," Kayleen muttered, whipping her blue blade up and tipping it in a salute. She flicked the switch to keep the blade color constant.

A dull thud reached her ears.

The man grinned but didn't advance. A line of blood trickled out of his nose.

Kayleen stared at him in shock but had little time to ponder her extended leases on life and freedom.

A soldier tackled her from the side.

The kerlinblade flew from her hand. Kayleen threw an elbow back into man's head, but he held on tightly. She wrenched her body back and forth, loosening his grip. Once free, Kayleen took two running steps. Seeing a dagger descend toward a familiar fallen form, she stopped short and tackled the man about to stab Lorian. He went flying to the left, and she bounced off his bony shoulder gasping for breath.

Groaning, Kayleen rolled over and half-rose. A kick caught her in the ribs nullifying her efforts to rise. She rolled onto her back too tired to continue fighting. Her vision clouded, and her thoughts turned to Teven. Another kick to the ribs brought an explosion of pain. Her body curled reflexively. More blows followed in rapid succession before she mercifully passed out.

***

After dodging the first energy beam, Teven yanked his banistick from its clip and flung it out. It opened directly into a man's head with a nice thud. The soldier fell over wearing
a stupid grin. Teven flowed through the crowd of RLA grunts, swinging his banistick back and forth. He ducked behind a dueling pair to avoid an energy beam, and it hit Gordon's man, ending the match prematurely.

Teven slammed the banistick into the dueling victor's stomach and brought his left hand down on the man's neck when he doubled over. A sharp shout behind him drew his attention. He spun to see a man with a hole in his head topple over. A group of four soldiers charged, and Teven raised his banistick defiantly, ready to meet them. Much to Teven's astonishment, they were cut down by serlak bullets while they were still a few paces from him.

My protector is still watching.

A kerlinblade sliced toward Teven's left leg. He knocked it away with his banistick, grateful Kayleen had modified the weapon to resist electricity. The young woman wielding the attacking blade grinned and swung at his neck. His eyes widened. Women were rare in Kezem's army. Teven moved without thinking, stepping close to her. His feet moved swiftly and surely, sweeping him into and out of danger several times during each heartbeat. Blade met banistick several times in rapid succession. Finally, a wild light came to the woman's eyes, and she swung with all her might. Teven dodged and brought his banistick up under her chin, knocking her out.

He turned and saw another soldier three meters away mercilessly pounding on a fallen rebel. Remembering the flingers Kayleen had given him, Teven whipped out three and hurled them at the soldier. The man straightened with an enraged scream as the flingers bit into his shoulders, back, and butt. The flingers didn't kill the man, but the distraction allowed the rebel to scramble away.

As Teven moved to engage the soldier, an exasperated cry reached his ears.

"Just die already!"

He turned to see a young rebel repeatedly slamming a body with a banistick.

"Stop it! He's dead!" Teven grabbed the young man's arm but was immediately thrown off.

"He killed my father!" the boy wailed.

"Then you won't do your father any good by sticking around to die!" Teven retorted. He traded his banistick for his kerlinblade and opened it as wide and flat as it would go. "We're falling back! Get out of here!" He caught an energy beam on his blade, directing it away from the distraught boy.

Though it hardly seemed possible, the boy's voice held more panic when he spoke again.

"Where's Anna? My sister! I've got to find my little sister!" The boy drove his banistick into a soldier's chest and began a frantic search.

"How old is she?" Teven asked, trying to follow the boy's erratic search pattern. The sooner they found the sister, the sooner the boy would leave the battlefield. Teven had known the rebels would lose this fight before they entered it, but he was determined to help them cut their losses.

"Six!"

"What's she—"

"There! Behind those soldiers!"

As they fought their way in the child's direction, Teven saw Kayleen disappear into the roiling mass of fighting soldiers.

"Kayleen!" called Teven.

With a wild cry, an enthusiastic soldier barreled at Teven, kerlinblade cocked over his head to strike.

Teven made the mistake of meeting the blade with his own. The blades trembled with the impact, and Teven went flying off balance to the right. He landed on his feet and traded his blade for his kerlak pistol. Three beams stopped the crazy soldier then Teven turned the pistol against others, systematically taking out enemy after enemy. He pulled the trigger one more time and a faint whine resulted. Tossing the useless gun aside, Teven reached again for his kerlinblade.

Get to Kayleen!

The thought burned through his brain on loop as Teven again rushed toward his friend, beating people aside with his kerlinblade. A little girl slipped through the line of soldiers, and her brother scooped her up and took off. Teven caught another glimpse of Kayleen brawling with some soldiers. Then, she disappeared again beneath a swirling mass of enemies. He tried to reach her, but something caught his shoulder. He whirled and swung.

Captain Alexi Gordon ducked.

"It's too late! We've got to retreat!" The rebel leader held a wounded child in one arm and Teven's right arm in the other.

"I'm not leaving her!" Teven declared, shrugging off the hold.

"Yes, you are!" said Captain Gordon firmly. "You're going to protect the children during the retreat."

Teven felt himself spinning around and being propelled away from

Kayleen. His heart nearly tore in two. His mind demanded he return to her, but he knew Captain Gordon was right. Commander Perit's troops had her, and if the rebels stayed much longer, they would die. He muttered Kayleen's name over and over as he fled. His despair turned to anger, which he took out on all who dared to follow Gordon's rebels.

Once they were safe, Teven looked about for Anabel, Marc, and Lorian.

I hope they're safe.

***

Zeri (June) 26, 1560
Same Day
Tryse's Camp, Kesler Plains

Tryse used a high-powered sniper rifle borrowed from Fort Riden to take out RLA soldiers. Like most sniper rifles, this one shot projectile bullets. He'd been following this rebel band for some time but hadn't revealed himself. Captain Alexi Gordon had once taught a kerlinblade class Tryse had taken.

Four soldiers approached a young rebel who waved a banistick boldly. Tryse took them out. He shot until the twenty bullets were spent. Then, he slammed in another cartridge and shot some more soldiers.

Tryse briefly mused at how far he had fallen from the ideal Coridian Assassin. Most in the special branch of the Royal Guard tended to scorn sniper rifles. Over the past few months, Tryse had come to appreciate the sleek weapon. He had followed derringers through most of the Kireshana, but then, he had taken to ambushing Fort Riden patrols. Hearing of Captain Gordon's plight caused him to seek out the rebels.

It helped that Tryse didn't much like Commander Perit. The opposing groups broke apart. Tryse continued to take out Perit's men. Shooting required some concentration, but he was still able to observe that the split had not been clean. Perit's men had prisoners. Tryse cursed. Kezem never had his men take prisoners unless he wanted something from them, and Tryse was determined to deprive Kezem of everything he wanted. He briefly considered shooting the prisoners but dismissed the idea. He would just have to follow Perit's men and hope he could help the prisoners escape.

***

Zeri (June) 26, 1560
Same Day
Kesler Plains

Hidden in a flimsy nalga tree two kilometers from the battle, Todd Wellum contemplated helping the rebels. He knew they were doomed, but he hoped they would defy the overwhelming odds. Knowing he would learn more by watching, Todd decided against interfering. He was curious. Commander Perit had committed an awful lot of men to destroy one tiny band of rebels.

Todd recognized one of the young rebels as a derringer. Although Todd had never bothered drawing close to those he protected, he knew he had seen this one before. The boy glided smoothly over the battleground, leaping into and out of danger. Then, another man stopped the young man from fighting and urged him to leave. Todd frowned and adjusted the field glasses for a close look at the young man's face. The enhanced view revealed a stream of tears and two syllables. It looked like a name. Todd's hand froze then trembled. He denied what he thought the boy was saying.

Kayleen.

Todd trained the field glasses over the boy's shoulder to a tangled mass of maroon uniforms that matched the color of the battlefield. A flash of red-gold hair floated among the soldiers. Todd's heart soared with hope, but the figure receded so quickly he doubted his eyes. He widened the field of vision, hoping to catch one more glimpse of her but found nothing.

The battle was over, and to Todd's amazement, Commander Perit's soldiers began to gather the prisoners. Miners and farmers were often pressed into joining the RLA, but whenever the rebels clashed with the RLA, the result was death to one side or the other.

Two soldiers lifted the young woman with flowing reddish blond hair from the depression. Todd focused the field glasses on her. The girl looked exactly like Kiata.

"Kayleen," Todd whispered in awe. A cry lodged in his burning throat. Every muscle strained to leap to his feet and fight for his daughter, but if he charged in now, he would only end up dead.

He had waited more than a decade to see his little girl again. A few days would not make a big difference, but they would certainly hurt. Silent sobs shook his body, as he watched the scene unfold.

The soldiers dropped Kayleen's limp form on the depression's edge and returned for more prisoners. A stab of pain and anger urged Todd to fly to the battle and kill every one of Perit's soldiers. Todd fingered his energy pistol but managed to keep his senses. Another young woman, this one with light brown skin, was dumped beside Kayleen.

Finding the sight of Kayleen too painful to face right now, Todd scanned slowly sideways, right to left. A visibly upset young man was yelling at a soldier placing stuncuffs on a pale young woman with a heavy layer of white cloth around her arm. A bright red stain indicated that the battle had reopened the wound. If the soldier activated the energy fields, the girl would probably faint from the shocks. The boy threw off the arms restraining him and punched the man hurting the girl. A stun beam ended his violent protests.

Todd shook his head and squashed another urge to help the rebels. He would never make it in time anyway.

A picture of the other young man, the one who had uttered Kayleen's name came to mind. Todd determined to have a chat with him. They would both be seeking a way to rescue Kayleen, so it was time to work together. Then, it struck him that he knew the young man.

Hello, Teven. You look like your father.

Chapter 34:
Hov Troubles

Zeri (June) 26, 1560
Same Day
Commander Perit's Camp, Kesler Plains

Kayleen felt sick when she woke up. She breathed slowly for several minutes and took mental notes on her condition. Her stomach ached, her head hurt, her ribs and back throbbed, and most of her muscles felt like they'd been pulled from her body and slapped back on haphazardly. She forced her eyes open and found herself in a tent. She lifted her right hand and was only mildly surprised to find it attached to her left arm. She let both arms flop back onto her stomach where they had been resting. A sore muscle in her abdomen twitched in protest, eliciting a groan from Kayleen.

"You have a way of expressing my feelings," Lorian Petole's voice said from somewhere to her right. "Thanks for the save, by the way. I'm sorry you got kicked for it."

Lorian's words brought the dull throbbing in Kayleen's lower right ribs to the forefront of her mind. She moaned again and rolled her head right to peer over at Lorian.

"No problem. Glad I could be of service," Kayleen muttered. She tried to sit up, but only managed to lift her head two inches before a wave of nausea flattened her again. She squeezed her eyes shut and willed her stomach to settle.

"I'd stay down if I were you," said Lorian. "You took quite a beating."

"Did anyone get away?" Kayleen asked, taking the good advice.

"Teven did."

Kayleen sighed with relief.

"Thank goodness. What about Marc and Anabel?"

"Right here," Anabel called from Kayleen's left. "Marc's unconscious because he tried to play hero when they arrested us."

Kayleen shook her head and immediately regretted it. Colorful spots floated behind her shut eyes. She felt the anotechs repairing some of the damage her body had sustained, so she stayed still to let them work.

"You talk in your sleep," Anabel said.

Kayleen grunted.

"You kept repeating that phrase from the other day," said Marc.

"Enuli asanti rimnula," Kayleen supplied with her eyes still shut.

"Right, that's the one, only this time you added 'edolin cumani' to the beginning," Lorian said.

"It is some sort of curse?" Anabel wondered.

Kayleen detected a note of pain in her voice.

"No," she said, making it a long word. She rolled the words over in her mind. *Edolin cumani enuli asanti rimnula.* "It's a healing charm, I think, but I don't know what it's for because I still can't make sense of the words."

She asked the anotechs for an explanation, but they remained suspiciously mute on the subject.

"Then, how do you know it's a healing charm?" asked Anabel.

"I just do," said Kayleen, knowing it was true but unable to explain why.

"It's hardly a useful charm," Anabel complained. "I could use a little healing here."

"Can you reach my hand?" Kayleen asked.

"Sure. Why?" said Anabel.

"I'm going to give you some more anotechs to help your arm heal faster," Kayleen explained.

A moment later, Anabel's cold hands wrapped around Kayleen's right hand.

Kayleen shut her eyes tighter in concentration. A brief inner battle ensued as the anotechs protested leaving their work on her aching muscles to go mend Anabel's arm. Kayleen won just as she heard the tent flap snap open.

"On your feet!" shouted a male voice. "Commander Isaac Perit present!"

Reluctantly, Kayleen opened her eyes but she didn't bother standing. She didn't think she'd make it anyway.

"Never mind formalities," Perit said gruffly. His stiff posture, gray hair, and grim expression spoke of a military background.

Perit appeared tall, but Kayleen attributed that to the deceptive view from the ground.

"Step away from the other prisoners!" barked the soldier who had announced Commander Perit. A swift stride brought him in striking range.

Instinctively, Kayleen shut her eyes and tensed, but the sound of a smack brought them open again. She caught a glimpse of Anabel collapsing next to her. The short, wheezing gasps hissing through Anabel's teeth told Kayleen that the soldier had struck the bad arm.

"Stand down, marksman," ordered the commander.

The young man looked disappointed but complied. He glared at the captives like it was their fault he got reprimanded.

"The hovs will be here within the hour to take you to the palace," said Commander Perit. "I'd like some answers before they get here."

"Good luck getting them," Kayleen challenged, drawing the hint of a smile from the grim commander.

"Your attire and kerlinblade claim you are a derringer, but my men say you fight like a Ranger," said the Commander. "I have orders to capture these three," he continued waving toward Anabel, Marc, and Lorian, "but you were never mentioned. That makes me curious."

He paused.

"Was there a question for me?" asked Kayleen, forcing a flippant tone. Having her head cocked to the side at an odd angle made it especially difficult to maintain a casual tone.

"Are you a Ranger?" Perit sounded impatient.

Kayleen felt it was useless to deny the accusation but wished to offer the commander no more help than she absolutely had to.

"I was raised by them," she answered carefully.

"Where is their hideout in the Riden Mountains?" asked the commander.

A flash of inspiration came to Kayleen.

He's testing me.

This was followed by a rush of anxiety for her friends in the Ranger camp. Captain Laocer came to mind and cold anger replaced anxiety.

"You already know the answer to that question," said Kayleen.

"Indulge me," said the commander.

"No."

Shock flashed across the commander's face. Obviously, he was not used to having his requests denied.

"If you have no information for me, then I have no use for you," Commander Perit said.

The marksman smiled and gave Kayleen an icy smirk. His hand rested lightly on his kerlinblade.

"But Lord Kezem does, and he would be displeased to know you killed a prisoner," said Kayleen.

"He would never know," Perit growled.

Kayleen knew, as he did, that Lord Kezem's spies were everywhere. A report of the entire battle had probably already reached him.

"You're a very bad liar, Commander," said Kayleen. It was time to go on the offensive. "Why were you ordered to capture my friends?"

Commander Perit regarded her cautiously. He must have concluded the information would do no harm for he answered. Something in his expression said he found the situation distasteful.

"Trouble at the palace. Lord Kezem needs to coerce Princess Rela into cooperating."

His statement made sense but didn't tell Kayleen anything new. She felt the vibration of approaching hov engines before she heard them. When she did hear them, it sounded like more than a few.

"Our ride approaches," said Kayleen.

At that moment, Commander Perit's comm unit beeped and spoke.

"Commander Perit, the Royal Guards have arrived to escort the prisoners to Rammon."

The commander nodded to his soldiers.

Kayleen and her friends were roughly hauled to their feet. Still disoriented, Marc
leaned heavily on his guards.

"Watch the arm!" Anabel protested.

The marksman who held Anabel squeezed her arm cruelly, making her grimace.

Propelled from behind, Kayleen had little choice but to exit the tent. She looked left and drew in a sharp breath. Twenty splendidly dressed Royal Guards stood at attention around four hovs arranged in a line. Their navy-blue uniforms stood out against the fields of light grain around them. Two klipper fighters hung in the air behind the line of hovs. Fear gripped Kayleen.

Lord Kezem really wants Lorian and the others.

Several kilometers into the journey to Rammon, Kayleen grew desperate. If they reached the palace, bad things would happen. The foursome had been split up. Marc and Anabel Spitzer had been taken in the first hov, and Kayleen and Lorian Petole had been tossed into the third. The second and fourth hovs each carried six soldiers, forming a small caravan. Sleek klipper fighters darted back and forth above them. The black and silver machines thrummed with angry-sounding power. The tinted windows made it impossible to see inside the cockpit.

Kayleen's arms remained bound in front of her. They had been traveling for four minutes now. At this rate, they would reach Rammon in a little under three hours. A gust of wind buffeted the speeding hov, throwing Kayleen into the side. As she reached out to steady herself, a crazy idea came to her. Willing some anotechs to slip through her fingertips, she sent them to the hov's engine compartment. A half-minute later, they returned reporting success. She silently cheered.

"What are you so happy about?" Lorian asked in a whisper.

The engine coughed and died, sparing Kayleen the obligation to answer. The surprised driver cursed and wrestled the steering stick. At Kayleen's bidding, a few straggling anotechs stung the pilot's arm. He jerked the steering stick back and to the left crashing into the fourth hov. Both hovs came to a grinding halt, pitching prisoners and soldiers against safety restraints.

Kayleen ignored the questioning glance Lorian cast her way.

"Hov Three, why are you stopping?" called a male voice through the hov's speakers.

"Don't you know how to drive?" fumed the irate pilot of the fourth hov.

"Why do you think I'm stopping?" muttered the pilot of Kayleen's hov, before activating his comm. He ignored the other pilot. "Engine difficulty, Predator One," he informed, managing to keep his tone civil.

"Well, fix it!" snapped Predator One.

The four soldiers, including the pilot, got out to inspect the damage. "It's done for," the pilot of Kayleen's hov concluded.

"What just happened?" demanded the fourth hov's pilot.

"How should I know?" snapped Kayleen's pilot.

Kayleen sent anotechs jumping from her hov to the fourth one. She tuned out the rest of the argument to focus on directing the anotechs from afar. Thirty seconds later, smoke began rising from Hov Four. She worked hard to keep a straight face.

Seeing smoke out of the corner of his eye, Hov Four's pilot whined. "Aw, now my hov's down too!"

Retrieving her anotechs, Kayleen bit her lower lip to hide a grin.

The rest of the convoy stopped and came back to join the two disabled hovs.

Predator One's annoyed voice came over both pilot's receivers.

"Move the prisoners to Hov Two, squeeze an extra soldier into each, and double bind the prisoners. Half the squad will stay here and wait for help to arrive from Meritab. The rest will finish the mission."

The soldiers obeyed. Kayleen winced as a second set of stuncuffs settled to the left of the first, giving her a solid line of metal for forearms. It was a pity she couldn't smack the nearest soldier with all that metal. A wave of guilt washed over her for the extra pain Anabel would suffer from the second set of stuncuffs.

Crammed in the back of Hov Two with a soldier between herself and Lorian, Kayleen waited impatiently for another fifteen minutes. She could have had the anotechs release her at any time, but that would not improve the situation. She needed to free Lorian, Marc, and Anabel and wanted to be well out of the range of any reinforcements before making another move. When she felt it was safe, Kayleen sent the anotechs to work their magic on Hov Two's controls.

"What the—" said the pilot.

"Hov Two slow down!" commanded Predator One. "You're flying erratically!"

"The panels are flashing, Captain! I have no control!"

"Well, get some control!" said the commander in Predator One.

Kayleen ordered the engine disabled but warned the anotechs not to break something vital. The hov sputtered and slid to a stop, so Kayleen recalled the anotechs.

A stream of curses came from the pilot's neck where the receiver was imbedded. The pilot grumbled and got out of the hov. Instead of going to the engine, he stormed up to her door, yanked it open, grabbed her by the collar, and pulled her close.

"What did you do to my hov, Ranger Witch?" growled the pilot.

Though she tried, Kayleen couldn't stop the smile that answered him. Her safety restraints were removed, and the pilot dragged her from the hov. A shove sent her flying toward Marc and Anabel's hov which had returned to help. She used the momentum to stumble into it, thrusting out her bound arms so her head wouldn't smash against the hov. The metal stuncuffs made a satisfying crunch on the hov's hull. Two strong shocks ripped along her arms, but she ignored the pain. Kayleen considered sending anotechs to bite the man who had pushed her, but she refrained. He had done her a favor. Knowing she wouldn't get another shot at this, Kayleen sent the anotechs zipping onto the final hov.

"Get her away from that hov!" screamed Predator One. The tortured cry came from a half-dozen comms at once, making it eerie and amusing.

The anotechs were back in seconds, duty done. Something akin to a machine sigh came from Hov One which gently settled to the ground.

Silence reigned over the Kesler Plains.

Kayleen straightened, turned, and smiled serenely up at Predator One. Her crossed arms made her appear smug. The Royal Guards eyed her with fear and respect. She could feel the intense glare Hov Two's pilot leveled at her back.

"What are your orders, Captain?" inquired a soldier.

A sigh came from the comm receivers.

"Predator Two, report our troubles to Rammon in person. The rest of you get out the emergency tents. We're staying the night. And someone restrain that Ranger!"

Predator Two hesitated, and Kayleen almost pitied the man who had to report failure to Lord Kezem.

"She already has two sets of stuncuffs on her, Captain Holeth," noted the soldier who had asked for orders.

"Restrain her feet, too," said Captain Holeth peevishly.

"That won't hold her, sir," the soldier lamented.

"Are you questioning my orders, Danub?" snapped the captain.

"No, sir, but Rangers are notoriously difficult to keep captive," said Danub.

"Separate her from the others and stun her. If she tries to escape, kill her."

Touchy, touchy.

Kayleen had no intention of escaping without her friends.

"Danub, hold her friend, the one with the broken arm," Captain Holeth ordered. "Reed, place your kerlinblade against the girl's neck. Meeks, restrain the Ranger. Ranger, you do anything stupid and your friend gets a very large hole in her neck."

Danub and Reed hurried to carry out their orders.

Kayleen's heart thudded in her chest and she watched helplessly.

Danub stood behind Anabel with his left hand around her waist and his right hand on her forehead, tilting her head up. Reed whipped out his kerlinblade with a flourish and pressed the tip against the side of Anabel's exposed neck.

Both men stared stonily at Kayleen.

She returned their gazes steadily but didn't fight as Meeks released both pairs of stuncuffs. She let her arms fall at her sides. Meeks walked behind her, grabbed her right wrist, twisted it, and wrenched the arm up behind her back. A hard boot slammed into her right calf just below the knee, causing it to buckle. Hot pain shot through her right arm and shoulder.

Meeks laughed. It was not a pleasant sound.

"Not so tough anymore, are you?" he mocked in her ear. "I'm gonna ask the captain for some quality time with you later. I love red heads."

Kayleen gritted her teeth, trying to hide the pain. Since two pairs of stuncuffs would not fit on Kayleen's arms while they were behind her back, one pair was reapplied and turned up high enough so that even slight movements set them off. As if that weren't enough, Meeks pushed Kayleen onto her face, so he could fit her ankles with restraints. As she fell, she instinctively twisted her head to the right to avoid breaking her nose. Kayleen winced as a shock coursed through her whole body.

"Is that really necessary?" Lorian demanded.

Kayleen shook her head and silently begged her friend to stay quiet. The soldiers picked her up, causing small electrical charges to run up and down her arms, making her teeth tingle. The failsafe mechanism stopped the charges just as the soldiers roughly deposited her in a hastily erected tent. She shifted position to something halfway comfortable before a stun beam helped her sleep.

***

Zeri (June) 26, 1560
Same Day
Throne Room, Royal Palace, City of Rammon

"The prisoner transport has been delayed, my Lord."

Kezem shook with rage.

The pilot in front of him, designation Predator Two, trembled with fear. Not knowing what else to do, the man rushed to explain.

"One of the prisoners is a Ranger. She disabled two of the hovs by crashing them into each other and then got the other two by …."

"By what?" Kezem asked.

"I d-don't know, my Lord. Magic, I think. D-dark magic," Predator Two stammered.

Kezem growled and made a violent slashing motion, which caused Predator Two to wisely fall silent.

"Kolknir!"

"Here, Excellency." Supreme Commander Kolknir looked annoyed that Kezem had neglected to include his title, but he stepped forward obediently.

"Send Captain Quedron and four more squads to fetch the prisoners. Sedate the Ranger until I can question her, but do not harm her. Leave that to me. Take the prisoners to Estra. I will meet them there." Kezem wanted to study the Ranger, question her, and discover more about this strange ability to conquer hovs. Once satisfied, he would kill her.

"Yes, Your Excellency. It will be done." Kolknir bowed and left to issue the proper orders.

Lord Kezem pondered his next move and wondered if he really needed those prisoners. Princess Rela was helpless to resist. He could have stuncuffs placed on her, and she would have to obey him. On a whim, he summoned the Azhel priest.

When the distraught man was brought before him with his robes not quite on straight and his hair mussed, Kezem felt nothing but contempt for him.

"The four months are almost over," said Kezem. "Tell me, priest, is it truly necessary to have Princess Rela's full cooperation in the matter of finding the treasure chambers in Loresh?"

"Oh yes, Favored One, if she does not wish to find the door, she will block its cry from her heart and mind," replied the priest.

"Where does this call come from? Why can only she hear it?"

The priest lifted a hand and stroked his chin. His gaze became distant. For a moment, Kezem thought the man might be stupid enough to ignore him. But at last, the priest spoke, "The cry comes from the departed spirits of House Minstel. They only call their own."

"Then, I will give her reason to hear that call," said Kezem darkly.

They could fly into Estra but would then have to hike the five kilometers to Loresh for fear that the heat from the hovs would collapse a vital tunnel. The quickest way to the Frozen North would be to go directly south from Rammon across the Kevil Plains and the Ash Plains. When they reached the coast, they would have to fly a hov over the South Asrien Sea or spend hours on a boat.

Kezem grunted. Neither option appealed to him. He disliked trusting hovs over water and outright despised boats.

Chapter 35:
An Ally Revealed

Zeri (June) 26, 1560
Same Day
Temporary Rebel Camp, Kesler Plains

The rebels certainly have amazing stamina, Todd Wellum thought after following them for almost six hours.

Relief flooded his weary limbs when the rebels finally stopped to make camp just as the sun began to set behind the Riden Mountains. If they traveled a little farther, they would run into the Lotrian fields. Todd could have gone a few more kilometers, but they would not have been pleasant ones, especially if they involved the Lotrian Fields.

He stopped about ten meters from the group, leaving the distance to avoid hastily released bullets. Todd waited for the rebels to finish setting up tents in a protective circle. When they settled down, he called to them.

"Hold fire! I am a friend!"

Immediately, a dozen weapons swung in his direction.

"Put your hands up and step closer!" ordered the leader.

"Tell your people to put down their weapons!" Todd called back.

A tense moment passed before the leader spoke again.

"We seem to be at an impasse!"

"I want to ask the boy next to you about one of his companions," said Todd.

"Kayleen?" the boy asked, perplexed.

"Yes! May I step closer?" asked Todd, voice trembling.

The leader nodded to his people who reluctantly lowered their weapons.

"Come slowly," he warned.

Keeping his hands well away from his weapons, Todd covered the distance between them as swiftly as he dared. His composure lapsed momentarily when he came within a meter of the boy who knew his daughter. He staggered forward. The boy recoiled.

The rebel leader's pistol snapped up.

"Stay where you are," said the rebel.

Feeling his knees giving way, Todd knelt. He didn't care that the pistol was still trained on his face. He stared desperately at the young man.

Tell me of my daughter!" he cried.

The young man nodded, and a flash of understanding entered his green eyes. The eyes were Queen Reia's, but the wavy black hair and finely structured features reflected King Terosh. Todd could almost see the thoughts whirling through the young man's head.

"Welcome, uncle," the boy greeted with a calm that reminded Todd of the queen.

"What's going on?" Confusion and anger were equally present in the rebel eader's tone, but he lowered the kerlak pistol.

Todd ignored him.

"Captain Alexi Gordon, meet my uncle, Ranger Todd Wellum," the boy announced.

Todd couldn't fathom how the boy had conjured his name or their family connection, but his next statements shocked him even more.

"He's been protecting derringers throughout the Kireshana," said Teven. "I … felt him watching."

"Prince Teven!" Todd said hoarsely. "I thought Lord Kezem had killed you!"

"He tried," Teven said with a faint grin.

"Your Highness, forgive me for not recognizing you," said the rebel leader, dropping to his knees before the boy.

"There's hardly a need for that out here," Teven noted, gesturing to the wide-open plains surrounding them. "I need to recover my friends before Lord Kezem gets them."

"We will help you," Captain Gordon promised.

"Thank you, Captain. We must cross the Lotrian Fields and get to Meritab. Then, we can take a hov from Meritab to Rammon."

"I'm coming with you," Todd said.

Teven nodded like he had suspected as much.

"Come, have a meal with us," Captain Gordon invited Todd. "Pitch your tent nearby. We'll start out in the morning."

Todd made no move to gather his things. Instead, he said, "Tell me about Kayleen. I've not seen her for more than thirteen years."

Chapter 36:
Shifting Loyalty

Zeri (June) 27, 1560
Princess Rela's Private Chambers, Royal Palace, City of Rammon

Kia stood perfectly still and watched Princess Rela Minstel sleep. Lord Kezem had not been joking when he said he wanted the Melian Maidens to watch over the princess constantly.

Whom do I serve?

The question came to her unbidden, as it usually did in these quiet moments of the night watch. Lord Kezem demanded weekly reports on the princess, and as head maiden, it fell to Kia to compose these reports. She didn't like spying on her young charge.

She thought over the last few months and found herself drawn to the princess by more than the need to protect her. One could hardly help liking the vibrant young woman who, despite the unseen chains, found ways to ease the suffering of others. Several times, Kia and the other Melian Maidens had found themselves conduits of good will, secretly carrying food, medicine, and clothes to families marked by Lord Kezem. A mark made trading nearly impossible and could be earned by offenses as small as wearing green or purple in support of House Minstel.

A soft thump brought Kia out of her reverie. Her bound brown hair whipped as she snapped her head around to glance at Jola who stood ready for battle with her hands hovering over her kerlinblade and banistick.

She must have heard it, too.

The assurance made Kia draw her banistick. She favored the weapon over kerlinblades because of its versatile nature. The lightweight piece of gilded metal could be snapped out in an instant to its full meter-and-a-half length or be made to partially unfurl for close quarters combat. Kia flicked her weapon out to its full length and slid the handle to the middle, so she could bat away any projectiles.

Peering intently at the corner where she heard the noise, Kia suddenly sensed danger from behind. She spun to see a black-clad figure drop noiselessly onto the end of Princess Rela's bed. Without thinking, Kia leapt onto the bed and interposed her body between the princess and the assassin.

Four in three weeks!

Kia couldn't believe the princess could have made so many enemies during her fifteen years of life. She didn't have time to dwell on that.

The assassin raised a pistol, but Kia's twirling banistick knocked it away before he could fire. The assassin cursed, tucked his right hand close to his body, and took out a throwing dagger with his left hand. Movement to Kia's left caught her attention. Relying on instinct, she closed her banistick and hurled it at the figure in the shadows. Then, she rushed the first assassin, throwing him from the bed. A clunk followed closely by a groan told her the banistick had struck her target. The one she had thrown leapt to his feet, but Jola was there to slam a hand across the back of his neck. He slumped in Jola's arms with a small, feminine cry.

Jola ripped the black mask from the assassin, releasing a mass of golden hair.

The prisoner moaned.

Jola stuncuffed the young woman and lowered her to the ground.

"Move and I kill you," said Jola.

"I am already dead," muttered the girl. Bitterness soaked the words.

Kia couldn't blame her for the attitude. She was correct. The attackers were as good as dead. After scanning the room for further signs of danger, Kia turned on the lights and moved to place restraints on the being she had beamed.

Princess Rela woke up and stared around her room wide-eyed.

"Again?" she asked. "Don't these people have anything better to do than try to kill me?" She threw off the blankets, revealing her shimmering purple night dress. It was one of the few items Kia had smuggled into the palace for the princess. Kezem had practically banned all forms of the royal colors.

A dagger flew toward Princess Rela. Kia watched helplessly as it whipped through the air. Rela threw herself to the left, but the dagger scraped along her right forearm. Kia flinched as Princess Rela winced. If the blade was poisoned, the princess would be dying right about now.

Jola flew across the room and dove behind the bed. A fierce wrestling match ensued. Kia rushed around the bed in time to hear a loud crack as Jola's boot met the man's lower right leg. His pained cry was cut short by a blow to the head. Jola dragged the limp man toward her first prisoner then returned for the attacker Kia's banistick had subdued. She added him to the line of prisoners and reached for her comm.

"I'll call Palace Security," said Jola.

"Wait!" Princess Rela and Kia shouted as one.

Kia's hazel eyes flew to the princess whose expression radiated pity. Intuition told her the princess would object to punishing the prisoners. Kia retrieved her banistick from the floor and braced for a verbal battle.

"We should question them," Kia told Jola, trying to buy time.

"Let them go," Princess Rela said in a tone that wavered between command and plea.

"That is impossible, Princess," Jola said. "They would only attack you again."

"You can protect me," said the princess.

"That is true, but it is less than ideal," said Jola.

"The interrogators will kill them soon enough," Kia said. "We might as well learn
what we can from them first."

Rela climbed off her high bed.

"Please, I do not want them to die because of me!" The princess sounded truly distraught.

"It's not about *you*," declared the girl from the floor. She spat in Rela's direction. The slimy projectile fell far short of the princess, but thankfully, it did stop her from approaching the prisoners. "If you die, he dies."

A look of horror crossed Princess Rela's face. She understood that if Lord Kezem experienced pain, she felt it and vice versa, but she hadn't considered dying.

"Who sent you? Is there a place we can send your bodies?" Kia asked gently. The second question was not unkind, merely practical.

The prisoners would soon be executed after unpleasant interrogations. Although sluggish in helping people, Kezem's government could be ruthlessly efficient when it wanted to be.

"Let my children go," said one of the masked figures on the floor.

At Kia's nod, Jola removed the black cloth masks. The young man who had caught the banistick across the forehead was still out cold.

The face of the older man was twisted with more than physical pain.

"I forced them to come with me to kill Lord Kezem." The man's voice trembled with fear and fatigue. "Do not hold that against them."

"No!" the girl protested. Her gray eyes flashed with passion. "Father, we have fought together to rid our planet of that monster. We will die together!"

"You do not need to die," Princess Rela said impatiently. After donning a dark blue robe with gold woven in an intricate pattern around the neck, waist, and sleeves, the princess moved forward to release the captives' bonds.

Kia moved to block her.

"Step aside!" A determined glint entered Princess Rela's blue eyes.

Kia couldn't guess where the princess had obtained the regal tone, but part of her rejoiced to see this new side of the young woman. Training took over, and Kia fell into step next to the princess. She would wait for her to release them, but as soon as they attacked, her kerlinblade would cut them down.

The father of the would-be assassins practically melted with relief as Rela reached for his daughter's bonds.

The girl looked ready to spit again.

"No, Lissa! Let her free you. Escape. Live to fight Lord Kezem another day!" His eyes begged his daughter to listen.

"I don't want her mercy or her pity!" said Lissa. A silent battle of wills raged for several long seconds. Then, her father's words finally reached her and horror replaced much of the anger. "What about you, Father? Why won't you escape?"

"My leg is broken. I won't be able to make it over the walls," said the father. His tone said accepted his fate. "Wake Brian and get out of here."

Princess Rela removed the stuncuffs, but Lissa just stared at her father.

Kia prepared to take the assassin down if she so much as twitched in the princess's direction.

"We can get you out," Princess Rela promised, turning to Kia. "You can take them down the servants' corridors and smuggle them out the waste room."

Her confidence told Kia that the princess had given escape plans much thought.

"Princess, these people tried to kill you," Kia said, letting her tone carry her disapproval.

"But they wanted to kill Lord Kezem," Princess Rela argued. "Even I have dreamed about that, Kia. Please, I am not strong enough!"

The statement about wanting to kill Kezem drained the rest of Lissa's anger and made Kia acknowledge that similar feelings had existed within her for quite some time. She had never considered attacking Lord Kezem, but she wasn't blind. She could see that his harsh rule was crushing the people. The thought that she, Princess Rela, and these attackers shared similar thoughts gave Kia pause. She cursed silently, knowing she was about to alter her life forever.

"Jola, you can stay here, leave, or take the boy," said Kia.

"This maneuver will be illegal," Jola commented.

"The Melian Maidens are not Lord Kezem's personal korvers. We swore an oath to trust, obey, and protect members of the Royal House. Furthermore, we swore to protect the people. I intend to fulfill my oaths tonight," Kia said, knowing the argument would appeal to Jola's sense of duty. She bent over to release the cuffs binding the older man. She paused for a final warning. "My commitment to your life ends the second you threaten the princess. Do *not* test me on this."

The man nodded solemnly, and once his hands were free, he meekly placed his left hand in her proffered right hand.

Kia grunted as she hefted the man and placed him in a comfortable position across her back.

"Lead on, Princess."

Princess Rela looked ready to protest but reconsidered.

"Hurry!" she urged.

A thrill of excitement rushed through Kia as she followed Princess Rela down several passages. It was a long way from the princess's seventh-floor suite down to the palace gardens. Near the end of their journey, Kia's shoulders began aching. She bumped the man's leg rounding a corner and winced sympathetically. His breath rasped in her ears, but he did not cry out. Eventually, they made it to the kitchen and then the waste room. Kia wrinkled her nose at the foul smell. The others clapped hands over noses or grimaced, but Princess Rela seemed unaffected.

They burst out the disposal room door and found themselves in a dense part of the palace gardens. As Kia set her prisoner on his feet, Jola's burden woke up and managed a small cry before his sister's hand clamped over his mouth.

"Hush, Brian, we're getting out of here. Father's hurt. If you scream, the guards will hear!" Lissa explained.

"Take this and buy passage out of Rammon," Princess Rela commanded. She took a small pouch on a string from around her neck and placed it around the older man's neck. It contained most of the kefs that remained from her botched escape attempt.

Tears came to the man's eyes.

Kia couldn't tell if the tears were from gratitude or pain.

"There is no way to hide the attack from Lord Kezem," Princess Rela continued. "He probably felt it when your dagger pierced my arm, and the guards could still come any moment! Go down this first path until you reach the wall. Follow it to the right until you reach the south gate. You'll have to stun the guards, but please don't kill them. That would only make things worse."

"Thank you, Princess. It is more than we deserve," said the man humbly.

"Kia, give me your pistol."

Kia reluctantly handed the princess the kerlak gun.

Flicking the pistol's setting to stun, Princess Rela handed it to the man.

"Use this on the gate guards and take it with you. They must not discover that the weapon of a Melian Maiden aided your escape. Now, go!"

Kia was wary of the prisoners. With the princess's permission, she followed them until they were safely off the palace grounds.

***

Zeri (June) 27, 1560
Same Day
Lord Kezem's Private Chambers, Royal Palace, City of Rammon

Lord Kezem awoke to find his white sheets marred with blood near his right forearm. He frowned and concentrated, trying to think. No one could have gotten close enough to harm him, and anyone who did would never have inflicted a mere scratch. That only left one possibility.

Rela has been wounded. The thought of the princess shot anger through him, but it faded as he thought, *Why didn't she tell me?*

After a hasty morning meal, Lord Kezem summoned the princess. She entered the throne room minutes later flanked by two of the Melian Maidens he had provided her. His breath caught in his chest and he did a double take, almost swearing it was Queen Reia who strode towards him.

Princess Rela wore a simple dress of royal blue shimmersilk that showed off her budding young figure. Her light brown hair was swept up away from her smooth features and woven in a manner that accentuated the few red strands.

"What happened last night?" demanded Kezem.

"There was a small incident," Rela answered, folding her hands in front of her.

"How were you wounded?" asked Kezem.

"Someone seeking your life threw a dagger at me. I failed to dodge quickly enough," she replied.

"Where were your maidens?"

"Fighting the other two aspiring assassins," said Rela.

"Why was I not given a report?" Kezem bellowed for the entire palace to hear. He leapt off the throne. "Where are these assassins? I will kill them myself!"

"They are gone."

"You let them go, didn't you?" Kezem glared at the princess. His left eye twitch with irritation.

After returning his gaze steadily for a few seconds, Princess Rela looked away and nodded.

"I did." Her answer was barely audible.

"What could possibly have possessed you to release them?" asked Kezem.

"You would have killed them," said Rela.

"Someone *will* suffer for this." Kezem's voice was low and tight.

"Why are you so angry? Why must there always be punishment? People would serve you if you served them!" The princess's face flooded with color.

Kezem flushed as well, for she had never spoken to him like that. He despised this new, independent streak.

"They will serve me because they fear me," said Kezem, stepping close to Rela.

The princess retreated a step but maintained eye contact. Only a tremor in her jaw betrayed her fear.

Still glaring at Rela, Kezem addressed his guards.

"Bind them and take them to the interrogation chamber. I have a lesson to teach the princess."

Chapter 37:
Royal Captive

Zeri (June) 27, 1560
Same Day
Princess Rela's Private Quarters, Royal Palace, City of Rammon

Twenty minutes after returning to her chambers, Princess Rela tried concentrating on a new food plan for Rammon's marked people, but her mind kept returning to Kia and Jola. She could almost feel Kezem's heavy hands on her shoulders. He had stood behind her lecturing while shocks tormented Jola and Kia.

Such a high price for defiance.

Rela blinked back tears and shuddered, remembering their pain.

Thankfully, Kezem had not been upset enough to kill them, but they would spend a week in the palace prison to appease his anger.

Linnea and Elia stood stiffly a few feet behind Rela. She didn't have to look to sense their burning anger. They blamed her for Jola and Kia's sudden absence.

I blame me too.

An empty feeling gnawed at her. She thought of the people starving for disagreeing with Lord Kezem. The subsequent anger helped her focus. She wrote a message asking Lory Pascal to send five bags of wheat to the Bann family. It was not what she had meant to do, but it would do for now.

"Elia, will you please take this letter to the Merchant Quarter?" asked Rela.

"We are here to protect you, Princess," Elia said stiffly. "We cannot do that and run errands."

"I regret what happened to Kia and Jola," Rela said softly, "but we cannot stop helping people because we might be hurt!"

"You never get hurt," Elia pointed out.

The comment stung, but Rela didn't fight the pain because she knew she deserved it. Frustrated tears slipped down her cheeks as she nodded agreement.

"I'll take the letter after dark, Princess," Linnea offered.

"Thank you." Rela wiped her eyes, reached into a drawer, rummaged around, and pulled out a ring with a small emerald in it. "Show this to Master or Lady Pascal to prove you act for me."

The Melian Maiden's green eyes widened, but she took the ring without protest.

Rela tried not to think about her mother's ring, the small link to a past she knew next to nothing about.

The door to Princess Rela's drawing room and private sanctuary burst open. Eight Royal Guards and ten Palace Security officers rushed in, the former in their dress blues and the latter in dark gray uniforms.

Experiencing a flashback to a few hours earlier, Rela leapt to her feet. "I demand an explanation!" she cried.

Linnea and Elia dropped into defensive positions at her sides.

Lord Kezem strode in wearing his usual dark ensemble and hard expression.

"Stand down," he barked at Linnea and Elia.

Confusion and conflicting emotions crossed their faces.

Linnea's blond hair bobbed as she shook her head. Elia just frowned and rested her hand on her kerlinblade.

"I said stand down," Kezem repeated slowly.

"Do as he says," Rela ordered. A sick, anxious sensation told her what was coming. "Thank you, but you cannot help me. There is no reason for you to be hurt."

"Disarm and arrest them," Kezem instructed his men.

His soldiers moved to obey. The first man to reach Elia was laid out flat on his back, clutching his jaw. Linnea's sidekick took out a second man. The rest reached for kerlak pistols.

"No!" Rela and Kezem screamed simultaneously.

Everyone froze.

"Go with them," Rela whispered, though it broke her heart. Her chest heaved, and she breathed shallowly, trying not to faint. She looked deep into each woman's eyes, willing her maidens to save their strength for better odds. "It will only be for a time."

"It will be for as long as I wish, Princess," said Kezem.

The Palace Security guards whisked the Melian Maidens from the room. Rela could only hope Captain Tayce's contact in the palace prison would hear of the incident. She had worked with the captain and his contact several times to smuggle extra medicine in for the prisoners. She didn't know Tayce's contact well, but the man had proven reliable thus far.

He'll know what to do.

We will tell him, if you wish it, Princess of the Chosen.

Rela flinched as if burned, but she refrained from crying out.

Please, tell him!

"Arrest her, but don't hurt her," Kezem said.

Rela backed up a step but bumped into her chair.

"Relax, Princess, the cuffs won't sting you. We're taking a trip to the Frozen North. Friends of yours will meet us there."

***

Zeri (June) 27, 1560
Same Day
Captain Tayce's Office, Fort Vik
Captain Tayce.

Tayce heard the mental call but dismissed it as a trick of his overworked mind. The prisoners had nearly rioted yesterday, and he'd spent most of the night solving subsequent problems. He leaned his head in his hands, elbows propped on his desk, and let his fingers massage his throbbing temples.

Captain Tayce. Princess Rela needs you. Read the palace reports.

What?

Receiving no response, Tayce figured it couldn't hurt to obey the child-like voices haunting his head. He dug his infopad out of a drawer and set it to review palace reports. It didn't take him long to find the reports on hov crews being readied and the arrest of the Melian Maidens assigned to Princess Rela. The day-old report of a battle on the Kesler Plains resulting in prisoners also surprised him, but the prisoner list itself cleared up that mystery.

Captain Tayce wasn't sure what it all meant, but he was certain Princess Rela was in danger. He placed a secure comm call to Marksman Cory Tiridan.

"Do you know where the Melian Maidens were placed?" asked Tayce, after pleasantries.

"Yes, sir, one moment. Let me check," the marksman said. "East Detention Block number forty-five through fifty, sir."

"Thank you." Tayce pondered his next words carefully before voicing them. "Cory, you know that matter we discussed at length? I'm due for a long vacation, and I think I'll take it now. Would you like to come? And if so, would you mind bringing the Melian Maidens?"

"What's wrong, sir?" Tiridan asked.

"Something's happening. Something big. I don't know the details, but Lord Kezem's on the move, and he has the princess with him. Whatever he plans for her, it can't be good."

"Agreed, sir. How shall I proceed?" asked the marksman.

"Have you placed trackers on the palace hovs?" asked Tayce.

"Yes, sir. I did that ages ago when you suggested it," Tiridan answered.

"Good, collect the prisoners as soon as possible and meet me on the eastern shore of the Crystal Lake."

"Yes, Captain," Cory said. "But what about—"

"I'll deal with the details and contact you when everything is ready."

Tayce spent an hour filling out forms to make sure Fort Vik could function without him for a while. Next, he left word with a junior officer that he would be unavailable for the rest of the week. With a final bracing breath,

Tayce used a code Princess Rela had given him to break into the palace prison system. Within minutes, he had quietly transferred several prisoners out of the East Detention Block and looped security vids so no one could witness the mass exodus. Finally, he forged orders for Marksman Tiridan, worded a brief private message to him, and sent it off.

"Ridenspeed, Cory," Tayce whispered.

***

Zeri (June) 27, 1560
Same Day
East Detention Block, Prison Level, Royal Palace, City of Rammon

Marksman Cory Tiridan moved down the dim corridors with a soldier's sure steps, but his heart raced triple time within him.

The checkpoint guards studied his orders closely but let him pass without comment. Supreme Commander Kolknir was not a man they wanted to question.

When Tiridan came to East Detention Block number forty-five, he paused and studied the occupant.

Observant hazel eyes swept up and down, measuring his threat level. The Melian Maiden was older than him by several years, yet she stood respectfully when he stopped before her cell. Her mass of brown hair was barely contained by clips. Her movements were stiff, reminding him of the unpleasant business conducted that morning.

It seems so long ago.

Cory didn't know what the maidens had done but doubted it was serious enough to merit the shock torture. He racked his brain for a name.

"Lady Kia, do you swear to protect Princess Rela of House Minstel with your whole being from now until death claims you?" he asked.

"I have sworn thus and still swear it," she answered.

"Then, you will help me rescue her," Cory announced, releasing the lock. He swallowed hard, keenly aware that she could snap his neck in a heartbeat. "Please, Captain Tayce needs your help. Lord Kezem has arrested the princess."

Without waiting for a response, Cory moved to the next cell and repeated his question.

"We have all sworn to protect the princess," Kia said. "We will follow you until she is safe."

Cory nodded and disengaged the lock. He continued down the line, releasing the Melian Maidens one by one. Introductions were exchanged, and they fell in neatly behind him as he rushed down the confusing prison passages to the hov lot.

"Half in this one, half in the other," Cory ordered, hopping into the hov's pilot chair.

Kia, Jola, and another maiden whom Cory recognized from Princess Rela's brief visits jumped in the back. He started the engine and waited for the vehicle to rise to its customary half-meter height. It seemed to take an eternity, but once that was accomplished, he tinted the windows and started at an unhurried pace through the gates. The other three maidens went to the other hov, also having the good sense to tint the windows.

"The next hov is with me," Cory called casually to the guard.

"I just received the orders. You're free to proceed, marksman." The gate guard hit a button on his control panel and the gates rose.

Cory nodded, resisting the urge to sigh with relief.

"Do you have a plan?" Kia asked.

Her tone told Cory he had better answer wisely.

"At the moment, we're getting out of Rammon," Cory replied. "Then we'll rendezvous with Captain Tayce. He'll know our next step."

"Elia and Linnea heard Lord Kezem say he will take Princess Rela to the Frozen North. We must go to Estra," said Kia.

"The meeting point is on the way to Estra," Cory said, speaking hastily lest she lose patience with him. He felt the intensity of her gaze and willed himself to concentrate on driving.

"Very well. The princess trusts your captain, so shall we … for now," said Kia.

"Lord Kezem's life is connected to Princess Rela, but I fear his emotional control over his physical self will fail when he discovers there is no treasure. He may try to harm the princess. That is unacceptable," said Jola.

Unacceptable indeed. Does she always talk that way?

They grew silent and remained so until they had safely passed through Rammon's West Gate, Glider. The name came from the legend of Kern Glider, the half-god charged with guarding Riden.

***

Zeri (June) 27, 1560
Same Day
Kevil Plains

The well-armed, heavily armored convoy carrying Lord Kezem and the unhappy princess across the Kevil Plains sped along at unhealthy speeds. Kezem scratched absently at his left wrist and watched the land slip by. A windstorm had recently flattened most of the fields. Gray clouds dominated the sky, but so far, no rain had fallen. His wrist bothered him again. Kezem glanced down at his reddening wrists and frowned. He activated the transmitter.

"Stop that!" he said.

"They bother me," Rela whined.

"Makil, remove Princess Rela's bindings," Kezem instructed, pinching the bridge of his nose. "She's about to rub my wrists off here."

"It will be done, Excellency," the faithful soldier promised.

"Does he come with any other lines besides, 'it will be done, Excellency'?" Rela mocked, doing a wonderful impression of Makil.

"Rela, stop tormenting Makil," Kezem said wearily.

"Do you honestly think this is the best way to gain my cooperation on your silly little treasure hunt?" Rela asked, overdoing the superior princess tone.

"Who told you that?" Kezem demanded, planning executions as he spoke.

"His High Fakeness, the great Azhel Priest Benali," Rela replied, sounding bored.

Lord Kezem sat up straighter.

How does she know he's a fake?

His informants had taken over three weeks to come up with that information. She'd been in a hov with the man for less than an hour.

"She lies, Favored One," Benali protested. "I have told her nothing!"

Kezem hit a switch and a screen popped down offering him a close view of Benali's nose hairs. Grimacing, Kezem adjusted the vid to a less offensive view.

"I have known you were a fraud for months now. I keep you around because you speak some truths about Loresh."

"It's a fable," Rela said in a sing-song voice. She primly smoothed out the sleeve of the bright blue smartcloth shirt. The fibers would automatically bind closer together to protect her against cold and wind.

"I have told her nothing!" Benali repeated.

"Then how does she know?" Kezem demanded.

"His thoughts are as transparent as they are ugly," said Rela.

Kezem moved the vid camera to get a closer look at the defiant princess. Her expression was angry and very disgusted, but her clear blue eyes spoke truth. She didn't know he was watching so she would hardly bother feigning innocence. He flicked off the comm transmitter and cursed in Bornovan.

She can read minds! As disturbing as that thought was, it didn't surprise him. After all, her mother had been a Ranger witch. He turned the transmitter and receiver back on. It was time he made her options and the consequences of defiance very clear to her.

"—not believe the nasty things he's thought about me. Even now, his gaze is murderous!" Rela ranted, unaware Kezem had cut off communication for a few seconds.

"Oh, I believe you, Rela, but do not concern yourself with Benali. When his usefulness has expired, I will dispose of him." Kezem enjoyed Benali's priceless expression.

Concern flashed across Rela's face, before disgust and anger returned.

"Do you ever get tired of threatening people?"

"No," Kezem answered honestly. "Just as I'm sure you never grow tired of undermining me." He sighed, trying to collect his scattered thoughts.

This is going to be a very long trip.

"But that is not what I wished to discuss with you. Benali may be a fraud, but Loresh's treasures are real and I *will* have those treasures. You will find the entrance to the lower levels or I will slaughter your friends before your eyes!" Kezem didn't think it was possible for Rela's eyes to get any bigger, but they did.

"You are absolutely insane," Rela muttered, sinking back in the seat.

"What if I cannot find the door because it does not exist?" She asked the question softly, staring out the window.

"For your sake, Princess, I hope you're wrong," Kezem hissed.

The gathering storm punctuated his statement. A lightning bolt flew from one end of the night sky to the other. Thunder crashed a second later. Rain fell so fast Kezem ordered his hovs to stop. It was unlikely they would crash into a rock or salt pillar so long as they stayed on the road, but staying on the road was difficult because rain reduced visibility to nothing. The storm delayed them for an hour, but Kezem calculated they would still reach Chara within four hours. Wearily, he rose and went to his sleep chamber for some much-needed rest.

Talking to Rela takes more effort than it should.

Chapter 38:
Crossing the Lotrian Fields

Zeri (June) 27, 1560
Same Day
Royal Guard Camp, Kesler Plains

Next morning, something kicked at Kayleen Wellum's ankles.

"Wake up. We're about to move out," Something in the man's voice told her their destination had changed.

Kayleen rolled over and realized her right arm was completely numb. An electric shock woke the arm up nicely. The jolt also provided her with enough incentive to sit up straight.

"Go where?" Kayleen asked, now fully awake.

"Wouldn't you like to know," retorted the Royal Guard.

"I asked, didn't I?" Kayleen said. She gave the soldier a knowing grin. "But you don't know, right? You're just a lowly marksman who catches the menial tasks."

"Shut up. I'm going to release the stuncuffs and the ankle restraints so you can eat and take care of necessities. If you try anything, I'll twist your friend's broken arm until she screams so loud—"

"I understand," Kayleen said, cutting him off.

He released the ankle restraints and then her arms.

Massaging feeling into her arms, Kayleen let the soldier help her up.

"Thank you," she murmured from force of habit.

He nodded curtly and released her arm.

"I'm not contagious, Marksman Reed. Promise," said Kayleen, reading his nameplate.

He ignored her comment but backed out of the tent looking like he would rather be anywhere else.

Kayleen followed him out of the tent and was dismayed to see a whole army camp arrayed around her. A sea of blue uniforms stained the otherwise pretty countryside. Buttons winked gaily in the sunlight.

Kezem didn't have to empty the palace of Royal Guards on our account.

The soldier led her to a wash tent.

A meal bar sat on one counter along with a bottle of water. She picked up the bar and tapped it lightly against the counter. It made a solid thunking noise.

Yummy.

Kayleen set the bar aside and used the primitive sanitation facilities that came with the new troops. Next, she scrubbed her hands and face until they gleamed, rinsed out her mouth, ate the brick of a meal bar, and drank some of the water. Afterward, she fixed the braid which had come loose during the night. When she had stalled as long as she dared, Kayleen stepped from the tent and took a deep breath of cool morning air.

"That's much better," Kayleen said to absolutely no one. She glanced left and caught sight of her young guard who held the restraints. "Not again."

"You'd be done with these if you hadn't broken the hovs," Reed reminded her.

"Yes, and I'd probably be dead, too. I'll take the stuncuffs, thanks." Kayleen held her arms out like a good little prisoner.

He applied the cuffs, shrugged as if to say he didn't care, and bent down to reapply the ankle restraints.

"I could walk to where we're going and save you the trouble of carrying me," she offered.

Reed didn't look big enough to safely carry her more than a meter. Nodding agreement, he escorted her to the big tent in the center of the small camp.

A man with light brown hair, a sour expression, and a stiff posture stood, arms akimbo, watching Kayleen and her guard approach.

"Marksman Reed, why is that prisoner walking?"

Kayleen recognized the voice.

Hello, Predator One.

"I thought it would be easier than carrying her here, Captain Holeth," said the soldier nervously.

"Well, she's here now. Bind her legs," snapped the captain. "And put her arms behind her back."

"That won't be necessary," said a man standing behind Captain Holeth. He wore the insignia of an aster captain above his heart.

"Captain Quedron, this prisoner is dangerous," Holeth protested. "She took out four of my hovs yesterday like it was nothing."

"My men will take care of her," Quedron assured Holeth.

That's ominous.

Movement to Kayleen's right drew her attention. She nodded to Marc, Anabel, and Lorian. Their clothes were rumpled, but they appeared mostly rested. Anabel even seemed comfortable in the stuncuffs.

They must have turned off the shocks.

"Shall I knock them out, sir?" inquired a soldier with a clipped Terab accent.

"No, just the one will do," said Quedron.

Kayleen felt several hands clutch her shoulders. Something small and cold was pressed against her neck. She fought against the hands holding her.

A hissing sound came from the instrument and coldness spread throughout her body. Her limbs suddenly felt heavy, and she wished to sleep.

Teven, help!

***

Zeri (June) 27, 1560
Same Day
Temporary Rebel Camp, Kesler Plains

"Kayleen!" Teven McKnight awoke with her name on his lips. His breath came in gasps. Cold fear coursed through him.

The anotechs were trying to tell him something.

Teven, help!

He threw off his blanket and scrambled out of the tent.

"You're up early," Todd Wellum commented from his seat beside some glowing embers he was attempting to coax into a fire.

"It's Kayleen. She's scared," Teven said, trying to still his racing heart.

"Do you know where she is?" Todd asked, frowning.

Teven silently asked the anotechs the same question and received an answer.

"East of us … and moving south in a hov," Teven told his uncle.

"How do you know?"

"A friend of ours gave her some anotechs. I think she's using them to call me. I'll explain while we move. We've got to hurry." Teven was speaking fast, as if that would help them get to Kayleen quicker.

Captain Alexi Gordon stepped out of his tent.

"What's going on? You look worried," said the captain.

"We've got to leave now," Teven said.

Gordon opened his mouth. His expression said he was framing an apology.

Teven waved a hand.

"I know you have obligations here, Captain. Good luck finding your followers."

"We will join you as soon as possible, Prince Teven," Captain Gordon promised.

"Captain, I must ask you and your followers to keep my identity a secret until it is safe," Teven said.

"Of course, Highness. May Riden swiftly bring that day," Captain Gordon replied.

Teven and his uncle broke down their tents, grabbed their packs, and began jogging toward the Lotrian Fields. On the way, Teven explained about the anotechs, too distracted to even realize that Todd Wellum didn't seem surprised. They reached the Lotrian Fields in a little less than an hour.

"Just what I need, a lesson in patience," Teven grumbled, glaring at the foul-looking land.

The Lotrian Fields were swamps infested with nasty reptilian carnivores called goritors. Both male and female goritors could grow to over five meters in length, a size that surpassed even zaloks. Practically blind, goritors relied on movement and scent to catch their prey. Their thick hides could stop energy blasts but were surprisingly vulnerable to metal blades at several soft spots.

Todd rubbed odor neutralizing spray on his arms and legs and offered Teven some.

"The anotechs will handle that," Teven said.

"Don't rely on them so much," Todd said. "One day it's going to get you in trouble."

Teven fingered his derringer dagger and considered the advice. The narrow road stretching across the Lotrian Fields was in poor repair because no one wanted to fight the goritors to fix it. Taking a deep breath and trying not to think about the danger, he stepped onto the path.

Todd didn't follow.

"Come on," Teven urged. "There won't be any goritors for a few miles."

"I'm going to make a call first," said Todd.

Teven didn't argue but looked at Todd impatiently. The comm chimed, confirming that the transmitter was seeking another signal.

"Ranger Wellum?"

"Greetings, Captain Tayce, I need your help. My daughter has been captured by Lord Kezem's men, and they are headed south. We need to follow them fast, but it'll take weeks on foot."

"She must have been part of yesterday's skirmish on the Kesler Plains," Tayce said.

"Correct," Todd confirmed.

"Then, I have good and bad news for you," said Tayce with a sigh. "The good news is that they will take your daughter to Loresh. I am heading there now with some Melian Maidens to try and save Princess Rela from Lord Kezem's wrath. Plug the comm into your infopad, and I'll send you the coordinates. The bad news is that Kezem will use her and the others to force the princess to find Loresh's hidden chambers. Where are you?"

Loresh! Mother mentioned Loresh. Rela's there?

The effort to absorb the information left Teven dazed. He forced himself to pay attention to Todd's conversation.

"Crossing the Lotrian Fields," Todd answered. He pulled out his infopad and plugged the comm into it.

"I'll send a hov to pick you up, but you're still going to have to hurry if you want to arrive in time."

"Thank you, Captain. Ridenspeed."

Teven and Todd moved down the narrow concrete strip as fast as they dared but not nearly fast enough for Teven. Anxiety ate at the pit of his stomach, reminding him he had neglected to eat anything.

"She's getting farther away!" said Teven.

"Slow down!" Todd warned in a loud whisper, pointing left where a goritor's trio of yellow eyes stared at them.

Teven nearly screamed but held the cry inside. Winding up a goritor's morning meal would not save Kayleen, and for his own sanity, Teven had to believe that he could somehow save her. Knowing she was his cousin only enflamed his protective instincts. Each passing second seemed an eternity to Teven as he and Todd inched forward one cautious step at a time. An hour later, the end came in sight. Though a half-mile off, the goal taunted Teven until he broke into a sprint.

"Teven, no!" Todd shouted, running after him.

A blur was Teven's only warning before a goritor's teeth-laden mouth snapped at his right leg. He leapt straight up, drew his dagger, and slashed downward, burying his dagger in a soft spot in the goritor's neck.

Todd's dagger flashed four times.

The goritor hissed and screeched, thrashing about until it died.

Teven slowly pulled his dagger out and stared at the black blood oozing down the handle. He stooped and cleaned the dagger on some nearby marsh grass, still acutely aware of the danger. Every goritor in hearing range would soon be lumbering over to feast on the fallen.

We need to leave! Teven thought, even as Todd pulled at his arm. Teven stumbled, but then, a picture of Kayleen's face came to mind with sudden clarity. Regaining his feet, he took off again toward the tiny glint in the distance that should be the ride Captain Tayce had promised.

They reached the yellow hov at the same time.

"I'm driving!" Teven and Todd both claimed.

"Have you ever driven a hov before?" Todd challenged.

Teven shook his head.

"Then, like I said, I'm driving."

"When was the last time *you* drove?" Teven shot back.

"Never mind that. Get in," said Todd.

Reluctantly, Teven obeyed. Todd started the engine and had the hov racing forward before Teven had the safety restraint fastened. Teven pitched forward and caught himself with his hands, scrambling to secure himself in the seat. A rock pillar loomed ahead. Todd swerved left to shoot around it.

Teven stared in horror as the rock passed inches from his face.

"We need to get there in one piece!"

"Quiet! I'm driving here!" called Todd.

"Rock! Rock!" Teven cried.

"Pipe down!" The hov swung right, this time partially scrapping a salt pillar.

"Just give me a second to get used to the controls."

Teven shrank into the hov's passenger seat, wishing Kayleen were there and hoping he didn't die before seeing her again.

Chapter 39:
Crystal Lake

Zeri (June) 27, 1560
Same Day
Northern Shore of Crystal Lake

"Great," Todd grumbled. "Just what we need."

"What's wrong?" Teven shook his head, trying to wake up from a nap.

"Low fuel." Todd pointed to an angry glowing button that grew bright orange and then faded to dull orange in an incessant cycle.

Instantly, Teven was wide awake.

"Where are we?" he asked.

"Nearing Crystal Lake, why?" asked Todd.

"Stay near the lake," Teven instructed. His expression said he had an idea he didn't really like

"If we crash, the last place on this planet I want to be is by this lake," Todd argued. "They say the water is—"

"Combustible," Teven finished with a reckless grin.

The hov sputtered, coughed one final agonized breath, and died but not before Todd Wellum wrestled it to the edge of the Crystal Lake. It settled onto the sand with a thump. The lake's water looked deceptively beautiful. The sun winked off tiny waves, but there was no sign of life in the lake. Any fish unfortunate enough to be washed from the Clear River into Crystal Lake had its flesh eaten off by the toxic chemicals.

"I hope you know what you're doing," Todd said.

"Trust me."

"Like I have a choice," Todd mumbled.

Teven searched the hov for the fuel port and found it on the side facing away from the lake.

"Help me swing this thing around."

Together, they managed to turn the hov. It was dangerously close to the water by the time they were done, but that had been Teven's intent.

"Okay, I see where your mind's at, but how are we going to get the water into the hov?"

Teven didn't answer Todd's question. Instead, he opened the fuel port, sat down, and gripped the edge with his left hand. Next, he stretched his right hand toward the water.

Todd gasped.

Teven's eyes shut against the pain as the chemicals chewed at his hand. An anotech shield prevented any damage real damage, but Todd found it painful to watch the process. Water flowed from the lake up Teven's right arm, over his neck, down his left arm, and into the hov's fuel tank.

Fifteen minutes later and only three quarters done, Teven's arms began to slump, hindering the fuel shuttle.

"Hold my arms up," he ordered. "We must save Kayleen."

Todd hesitated but knew Teven was serious, so he did as asked.

The process took twenty-three minutes, and when it was over, Teven slumped in Todd's arms in a semi-conscious state.

"You did good, kid," Todd said hoarsely.

He knew it would take just under two hours to reach Chara. They would have to stop for supplies and a water hov or wait an hour to get the land hov fitted to handle water. From there, they could make Estra in another two hours and hike to Loresh.

Todd gently picked up Teven and placed him in the back of the hov so he could sleep while they traveled. As he fixed the safety straps, Todd studied his nephew who knew his daughter better than he did. They had spoken briefly the evening before, enough so that Todd could see the boy was in love with his daughter. He assumed such deep devotion could not develop unreciprocated. His heart ached for them. It had been cruel of fate to throw them together without warning.

He will always be a royal, and Kayleen will always be a Ranger.

As he climbed into the driver's seat and started the engine, Todd shuddered at just how disastrous the last such relationship had turned out. Reia's defiance of the ancient codes against intermarrying with House Minstel had split the Rangers along ideological lines. Not wanting to think about that, Todd turned his thoughts to his daughter.

What is Kayleen like?

The last time Todd had seen Kayleen, she had been a strong-willed child with untamable fiery hair. The mental picture of her rosy cheeks and constant smile made him grin. The brief picture of her during the battle on the Kesler Plains was quite different but no less special. There she showed only grim determination to fight and live.

She's alive but a captive!

The thought brought both comfort and grief.

I must save her. Kiata would kill me if I let anything happen to our daughter.

Todd programmed the hov to pilot itself while they reached a long, straight section of open road. Then, he let his thoughts turn to his long-dead wife, Kiata Antellio Wellum, who had been very close to her younger sister, Reia. Todd had grown up with them in a Ranger camp in the Riden Mountains. Their parents had been murdered by people wanting to steal their tosh mines. For a moment, Todd wondered if Basil and Sela Antellio weren't luckier having perished long before things turned so dark for their daughters. He regretted the thought. There might be pain in the knowledge, but he'd

rather know his daughter's fate than wonder forever.

Maybe Teven and Kayleen trained in the same camp.

He fondly recalled how the sisters had tormented him by speaking Kalastan backwards. He didn't even know how they managed that. Kiata had always been ready to fulfill her Ranger duties. Her heart had been wounded when the Ashatan Council cast out her sister for loving Prince Terosh. The meandering path of Todd's thoughts turned again to Reia.

She was always more serious than Kiata. Almost as beautiful as well.

His thoughts flew past the rift over Reia's choice, the secret marriage he and Kiata had attended, the death of King Teorn and Prince Tate, Prince Terosh's rise to the throne, and Reia's rise with him. The years had been both sad and happy. He and Kiata had moved to Rammon to be ambassadors to the palace. There had even been peace for several years.

He wanted to pause his thoughts in those good years, but more images flooded Todd's mind. GAPP's initial clumsy overtures to tempt Reshner to join them, Queen Reia's Safe Service Act, Rorge II's plight, more discussion over joining GAPP, King Terosh's disastrous duel with Kezem, the Colza Star explosion, Teven's birth, Rela's birth, discussions deteriorating to debates, Tavel's birth, Terosh's assassination, and finally, Kezem's attack on the palace. In one night, Todd's wife and her sister had been murdered and he had been thrown into prison where he spent many dark years. The thought of prison brought him back to his daughter.

If anyone touches her, I will end them.

Chapter 40:
Glass Coast Mercenary

Zeri (June) 27, 1560
Same Day
Ash Plains

Teven silently willed the hov to go faster. The anotechs, taking him literally, sent a detachment to enhance the hov's engine.

"Whoa!" Todd exclaimed as the machine jerked forward with a power surge. "Did you do that?"

"Sorry." Teven called the anotechs back.

"No, no. We can use all the power we can get," Todd said.

They reached Chara, a city on the Glass Coast, without serious incident, but Todd's driving bordered on reckless.

"Can I drive to Estra?" Teven asked.

Todd slipped the hov left to miss an angry pedestrian.

The blue-skinned being twirled its tentacles at them in a gesture Teven guessed was meant to be rude.

"Watch it!" Teven shouted.

Todd weaved and missed a young couple who had been gazing into each other's eyes. Now, their eyes were just wide with fright.

"Slow down. We don't want to kill somebody by accident," Teven said. As the city flew by, he gripped the seat so hard his knuckles turned white.

"Let's see how long it's going to take for them to outfit our hov to handle water," said Todd. "I'd like to keep the enhanced version."

It took Todd several minutes to maneuver the hov through the narrow streets to the marina where the necessary modifications could take place. After a vigorous bartering match with the squat owner of Teague's Water Wonders, Todd worked out a deal to have their hov modified for two thousand kefs. Another thousand kefs on top of that bought them top priority and a promise to cut the time down to forty minutes.

Teven had to use almost all the kefs he had left.

It's a small price if it'll pay the way to Kayleen.

They entered a local tavern to pass the time and get something to eat.

Todd ordered a fried nefletch fish on rye bread and an ale that looked and smelled like it would be fine fuel for their hov. The anotechs couldn't decide if the sickeningly sweet, sharp smell was offensive or not, but Teven cleared up that point by instructing them to filter the ale odor. He ordered tropher cakes and lila juice.

While they waited, Teven listened to the conversations around them. He closed his eyes, released a few anotechs through his fingertips, and sent them to nearby tables. If Todd noticed anything strange he said nothing. The first dozen conversations that flooded Teven's mind were mundane, covering everything from the recent rash of storms to Glass Coast Water Tower's fight with Meritel Power Plus over rights to Crystal Lake. Teven sent the anotechs to another table. He continued in this manner until reaching a corner table where one word caught his attention.

"—ing to Loresh! I no care it pay well. I no work for that man!" said an irritated male voice.

"Keep your voice down! What difference does it make who we work for?" asked another male voice, slightly louder than the first.

"He betray king!"

Teven could almost picture the second man rolling his eyes.

"Are you ever going to get over that? It's been more than a decade. Move on. Your crazy theories are standing in the way of good money."

"I no go against conscience," declared the first man.

"I'm not missing out on that many kefs! I'll be back when the job's done." A rustling sound indicated the second man was leaving. Four seconds later, he brushed past Teven and Todd's table and exited the tavern.

"Be right back," Teven promised. He jumped from his chair like it had suddenly grown hot and charged to the back corner where the two mercenaries had been talking. Placing both hands on the table, he called the anotechs back. A bald man looked up surprised. He barely glanced at Teven. Instead, he scanned the room for danger.

His voice made him sound so much older.

The four digits on each of the being's hands kept tapping his bottled ale, but Teven's danger sense was aroused. Soon, he realized that two more hands were under the table pointing pistols at him.

"Who was offering that job you refused?" Teven asked.

"Who ask?" inquired the man, returning to his drink. Though it appeared as if the man wasn't looking at him, Teven got the distinct impression that he was under intense scrutiny.

"Does the name Ectosh Laocer mean anything to you?" asked Teven. "What makes you think he betrayed the king?"

The man's orange eyes flashed with anger.

"As Royal Guard, I see traitor talk to Kezem. I in prison many years. I shave head since king murdered!" The man had a way of cutting out inconsequential words, but Teven had understood him well enough. "I feel king die! Elish see things you not dream of."

"You were a Royal Guard?" Teven inquired, surprised.

The man's eyes narrowed.

"Once, many species Royal Guard. We fought for honor and peace, but no longer."

"Fight for peace again," Teven said.

The man, who had been staring deep into his drink, lifted his gaze to Teven and shook his head to clear the ale-induced fog.

"Voice," he said hoarsely. "You royal!"

"Shhh! It's not safe to say that here," Teven said. "I have no money to hire you, but my sister and friends are at Loresh. Help me save them, and I will do everything I can to compensate you."

"For peace, honor, and slain brother, Covin, I serve you," the Elish said, putting the pistols back in their holsters.

Does he speak the truth?

Zareb is a friend of House Minstel. Trust him.

Teven led his new friend to the table where Todd sat. By the time he returned, the food had arrived.

Todd had finished his nefletch fish and was working on a second container of ale.

"You haven't aged a day," Todd said upon seeing their guest.

"Elish age different," Zareb replied. "Look same fifty year then change. Look same second fifty then die."

"I had forgotten," Todd murmured.

Zareb and Todd continued to talk while Teven ate his tropher cakes. The forty minutes passed quickly. They returned to Teague's Water Wonders where their modified hov sat ready to take on the South Asrien Sea. Extra steering fins, a pointed front piece, and waterproof engine covers had transformed the land hov into a sleek water hov.

To Teven's relief, Zareb drove the hov and knew exactly how to handle it in rough waves. Along the way, the Elish explained what he knew.

"Captain Laocer call many mercenary. He says camp in Loresh from day past to two day forward. I no know how he lure him, but he expect Lord Kezem soon."

"Whatever he did, it worked," Teven said, only partly listening. As usual, his thoughts dwelt on Kayleen. He could still hear her call for help. Her anotechs seemed upset about something.

We must go faster!

He again enhanced the hov's performance with anotechs.

They reached Estra in just under two hours. The ice-covered city twinkled under the sun, but Teven couldn't enjoy the beauty.

They rented a room in southern Estra.

The owner, a petite woman with flowing white hair, frowned at their arsenal.

"Great, more mercenaries," she muttered.

"We fight for honor, Lady Brina," the Elish said solemnly.

"That's what they all say, honey," the woman responded.

"One time, Zareb fight for kef. Now fight for son of king."

Brina gave Zareb a look that said he was crazy.

Teven tugged on Zareb's lower right arm and pulled him toward the room where they would stash their supplies. Teven changed into warmer clothes and strapped on a weapon belt. The weight of his banistick and kerlinblade balanced a serlak pistol taken from Todd's stash. He added a pouch of flingers.

"You're going to fall over," Todd said. "Maybe you should leave the banistick."

"I'm used to it by now," Teven replied.

They left Estra and headed south to Loresh. Teven ran, relying on the anotechs for extra traction. They had no time to waste.

Kayleen's in there. We must find her!

Chapter 41:
Escape in the Frozen North

Zeri (June) 27, 1560
Same Day
Loresh Cave System, Frozen North
The twenty-kilometer system of tunnels and caves known as Loresh best resembled a cross sectional slice of passion fruit stuck in the snow at a forty-five degree angle. The main tunnel, wide enough to squeeze a hov tank through and high enough to accommodate claustrophobic humans, sloped down into a large central cavern before angling deeper into Reshner via a twin. Two minor tunnels, flanking the main one, also emptied into the central cavern. Smaller tunnels branch off seemingly at random, leading to various side caves. Cheerful glowcrystals embedded in the walls have witnessed many explorers die seeking treasures as exotic as youth gems and as simple as gold.

The mercenaries arrived first and spent their time staying warm and preparing ambushes. Typical for their kind, the mercs didn't trust each other. Everyone's desire to kill Lord Kezem resulted in much counterproductive activity. Their master had been clear on only one other point: do not kill Princess Rela until after Loresh's secrets are unlocked. That ruled out most traps, including mines. No one would have used mines anyway for fear of collapsing the system and condemning everybody. Most specialized in brute force anyway.

Lord Kezem's soldiers escorting the Kesler Plains captives arrived second. At Captain Quedron's order, they spread out to prepare Loresh for His Excellency. More squads of Royal Guards and RLA soldiers were slated to arrive throughout the day.

The Royal Guards deposited the prisoners in a small side cave immediately off the main tunnel. An ancient door preserved by ice converted the cave into a cold prison. The door was currently swung inward. Strategically placed portable lamps brightened the cave above the eerie light from glowcrystals.

"Kayleen, wake up!" Lorian Petole called, nudging her friend with her boot.

The guards had carried Kayleen on a hov sled, but now that they were in Loresh, they wanted the prisoners awake to meet Lord Kezem. Lorian had begged the guards to let her wake Kayleen naturally. She didn't know what chemical they intended to inject her friend with but the fewer chemicals involved the better. Kayleen shivered but remained stubbornly unconsciousness.

"Step aside," ordered a soldier. With his short military haircut, clean shaven face, and constant frown, the soldier looked like the rest of his squad.

Lorian didn't have to look to know he held the same nasty instrument that had knocked Kayleen out in the first place.

"Give me a few minutes," said Lorian. "This would go faster if my arms weren't behind me."

"Captain Quedron's orders," replied the soldier without inflection.

Lorian almost spoke the words with him, for that's all her complaints ever earned her. She carefully lowered herself to her knees.

"Kayleen, please wake up. Lord Kezem will be here soon. You wouldn't want to miss that, would you?"

Kayleen slowly opened one eye, consequently raising an eyebrow, forming a questioning expression.

Lorian chuckled.

"That got your attention." To her relief, the soldier went away.

The door crunched back into place, leaving them alone. At least, they could talk freely now.

"I have got to stop waking up like this," Kayleen muttered, opening her other eye. "Where are we? I'm freezing."

"You *are* lying like a slab of preserved tretling meat on a hov sled in the Frozen North with half a sleeve missing," Lorian said, suppressing a shiver. The derringer attire of simple beige cotton shirt and comfortable brown trousers was not keeping much of the Frozen North out. Lorian wished she could help Kayleen climb to her feet, but the stuncuffs nixed that option.

Kayleen groaned with the effort to sit up.

It's a start, thought Lorian.

The soldier returned carrying a black stack of clothes.

"Captain Quedron says you should put these on," he said, throwing some warm shirts at them. He turned to leave.

Lorian cleared her throat. He glanced at her, and she turned sideways so he could see her bound arms.

"I'm not authorized to release you," he said, flustered. He left, presumably to seek out permission to remove the stuncuffs. The metals in the tunnel and cave walls wreaked havoc with communications.

"Are they always that inefficient?" Kayleen asked.

"Unfortunately, yes and no," Anabel answered.

"You missed the morning meal," Marc added. "That was a fiasco. They served tretling stew ration packs, and no one was authorized to give us utensils for fear we'd turn them into weapons. Then, when we did get spoons, no one was authorized to release our hands. They ended up spoon feeding us like babies!"

The soldier returned.

"I have acquired authorization to release you one by one to change," he said.

Kayleen was first. The soldier removed the stuncuffs and ankle restraints as quickly as possible, then stepped back and stared at her. She climbed to her feet and managed to slip the warm, smartcloth shirt under her derringer shirt. The soldier frowned, obviously wondering if that was authorized or not, but he said nothing as he settled the stuncuffs and ankle restraints back into position. This time though, Kayleen's hands were bound in front of her. Next, he released Lorian who followed Kayleen's example of slipping the warmer shirt under her own. After Marc and Anabel were changed as well, the soldier left. They waited for the door to completely shut.

"Are you really that cold?" Lorian asked Kayleen.

"No, but black comes fairly close to blue in the shadows, and I am not looking like a Kezem lackey when the shooting starts," Kayleen declared.

They were silent for about thirty seconds.

Kayleen appeared deep in thought.

Lorian didn't want to disturb her, so she waited.

"What do we do?" she finally asked, glancing at each of her companions.

"I'd rather not wait around for Lord Kezem to come kill me," Kayleen said.

As Lorian watched, Kayleen's stuncuffs flew off, hit the far wall in between Marc and Anabel, and thudded to the ground at their feet.

Everyone stared at Kayleen with mouths open.

"Sorry. Guess I overdid that," Kayleen said with an apologetic grin. "The anotechs and I are still working on communication." The ankle restraints also fell off.

At Kayleen's touch, Lorian's stuncuffs promptly unfastened. She wriggled free of them and rubbed her hands up and down her arms to enhance circulation. Even with the smartcloth shirt the cold air nipped at her skin.

"Next move?" Marc asked, after Kayleen had released his cuffs. He looked to Kayleen whose Ranger skills made her the obvious leader in this strange environment.

Lorian didn't mind. Loresh was a long way from the Rammon palace, and Kayleen seemed capable. Despite having traveled with her for several weeks, Lorian realized she knew little about the Ranger turned derringer.

"First question: how are you?" Kayleen asked in a no-nonsense manner. "Second question: can you fight?"

"Fit to serve, Captain Kayleen," Marc said with a grin. "Requesting authorization to engage the enemy."

Lorian glared at him.

"I'd prefer to avoid hand-to-hand encounters, but I can still blast things," Anabel offered.

"I'm good to go," Lorian said.

"How many guards are there? Where are our weapons?"

No one had a chance to answer Kayleen's questions because their young guard opened the door. Seeing them free of restraints, he reacted like any good soldier and opened his mouth to shout a warning. Fear overcame cold, and Lorian snapped into action. She leapt toward him, flattened her right hand, and slammed it none too gently into his throat. A strangled noise escaped him, as he collapsed, drawing the other guard's attention.

Marc and Kayleen dodged Lorian and the first guard to reach the second. Marc grabbed the man by the shirt and pulled forward while Kayleen slipped behind the man and put him in a chokehold. She applied enough pressure so the man would concentrate on breathing and not screaming but not enough to knock him out. It helped that she was shorter, and thus, his back was already arched.

"Marc, get the door," Kayleen said. "I think we have the answers to our questions."

"Where's the armory?" Lorian asked. Lord Kezem's troops always kept a temporary armory or two in their camps.

"I'm not—"

"This *is* your authorization," Kayleen said, giving his throat a squeeze.

The man had a pretty thick neck. Lorian was impressed Kayleen's relatively small arms could keep such a firm grip around the neck.

"Cave!" the man gasped.

"Could you please be a little more precise? There's nothing but caves here," Lorian continued, folding her arms impatiently.

It feels good to be in control again.

"Two down to the left," their prisoner answered.

"How many soldiers will be there?" Anabel wanted to know. She fingered the kerlak gun she had acquired from the first soldier.

Lorian took over the man's kerlinblade.

Marc retrieved the weapons from the man Kayleen held.

"Don't be sad because you're second best," Marc said addressing the prisoner. "We're derringers of the Royal Guard."

"Marc, he *is* a Royal Guard," Anabel pointed out. "Besides, that kind of talk gets people killed."

"Answer the question," Kayleen ordered.

The soldier glared at Marc but said nothing.

"Wrong choice." Kayleen squeezed the pressure point on the man's neck until he passed out.

"Blade or gun?" Marc asked, once Kayleen's hands were free. He managed to make the choices sound exciting.

"I'll take the blade, thanks."

The small band of escapees cautiously entered the main tunnel. Marc slid the bar across the door, sealing the hapless guards inside. Lorian took off after Kayleen at a slow jog. They took turns searching side caves for weapons caches. It would have been ideal if they could find their own weapon belts. All derringers became sentimental when it came to their banisticks. Any quality merchant sold banisticks, but long hours on the Kireshana usually resulted in personal modifications. Also, the banisticks and kerlinblades they had acquired in Fort Riden had been recently updated.

Lorian hoped to avoid patrols, but wishful thinking was no match for fate. Barely a half-dozen meters from their prison, a patrol of four emerged from a side tunnel. Marc and Anabel shot without hesitation. Anabel's aim was a little wobbly but three of her four shots hit the front man in the left shoulder, spinning him around. Marc's blast caught the second man in the throat. Kayleen and Lorian leapt forward and cut down the third man. The fourth hastily retreated, racing down the tunnel. Marc and Anabel sent energy beams streaming after him, but he escaped around a corner.

Marc took two steps in pursuit before Kayleen halted him.

"Stop! We need to find more weapons before we take on the entire Royal Guard."

"We have to stay together," Lorian added.

"We should move the bodies," Anabel said. Everyone nodded but no one moved. "Don't look at me," she said, raising her broken arm.

Lorian, Marc, and Kayleen each grabbed a corpse and dragged it to the last side cave they had passed. Anabel got the door. When the bodies were safely stowed, Anabel closed and locked the doors. Lorian considered going back to kill the first two soldiers but dismissed the thought with a shrug.

"Shouldn't we hunt the patrols while they're vulnerable?" Anabel asked.

Kayleen and Lorian shook their heads.

"We're going to run into enough of them as it is," Kayleen explained.

"No use seeking more trouble," Lorian agreed.

Chapter 42:
The Search for Turgot's Treasure

Zeri (June) 27, 1560
Same Day
Loresh Cave System, Frozen North

Lord Kezem glared at Aster Captain Quedron. The brilliance of Princess Rela's smile would have outshone all three full moons.

"We will find them, Lord Kezem," Quedron promised. "The guards they attacked were found almost an hour ago and are being treated—"

"I don't care about the guards," Kezem interrupted. "I want my prisoners back!"

"Yes, Lord Kezem, it will be done."

Rela watched with distaste as Quedron bowed to Lord Kezem and barked orders to his soldiers who retreated into the side tunnel they had appeared from only moments before.

"You underestimated them," Rela taunted. "Three derringers and a Ranger are not to be trifled with." She didn't understand why she knew the information, but something had whispered it into her mind. An artery in Kezem's forehead ticked, and Rela managed to suppress another grin.

"They will come for you, Princess," Kezem sneered, turning to face her.

"Without them, your threats mean nothing. You cannot kill me without harming yourself," Rela said. She was getting sick of this invisible link between them, and she didn't like this creepy place either. Loresh gave her chills in several different flavors. It was like a thousand soft, jumbled whispers called to her from every direction.

"It doesn't matter. They are drawn to you by misguided notions of rescue. When they come, my men will take them. In the meantime, I suggest you start searching for my treasure. For every day that passes, I will kill one of your friends as slowly and painfully as possible."

"It could take weeks to search every cave!" Rela protested.

"Find my treasure!" Kezem shouted like a petulant child.

"Turgot's treasure," Rela replied, surprising everyone.

"What?"

Lord Kezem drew uncomfortably close, breathing foul breath into her face. But just as soon as the stench hit her, it vanished.

"You seek Jaspen Turgot's treasure." Rela closed her eyes and frowned. "But I do not think you will like it." She bit her lip thoughtfully.

"I'll be the judge of that. You just find it!"

"Please stop shouting," said Rela.

"There will be shouting and pain if you don't move it," Kezem vowed.

Part of Rela wished he would hurt her just for the pain it would cause him.

"Might as well start searching," Rela said.

Kezem spun on his heel and stalked down the main tunnel.

Rela followed, desperately trying to think of a way to escape. As they walked deeper into Loresh, Rela was surprised to find herself in the lead. She stopped suddenly.

"Keep moving," Kezem ordered.

Rela swallowed a retort. Maybe if she found this secret chamber and proved that it held nothing, the nightmare would end. She let her feet take over.

The voices returned, beckoning her straight ahead.

The main tunnel dumped the party into the central cavern which spanned fifty meters in front of them and thirty meters to their left and right. The cavern itself ended prematurely. Solid rock walls rose to either side of the main tunnel's twin which began a few meters behind a small stone pillar. The ceiling was so high that it disappeared into the darkness above, a place no glowcrystal bothered growing. Like everywhere else in Loresh, the glowcrystals provided ample lighting along the walls and paths. The naturally good acoustics turned the cavern into an amphitheater. On either side of the downward sloping main path, a series of wide stairs were carved into the rock and ice.

"Beautiful," Rela murmured. She felt a familiar presence press close around her. A shove started her down the path. Soon, she approached the stone altar and read the strange symbols on it. "Etmani coress cherimon. Dantel corla asmenai."

The excited, indistinct voices inside her whispered the meaning.

"What's she saying, Lord Kezem?" asked a young soldier.

Luckily for him, Lord Kezem wondered that as well and was too shocked to punish the man.

"It means 'Here lies the gate. Enter to seek wisdom.'" Rela stretched out her hand and touched the pillar. A small cry escaped her as some anotechs left her for an instant to unlock the hidden chamber.

Having experienced the same tiny prick of pain she did, Kezem frowned and stared down at his right hand.

Large portions of the rock walls flanking the second half of the main tunnel behind the pillar swung in slowly with a loud grinding noise.

Excitement and horror battled inside Rela as she waited to see what treasures lay ahead.

***

Teven McKnight charged down a side tunnel.

Kayleen's ahead.

Lord Kezem's guards at the entrance had put up a pitiful fight. Zareb and Todd Wellum flanked Teven left and right respectively. Zareb brandished two kerlak guns and two serlak guns. As their loud nature made them poor stealth weapons, the serlak guns were only present in case the situation turned desperate.

Suddenly, a violet kerlinblade flashed toward Teven's head. He whipped out his own blade and met it. The other blade immediately turned white, and Teven found himself staring into Kayleen's gorgeous silver-blue eyes. Even with an intense expression, she was more beautiful than he remembered. Next instant, their blades were back on their belts, and they were in each other's arms.

Not caring whether or not they ought to fall in love, Teven leaned down and kissed Kayleen. Her lips were cold and soft and sweeter than anything he had ever tasted. Teven never knew how long that wonderful moment lasted. The next thing he became aware of was Todd Wellum's trembling voice whispering Kayleen's name. Teven stepped back, feeling guilty but still gripping Kayleen's hands.

"This is not a good place for a reunion," Lorian said tersely.

The group of seven ducked into a semi-private cave. Marc, Anabel, Zareb, and Lorian settled themselves by the door and spoke softly. Todd, Teven, and Kayleen moved to the back. An awkward pause ensued. Todd stared at Kayleen like a man suddenly thrust into the presence of a goddess. His breath came shallowly, and his expression clearly said he had about a thousand things to say. Kayleen returned the steady gaze with a measured one of her own that covered Todd's face. Teven could almost feel the warm familiarity that slowly spread through his friend. He took the opportunity to openly stare at her.

"Father?" Kayleen finally asked in wonder and disbelief. Her eyes sparkled to life in a way Teven adored. Todd and Kayleen's hands clasped with desperate strength. Then, Kayleen practically tackled her father. "I don't believe it!"

"It's been near forever, Kaylee," Todd murmured into her hair. Tears flowed down his worn face. His story poured out almost faster than Teven could absorb. "I was captured when Rammon fell. Lord Kezem sent men to capture or kill every Ranger, especially those of us loyal to the queen. Your mother—" Todd's voice hitched. He took two quick, ragged breaths and continued, "Your mother was killed before I reached home, but she must have sent you away with Nils. I spent many years in the prison below the palace, but thoughts of you kept me alive! I knew I would find you if given the chance, and Captain Tayce gave me that chance."

"Nils died, Father. He was murdered," Kayleen said. Her voice was muffled because her face was buried against Todd's chest.

"Kayleen, listen to me," said Todd. "There's something more you need to know. Your—"

A shout from Lorian broke up the happy reunion. Kayleen and her father released each other and reached for weapons. Teven's kerlinblade was in his hand in an instant. Zareb, Anabel, and Marc gunned down a group of mercenaries.

"We need to leave!" Lorian called.

A strange feeling swept over Teven.

The anotechs were very excited.

"Princess Rela is near," said Teven.

"Then let's find her," Marc said impatiently.

"No, Lord Kezem wants you three as hostages. Stay here," said Kayleen.

"No way!" Marc, Anabel, and Lorian declared as one.

"You're going to need our help," Lorian explained. "Lord Kezem will use anyone against the princess. Nobody can get caught. We all go."

Teven nodded and followed his instincts through the maze of side tunnels back to the main tunnel. The four patrols they met along the way scattered in disarray. Nothing was going to stop Teven from reaching his sister.

Chapter 43:
Fight for the Crash Site

Zeri (June) 27, 1560
Same Day
Central Chamber, Loresh Cave System, Frozen North

"Halt!" The commanding young voice bounced around the cavern in a creepy manner.

Lord Kezem had been savoring the sweet taste of victory. The treasure lay just beyond wide open doors. Nothing could stop him from claiming it. He glared resentfully at the pest who stood at the top of the path.

"Kill them!" he barked.

"I thought you wanted them alive," Captain Quedron said from Kezem's left.

"We don't need them now," Kezem insisted.

Before he could stop her, Rela touched the stone pillar again, and the stone doors began closing.

"No!" Kezem pressed the princess's hand against the pillar.

Nothing happened.

"Release the princess!" shouted the irritating boy. He began descending the path with a small group of well-armed backup.

"I was right! It does depend on her willingness!" Benali exclaimed.

Kezem ignored them all. He threw his left arm across Rela's neck and pressed her right hand harder against the pillar. He could feel an invisible hand painfully grasping his arm, but he refused to acknowledge the pain.

"Open the doors!" he ordered.

"You will never get in if you harm them," Rela promised. Her voice betrayed nothing but determination.

"Seize them!" Kezem screamed. His men scrambled to obey. Energy beams began flying, and Lord Kezem turned to use Rela as a shield. Realizing how ridiculous that was since their lives were linked, he growled and flung her at Captain Quedron. "Protect her!"

Lord Kezem snatched his kerlinblade off his belt and batted away several beams. He charged up the path at the newcomers. As he did, twenty mercenaries rushed into the main cavern and attacked both his men and the intruders. He threw himself into the fight, slashing left and right with his two-toned blade. The thin core was red, matching his anger, and the outside was bright orange. Two mercenaries fell in pieces. One of the young intruders stumbled toward him. He could have shoved his blade right through her, but he refrained for the sake of Rela's favor. Instead, he slashed the throat of the mercenary who had sent her flying.

"Kill the mercenaries! Capture the others!" Kezem commanded.

Three mercenaries blasted at him with energy guns. A four-armed intruder shot them repeatedly from behind and nodded at Lord Kezem before turning his guns on the next poor mercenary.

Kezem nearly tripped over the young intruder he had saved. She was struggling to her feet, clutching one arm protectively. Seizing her by the shirt, he tossed her down the path toward Quedron. He could not win this chaotic battle. He had too few men.

"Captain, retreat to the base! We will return with more men!" shouted Kezem.

Quedron nodded and barked orders to the men. Slowly, Kezem's soldiers forced their way through the crowd and withdrew from the battle, taking Princess Rela and one of the intruders with them.

***

Rela! No!

Lord Kezem was escaping. Teven caught a glimpse of Rela repeatedly treating her current protector to both fists, but then, he had to duck and roll away from a kerlinblade. For the next few minutes, a duel with one mercenary occupied Teven's thoughts and energies. Fear for Rela and Kayleen drove him to strike hard and fast. Once upon a time, he would have conserved his strength, worn his opponent down, danced about gracefully, and finally struck for the win, but this was different. Time he could not afford to lose slipped by while he dueled.

A kick to his left shin surprised him. He began falling toward his enemy's hungry blade. With all his might, Teven swung his blade up. The mercenary had not expected the move. When the man's weapon was neutralized, Teven whipped his blade back down and across the man's chest.

A scan revealed Kayleen dueling two mercenaries. They cautiously struck at her from opposing sides, seeking an opening for a killing blow. Kayleen fared well enough but spent her time catching strikes from one mercenary or the other. Teven went to even the odds. He maneuvered himself beside Kayleen and challenged the mercenary on the right.

"Thanks!' she called, before turning her attention to the mercenary on the left who wisely fled.

Seeing his partner flee, Teven's opponent also abandoned the fight.

A barrage of energy descended upon Kayleen and Teven. They threw themselves off opposite sides of the path, rolled, and rose swinging. One of the energy beams bent around Teven's kerlinblade and struck a mercenary in the back. The man's scream was cut short by a serlak bullet from Zareb.

Kayleen helped Lorian battle four mercenaries hand-to-hand.

Teven thought about entering the fight but feared to break their concentration. He contented himself with cracking the handle of his kerlinblade across the back of an already stunned mercenary. When he looked back again, a large soldier had his big arm wrapped around Kayleen's neck. She used her lower center of gravity to heave the man over her shoulder. He landed on his neck funny and didn't rise. Another man Kayleen had been fighting was already down, and yet another man lay in front of Lorian who grappled with the final mercenary. She almost had him in a chokehold, but he threw her arms off. The combatants glared at each other over the fallen mercenary.

"Yield," Lorian demanded, motioning around them.

Marc, Kayleen, Zareb, and Teven looked on.

"You're outnumbered," said Lorian.

"Never!" said the mercenary.

Marc shrugged, raised his energy gun, and shot the man in the ankle.

"I'd get that checked out if I were you," said Marc.

Muttering curses, the mercenary hobbled up the path to the main tunnel.

"Is everyone okay?" Teven inquired.

"Flesh wound," Marc reported. He turned his left leg so they could see the gruesome spot of charred skin and muscle framed by tattered trousers.

"A few bruises," Lorian responded.

Zareb and Kayleen merely nodded.

Kayleen tensed, and her voice reflected alarm.

"Where's my father?"

Everyone scanned the cavern.

"There!" Marc shouted, hobbling in the direction of the fallen Ranger.

Teven ran where Marc pointed, but Kayleen beat him to the Ranger by two strides. She fell to her knees next to her father at a loss for words.

"Kaylee, I love you!" Todd Wellum whispered. The simple sentence drained much of his strength.

Teven placed his hands upon Todd's chest where three energy beams had burned their way through flesh and bone.

"It's too late." The words were fainter than his first.

Teven refused to accept that. He poured anotechs into his uncle.

"Hang on!" he said.

They returned almost immediately, telling him there was nothing they could do to heal the damage.

Tears streamed down Teven's face. His hands rested uselessly on Todd's chest.

"Don't die!" Kayleen pleaded. She placed her hands next to Teven's, sending anotechs into the wound. Teven could tell by the way she jerked her hands away that hers too had returned and reported that Todd was correct.

"Kaylee, the game! Remember your mother's game!" Todd

instructed. He continued looking up at Kayleen with love in his eyes before closing them and relaxing into death.

Teven opened his arms and hugged Kayleen who collapsed into his embrace, sobbing. More silent tears coursed down Teven's cheeks. It had been too good to dream that everybody would make it out of Loresh alive, and the shattering of that dream left him stunned. The others stood back with solemn expressions.

For several minutes, only the sound of Kayleen's sobs broke the silence.

***

When no more tears would come, Kayleen Wellum sucked in deep, cold breaths and waited for her heart to stop racing. Finally, she released Teven and moved to stand up. The sight of her father's body tore at her heart again, but she concentrated on her anger.

It's not fair! She had only reunited with her father, spoken a few words, and now he was gone again. *This time forever.*

During the many years of not knowing, Kayleen dreamed of the conversations they would have, pictured his face, and imagined what he was like. Briefly, she thought it might have been better had he never shown up, so she could keep her dreams. But she concluded that those few moments with him were far more precious than countless hopeful dreams. The pain would pass, but she would always carry this image of her father: the hero who had traversed the planet to find her.

His last words confused her, but she lacked the energy to think about them.

"We'll honor him later," Kayleen said, getting to her feet. "Let's deal with Kezem first."

"Right," Teven answered. He rose and took a step up the path up to the main tunnel then stopped. He turned and cast a puzzled glance at the stone pillar. "Let me just check one thing." He jogged over to the stone pillar and ran his fingers over the words inscribed on it.

The small band gathered around Teven.

"What does it say?" Marc inquired.

Kayleen glanced at it. She recognized some of the symbols, but it had been years since she'd read Kalastan.

"Etmani coress cherimon. Dantel corla asmenai," Teven read.

"Here lies the gate. Enter to seek wisdom," Kayleen translated for those who didn't understand.

Teven hesitated.

"Go on. Touch the pillar, Teven," Kayleen urged.

They had seen Princess Rela open and close the stone door. Kayleen hoped it worked for all members of House Minstel.

Teven slowly touched the pillar, and a grinding noise told them it worked.

Kayleen watched in awe as whole sections of the walls to either side of the second main tunnel swung inward.

Two doors!

The momentarily thrill burned through her grief.

"Which one do we go in?" Marc asked.

Teven approached the doorway on their right. The others followed him.

Kayleen wanted to rush through and see what lay beyond, but Lorian's hand gently rested on her arm, telling her to wait. She understood. This was a private moment for Teven.

"I'll wait here and call you back if there's trouble," Marc offered.

"I wait," Zareb announced.

"I'll be here," Lorian promised. She released Kayleen's arm. "Go with him."

Teven didn't acknowledge any of them. He simply kept walking toward the open doorway in a daze.

Chapter 44:
History Lesson in Loresh

Zeri (June) 27, 1560
Same Day
Chamber of Enlightenment, Loresh Cave System, Frozen North

Teven McKnight stepped through the doorway with reverent slowness. He wanted to run, but something pressed the importance of this place upon him. Two steps inside, he halted. The anotechs were alive with excitement, causing a disconcerting flutter in the pit of his stomach. Before him, resting peacefully on a raised mound of rock and debris sat a small ship cocked at a downward angle where it had crashed. The front end was smashed, but surprisingly, the rest of the ship seemed to be in good repair.

A small stone pillar marked the ship's side entrance. Teven walked to the pillar and rested his hand upon it. A translucent, wispy figure about the size of his forearm appeared above the stone and tipped its head forward in a bow. The man's expression was strained.

"Greetings, I was once Jaspen Turgot, chief aide to anotech creator Sebastian Seltan," the figure said.

Teven sucked in a sharp breath at the name *Seltan*.

"We had hoped to right the universe's wrongs, but the power was too much for Sebastian. He turned on us. I escaped before things got too bad, but I am afraid for my planet. I don't know how long I lay unconscious, but when I had awakened, the anotechs had carved their way through this frozen land. They initially told me we were on the top of this world, so I called it the Frozen North, but now they say the planet has been flipped. I think it more likely they were mistaken and reluctant to admit such." The figure fell silent.

"There must be more," Kayleen murmured.

Teven touched a spot on the stone pillar below where he had touched before. The figure spoke again.

"This place I have fled to is beautiful, but I fear I too will abuse the power of the anotechs. The locals already think I am a god for surviving the crash. I had to accept a royal appointment or risk horrible death. I have chosen the surname Minstel, meaning 'eternal ministry' for my old name has become bitter to me."

"I never thought about the meaning of the name," said Teven.

"It means more now than ever, Teven," Kayleen said.

"What do you mean?"

"Reshner has suffered too long. It needs your family's guidance," Kayleen explained.

Teven reached for the pillar again.

"It has been three years since my rebirth," said the figure. "The anotechs have taught me much and taken my dreams and made them reality. I now have a wife and two sons to live for, but thoughts of immortality repulse me. I will live a natural life and serve this trusting people. Anotechs will fill the blood of my children and their children forever, but when one life is spent, they shall return to this place for restoration. This site will be open to my bloodline to seek the wisdom of those before them."

"I see you have found the Chamber of Enlightenment," Jalna Seltan noted.

Kayleen and Teven spun to face her. The three sentries also whirled, astonished. Jalna looked and sounded like the young girl Teven had met in the Ranger camp all those years ago.

"Who are you?" asked Lorian.

Teven handled introductions.

"How did you get past us?" Marc demanded.

Chuckling, Jalna waved to some steps behind her.

"The Chamber of Wisdom," she answered. Noticing Teven's questioning expression, she continued, "Jenell and Karric are safely in the care of Master Niklos. The anotechs called me here. There will be time for explanations later, but for now, we must save your sister."

"Lord Kezem will bring her back here," Marc pointed out.

"We wait; he come," Zareb agreed.

Kayleen, Lorian, and Teven shook their head vigorously.

"I'm not fighting Kezem on his terms!" Kayleen said. She gripped her kerlinblade with a white fist.

"We may not have a choice," Jalna said. "Let us seal this chamber and move the bodies to the sides of the main cavern. Another fight approaches."

About a half-hour passed while the small group handled the grim task of stacking the bodies. Teven helped Kayleen carry her father's limp form. She moved stiffly, and he could have done a more efficient job by himself, but it was a task he could not deny her. They carried Ranger Wellum a little farther than the others and laid him in a sleeping position on his back. Tears worked their way down Kayleen's face.

"What did your father mean about a game your mother played?" Teven asked, trying to take her mind off the aching loss.

"I don't know. I've been thinking about that," she replied. "I was only four when my mother died, and I think she blocked some of my memories."

The small group had gathered in front of the stone pillar that unlocked the Chamber of Wisdom and the Chamber of Enlightenment. Teven and Kayleen joined them. Everyone appeared tired and disheartened. Teven's touch sealed the chambers with a grinding noise that echoed about the main cavern.

"Come on, come on, we've got to find Anabel and the princess," said Marc.

"You are in no condition for a confrontation," Jalna said. "Sit down."

Marc obeyed, but his irritation showed up in his expression. Teven understood Marc's feelings but knew Jalna was right. Marc had been standing on his festering leg for far too long. Jalna placed her hands over Marc's wounded left leg. Soon, she had the wound cleaned and wrapped in sterile cloth taken from a dead mercenary's supply pack.

"Thanks. That feels much better," Marc announced, climbing to his feet.

Jalna poked him in the chest.

"The painkillers do not change the fact that your wound is grave. Do not overexert yourself."

"I agree. Take it easy, Marc," Lorian said.

"But Anabel—" Marc began.

"Will remain Lord Kezem's captive until we can free her," Jalna finished. "We have a much better chance of rescuing the young women when everyone is rested."

"There's no time!" Marc insisted.

"But there is," contradicted a voice Teven recognized.

Teven's head snapped up to where Captain Ectosh Laocer stood flanked by a large group of mercenaries.

"Who are you?" Marc challenged.

"Perhaps a former Captain of the Royal Guard," Lorian surmised.

"Very good, derringer," Laocer mocked. He slowly led his group to within twenty meters of Teven and his friends.

The well-armed mercenaries brandished their weapons.

"Far enough," Zareb said, resting his four hands on pistol grips. He stepped forward to protect Teven.

"Zareb. Can't say it's a pleasure to see you again," Laocer commented.

"You remember?" Surprise rang through Zareb's words.

"Of course, there weren't too many four-armed freaks under my command," Laocer said. His voice lost some of its edge when he added, "But you were Taytron's pet before I took command, and Queen Reia insisted we open the ranks to other species."

The anotechs reminded Teven of the epiphany he and Kayleen had had two days ago.

"You helped Lord Kezem take the palace!" Teven fired the accusation again with his eyes.

Laocer's answer surprised the prince.

"I did a lot of regrettable things," said Laocer. "King Terosh was a good friend, but he stood between your mother and me. My first duty was to our love."

"You lie!" Zareb yelled, clearly as incensed as Teven over Laocer's obsession with the queen. "Queen Reia always love king!"

"Step aside, Captain," Teven ordered. "Lord Kezem—"

"Will find you," Laocer finished, echoing earlier sentiments. "We will wait here until he arrives. Then, you will help me kill him, and I will take my rightful place as king."

"Rightful?" Kayleen scoffed. "What happened to restoring the throne to *Prince* Teven?"

Teven winced at her emphasis on his title.

"He's just a boy," Laocer said. "Reshner needs a strong ruler."

"Already got one. He's terrible," Marc growled.

"He will die soon," Captain Laocer promised.

Teven wondered whether Laocer heard a word of what they were saying or if an entirely separate conversation played inside the man's head. The point became moot when two serlak bullets slammed into Laocer's back just below the neck, killing him instantly.

Chapter 45:
Heroes and Villains Collide

Zeri (June) 27, 1560
Same Day
Loresh Cave System, Frozen North

Kezem hated retreating, but he found fresh RLA soldiers waiting for him halfway up the main tunnel. Knowing the enemy would be prepared for his return, Lord Kezem ordered his men to get fresh weapons, eat, and rest. Benali, the coward, had slipped off, but Kezem didn't care. He would dispatch some men to kill him later, but for now, he had far more pressing matters to deal with.

The delay had been worth the wait. The traitor stood before him talking to the intruders.

Lord Kezem hardly dared to believe his luck.

"Kill him," he ordered.

Captain Quedron's response was to take out his sidearm and fire on the mercenary leader. Laocer's body fell forward and rolled down the slope twice before sliding to a stop.

Everyone raised their weapons and discharged them at once.

The mercenaries in the back whirled and fired on Lord Kezem's soldiers. The rest opened fire on the young intruders. A sideways glance revealed that Rela was safely tucked behind a wall of his finest soldiers whose only orders were to protect her.

Kezem didn't bother with energy guns. He flicked on his kerlinblade, spun the color dial, and raced forward with a yellow and green blade. Once in the center of the fray, Kezem swept the kerlinblade across two mercenaries. Then, he whipped his banistick out and thrust it into another soldier's throat with the electric shock set high enough to scramble the man's brain. Kezem returned the banistick to his belt.

A kerlinblade-wielding mercenary caught two of his strikes. Then, a kick struck the man low in the stomach, doubling him over right into Kezem's blade. He yanked the blade out and punched the man for good measure, before selecting another target. Suddenly, he found himself blocking banistick strikes from a Melian Maiden. A wave of surprised anger shot through him.

You're supposed to be in prison! Someone will die for this treachery.

"Yield! You are *my* servant!" Kezem screamed. He took out his banistick again, knowing he would need the extra edge against this enemy.

"I serve the Royal House!" Kia declared.

Kezem pounded at her flawless defenses, ignoring the bullets and kerlak beams flying around them. She backed down the slope, and he followed, battering her banistick with both of his weapons. Finally, the electric impulse from his banistick shorted the shock nullifiers protecting her weapon. She dropped it to avoid the electric charge. He lunged forward for a killing blow and met the back of her hand as she spun up the slope toward him. The blow surprised him more than hurt, but it was enough for her to scramble away.

Frustrated, Kezem smashed his banistick against a mercenary's chest and held it there for several seconds longer than necessary. The man's screams only fueled Kezem's bloodlust. He relished the feeling of power coursing through him as he roamed the battlefield seeking new opponents. The mercenaries—who had never been a coherent fighting group—scattered and ran for their lives. Kezem took great pleasure in cutting them down.

***

After having her banistick shorted by Lord Kezem, Kia split her attention between trying to stay alive and searching for Captain Tayce.

That man is infuriating.

His noble spirit and sense of duty were going to get him killed. He possessed decent fighting skills, but his administration post left little time for real combat experience. A flash of short blond hair to her left caught her eye. Kia punched out the mercenary who had a serlak pistol partially raised to shoot her. Two strides brought her up behind a soldier choking the life out of Tayce. A hard smack to the back of the neck stopped the soldier. She reached down and yanked Tayce to his feet even as she relieved the unconscious soldier of his blade, ignited it, and blocked an energy beam headed for them.

"Captain, get out of here!" Kia shouted. She didn't wait for a reply but paused long enough to see Captain Tayce shake some sense back into his head.

Three soldiers fell upon them. The first tackled her, knocking the blade away. The soldier had strength on her, but she had years of hand-to-hand combat training. They tumbled down the slope a ways before rolling off the main path and onto a flatter, more fight-friendly surface. His fist came at her face. She turned her head and took the glancing blow to the side of the head, causing her ear to throb painfully. Kia lashed out with her left foot, catching his ankle. He grunted, but she didn't give him the chance to recover. A roll brought her to her feet and a spin kick to the man's side ended the fight. She didn't bother killing him.

Tired, dirty, and far from done, Kia grabbed a kerlak pistol off the ground and shot two blue soldiers and a maroon one. The gun whined, telling her it was done for. She tossed it aside and picked up another. A bullet grazed her side. Stinging pain spread from the area. She felt herself falling. With considerable effort, she twisted around to avoid landing on the wound. The frozen ground knocked the breath from her.

I've failed the princess.

The mercenary who'd shot her smiled as he lined up his weapon for the kill shot. Her salvation came from the most unlikely of sources: an RLA soldier.

No, not a soldier, a Coridian Assassin. Interesting.

Kia recognized Tryse from training camps they'd both attended. She couldn't remember if they had ever met, but there was little time to dwell on that now anyway.

Tryse slammed his banistick down on the mercenary's gun arm then brought the weapon up under the man's chin. Clearly, he too had decided that Lord Kezem was a disease that needed to be cut out of Reshner. Unfortunately, Kia didn't know how to do that without harming the princess.

Before Kia could rise to help Tryse with his crusade against Kezem's forces, four energy beams struck the assassin high in the chest.

Tryse! No! Kia's mind screamed.

She had no energy to make the cry real. She could only watch as realization dawned behind his eyes. He met her gaze and nodded at her. Then, he grabbed his pistol and shot the three soldiers nearest him. With the last of his strength, he dropped the gun, drew his kamad dagger, and hurled it at the last soldier standing near Kia. Sighing, he fell forward and closed his eyes, a small smile forming on his lips.

***

Teven's arms ached from the half-dozen mini-duels he had waged and won. This current one was by far the toughest. A hard strike knocked him off balance and caused his right shoulder to throb with pain. Kayleen whirled in front of him and caught the next three blows on her shining green blade. The soldier stepped close and slammed his fist into her head. Next, the man slashed wildly and scraped his blade across Kayleen's left arm. She didn't flinch. Terror for Kayleen shocked Teven into hefting his blade and hurling it over her shoulder into the man. He followed the blade, pulled it out, and looked around for more danger.

Jalna and an opponent sailed by. The man was backpedaling as fast as he could, but her strikes were quicker than he could handle. Marc had traded his kerlak gun for a blade and was in the midst of an intense contest with a mercenary. Teven didn't see Zareb anywhere. A beam flashed toward Teven, and he dove instinctively.

When he was halfway to his feet, Teven saw a white blade out of the corner of his eye. The thought of impending death didn't disturb him so much as deeply sadden him. He knew Kayleen cared for him and did not wish to add to her pain today. To his surprise, the blade failed to strike him. Instead, it knocked down an energy beam that would have struck his head. Looking up, Teven found a tall woman with dark brown eyes and a playful grin staring at him. Her skin tone was complemented by the soft colors of her flowing light blue robes. She looked completely out of place.

"Energy beam to the head would be painful," she commented before turning and disappearing into the thrashing crowd.

Teven almost felt like the beam had struck him. Then, Kayleen was next to him, helping him stand. By this time, the mercenaries were either dead or gone.

Teven and Kayleen were about to pick another fight with an RLA soldier, when Lord Kezem's voice rang out.

"Stop fighting!"

Everyone froze.

Marc yelped.

"No!" shouted Princess Rela. She struggled to approach Lord Kezem and her friend.

Two RLA soldiers held Anabel whose arms were stun-cuffed in front of her. This time, the shock feature was definitely activated. Lord Kezem's blue and green kerlinblade blazed at her throat. The light reflected off her pained expression.

"I'll open the door!" Rela cried. Her voice was high with the intensity of her fear for Anabel. Tears slipped down her flushed cheeks. She almost broke free from the soldiers, but they caught her arms and held her fast.

"I know you will," Kezem said darkly.

"Please don't kill her!" Rela's voice, though barely a whisper, carried in the cavern.

"There is only treasure beyond for those who seek wisdom," Jalna said. "You will not find power or riches here."

Teven saw Jalna close her eyes as she spoke, but Lord Kezem was too far away to see.

"The treasure is mine!" Kezem shrieked.

Teven worried he might let the blade slip and cut Anabel. Then, he remembered Jalna's lessons on surroundings. He reached out with the anotechs. A steady stream of them flowed from Jalna to Lord Kezem. Suddenly, he understood.

When he was sure Anabel would be safe, Teven shouted and launched himself at Kezem who reacted faster than he thought possible. The blade in Kezem's hand raked across Anabel's exposed neck, but only a thin line of blood spread for the effort. Kezem howled with rage and turned his anger on Teven.

Their blades met with a crash and locked. Teven bolstered his strength by calling on the anotechs for help. They swirled through him, rejuvenating his exhausted muscles. Recognition flashed behind Kezem's cobalt eyes when they were face to face.

"A blade did not save your mother! It will not save you!"

"She defeated you that day!" Teven tossed back.

None of Kezem's men dared to interfere, and Teven's friends stood back as well. Everyone understood that this confrontation had to take place.

Lord Kezem reached for his banistick. Teven had seen what that banistick could do so he disengaged. Lord Kezem swung the banistick with all of his considerable might. Teven leapt out of the way. The banistick passed close enough to raise the hairs on Teven's arm.

While Lord Kezem was slightly off balance, Teven kicked the banistick from his hand. Kezem growled and swung his kerlinblade with both hands. Teven had no choice but to block the blade. The blow landed with enough force to knock Teven back a meter. He twisted his neck aside to keep from cutting his own throat.

"Teven!" cried Kayleen.

Teven caught a glimpse of Lorian and one of the Melian Maidens holding Kayleen back. He was grateful. He tripped over some pebbles on the slope and started falling but managed to turn the tumble into an over the shoulder roll. Somehow, he held on to his kerlinblade without impaling himself. Lord Kezem pursued. Teven expected to feel the bite of Kezem's blade any second. As Kezem heaved a devastating blow, Teven steeled his nerves and stood his ground. At the last possible moment, Teven pivoted on his right foot, letting Kezem's blade pass within two centimeters of his body. He finished the spin and planted his left foot on Kezem's back.

Lord Kezem recovered quickly, but Teven was several meters up the slope. They were back to the main group. Teven stopped running because there was nowhere to run. Lord Kezem's men completely blocked the main tunnel out of Loresh. Besides, he would never abandon his sister or friends. Teven turned to face Lord Kezem again.

Even with the anotechs' aid, Teven could barely stand. He rallied enough strength to parry the first dozen of Kezem's strikes. Then, a kick caught him in the stomach and knocked him to the ground. A triumphant smile lit Kezem's face. He threw down his kerlinblade, lifted Teven by the shirt, and slammed him hard against the ground. Two more similar assaults left the prince gasping. A series of hard punches caught Teven's face, neck, and shoulders. Then, Kezem's fingers were at his throat squeezing.

***

Princess Rela Minstel watched the young man fight Lord Kezem, knowing she should recognize him. Partway through the fight, Kezem ranted something about the boy's mother and the answer struck Rela with a near physical blow. Then, somebody shouted the boy's name, and the connection solidified. Rela's visions of her mother had spoken of the young man, her brother.

Teven!

Her mind frantically tried to conjure a means of escape. Teven kicked Lord Kezem, and Rela cheered. The soldiers gripping her shoulders did not release her, but their grasps loosened as the duel distracted them. She didn't know how Teven could fight on so long and hard, but he parried Lord Kezem's fierce strikes time and again. She silently willed him to win even if it meant her death. The air was thick with anticipation of the duel's end. To Rela's dismay, her brother's reflexes slowed ever so slightly.

Lord Kezem knocked him down and attacked with his hands. Rela's hands hurt. Kezem's hands were bloody from beating her brother. The solution came to her with such sudden clarity that she gasped.

If she thought about it too long, she would lose the nerve to do what was necessary. Dropping to her knees, Rela seized the dagger tucked into the left boot of the man to her right, scrambled away, and fell upon the blade. It pierced her right side between the bottom two ribs and sank into her up to the hilt. A sharp cry flew from her lips as she rolled onto her back, inadvertently twisting the blade deeper. Pain like she had never experienced before radiated from the wound. With monumental effort, Rela yanked at the dagger. In her haste, she pulled the blade down as well as out, further splitting her side open. Tears flowed as easily as the blood, but Rela had some small comfort in knowing Lord Kezem would feel every bit of pain.

The loud crack of a serlak gun echoed in the nearly silent chamber. A different kind of pain exploded in her stomach, and Rela passed out.

Chapter 46:
Broken Code

Zeri (June) 27, 1560
Same Day
Loresh Cave System, Frozen North

Lord Kezem felt like his insides were being ripped out. He had suffered wounds before but never like this. He stopped choking the boy and fell back in shock. Something thudded into his gut increasing the pain tenfold. The sound of the shot reached his ears ages later. Looking up, he spotted a being pointing four guns at him.

***

"No! No! You'll kill the princess!" Marc screamed, clutching at Zareb's arms.

"What mean?" asked Zareb.

"She's linked to him! If he dies, she dies!" Marc explained. His tone neared hysteria.

Kayleen observed everything with a numbness that comes from seeing too many people die. Teven lay so still that she didn't know if he still lived. That thought was too painful to follow. Kezem's men looked at each other wondering how to react. Marc was still screaming at the man who had come to Loresh with Teven and her father. Anabel watched everything in horror. Princess Rela lay on the ground with blood pouring from her side. Finally, Kayleen couldn't take it anymore. She separated herself from the pain. In that moment, the walls surrounding her memories melted.

Her mind wandered to happier times. She remembered her childhood home, the one before Nils took her to the Ranger camp. Mother had always kept a neat house. The unit had been small but very comfortable and safe. Father had been away often, but he would always come back with trinkets and stories for Kaylee even though Mother scolded him for spoiling her. He always answered with a kiss and a promise to be stricter when Kaylee grew older. Then, the trouble in Rammon had started. News of rebel soldiers brought a sad look to Mother who summoned Nils Clavon. He was okay as a friend, but Kayleen didn't want to go with him.

Go with Nils, Neelyak, my beautiful baby.

Mother had often called her Neelyak, but only when they were alone.

Kiata.

That had been Mother's name. She had been everything Kayleen wished to be. Her long, light brown hair used to hang freely in front of her face, as she leaned over Kayleen's tiny bed. Batting the soft hair had been a favorite pastime for Kayleen.

Edolin cumani enuli asanti rimnula. Remember these words, Neelyak. They are very important.

Kayleen had cried so loudly she barely heard Mother, but the words had always stuck with her. Mother had opened her mouth to say more, but Nils took her away to escape the soldiers. He took nothing but a small pack of provisions and ran for his life, carrying Kayleen away from danger.

Remember your mother's game!

The full meaning settled upon Kayleen, snapping her out of the escapist thoughts. Mother had often spoken Kalastan backwards, especially when addressing her sister—Queen Reia. Kayleen was beyond shock at this point. She merely nodded and concentrated on the words her mother had told her to remember.

Edolin cumani enuli asanti rimnula became *alunmir itnasa ilune inamuc nilode. The time has come; break foul curse, release the royal to new birth.*

Kayleen moved before her mind officially gave the order. The soldiers had backed away from the fallen princess. Kayleen knelt over Princess Rela and took her cold, bloody hands in her own.

"Alunmir itnasa ilune inamuc nilode!"

Nothing happened.

She leaned closer and repeated the message.

Rela's shallow and ineffective breathing began to even out. She was still unconscious, but Kayleen could almost imagine color returning. She felt a hand on her shoulder and glanced up to see Jalna.

"She will live," Jalna said.

"Perhaps," Kayleen replied.

"She killed Lord Kezem," a young soldier hissed. "She dies."

Before anyone could stop him, he raised his kerlak gun and blasted Princess Rela from two meters away. Kayleen dove across the princess. Other soldiers and Marc gunned the man down instantly, but five shots had been released. One hit the ground near the princess. One struck the princess and the other three caught Kayleen across the back. By all rights, she should be dead, but the anotechs had isolated some of the energy.

Throwing out her left hand, Kayleen touched Rela and willed the anotechs to draw the excess energy away from the princess. She knew that the anotechs could either save her or Princess Rela, not both. They disagreed. Tears streamed down Kayleen's face as she willed the anotechs to ignore her wounds. She began pouring anotechs into the princess. She felt Jalna's silent protest.

"Save her!" Kayleen commanded.

Jalna nodded solemn acquiescence to Kayleen's wishes and turned her full attention to Princess Rela.

When she finished transferring her anotechs to the princess, Kayleen felt strangely alone. Every ache in her body was magnified. A deep gash on her arm, which she hadn't even noticed, began throbbing. Something soft was placed under her head.

"Kayleen, don't die. Keep fighting!" Teven's warm hand squeezed hers and anotechs rush in to heal the damage, but Kayleen knew it was too late.

"We have to finish the Kireshana!" said Teven.

Kayleen forced her eyes to fix on her friend's face.

"Teven, you'll always be Reshner's Royal Guard to me," she whispered with her dying breath.

***

Do you wish to be saved?

Of course, Kayleen answered. *Why wouldn't I want to be saved?*

You would not be the same.

Why not?

Your body is dead. We can only preserve the essence of you.

At what cost? What's the catch? Will it harm anyone?

Living beyond death can be … disconcerting. You would be more us than you, though in time we may find a suitable body for you.

I'd be like Jalna.

Yes, you would be like the Maker's Daughter. What say you?

Do it, but only if Teven, Jalna, and the princess agree.

A war is coming. They will need every ally they can get. Sleep. Heal. Rest.

***

Teven couldn't believe it. Two minutes ago, he was dying while Kayleen watched. Now she was dead, his sister was dying, and dozens of soldiers stared down at his back ready to finish what Lord Kezem had started. He was still trying to absorb Kayleen's death when a soldier asked the key question.

"What happens now?"

"You surrender," Zareb replied.

Teven didn't have to look to know all four of Zareb's guns would be trained on the soldiers. He sensed more than saw his other friends tense for another round of chaotic battle.

"Who will rule?" the young soldier inquired, sounding lost. "Lord Kezem's dead!"

"The princess still lives," said one of the other soldiers.

"But we served Lord Kezem! We're done for if she rules," insisted the first soldier.

"The princess is not above forgiving," one of the Melian Maidens offered.

"She cannot rule!" cried the first soldier.

"Don't even think about it," warned the second man.

"You can't stop me!" Receding footsteps said the first soldier was retreating. A few others followed, but the majority stayed in the main cavern.

Teven wearily climbed to his feet.

"Put down—" Zareb began.

"Not a chance," the second soldier cut in.

"Their weapons are inconsequential," said a fair-haired Melian Maiden. "They will need them to serve the princess."

"Unhand my sister!" Marc snapped.

The soldiers reluctantly obeyed, releasing the stuncuffs and standing back looking suddenly shy. Anabel ran to Marc and hugged him. Teven envied their happiness.

Rela stirred.

The Melian Maidens gathered close to her, edging Teven away.

"He will do her no harm," Jalna informed the maidens.

"Enough harm has already been done," the head maiden replied, keeping her eyes on Teven.

"Let me take some of her pain," Teven requested.

"Do you not recognize him?" Jalna inquired.

One of the older soldiers broke ranks to move closer to the princess and gasped.

"King Terosh," he said in an awed whisper.

"Not quite," Teven answered. The right side of his face twitched up for a second, the closest he could come to a smile. "Teven."

Through the anotechs, Jalna silently urged him to go on.

Teven squared his shoulders and wiped most of the grief from his expression.

"I am Prince Teven, born of House Minstel, son of King Terosh and Queen Reia, brother to Princess Rela and Prince Tavel." His announcement left everyone stunned, even those who had previously known.

"Teven was the firstborn," the veteran soldier said. "You are king." He dropped to his knees.

"That has yet to be decided. We must save my sister first," Teven said. He approached Rela again.

This time the Melian Maidens parted respectfully.

"How can you help her?" wondered the head maiden.

Aster Captain Kia Meetcher of the Order of Melian Maidens, the anotechs said.

Teven didn't reply. Instead, he sat on the ground next to Rela, touched her neck with his left hand, and laid his right hand across her gruesome side wound. He winced as some of her pain transferred to him. Her skin was hot to the touch. He felt the anotechs working frantically to knit her torn flesh together.

Please live, Rela, I've lost so much. I can't lose you too!

When he had done everything he could for her, Teven struggled to his feet.

"You need rest," Jalna observed.

"I need answers," Teven said peevishly.

"What are your orders, Prince Teven?" asked a soldier. "With Lord Kezem dead and the princess unconscious, you are our leader."

Teven dispatched half the troops to gather supplies from the base so they could spend the night and ordered the other half to gather the bodies to be taken out of Loresh.

A chorus of "It will be done," answered him.

He eyed the departing troops warily.

"Can we move her?" Teven asked Jalna.

"I doubt it would do much good, Prince Teven," Jalna said.

Teven got the impression she was trying to get him used to the title.

"She should awaken by the morning, but sleep is good for her."

"I'd like to speak to her in private when she wakes up," Teven explained.

"In that case, we can try, but let's wait for a hov sled."

"I know where to find one," Lorian offered. "We need to collect the prisoners there anyway. Uh, that is, if they're still there."

An uneasy truce settled between the soldiers and Teven's friends. He sensed treachery, so he did not rely on them to guard him. The Melian Maidens and an RLA officer, Captain Ethan Tayce, hovered within arm's length constantly. It both pleased and irritated him.

Marc, Anabel, Kia, and Lorian had their injuries addressed. Jalna finally got a good look at Anabel's arm. A half-hour session of anotech therapy worked wonders for the broken arm. Teven was glad to see Anabel's skin tone return to a normal color.

The biggest surprise came when Teven carried Kayleen's body over to her father. He found Todd Wellum breathing.

How is he still alive? I watched him die!

Queen Reia's last gift, replied the anotechs.

What do you mean? What did she do?

She instructed us to fake his death if he ever came gravely near it. Then revive him later. He will live but recovery will be slow. His wounds would be fatal several times over.

Dizzying hope shot through Teven.

Did my mother protect Kayleen too?

Regret clung to the anotechs' words. **Yes, but Kayleen already died the day her caretaker did. We saved her body once.**

Can't you do it again? Teven pleaded.

Her body is beyond us now, Prince of the Chosen, but if the Maker's Daughter is willing, we can save her mind.

Please ask her.

Teven wept.

Chapter 47:
Anotech Deal

Zeri (June) 28, 1560
Loresh Cave System, Frozen North

When Princess Rela regained consciousness twelve hours later, she felt nothing and couldn't pick up her head.

That's odd.

She frowned, blinked, and slowly moved her jaw to see if it worked. Something stirred at her side, but she couldn't turn to see it. At least, she felt no threat from that direction.

Why am I lying on the ground, why can't I feel anything, and why am I not panicking?

"Princess Rela?" Kia called her name gently.

Rela's mouth was dry, her tongue thick, but in happier news, her jaw worked. She slowly opened and closed her mouth a few times.

"Kia," she managed to say finally. It came out barely above a whisper, but Rela could almost feel the woman's pulse quicken with joy.

"Linnea has something for you, Princess," said Kia.

Rela felt something slip onto her right ring finger. She flexed her fingers.

Well, at least feeling has returned.

"Welcome back, Princess," Linnea greeted. "I was unable to complete the mission to Master or Lady Pascal, but I'm sure the Bann family will be all right. Captain Tayce sent them some help as soon as we were safely on our way here."

"Thank you," Rela whispered.

"There's someone who wants to meet you, Princess. Are you well enough for an audience?" Linnea asked.

Rela nodded weakly.

I doubt I shall go anywhere for a while anyway.

"Prince Teven! The princess will see you now!" Kia called.

Prince Teven?

A thrill ran through Rela. In another moment one of the young men Lord Kezem had cursed knelt at her side and leaned over her. He was handsome, even sideways. His black hair appeared wind tossed, and his brilliant green eyes shone with concern. He looked exactly like her mother had described her father.

The longer he stared at her the softer and more peaceful his expression became.

"Nice to finally meet you, Rela," Teven said with a crooked grin that made him appear younger.

Rela sensed her maidens slip a respectful distance away.

"Teven!" she whispered fiercely. Saying his name made her want to throw her arms around him.

He partially picked her up in a warm embrace.

She felt his heartbeats tap a soothing cadence in her ear. Gradually, as mobility was restored to the rest of her, Rela returned his hug with desperate strength.

"You have a very healthy grip," Teven commented. "That won't last when the pain returns."

"Returns?"

Teven pulled away and looked at her with a teasing smile.

"You've probably got more anotechs in you than blood right now."

"Dare I ask what anotechs are?" asked Rela.

"It's a very long story. I'll tell it to you sometime, but I wanted to talk to you about something else right now." He paused, waiting for permission.

"I am sort of a captive audience here," Rela pointed out.

"The anotechs have a deal they wish to offer Reshner's ruler," Teven began.

"Which is you, if you're my older brother," Rela broke in calmly.

"We can deal with that mess later, but I think you should consider their offer," Teven advised. "Can you stand up? It's best if the anotechs present their case directly to you."

"Are you willing to be a crutch?"

"Sure. I'm sorry we don't have the hov sled anymore, but the soldiers are using them to carry bodies out of Loresh," Teven explained. "I needed to talk to you alone."

Rela sucked in sharply when Teven moved to help her stand.

Ouch! Pain's back.

"I see what you mean about the pain returning. What happened?"

Ceasing efforts to help her up, Teven stared at her incredulously.

"You don't remember stabbing yourself to stop Lord Kezem from killing me?"

Suddenly, Rela remembered everything: the battle, the screams, the wounded, the dying, the dead, the helpless feeling of being held by the soldiers, the pain from the dagger, and the shock of being shot. Her gaze dropped to her right side, which was dominated by a large blood-soaked bandage. A faint burning sensation spread around the spot on her side where the energy blast hit. She grimaced.

"I remember."

"This is really going to hurt," Teven warned. He must have changed his mind about wanting her to stand, for without giving her a chance to respond, he scooped her up in his arms.

The burning sensation spread, but she willed it to diminish.

"Good, you're doing fine," said Teven. "The anotechs are machines tinier than cells. They can repair and rejuvenate your tissues and rally your natural defenses. Jalna taught me how to live with them. You'll get to meet her later." He carried Rela like a child.

She rested her head against his shoulder.

"That wasn't a very long story," said Rela.

"Like I said, it's best if they explain." Teven touched the pillar then settled Rela as gently as possible on the small stack of bedrolls placed there for that purpose. "We are ready for your offer."

A translucent figure of a man appeared above the stone pillar.

"Greetings, if rulers of the Chosen not mind, we will use the figure of Jaspen Turgot who became Minstel."

Rela stared at the figured utterly lost.

"Better give her the beginning messages, too," said Teven.

Rela listened raptly to the figure's first three messages. Then, a fourth message played.

"I call this place the Chamber of Enlightenment. Here, I shall lay out the chronicles of my life. The second room shall be the Chamber of Wisdom. There, I have asked the anotechs to protect any pieces of wisdom my posterity wish to put there. It is my hope that such a collection will protect them from bringing further harm upon the universe through the power they wield. I could cut them off from all knowledge of the anotechs but that would be wrong. The anotechs are not evil, only powerful. Power can be used for great good, but only the tragedies are remembered."

"Did our parents leave messages in the Chamber of Wisdom?" Rela asked. Her blue eyes shone with excitement.

"We can check later," Teven promised. "Are you ready for the anotechs' offer?"

"Yes," Rela said, grinning as a fluttering sensation filled her stomach. "Their impatience is quite apparent."

Teven touched the pillar again and the figure of their mother appeared, complete with the voice they knew so well.

They gasped.

"Greetings, think us not cruel for taking this form. We sense you both miss her much. Perhaps seeing her and hearing her will ease that pain. We seek promises from you who are destined to lead the Chosen. Use your power well. Great factions run over Reshner, spreading animosity and corruption. You have already defeated the greatest of these threats.

"Jaspen Turgot, who built House Minstel, sought peace as did his son and his son's daughter, but several generations down the line that goal was sacrificed for greed and comfort. Restore peace. We will help you by fixing the damage we wrought in our distress. The rains will no longer eat the flesh, the wind will no longer gather so strongly, and the waters of the Crystal Lake will be clean again."

"You can do that?" Rela asked breathlessly. "Why have you not done so already?" She felt her ire rise against the anotechs.

"Destruction and hardship bind people together, we had hoped to unite Reshner, but evil persisted and so punishment persisted."

"It's cruel!" Rela protested. Her side ached and burned. "How can we judge these people?"

"You are Princess Rela of House Minstel. You must instill discipline, or more will die from the chaos. We have seen this. Our old home, Kalast, was lost to such chaos. We do not wish to lose this planet as well. Please help us," their mother's figure begged.

Rela slowly nodded.

"Life has never been fair," she reflected, "but how shall we set things right?" She felt a heavy burden descend upon her as she thought of the task ahead.

"Punish the evildoers, feed the hungry, help the lost, defend the innocent, and never compromise peace."

Teven whistled.

"Right, like that's ever going to happen. Countless generations have passed, and people still haven't figured out how to do all that."

"Never stop fighting for right!" An edge crept into the voice coming from the form of Queen Reia Minstel. "We did not ask for this task, but it is here. To not act would be wrong."

"I can only speak for me, but you have my word that my life will be spent in the service of this planet," said Rela.

"I have already sworn my service." Teven grinned crookedly again. "Welcome to the team, Princess Rela. Shall I escort you to the Chamber of Wisdom now that you have been enlightened?"

"Please." Rela barely noticed the pain this time as Teven scooped her up again. She felt comfortable in his arms. Only Sarie had ever dared to hug Rela, and Lord Kezem had driven her away many years ago. The touch of another human was both wonderful and strange.

Chapter 48:
Chamber of Wisdom

Zeri (June) 28, 1560
Same Day
Chamber of Wisdom, Loresh Cave System, Frozen North

Teven McKnight felt some emotional pain fade as he carried his little sister down the stairs through the short hall and up the next set of stairs into the Chamber of Wisdom. His heart ached to have Kayleen back, but the knowledge that she had died saving Rela made his sister's presence that much more precious to him.

This chamber lacked the ship that made the Chamber of Enlightenment seem cramped. From the stairs, it was about thirty meters to the opposite wall, two meters to the left wall, and twenty-five meters to the right wall. The far wall curved gracefully after about fifteen meters, lending a comfy atmosphere to the cave. A line of meter-high stone pillars started at the far left wall and continued around the curve until it reached the wall which composed the second half of the main tunnel. A second line stood in front of it, and a third in front of that. A forth, unfinished row ended approximately halfway around the curve. Each stone pillar was about a tenth of a meter thick and stood a short distance from its neighbor.

"There must be hundreds of pillars in here," said Rela.

"Where do you want to start?" Teven asked, though he could guess her answer.

"With the end ones."

He carried her to the last stone pillar. As they drew near, the frozen dust and stone began swirling. Within minutes, two new pillars would decorate the Chamber of Wisdom.

"Impressive. I think this is a gesture of friendship," Teven guessed.

"I don't have any wise words to say now," Rela said.

"Don't worry. The first message is always an introduction."

"Always? You've only heard Jaspen Turgot's pillar," Rela reminded.

Teven stopped walking toward the pillars.

"I know many things," he said, solemnly meeting her eyes. "I am the wise, all-powerful older brother here."

"Remind me to smack you when my arms function properly."

"Of course, Princess. It will be done," Teven promised, doing his best impression of an RLA soldier.

They chuckled.

"Owww! Stop making me laugh!"

"Don't stab yourself next time," he retorted.

"I'm never going to live that down, am I?"

"Not if I can help it."

"Oh, just carry me to the pillar," she ordered.

He opened his mouth.

"Less talk more forward movement."

He smiled.

When they reached the last stone pillar besides the two new ones, Teven let Rela run her hand along the top of it. A holographic form of their mother appeared.

"Greetings, I am Reia Antellio Minstel, younger sister to Kiata, daughter of Sela and Basil Antellio, wife of Prince Terosh Minstel. Once a Ranger, now an outcast, I confess choosing love over duty and the life I was bred for." The figure fell silent and disappeared.

Rela touched the pillar again.

"Doesn't this thing have a play all button?"

"Guess not. Life's rough, Princess."

Their mother appeared again. Her expression radiated joy.

"We have a son! Terosh could not come with me this time because one of us had to stay to receive the representatives from the Galactic Alliance of Populated Planets. But I had to come. Teven is beautiful. He has his father's black hair, my green eyes, and a scream that can penetrate every corner of the palace! I know I am supposed to be recording bits of wisdom here so here is my lesson for future generations: enjoy every moment you can basking in the love of family." Her smile was steady as she slowly faded.

Teven gently pressed his right hand to the pillar then squeezed Rela's arm.

"She's speaking to us."

When their mother appeared this time, she was distraught. A haunted, far-off look lurked in her expressive eyes. She began speaking softly, but her voice got faster as her emotions raced.

"My beloved Terosh is dead. We suggested joining the Galactic Alliance of Populated Planets so we could offer further aid to neighboring planets suffering from the Colza Star explosion, but our suggestion was ill-received by the Senate and the Governors Council. Lord Kezem, Governor General Third Lord of Idonia, protested most vehemently. The debates stretched on from months into years. Terosh suspended the meetings for a time to let tempers cool but it did not help. A few days ago, Terosh received an offer of information from an unknown woman. A meeting was set up in Estra. Terosh was ambushed, and now he is gone." Queen Reia continued staring straight ahead, pausing so long Teven and Rela thought she had finished.

"So that's what happened," Rela said. "I wish I had known them."

To their surprise, their mother wiped at some tears, took a deep breath, and continued speaking. Her voice wavered with emotion.

"I fear for my children. We have three now: Teven, Rela, and Tavel. What will become of them? Lord Kezem is quickly gaining support. He will strike sooner or later, and I fear I shall not survive the confrontation. I do not fear death, but I fear not knowing what will become of my children. They are innocent. They should not pay for decisions Terosh and I have made. But they will. GAPP deceived us. They will force a joining when it suits them. I can only hope I can prepare my children for all the dangers they will soon face. The anotechs are a powerful gift. I bid future rulers to use them unselfishly. Selfish actions only cause pain, and it is better to suffer than cause suffering." Queen Reia looked like she wanted to say more, but then, she turned away and disappeared.

Rela touched the pillar again but nothing happened. After a moment, their mother's first message played again.

"Shall we hear what Father has to say?" Teven questioned, wondering if Rela had the strength to hear more. His arms were getting tired.

"Yes, I would like to see him," Rela murmured.

Teven sidestepped left so Rela was in front of their father's stone pillar. The holograph showed a boy of about twelve or thirteen who looked strikingly like Teven.

"My name's Terosh." The young man looked somewhere off to his left and rolled his eyes. His voice contained equal parts annoyance and arrogance. "Yeah, yeah. I'm getting there. Greetings, I am Prince Terosh Minstel, brother of the obnoxious I-am-great Prince Tate, second son of Kila and Teorn Minstel. I cannot sing, and I'll never be king so lots of me will you hear."

Rela laughed.

Teven chuckled as well. He'd always pictured his father as a serious man.

"Play that one again," Rela instructed.

"You like being in pain?"

"I want to see him as a child," Rela insisted.

"It'll cycle around eventually. Somehow, I don't think he has as many messages as he thought he would."

At Rela's touch, Prince Terosh returned a few years older and beaming with happiness.

"I am in love! I have come with my new wife so all future generations may learn from her as I have. She is wonderful in a hundred thousand ways which I have no time to record. Besides, I'd rather spend my time with her than this machine anyway." He winked and vanished.

Another touch to the pillar brought forth the figure of a much graver Prince Terosh.

"My father and brother are dead. They went to Mitra to help Princess

Alikai avoid the Blood Harvest. Their bodies returned a few days ago, and the anotechs with them have quite a story to tell. I can barely believe them, though I know they would not lie. It now falls to Reia and me to lead this people. I never realized how much pressure Tate took upon himself, ruling the planet while our father grieved for our slain mother, the queen. It is now my task and burden. Riden help us."

"Now it is our task and our burden," said Rela. "I wonder when Lord Kezem decided to turn on our parents."

"He was ambitious, smart, and ruthless," Teven said. "I'm not supposed to rejoice over death, but I am relieved he is gone."

"Me too. Try having your life linked to him," Rela said.

"You've got me there."

Rela touched the pillar and the young Terosh appeared again and delivered his message.

Teven frowned and a sense of sadness spread through him. The three messages left so much unsaid. They fell silent, thinking of all that had transpired and silently mourning the lost years.

"Rela, I've been thinking about what our cousin said just before she died," Teven said thoughtfully.

The title—cousin—still felt strange to him.

"Who?"

"Kayleen Wellum. Her mother and our mother were sisters. She said I would always be a Royal Guard. Is that possible?"

"What are you asking?" Rela's tone mixed curiosity and fear.

"Will you take Reshner's throne?" asked Teven.

"You do not wish to be king?" She stared at him in disbelief.

"We're going to need all the help we can get to ferret out the deeper levels of corruption. I cannot do that as king. If you became queen you could put formal pressure on the Senate and the Governors Council to get their act together, and I would be free to apply my own pressure from another direction," Teven explained. When she didn't answer immediately, he hastened on. "I would always be nearby to help you as necessary. That's what Royal Guards do anyway."

"Don't make promises you don't know if you can keep," Rela said gently.

"Words of wisdom, Princess, you should record that," Teven said.

"Promise me you'll try to not die."

"I promise."

"Then I will accept the throne and serve the people for as long as I can," Rela vowed.

Teven waited, knowing she had more to say.

"But do not think you have escaped politics, Prince Teven. State dinners and formal wear await you."

She was joking but he protested anyway.

"I think it would be best if the people believed me still lost or dead." His frown deepened. "It would put you in more danger but hopefully not for long."

"That is why I have Melian Maidens," Rela said with a weary sigh.

A new idea occurred to Teven. His frown softened.

"Rela, could you make me a Royal Guard captain, so I could stay with you?" He felt her studying his face.

"That is a high promotion for a first-class derringer," said Rela, pulling his current rank from his mind.

He didn't care. It was comforting to share thoughts with her. Now, it was her turn to think. He took the time to absorb her soft brown hair, smooth features, and passionate blue eyes.

The protective instincts stirred.

"I do not wish to be the Captain of the Royal Guard. I want to be just an ordinary captain. They can get places full commanders cannot."

"You have a devious mind, Teven. Are you sure you don't want to be king and level that deviousness against the Governors Council?"

"Positive. I can be more devious if they don't know who I am. Teven's a common enough name. No one will think twice about Teven McKnight. I could protect you and slip away to investigate our enemies as well."

"But most of the soldiers already know who you are," Rela pointed out.

"The anotechs can fix that," Teven said seriously. The thought was troublesome but necessary. "There are several others that will have to be dealt with as well. Jalna can arrange it."

Rela shuddered.

"Please do not talk like that, you sound like Lord Kezem."

"I'm sorry," replied Teven.

"What about your face?" Rela asked with a concerned expression.

"What's wrong with my face?" Teven demanded, pretending to be miffed. A twinkle in his eyes gave him away. He knew she referred to his uncanny resemblance to their father. "I think the anotechs could fix that as well."

Rela blew out a long breath.

"I do not like it, but it will suffice as a plan for now," said Rela. "Modify your face and alter their memories as needed but leave the Melian Maidens and Captain Tayce alone. They are trustworthy and someone must know the truth in case something happens to me." She sighed and tapped her fingers on Teven's shoulder. "You win, Captain McKnight, but we must forgo formalities until my legs stop rebelling."

"As you wish, Princess," Teven said. There was a tender quality to his voice. He cleared his throat. "With your permission, Highness, I'd like to put you down now. My arms hurt."

She leveled an imperious gaze at him.

"You have my permission but know that I will be relying heavily upon your advice on royal matters. You will be a hidden king. If you do not like my terms, tough."

"You would have driven our father mad," Teven commented, shaking his head.

Her expression said she took that as a compliment.

Chapter 49:
Perilous Return to the Palace

Zeri (June) 29, 1560 - Temen (July) 5, 1560
Loresh, Frozen North to Royal Palace, City of Rammon
Two days were spent in Loresh. Teven divided his attention among sitting by his sister, viewing messages from their ancestors, subtly adjusting his features, selectively modifying memories, hovering near his uncle, and helping the RLA soldiers clean up the battlefield. The anotechs cleaned the blood that had fallen on the cold ground. Most of the bodies were taken out of Loresh and burned traditionally.

Teven took care of Kayleen personally. He conducted a small Ranger ceremony with only Todd Wellum, Princess Rela, the six Melian Maidens, Rela's three friends, and Jalna present. Teven felt older and wearier than his new face could ever convey. He had the anotechs add cells to the bottom of both cheeks, making his face squarer, and then, he grew a beard to add false years to his life. His heart broke all over again when he spoke the ritual words.

"Resmundel resmunsi rel ihala ental mieltsom."

Jalna translated for the others, "Return to dust, return to spirit, rest, I hold you forever in my heart."

When only ashes remained, Teven and Todd buried them in the small cave where Kayleen had reunited with her father. With the unpleasant tasks finally done, they could return to Rammon. Teven knew Rela would face a tough battle to reach the capital, but he was determined to see her there safely.

The return journey took five days instead of one because they had to travel slowly for Rela's sake. Even with the anotechs controlling the pain, she could not be moved fast.

Princess Rela slept a lot, first on the hov sled ride to Estra, and then, in the modified hov to the coast. Teven had them camp beside the Asrien Sea for several days, reluctant to put Rela through the rough waters. At her insistence, they finally proceeded. Throughout the Frozen North, the defectors from the RLA and Royal Guard formed a perimeter. Inside, the six Melian Maidens, the recently minted Aster Captain Ethan Tayce, Jalna, and Teven formed another perimeter around Princess Rela. Marc and Lorian stuck close to Anabel, who despite protestation was also forced to rest.

Escapees from the Battle for Loresh had informed the rest of the RLA of Lord Kezem's demise. In addition, the word spread to the Senate and the Governors Council. Supreme Commander Kolknir was the most logical choice to succeed Lord Kezem, but other Royal Guard, Melian Maiden, and RLA officers vied for control. Senators and governors broke and formed alliances constantly, hoping to curry favor with Reshner's next ruler. Rumors circulated that Princess Rela might have survived, but they chose to ignore the whispers.

Three times, the Princess's entourage was attacked, once by desperate mercenaries and twice by remnants of the RLA still loyal to Lord Kezem. Teven was awed and comforted by the Melian Maidens' fighting skills. Kia whirled her banistick so fast he could barely see it. Energy beams flew away from her and the princess. Jola, Elia, and Clara seemed to be everywhere at once slashing attackers with their blazing white kerlinblades. Linnea and Nalana stood their ground, protecting themselves with banisticks and simultaneously returning fire with energy pistols. Each fight was finished in moments, but the repeated nature of the attacks annoyed Teven.

They arrived in Rammon at dawn, neutralized the guards at the southernmost gate, and headed directly to the Senate Great Hall. A scout reported that Supreme Commander Kolknir had barricaded himself and his command inside the palace. The senators were summoned because they could request an immediate audience with the ruler. If Supreme Commander Kolknir came, they would have a much easier time of dealing with him. As expected, he refused to come. His spies had reported Rela's return.

A subsection of the Senate foolishly tried to have Rela arrested. Teven and the Melian Maidens put a stop to that. A loud debate raged back and forth for a few minutes. Rela stood to the side and observed the scene serenely. Teven stood by her side, like a good Royal Guard. Her carefully controlled expression hid the pain she must be in. Teven admired her grit.

"She is the only heir left to House Minstel," Senator Morren said reluctantly. "We have to have a ruler, and I will not serve a common soldier!"

"She's not even of age yet!" argued Senator Keel.

"We must wait for the prince to be found," Senator Rorian insisted, nodding agreement.

"If she becomes queen our positions are forfeit!" reminded Senator Keel.

The arguments continued in circles, until Rela lifted her chin and cleared her throat. They fell silent once they realized she would not bother to shout above them.

"It is not your choice. With or without your permission, I *will* take back the throne and appeal to the people. Many of you gained your positions through favoritism, not merit. That is to be expected. It is time you earned your place in this government. Many changes must be made as to how trade is conducted. There will be no more marks. Criminals will have fair trials and pay for their crimes accordingly. You will no longer be above the law. I will not tolerate graft or abuse. If you cannot abide by the laws, then leave." Rela spun away and strode out of the Great Hall. The anotechs reported great pain rolling off her.

"How are you still walking?" Teven murmured. He felt a tingling in his side just being near her.

"We need to retake the palace, right now," Rela stated, instead of answering his
question.

Teven was becoming more alarmed by the second. Rela was walking awfully fast for someone with a dagger slash down her right side.

Of course, we must retake the palace, but we should infiltrate it at night not midmorning.

"We can handle that, Rela," Teven said earnestly, referring to the Melian Maidens and the soldiers they had acquired in Loresh.

Rela shook her head and talked as she walked toward the center of the city and the front palace gates.

"Reshner politics have changed very little over the years. We can still appeal to ancient customs. If I am to be accepted as queen, I need to physically take the palace *without* bloodshed. Lord Kezem never became king because his birthright was forfeited when his mother was cast out, and he took the throne by massacring half the palace staff, not to mention our mother."

"But Kezem controlled the Senate and the Governors Council. How could he not have controlled the people?" Teven asked, still following her closely.

The streets were disturbingly quiet. Having heard the news of Lord Kezem's death, most people waited inside secret chambers for the power struggle to end. They knew violence was likely.

"He *did* control the people. He controlled every aspect of their lives so rigidly that their only small revenge came in denying him the title."

"What's your plan?"

"March through the front door," Rela replied.

"Oh, they'll never expect that," Teven said.

It's going to be a very long day.

"Anabel!" Rela called.

"Yes, Princess?" said Anabel.

"Stay near the back and stick to a kerlak gun," Rela instructed. "If it comes down to a blade battle get out."

Teven guessed that was the best advice. Telling Anabel she couldn't help capture the palace would have been asking for trouble.

"Yes, Your Highness," Anabel answered, dropping back a few steps.

They came to the palace gates fifteen minutes later.

"Halt!" shouted a soldier.

"Get in line or get out of the way. Those are your options," Rela said, stopping two meters from the gates. She leveled her energy gun at the man who had spoken. A second guard slowly walked away from his post.

"Where are you going?" the first guard demanded. "Supreme Commander Kolknir will kill you for deserting."

"Exactly. The princess will not," the second guard said, pointing at Rela.

The first man struggled with that logic before lowering his weapon, opening the gate, and waving them through.

"I never liked the supreme commander anyway," the second guard mumbled.

"Set your weapons to stun if you want to come," Rela ordered. "No one is to die today."

"Yes, Highness, it will be done," answered the first soldier.

Teven sensed deception from the man. Rela gave him the mental version of a wink via the anotechs. She felt it, too. They entered and jogged down the main path. Soldiers fanned out in front and to the sides of them, and the Melian Maidens remained in a loose circle around Rela. Their array left plenty of room for them to maneuver with their banisticks and gave Teven and Rela space to shoot. Teven checked the setting on his kerlak pistol and took out his banistick.

A pair of snipers perched in the second-floor balcony above the front doors took several shots at them. Teven traded his pistol and banistick for his kerlinblade and turned the power up to full. He batted away beams that came too close to Rela for comfort.

At a nod from Kia, Linnea lengthened her banistick farther than normal and sprinted in an unpredictable zigzag pattern toward the balcony. When she was two meters from her target, she stabbed the ground with her banistick and launched her body into the sky. She sailed over the railing and landed feet first on one of the snipers. The second sniper surrendered and was promptly chucked from the balcony. Linnea leapt down gracefully and rejoined the group. Seconds later, a squad of twenty Royal Guards charged from the ornate double doors in four lines of five.

"Halt! Surrender or be shot!" shouted the lieutenant.

Teven felt uncomfortable with twenty energy guns leveled at his sister.

Aster Captain Tayce took two steps closer to the Royal Guards.

"Stand down! I am your new commander!" shouted Tayce.

"Supreme Commander Kolknir—"

"Is a traitor and will be dealt with. Join us or be tried for treason," said Rela.

Doubt crossed the faces of two or three of the soldiers.

"My time is short. If you join me, nothing further will be said about your service to Kezem or Kolknir, but you must decide now." Rela waited two seconds for them to comply. "Very well," she said with a sigh. Turning to her companions, she said, "Deal with them."

A barrage of twenty deadly energy beams flew at them. Teven's heart climbed up into his throat. He needn't have worried for Rela's sake. Two of the front soldiers took the brunt of the attack and died instantly, but the

Melian Maidens, Kia in particular, turned back the rest of the beams with swift strikes from their golden banisticks.

The rest of the hours-long, on-and-off battle for the palace passed similarly to the first few seconds. Teven and the Melian Maidens spent the bulk of their efforts keeping a hail of energy beams away from Rela. The princess and her loyal soldiers, including a few new additions, poured stun beams back at Kolknir's men.

The throne room door was code locked, and the guards in front of it were a bit more challenging than the last two hundred or so.

"Kia, Elia, I trust you can clear that door," Rela said calmly, slowing to a walk.

Kia and Elia leapt forward and engaged the guards. While they fought, Teven and Rela exchanged a glance, shared a thought, and placed both hands on the doors. The anotechs flowed from their fingertips. Within seconds, the anotechs had the doors unlocked and the bomb attached to the doors disabled. Teven and Rela retrieved their anotechs and stepped back. Linnea kicked one door in and Jola kicked in the other. The group burst into the throne room to meet the astonished crowd of soldiers beyond.

Teven didn't like the situation. A few hundred soldiers crowded into the throne room. If it came down to a fight, everyone would be hard-pressed to stay alive. The problem was magnified by Rela's insistence on not killing. The weakened energy beams would wear off soon and the soldiers spread throughout the palace would be called to the throne room to trap the intruders.

"Give me one reason—" Supreme Commander Kolknir began.

Rela's energy beam caught him in the throat. Teven saw her flinch at having to shoot him in such a vulnerable spot, but the rest of him was covered by black body armor, leaving her little choice.

Where'd she learn to shoot like that?

Rela addressed the soldiers before the shock wore off.

"Lord Kezem is dead. I am Princess Rela of House Minstel, and as such, I have the right and duty to claim Reshner's throne. Whether I become queen or not rests in your hands and the hands of every citizen. Those who lay down arms will be reintegrated into the army under new leadership. You will also have the choice of resigning and joining civilian service branches or going home and pursuing a legal trade. Either way you will help rebuild this war-torn planet. Whether you do so from a prison post or as free people is your choice. Choose carefully."

Teven held his breath. The soldiers eyed one another. A tense half-minute passed without sound. Finally, a young female soldier slowly removed her kerlinblade and placed it on the ground. Then, she reached for her energy pistol, placed it on the ground beside the blade, stood up, and bowed to Rela. Others followed the example.

"No!" shouted the first gate guard who stood to Rela's left. He lifted his energy gun to shoot Rela.

Teven's heart skipped a beat. He couldn't get through Rela in time to intercept the shot.

Kia—who was on that side—reacted with speed born of good reflexes and plenty of practice. She knocked the weapon up and twisted it from the man's grasp. In the next instant, he was on the ground kneeling before Rela with head bowed and arms twisted up behind his back. Kia hauled him to his feet and tossed him at some guards who caught him and applied stuncuffs. Her quick actions convinced the remaining soldiers to surrender peaceably.

The Rammon palace was finally secure.

Chapter 50:
Reshner Approves

Temen (July) 10, 1560
Royal Palace, City of Rammon

The next several days passed like a heartbeat. Princess Rela had never dreamed of the amount of energy it took to deal with politicians and commoners. Already their pettiness tore at her spirit.

The General Council, composed of commoners from across Reshner, had held their first meeting yesterday to discuss her bid for the throne. No one could deny that Princess Rela belonged to House Minstel and had taken the palace bloodlessly, but the Senators had rubbed off on the General Council. Part of her found it amusing to hear the same arguments, which called her competence into question, coming from a farmer with the same words used by a senator. The General Council met again this morning to make a decision.

Rela paced the throne room, waiting for an answer. She tried to convince herself she would be okay without the title.

You're lying.

She drew a deep breath and held it for a few seconds before releasing it.

"You're going to give yourself the hiccups," Teven said from behind her.

Rela turned sharply and winced as the wound stretched. She still relied heavily on the anotechs to ignore the pain from her side. Even the slightly quickened breaths caused her some discomfort.

"Do not make a habit of that," she said, annoyed. Rela checked the bandage attached to her side to make sure her blood was staying inside. This was her first day with just the bandage. She had removed the anotech barrier in favor of using them to enhance her perceptions. She needed every advantage when it came to the slippery councils.

"Your pardon, Highness, but the delegate from the General Council approaches," Teven said.

"You know something," Rela said, catching a gleam in his eyes. She hurried back to her throne to be properly seated.

"I know something," Teven confirmed in a whisper, as the throne room doors swung open.

A woman in a flowing white dress entered. She was plain in terms of beauty but held herself with impressive dignity. Her steps were swift but sure. Upon reaching the dais steps, she stopped and knelt.

"My Queen, you have the confidence of the General Council and the support of the people. May Riden give you wisdom to rule as fairly as King Jaspen of House Minstel."

Rela's heart soared with triumph.

"Thank you, Lady Zelene, I shall do my best to earn the trust placed in me, but our future is as much in the hands of the General Council, the Senate, the Governors Council, and the people as it is in mine."

"How may I serve you, Your Majesty?" asked Lady Zelene.

"My first request is a thorough report from each region," said Rela. "The governors can help you with that. I need to know what each region needs if I am to address their problems. Also, I shall require good intelligence on the movements of dissidents. Rebuilding Reshner will be hard enough without having the civilian engineers attacked. The RLA and Peacekeepers will provide some protection, but the last thing I want to do is return Reshner to the military state it has been for the last thirteen years."

Why can't I just browbeat everyone into behaving?

"I will convey your wishes to the council at tomorrow's meeting. Tonight, we eagerly await your address. Infopads will carry your message to every settlement, including Ritand, though only a few refugees have returned after the floods."

Rela had determined to address the people regardless of the council's decision. She wanted to put rumors to rest and extend her offer to help.

"Is Ritand in your region, Lady Zelene?" Rela inquired.

"Yes, Your Majesty, my home is in Resh, but I went to Ritand many years ago to help the refugees when the Ashasten nearly swallowed the island. My father was once the governor of Resh. Thus, I am one of the only people trusted by both the citizens of Resh and the Ritand people. That is why they have honored me with the council post."

"You have earned their trust, Councilor," Rela said, motioning for the lady to rise. "Guard it well."

"I shall," Lady Zelene said. She recovered her feet and waited.

An awkward silence fell before Rela realized the woman was waiting to be dismissed.

"Forgive me, Councilor, I am a little new at this. You are dismissed unless you have anything else you wish to add or ask. Please, do not hesitate to voice your requests."

"You are kind, my queen, a quality both your parents possessed in abundance. They would be proud to see their daughter on the throne. With your permission, I shall impose upon your time later." The ease with which the woman spoke of Rela's parents suggested familiarity.

Rela wondered how familiar but decided it was a conversation for another day.

Lady Akia Zelene bowed and left.

"You scared her, Highness," Teven said, clearly amused. He usually addressed her that way even when they were alone.

Kia and Jola flanked the throne and Aster Captain Tayce stood like a statue next to Kia.

Sometimes, Rela wished Teven would just call her by name, as he had done in Loresh, but she understood the necessity of the charade.

"How so?"

"She was tenser than a tretling in a korver den," said Teven.

Rela groaned.

"I don't want to scare them."

"Do not dwell on it, Your Majesty," said Kia. "Lord Kezem's reign was long, and he cultivated fear. It will take time to correct the perception of leadership."

Rela was pleased that her maiden spoke. It had taken a long time to get Kia to see that she was more than a glorified shield to Rela.

"Thank you, Kia," said Rela. "It is good to know I am not that intimidating. Just don't tell the Senators. A few of them could use a little more fear."

"Leave that to me," Teven advised.

"I have a speech to prepare, but I want an explanation for that statement later," Rela said.

I could get used to ordering Teven around.

"Of course, I shall now blend into the walls like a good Royal Guard," said Teven.

Rela suppressed the giggle at seeing Captain Tayce's confused expression. She began pacing back and forth across the small platform that held the throne, pondering what to say to her people. Every time she looked up she saw another statue of Lord Kezem's head staring at her.

That is disturbing.

"Those have got to go," she muttered.

"The ugly statues are slated for destruction three days from now, Highness," Teven said cheerfully. "The replacement heads in your likeness are already on their way."

Rela sucked in sharply, horrified for the full second she believed him. Then, she caught the gleam in his eye.

"Teven, that was very cruel." Despite herself, Rela chuckled at the mental picture of walking past her likeness every day.

"Perhaps, but I have a gift that can make you forget just about everything," Teven teased.

"What is it?"

"You'll find out later," Teven promised.

***

Two hours after the evening meal, Queen Rela stepped out onto the third-floor balcony above the palace's double doors. The huge crowd on the lawn shifted restlessly, standing shoulder to shoulder. Rela shivered under the intensity of their collective gaze.

Talk about intimidating!

The expansive palace grounds were a security disaster waiting to happen. A wall of blue Royal Guards lined the walls, giving Rela a mixture of comfort and sadness. Both Teven and Captain Tayce had insisted on the visible security, but their presence undermined what she wanted to say.

Rela slowed as she neared the balcony railing, fearing her knees would fail and pitch her into the crowd. Flattening a dozen spectators during her first speech would be a poor first impression.

Seeing the stars and the three crescent moons shining above the crowd, Rela wondered how her mother's crown fared against those night jewels. Rela's breath hitched as she imagined her mother standing on this balcony preparing to address the people. Her heart nearly broke under the strain of longing for her father to present her to the crowd as would have been his right. Rela would have gladly traded all the crown jewels for a simple farewell to her parents, but they were gone. Knowing she must carry their legacy of strength, compassion, and wisdom, Rela felt completely inadequate.

A cheer rose from the crowd as people realized she had arrived. Heart pounding, Rela stepped to the voice amplifiers set up by the railing. The deep purple gown she had commissioned for the occasion sparkled under the bright lights as she moved. She gripped the balcony railing with both hands to keep them from shaking and leaned forward. She spoke softly, relying on the voice amplifiers to carry her message.

"Greetings, I am Queen Rela Minstel. You know who my parents and brothers were. You know what happened to them," she began, already deviating from her planned speech. "You also know what it is like to suffer under a tyrant. Yet by granting me the title of queen, you have demonstrated much trust. Thank you. I have not done much with my life, but much has been destroyed and now needs rebuilding. With your cooperation, we can return Reshner to peaceful days. It may last a day. It may last several lifetimes. We can only control our own actions and hope the next generation will learn from our wisdom and our mistakes. Tyranny was a mist—"

"What about the soldiers?" a man shouted. "You have more guards than Lord Kezem ever did!"

"The soldiers you see and feel around you are there for your protection and mine," Rela explained. "For as many of us who want peace, there are those who still want war. Many feel threatened by this change in government. Threatened people act rashly. Until the broken pieces of our cities are picked up and the scars are removed from the land, soldiers will be present, but they will be you. The Peacekeepers will be a branch of the army composed of citizens. Those who do not wish to serve in this manner may choose some other—"

"So now *you're* telling us what to do?" the man challenged. He sounded triumphant.

Stop interrupting!

Rela clamped down on her temper. A display of anger would not help her cause. She tried again.

"For three years starting at the age of sixteen, everyone who wishes to be a citizen will serve in some way. That does *not* mean you have to disrupt your lives. In fact, most of you are already public servants. There will be abundant opportunities. Teachers, doctors, peacekeepers, ship builders, hov designers, scientists, artists, disaster workers, and street cleaning crews all serve. The point is not to make you miserable but to get you to do something unselfish for a time."

A low murmur buzzed through the crowd as the people quietly discussed Rela's proposition. Slowly, a cheer started from the back corner and worked its way forward growing louder every second. Rela listened carefully, a smile spreading across her face.

"Etvi vental la creshon!"

Long live the servant queen!

***

Teven McKnight watched his sister proudly.

She won.

Queen Rela had emerged victorious in the battle for the people's hearts. Teven smiled to himself and thought of the surprise he had for her once the crowds had gone and Rela had a moment to herself. His guest waited in the throne room. The surprise was Lorian Petole's idea, but it had been Teven who made the countless calls and finally tracked down the elusive woman. He only hoped he would have as much success when he tried to find his brother.

That's a task for another day.

By the time Teven finally steered Rela back to the throne room, he'd grown so impatient he practically danced circles around her. First, he was on one side of her then he was on the other.

Seizing his arm, Rela leaned close.

"What is wrong with you?"

"My surprise is near." Teven twisted out of her grasp and flung the throne room doors open with a flourish.

A large, dark-skinned woman opened her arms to receive the young queen.

Rela froze and stared.

"Sarie!" she cried, rushing forward to meet the embrace.

Despite the six silent, ever-present Melian Maidens observing the happy reunion, Teven felt his presence was an intrusion. He slowly backed out and shut the throne room doors quietly, pleased to have restored a little peace to his sister.

THE END

Thank You for Reading:

I hope you enjoyed this epic science fiction saga. It's by far my most ambitious project. One day, I hope to return to Reshner and continue chronicling the adventures of the Royal House. I would love to hear your thoughts on these stories. Please consider leaving an honest review for them, individually or as a whole.

Although there are no more Reshner tales, you may wish to try a different brand of science fiction (Devya's Children) or switch over to some fantasy. There are 7 stories set on a different planet, Aeris. I hope to have a litRPG series connected to Aeris soon.

If you want to keep up with any of my series or get bonus content, sign up for my newsletter **(https://www.subscribepage.com/n7e8l8)**.

Sincerely,

Julie C. Gilbert

Expanded Cast of Characters Combined
(contains spoilers)

Adrik Bentanner – RT agent working under Gareth Restler

Airiel Archer – pregnant wife of Derk; captive

Akia Zelene – daughter of Resh's governor; representative of the General Council

Alden Tarpon – son of Vera and Tyko; RT agent

Alexi Gordon – rebel leader

Alikai Deleur – Mitran princess who marries Taytron Minstel to avoid the Blood Harvest

Ariman Keldor – RT agent; Taly's father; Niktrod's

Arista Restler – mother of Gareth and Nera

Anabel Spitzer – friend of Princess Rela Minstel

Atien Belcross – former scientist; worked in the palace once upon a time

Aveni – Ranger born on the planet of Wirsh

Bairok – RT agent; works for Donovan Meetcher

Benali – an actor hired by Laocer to manipulate Lord Kezem

Bova – Ranger from the planet of Rorge II

Brook Tarpon – eldest son of Vera and Tyko; Nera's husband

Cadrish – speech tutor for the Royal House Minstel

Carla Etan – former servant in the royal palace

Clara Arganon – a Melian Maiden assigned to Princess Rela

Clive Weldon – marksman assigned to Fort Riden

Coleth Timmer – mercenary, works for Gareth Restler

Cory Tiridan – marksman; helps Ethan Tayce

Covin – Elish male; twin of Zareb; Royal Guard; serves King Terosh

Dalonos – "dark ones"; anotechs who have a proclivity to pursue evil intent

Dantrel – Lord Kezem's servant

Dariad – RT agent; works for Donovan Meetcher

Darmon Zelene – Governor of Resh; Akia's father

Deanna Koffrin Minstel – deceased scientist; wife of Crown Prince Taytron Minstel; mother of Elia

Dennel – servant for Kezem Altran

Dennin Molik – one of the Royal Guards assigned to guard Prince Terosh during the Kireshana

Dentelich – doctor for the Royal family

Derk Archer – husband of Airiel; captive

Derna Praem – tretling herder

Dillain – Royal Guard

Dravid Altran – Kezem's father; deceased

Dryse – Coridian assassin candidate

Ectosh Laocer – Royal Guard captain; secretly loves the queen

Einer Akurin – RT agent working under Gareth Restler

Eldon Altran – eldest son of Mavis and Dravid Altran, Governor Lord and First Lord of Idonia; brother of Kezem; Calia's husband, father of Emry and Jaedin

Elia Koffrin (Minstel) – daughter of Prince Taytron Minstel and Princess Deanna Koffrin Minstel; one of the maidens assigned to protect Princess Rela

Ethan Tayce – soldier in the Reshner Liberation Army; has a change of heart and helps Princess Rela and Todd Wellum

Erik Restler – uncle of Gareth and Nera

False Jalna – a form assumed by Dark Ones, anotechs devoted to power as the goal

Gareth Restler – eldest son of Arista, Merisia's husband

Gemon Dravir – farmer who meets Reia early during the Kireshana

Geroli Rikk – new king of Mitra when Hinoli Brek declares denulan on House Deleur

Gina Kelter – Aster Captain of the Melian Maidens; personal guard to Crown Prince Taytron

Herik Lezan – RT agent working under Ariman Keldor

Hinoli Brek – would have inherited the Mitran throne

Hiram Alikron – former speaker for Ashatan Council; deceased; secretly served Lord Kezem

Irek Praem – tretling herder

Jaidir Drisher – neighbor of Derk and Airiel Archer; Vel's son

Jalna Seltan – daughter of the anotech creator; trains Kayleen and Prince Teven to use anotechs

James Celdin – Ranger originally assigned to guard Terosh during the Kireshana

Jenell – a derringer on the Kireshana; travels with Kayleen and Teven

Jola Westin – a Melian Maiden assigned to Princess Rela

Jolinda Ekris – Ranger Master of Healing, Ashatan Council member

Jos Millard – a Royal Guard assigned to Prince Terosh during the Kireshana

Kale Corida – Ranger Master of Tracking, Ashatan Council member

Karric – a derringer on the Kireshana; travels with Kayleen and Teven; was trapped in the Huz Mon salt mines for a time

Kel Kiren – smuggler on Reshner to research his past, charged with raising Prince Tavel

Kezem Altran – youngest son of Mavis and Dravid Altran; Governor General of Idonia; Third Lord of Idonia

Kiner – servant for Meetcher family; RT agent involved in the korver enhancement project

Kovit – RT alliance agent; killed just before Kireshana

Lara Vireth – RT alliance agent

Liam Deliad – Ranger Master of Arms, Ashatan Council member

Linnea Price – a Melian Maiden assigned to Princess Rela

Lucas Telon – former Ranger master, serves the Lady; trains with Kolknir; in love with Reia

Gareth Restler – eldest son of Arista, Merisia's husband

Kayleen Wellum – daughter of Kiata and Todd Wellum; Ranger apprentice; Teven's friend

Kezem Altran – youngest son of Mavis and Dravid Altran; Governor General of
Idonia; Third Lord of Idonia

Kia Meetcher – daughter of Meralla and Donovan Meetcher, deceased members of the RT Alliance; being raised by Lord Kezem; head of the Melian Maidens assigned to protect Princess Rela

Kiata Antellio Wellum – Nareth Talis Ranger; Reia's older sister; wife of Todd

Kila Creston Minstel – deceased queen of Reshner; assassinated by Niktrod Keldor; mother of Terosh

Kira McNoughten – mother of Teven, who died of Heskrin during Terosh's Kireshana

Kolknir – Kezem's agent; mercenary; former Ranger master; serves the Lady as well; trains Lucas Telon

Liam Deliad – Ranger Master of Arms, Ashatan Council member

Lorian Petole – servant in Kezem's palace, friend of Princess Rela Minstel

Marc Spitzer – friend of Princess Rela Minstel

Maledek – part played by both Lord Kezem Altran when he doesn't wish to reveal his identity **Mavis Mavis Altran** – mother of Eldon, Mitrek, and Kezem; former princess; disowned by her father when she married Dravid Altran to escape an arranged marriage to a Gardanian prince; Teorn's elder sister; also known as the Lady

Meralla Meetcher – mother of Kia; wife of Donovan

Merek – Lord Kezem's adviser, tries to understand the anotechs by studying Princess Rela

Merisia Restler – daughter of Vera and Tyko; Gareth's wife; ran away from the RT Alliance to protect her unborn child

Miscel Endelbaum – RT agent; friend of Alden Tarpon

Mitrek Altran – middle son of Mavis and Dravid Altran; Governor Judge and Second Lord of Idonia; brother of Kezem; husband of Delia; father of Silvia, Arabeth, and Sullivan

Morgan Pavron – RT agent working with Lucas; assigned to capture Prince Terosh

Nala Wellum – wife of Terik Wellum

Nalana Vastel – a Melian Maiden assigned to Princess Rela

Nathan McKnight, Jr. – called Nate, raised as the brother of Prince Teven, son of Pria and Nathan McKnight

Nera Tarpon – daughter of Arista and Tobias; Brook's wife

Nicholas Riggs – servant in Royal Palace in Rammon, friend of Princess Rela

Niklos McGreven – Ranger Healer master; substitute father for Reia and Kiata

Niktrod Keldor – man who assassinated Queen Kila; father of Ariman; grandfather of Talyon

Nils Clavon – servant and friend of Kiata and Todd Wellum

Pria McKnight – palace servant who smuggled Prince Teven out before the coup

Quasim – derringer on the Kireshana

Quedron – Aster Captain in Kezem's army

Reia Antellio Minstel – Ranger's new queen; Kiata's younger sister; adopted by Antellio family

Sarie Verituse – Melian Maiden; caretaker of Princess Rela

Talyon Keldor – RT agent; Ariman's son; Merisia's friend; Niktrod's grandson; also Peter Estan, the man who trains Princess Rela how to fight

Taytron Minstel – deceased elder son of Kila and Teorn Minstel; Terosh's brother

Teorn Minstel – deceased father of Taytron and Terosh; Mavis's younger brother

Terik Wellum – brother of Todd Wellum

Terosh Minstel – Reshner's king, son of Kila and Teorn Minstel

Todd Wellum – Nareth Talis Ranger, often works with his wife, Kiata

Trina Kiren – wife of Kel, agrees to raise Prince Tavel when they escape Reshner

Tryse – Coridian assassin in training

Tyko Tarpon – father of Brook, Alden, and Merisia; works for the Lady; husband of Vera

Tyler McDooley – personal messenger working in the South Quarter; healed by Reia after he scraps his knees in a fall

Semon McNoughten – husband of Kira; father of Teven, Dable, Kesella, Arel, Nicella, Azer, and Torkrin

Surd Antar – Aster Captain; head of the Royal Guard; works for Kezem

Vel Drisher – mother of Jaidir; temporary captive caught while looking for her son

Vera Tarpon – mother of Brook, Alden, and Merisia; wife of Tyko

Zareb – Elish male; twin of Covin; messenger for Prince Taytron

www.ingramcontent.com/pod-product-compliance
Lightning Source LLC
Chambersburg PA
CBHW081137020726
47504CB00009B/1890